The Cinderella Ball

Books #1 – 4

by

Day Leclaire

USA Today Bestselling Author

For more information, visit my website at: http://www.DayLeclaire.com

Thank you!

Book Descriptions

Married by Midnight!
You're invited to a wedding . . . your own!
Come to the Cinderella Ball single . . . leave
happily wed.

The Cinderella Ball is the chance of a lifetime for individuals to come together to find their special someone. Their one and only. Their soul mate. Obtaining a ticket isn't easy, but for those select few, it offers the chance at a lifetime of happiness.

Fairy Tale Husband:

Lone wolf, Jake Hondo has lived his life on the outside. An outcast. A bastard. Now he has a shot to change all that. In order to secure his inheritance, all he needs is to wed and bed a woman. *Any* woman. After that, he and his bride can go their separate ways, which is exactly how he wants it.

Kind-hearted waif, Wynne Sommers, longs for happily-ever-after, love at first sight, and knights in shining armor. The Cinderella Ball offers her all of that . . . and more. All she needs is the right man to accept that her love comes as part of a "package deal," a package that includes her young niece and nephew.

But as much as Wynne longs for love, Jake wants nothing to do with the unwelcome emotion. Or so he thinks until his new life is threatened. Will he be able to save his family from the forces marshaling against them? Or will he lose everything—his home, the children he's sworn to protect, and the woman who's become the most important person in his life?

Fairy Tale Wife:

Brilliant businesswoman, Nikki Ashton is in a desperate situation. In order to hold her young, smitten boss at a safe distance, she invented a husband. Now she needs to produce her absentee soul mate or risk being outed as a liar, something that could bring a fast end to her stellar career. The Cinderella Ball offers the perfect solution. All she has to do is find a strong, alpha male willing to marry her ... temporarily.

Tough, take-charge businessman, Jonah Alexander, will do everything necessary to protect his family, including marrying the gorgeous gold-digger who's set her matrimonial sights on his baby brother. When he discovers the two are planning to attend some sort of marriage ball in order to tie the knot, he swoops in, his world upended by the gorgeous, desperate redhead.

What neither expects is the passion that explodes between them. Then Jonah discovers Nikki is keeping secrets, secrets that threaten to destroy his Fairy Tale Wife on a personal and professional level, and put a permanent end to their temporary marriage.

Fairy Tale Wedding

Five long years ago, shy, passionate Ella Montague fell in love with tough, Costa Rican businessman, Rafe Beaumont. She thought he loved her, too. But that was before her family's Cinderella Ball tore them apart. Now he's back and insisting they marry at this year's ball. If she refuses, he'll destroy her family. His plan? To wed her and bed her, then leave her, which will prove once and for all that the "magic" of the ball is sheer fantasy.

What Rafe doesn't count on is reigniting the passion they experienced all those years ago. Leaving Ella and returning to Costa Rica is the hardest thing he's ever done. Then Ella shows up on his doorstep, determined to make their marriage a real one—no matter what it takes.

Will Rafe drive away his Cinderella bride or will he surrender to the magic of his Fairy Tale Wedding?

Fairy Tale Marriage

At the tender age of seventeen, sweet, innocent Shayne Beaumont attended the Cinderella Ball and fell in love with rough-and-tumble wrangler Chaz McIntyre. But their marriage only lasted one night before her brother, Rafe (the hero from *Fairy Tale Wedding*, Book #3 in **The Cinderella Ball Series**) ripped them apart and had their marriage annulled. Now, she's back—older, wiser, and determined to find love again.

Cold, hard-hearted Chaz McIntyre has no choice. If he wants custody of his daughter, he must marry immediately. And though he hates the idea of returning to the Cinderella Ball, it's the only option if he wants an instant wife. And he finds one, a masked beauty who seduces him into marriage. It's only after the fact that he discovers it's the one woman he least wants to marry. His ex-love, Shayne.

But need outweighs all other considerations and he returns to his ranch with his wife, tasking her with putting together a home that will guarantee custody of his daughter. What he doesn't expect is for Shayne to peel away the wintery layers surrounding his heart, bit by painful bit. While Chaz struggles to deny love, his wife and daughter are equally determined to unleash the miracle of Christmas, the one holiday he swore he'd never again celebrate.

Other Titles by Day Leclaire

The Cinderella Ball Series:

Married by Midnight!
You're invited to a wedding . . . your own!
Come to the Cinderella Ball single . . . leave
happily wed.

Fairy Tale Husband, Book #1
Fairy Tale Wife, Book #2
Fairy Tale Wedding, Book #3
Fairy Tale Marriage, Book #4

The Dante Inferno:

The Dante Dynasty Series

Some blazes, once ignited, can't be
extinguished. Just one burning touch
connects a Dante with his soul mate.
The Inferno ... curse or blessing?

Sev's Blackmailed Bride, Book #1
Marco's Stolen Wife, Book #2
Nicolò's Wedding Deception, Book #3
Lazz's Contract Marriage, Book #4
Luc's Unwilling Wife, Book #5
Rafe's Temporary Fiancée, Book #6
Draco's Marriage Pact, Book #7
Gianna's Honor-Bound Husband, Book #8
Becoming Dante: Gabe, Book #9
Dante's Dilemma: Romero, Book #10
Forever Dante: Lucia, Book #11

The Wacky Women Series

*In the world of Wacky Women,
nothing ever goes according to plan!
From one disaster to the next, these
women will do anything to find
true love.
Heartwarming, hilarious, and
unexpectedly poignant,
Fall into laughter while you fall
in love.*

Once Upon a Cowboy, Book #1
Once Upon a Jinx, Book #2
Once Upon a Time, Book #3
Once Upon a Ghost, Book #4
Once Upon an Enchantment, Book #5

Table of Contents

Fairy Tale Husband

The Cinderella Ball Series:
Book #1

by

Day Leclaire

USA Today Bestselling Author

Dedication

In memory of Robert M. Totton. We'll miss your humor, your wit and your wonderful stories. Mostly, we'll miss you just being there.

Prologue

Towson, Maryland

Wynne Sommers sat on the floor of her apartment and cupped her chin, her pale brows drawn together in thought. "Do you know what I really need, Laura?"

Her friend snorted, folding clothes into a large moving box. "Sure I know. You need to have your head examined if you still intend to go through with this ridiculous idea."

"No . . . What I really need is a knight in shining armor. A protector."

Laura shoved the box to one side and threw her hands up in despair. "Oh, for crying out loud! Why don't you just wish for Prince Charming, a palace, and a million dollars while you're at it? It's just as realistic." She shook her head with a groan. "And listen to me talking about realism to you of all people. A woman planning to marry a complete stranger wouldn't recognize reality if it bit her on the—"

"Yes?" Wynne asked, amusement clear in her voice. "Bit me where?"

"Oh, forget it," Laura muttered. "Why do I bother?"

Wynne smiled, not the least offended by her friend's bluntness. "Because you care. And in case you've forgotten, I know all about reality and being realistic. It hasn't worked for me, which is why I'm willing to give the alternative a try."

"I know," Laura said contritely. "But to marry a complete stranger . . ."

"My point exactly. Since I am going to marry a complete stranger, why not pick one with all the qualities I need?"

"Because it's crazy. It's just asking for trouble." Laura's gaze grew concerned. "Please, don't do this. There has to be another solution."

"You know there isn't," Wynne said with calm finality. "I've lost my job, my apartment, and I'm out of money. This is the only option left. It'll work out, you'll see."

Laura frowned. "What do you mean you're out of money?" she demanded. "What happened to your savings?"

"I spent every last penny on my ticket to the ball. I had to. It was the only way to find a husband by the end of the month."

A long silence stretched between them. Wynne knew she'd upset her friend, but she had no choice. From the moment she'd heard about the Cinderella Ball, she'd known it was the answer to her prayers. It had been a fluke that she'd seen the advertisement at all—a newspaper left at the restaurant where she'd worked, a gust of wind from an open doorway, pages of newsprint blowing to the floor and . . . And there it was. A small, elegant ad that had caught her eye and offered a chance of a lifetime.

The Cinderella Ball
Where you'll be married by Midnight!
You're invited to a wedding . . . your own!
Come to the Cinderella Ball single . . . leave happily wed.

And it had given a phone number, a number she'd called that very night. A ticket to the ball had been exorbitant, the application form detailed and thorough. But she'd apparently passed the intensive investigative process they required and been accepted as a guest to the ball.

Unable to resist, Wynne crossed to the scarred dining table at the far end of the room and stared down at the intricate gold-embossed box she'd placed on her best remaining china plate. It had arrived earlier that day, hand-delivered by a liveried messenger along with a card that read, *"The Montagues wish you joy and success as you embark on your search for matrimonial bliss."* Taking a deep breath, she opened the wooden box again and removed the white velvet pouch inside.

Reverently she ran a callused fingertip over the pouch, then slid the surprisingly heavy gilt "ticket" from its nest. The metallic wafer caught the light from the overhead bulb and shimmered as though alive, flooding the drab room with a brilliant, golden promise. She'd made the right choice, she assured herself, made the only possible decision. Just holding the engraved ticket filled her with that certainty.

Laura came to stand behind her, peering over her shoulder. "I'm sorry, Wynne," she said. "I didn't mean to criticize. I'm just worried about you. You don't always see people the way they really are, and I'm afraid one of these days someone will take advantage of you."

"I guess that's all the more reason I should get married. My husband can make sure that doesn't happen."

"What if *he* takes advantage of you?"

Wynne laughed. "I wouldn't marry a man like that. That's why I'm going to the Cinderella Ball. The man I find will be special." She smiled with dreamy certainty. "He'll be good and kind, patient and loving. Strong. Fair."

"Yeah, right. A knight in shining armor. A protector."

A small frown creased Wynne's brow. "I know women aren't supposed to need protection. They're not even supposed to want it anymore. Do you think he'll mind? It won't be for long. Just until Mrs. Marsh is taken care of. And then I'll be happy to take care of him."

"You aren't going to tell him, are you?" Laura demanded bluntly. "Not everything?"

"It's only fair that I do."

Laura planted her hands on Wynne's delicate shoulders and turned her around. "Listen, my friend. I'll go along with this crazy scheme. I'll even help in any way I can. But there's one condition."

"Only one?" Wynne teased.

"Just one. You aren't to tell him the truth until after you're married."

"But—"

"Look what happened when Brett found out. He ended your engagement."

Wynne grimaced. "He obviously wasn't the man I thought he was."

"Nor was Jerry. Nor was Kevin. The minute they found out, they both dumped you, too."

"All that means is that knights are in scarce supply these days," Wynne insisted.

"My point exactly. Take my advice and pick out your knight. Wed him, bed him, then tell him the truth. That way he won't have any choice but to help you."

Reluctantly Wynne shook her head. "I can't lie, Laura. You know I can't."

"Fine. Just don't give him all the details. Be vague." Laura glared. "You can be vague, I know you can. I've seen you do it often enough."

Wynne peeked up at her friend. "I believe that's thoughtful, not vague," she offered.

"Trust me. I know vague when I see it and you're vague."

"Okay, but I can't lie."

"I'm not asking you to lie. Just be selective in what you tell him. I'm not joking, Wynne. I want your promise. I know how seriously you take promises. Swear to me that you'll keep your mouth shut until the ring is on your finger."

Wynne frowned, hesitant to commit to something so contrary to her nature. "I promise I won't tell him until after we're married . . . *unless* he asks." She lifted an eyebrow. "Is that good enough?"

"I guess it'll have to do." Laura sighed. "Let's just hope he's so enthralled by big green eyes and white-blond hair he doesn't think to ask too many questions."

"It'll work out, you'll see," Wynne consoled. "Why, with any luck at all, he'll be vague, too."

Chesterfield, Texas

Jake

Hondo glared at his attorney—even though said attorney was his best friend. Correction. His *only* friend. "You told me you could get that stipulation in the will overturned," he said in a furious undertone, yanking open a massive oak door reading, Dodson, Dodson, and Bryant, Attorneys at Law.

Peter Bryant shrugged, practically jogging to keep up with his client. "I didn't expect your cousin to contest it. If it hadn't been for Randolph, the judge might have let the condition slide. But that's not possible now. I'm sorry, Jake. I did my best."

"Your best, huh? Well, your best means that I have seven days to find a wife or I lose my inheritance." He thrust a hand through pitch-black hair and gritted his teeth, struggling to control his anger. "Marriage. What a joke."

"It's not a dirty word. Marriage can be quite pleasant."

"It's a state of pleasantness I've managed to avoid for thirty-five years. Why spoil a perfect record at this late date?"

"Come into my office where we can discuss it in private," Peter suggested, opening a door leading off the plush corridor. He dropped his briefcase onto his desk. "Can I get you something to drink?"

"Only if it's a hundred proof. Damn it, Peter. What the hell am I supposed to do now? What about a temporary deal? You know, one of those marriage of convenience things?"

Peter poured two fingers of whiskey into a glass tumbler and handed it to Jake. "Assuming you could find someone agreeable, there's still one detail you should keep in mind."

Jake swallowed the whiskey and lifted an eyebrow. "What's that?"

Peter crossed to sit behind his desk. "I believe your grandfather's exact wording is 'wedded and bedded,'" he clarified.

"I know his exact—" Jake ground to a halt, slamming his empty glass onto the oak table top. "You can't be serious! Tell me you don't mean what I think you do."

"'Fraid so. I gather your grandfather must have anticipated our creating a loophole with a temporary arrangement. He hoped for a real marriage with a real wife and real kids."

Jake waved an impatient hand. "I don't give a damn what he hoped. Just explain the specifics. How the hell are they going to prove the marriage is consummated? Don't tell me they're going to have a doctor—"

"No, no," Peter hastened to assure. "Though if your cousin had his way it might have come to that. The lady's word will be sufficient."

Jake balled his hands into fists, wishing he were still young and impetuous enough to give physical expression to his fury. "Any other details I should know about?"

"Not as far as the will is concerned, no. But I did suspect Randolph might try something devious, underhanded, and unfortunately legal. So I devised a counter measure." Peter smiled expansively and centered an ornate box in the middle of his desk. Opening the lid, he removed a thick, gold-embossed envelope. "I believe this will help you find a temporary bride."

Jake raised an eyebrow. "What is it? A list of candidates?"

"Close." Peter patted the envelope. "I took the liberty of arranging for this the minute Randolph fired off his first salvo."

"Get to the point, Bryant."

"Sit down and I'll explain." He waited until Jake had complied before continuing. "Have you ever heard of the Cinderella Ball?"

"No. Nor am I in the mood for fairy tales."

"This isn't a fairy tale. Not exactly." Peter grinned. "Though it is sort of sweet."

"Please. Spare me."

"You're such a cynic," the attorney observed, then held up his hands as though hoping to calm a threatening storm. "Relax. Since you're not in the mood for a lengthy explanation, I'll give you the short version."

"Smart move."

"I heard about this ball back in my college days. It would seem a couple by the name of Montague throws one of these affairs every five years because that's how they first met—at a ball. One look and they fell madly in love. They were married by dawn the next day and have, according to them, lived in wedded bliss ever since. By holding this Cinderella Ball, they're hoping to give other couples a similar opportunity."

"Sounds like a bunch of bull," Jake stated bluntly. "I find it hard to believe anyone would be interested in attending something so ridiculous."

"You'd be surprised," Peter replied. "There are a lot of lonely people in the world. They want marriage and they want a partner who shares the same mindset. All the guests who request a ticket are investigated by a security company to weed out the psychos and weirdos. Those that pass scrutiny pay a hefty fee to attend. That alone culls the mix even further."

"So you sent in my name?"

Peter nodded. "If we hit a snag with the will, I thought this might be a viable alternative."

"Well, you're wrong." Jake stood and crossed to the liquor cabinet, pouring himself another drink. "There has to be some other way. Find it."

"As your lawyer, I'm telling you this is the only alternative. As your friend, I suggest you walk away. Forget the inheritance. Let Randolph have it."

Jake's expression hardened. "Not a chance."

"Then you must marry." He leaned hard on the word *must*.

His statement hung between them for a long moment. With a sigh, Jake nodded and sat down again. "Give me the details."

"By attending this ball, you're able to cut through all the usual first meeting nonsense and get right to the basics. Everyone who attends wants to marry, so it's just a matter of finding a compatible spouse, one who shares your interests. In just a few minutes, you can discuss and settle all sorts of issues, from finances to children. And no one is offended by such frankness."

"They don't have time to be," Jake inserted.

Peter nodded. "Exactly."

"So I wander around this place canvasing women to see who'd be willing to marry me, sleep with me, and then walk away. Is that it?"

"That's it, though fair warning. The odds of finding someone who's agreeable are next to nil."

Privately Jake agreed. "And if I don't find myself a wife?"

Peter shrugged. "Then I won't make you reimburse me for the ticket."

Jake actually smiled. "Fair enough." His smile faded. "What about a prenuptial agreement? There's not much point in gaining my inheritance if some greedy little viper's going to snatch it away again."

"I can draw up a document. Getting her to sign it will be your problem."

A cold light entered Jake's eyes. "She'll sign it," he assured curtly. "Or she'll look elsewhere for a husband."

"Then let me also warn you that without her having a lawyer representing her interests, the legality of the document may be at issue. She could contest it."

"She won't," Jake stated with absolute certainty. "Otherwise she'll find herself grabbing hold of more trouble than she can handle. The woman I marry won't be some starry-eyed dreamer with visions of Prince Charming and fairy castles and happily-ever-afters dancing in her head. She's going to be plain, practical, and levelheaded. And once the terms of the will are met, she's going to walk away without a backward glance. I guarantee it."

Chapter One

The moment Wynne saw him, she knew she'd found her knight. If she hadn't already believed in love at first sight, she would have in that instant. He stood tall and broad and indomitable against the dusk-filled November sky, everything about him suggesting Prince Charming, fairy castles, and happily-ever-afters all rolled into one.

He was, as far as she could tell, perfection.

She first noticed him as she approached the "palace," a huge mansion that rose out of the Nevada desert like a great white beacon of hope. He stood in the center of the flagstone walkway, taking in the whimsical, wedding cake design of the house with an expression of cynical disdain. Clearly he considered the overall effect pretentious.

She considered it a dream come true.

Not that she'd hold his attitude against him. Heavens, no. The man she married needed to be in touch with the real world, to have a tough, no-nonsense edge. He needed to be a match for Mrs. Marsh.

She slipped closer hoping to get a clear look at him. As though accommodating her, he turned slightly so the floodlights lining the walk stabbed across his face, revealing in brutal detail every austere plane and angle. What she saw stopped her cold. This was no Prince Charming boldly blocking the path, but a Prince of Darkness.

The man might have been hewn from solid rock, as starkly beautiful and as fatally dangerous as the desert surrounding them. Hair as black as coal swept back from a broad furrowed brow and framed high, arching cheekbones and a firm, squared jaw. His features were too bold to be called handsome, but she didn't mind. The harsh, craggy planes appealed to her.

He looked down then, as though surprised to find her at his side, and lifted a dark eyebrow. She caught her breath, captured within the austere glare of his bright golden eyes. "Getting a jump on the competition?" he asked, his voice reminding her of the rumble of distant thunder.

She tilted her head to one side. "Excuse me?"

"You're looking for a husband, aren't you?"

"Yes."

"Then run along inside, elf. I'm no one you'd want to marry."

He was accustomed to instant obedience, she realized. She suppressed a smile. He'd soon discover she didn't skitter away at the first flash of lightning or crack of thunder—for that's what his expression reminded her of, the threat of a fast approaching storm. "I need a strong man. You look strong," she said instead.

"I need a wife to share my bed. And then, after a brief-as-possible marriage, to go away." He folded his arms across his chest and lifted an eyebrow. "Is that what you want, too?"

"I want a man who likes to win," she said, evading the question. "Someone who's a fighter."

"You waging war?"

She frowned, considering. "I guess you could call it war. All right, yes. I'm waging war. But I also need someone fair and reasonable and patient. A . . . a gentle warrior."

He laughed at that, amusement lightening his eyes, but doing nothing to ease the hardness of his features. "You have the wrong man," he stated and walked away.

She watched him go, taking in his easy, long-legged gait, not in the least surprised when people quickly made room for him, giving way to the stronger force. That was how he'd be with Mrs. Marsh, she didn't doubt for a minute. And though he claimed he wasn't fair or reasonable or patient, she suspected he lied. Oh, not deliberately. He wasn't the type. He just didn't see his own goodness.

But she did.

"You'll do," she whispered with a wide grin. "In fact, you'll more than do."

Jake wended his way through the crowd streaming toward the mansion. One down, he thought grimly, and only a few hundred more to go.

With nine or ten hours available to him, that meant he had to interview about a dozen or two women an hour. That gave him three and a half minutes per candidate. He shook his head in exasperation. This was crazy. Three and a half minutes to choose a wife. Great. Just great.

What the hell could Peter have been thinking? Better yet, what the hell was he thinking to have gone along with such an asinine plan?

He climbed the sweeping steps leading toward the entrance hall and glanced back. His elf still stood where he'd left her, her dress a pale splash of bridal white in the gathering dusk. Too bad she hadn't worked out. She'd been a tempting little morsel.

Unfortunately, the instant he'd spotted her hovering at his elbow, he'd known she was all wrong. For one thing, she looked the type who expected a Prince Charming and fairy castles and happily-ever-afters. And for another, he found her too damned attractive. One look at all that white-blond hair tumbling into eyes the color of new spring leaves and he'd known he'd have to put a whole lot of space between them. Otherwise he'd end up slinging her over his shoulder and heading for the nearest exit. That would never do.

A damn shame, but still the God's honest truth.

He frowned, turning from the sight of her, shaking off the memory of her wide, pixie-like smile. She had too open a face—mischievous, intelligent, and vulnerable. The sort of face that threatened to creep into a man's heart and soul and poison him with impossible fantasies. Fantasies he'd given up eons ago. Fantasies that would never come true.

Besides, she was a complication he couldn't afford. Not if he wanted to gain his inheritance.

A nudge from behind woke Wynne to her surroundings and she started, realizing she stood in the middle of the walkway lost in thought. She'd been picturing the sweetest of fantasies—one that involved a dark, handsome prince and a real house and children. It was a fantasy that could be hers, once she got past a certain masculine stumbling block.

She eyed the retreating back of the stumbling block in question, pleased beyond all measure when he hesitated and glanced over his shoulder in her direction. He needed her. The instinctive knowledge grew stronger with each passing moment. She sensed a gaping emptiness in him and knew she could fill it, a raw hurt she had the power to heal. He needed someone who could see the inherent goodness in his character, who wouldn't be fooled by his stormy expression and searing gold eyes and tough, independent attitude. He was a man plagued by demons, demons she could destroy.

He needed her.

Gathering up the long sweep of her skirt, she started toward the mansion. She didn't want to get too far behind her future husband. Heaven only knew what trouble he'd get into if she did. He might even pick the wrong woman through sheer ignorance. She grinned. Or sheer bullheadedness.

Stepping through the double doors leading inside, she stopped dead, staring around in amazement. The marble entrance hall seemed to stretch endlessly, the huge support pillars decorated for both Thanksgiving and Christmas with pine garland, fairy lights, and white satin bows. A massive chandelier, glittering with thousands of tiny prisms, caught the setting-sun and scattering a dancing circle of rainbows in joyous welcome. Twin, curving staircases on either side of the hallway led to the upstairs ballroom, joining at the top to form a perfect heart.

Wynne climbed the steps, feeling more like Cinderella by the minute. Reaching the upper landing, she joined others in a short receiving line, holding her invitation in a white-knuckle grip. All her hopes and dreams lay in this thin, gold metallic wafer. She closed her eyes for an instant and made a wish, a wish that all who came that night would find their heart's desire.

"Welcome to the Cinderella Ball."

With a start, Wynne opened her eyes, realizing she'd reached the front of the line. Standing before her was the most beautiful woman she'd ever seen.

The woman's hair was richly black, pulled away from her face and fashioned into an intricate knot. Her eyes were huge and a clear, rich amber, thick lashes shading the innate reserve that lurked in their depths. She held out her hand and offered a warm smile. "I'm Ella Montague."

"Wynne Sommers. It's a pleasure to meet you." She shook hands, gazing in open admiration. It might be interesting to look like this for a day instead of like the "pocketful of nothingness" Mrs. Marsh had once called her. Somehow she couldn't see Ella Montague allowing anyone to intimidate her, certainly not the beastly Mrs. Marsh. But then, everything had a price. Even beauty, judging by Ella's wary expression.

"I hope you enjoy yourself this evening," she murmured, taking Wynne's gold ticket and dropping it into the velvet-lined basket she held. "You're free to explore any of the rooms on the first two floors. Buffet-style dinners are available downstairs, and the gardens are open for your enjoyment. Once you find a partner, marriage ceremonies are conducted in the salons off the main ballroom. If you have any questions or problems, there are footmen who can assist you. They all wear white-and-gold uniforms, so you can't miss them."

"Thank you," Wynne murmured and moved further down the line. An older couple stood together, their expressions as guileless as newborn infants.

"Welcome, my dear," the woman said in greeting, taking Wynne's hand in hers. "I'm Henrietta Montague. And this is my husband, Donald."

Wynne glanced back over her shoulder at Ella, a mesmerizing flame of gold in her Grecian-style gown, and then back at the Montagues. "Ella is your daughter?" she asked tentatively.

"Our one and only," Henrietta confirmed cheerfully. "A bird of paradise raised by wrens."

Wynne smiled. "I quite like wrens. They're quick, cheerful, and always have something to say for themselves."

Henrietta beamed. "What a lovely description. Did you hear, Donald?"

"I heard, my sweet." He took hold of Wynne's hand and squeezed it. "Now you look around carefully tonight. Only the best for you."

"Oh, I've already found him," Wynne hastened to say. "And he is the best. The very best."

Tears glittered in Henrietta's eyes. "I'm so pleased. Much happiness, my dear. And with luck we'll see you again next year."

"Next year?" Wynne asked in confusion.

"That's when we hold our Anniversary Ball. All those who meet and wed at the Cinderella Ball are invited to celebrate their first anniversary with us."

Wynne gave a definite nod. "Then I'll see you again next year." With that, she moved into the ballroom and scanned the crowd for coal-black hair and a distinctive set of broad shoulders.

Time to find her husband-to-be.

Jake lounged against a wall and watched the crowd with weary impatience. Damn it all! Four miserable hours had passed since he'd arrived. Four hours spent stampeding from woman to woman like some sort of lust-crazed bull in a field full of bashful cows, and he didn't have a single prospect to show for it. Oh, there were plenty of women, available in every shape and size, but they'd all come with a list of wants he couldn't care less about, let alone had a hope in hell of fulfilling.

And not one of them was interested in a temporary relationship.

A hard-eyed brunette approached just then. It didn't take long to discover the size of his bank account interested her far more than marital bliss. After two minutes of conversation, he knew she'd never sign his prenuptial agreement. After another two he managed to convince her he wasn't interested in purchasing the goods she had for sale. The instant she left, an auburn-haired woman replaced the brunette. She practically shook in her ivory heels and he suspected it took every ounce of gumption for her to even approach.

"Nikki Ashton," she introduced herself and offered her hand.

"Jake Hondo."

An awkward silence descended and she visibly scrambled for something to say. "I—I'm looking for a husband," she finally announced.

"Really?" he murmured dryly. "What a coincidence. I'm looking for a wife."

She stared at him in dismay, bright color sweeping into her face. "Oh, I knew this would never work. Coming here was a mistake." A hint of violet glinted within the pansy-blue of her eyes. "I'm sorry to waste your time. It's just that I've never done this before. And I thought . . . Or rather, I'd hoped . . ."

He released his breath in a gusty sigh, afraid that if he didn't say something nice—and quick—she might burst into tears. "You want to start over?"

She gave a forlorn little shrug. "Is there any point?"

"Could be. I'm looking for a temporary wife. You interested?"

That caught her attention. "Yes. As a matter of fact, I am." A small smile crept across her full mouth and she relaxed minutely. "I wouldn't mind a temporary arrangement in the least."

He lifted a sooty eyebrow. "You serious?"

"Very. I just need a husband long enough to convince my sister I'm happily married."

"Happy, huh?"

"Ecstatically happy." Her eyes narrowed. "You can fake ecstatic, can't you?"

"I suppose." He waited a beat before adding, "If you're willing to sleep with me."

Her mouth fell open. "Excuse me?"

"I have to be legally wedded and bedded to inherit my grandfather's property. And my wife will need to stand up in court and admit as much to the judge." He rocked back on his heels. "Can you handle that?"

He watched as she mulled it over. If she hadn't claimed she'd be interested in a temporary marriage, he'd have brushed her off. One glance had told him she'd never do. For one thing, she was too beautiful, as lovely as his little elf, though perhaps more colorful and vibrant. If he'd learned nothing else in his thirty-five years of existence, it was to give beautiful women a wide berth.

For another, Nikki's soft, white hands hadn't seen a lick of work since the day she'd tumbled into this world. She'd be about as useful on a ranch as a silk-covered saddle.

Still, he was fast running out of options. He could tolerate the woman, if push came to shove. Let her sit in the parlor and look as gorgeous and helpless as she wanted, so long as she warmed his bed. Check that. So long as she warmed his bed and confirmed she'd done her wifely duty before the judge, along with various and sundry witnesses.

"Well?" he prodded.

"There's no other option?"

"No other option and no other conditions. How about you?"

"Just one other detail. In addition to my sister, I have a boss to convince. You'd have to act the part of the loving-husband whenever we attend business functions together or whenever my family's around."

Damn. "Whoa. Time out. Where were you planning on conducting this ecstatically happy marriage of ours?"

"New York," she answered. "Why?"

"Because I have a ranch to run. I need my wife living with me in Texas."

She shook her head. "I need my husband living with me in New York." Her mouth tilted into a rueful smile. "This isn't going to work, is it?"

"Doesn't look like it."

"Thanks anyway." She offered her hand again. "And thanks for helping me through this. It should be easier from here on out." With that cryptic remark, she disappeared into the crowd.

"Wasn't she right for you?" a friendly voice questioned from behind.

He turned and glanced down, both intrigued and irritated to discover that his elf had reappeared. "I thought I got rid of you earlier."

She shrugged, the graceful movement drawing his attention to the fine, sculpted lines of her neck and shoulders. Her short, layered hairstyle further emphasized the most exquisite bone structure he'd seen in a long time. She reminded him of a thoroughbred, lean and delicate and fluid.

"I'm hard to get rid of," she replied, not in the least offended by his gruff comment. "I'm persistent."

A small smile eased the corners of his mouth. "Annoying."

"Tenacious."

"Pesky."

"Determined."

"Clingy."

She laughed up at him. "In that case, I'll grow on you."

"That's what I'm afraid of," he muttered wryly.

Tilting her head to one side, she gave him a sympathetic look. "Not having any luck?"

"Not much. How about you?"

"Oh, I haven't given up, yet. These things take time."

He grimaced. "Something we're fast running out of."

"Unfortunately."

She brushed a lock of hair from her eyes and peeked up at him. To his amusement, the look held a contradictory element of both caution and daring, and he folded his arms across his chest. "Spit it out, munchkin. What do you want?"

She took a deep breath and offered an engaging smile. "I don't believe we've introduced ourselves. I'm Wynne Sommers."

The name suited its owner. They each had a fey, almost arcane feel about them. "Jake Hondo," he replied with notable reluctance.

"Are you hungry?" she asked. "I'm starved. Why don't we visit the buffet table and you can tell me what it is you expect in a wife."

"We've already covered that ground," he said, a hard edge invading his tone. "I want a temporary arrangement. You want permanent."

"I prefer permanent," she said, correcting him. "But I'm willing to compromise."

His eyes narrowed. "I want someone who's not afraid of hard work. You'd blow away in the first gust of wind."

"Oh, I'm not that easy to blow away. And as for hard work . . ." She held out her hands, palms up. They were marred by calluses, the skin red and chapped. "I know my way around a bucket of soapy water."

He gritted his teeth to prevent an exclamation of fury. She shouldn't have hands like that. They should be like the redhead's hands, silky and white and pampered. He eyed her with a frown. His elf worked hard for a living. Is that why she'd come? To escape a life of drudgery?

"You want a gentle warrior," he reminded. "And I'm not even close to gentle."

She tossed him a gamine-like grin. "Aren't you?"

"No," he said with pointed finality and turned away.

She didn't leave. Instead she stood quietly at his side and waited. Reluctantly he glanced down at her. A band of pearls decorated with a small sprig of flowers peeked through her pale hair, the spring green of the leaves a near perfect match for her eyes. Her dress was made of some sort of lacy material, the strapless bodice hugging her slender curves. He suppressed the savage urge to steal her away to a dark, private corner and become intimately familiar with those curves. Curves, he suspected, that would prove to be a hell of a lot softer than her hands.

"You don't want me," he told her in a harsh undertone. "I'm not the right sort of husband for you."

He might as well have saved his breath. "If you won't eat with me, will you dance with me?" she asked.

Take her into his arms? Feel that pale, velvety skin beneath his hands, breathe in her scent, and mold her body to his? He gritted his teeth. What the hell did she think he was made of? Stone?

"Not. A. Chance." He grabbed hold of her work-roughened hand. "It's the buffet or nothing."

He towed her through the crowds, calling himself every kind of fool for not avoiding the trap closing around him. But he couldn't. Something in the way Wynne looked at him, the unquestioning faith he read in those candid green eyes made him want to take her under his wing and ensure that nothing ever harmed her.

He didn't stop to analyze his reaction. He only knew that for the past four hours he'd caught distracting glimpses of her, not to mention the men stalking her like a pack of feral dogs. Each time he'd thought her on the verge of selecting one for a husband, it had felt as though he'd been mule-kicked square in the gut.

He was doing her a favor, he decided. He didn't know why she felt the need to go to this extreme, why she believed marriage represented salvation, but he suspected she only saw the dream, not the reality. If he married her, she'd be free in a short amount of time. By then, she'd have realized that marriage didn't solve problems, it only added to them, and she'd be only too happy for an opportunity to escape.

His mouth tightened at his feeble attempts to rationalize a way around the truth. If he were honest, he'd admit that he cared about just two things—gaining his inheritance and having this woman in his bed. He wanted her. He wanted her silken limbs wrapped around him. He wanted to see her in the full flush of passion. Most of all, he wanted her to continue gazing at him with such blatant adoration and trust. She was a fool to assume him worthy of either.

And he was a bigger fool for condoning it.

Wynne hesitated at the doorway to the dining area, staring in wonder at the feast laid out before them. "I've never seen so much food in all my life," she whispered.

Jake glanced at the damask-covered tables, piled high with every imaginable delicacy. The Montagues had spared no expense. His mouth twisted cynically. Considering what they charged for tickets to this ridiculous party, they could afford a decent spread.

"What would you like?" he asked, amused by the hungry greed she made no effort to conceal.

"Some of everything," she answered promptly. "Let's start with the desserts."

He laughed in genuine amusement, amazed that he still remembered how. "Not worried about calories?"

"Oh, no," she assured blithely. "I find plenty of ways to burn them off."

He lifted an eyebrow, wondering if she meant her comment to sound so suggestive. "Burn them off, how?" he probed, handing her a china plate. "Busy nights?"

"Very." She helped herself to a huge slice of fudge cake, then took a deep breath and glanced at him with a stoic expression. "I work as a waitress and dishwasher," she informed him with determined frankness. "Correction. I *worked* as a waitress and dishwasher. I'm not even that anymore."

Which explained the hands. As for his innuendo, she hadn't picked up on it at all. Surely, she wasn't so naive. He frowned. Or was she? What if she were—he blanched—a virgin? Hell, he couldn't handle that.

Virgins expected permanency. Commitment. Romance. Virgins expected forever. He needed someone experienced. Someone who knew what she was getting into. Someone who wouldn't balk when it came time to perform her marital duties and would have the gumption to admit as much to Judge Graydon.

Someone who'd walk away from him without a backward glance.

"How old are you, anyway?" he asked suspiciously.

"Twenty-six."

He couldn't hide his relief. Twenty-six. That was encouraging. There couldn't be many twenty-six-year-old virgins left in the world. Still, there was something about her. Something pure and innocent and fresh that made him as skittish as a stallion with his first mare. "You ever slept with a man?" he demanded bluntly.

She didn't appear anywhere near as stunned as the diners who'd overheard his question. She tilted her head to one side and blinked up at him. "Should I have?"

"Yes. Without question."

"Oh." She slipped a raspberry tart onto her plate. "Well, if it helps any, I've been engaged three times."

His hands tightened on his plate. Damnation. Three times. Three men. Three engagements' worth of opportunity to lure his little elf into someone else's bed. He should feel relieved. Instead, he felt murderous.

"Three times, huh?"

"Yes."

She looked at him and he read the truth in her eyes. Three men had had her within their grasp and not held on. Were they blind, stupid, or just crazy? He took her plate out of her hands and jerked his head toward an open doorway.

"Come on. Let's find somewhere private to talk. I want to get this settled."

She cast a wistful glance toward the desserts they'd missed and then accompanied him out a set of French doors and into the garden. The November desert was unseasonably warm, the evening chill barely penetrating. Shrubbery glittered with fairy lights, a full moon splashing the pathways with interesting patterns of illumination and shadow. Tables and benches peeked out of dark little nooks. And incongruous for a desert setting, imported trees strung with more fairy lights towered over some of the benches. Wandering deeper into the garden, Jake found an empty one.

"Tell me why you want to marry," he began peremptorily, setting their plates on the table.

She sat, her gown shimmering softly in the subdued starlight, her hair and eyes burnished with silver. "I was afraid you were going to ask that." She shot him a hopeful glance, nibbling at a morsel of rum cake. "I don't suppose you'd care to go first?"

"Okay," he consented, shoving his plate to one side. "It's quite simple. I have an inheritance at stake. I either marry or I lose it." His voice deepened, grew cool and stark. "And just so you know, I don't intend to lose it."

She lowered her fork and stared at him in astonished delight. "That's wonderful."

He leaned across the table, pinning her with a look of cold displeasure. "I'm about to lose my inheritance and you think it's wonderful?"

"No, no. You don't understand."

"Then explain it so I will."

"I have an inheritance, too. And the only way I can keep it, is if I marry." She peeked up at him. "Quite a coincidence, don't you think?"

He lifted a skeptical eyebrow, thinking it a little too convenient a coincidence. "Then why do you need a permanent marriage?"

"I told you. It doesn't have to be permanent. It's just . . ." She hesitated, as though choosing her words carefully, something he suspected she didn't bother with very often. "You see, there's this woman. Mrs. Marsh. She wants my inheritance and she'll do whatever it takes to get it away from me." She frowned, her expression turning fierce. "She's already scared off three fiancés. That's why I need someone strong, someone who'll help me fight her."

That explained a lot. Her previous fiancés sounded like total bastards, making promises they had no intention of keeping. All so they could entice her into their beds, he didn't doubt. "I don't scare easy," Jake commented. "And I've never yet failed to keep my word."

She grinned. "I hoped you'd say that. Which leaves only one problem."

Of course. While he'd been distracted by the more pleasurable aspects of having her as his wife, she'd been baiting her trap. A trap he'd almost fallen into. When would he learn? Nothing ever came without a price.

"What's your problem?" he asked grimly.

"You want a brief marriage. But I don't know how long it will take to get rid of Mrs. Marsh, to convince her that she can't take my inheritance away from me."

"I don't understand. Once you marry—"

"The inheritance is mine. Legally. But if she finds out it's only a temporary marriage, she'll never give up. She'll try to get her hands on it after we divorce. She'll argue that the marriage was just a ruse."

He shrugged. "Then we'll have to make sure she doesn't learn about the divorce."

Wynne nibbled on her lower lip. "If she does, I guess I could find myself another husband."

Jake stilled, fighting the surge of displeasure her comment stirred. He had no right to feel that way. Once she'd fulfilled her marital duty, it wasn't any of his business what Wynne chose to do. He'd help her get rid of this Marsh woman for now. Later could take care of itself. He hesitated, aware their deal wasn't the least equitable. He hadn't even warned her about having to stand up in court and confirm that they'd consummated the marriage. She still had the chance to find someone else, someone who'd stick around longer, who could guarantee Mrs. Marsh would never be a problem.

"I'm not right for you," he said in a low voice. He stood, pulling her to her feet. "Go back to the ballroom and take another look around. Maybe you'll find the perfect man, a permanent sort of man."

She shook her head and smiled. "I've already found the perfect man."

He'd give her one final chance to escape. If she stayed, she'd seal her own fate. It would be out of his hands and he could take her with a clear conscience. "Run away, little elf," he insisted curtly. "Go now, while you still can. You don't want me for your husband. I'll only hurt you."

"You could never hurt me," she said, lifting her face to his.

"You don't think so?" His hands closed on the narrow bones of her shoulders and he tugged her into his arms. "Let's find out."

And unable to resist any longer, he took her mouth with his.

Chapter Two

Wynne stood clasped in Jake's arms, reveling in the most incredible kiss she'd ever received. She'd known from the grim set of his jaw and the hard grasp of his hands he'd meant for it to be ruthless. He'd meant to scare her off. But somewhere between the time he'd pulled her close and the time he'd kissed her, his intentions must have changed.

He groaned, his mouth moving over hers with gentle warmth, probing, sampling, tasting at will. It was as though he were indulging in a leisurely exploration, stirring her in ways that emptied every thought from her head save one—to experience more. He must have sensed her total capitulation, for his touch grew more assured, firmer, coaxing a response unlike any she'd known before.

Did he suspect how thoroughly shaken she was by his kiss, how new and wonderful she found it? He'd been so concerned about her level of sexual expertise earlier, so appalled that she might still be a virgin. And yet, his kiss seemed to take that possibility into consideration, easing from the lightest of caresses to a more potent, heady embrace.

She stood on tiptoe, pressing closer, determined to enjoy every aspect of this unexpected treat. In response, he molded her against him, his body hard, his arousal blatant. His hands swept over her with unmistakable skill, as though committing each curve to memory. His touch burned, igniting a reaction that grew more intense by the moment. She trembled uncontrollably, desire overriding every other thought and emotion.

"Jake, please!"

The cry escaped before she could prevent it. For a crazed instant she thought he'd tumble them into the bushes and take her right then and there. Instead, he tensed and pushed her away, cool air replacing the unbearable heat of seconds ago. She fought him, refusing to leave the protective warmth of his arms.

"We can't take this any further, Wynne," he murmured close to her ear. "This isn't what I'd planned."

She clung to him, shivering, struggling to regain her equilibrium. "What did you plan?"

"To drive you off." His response was stark, yet painfully honest.

"Oh." She snuggled deeper into his arms, burying her face in the curve of his shoulder. She fit as though made for him. "You didn't succeed."

"I can see that," he said with a soft laugh. "Does this mean we're committed?"

She forced herself to consider his question rationally, to control the emotional upheaval clouding her mind. Her mouth curved in a wry smile. It was an impossible task. How could she think when all she wanted was to lose herself in his embrace? She'd never fallen in love before, certainly not with a man she'd only known for a few brief hours. She didn't have a clue how to separate reason from sentiment.

"Wynne?" Tension rippled through him and his arms tightened around her. "Have you changed your mind?"

She shook her head. "No. I haven't changed my mind." Pulling back, she looked up at him. "You said 'committed.' Is that a proposal, by any chance?"

He hesitated. "It's a proposition for a temporary marriage."

She wouldn't get any more from him than that. At least, not yet. Not that it mattered. She'd have plenty of time to prove he needed her on a permanent basis. After all, who knew how long it would take to convince Mrs. Marsh that their marriage was real? A week, a month, six months? Those six months could become six years, she was certain of it. And six years could become sixty.

"In that case, I accept," she agreed. "Though I'll be happy to stick around longer if you want."

"I won't." Steel had crept into his voice. "Don't think you can alter my decision about this, Wynne. It won't happen. This marriage is a temporary arrangement."

"Whatever you say." She sighed, sliding her fingers through his crisp, dark hair. "Would you kiss me again? I rather liked it. It was nice."

He frowned. "Nice, huh? Remind me not to ask you for a reference."

Color tinted her cheeks. "Well, I liked kissing you enough to want it to go on for the rest of the night."

"It can."

If he meant to alarm her with his bluntness, he failed. Miserably. She stared in wonder, lifting her mouth to his. "Really? All night?"

He set her from him, his fierce gaze telling her all too clearly how much of a temptation he found her, a temptation he intended to resist. "All we have to do is get this farce of a wedding over with. I have a room at the Grand Hotel and we'll go there the minute we're married. Once that's out of the way, we can make this night last as long as you'd like."

Her smile grew luminous. "That's just perfect. I'm staying at the Grand, too."

"Listen to me, Wynne . . ." His tone cut through her euphoria, sounding deadly serious. "There's one or two details we need to discuss."

"Is that all?" she teased in an effort to hide her nervousness. "Just one or two?"

"When we get to the Grand . . ." He hesitated as though searching for words, then stated flatly, "I expect to consummate the marriage. If you're not certain you can handle that, now's the time to back out."

"I won't back out," she replied instantly.

Why would she? He was perfect. He was everything she'd always wanted in a man. She'd discovered her knight in shining armor, just as she'd known she would. No. Without a doubt, she'd find joy in this marriage and with this man, no matter how long their time together might last. An impish smile played about her mouth. Of course, she intended it to last a bit longer than he did.

"That's one detail taken care of." She tilted her head to one side. "What else is there?"

"I have a prenuptial agreement I want you to sign."

She shrugged. "No problem. Give me a pen and I'll sign it."

His mouth tightened. "You won't sign a damned thing until you've read it,"

"Fine, I'll read it. Why? What does it say?"

"That when we divorce, my inheritance stays with me." His gaze met hers, his eyes direct and unflinching in their regard. "All of it."

"Well, of course. That's the whole point of the marriage, right?"

He gathered her hands in his. "It occurred to me that you might be marrying for more than just an inheritance."

She stared down at their joined hands. Hers were engulfed in his, and she frowned at how red and chapped her skin remained despite all the moisturizer she'd used. Did he despise the roughness? She'd always thought it a small price to pay when balanced against all she stood to gain.

"I told you why I need a husband," she said, not quite certain what he was implying. "What more could there be?"

"Maybe you're tired of working so hard to make ends meet and are looking for someone to help ease your burden." It was the gentlest of accusations and carefully phrased. Quite out of character for such a blunt, cut-to-the-chase type man.

"I see," she murmured. "You think because I work hard, I'm unhappy."

He shook his head. "Not unhappy. Just anxious to start a new life. Marriage can look damned appealing if it means escaping a lifetime of drudgery."

She smiled in relief. "I can understand why you might think that. And you're right. I do work hard to make ends meet." In fact, if he knew the whole truth, he'd consider her situation quite desperate. No money. No job. No place to live. But that was only a temporary condition.

"Is that why you're marrying, to escape your current life?"

"No," she stated without hesitation. "Some people might see marriage as a way out. But I'm not one of them. I have my health. I've never been afraid of hard work. And when things go wrong, I do whatever it takes to right my situation. Marriage only ensures I hold onto my inheritance."

She'd deal with the rest of her troubles when the time came When her marriage ended. If her marriage ended, she couldn't prevent the wistful thought.

"That's it? You're marrying in order to gain control of your inheritance. No strings attached?"

"I don't need your money," she said with absolute sincerity. "Or whatever else your inheritance might be. I just need you. If you'll give me the paper and a pen, I'll be happy to sign the agreement."

He studied her for a long moment, then nodded. "Fair enough. That's the last of my conditions. This would be a good time to name any you might have."

"All I want is your help fighting Mrs. Marsh," she said. "Once we're married, I expect you to stick by me."

A sardonic smile edged his mouth. "You have my unconditional support for the length of our marriage. Guaranteed."

She eyed him keenly. "Even if that isn't as short a time as you'd prefer?"

He didn't like the implication, but to her relief, he didn't argue. "Yes."

"I hope you mean that."

"You doubt my word?" he asked ominously.

She gave an awkward shrug. "It's not that. It's just that none of my former fiancés lived up to their promises. Mrs. Marsh scared them all off."

"I'm not those other men," he snapped. "I keep my word."

She prayed he'd still feel that way once he knew the complete truth. But somehow, she doubted it. "Do we have a deal, then?"

"We do."

She smiled up at him, daring to tease. "Shall we seal it with another kiss?"

His eyes glittered dangerously. "Not wise, elf."

"Maybe not." Her smile grew to a teasing grin. "But it is enjoyable."

He shook his head. "I prefer we do this by the book. First, we'll take care of the prenuptial agreement. Then we'll have a wedding."

"And the kiss?"

Passion marked his expression, burning in the fevered gold of his eyes. "Once we're back at the hotel and in the privacy of our own room, you can have as many as you want."

As many as she wanted ... The thought fired her imagination. It seemed too good to be true. Soon she'd be married to Jake, she'd make love to him. Excitement stirred, and with that excitement came a fragile hope that their relationship would be blessed, that she could fill the emptiness he carried like a leaden weight and vanquish his demons. That a special joy would come from their joining, a joy unlike any they'd known before.

He needs me, she repeated silently. And I need him.

"Sit down and take a look at these papers," he requested, spreading them out on the table.

She resumed her seat and tilted the documents so the glow from a nearby lantern fell across them. To her relief, the agreement appeared simple and straightforward. Jake stood over her, insisting she read every word. Once done, she signed without a qualm, then glanced up at him.

"What's next?"

"We have to fill out an application before we can marry. There's a county clerk stationed in the library with the necessary documentation."

Wynne smiled. "Which means all we have to do is find the library."

Footmen were quick to direct them and they discovered the county clerk seated behind a massive oak desk processing marriage applications. Her nametag read, Dora Scott, and she'd propped a sign next to her that announced, "For faster service, feed me hors d'oeuvres."

"Cute," Jake murmured, amused. He gestured for a footman and inclined his head toward the sign. "Bring a tray of your best."

Dora overheard and grinned. "I appreciate that. You two in a hurry or just kindhearted?"

Jake propped a hip on the desk. "No one has ever accused me of being kindhearted."

"Which leaves in a hurry," the clerk said with a laugh. "Well, it just so happens you've caught me during a lull. Let's see what I can do." With a speed that left Wynne breathless, Dora whipped through the formalities. Completing the paperwork, she explained each in detail and handed them a pretty blue-and-white envelope. "Give these forms to whomever you choose to officiate the ceremony. The gold sealed certificate is a souvenir for decoration only. You can frame it, hang it on your wall, or throw darts at it for all I care. But it's not a legal document, so don't go trying to palm it off as one."

"No problem," Jake said. "Thanks for your help."

"My pleasure. Just do me one favor."

"Sure."

The clerk held him with a piercing gaze. "Be happy. That's all I ask. Now go on and get out of here. I've got another couple waiting and by the look of the hors d'oeuvres he's carrying they're in an even bigger hurry than you two."

Documents in hand, Jake and Wynne crossed to the salons set aside for the wedding ceremonies. "It seems we have a choice," she murmured. "Religious, civil—"

"Or anything in between," Jake finished for her, his voice unexpectedly harsh. "Which do you prefer?"

She glanced at him, about to answer, then caught her breath in dismay. He stood unmoving, his jaw set in rigid lines, his shoulders tensed as though in anticipation of a blow. He dreaded this next part, she realized in dismay. She could see it in the turbulent glitter of his eyes and the rigid line of his mouth. Of all that had gone before, this would be the most difficult for him. Why? What painful memories lay beneath that stoic expression?

Tears of sympathy gathered in her eyes and she blinked to clear them before he noticed. He wouldn't appreciate her compassion. In fact, it might very well drive him away. If she wanted to help, she'd get this next part over with as quickly as possible. She sighed. All her life she'd dreamt of walking down the aisle of her hometown church. At the very least, she'd hoped for a quiet, religious service, its simplicity both moving and memorable. Now she knew she'd have neither. It would be asking too much.

"Why don't we have a civil ceremony," she suggested gently.

Jake nodded in agreement, relief easing the tension consuming him. He led the way into the appropriate salon, hesitating once inside the room. A frown creased his brow. She looked around, wondering what had caused his displeasure. The room was decorated in an elegant, if rather formal fashion. A pale blue silk couch and chairs stood in a group to one side of the room with small dried flower arrangements gracing the walnut end tables. At the opposite end of the room was a podium in front of drawn drapes, a justice of the peace officiating an unpretentious ceremony.

"Is there something wrong?" she whispered.

His frown deepened. "Let's take a look at the other rooms." He didn't wait for her response, but turned and led the way to the next salon.

Wynne stepped through the open doorway of the next chamber and caught her breath in delight, feeling as if she'd just escaped from the bleakness of a wintery landscape into the comforting warmth of a summer evening.

Subdued lighting flickered across a vaulted ceiling trimmed in cypress wood, a bank of windows stretching across one full wall of the room. Brass containers lined the base of the windows, overflowing with fresh flowers, their heady scent filling the air. In the middle stood the altar. Vivaldi played softly in the background like a benediction, and in that moment she knew. She wanted to be married here. It was the perfect place for a perfect wedding.

"We could look at the other rooms," she offered reluctantly. "See what other choices are available."

Jake shook her head. "No need. This will do."

Once again they'd arrived during a lull and the elderly minister motioned for them to approach the altar. She could see their reflection in the windows, pale and ghostly. And she could see beyond the glass, to a midnight sky lit by the moon and stars. Far below, the fairy lights twinkled among the trees and shrubs.

"It's like standing between heaven and earth," she whispered, tucking her hand into the crook of Jake's arm.

The minister smiled at her comment. "It is, isn't it? I think this is my favorite room for just that reason. Do you wish to be married?" he asked.

"Yes, please," Wynne said, as Jake handed over the necessary papers.

"Before we start, I'm required to ask that you give careful consideration to what you're about to do," the minister began, his gentle blue eyes turning somber. "Marriage is a serious commitment, not to be entered into lightly. So I ask that you face each other and look carefully at your partner. Make sure your choice is the right one."

Wynne turned and stared into Jake's eyes. They had darkened in color to a deep, rich shade of honey, all emotion held carefully in check. He was such a bewildering contradiction, confronting the world with uncompromising aggression and a fierceness that defied resistance. Even his eyes were those of a wild animal, spirited and untamed and predatory. And yet, his face suggested an austere nature, his expression stern and unapproachable, giving even the most combative personalities pause. He made his home in darkness and shadow, and she wondered if some painful incident in his past had forced him to turn his back on the light of human warmth.

Or was it that he wanted people to think the worst? came the stunning thought. Not that she ever could.

She offered a reassuring smile. He might intimidate some, but she'd sensed the goodness he worked so hard to conceal. From the moment she'd first seen him, she'd sensed his strength of character, his innate decency, and had known he'd make the perfect husband. She'd been so worried the man she selected would be getting the raw end of the deal and she would receive far more. But with Jake there was no cause for concern. She could give him his dream. His inheritance. Better yet, she could give him what he lacked most in life.

Love.

She glanced toward the minister. Was she certain of her choice? Without question. The answer was yes.

Jake stared at the woman clinging to his arm and then at the minister, dread balling in the pit of his stomach. Was he certain of his choice? Without question. The answer was no.

He found Wynne a bewildering contradiction—soft and sweet, and yet surprisingly sensuous. Her smile alone made him lose every thought in his head. She was a glorious mix of fire and innocence. A volatile combination. He frowned, realizing he hadn't been so rattled by a woman since adolescence. That alone should make him wary.

But what disturbed him the most were her eyes. A vivid green, they appeared as open and compelling as a child's. They shone with an inner purity his touch would surely corrupt. Worse, they held a shrewdness that swept past all barriers and stripped bare the blackness of his soul. He didn't understand it. If she saw him so clearly, why did she stay? He glanced at her again, stared into those huge, beautiful eyes, and what he saw made his chest tighten.

She may have agreed to temporary, but her eyes promised forever.

"Have you reached a decision?" the minister asked.

Jake started to answer, to end this farce before it went any further, but then realized he wasn't the one being addressed. Apparently the minister didn't doubt that Wynne would make an acceptable bride. No. His concern was whether the bride would regret saddling herself with such an unlikely husband. It shouldn't surprise him.

"Please begin the ceremony," Wynne said, perfectly calm and collected. Perfectly willing.

For an instant, Jake wavered between making the noble choice by backing out or remaining silent and letting her pay the ultimate price for her folly by marrying him. He gritted his teeth, torn. How could he allow her to commit such an ill-advised act? This marriage wouldn't be fair to her. She wouldn't get anything out of it other than a wealth of heartache. Hadn't he caused enough heartache without inflicting more?

What about the inheritance?

If he didn't marry Wynne, his chances of finding another bride before the deadline were next to nil. Besides, he wanted her. He wanted her in his bed and in his home. In that moment, he wanted her almost as much as he did his inheritance.

An instant later the choice vanished like darkness before dawn.

"I do," he heard her say.

She smiled up at him as she said it, her eyes shining, trapping him in a pool of glorious green sunshine. He stared back, his own responses to the minister barely registering.

"Before I pronounce you man and wife, would you care to exchange rings? We have them on hand," the minister offered, peering at them from over his spectacles. "They're tokens, really. Just something to use until you're able to replace them with the genuine article."

"That isn't necessary," Jake replied, digging into his pocket and pulling out a simple gold band. He'd picked an average-size ring, but to his amusement, it proved far too large, forcing Wynne to make a fist in order to keep it on. Not that it seemed to bother her.

"It's beautiful," she whispered. "I'll treasure it forever."

"You'll treasure it for the brief length of our marriage," he retorted in a hard voice.

She shook her head, leveling him with another of those bewitching smiles as sensuous as it was innocent. "No. I'll treasure this ring for the rest of my life because it's given me everything I've always wanted." Then her brow wrinkled in concern. "But what about you? Where's your ring?"

"I don't need one." Their marriage was a temporary measure, not worthy of a ring to symbolize the event.

Understanding dawned in her eyes and with that understanding came a terrible sadness, one that totally devastated his defenses.

And as the minister pronounced them husband and wife, Jake realized he was in deep, deep trouble.

Wynne knelt on the carpet, eyeing the hotel door in disgust. For the tenth time she stabbed the card into the locking mechanism and for the tenth time a red button flashed its rejection.

"Whatever happened to keys?" she muttered. "I liked keys. And keys liked me. At least they unlocked the—" The door opened and she practically tumbled into the room.

Laura stood there, dressed in a nightgown and robe. "Oh, thank goodness! I thought I heard you. I was getting worried." She frowned in concern. "What are you doing on the floor?"

"I'm trying to get this stupid thing to work," Wynne said, holding up the card key as she struggled to her feet.

Laura froze, staring at Wynne's hand. "You're wearing a ring! You did it, didn't you? You're married."

"Yes, I'm married." Wynne smiled, wriggling her fingers so the light flickered across her wedding band. It slid off her knuckle and she hastened to push it back in place. "Oh, Laura, I'm so glad you came with me. Now I can tell you all about him. He's wonderful. He's everything I'd hoped."

Laura grinned, tears leaping to her eyes. "I'm so relieved. I've spent the night worrying that some fast-talking rat would take advantage of you. Who is he? What does he do? How old is he?"

Wynne stared at her blankly. "I'm not sure. But, his name is Jake . . . Jake . . . Good grief. Considering we're married, you'd think I'd remember his last name," she muttered, then quickly corrected, *"Our* last name. Oh, never mind. His name's not important. It's Jake something-or-other."

Laura's tears evaporated, along with her smile. "Jake something-or-other? You can't remember your own husband's name and you don't think that's important?" she questioned ominously.

"No. What is important is that he's perfect. Absolutely perfect. And he's the sweetest man in the world." She hesitated. "Well, to be honest, I suppose he isn't all that sweet. No, sweet's the wrong word."

Laura groaned. "What's the right word?"

"Tough. Strong." Wynne smiled cheerfully. "Hard as nails would be a pretty accurate description. Mrs. Marsh doesn't stand a chance against him."

"Hard as nails, huh? That's good. I guess." Laura's voice held a marked lack of enthusiasm. "Where is he from?"

Wynne shrugged. "I never thought to ask. Someplace further down south, I think. He has an accent. Or rather a drawl."

"I don't believe this! You don't remember his name, never bothered to ask where he's from, or what he does for a living. Nor do you know how old he is. Is it just me or is there something wrong with this picture?" She tightened the belt of her bathrobe and glared at Wynne. "What, precisely, do you know about this man? Why does he need a wife?"

Wynne smiled in relief. "Now that one I can answer. He needs a wife in order to keep his inheritance."

"And what's his inheritance?"

"I . . . I don't know. Does it matter?"

"Of course it matters! What if—" Laura paused, her eyes narrowing. "There's something you're not telling me. What is it?"

Wynne peeked at her friend from beneath her lashes. "I'd really rather not say."

"I'd really rather you did." Laura folded her arms across her chest. "Please. Tell me. What are you hiding?"

"Just wait until you meet him. You'll think he's perfect, too," Wynne hastened to assure. "And he's a good man, though I suspect he wouldn't agree."

"He wouldn't agree? Wynne! What sort of person did you marry? Tough, hard, strong. He sounds like some sort of brute. And you still haven't answered my question. What have you left out?"

Wynne cleared her throat. "Not much. And he's not a brute! He's the kind of man who can take care of Mrs. Marsh. He's more than a match for her, even if he only wants a temporary marriage." She could see this latest piece of news didn't go over well.

Laura looked stunned. "A temporary marriage? You spent all your money on a *temporary marriage?* I can't believe this! What happens when it ends? You'll be right back where you started. No job. No money. No place to live. How will that help? Mrs. Marsh still wins and you'll have gone through all this for nothing."

"Jake won't let that happen," Wynne insisted stubbornly. "He says he isn't interested in a permanent relationship, but I think he'll change his mind."

"You're willing to gamble everything on a bunch of maybes? You're willing to risk losing—"

"I won't lose a thing," Wynne interrupted, her voice sharper than she'd intended. She took a deep breath, fighting for composure. "Please, Laura. Let's not argue. This is my wedding night and I'm so happy. Wait until you meet him. You'll see what I mean. You'll understand why I'm so certain he's the right man."

"You're spending the night with him?" Laura demanded apprehensively.

Wynne nodded. "He's asked me to and I've agreed. I came by to pick up my overnight bag and check on you. Is everything all right?"

"Oh, everything's fine here," Laura claimed. "Blissfully quiet. But what about you? Maybe you should—"

Wynne cut her off. "Maybe I should get my bag and join my husband," she said with gentle finality.

Laura raised her hands in surrender. "Okay. I give up. It's your life to live as you see fit."

"Don't be angry," Wynne pleaded. "You're my best friend. Try to be happy for me. I've been dreaming of this moment all my life. I have an incredible husband and a whole new life ahead of me."

"Right. Besides, look at the bright side," Laura said dryly. "If things don't work out, you have an automatic escape clause."

"Oh, I won't need it," Wynne claimed, flashing an impish smile. "And if I have anything to say about it, neither will Jake."

Chapter Three

Jake stood in front of the hotel window looking out at a starlit night, lost in the darkness of his thoughts. Would Wynne come? Or would she have second thoughts about the wisdom of their marriage and run?

He didn't want to care one way or the other. But he did. His future hung in the balance, the choices made by a pint-size elf the determining factor. He clenched his hands, jamming them into the pockets of his robe. Damn. He'd never felt so out-of-control in his life.

And he didn't like the feeling.

A knock sounded at the door. Not a soft, tentative rap, but a rapid, eager tattoo. Suppressing a smile of satisfaction, he strode to the door, flinging it open.

Wynne stood on the threshold, her green eyes peeping at him from beneath wispy white bangs. "Hi," she said.

He lounged in the doorway, his tension fading beneath the sunny warmth of her smile. "Hi, yourself."

She tilted her head to one side. "Were you afraid I wouldn't show?" she asked gently.

Was he so transparent? "The thought crossed my mind." He forced out the admission, and stepped aside so she could enter.

"You'll find I'm really quite trustworthy," she assured, glancing around the suite with interest. "But since you don't know me very well, I can understand you not realizing that."

"Thanks for filling me in," he retorted dryly, taking her bag.

Her gaze settled on him, the passion and vitality in that one look as powerful as a physical blow. It never ceased to amaze him how different she was from all the other women he'd known. How had so much zeal been bundled into such a tiny package?

"You've showered," she said, stating the obvious. "Would you mind if I did, too?"

"Be my guest. There's another of these hotel robes hanging on the door. Feel free to use it."

"Thanks, but I have a nightgown." She gestured toward the case he held. "If you wouldn't mind?"

"I don't mind." He tossed the bag to her. "But you won't need it. Not for long."

A hectic flush chased across her cheekbones and Jake regretted the crassness of his remark. There were times he felt like the proverbial bull in the china shop. This was definitely one of them. She gave a shrug that showed amazing sangfroid considering her obvious embarrassment, and crossed to the bathroom.

She seemed so young and fragile from the back, her shoulders fine-boned, the graceful sweep of her neck highlighted by the short pixyish cut of her hair. He'd never realized the nape of a woman's neck could look so vulnerable. A sudden urge to protect her gripped him, until he realized the only protection she needed was from her husband.

She hesitated at the doorway to the bathroom and glanced over her shoulder. "Oh, I meant to ask when I first arrived," she said unexpectedly. "What's your . . . *our* last name? I'm afraid I've forgotten."

His mouth tightened. "Hondo." He paused for a moment, then stated with cool deliberation, "It was my mother's name."

He couldn't tell whether she'd discerned the significance of his comment or whether she deliberately feigned ignorance. Or didn't it matter to her? He shook his head, unwilling to believe she found his parentage inconsequential. The people of Chesterfield considered it of critical importance.

"Hondo," she repeated. A tiny smile played around her mouth and his gut clenched at the guileless sensuality. "Wynne Hondo," she said, as though tasting the words. Then she laughed aloud. "It doesn't fit me half as well as it does you. But maybe it will in time."

She shouldered her overnight bag and disappeared into the bathroom, leaving him to mull over what she'd meant by "in time." It had better mean damned short and not a second longer. The splash of the shower interrupted his thoughts and he became instantly aware that every sound she made reverberated through the thin walls.

He could hear the material of her gown rustle as she removed it and pictured her stripping, baring soft, pearly skin. He knew the minute she stepped beneath the steamy spray, her murmur of pleasure as seductive as a siren's song. It took every ounce of willpower not to thrust open the door and join her. Would she complain, or would she welcome him? He reached for the knob, determined to find out.

She'd be slippery with soap, wet and sleek. If he found her willing, he'd take her in his arms and make her his wife in fact as well as name. But before he could follow through, the water stopped and he hesitated, annoyed the choice had been taken from him. He released the knob and stepped back and after a few short moments she emerged from the bathroom.

He froze at the sight of her, unable to draw breath, feeling as though someone had smashed an iron fist into his chest. He seesawed on the edge of control, rock-hard with desire, passion driving him to the point of no return. Only one thing kept him from plunging over the edge and taking what he wanted . . . .

Wynne's nightgown.

His wife stood uncertainly in the doorway, enveloped in whisper-thin cotton. The nightgown floated around her like mist, clinging for a moment as it caressed the pure, graceful curves of her body before swirling away. One detail in particular stopped him dead in his tracks. The damned thing was white. Stark white. Snow white. Unadulterated, unsullied, virginal white, the color as untainted as the woman who wore it. Three men, he struggled to remind himself. She'd said three men. He shook his head in disbelief. It couldn't be. It wasn't possible.

Because once they'd touched her, how the hell could they have walked away?

She moved into the room. Light from the bedside table threw her body into silhouette, almost bringing him to his knees. It was the most erotic sight he'd ever beheld, crippling in its impact. For such a little thing, her figure was all woman. She had a narrow waist that flared into sweetly rounded hips, her backside exhibiting just the right amount of curve. Her breasts shifted beneath her nightgown, the nipples dark shadows that pearled before his eyes. With a muttered exclamation, he forced his attention upward and away from temptation.

She stood quietly, staring at him, her eyes huge and wary, her hair tousled and damp from her shower. He didn't say a word, but simply held out his hand. After a momentary hesitation, she slipped her fingers into his.

"I see why you wanted to wear this instead of a robe," he said, his voice husky with need. "It's very provocative."

"Really?" She glanced down, her brows drawn together. "I always thought it rather modest."

He chuckled. "Your definition of modest must differ from mine." He reached for her, running his index finger along the curve of her breast, pausing at the peak to draw lazy circles around the rigid tip.

Her head jerked upward and she stared at him, her eyes enormous, the green turning as dark as a shadow draped forest. She moistened her lips. "Could we turn off the lights?" she requested anxiously.

"The lights stay on. I want to see you when we make love."

She didn't argue, but some of the color ebbed from her face. "I didn't expect to feel this nervous," she confessed. "But I can't seem to stop shaking. Are you sure we can't turn off the lights? Just this once?"

His mouth tightened and he left her for a moment, flicking the switch on the bedside lamp. The room plunged into darkness, relieved only by the faint illumination from a fast sinking moon. "Better?"

"Much, thank you." She drifted across the room, the conspicuous white of her nightgown marking her progress. "Should I get into bed?"

She marked the question with an undercurrent of breathless uncertainty and he bit back a caustic comeback. Something was out of kilter but he remained too hard-ridden by desire to analyze what it might be. "Sure. Get into bed if it makes you more comfortable."

"Actually I'm thirsty," she said, veering toward the bathroom. "I think I'd like some—"

He blocked her path, catching her off guard. She looked at him, startled, and her breath came swift and uneven. He didn't hesitate, but took her mouth in a demanding kiss. He felt, rather than heard, her small murmur of protest. She stiffened, not quite fighting him, but not responding as she had at the Montagues'.

He lifted his head and stared down at her. "Relax," he murmured, stroking his thumb along the tender curve of her cheek. "You want this as much as I do."

"I thought I did," she said, a tiny catch robbing the certainty from her voice. "I seem to be having second thoughts."

"You won't for long."

His mouth dropped over hers once again and he molded her closer, exploring the shapely curves beneath the thin cotton nightgown. If he'd had any lingering qualms about taking advantage of her, they vanished, dissolving beneath his desperate need to possess the woman in his arms. She belonged to him now, and he meant to take what was his.

He released the buttons fastening the bodice of her nightgown and swept the material from her shoulders, baring her to his intent gaze. Moonlight lanced across the paleness of her skin, carving tempting shadows between her gently rounded breasts. He groaned, lowering his mouth to taste her perfection.

She seemed to shudder, though she didn't make a sound, merely lifted a hand to brush the hair from his brow. The muted gleam of her wedding band distracted him and he pulled back, looking at her, seeing her clearly for the first time that night.

And what he saw stopped him cold.

A solitary tear traced a path down the waxen curve of her cheek, and he took a quick step back, disgusted by what he'd been about to do. Despite that disgust, every instinct he possessed railed at him to finish what he'd started, to put his mark on her in the most basic way possible.

He'd never considered himself noble or honorable or decent. Tonight confirmed that beyond any doubt. Only one problem rooted him in place. He looked into Wynne's wide, unflinching eyes and saw not passion or excitement or even curiosity. Definitely not lust. Instead he caught the damp glitter of stoic acceptance. The sight very nearly unmanned him.

What the hell had he done, marrying her like this?

He took another step back and then another and another until he'd put as much room between them as he could. "Get in the bed," he whispered harshly.

Still she didn't speak, merely drew her nightgown back in place and obeyed. She clambered onto the mattress, and in that moment, he knew. He couldn't touch her, couldn't risk hurting her. Not now. Not even if it meant losing the inheritance he'd fought so hard to win.

He forced himself to turn his back on her, staring instead at the desert skirting the hotel, feeling oddly at one with the bleak beauty. Slowly the serenity of the landscape crept into his soul, calming him, and he gained a small measure of control. Only the strongest and most determined survived in such an arid section of the country, just as only through sheer strength and determination had he survived the aridness of his youth. But his survival had never been at anyone's expense but his own.

Until now.

"Jake?"

He didn't turn around. "Go to sleep, elf. We'll talk in the morning."

He heard the rustle of sheets as she left the bed and approached. Her icy hand slipped part way around his bicep. "Have I done something wrong?" she questioned quietly.

His laugh rang out, cold and humorless. "Yeah, you did something wrong. You married me."

"No," she protested. "Marrying you was the smartest thing I ever did."

He spun around, grabbing her shoulders. "Don't you get it? Don't you realize what happened here tonight? I almost . . . I almost . . ." He couldn't speak the words, couldn't admit he'd nearly committed such a vile act.

"Don't say it," she urged, pressing her fingertips to his mouth. "You did nothing wrong. I'm your wife, remember? You could never hurt me."

"If that's what you believe, then you're setting yourself up for a mighty big fall." He stepped away, warning, "It's not wise to stand this close, not the way I'm feeling right now. Wife or not, it's clear I can't be trusted."

She stood her ground. "Don't be ridiculous. I'd trust you with my life. Please come to bed with me, Jake. I don't want to sleep alone on our wedding night."

He shook his head. "You don't know what you're asking."

"No, I don't suppose I do. Come, anyway." She tilted her head to one side and a smile trembled at the corners of her mouth, erasing all vestiges of her earlier tears. "I promise I won't take advantage of you."

Not bothering to argue further, he swept her into his arms and carried her to the bed. Tucking her carefully beneath the covers, he started to return to his stance by the window, but found it impossible to leave her side. Instead he stripped off his robe and joined her between the sheets. More than anything he wanted to pull her into his arms, even though it would be begging for trouble. He'd narrowly escaped their last encounter with his sanity intact. He'd never escape this time if he gave in and held her again.

"Jake?"

"I'm right here," he murmured gently. "Try to get some sleep."

"What about your requirement? That we make love tonight?"

"Forget it," he said, slinging an arm across his eyes. He suddenly realized he'd never explained about the condition in his grandfather's will—that their marriage be consummated and she testify to that fact before a judge. Not that it mattered now, because clearly, there wouldn't be any consummating. "It was an unreasonable demand."

"If you say so. But if you change your mind—"

"I won't," he cut her off.

Silence reigned for a moment or two, then, "Jake?"

"What is it?"

"I really am glad I married you."

He swallowed the thickness blocking his throat. "Me, too, elf. Me, too."

Jake awoke in that timeless moment between the black of night and the first light of dawn, not quite certain what had disturbed him. A whispery sigh drifted from the other side of the mattress and he turned his head. Wynne lay facing him, sound asleep. In that instant reality came crashing down.

He was married, a condition he'd sworn he'd avoid, and this slip of a woman was his wife. He gritted his teeth, calling himself every kind of a fool. What had he been thinking, marrying someone so clearly out of her element? He must have lost his mind.

She murmured a name, his name, perhaps, and he propped himself on one elbow, studying her. She'd kicked off her covers during the night and her nightgown had ridden up, hugging her slender hips. She had beautiful legs, lean and lightly muscled, legs that begged to be touched. He gave in to their allure, stroking the silken skin of her thigh, inching his hand ever upward. Slowly, carefully, he slipped beneath the thin cotton nightgown, his palm caressing the curve of her hip.

She felt like heaven.

He closed his eyes, overwhelmed by the need to make this woman his. He wanted her. He wanted her as desperately now as he had last night.

She was his wife, damn it all. He could take her and no one would object, including his lovely bride. But to fondle her as she slept, when she wasn't in a position to object . . . What sort of lowlife was he? Using every ounce of strength, he removed his hand and opened his eyes.

Wynne's sleepy gaze met his.

Her expression held open curiosity and he stilled, reining in his desires, forcing his features into an impassive mask. His control was pointless. She inhaled sharply, comprehension dawning with the first glimmer of morning light. Her spring-green eyes never wavered, hope shimmering in their depths, and she shifted closer, trapped within the stream of scarlet rays just peeking over the windowsill. Sunrise bathed her in a russet glow, licking across her hair and skin like a flame.

She greeted him with a shy smile. "Good morning, Mr. Hondo."

"Mornin', Mrs. Hondo," he replied gruffly. "How did you sleep?"

"Not bad. Thank you for joining me. I was afraid you wouldn't."

"I almost didn't."

"What changed your mind?"

"You asked so nicely. How could I refuse?"

She grinned in response and brushed a lock of hair from her eyes. The unstudied movement caused the bodice of her nightgown to gape, exposing her breasts. They were lovely, pale and round, the nipples the color of sun-ripened peaches. Unable to resist, he reached out and filled his palm, anticipating some sort of protest. It never came. Her only reaction was a muffled gasp, while her eyes grew dark and slumberous.

He glanced down at his hand, his copper-tinged skin a sharp contrast to the pure whiteness of her breast. She was beautiful, beautiful to the eyes and exquisite to the touch. As one timeless moment followed another, he silently raged at himself for allowing lust to overrule common sense. With a bitten off curse, he released her.

"Don't stop," she murmured shyly.

His mouth tightened. "You're joking, right?"

"I'm not afraid anymore."

He jackknifed upright, looming over her, infusing his voice with a strong warning. "You will be if I don't stop. I guarantee it."

"You wouldn't hurt me."

"Oh, no?" He laughed at her naïveté, the sound barren and humorless. "We've had this conversation before, remember? I'm not capable of doing anything else."

"Others may believe that, but I don't." She reached for him, stroking the tense muscles of his arm. When he didn't protest, she leaned closer, emboldened, pressing feather-light kisses the length of his raspy jawline.

He managed to shove a single word past tightly clenched teeth. "Don't."

"I just wanted to show I wasn't afraid."

"Aren't you?" It would be so easy to prove her wrong. His resolve hardened. Maybe if he did, it would settle the situation between them once and for all. He didn't delay any further. In one lightning-fast move, he tossed her backward. Crouching above, he planted his hands on either side of her head, settling the lower half of his body on top of hers. Only her cotton nightgown separated them. It was a flimsy barrier, about as flimsy as his self-control. "Afraid now?" he demanded.

She shook her head, but he noticed that some of her confidence had fled.

"You should be."

Shadows briefly marred the serenity of her expression before vanishing in the face of absolute certainty. "I need you, Jake." She reached for him, tracing the taut angles of his face from cheekbone to chin. "And you need me."

The wild animal came roaring back, feral gold eyes glaring down at her. "Why are you doing this?" he snarled. "Don't you understand? Don't you get it? This marriage should never have happened. I'm not a safe man to be around."

"Do you want to hurt me?" she asked curiously. "Does it give you pleasure to hurt people?"

A muscle jerked in his cheek. "No."

"Then don't."

"It's not that simple."

"Isn't it?" Her other hand settled on his hip, gliding upward, tracing the contoured muscles from abdomen to chest.

His breathing grew strained and he caught her hand, stilling its insidious exploration. "I can't . . . I don't . . . Damn, but you're pushing your luck."

"I guess I am. But tell me something. If I said you were hurting me, would you stop?"

His throat worked for a moment as though answering were a struggle. Finally he nodded. "Yeah. I'd stop."

She smiled, her expression so radiant, it blinded him to everything else. "Then I'll make a deal with you. The minute you do something that hurts me, I'll ask you to stop. And if I do anything that hurts you, just say the word. All right?"

A harsh, disbelieving laugh burst from him. "You can't be serious—"

"I'm very serious." She gazed at him, her eyes clear and direct. It was a probing look, one that threatened to pierce straight to his very soul—assuming he still had anything worthy of such a name. And then she said something that knocked him over the edge. "I trust you, Jake."

So simple. So absolute. So innocent and trusting. And so devastating. It broke him, splintering the rock-solid shell he'd spent his entire life erecting.

From the first moment he'd seen her, he'd wanted her. Of course, it had been sheer desire, a physical need, savage and elemental and basic. He hadn't tried to fool himself about that, had never held with the sort of man who wrapped lust in pretty lies. No, he'd always been blunt and honest, both with himself and with his women. He took what he wanted without concern for the consequences before walking away, heart-whole and fancy-free. It had been his credo as long as he could remember.

But with Wynne . . .

He couldn't. He couldn't take her with the same thoughtless disregard. She wasn't like the other women he'd had. They'd all known the score. If they'd secretly hoped to change his mind, he'd been quick to disabuse them of the notion.

"Jake?"

He fought for strength, fought harder than he ever had before. If he never committed another noble or honorable act again in his life, so help him, he'd get this one moment right. "Are you sure?"

"Positive."

"If you want me to stop, say the word and I'll stop." He hoped. With infinite care, he gathered her close. "Just do me one favor."

"What?"

"Don't wait too long. My off switch isn't all that trustworthy."

Her soft laugh stroked across him, as arousing as a caress. "You won't need it. I promise."

"I hope you take your promises seriously," he muttered and lowered his head, kissing her with unchecked passion.

He'd finished talking. If he frightened her, it would be best to know now while he still had the self-possession to leave her untouched. Instead of pulling back, she wrapped her arms around him and gave him kiss for kiss.

Wynne was lost. Lost in a sensuous haze of mouths and tongues and tender caresses. She lay on her back, the hem of her nightgown drifting ever upward, the neckline falling further open while Jake explored at will, touching, caressing. His mouth and tongue skating over her bared skin, nudging aside the thin cotton until he found her breast. He captured her nipple between his teeth and tugged gently.

"Yes!" The small cry escaped unbidden, filled with eager passion.

"Too many clothes," he muttered, the warmth of his breath spreading across her breast.

The next instant there weren't any clothes.

"Jake . . ." His name came out half-strangled. "Please."

"I want to please you. Tell me it's what you want, too." He surged upward, lifting half off her. Cool air swirled into the breach, a biting foil to the explosive heat simmering between them. "What's your final answer, wife?"

"Wait."

She groaned in dismay, knowing that wasn't what she'd meant, that she'd only said it to keep him from leaving her side. Everything was so mixed up. So confused. Words didn't make sense any more. Nothing made sense.

Except for Jake.

"You want me to stop?" His voice sounded strained, urgent. "Don't play games with me, damn it!"

Her head shifted restlessly against the sheets. "No. Don't stop." Finally the words came out right, fervent in their demand. With an aggression that amazed her, she pulled him back into her arms, shifting to accommodate his weight. "Don't ever stop."

His mouth found hers, absorbing her whimpered pleas before slipping downward. He anointed her rounded contours with his tongue, savoring each gentle dip and curve as though it were an exotic spice. His touch left behind a trail of insidious devastation as he explored places never seen by a man, let alone kissed. And all the while a burning need licked at her. She trembled helplessly when Jake fed that fire, building it higher and brighter and hotter. Desire became a ravenous hunger unlike any she'd ever known, a hunger she'd do anything to sate.

"Jake!" She sobbed out his name, begging for that ultimate gratification.

"It's coming, sweetheart. I promise, it's coming."

Still his hands played, tripping along nerves stretched to the brink. As though sensing she'd reached the end of her endurance, he positioned himself between her thighs. For an endless moment she lay spread beneath him, trembling helplessly on the verge of some great cataclysm. Then he drove into her with one surging thrust.

He tensed as he absorbed the shock of her innocence, his eyes blazing like golden flames through a tumble of black hair. "What—"

"It's all right," she tried to reassure. "Please, Jake!"

Didn't he understand? The pain of his taking was nothing in comparison to the urgent need his possession had sparked. She smoldered with it. Desperate to convince him, she rocked her hips upward in silent appeal, begging for the completion hovering just out of reach. He wanted to pull away, she could tell, and she watched helplessly as he fought an inner battle, struggling to subdue the most powerful of nature's urges.

It was a battle he had no hope of winning.

"I can't," he muttered. "Heaven help me, I can't."

He shut his eyes, fighting for restraint, fighting to make her passage as painless as possible. But restraint was also beyond him. The breath exploded from his chest and he drove into her heat. "Forgive me, elf," he gasped out the words. "I never meant for this to happen."

They rode the crest together, out of control and not caring. It was a magical experience, a melding of heart and body and soul. And just as the sun loosened its full glory on the pair of lovers, they found sweet deliverance within its circle of golden light.

Wynne couldn't tell how much time passed or how long they lay entwined in each other's arms. With the sating of their passion, sanity slowly returned. Jake recovered first.

"You were a virgin," he accused, rolling free of her embrace.

Suddenly self-conscious, she tugged the sheet around her. Not that he seemed terribly concerned about modesty. "I didn't think you'd notice."

"You didn't think I'd . . ." Outrage battled disbelief. "Take my word for it, I noticed!"

"Does it matter that much?"

He came off the bed, snagging his robe from the floor as he did so. "We discussed this last night at the Montagues'," he said, thrusting his arm into the terry-cloth sleeve. "I told you flat out that I didn't want to be married to a virgin."

"You're not. At least, not anymore."

His scalding invectives brought a rosy glow to her cheeks. "Don't split hairs with me, lady. Damn it all, I don't want to be saddled with a virgin. I wouldn't know what to do with one."

She lifted onto her elbows and gave him a mischievous grin. "What you just did suits me fine. And as I keep pointing out, it's no longer an issue."

"That's not what I meant!" His anger simmered visibly, like heat roiling in the desert air. "You lied to me. You said you'd been engaged three different times."

"I didn't lie. I was engaged three times."

"And not one of them . . . They never . . . ?"

"Not one of them," she confirmed. "Ever."

"It staggers the imagination." He planted his hands on his hips and grimaced. "That doesn't change the fact I need an experienced woman. I need someone who's willing to admit in open court that I . . . That we . . ."

She tilted her head to one side. "Yes? That we what?"

"That we—"

A loud banging sounded at the door. "Aunt Wynne! Aunt Wynne! Wake up."

Jake stiffened. "Now who the hell is that?" Laser-sharp eyes focused on her. "Something I should know about?"

Wynne swallowed nervously. She really wished she'd had a little more time to prepare him. Because she suspected his annoyance over her innocence would be nothing compared to his annoyance over this next bit of news. Gathering every ounce of self-possession, she offered a tentative smile.

"That," she announced, "is my inheritance."

Chapter Four

Not waiting to see Jake's reaction to the news, Wynne jumped out of bed, dragging the sheet with her. Unlatching the door, she opened it a scant inch. "Hey, brat," she teased the boy planted squarely in front of the threshold. "You're up early."

"It weren't me," scorned Buster, hauling a younger boy out from behind him. "It was Chick. He got scared when he woke up and couldn't find you."

"What about Laura?" Wynne asked in concern. "She was there, wasn't she?"

Buster shrugged. "He didn't want Laura."

She switched her attention to the smaller of the two, and offered a reassuring smile, not at all surprised to see Chick's thumb firmly planted in his mouth. "Well, I'm here now. Just give me a minute to dress and I'll let you in so you can meet your new uncle, okay?"

That sparked some interest. "An uncle?" Buster questioned cautiously, exchanging a quick look with his brother. "How'd we get an uncle?"

"I married him last night. Remember? I told you I might. Now don't move. I'll be right back."

She decided not to introduce the boys to Jake until she'd changed into something more appropriate than a sheet. Leaving the door slightly ajar, she snatched up her overnight bag before shooting Jake a brief, nervous glance. He stood by the window facing her, his arms folded across his chest. His expression did not bode well for her future health.

Fleeing into the bathroom, she slammed the door closed. This was not good. Not good *at all*. She leaned against the cool, painted surface and nibbled her lower lip. How much had he heard and just how mad had it made him? Enough, she decided, and plenty mad. If she read that glitter in his eyes correctly, he was seriously ticked off. She sighed.

This was not going at all as she'd planned. Well, except for last night and this morning. That had exceeded every dream she'd ever envisioned and then some. She shoved her wedding band more securely onto her finger, her movement reflected in the mirror over the sink. Curious, she dropped her bag and crept closer, studying herself for any changes the past few hours had wrought.

Her hair couldn't have been more rumpled if she'd just come in from a fast ride in an open convertible. Beneath wispy bangs, her eyes glowed a vivid green, brimming with happiness and startling in their intensity. She looked as though she'd found the key to all the secrets in the universe and then some. Well, maybe she had. She'd certainly found a whole new world locked within Jake's arms.

She adjusted her grip on the sheet and it dipped lower, exposing a small patch of reddened skin. It was a brand of possession. Jake's possession. She swallowed, remembering the delicious rasp of his stubbled cheek against her breast.

Three different fiancés had attempted every wile under the sun to lure her into their beds and not once had she been tempted. But with Jake ... No wiles. No lures. Just a passionate, irresistible man with wicked gold eyes and a touch that drove every thought but one from her head. And look where that one thought had led her. Straight into marriage and then into his bed.

Had it been a mistake? She shook her head without a moment's hesitation. No. She hadn't made a mistake. She'd chosen a warrior to fight Mrs. Marsh and a husband who'd made her passage into marriage a memory more precious than anything that had gone before.

Jake pounded on the door. "Move it, elf," came his muffled order. "You can't hide in there forever. Get your tail out here and face the music."

She sighed. So much for precious memories.

Catapulted into action, she took the fastest shower on record and scrambled into her clothes, happiness gripping her despite her worries. The past twenty-four hours had been the most wondrous, enchanted moments of her entire life. The idea of a future filled with equally wondrous, enchanted moments brought a silly grin to her mouth.

It disappeared the instant she stepped from the bathroom.

"Who the hell is the kid at the door?" Jake demanded.

She hesitated, casting him a quick, sidelong glance, noticing he'd also taken time to dress. Well-worn jeans clung to his lean hips, delineating the powerful length of his thighs. His unbuttoned shirt proved more distracting since it did nothing to conceal the impressive breadth of his darkly furred chest.

"He's my nephew."

Jake's eyes narrowed as he shoved his feet into boots. "He has something to do with your inheritance?"

She shot a quick look at the gaping door, certain the boys were eavesdropping on every word of their conversation. "He *is* my inheritance, but, ah . . ." She wavered, torn between the desire to answer Jake's questions and her anxiety over leaving the boys standing in the hallway unattended. She'd learned from experience they didn't do well on their own. In fact, it was amazing they hadn't already lost patience with the delay and erupted into the room. "Could we discuss this later?"

"No. We'll discuss this right now."

"Then, could we make it fast? The boys are waiting."

"Tough," he retorted, then froze. "Whoa. Time out. You said *boys*. As in plural? There's more than one of 'em?"

"There's two. Buster and Chick." She edged toward the door. "Look, they're my sister's kids. She and her husband were killed a year ago and I'm their guardian. At least they were left to me in Tracy's will. Unfortunately, Mrs. Marsh—that's their other aunt—is doing everything in her power to gain custody of them. So, I married you to prevent her from succeeding. Okay?"

She never learned if he thought it okay or not. Another knock sounded at the door and Wynne flung it wide before

Jake could gather breath to protest. To her relief, Laura had joined the boys.

"About time," she groused, stepping into the room, a decidedly grumpy expression marring an otherwise pretty face. "The minute I turned my back, these two took off. Though how they found your room is beyond me."

"We asked the front desk," Buster explained. "They wouldn't tell us till I pinched Chick and he started hollerin'."

Chick sniffled in response, rubbing an apparently sore arm.

Jake took a step in their direction. "Would someone tell me what the hell—" Four sets of outraged eyes nailed him on the spot and he made a quick adjustment to his vocabulary. "What the . . . the *heck-fire* is going on?"

Laura gave Jake one long, horrified look before spinning to confront Wynne. "Please. Tell me this isn't your husband. He's not, is he?"

"Of course he's my husband." Wynne frowned. "Why?"

"Oh, no. This will never do."

"Finally," Jake said in satisfaction, folding his arms across his chest. "Someone who agrees with me."

"Why won't he do?" Wynne questioned. She stared at the man she'd married, searching for any visible flaws she might have overlooked the night before. As far as she could tell, there were none. He was as perfect now as he'd been when she'd first laid eyes on him.

"He's a Texan!" Laura stated as though that were explanation enough. "I'd know that accent anywhere."

"Now wait just a damn—darn minute," Jake growled, clearly insulted. "What's wrong with Texans?"

"Good question. What is wrong with Texans?" Wynne asked.

"What's wrong with them?" Laura grasped her friend's arm and hustled her to one side of the room. "Have you lost your mind?" she questioned in a distressed voice. "You can't throw a rope around a Texan and expect to lasso anything other than trouble."

"Don't be ridiculous," Wynne said with a laugh. "Jake won't give me a minute's trouble. He's here to help."

Jake stared at her in disbelief before informing her grimly, "Trust me, wife. The minute we're alone I intend to give you a sh—*truckload* of trouble. You lied to me. And I don't take kindly to lies."

"I didn't lie," she protested.

"Then you did some mighty fancy two-steppin' around the truth. In my book that's as good as a lie."

She sighed. "I just omitted one tiny detail."

"That detail being that your inheritance comes with arms, legs, and a whole lot of aggravation in between. Why didn't you 'fess up last night?" He nailed her with a hard glare. "I'll tell you why. Because if you had, you knew I'd walk away. Hell, I'd probably have run."

Laura groaned. "You are in way over your head here," she warned.

"Everything will work out," Wynne insisted, glancing pointedly at the boys. She offered a bracing smile in the hopes of easing their worried expressions. "Jake and I just need to talk this through. Alone and in private."

Laura gave a little snort. "A fat lot of good that'll do. You don't talk things over with Texans. They bark and you start jumping or suffer the consequences. I should know. I'm sorry to say I was married to one." She fixed Jake with a sour look. "Fortunately for my mental health it was brief. *Very* brief."

"Ah, jeez," Jake muttered in disgust.

"Just look at him," Laura continued as though he hadn't opened his mouth. "In case you failed to notice, this is one tough cowboy. He's more outlaw than savior. Why, I'll bet the man eats nails for breakfast, shoe leather for dinner, and bullets for between meal snacks."

"He hasn't eaten a single bullet that I'm aware of," Wynne retorted mildly. "Unless they were buried in the chocolate cake we had last night."

"They weren't," Jake reassured.

"You know what I mean," Laura snapped, glaring at him before returning her attention to Wynne. "He'll make mincemeat out of you in no time. And what about the boys?"

Wynne wrapped her arms around their shoulders, hugging them close. "What about them?"

"What sort of influence will he be on Chick and Buster?"

"A bad one," Jake admitted.

"Terrible," Laura concurred. "I suggest an immediate annulment. We'll find some other way to take care of Mrs. Marsh."

"Forget it."

"Not a chance."

Wynne smiled at her husband, pleased they were in temporary accord. "There, you see?" she said. "He's a man of his word. He promised to help me keep my inheritance and that's what he'll do. He's just a little surprised at what it entailed."

"That's the understatement of the century," Jake said.

"And how do you know that the minute Mrs. Marsh shows up, he won't dump you like all the others?" Laura questioned sharply.

"Because we made a deal." Wynne's voice reflected her absolute faith. "He has too much honor and integrity to leave me and the boys at the mercy of Mrs. Marsh. Right, Jake?"

He shut his eyes and rubbed a spot between his brows with his thumb. "I knew I should have kept walkin' the instant I saw her heading my way," he muttered. "Why didn't I?"

Wynne smiled. "Because I needed you and you needed me."

"No." Eyes as bright and golden as the midday sun seared her with unrelenting heat. "It's because I let the wrong part of my anatomy do my thinking for me."

"Wynne, get out of this marriage before it's too late," Laura pleaded.

"I can't." Her gaze never left Jake's. "If I leave him, he'll lose his inheritance."

"So what? Let him. He's strong. He's hardheaded. He can take care of himself."

"I'm sure he can," Wynne admitted.

"Then why go through with this?" Laura pressed. "Because you're kidding yourself, you know. He doesn't need you. His sort doesn't need anyone."

Wynne jabbed a finger in her friend's direction. "That's where you're wrong. He may not know it, but I have something he lacks, something he wants."

Laura groaned in frustration. "Open your eyes. Look at all you stand to lose if you go through with this. If you won't do what's best for yourself, then at least think about what's best for the boys."

Wynne spared her friend a brief glance. "I am thinking of the boys," she said gently. "In fact, they're my sole consideration. They need a man in their life, a role model. Someone they can look up to and emulate. Someone who can protect them." Her gaze swung back to Jake. "And that's exactly what I've gotten."

He flinched as though she'd struck him. "You don't know what you're talking about."

"Don't I?" She came to a decision. "Laura, please take the children back to our room," she instructed. "Jake and I need to discuss this privately. I'll join you there as soon as I can."

Laura planted her hands on her hips and shook her head. "And leave you alone with this . . . this *Texan?*" She spat the word like an imprecation. "Not a chance."

"There's nothing he can do to me that hasn't already been done."

"Don't count on it," Jake inserted.

"What about us?" Buster asked, dropping into the conversation. "Is that man gonna be our uncle or what? Chick wants to know."

"And I'll have an answer for Chick in a little while," Wynne replied. "But first I need to talk to Jake."

Laura took a deep breath and slowly released it. "All right, Wynne. We'll do it your way. The boys and I will go back to the room on one condition."

"Which is?"

"I want you to take a good, long look at Mr. Texan over there. You told me you were going to marry a Prince Charming." She stabbed a finger in Jake's direction. "Well, that's not him. And if you give him half a chance, I'm sure he'll prove it to you." With that she grasped each boy by the hand and hustled them through the door, slamming it behind her.

A tense silence descended, and Wynne took the opportunity to do as Laura had requested. She studied Jake curiously, wondering what qualities her friend had seen that had escaped her own discerning gaze.

True, at first glance he was an intimidating man. His height and breadth alone might give some people pause, especially when combined with his strange golden eyes—eyes that could change from arctic cold to broiling heat in the space of an instant. She also supposed his shadowed jaw and rumpled hair gave him the appearance of a man more comfortable living outside the boundaries of convention. Despite that, where Laura saw a hard, ruthless Texan, Wynne saw a strong, determined protector.

In fact, the only difference she noticed since last night was the distrustful expression glittering in his eyes. A deep-seated wariness mixed with jaded cynicism. She recognized that look. Jake had close and personal experience with bitter disappointment and expected to again in the near future.

From her?

He stood off to one side of the room, his jaw set at a combative angle, his body tensed in anticipation of a blow. It struck her as a customary stance for him, one he'd probably assumed with distressing frequency. He was demon-ridden, she sensed, battling both outer and inner conflicts. It saddened her. Had he always been a loner, at odds with the world, forced to fight his way through life? Somehow she suspected he had.

"Why would you be a bad influence on the boys?" she asked abruptly.

"What?"

She crossed to the bed and perched on the end of it. "Laura said you'd be a bad influence on Buster and Chick and you agreed with her. Why?"

"Because I don't know anything about kids or how to raise them."

"You were once a boy. Why can't you—"

"Take a page from what passed as my childhood?" Darkness descended on him. "You wouldn't want that. Not when it comes to my fathering someone you cared about."

She regarded him curiously. "Would you hurt the boys?"

"Not on purpose."

"Then—"

"That's not the point." He ran a hand through his hair, impatience edging his voice. "I attended that asinine party because I needed a temporary wife in order to gain control of my inheritance. To be brutally frank, I didn't give a damn who I married so long as she'd stick with me until the terms of the will were fulfilled."

"No problem."

"Big problem," he corrected. "You need a real husband. A full-time, forever type to give those kids a stable home. Well, I'm not it."

"You could be."

He shook his head in disgust. "Boy, are you barking up the wrong tree," he muttered. Taking a deep breath, he fixed her with a stern, no-nonsense stare. "This isn't some sort of fairy tale wedding, you know. There aren't any happy endings waiting around the next bend in the road. If you'd been straight with me from the beginning, told me what your inheritance was, you'd have saved us both a lot of trouble."

"This may not be what you initially anticipated, but—"

"It's nothing like I anticipated," he cut in. "I require a wife in my house and my bed for a brief stint. Period. End of relationship."

"And I've agreed to that," she insisted doggedly.

"Have you?" In two swift strides, he ate up the distance separating them. Clasping her shoulders, he hauled her to her feet, looking every inch the menacing outlaw Laura had accused him of being. "I want a woman in my life for as long as necessary and then I want her gone. No complications. No regrets. And no future. When our time is through, I'm walking away and I won't be looking back."

She nodded, her wide gaze glued to his. "You told me that already."

His mouth thinned. "But you weren't listening, were you? You've had your head in the clouds for so long, you couldn't find the ground if you landed on it face-first. And now I'm saddled with a wife who believes in fairy tales and a couple of kids in desperate need of a father."

"That's what I'd have preferred," she admitted, "but I'm willing to—"

"To what?" he demanded. "Continue playing your little games after I take you home with me? What's the plan now, to try to get me to agree to something more permanent over the next few months?"

She didn't dare admit the truth. Instead she gave a forlorn little shrug. "It doesn't matter what I'd hoped, Jake. I realize now it was a foolish dream. We'll do it your way."

"You're damned right we will. But just to set the record straight, let's hear the truth." He grasped her chin and forced her to meet his eyes. "You deliberately kept silent about those kids. And you did it because you knew it would be too risky to explain their existence before that wedding band hit your finger. Have I missed anything?"

Guilt swamped her. Her expression must have given her away because his eyes iced over. Misery filled her. Why, oh why had she agreed to Laura's stipulation? Judging by the look on Jake's face, it had been a costly error. She took a deep breath. "Yes, I deliberately didn't tell you about Buster and Chick. I would have been up-front about it, I swear. At least, I would have if I hadn't already lost three fiancés as a result of that sort of honesty."

His hands tightened, anger rippling across his countenance. "You didn't tell me about those kids because you accurately guessed that I'd never have married you. Then you wore that damned nightgown in an attempt to seduce me, knowing full well I'd do anything to have you. And once I'd had you, I'd be stuck with our bargain. Isn't that right, my sweet little virgin?"

She shook her head frantically, appalled by his reasoning. "No. That's not true. You said you needed to consummate the marriage. I was just—"

"Sacrificing yourself for the sake of the boys?" His mouth curled to one side. "How noble."

Tears gathered in her eyes, but she stubbornly refused to let them fall. "I've done everything you've requested. You warned me our marriage would only be temporary and I've agreed. You asked that we consummate the marriage and I did. What more do you want from me?"

His gaze turned steamy. "It isn't complicated. You figure it out."

"I mean, does our marriage stand or not?" she asked bluntly.

With a muttered exclamation, he released her. "I don't have much choice. If I let you go, I lose everything. And I'm too close to winning to allow that to happen." He crossed to the window and stared out at the landscape for endless moments before swinging around to face her. "Okay. The marriage stands, but fair warning. You deceived me once. Don't let it happen again. You won't like the consequences."

His threat barely impinged as she struggled to conceal her jubilation. "Fine," she agreed. "And just so you know, I would have been frank about the boys if you'd asked." She lifted her chin. "But you didn't."

His eyes narrowed, reflecting his skepticism. "I guess we'll never know for sure, will we?" He didn't give her a chance to debate the issue. "Well, wife, what now? I can't say this is a very auspicious beginning to our relationship."

Wynne reluctantly allowed him to change the subject. Besides, what good would debating the point do? He'd never believe her. "All I have asked, and still do ask, is that you protect us from Mrs. Marsh."

He released a gusty sigh. "I'm supposed to slay your dragons, is that it?"

Wynne nodded. "That's it."

"Tell me about this Mrs. Marsh. Who is she?"

"She's the boys' aunt, my brother-in-law's sister."

"And you call her Mrs. Marsh?"

"She discourages familiarity," Wynne explained wryly. "And she has both the money and the power to indulge her preferences. Right now, the preference she's indulging is a powerful maternal streak, and she's not happy that Tracy and Rob appointed me the boys' guardian."

"How did they die?"

"In a car crash." Her expression turned somber. "Chick was with them when it happened. He hasn't spoken since—except to Buster."

"Poor kid." Sympathy intensified the grim lines bracketing his mouth. "What's with the odd names? Or are they nicknames?"

"Nicknames. Benjamin Curtis and Charles William, alias Buster and Chick. Buster is eight and Chick just turned five. They're very close."

"I noticed. They never strayed more than a foot apart." He hooked a thumb through his belt loop and eyed her intently. "You ever have them in for counseling?"

She nodded. "Buster seems to have made quite a bit of progress, but Chick . . . Aside from the trauma of the accident, I think he's also afraid Mrs. Marsh will get hold of them again."

"Again?"

"She took care of them for several weeks right after the accident."

"Is she really that bad?"

Wynne shrugged. "She means well, I suppose, but we have our differences. One problem is that I've been home-schooling them this year because they couldn't bear to be separated. Mrs. Marsh objected. She feels the boys would be better off in a private school. It's one her brother attended, but neither of them wants to go. Nor do I think it would be a smart choice right now. Plus, she's . . . Well, she's rather strict."

"Strict isn't bad."

Wynne sighed. "You'd have to meet her to understand."

"I gather she wants custody?"

"Yes. After her brother died, she threatened to take me to court in order to keep the children. I've spent the last year doing everything I could to prevent that from happening."

"Not an easy task."

"No." That one word spoke volumes. "Besides the issue of school, finances are tight. Rob and Tracy left some insurance money in trust for the boys." Wynne made a face. "Mrs. Marsh had it frozen. Even if she hadn't, I wouldn't have wanted to dip into the money. Better to save it for their education."

"But it's made supporting them difficult," he guessed.

"I've managed."

"You're working like a dog and are broke. Is that about the size of it?"

He saw far too much, she realized uneasily. "Yes," she admitted. "I'm afraid it is."

"So your solution is to marry?"

She shot him a direct look. "I wasn't after a meal ticket, if that's what you're suggesting. The reason for the marriage was Mrs. Marsh. If I have a husband, she no longer has grounds for going after the children."

"And without one?"

"She has a case," Wynne admitted grudgingly.

He took a minute to absorb the information before nodding. "Okay. If this marriage is going to work, even temporarily, we'll both have to do our part. So, for the length of our association I'll do my best to protect you and the boys from Mrs. Marsh."

"And I'll uphold my end of the bargain, as well."

He cupped her face between callused hands. "This isn't what I'd planned. You know that, don't you?"

She could hear the frustration underlining his quietly spoken question, the thread of anger he still hadn't mastered. All the while, his eyes revealed another emotion altogether, one of blatant desire, a potent, overwhelming need he seemed helpless to control. Her reaction followed swiftly. Warmth pooled in the pit of her stomach, spreading outward with each beat of her heart. A helpless lassitude paralyzed her limbs, holding her in place. Even if she'd wanted to, she couldn't have pulled free of his grasp.

"Jake," she whispered.

His laugh was half groan. "I know, elf. I know. I don't understand it, either."

He nuzzled the curve of her throat, just below her ear and she gasped, her eyes falling closed. He hadn't buttoned his shirt and she spread her hands across his chest, fanning her fingers through the generous mat of hair. Her palms tingled from the delicious abrasion and she followed the compact line of muscles from shoulder to abdomen. He felt wonderful, strong and hard and deliciously male.

"You drive me crazy," he muttered.

Thrusting his hands beneath the bottom of her blouse, he skimmed the length of her spine until he found the fastening for her bra. With one quick flick, he unhooked it, freeing her breasts for a more thorough exploration. It was still too restrictive, the fitted blouse too great a barrier. He didn't waste time unfastening the buttons, but simply yanked her top over her head, baring her to his heated gaze.

"Jake—"

Dark color emphasized the high arch of his cheekbones. "Don't fight me. Not now."

"We can't." The objection sounded reluctant even to her own ears. "Laura and the boys are waiting."

"Let 'em wait."

"They might come back."

"I'll lock the door." He cupped her softness, his eyes a molten gold. "They'll get the message when we don't answer."

She struggled to think, to put words into a coherent whole. "You don't know Laura," she managed to say. "She's tenacious."

"We'll hang up the Do Not Disturb sign. She's no fool. She'll understand."

"That's what I'm worried about."

"Forget Laura," he demanded, passion adding a husky edge to his voice. "I have something more interesting in mind."

With that, his mouth closed over hers and all thought ended. Desire blossomed with stunning speed, returning more swiftly than before, burning higher and with greater ferocity. How was it possible to feel so at one with a man she'd only known for a few short hours?

"I've never seen a more perfectly made woman." His heated breath mingled with hers. "If it weren't for those kids, our time together would be downright perfect."

With those few heartfelt words he destroyed all her illusions, proving beyond a doubt how wrong she'd been about their relationship. Having a bucket of ice-cold water tipped over her head couldn't have sliced through her sensuous haze any more thoroughly. The air escaped her lungs in a harsh gasp. "Say you don't mean that," she whispered, distressed beyond measure.

It took him a minute to hear the misery in her voice, to realize she no longer actively participated in their lovemaking. He fought to control his desire, his muscles tense. Taking a deep breath, he pulled back, a rush of cool air filling the chasm between them.

"What?"

"Your comment about the children. Say you didn't mean it."

"You want me to lie?" he questioned sharply. "You want me to say that I'm thrilled to be saddled with a wife and two kids I'd never planned on having? Sorry. I'm not putting a pretty face on an ugly truth. I want you. No question about that. But I'd have been a whole hell of a lot happier if there weren't any strings attached."

She jerked free of his hold and swept up her blouse. "Everything comes at a price," she informed him tautly, dressing with more speed than grace.

"I'm well aware of that." A wealth of meaning lay buried in his retort, a history she could only guess at. "But you didn't tell me the cost until it was too late for a refund."

"Or you'd never have made the purchase?" she asked, bracing herself, as though in anticipation of a blow.

He didn't answer. Crossing the room, he picked up a canvas tote and his Stetson. "You ready to leave? Looks like we're done here."

She didn't bother arguing. Grabbing her overnight bag and purse, she nodded. "I'm ready," she said, following him to the door. "Though you haven't told me where we're going yet."

He paused. "Texas, as your friend so accurately guessed. Chesterfield, Texas, to be precise. I own a spread there."

She stared in wonder. "A ranch." It was almost too good to be true. "What a wonderful place to raise children."

His face darkened, his eyes deepening to a tarnished bronze. "I'll have to take your word for it. I was raised in the city." He yanked the door open, then hesitated, tossing the words over his shoulder. "Fair warning, wife. I'll do whatever's necessary to make this marriage as comfortable for you as possible. But don't expect me to give you what I don't have."

"You mean love?" she dared to ask.

"Love's an illusion," he retorted coldly. Then his voice dropped, turning gritty with tension. "Funny thing, illusions. No matter how hard you work at it, you can't believe them into existence. Try it and you'll end up with a world of hurt."

With that, he walked out the door.

Chapter Five

They flew to Texas on a large, commercial carrier, switching to a private puddle-jumper for the flight to Chesterfield. Jake had an extended cab pickup waiting for them at the tiny landing strip.

"Boys, hop in the back," he instructed, opening the door for them. He dumped their three small suitcases in the bed of the truck and opened the front passenger side door for Wynne. "You didn't bring much with you."

She shrugged, her attention focused on Chick. He still had trouble riding in cars, and she wasn't certain how he'd take to the pickup. "I thought it would be easier to travel light. The rest of our belongings are packed and ready to be shipped once I supply the moving company with an address."

"You can phone them as soon as we get to the house," he said. "Come on boys, shake a leg. Climb in and fasten seatbelts."

She held her breath, waiting to see what Chick would do. To her relief, he clambered inside without hesitation. Apparently, the truck didn't rouse the same frightening memories as a car.

Jake turned to face her, lifting an eyebrow in question. "What's the matter?" he asked in an undertone.

She looked at him, startled. "You don't miss much, do you?"

His mouth curved into a wry smile. "Depends on how distracted I am. Is there something wrong with Chick?"

She shrugged. "Cars don't always agree with him," she explained quietly. "They upset him."

Jake didn't appear surprised by her comment. "No problem. I don't own a car." He helped her into the cab. "And, since the pickup doesn't cause the same reaction, I'll let you drive it while you're here."

She poked her head out of the window. "But, what about you?"

"I have an old rust-bucket that I can use in the meantime. Or there's always my horse." With that he circled the truck and climbed behind the steering wheel. "Everybody ready? Seat belts fastened?"

"We're set, Uncle Jake," Buster said. "Where's your ranch? Chick wants to know."

"Not far. It'll take about a half hour to get there."

The time passed quickly, the boys watching every move Jake made with avid interest. Two minutes from the airport, the questions began, questions he answered simply and directly. Despite his annoyance over having acquired a ready-made family, he had been kindness itself to the boys on the flight, showing amazing patience while holding Chick's hand and listening to Buster's endless running commentary.

Clearly the boys had developed a severe case of hero worship. It worried her. Although Jake took naturally to the role, he wouldn't be in their lives for long. She sighed. She'd taken great pains to explain that their new uncle was only a temporary addition to their family. But she wasn't convinced they'd believed her. And why should they, when she didn't believe it herself?

Twenty minutes later, they passed through a small town. "This is Chesterfield," Jake volunteered with notable reluctance.

Wynne looked around eagerly, deciding the town had an abundance of character. It was small, but attractive, with all the shops freshly whitewashed and accented with either shutters or awnings or flower boxes. A clapboard livery with tall barnlike doors was sandwiched between an old-fashioned barber shop and a contemporary boutique. Across the street a general store with a two-story nineteenth-century facade stood cheek and jowl with a brand-new stucco bank. Most incongruous of all, a modern brick and glass structure housing a law firm sat opposite an outdoor market selling everything from flowers and produce to Mexican blankets and straw baskets.

It was unlike any place she'd ever seen. Horses stood placidly, hitched in parking spaces alongside cars. A huge bronze statue commemorating the Texas Rangers held a place of honor in the middle of the road. And an honest-to-goodness saloon with real swinging doors graced one end of town. It even had a cowboy lounging outside in a rocker. Best of all the Lone Star flag snapped proudly above the small courthouse.

"This is Chesterfield?" she questioned in wonder. "It's beautiful."

"Avoid it," Jake retorted with a sharp edge. "There's a sizable town about forty minutes south of the ranch called Two Forks. It has everything you need. Lots of malls and movie houses and such. You can go there whenever you get an itch to explore."

She twisted in her seat to catch a final glimpse of Chesterfield as it disappeared from view. "But why would I want to go to Two Forks when I could come here instead?"

"Because I said so."

His implacable tone ended the discussion. She frowned. He'd have to get over his autocratic ways and soon. She'd been remarkably tolerant, considering he'd taken on far more than he'd planned when he'd married her. Still, that didn't mean she'd jump every time he barked a command, or obey without question or comment.

"Is that it?" Buster asked just then. He leaned forward, staring out the windshield. "Is that your ranch?"

"Yeah. That's it. Welcome to Lost Trail Ranch." Jake spared Wynne a quick, cryptic glance. "I know it needs some repairs—"

"I think it's wonderful," she exclaimed.

"Look, Chick. There's a barn and everything," Buster said, pointing. "You have horses, Uncle Jake? And cows and pigs?"

"No pigs. It's a ranch, not a farm. But there's plenty of cows and horses."

He turned down a long dirt driveway dividing an endless expanse of pastureland and parked outside the ranch house. The boys tumbled from the truck and scampered up the sagging porch steps while Jake unloaded the suitcases. Wynne followed behind, bemused by her good fortune.

She'd married a man with a house. How lucky could she get? They'd be living in a real two-story, multi-room residence instead of a cramped apartment. She fought to control the surge of tears stinging her eyes.

"It even has an upstairs!" Buster informed his brother. "Come on." He grabbed Chick's hand and disappeared into the cavernous interior.

Jake stepped across the threshold and glanced her way. His set jaw and rigid stance spoke more loudly than words. He didn't like having her here. With a tiny sigh, she entered the house and looked around. The glaring afternoon sunlight followed them through the open doorway, cruelly accentuating the scarred pine floor and peeling wallpaper. Cobwebs trailed from the ceiling corners in ghostly tendrils and dust lay like a dingy gray blanket on every conceivable surface. Even the furniture appeared secondhand, mismatched and faded from use.

The house reminded her of a woman who, tired and careworn after years of hard living, had given up the effort.

"Look," he began in an undertone. "I know it's run-down—"

"It's beautiful," she whispered, seeing only the possibilities. "It just needs some tender loving care to give it new life."

"It's a dump. I just moved back in and haven't had a chance—"

"Look at the size of the rooms. Compared to where we were living, it's a palace." She craned her neck. "And those ceilings! They're so high."

"I know you're upset," Jake began.

"Where's the kitchen?"

He pointed to the right and trailed behind her as she continued to explore. "But it's only for a short time."

She dropped her purse on a scared kitchen table and made herself at home. "You've got plenty of food supplies," she said, checking the cupboards. "Rags?"

"Through that far door. In the mudroom." He stood in the middle of the kitchen, looking around in distaste. "I can hire some people to come out and help clean up a little."

"You even have a washer and dryer! I can't believe it." She practically danced across the kitchen floor. "And is that a fire-burning stove? I've never seen one before. How does it work?"

"Wood-burning," he said, correcting her. "It's a wood-burning stove and I'd rather you not fool with it. I'll get a microwave in here and you can cook with that."

"Oh, Jake. This is wonderful. A little soap and elbow grease and you won't recognize the place."

"I didn't marry you because I wanted a maid," he said more sharply than he'd intended.

Her smile didn't dim. "I know why you married me." She threw her arms around his neck. "A clean house will be my way of thanking you. I couldn't have asked for a more perfect home."

He muttered something beneath his breath and wrestled free of her stranglehold. Grasping her hands in his, he held her at a safe distance. "You don't need to put on an act for me. I know what this place looks like. It's a wonder you haven't turned tail and run." His mouth tightened. "But then, where would you go?"

She shrugged. "I haven't a clue. But fortunately, that's not a problem." She gazed up at him with eyes as clear and vivid as spring grass, and a face as open and innocent as a newborn. "You couldn't have given me anything nicer than this."

Feeling like a total heel, he released her and stepped back. "I'm going out," he informed her gruffly.

"Okay. When will you return?"

"I don't know."

"Well, while you're gone I'll just run into town for supplies."

"No!" His hands balled into fists as he fought for control. "I mean, you can get supplies at the supermarket in Two Forks. When you get to the end of the driveway, turn left."

"Right."

"No, left. Got it? Left."

She grinned. "Gotcha."

He thrust a hand through his hair. "I'll hire some people to clean the house. And I'll pick up dinner at the local takeout. You don't need to worry about a thing."

It was the least he could do, considering his duplicity. A tight knot formed in the pit of his stomach. Why was he doing this? Why drop her in a house that should have been condemned years ago when he could put her up in a place worthy of a queen? He knew why. If he took her anywhere else, it would give her false hope. It would suggest a permanence he could never allow. Didn't she understand? He wasn't the marrying kind. Eventually he'd let her down. He'd shatter every hope and dream she'd ever possessed. And he couldn't bear to look into those huge, limpid eyes of hers when he destroyed that final illusion. No. Once she'd existed in this hellhole for a while, she'd be desperate to leave.

And maybe one or two of those dreams would remain intact when she did.

"Why don't you look the place over and make a list of what you need?" His voice grated like steel wool on rust. "If you hit a snag, Dusty can help out. He should be around here someplace."

"Dusty?"

"My foreman. Big hat, little guy. Spits a lot. You can't miss him."

She grinned. "He sounds like quite a character."

"Yeah. He's a character, all right." Unable to help himself, he swept her into his arms and kissed her with unmistakable desperation. "You shouldn't have married me," he muttered when he finally released her. "You'll live to regret it. I guarantee."

"The only regret I'll have is when it's time to leave."

He closed his eyes. "But you will leave," he told her in an inflexible voice.

"Do I have a choice?"

He hardened himself against the wistful plea tugging at the chip of stone that had once passed for his heart. "No. You don't," he said and walked out the door.

"Uh-oh," Wynne murmured as she gripped the steering wheel and stared at her feet.

"What's wrong?" Buster demanded.

Chick pointed at the pedals on the floor.

Buster frowned. "There's three." He eyed his aunt, a concerned expression creeping across his face. "You know how to drive a three-pedal car?"

She sighed. "'Fraid not."

"That's okay. I watched how Uncle Jake did it. And Dad's car had an extra petal, too." He stabbed a finger toward the first one. "That there makes it go. The middle makes it stop. And you push in that last one when you move this stick." He yanked on the gear shift to demonstrate.

"I had that much figured out." She gnawed on her lower lip. "Maybe we should wait until Jake gets back. I don't think I can make it all the way into Two Forks on my own."

"I don't wanna go to Two Forks, anyway," Buster retorted. "And neither does Chick. Let's go to that other town. The one with the cowboy statue. We like that town."

"Me, too," Wynne confessed.

"It's not far. You can do it."

Chick nodded enthusiastically.

"Okay," she said with as much optimism as she could scrape together. "Here goes."

She pushed in the clutch and turned the key, giving the engine some gas. It roared to life. But the second she lifted her foot off the clutch the car lurched to a stop and stalled.

"You gotta push hard on the gas and let that other one out real slow," Buster instructed.

Wynne shook her head. "I don't know. I'm not sure about this."

Chick patted her on the shoulder, his big blue eyes mirroring his absolute faith in her ability. With a sigh, she tried again and managed to keep the truck going long enough to turn it in a wide half circle. Engine screaming, they bounced down the dirt driveway.

"Move the stick!" shouted Buster.

Pushing in the clutch, she jerked the stick into a new setting. The pickup bucked angrily and stalled yet again, rolling to a halt at the end of the driveway.

"You're...ah...you're getting better," Buster lied unconvincingly.

"But not good enough to risk going all the way to Two Forks, right?" she said dryly.

"No way."

Chick shook his head emphatically.

"I guess that narrows our choices down to one. Chesterfield. Agreed?"

"Agreed," Buster confirmed.

Restarting the engine, she ground her way into first and turned to the right. Four stalls later, they reached the outskirts of town. The pickup jerked to a stop in front of the outdoor market and, deciding she'd pushed her luck as far as it would go, she coasted into a parking spot.

"Made it," Wynne said with undisguised relief. "But there's one small problem."

"What's that?" Buster demanded.

"I don't know how to do reverse. We may be stuck here a while." She brightened. "In the meantime, let's find that general store. We have shopping to take care of."

Jake turned his back on the window overlooking the colorful booths of the outdoor market and thrust his hands into his pockets. "It isn't going to work, Peter. This marriage is a total disaster."

Alarm appeared on the lawyer's face. "What happened? Wouldn't she sign the prenuptial agreement?"

"She signed it."

"She knows the marriage is temporary? Is she going to create a scene when it's time for a divorce?"

"She's agreed to the divorce, and she won't kick up a fuss."

"What about fulfilling the conditions of the will? You two are . . . ah . . . wedded and bedded, right?"

Jake gritted his teeth, pushing the words out with an effort. "It's been taken care of."

"And she'll admit as much? In open court?"

Jake's mouth tightened. "We haven't discussed it, yet. But knowing Wynne, she'll do anything I ask."

Peter stared, nonplussed. "Even a real wife wouldn't do that. Where's the problem? Your bride sounds damn near perfect to me."

"She's . . ." He searched for the appropriate word. So many occurred. Sweet. Adorable. Innocent. Sexy as hell. He didn't dare use any of them. He settled for the blandest suitable description, even if a wholly inadequate one. "Nice. She's nice."

"Hell. That *is* a problem."

"I don't need your sarcasm, Bryant," Jake growled. "I'm serious. I'm in a real fix here."

"How? You wanted a plain, practical and levelheaded woman who'd agree to a temporary arrangement. Isn't that what you got?"

Jake frowned. "She isn't exactly plain," he admitted.

"No? You roped a pretty one, huh? What did you say her name was? Wynne?"

"Wynne Sommers. And she's . . ." He pictured her on their wedding night, reaching for him, eyes drugged with passion, lips full and ripe and moist, her body trembling with desire.

"Practical?"

Jake couldn't help smiling. "Not that I've noticed." Determined. Whimsical. Adorable. A starry-eyed dreamer.

"But at least she's levelheaded."

When her head wasn't in the clouds—a rare occurrence he suspected. "She's hard to describe."

Peter didn't bother to hide his confusion. "Uh-huh. Give it a shot, anyway."

"She's . . ."

"Nuts. Wait a minute, boys. We have another problem." Wynne opened her purse and thumbed through her wallet, counting the last few dollars she had to her name. "Thirteen, fourteen, fifteen. Fifteen dollars and sixty-seven cents. That's not going to go very far."

"Can you write a check?" Buster asked, ever practical.

"I closed my Maryland bank account. But maybe we can get some help." She grasped the boys by the hand and marched toward the front of the store. "Excuse me," she said to the woman behind the cash register. "Is the owner here?"

"You're speakin' to her, honey. Belle Blue's the name. What can I do you for?"

"I'm Wynne Hondo. And these are my nephews, Buster and Chick. We just moved to Chesterfield and I came shopping while my husband ran errands and—"

"Did you say Hondo?" Belle repeated sharply.

"That's right." Wynne smiled in delight. "Do you know Jake?"

"Black hair, a heart of stone, and the devil's own eyes? Sure, I know him."

Wynne frowned. "I think you must have him confused with someone else. Jake does have dark hair, but he's the kindest man in the world. And his eyes are the most beautiful shade of gold I've ever seen."

Belle stared in disbelief. "Somebody's confused, that's for darned sure. Who did you say you were?"

"Wynne Hondo."

"And you're Jake's . . ." She seemed to have trouble getting the appropriate word out.

"Wife. Yes. We just got married."

The woman eyed her suspiciously. "You have proof of that?"

"I think so." Wynne dug in her purse, searching for the envelope the county clerk had given her.

"Asa, come over here and listen to this," the woman called out. "Jake's gone and got himself a wife." She shook her head in wonder as a tall, gray-haired man joined them. "And Randolph claimed there wouldn't be time enough. He is gonna be fit to be tied."

Locating the gold-leafed certificate, Wynne offered it to Belle, aware that a small, curious crowd had started to collect around the register. "This is just for decoration, you understand. It's not a legal document and I'm not supposed to pass it off as one, but—"

"Honey, any woman brave enough to throw a lasso around a man like Jake Hondo deserves a frame for that piece of paper—legal or otherwise. Consider it a wedding present from me and Asa."

"Why, thank you. That's very kind of you." Wynne's smile wavered. "But I still have a small problem."

"How can I help?"

"I only have fifteen dollars and sixty-seven cents on me and I wondered—"

"We'll put your purchases on Jake's tab. No problem." She winked. "It's not like we won't know where to find you when the bill comes due at the end of the month. That Chesterfield spread sure is a beauty, isn't it?"

Wynne stared at the woman in bewilderment. "Excuse me?"

"The Chesterfield spread. The ranch house where you're living."

"Oh, you must mean Lost Trail. The boys and I love it."

Belle gave her a strange look. "You're stayin' at Jake's old place?"

"Well, it does need a lick and a shine." A small murmur ran through the crowd of shoppers. "But we'll get it into shape in no time," she hastened to reassure.

"Oh, you will, will you?" Belle shook her head and muttered, "That Jake Hondo is some piece of work."

Wynne laughed. "He's something else."

"She's . . . She's something else," Jake finally said.

"And this *something else* is a problem?" Peter guessed, struggling to uncover the source of Jake's displeasure. "I don't understand. Didn't she like the Chesterfield spread?"

"I don't know. We're living at my place."

Peter stared, openmouthed. "You took her to that dump? Have you lost your mind? No wonder she's upset. Take her to Chesterfield Ranch. She'll cheer right up."

If he took her to his grandfather's house, she'd never leave—an untenable situation. Because one day soon the knight's armor in which she'd sheathed him would begin to show its tarnish. He couldn't bear to live with her eventual disillusionment when she finally saw the man beneath the chain mail. The real man.

"Wynne's not upset," he retorted. "In fact, she likes my place. She's thrilled to be living in a house instead of an apartment. She's even going to clean it for me."

"What!"

"Not that I'd let her," he added defensively. "Which reminds me. I need to hire somebody to knock the place into shape. Give me some recommendations, will you?"

Peter's brow wrinkled in confusion. "Let me understand. You don't like this woman, right?"

"I didn't say that."

"But you're not in love with her."

Jake turned his back on Peter and poured himself a drink. It took a quick swig and several minutes of intense concentration to throw off a cool and adamant, "No."

"And she's thrilled to be living in that pigsty you call a house? She'll even clean it for you?"

Jake shrugged. "I gather her previous accommodations weren't as spacious." He thought of her labor-roughened hands. "Nor is she afraid of hard work."

"And she's not bad looking?"

Hair the color of moonlight, skin as pure and soft as virgin wool, eyes as serene as a forest glade. "She's beautiful," Jake admitted roughly.

"I want her."

"What!"

"After your divorce, I want her. She sounds like a dream come true."

"Go to hell, Bryant," Jake snapped, and turned to stare out the window.

Wynne shook hands for the umpteenth time, introducing herself and the boys to yet another resident of Chesterfield. "This has to be the friendliest town in the whole world," she marveled as she pushed her cart down the aisle.

"Kinda crowded," Buster observed, dodging another shopper.

"I guess they didn't feel like driving all the way into Two Forks any more than we did."

"How come everyone wants to shake hands with us? Nobody ever did that when we went shopping in Maryland."

"I guess that's the way people do things in Texas." She paused by the local bulletin board and studied the various announcements. "There's a charity craft fair next weekend. I wonder if Jake's donated anything. Maybe I can bake a cake if he hasn't."

Chick tugged on her arm and Buster said, "Chick wants you to bake cookies instead of cake. That way we can help fix 'em."

"Help eat them, you mean," she said with a laugh. "Well, grab a couple bags of chocolate chips and walnuts. They're on that bottom shelf over there. In fact, grab several. Thanksgiving is just around the corner and that means lots of baking. Just remember cleaning the house comes first, okay? I promised Jake. Cookies are a solid second."

Jake tried to ignore the annoying buzz of Peter's unending string of questions and stared moodily out the office window. Gradually he focused on the pickup parked across the street—a familiar-looking sleek, black, mud-spattered pickup. He frowned, suddenly realizing just why it looked so familiar. Damn it all! That sleek, black mud-splattered pickup was *his*.

"Hell and damnation," he swore. "She lied to me. That blasted woman promised she'd go to Two Forks and it was all a lie. I'm going to strangle her. I swear I will."

"What? What's she done?" Peter demanded.

"She's here. In town."

"So?"

"So, I told her to go to Two Forks, and she's deliberately disobeyed me."

Peter grinned. "I can't wait to meet this wife of yours. I'm really starting to like her."

"Go to hell, Bryant." Jake slapped his Stetson on his head and strode toward the door. "I'll finish with you later. Right now, I've got to find my wife before she gets into trouble. Though knowing her, I'm way too late."

"Wait a minute. Jake! What about your grandfather's will? We need to set a court date. Wynne needs to—"

Jake stopped dead in his tracks and stomped back into the office. "I've changed my mind. I'm not having my wife stand up in open court and tell the whole of Chesterfield about our wedding night." He refused to turn such a private, soul-altering moment into fodder for Chesterfield's rumor mill. He couldn't do that to Wynne or to himself. "You get Judge Graydon and Randolph to agree to a more private get-together. A dinner party or something, where we can all discuss it casual-like."

"A dinner party," the lawyer repeated in disbelief. "What's the plan, have her serve up the main course and say, 'Oh, by the way, Jake and I did it on our wedding night. Pass the salt and let's eat.'? I can just see that."

Jake scowled. "I won't allow Wynne to be embarrassed or humiliated in any way, shape, or form. Understand? Can't the judge just ask how our wedding night went? She can tell him it was great and that'll be the end of it."

"And was it? Great, I mean?"

Fury darkened Jake's face. "If you weren't my lawyer, I'd knock your teeth down your throat."

Peter grinned. "Good thing I'm your lawyer then, isn't it? Wait a minute. One last question before you go."

"What?"

"This is your temporary wife, right? The one who's leaving you once the terms of the will are met? The one you're not in love with?"

Jake scowled, pulling the brim of his hat low over his brow. "That's three questions, Bryant, and not one of them is any of your business. Just arrange for the dinner. Got it?"

"Fine, but you'll have to talk to Wynne, explain what's expected of her."

"I'll tell her."

Maybe.

Or maybe he'd arrange for the judge to ask a few subtle questions over after-dinner coffee. He strode down the hall and out into the warm November sunlight, considering the matter. Wynne would never have to know the true purpose behind the get-together. He could keep it a secret. He'd just warn her that the judge was a nosy old man and she should humor him. It might work, if he planned carefully.

He shook his head in disgust.

Wynne's idealism must be rubbing off. Why else would he be casting himself in the role of her personal protector? When would he learn? He was the villain of the piece, damn it all, not the hero.

After signing the receipt for the groceries she'd purchased, Wynne offered Belle a cheerful farewell and pushed the loaded cart toward the exit. Before she'd reached it, a man planted himself square in front of her, blocking her path.

"Rumor has it you're married to Jake," he said by way of greeting. "Is that true?"

An unnatural silence descended and Wynne studied the man. Anger marred what might have been an attractive set of features and she wondered what she possibly could have done to antagonize him. "If you mean Jake Hondo, I'm his wife, yes," she admitted and offered her hand. "My name's Wynne." He pointedly ignored her gesture, instead hooking his thumbs in his belt loops and rocking back on his heels. She slowly dropped her arm.

"Jake only married you to get his hands on my inheritance," he announced, eyeing her belligerently.

She lifted her eyebrows in surprise. "Your inheritance?"

"Randolph, please," a sad-eyed woman behind him murmured, tugging on his arm. "Don't cause a scene."

He shook her off. "I'm Randolph Chesterfield and that ranch land he's after rightfully belongs to me."

"This land . . . it's his inheritance?"

"Only if he's properly wedded and bedded."

Wynne laughed. "Then there's no problem."

It was the wrong thing to say. Her comment only served to infuriate him. His hands closed into fists and he stepped closer, shoving her shopping cart to one side. "You can't know the man very well, or you wouldn't say that."

She lifted her chin, refusing to be intimidated. "I know Jake quite well and—"

"Then you know the conditions of his grandfather's will." The comment shot like a bullet. "He married you to get my land."

"*His* land," she corrected with a sunny smile. "And of course I know why he married me. Not only is Jake an honest man, he's also the sweetest, kindest, most generous husband a woman could want. If it weren't for him, I wouldn't be able to keep my nephews." She wrapped her arms around Buster and Chick's shoulders. "Why, as far as I'm concerned, he's an angel!"

Randolph's mouth opened and closed as he fought to digest her analysis of Jake's character. "He sure has you buffaloed," he said at last. "I don't know whether to pity you or congratulate him. But I'll give you fair warning. He doesn't give a plugged nickel for either you or those kids. You're nothing more to him than a means to an end. Once he gets what he's after, you and those kids will be out on your collective backsides."

"Randolph, please," the woman behind him said. "Let her be."

"Hush, Evie. I'm only speaking the truth. Someone ought to tell her about Jake. Explain what a low-down, rotten snake he is before he hurts her or one of the kids."

"Uncle Jake's not a snake. And he wouldn't hurt us, neither. He loves us!" Buster shouted, his face turning red with indignation. "Don't you say anything bad about him or I'll kick you."

Wynne squeezed her nephew's shoulder. "It's all right, sweetheart. Mr. Chesterfield doesn't know Jake the way we do." She glared at Randolph. "You're wrong, mister. My husband is an honorable man, and one of these days he'll prove it to you. In the meantime, don't you say another nasty word about him or you'll regret it. Now, stand aside. It's time we left." She grabbed the cart and shoved it in his direction, deciding that if he didn't move out of the way, she'd run right over his toes.

With an exaggerated sweep of his arm, Randolph stepped back. "Don't let me keep you," he said as she stalked past. "But just out of curiosity . . . How much is he paying you to crawl into bed with him? It must be a bloody fortune."

A collective gasp ran through the store and Wynne felt her own anger skyrocket, though it was nothing compared to the fury that exploded across the countenance of the man lounging quietly in the doorway.

Chapter Six

Jake straightened, his eyes burning brighter than the fiery pits of hell. "I see you've met my wife, Chesterfield," he said, his voice all the more terrifying for its deadly control.

Startled, Randolph whipped around and blanched. "Hondo! I—"

Jake stepped closer, crowding the man against the wall. "You speak to her again without my permission and I'll permanently rearrange those pretty-boy features of yours. You got that?"

"Listen, Jake, I was just—"

"I didn't catch your answer." He grabbed a fistful of Randolph's shirt. "Are we communicating, cousin? You don't speak to her. Hell, you don't even look at her. Understand?"

Sweat beaded Randolph's brow as he gave a tight-lipped nod.

Jake released his grip. "Smart answer. Because if you ever interfere in my business again, I'll put paid to your future existence. You have my personal guarantee." His attention switched to Wynne and he jerked his head toward the door. "Get goin'."

Without a word, she swept by. Buster followed in her wake, poking his tongue out at Randolph as he passed. Not to be outdone, Chick stopped and gave the man a swift kick in the shins before darting after his brother.

Jake's gaze swept the crowd of shoppers gathered. He didn't doubt they were all there to catch a glimpse of his wife.

He wasn't surprised when few met his eyes. "Just so it's clear," he announced in a carrying voice. "I protect my own."

"No one doubts that," Belle retorted in a dry voice. "And don't you worry about Wynne. She made quite a hit the short time she was here."

Jake inclined his head. "Glad to hear it." Noticing Randolph's wife for the first time, he tipped his Stetson. "Always a pleasure, Evie."

"Damn you, Hondo. Leave her alone or I'll do some damage of my own," Randolph snarled, recovering a modicum of his aplomb. "You've got a wife now, remember? You don't need mine."

Tears sprang to Evie's gentle blue eyes and Jake instantly regretted turning his cousin's rage in her direction. He could handle it. She couldn't. But then, he hadn't expected his cousin's show of mettle. It had been a long time since Randolph had worked up the backbone to issue such a blatant challenge. Desperation must be riding him hard.

Jake inclined his head. "For the first time in your life, you're right, Chesterfield. I do have a wife now." He glanced over his shoulder at the gracefully swaying bottom disappearing down the sidewalk. "Our conversation can keep. She can't."

With that, he stalked from the store, his swift stride narrowing the gap between him and his troublesome wife. He caught up with her by the truck.

"What are you doing here, Wynne?" he asked as he helped dump bags of groceries into the bed of the pickup. "I thought I told you to go to Two Forks for supplies."

"You did."

Her back was to him and a cool breeze stirred the white-blond hair at her nape. A sharp pang of desire twisted his gut in knots. She was so delicate, so vulnerable. And so damned unpredictable. "Then why didn't you?" he demanded.

She glanced over her shoulder, her green eyes reflecting her surprise at his vehemence. "It was too far. I didn't think I could make it."

"What do you mean, couldn't make it?"

"It's the three pedals," Buster offered. "I tried to help, but she's not very good at it."

"Three—" Understanding dawned. "You don't know how to drive a stick shift?" he questioned ominously.

"I do in theory. I'm just not so great at the 'in practice' part," she confessed.

He swallowed the multitude of retorts that leapt to his tongue. "Get in the truck," he instructed. "I'll follow you home."

Chick sighed.

Buster rolled his eyes and groaned. "Uh-oh."

Jake glared. "What's wrong now?"

"I don't do reverse," she explained.

"You don't—" He bit off an exclamation. "But you can go forward, correct?"

She grinned. "Well enough to have gotten us here."

"Well enough to get you back home again, too?"

"I think so."

He yanked open the cab door. "Stand on the sidewalk. I'll back the truck out."

Buster tugged on Wynne's arm. "Uncle Jake sounds funny again," he whispered. "Like when he was in the store."

"I think that means he's annoyed," she whispered back.

"I'm not annoyed." Jake corrected her grimly. "I'm mad enough to spit nails. Now go stand on that sidewalk like I told you."

Silently they did as he asked. Or rather, ordered. Starting the engine with a roar, he spun out of the parking space and left the pickup idling in the middle of the street. "Hop in and start for home," he called to Wynne. "I'll be right on your tail."

The three climbed into the truck. With an earsplitting grinding of gears, Wynne popped the clutch into first and coughed her way down the road. Jake winced. His mechanic was going to love her. At a transmission a month, Billy Dee would soon be able to afford that Ford F-450 he'd been eyeing. Shaking his head in disgust, Jake climbed into an ancient Jeep and planted his front bumper inches off her back one. The first time she stalled the engine, he almost rear-ended her. After that, he kept a respectable distance between them.

Ten minutes later they reached the driveway to Lost Trail. It took three tries for her to find the right gear and keep the engine running long enough to make the turn. Jake released a gusty sigh. He had a horrible feeling this was only the beginning of his tribulations with his adorable wife. Unfortunately, he had a tough time working up any real irritation with her, especially after her spirited defense of him in the general store.

Dusty emerged from the barn to greet them as they pulled into the yard. He eyed Wynne and the children with trepidation. "That her?" he questioned, poking his head in the open window of the Jeep. "Where'd the kids come from? Don't remember you sayin' anything about kids."

"I told you my wife packed a few surprises. They're just one of them. Come on and I'll introduce you."

Dusty held up his hands and started backing toward the barn. "That's not necessary. Any ol' time will do. Next week. Next month. How 'bout while they're packing to leave?"

Jake shook his head. "Not a chance. You'll meet them now. That way you can keep an eye on the kids while I teach Wynne how to drive a stick."

"I'm no babysitter," Dusty protested.

"Yeah? Well, you're not much of a foreman, either. But that's never stopped you from collecting the wages of one. Now shut your yap and come on." A sudden thought occurred and he swiveled to glare a warning. "And don't spit on her."

Wynne turned her attention from the endless expanse of pastureland flying by the truck window and glanced at Jake. "I appreciate your teaching me to drive the truck."

"You should have told me you'd never driven a standard transmission before."

She shrugged. "I didn't notice it was standard until we were ready to go shopping."

"Once you did notice, you should have waited until I returned. You could have caused an accident."

Silence descended again and she twirled her wedding band around her finger, scrambling for something else to say. "The people of Chesterfield are really nice," she volunteered. "Belle sure does have a busy store. I guess that's why you wanted me to go to Two Forks, right? Because it isn't as crowded there?"

"Wrong. Belle's place was so packed because word spread that a Mrs. Jake Hondo had wandered in to do her shopping. They were all curious to meet the woman brave enough to take me on." A muscle worked in his jaw. "I wanted you to go to Two Forks to avoid all those nice, curious people. In particular, I'd hoped to avoid Randolph."

She blinked. "Oh. Well, except for him, Chesterfield's an awfully friendly town. I probably met just about everyone. What a wonderful place to celebrate the holidays." She slanted him another look. "I wonder why Randolph took such a dislike to me."

"I believe he explained that."

"Then he wasn't lying about the inheritance?"

"No."

Another thought occurred to her. "You must have been standing there a long time to have heard all that."

"Long enough."

"Jake—"

His hands tightened on the steering wheel. "Although he denies the relationship, Randolph's my cousin. A distant cousin, but a cousin nonetheless. Is that what you wanted to know?"

"Why?"

He sighed. "Why what?"

"Why does he deny the relationship?"

"Because my father, Weston Chesterfield the third, wasn't married to my mother. Ours is an accidental connection, not a legitimate one and he resents it like hell. I may carry the blood of a Chesterfield, but I'm not one according to the law."

"But that's not the only reason he resents you," she guessed.

"No. His anger intensified when my grandfather left his ranch to me. With one small condition, that is."

"Marriage?"

"You got it."

"And if you hadn't married?"

"The ranch would have gone to Randolph."

"Why would your grandfather add such an odd provision?" she asked. "Why force you to marry?"

"Because he was a meddling old fool who wanted great-grandchildren."

"But—"

"This discussion is over." He spun onto a gravel shoulder beneath a huge cottonwood tree and switched off the ignition. Open ranch land stretched in all directions. "It's your turn to drive."

Wisely abandoning her previous line of questioning, she asked, "Where are we?"

"Close to the north end of my property. No one ever comes this way except my men, and they're several clips west of here working my grandfather's spread. We should have this stretch of road all to ourselves."

"No one to run into?" she teased.

He didn't deny it. "It'll be a hell of a lot safer teaching you here than on the road into Chesterfield, that's for sure."

"Trying to mitigate damages?" she asked wryly.

"Somebody better. My insurance coverage only goes so far. You ready?"

To her surprise, instead of exiting the vehicle, he slid over until they were joined hip to thigh. In the next instant, he'd pulled her onto his lap, cradling her in his arms.

"I'm not complaining, you understand," she said, snuggling deeper into his embrace. "But I thought you were going to teach me to drive a stick shift."

"I am."

She grinned. "I might find it a little difficult learning while sitting like this."

"Fat lot you know. I think this is a perfect learning position."

"But I can't reach the clutch from here." She stuck out her foot to demonstrate.

"You don't need to reach it. You already know where all the various parts are. It's how they work together that you need to learn."

She swallowed. "We're still talking about driving, right?" she asked in a husky voice.

He lifted a sooty eyebrow. "What else would we be talking about?"

She had no intention of answering that one. "Maybe we should get started," she murmured.

"Fine. Let's talk about first gear." He settled her more comfortably on his lap, his warm breath caressing her mouth. "First gear is where you start off. It's sort of like . . . Well, like a first kiss."

"A kiss."

"A *first* kiss," he said, correcting her.

She tilted her head to one side and frowned. "There's a difference?"

"You better believe it. If you're smart and want to keep everything running smoothly, you ease into a first kiss, slow and gentle. Like this." His mouth brushed hers, lingering, probing.

Her eyes drifted closed. "Slow and gentle," she managed to repeat.

"That's right. If you begin with a light, easy touch, you'll slip right into gear without any resistance." His tongue eased past her lips, caressing the softness inside. "See?"

She moaned. "I think so. Maybe we better make sure. Why don't you show me again?"

He didn't need any further prompting, but gave her a thorough grounding in the complexities of first gear. "I think we're moving toward second," he murmured after several minutes.

"How do you know?"

"The closer you get, the more the engine hums. When it starts to strain, it's a warning that first isn't getting the job done. Then you drop into the next gear."

"Second, right?" She tilted back her head, giving him access to the hollow at the base of her neck.

"Right." His mouth followed the length of her throat. "Now if first is a kiss, second is a touch." His hand slid from her shoulder downward. "It's just a tease, really. A prelude to more exciting things to come."

She shivered beneath his playful fingers. "Does it last long?"

"Depends on where you are." He fumbled with the buttons of her blouse. "And what sort of impediments are in your way. If your progress is interrupted, you might even have to go back to first."

"And if there aren't any?" The edges of her shirt fell open. "Impediments, I mean?"

He stroked his index finger along the line of her bra. "You hit the gas to get things moving faster. When the engine starts to strain again, then you push for third."

It was an effort to breathe. "What's third like?"

"Third is a bolder caress."

She licked her lips. "How bold?"

He unhooked the front of her bra and parted the silky cups. "This bold." He demonstrated and her breath stopped completely. "You're picking up speed, moving faster down the road. The tempo accelerates with third."

"I remember." She shuddered beneath his touch, burying her face in his shoulder. "But I never went past third. I was afraid to go any faster."

"Then we'll shift into fourth together." He turned her so she faced him, her knees hugging his hips, his corded thigh muscles like taut ropes beneath her bottom. "Fourth is all the way, sweetpea. There's no turning back. It's a hard, fast ride with the engine wide open. It feels great. And for a while you think it's right where you should be. Where you belong."

His hands had slipped to places better suited to the velvet darkness of a moonlit night. The breath sobbed from her lungs. Even as she surged toward some unobtainable peak, she knew she'd never reach it. Not here. Not now. Her fingers dug into his shoulders. "It's not enough!"

"That's when you shift into fifth." He pulled her tight against him so every move he made, every breath he took was echoed by her own body. "Fifth is that final release. Fifth takes you to the end of the road."

She squeezed her eyes closed, his scent filling her nostrils, his breath hot against her ear, his taste sweetening her tongue. She was afraid to move, afraid to break the connection pulsing between them. "And after fifth?" Her words were labored, her voice nearly inaudible.

"There's nowhere else to go after that and only one possible option."

"What option?"

His mouth sought hers, his tongue breaching her lips in a soft, gentle caress. "You can throw it into reverse and start all over again."

"Oh, yes!" The words escaped on a sigh. "Take me for another ride."

"What the hell is going on?" Jake came out of the truck in one fluid motion. Dusty, Buster, and Chick stood in a row, all three scuffing dirt with their toes and avoiding his eyes. "I just passed Mad Dog burning up the field a mile north of here. How did he get out?"

No one said a word.

"My prize stallion is in the same pasture as my prize bull and you three have nothing to say? What do you suppose the odds are that one or both of my animals will end up as hamburger meat on tonight's dinner table?" He glared from one set of guilty features to the next. "Well? Who's gonna start talkin' first?"

Dusty cleared his throat. "Guess that's me. It was . . . ah . . . It was an accident."

Jake's eyebrows arched skyward. "Mad Dog escaped out of a padlocked stall by accident? How'd he manage that? Sprout wings?"

Wynne climbed from the truck and joined Jake. "Buster? You were asked a question. What happened?"

Buster raised tear-filled eyes. "I'm sorry, Uncle Jake. I just wanted to show Chick how to ride a horse."

The color bleached from Jake's face and he fought to keep his knees from buckling. "You let that horse out? *You?*"

Buster nodded miserably. "I saw where the key was hanging and thought I'd see if your horse would let me ride him. He was real sweet. He followed me outside just like a puppy dog."

"That . . . that puppy dog is the meanest son of a b—*gun* on this ranch. If he didn't sire such prize-winning offspring, I'd put a quick end to his sorry existence. You could have been—" He closed his eyes, fighting not to think about the could-have-beens.

Chick released a hiccupping sob and launched himself at Jake's knees, nearly toppling him.

"It was my fault, boss," Dusty muttered. "When I saw the kid with Mad Dog, I sort of lost it. I started hollerin' and that crazy hoss rolled back his eyes and kicked up his heels. I gotta confess, though. The kid has real good reflexes. He rolled clear of Mad Dog's shenanigans, grabbed his little brother by the scruff of the neck and skedaddled onto the porch."

Jake's hands balled into fists. "I thought I asked you to watch them, Dusty. You call this watching them?"

"I only turned my back for a minute. I swear. Was showin' them around, 'splaining how stuff works and the next thing I know, they took off on me."

"Oh, Buster," Wynne said with a sigh. "You know better than to disappear without telling the person in charge where you're going. You also know better than to touch someone else's property without permission."

"And if he didn't before, he's sure going to learn now," Jake stated in no uncertain terms. He stabbed a finger first at Buster and then at Chick. "Both of you. Get to the barn and wait for me."

"What are you going to do to them?" Wynne asked apprehensively.

"We're going to have a man-to-man talk. And if they're lucky they'll be able to sit down sometime next week." He didn't wait for a response, but turned to Dusty. "As for you . . . If you want to keep your job, not to mention your hide, you'll round up the men and go corral that horse."

"Yessir, boss. I'll get right on it," he said and raced toward the Jeep as fast as his stubby legs would take him.

"Jake?"

Wynne touched his arm and he deliberately kept his back to her. If he looked at her, he'd never be able to discipline the boys. One glimpse of her huge, pleading eyes and all his good intentions would melt like ice beneath a noonday sun. "What is it?"

"Make sure they understand what they did wrong. Otherwise they'll never learn."

It took him a minute to digest her words. "What did you say?" he whispered.

"A ranch in Texas is a lot different from an apartment in Maryland. I don't think they quite realize that yet."

Slowly he turned to look at her and the trust he read in her calm expression left him fighting for control. "You're not afraid I'll hurt them?" he questioned roughly.

She actually laughed. "Don't be ridiculous. I know you'd never do that, despite what Randolph said. Buster shouldn't have touched Mad Dog. And as you said, if he doesn't realize it now, he will as soon as you speak to him."

He cleared his throat. "I won't be long."

"There's no hurry," she replied. "I'll start dinner while you deal with the boys."

He couldn't answer. Instead, he nodded and headed for the barn. The boys were waiting just inside the door. Buster stood in front of his brother, his expression one of stoic resolve. The phrase "taking it like a man" leapt to mind and Jake studied them in silence, waiting. Buster broke first.

"We're sorry for what we did, Uncle Jake. And it won't never happen again. We promise."

Chick peeked apprehensively around his brother and nodded, before popping his thumb into his mouth and sucking furiously.

Jake inclined his head. "That's good to know. Because if I can't trust your word, I'll have to restrict you to the house instead of having you help around the ranch."

Surprise warred with exhilaration on their expressive faces. "Really? You mean it? We can help you?"

"I wouldn't have said it if I didn't mean it."

"We promise!" Buster stated fervently. "We'll do everything you say."

Chick tugged on his brother's arm and whispered something.

"Okay, I'll ask." Buster glanced at Jake. "You want both of us to help, right?"

"Yep. A ranch this size needs every pair of hands available." He gave Buster a stern look. "But there's a lot of dangerous animals and equipment on a ranch. One thoughtless mistake can get you seriously hurt, like with Mad Dog. I know you wouldn't want Chick injured through your carelessness."

"No, sir," came the somber reply.

"That means you can't do anything without asking permission first. You got that?"

"Got it."

Chick gave a decisive nod of agreement.

"Okay. The only problem is, your little stunt today has caused Dusty and my men a lot of extra work, which means they're going to have trouble getting all their chores done."

Buster didn't hesitate. "Maybe we could do some of those chores."

Jake pretended to consider. "You know, I think that's an excellent way to make amends." He hooked a thumb toward a pair of pitchforks propped in the corner of the barn. "Let's see how good you are at pitching hay." He watched in satisfaction as the boys scrambled to obey. A little hard work and they'd be too worn out to get into any more mischief.

He hoped.

Which just left Wynne. He rubbed a hand across his jaw and grinned. That shouldn't be much of a problem, either. If he put his mind to it, he didn't doubt he could think of one or two activities to keep her occupied. Like reviewing what she'd learned about driving a stick shift. Only this time, he'd make sure they didn't just talk about fifth gear.

He'd make sure they experienced it, as well.

Chapter Seven

Jake sat at his grandfather's desk and stared at the bills and correspondence littering the oak surface. Just over a week had passed since he'd returned home and a veritable mountain of work had piled up. He'd hoped that by coming to the Chesterfield ranch he'd find the peace and quiet to accomplish it. No runaway horses. No grouchy foreman. No hero-worshiping kids. And no starry-eyed wife who thought the sun rose and set at her husband's behest.

But instead of settling down to business, he found himself gazing off into space, picturing an impish smile, winter-white hair, and impassioned green eyes. In the past week he'd developed an uncontrollable need to steal Wynne away as frequently as possible and review the finer points of driving a standard transmission. Worse, when he wasn't preoccupied with his wife, his mind turned to what new activity he'd introduce to the boys and how he might wheedle one, tiny word out of Chick.

The phone at his elbow rang and he snatched it up with relief. Anything to block such appealing, impossible daydreams. "Hondo."

"Thought I might find you there," Peter's satisfied voice echoed down the line. "I just spoke to Judge Graydon. He approved the dinner party."

"Glad to hear it."

"I don't think he liked the idea of a public hearing, either. As for a date, he's available Saturday night. Randolph, needless to say, is protesting for all he's worth. Not that it's done a lick of good. Graydon supports you in this instance."

"I assume my cousin has to be there," Jake stated with a marked lack of enthusiasm.

"'Fraid so. I did suggest he bring Evie. I'm hoping she'll help control that temper of his."

"Not likely. But I trust you impressed on him the importance of keeping his mouth shut around my wife."

"I did, and I sincerely doubt he'll start any trouble. I think the incident at Belle's was a sufficient deterrent. He won't be interested in a repeat performance."

"Let's hope you're right."

"So, that just leaves Wynne. I assume you've talked to her? She knows what to expect?"

"I'll deal with that end of things, you worry about the legalities."

"Fine." There was a significant pause. "I'm curious to meet her, considering the impression she's made around here. People in town have been talking about little else. Seems everyone has a story involving her."

"Involving her how?" Jake demanded.

"You know. Her contributions to charity, how she visits the shut-ins, the way she cares for her nephews, her nonstop defense of you." Peter chuckled. "Anyone who speaks ill of her husband better watch out. She lets them have it with both barrels."

"Does she?" Jake murmured, grinning.

"Sure does. When the time comes, you'll have to fight off her suitors with a stick."

"When the time comes?" Jake's brows drew together, his grin dying a rapid death. "What time? And what suitors? What the *hell* are you talking about?"

There was an uncomfortable silence. Then Peter admitted, "Randolph's continued to spread the rumor around town that your marriage is a pretense. That as soon as the judge gives his final approval, you'll divorce her. Though in all honesty, it's not much of a rumor, is it?"

"The length of my marriage is nobody's business but mine."

"And Wynne's," Peter retorted coolly. "Anyway, every bachelor within sixty miles who's exchanged so much as a word with her, is hot to cozy up to the soon-to-be ex-Mrs. Hondo. They all think she'd make the perfect wife. I probably would, too, if I'd ever met her."

Jake's hand closed into a white-knuckle fist. The soon-to-be ex-Mrs. Hondo? *Ex*-Mrs. Hondo? "You so much as look at her funny," he snarled, "and not only will you be my ex-lawyer, you'll also be my ex-friend carrying around a handful of ex-teeth."

He banged down the phone and thrust back his chair. Damn Peter for stirring up such disturbing images. The problem was, he was probably right. Most men would consider Wynne the answer to their dreams, kids and all. If she'd come to Chesterfield looking for a husband, instead of to the Montagues' ball, she'd have had potential husbands lined up and begging for her hand. And they wouldn't have been interested in any temporary arrangement, either. They'd have been every bit as intent as Wynne on having a happily-ever-after marriage.

Unable to contain his restlessness, Jake wandered through his grandfather's ranch house, picking up the occasional knickknack before setting it back in place. As reluctant as he was to admit it, he loved the ranch almost as much as he'd loved his grandfather. But it was a love mixed with anger and resentment, stirring to life demons better left undisturbed. Chesterfield Ranch represented all he'd been denied as a child. Hell, he'd never stepped foot inside the house proper until he was practically an adult. And then, when it was far too late, he'd been offered it all.

It was a beautiful place, he reluctantly conceded, one that cried out for a family. His grandfather had often said it would never be a true home without the ring of youthful voices bouncing off its high, sweeping ceilings. For the first time, Jake understood what that meant.

The house seemed to be holding its breath, its walls achingly empty of the plethora of childish artwork it needed to accent the knotty juniper trim. The air smelled stale and unused without the scent of cookies baking in the kitchen or the light tantalizing fragrance of a woman's perfume. He glanced around. The rooms were too neat. No cookbooks left in an open pile on the table, no toys scattered haphazardly across the carpet, no woman's accessories cluttering the bathroom. If he closed his eyes, he could almost picture how it would react to Wynne and the boys.

He found the image all too appealing.

With a muttered exclamation, he returned to the office and snatched his Stetson off the hat rack. Not only was he a fool, but he was also the grandson of a fool. If he didn't get out of here right now, he'd do something stupid. Like pack up Wynne and the boys and turn this house into the home it was meant to be.

"Wynne? You there?" Jake yanked off his muddy boots, something he'd never have done until a week ago, and opened the door to the kitchen. "Elf?"

"Look out, Jake!" he heard her panicked shout. "Don't come in."

"Why not?" Already in the room, he stared at Wynne in disbelief. "What the hell are you doing on the counter?"

Buster peeked down from the top of the refrigerator. "Hey there, Uncle Jake."

He stared from one to the other. "Mind telling me what's going on?"

A cupboard door swung open and from his curled-up perch on the shelf, Chick pointed toward a splash of sunlight on the floor.

Jake turned to look and jumped back, cutting loose with a blistering expletive.

"I did try to warn you," Wynne said meekly.

"Next time forget all the 'look out' and 'don't come in' stuff and just scream, 'snake.' Trust me, I'll get the message."

He stared at the reptile coiled on the floor and let out a long, low whistle. "That has got to be the biggest damn—*darn* rattler I've ever seen in my life."

"We weren't certain that's what it was, but we didn't want to take any chances."

"Smart move, sweetheart." He shot them a quick look, tension gripping him. "Everybody all right? Anyone bit?"

"We're fine," Wynne reassured.

"Chick needs to pee real bad," Buster chimed in. "I thought about havin' him wet down the snake, but figured it would only make the thing madder. Maybe mad enough to slither up here and get even."

Jake fought to keep a straight face. "I appreciate your restraint."

As though tired of being left out of the conversation, the snake swung its spade-shaped head in his direction, its tail quivering an ominous warning. Jake froze, knowing better than to make any sudden moves.

"Would you mind putting it outside?" Wynne requested nervously.

"Would I mind—" He eyed the distance between him and the snake. "No, sweetpea. I wouldn't mind. As a matter of fact, I'll get right on it." Deciding he was far enough away to avoid an unexpected strike, he backed slowly toward the mudroom. Scooping up his boots, he donned them with due speed.

He poked his head around the door. "Care to explain how you came to be entertaining a diamondback?"

"It wasn't by choice, believe me. It must have been hibernating in the woodbox by the stove. We were going to try baking cookies on the fire-burner and I opened the box to get some wood and—"

"It's a wood-burner and I get the picture." His shut his eyes. In fact, it was all too vivid a picture, almost crippling in its impact. It was also an image he'd have to hold at bay if he were to be of any use. "Listen to me, Wynne. I need to get to the den and since I don't think our friend here is going to let me by without payin' a stiff penalty, I'll have to circle around. I'll be back as quick as I can. Stay put, okay?"

"No worries there," Wynne replied, attempting a smile.

Not wasting another minute, he exited through the mudroom and ran like hell for the front of the house. In thirty seconds flat, he'd beat a path to the den, had the gun case unlocked, and his rifle loaded. Ramming home the shells, he headed for the kitchen. At the doorway, he paused, checking cautiously for the snake. It hadn't moved, but lay coiled in the sunlight, warming itself.

"All of you, turn around and don't look," he ordered.

"What are you going to do with the gun?" Wynne asked apprehensively.

"What do you think? I'm going to blow that critter to kingdom come."

"Here?" she questioned, appalled. "In the kitchen?"

"Right here and right now." He shouldered the rifle. "Close your eyes. It's gonna be messy."

"Jake, no. You can't."

He sighted along the barrel. "What do you mean I can't? I'll have you know I'm a dead shot."

She lowered her voice. "Not in front of the children, you aren't."

"Why not?" Buster demanded. "We want to see Uncle Jake blow the snake to kingdom come."

Chick nodded, his powder-blue eyes gleaming with bloodthirsty enthusiasm. He popped his thumb from his mouth and took aim with his index finger. "Pkkkww."

Wynne stared at him in delight. "Chick! You spoke."

Buster made a sound of disgust. "Pkkkww isn't a word. It's a noise. You know, like a gun blast."

"Oh." She looked crestfallen for an instant, then brightened. "That's okay, Chick," she said with an encouraging smile. "You'll talk when you're good and ready."

"Excuse me, but could we please focus on the problem at hand?" Jake interrupted, an exasperated edge to his voice.

She frowned. "Right. The snake. I'd really rather you not shoot it in the house. In fact, I'm not sure I want it shot, period." She gazed hopefully at Jake. "Can't we just move it someplace else?"

He lowered his rifle. "You don't have a clue, do you?" He pointed. "For your information, that snake is a western diamondback. It's the second most venomous reptile in the U.S. Know what that means?"

Eyes enormous, Wynne shook her head.

"It means that this snake's gonna meet its maker and I'm the one who's sending it there. And if I find any of its brothers, sisters, or cousins hanging around, they'll join 'im in snake heaven." He shook his head in disbelief. "Why the hell—*damn!—heck* am I even standing here discussing this, when I should be taking care of business?"

"But—"

"Forget it," he said flatly. "Do you really want to risk one of the kids getting bit? Because that's what could happen if I don't kill it."

"Of course I don't want the boys put at risk. But, can't you kill it outside?"

"How do you expect me to get it there? Say 'Hey, pardner, would you mind slitherin' outside so we can discuss this problem man-to-reptile?'"

"You don't have to be sarcastic."

Dusty burst through the mudroom door. "What's all the excitement?" he demanded, panting for breath. "Saw you running like your britches were afire." Spotting the snake, he squawked and scrambled backward.

Apparently Dusty's arrival was one human too many. With a furious shake of its tail, the rattler slithered toward him.

"What the hell are you waiting for, boss?" Dusty shouted. "Shoot the sucker!"

"Sorry, old friend. My wife won't let me. And watch your language in front of the boys."

"This ain't funny, Jake. Come on! Shoulder that blowpipe and let 'er rip, will ya?"

"Not unless Wynne agrees."

"I'm runnin' short of options here," Dusty bellowed as the rattler rapidly closed the distance between them. "What do you want me to do? Spit on the dang thing? Fire, I say. Fire!"

"Wynne?"

"Boss!"

"Okay! Shoot it! Shoot it!" Wynne yelped, tumbling off the counter.

The snake swung in her direction, preparing to strike. It was the last move it ever made.

The rifle blast practically deafened them. Peeking through her fingers, Wynne saw Dusty flat on his back, a cloud of dust and debris hanging over him. The snake lay in a small crater nearby, unmoving.

She fought for breath. "Dusty." His name escaped in a panicked whisper. "Oh, no. What have I done? Dusty, speak to me. Are you bit? Shot? What's wrong?"

"He passed out," Jake informed her dryly. "Too much excitement, I guess."

With a groan, the foreman sat up and looked around. Spying the dead snake, his face split into a wide grin. "Looks like I got me a new belt. Maybe a hatband, too." He picked up the snake by its tail and glanced at Wynne, offering generously, "Want the rattle for a key chain?"

Jake didn't give her a chance to reply, but dropped his rifle onto the table and literally snatched her off the floor, enfolding her in a fierce embrace. "You scared the life out of me, you know that?" he muttered. "I can't leave you alone for five seconds without your getting into some scrape or another."

She wrapped her arms around his waist, giving him a reassuring hug. His heart pounded against her cheek, his rapid breath stirring the hair at her temple. A familiar lethargy stole over her, leaving her deaf and blind to everything but Jake. It was always this way when he touched her and she couldn't help but wonder if he felt the same.

"Maybe next time you'd better just shoot it," she offered generously.

"Instead of listening to my wife? Thanks. I'll do that." He glanced at the boys. "Hop down. The show's over."

"That was cool!" Buster enthused. "Will you teach me how to use a gun like that?"

"Absolutely not," Wynne answered, reluctantly leaving Jake's arms.

"You'll be far too busy packing," he added smoothly.

"Packing?" All four turned to stare at him.

He folded his arms across his chest, his chin set at a familiarly stubborn angle. "It's not safe at Lost Trail. So, we're moving over to my grandfather's ranch."

Dusty's jaw dropped. "Have you lost your mind?" he asked. "You're movin' them over to the Chesterfield spread because of one little ol' snake?"

"Yes."

"What for? That diamondback happens to be the most common in the whole da—" His gaze swung toward the boys and he cleared his throat. *"Gol' dern* state of Texas. It's not like you can put up No Trespassing signs to keep them off Chesterfield property, you know."

"We're moving and that's final." Jake glared at his foreman, daring him to argue further. "Any other objections?"

Wynne cleared her throat. "What about my cookies?"

He stared at her blankly. "Come again?"

"We have cookies to bake for Mrs. McCracken." She gestured toward a large ceramic bowl sitting on the table. "I have the dough ready and everything."

Jake frowned. "Who's Mrs. McCracken?"

"You know," Dusty said. "That cranky ol' bitty who lives next to the schoolhouse. Enjoys poor health. Always has some ailment or other to moan about."

"She's laid up with sciatica. I saw a notice at Belle's. I thought the boys and I could take a few things over to her. I'm sure she'd enjoy the company."

"You're jes a regular ol' Polly-butter-wouldn't-melt-in-her-mouth-anna, ain't you?" Dusty muttered. "Cookies for this charity, brownies for that. Cakes for the poor little orphans."

Wynne looked alarmed. "What orphans? I didn't hear about them."

"There aren't any orphans, ya dang . . ." Dusty yanked his hat so low it hid half his face. "Never mind."

She tilted her head to one side, a sudden thought occurring to her. "You know, I think I made way too large a batch. I just might have a few cookies left over. I don't suppose . . ." She heaved a sigh. "No, I guess not."

Dusty clutched the limp snake to his chest, a greedy expression creeping across his wrinkled countenance. "Don't suppose, what?"

"That you and the men might like some." She gave him an innocent look. "Or don't cowboys eat cookies?"

Dusty scowled, clearly fighting a battle between pride and stomach. "Wouldn't want to hurt your feelings by refusin'," he said at last. "I guess we could rid you of them if nobody else will."

"I'd appreciate that," she said, deciding then and there to have extra cookies available on a regular basis. "Oh! I almost forgot." Crossing to the ceramic bowl, she fished out her wedding ring and slipped it back on her finger. She peeked over at Jake. "That snake distracted me so badly, I'd almost forgotten it had fallen off."

"We should have that sized before you really lose it." He turned to scowl at the woodbox. "As for your cookies, load your dough into the truck. You can bake them over at my grandfather's." That should help the ranch house smell like a home. That and Wynne's heady brand of scent. "Let's move, people. We have work to do."

Dusty shook his head, muttering, "First we live here for a spell. Then we up and move to Mr. Chesterfield's place when he got hisself sick. Then we move ev'rbody to Lost Trail 'cause you're gettin' married. Now we're goin' back again after jes ten bitty days." He stomped toward the door. "I wish you'd make up your blasted mind, Boss. I'm gettin' dizzy."

The shift from Lost Trail to the Chesterfield ranch took longer than anticipated, the move not finalized until the day of the dinner party. Wynne didn't bother unpacking her personal possessions, instead focusing on getting ready for the evening. Carrying a stack of plates into the dining room, she placed them on the sideboard and glanced around in satisfaction. The table could seat a dozen people, which was more than adequate for their plans. It would also be perfect for Thanksgiving.

"Hello? Anybody home?" A man carrying a huge bouquet of flowers appeared in the doorway, stopping dead at the sight of her. "You're Wynne?" he demanded. "Jake's wife?"

"That's right," she confirmed, wondering why he found her identity so amazing. "And you're . . . ?"

"Sorry." Recovering swiftly, he offered an engaging grin. "Peter Bryant, Jake's lawyer and occasional friend. I didn't mean to stare, but you aren't quite what I expected. I didn't know Jake had such good taste."

"It's a pleasure to meet you." She tilted her head to one side. "Why occasional?"

"Pardon?"

"You said, 'occasional friend.' Why?"

"I have this annoying habit of ticking him off," he confided.

Her mouth twitched. "And when that happens you're not his friend anymore?"

"So he claims."

She eyed the flowers. "Are those for me?"

"Oh, right." He held them out. "It's a welcome to the neighborhood gift. A little late, I'm afraid. But they're actually just an excuse to meet you before dinner tonight."

Wynne laughed. "You didn't need an excuse. And you certainly don't need flowers. You're welcome anytime."

"In all honesty, I wish I could claim I'd brought them out of the goodness of my heart. But the truth is I wanted to make sure we're ready for tonight."

She shot him a startled glance. Was this evening more important than she'd realized? "I think we are. Everything's sort of hit at once—the move, the dinner party. Did you know this will be our first night staying here?"

"Jake mentioned something to that effect. I couldn't believe it when he said he planned to move you all over here." Before she could ask why, he added, "But you haven't answered my question."

"About whether I'm ready for tonight?" She gestured toward the sideboard. "I'm setting the table right now. The meal won't take any time to put together and—"

"The house looks beautiful, and I'm sure dinner will be perfect," he interrupted, a small frown furrowing his brow. "I guess what I really meant to ask was how you're doing. You're not worried about the real reason for tonight's gathering, are you?"

"The real reason." She stilled, something in his tone warning her to tread cautiously. "Would you care for a cup of coffee?" she offered.

"And some of those cookies I've heard so much about?" he suggested with boyish eagerness.

She managed a smile. "They certainly have helped cement my relationship with Dusty. It's amazing what a man will do for a plateful of cookies."

"They must be some cookies." He followed her into the kitchen. Opening a cupboard with obvious familiarity, he removed two mugs and filled them with the coffee she'd just finished brewing. "How do you take it?"

"With cream and sugar."

He poked his head in the refrigerator and removed the creamer. "I assume Jake spoke to you about tonight?"

"Sure." She loaded up a plate with cookies and joined him at the table. "I was a bit surprised to hear Randolph is coming."

Peter helped himself to an oatmeal raisin. "He wouldn't miss it for the world. He still lives in hope that he can do Jake out of his inheritance." He waved the cookie at her. "Hey, these are great. No wonder Dusty's been jumping through hoops."

"Thanks. So long as I keep the cookie jar filled, we're the best of friends." She hesitated. "I don't understand something. Jake and I are legally married, right? So why would Randolph think he could win at this late stage?"

"Because Judge Graydon hasn't recognized the marriage. He can't until after he talks to you tonight and confirms that you . . . That you and Jake . . . You know." He snagged another cookie. "I thought Jake explained all this."

She buried her nose in the coffee cup, suddenly aware there was a whole lot she didn't understand. "It must have slipped my mind."

"If there weren't so much at stake, it would be funny. Before Jake married you, it was all cut-and-dried. He'd pick out a plain, practical, levelheaded woman, marry her and then march her into court."

"Practical? No wonder you were surprised when we first met," she murmured.

"You don't exactly fit the criteria," he admitted, before hastening to add, "Not that it matters. The only vital requirement was that his wife be willing to stand up in front of the judge and half the world and make the necessary statement. But ever since he brought you home, he's been all hot and bothered about fulfilling that particular condition."

What condition? And what statement? She wished she could come right out and ask, but she didn't dare. Peter obviously assumed Jake had explained it all to her. Which prompted yet another question: Why hadn't he? "You said Jake was concerned about this part of the will. Why?"

"He doesn't want you embarrassed. Told me to get the judge to agree to something more private." Peter shrugged awkwardly. "At least you won't have to stand up in court and inform the whole of Chesterfield that you consummated the marriage. Although doing it over dinner is bad enough, I suppose."

She paled, her mug clattering against the table. "I have to—"

"Unbelievable isn't it?" Peter shook his head. "Mr. Chesterfield sure was a crazy ol' coot. But he was desperate to have Jake married in every sense of the word."

"Why?" she asked again.

Peter shifted uncomfortably. "You'll have to ask Jake about that." He finished his coffee and stood, snitching an extra couple of cookies. "Well, sorry to eat and run. But as I said, I just needed to confirm that everything's set."

"I appreciate your stopping by." More than he'd ever know.

"Thanks for your hospitality. I'll see you later tonight."

For the hour following Peter's departure, Wynne finished setting the dining room table, turning their conversation over in her mind as she did so. She kept coming back to the same concern. Why hadn't Jake told her what to expect? Was he just going to drop it on her right before their guests arrived? It didn't make sense.

By midafternoon, everything was ready. The silverware shone, she'd polished the fine cherry wood table to a lustrous finish and arranged the flowers Peter had given her in a silver bowl as a centerpiece. All she had left to do was shower and dress.

Jake entered the bedroom just as she emerged from the bathroom. "I saw the table. You've done a wonderful job. Thanks."

"I wouldn't want Randolph to have room to complain."

He grinned. "That won't stop him. But I appreciate it, even if he doesn't."

"Have Dusty and the boys left?" she asked.

"Just now. They're thrilled at the idea of camping overnight with real cowboys. Chick was so excited, I thought the words would bust right out of him."

"He's going to talk soon. I know he will." Every day the knot of tension and grief that gripped his small body eased a little more. She literally lived for the day when the dam holding back his words finally burst wide open. "Everyone's been so good to him. You. The townspeople. Dusty and the other wranglers. He feels comfortable with all of you. More importantly, he feels safe."

"I'm glad. He's a good kid who's had a rotten break." He took a deep breath, as though gathering strength, and approached. "Listen, I need to talk to you," he said, coming up behind and slipping the towel from her head.

Here it comes, she thought. Now he'll tell me the truth about this dinner. "Is there a problem?"

"No problem. But I think you should know. Judge Graydon may ask you some questions."

"What sort of questions?"

"About our marriage." He combed his fingers through her damp hair, caressing her nape. "He's a nosy old man, so just humor him, okay?"

"But you want me to answer his questions?"

"Yes. I'll cut him off if he goes too far."

She turned around, about to reveal what Peter had told her. Then she looked into Jake's eyes, the words dying on her lips unborn. Fierce pride and determination glittered within his golden gaze and in that instant she discovered the answers to all her earlier questions. He hadn't told her the truth about the dinner because he was protecting her, she realized with a sense of wonder, trying to shield her from potential hurt, just the he had when Randolph had accosted her at Belle's. Just the way he had with the snake. He hoped to pull off tonight without her ever having realized the true purpose of the evening.

Her knight was geared for battle.

"Oh, Jake," she whispered. "Have I ever thanked you for coming into my life?"

He shut his eyes, the muscles knotting in his jaw. "Every day, elf."

She slid her arms around his neck. "It can't possibly be often enough." More than anything she wanted to whisper three tiny words. Three precious, life-altering words. *I love you.* Though it would give her intense joy to speak them, it would cause him intense pain and conflict. And she wouldn't make his life more difficult, not after all he'd done for her and the boys. Unable to resist, she gave him a soft, gentle kiss.

He groaned, his arms tightening around her. "We don't have time for this, do we?"

"Not really. Not if we want to greet our guests when they arrive."

"We could always leave the front door open and put out a make-yourself-at-home sign. If we're long enough, the judge won't even have to ask—" He shut his eyes, his mouth forming a thin, taut line.

"What we've been up to?" she finished lightly.

He released his breath in a gusty sigh. "Yeah."

"How could they doubt it?" she teased. "What woman could possibly resist a man like you?"

His laugh rumbled close to her ear. "You're pretty damned irresistible yourself. Put some clothes on, wife, while I take a shower. Otherwise, I'll say to hell with our guests and take you to bed for the next twenty-four hours."

"Tempting, Mr. Hondo. Very tempting."

He kissed her, an intense, passionate kiss that told her more clearly than words how much he wanted her. It gave her hope.

Or was it false hope?

Chapter Eight

"YOU must have been in quite a state when you saw that diamondback," Judge Graydon said, shaking his head in amazement.

"About the same state I was in when Buster tried to ride Mad Dog," Jake retorted dryly. "I think it's called sheer unadulterated terror."

The judge stirred his coffee, his gaze shrewd beneath heavy gray brows. "Having a family is quite a responsibility."

"So I've discovered."

"But worth it?"

Jake glanced at Wynne, the words torn from him. "Yes, it's worth it."

"Oh, please," Randolph muttered in disgust. "What else is he going to say? He'll do whatever it takes to inherit this place. Even lie."

Wynne's coffee cup clattered onto the saucer. "He doesn't lie," she informed him fiercely. "Nor do I. And just so you know, Jake and I did sleep together on our wedding night." She hesitated, then grudgingly conceded, "Actually it was the next morning. But the point is, we're a duly consummated couple. There. Now that we have that out of the way, how about cake?"

"Who told her?" Jake shot to his feet, his scorching gaze pinpointing each dinner guest in turn, before keying in on Peter. "You. This is your doing, isn't it?"

"I—I came by earlier, sure," the lawyer confessed. "But just to make certain everything was set for tonight."

"You son of a—"

"Wait a minute," Peter protested. "Why are you so upset? Didn't you tell her what to expect tonight?"

"No, I didn't," Jake snapped.

"But, you said you would."

"I lied!"

"See, he does lie," Randolph said, adding his two cents' worth.

"Why the hell didn't you explain it to her?" Peter questioned in exasperation. "What did you expect to have happen tonight?"

Jake folded his arms across his chest. "I expected a few subtle questions from the judge. Subtle enough that she wouldn't catch on to the real reason behind his queries."

Judge Graydon frowned in concern. "Why would you keep such a thing from her, Jake?"

He remained silent a long moment, then reluctantly admitted, "I'd hoped to spare her feelings."

"He wanted to protect me," Wynne explained, giving her husband a dazzling smile. "He's just being his usual noble self."

Randolph leapt to his feet, leveling a finger at Jake. "That man hasn't got a noble bone in his body. Nor does he care about your tender feelings. I'll tell you why he kept quiet about that clause. He knew you'd leave him. Any normal woman would, rather than be forced to discuss such intimate details in public."

"Leave him?" Wynne shoved back her chair, her eyes flashing like gemstones. "You think I'm embarrassed or humiliated to admit I'm Jake's wife in the truest sense of the word? I'm proud of it. I'd announce it to the entire world, if he asked me."

"He's just using you," Randolph retorted, resentment gathering in his voice. "You must be blind not to see it."

"If that's what you believe, you can't know Jake very well," she stated with absolute conviction.

"I've known him for years. Unfortunately." He glared at her in frustration. "You seem to have the mistaken impression that he's some sort of domesticated lap cat. Well, you're wrong. The man is a vicious predator who wandered over from the wrong side of the tracks. And the minute you turn your back on him, he's going to rip you to shreds."

Jake returned to his seat, a lazy smile creeping across his face. "Please, Chesterfield. Don't bother to pull your punches." He tipped the chair back onto two legs. "You've been dying to tell me what you really think for years now. Well, here's your chance."

"You're right. I have wanted to tell you what I think." Randolph's jaw clenched, his entire body tensing in anticipation. "And with the judge as a witness, you wouldn't dare attack me for speaking the truth."

"Your version of the truth." Jake corrected him mildly.

"Mine and everyone else's in this town." Randolph planted his palms on the tabletop. "You're a no-good louse, Hondo, with an eye on the main chance, just like your mother. The only difference between you two is she didn't have your luck. If the old man hadn't been so desperate for a grandson, he'd never have taken you in."

Jake shrugged. "Old news, Chesterfield. My grandfather made that very clear when he came for me. If he'd had any legitimate grandchildren, I'd have been left in the gutter where he found me. So what? I never wanted to go with him in the first place. If the courts hadn't enforced his request, I'd have stayed put. At least I knew where I stood on the streets."

"But you did come back with him. And then you rode into town intent on getting even with anyone who'd known your mother—"

The front legs of Jake's chair crashed to the wooden floor. "I didn't ride in, I was driven. Or should I say hog-tied and dragged, fighting every damned inch of the way? It'd be more accurate."

"You wanted to get even because we all stood by while Chesterfield threw your mother off his land."

Jake laughed, the sound more chilling than a bitter arctic wind. "He didn't throw her off. Hell, he didn't have to. All it took was a few coins chucked into the dirt and she left of her own accord, grateful for that much."

"Nonetheless, you came back to get even because no one lifted a finger to help her. You blackened every eye that looked at you sideways and forced yourself on every woman who wandered within reach."

Evie stood and crossed to her husband's side. "Randolph, stop. You don't know what you're saying."

"I know exactly what I'm saying. And it's time the sweet, faithful Mrs. Hondo knew, too." He shot Wynne a mocking look. "How do you like the truth so far?"

"Which truth? That Jake's illegitimate?" She shrugged. "He told me. Since that's not his fault, I can hardly hold him responsible. Though apparently you do."

"I hold him responsible for his actions since coming to town. Or doesn't it bother you that he speaks with his fists and can't be trusted around any decent woman?"

"If you think I'm shocked that Jake has been in a few brawls, you're sadly mistaken. Of course he gets into fights. All you have to do is look at the man to know that you provoke him at your own risk." Wynne smiled proudly. "He's a natural-born warrior. That's one of the reasons I married him."

"You can't be serious!"

"I'm quite serious. And as far as women are concerned, I assure you, he would never force himself on anyone. He wouldn't have to."

A harsh laugh burst from Randolph. "I know for a fact that he's done just that."

"Please, don't say more," Evie urged her husband. "It won't change anything."

Wynne refused to back down. Randolph was maligning her husband, and that was one challenge she couldn't allow to pass uncontested. Slowly rising to her feet, she flung her linen napkin onto the table as though it were a gauntlet. "Women may claim they were forced," she informed him in clear, precise tones. "But only because they didn't have the nerve to admit the truth."

"And what truth is that?"

"That they allowed themselves to be seduced by the town's black sheep."

She'd clearly struck a chord. Hot color washed into Randolph's face. "That's a lie!"

Jake didn't say a word, simply raised his wineglass in a salute, the tender expression in his eyes tearing at her heart. It was all the encouragement she needed.

"It's not a lie, but a shameful truth," she retorted. "I wonder, how many women wouldn't give my husband the time of day in public, and yet slipped eagerly into his bed in the dead of night? Five, ten . . ." She glanced at Jake and lifted an eyebrow. "More?"

"It was before I knew you, elf," he said without apology. "I hope you're not offended."

"I'm not the least offended. It was their loss, not mine. They only knew half the man. I intend to know the whole."

"When's the next Cinderella Ball?" Peter demanded. "I want a wife like her."

"She's lying I tell you!" The words burst from Randolph, laden with helpless fury. "She's so hot for Hondo she'll make up any story to protect him." He scowled at her. "You may have been an easy tumble for him, but my wife never was!"

"Randolph!" Evie cried.

Wynne didn't waste her breath trying to stop the fight brewing. She could tell Jake was blind to everything but the overwhelming urge to get at his cousin. Instead, she darted around the table and threw herself at Jake, physically restraining him. His muscles bunched beneath her hands and he caught her shoulders as though he intended to force her from his path. It was Evie's plea that ultimately checked his threatening move toward Randolph.

"Jake, I beg you. Don't touch him," she whispered. "He doesn't know what he's saying."

The breath shuddered through his body and he fought to bring his anger under control. "Get out of my house, Chesterfield. Quick," Jake warned in a low, grating voice. "And don't come near me again for a long, long time. Otherwise you'll pay a hard price for that crack."

Randolph didn't need any further encouragement. Wrapping an arm around Evie, he fled the room.

"Make sure he leaves without causing any more trouble," Jake said to Peter. "I'll talk to you in the morning."

"No problem. Time I was getting home, anyway."

Jake turned on Judge Graydon next. "Have you heard what you came for?" he demanded. "Because as far as I'm concerned, you can all go to hell. I'm not answering any more questions, and neither is my wife."

"Easy, son," the judge said, holding up his hands. "You and Wynne have satisfied the terms of the will. The property is legally yours." His gray brows pulled together. "I hope for your sake, however, that Randolph is wrong."

"Wrong about what?"

He nodded toward Wynne. "This wife of yours is good for you, Jake. You won't find better. It's none of my business, but I sincerely hope that this marriage is more than just a sham."

The muscles in Jake's jaw tightened. "You're right. It's none of your business. My grandfather had no call putting such an unreasonable condition in his will. You can safely assume that any loopholes I find are fair game."

"He put that marital clause in there for your sake, my boy."

"*Bull!* He did it to ensure the continuation of his line. He was obsessed with siring a dynasty."

"Knowing Weston, that probably played a part in his decision," Graydon conceded. "But that wasn't the real purpose. There was another, more important reason."

Jake's expression turned derisive. "Yeah, right. Why don't you tell me what his *real* reason was? It ought to be good for a laugh, if nothing else."

Graydon sighed. "He wanted to give you the one thing you've never had."

That gave him pause. "And what was that?"

"Sorry, Jake. I'm not going to make it easy for you." The judge glanced at Wynne. "Besides, if you don't figure out the answer soon, then Weston failed and it won't matter anyway."

"He wanted to give me a wife?" Jake demanded in frustration. It didn't make sense. "Legitimate children? I could have taken care of that myself. It wouldn't have been difficult to arrange."

"Oh, Jake," Wynne whispered. "You don't just buy those things."

"No?" He gave a cynical laugh. "My grandfather spent a lifetime demonstrating just the opposite. He took great pleasure in proving you can buy anyone and everything."

"No, not everything. And that's what your grandfather finally did learn," she responded quietly. Arguing with him would be fruitless, she realized then. Judging by the set of his jaw, she didn't have a hope of altering his stance on the subject. She turned to the judge and offered her hand. "Thank you for coming. I apologize that the evening got a little heated."

"Only to be expected." He gathered her hand in his. "It's been a real pleasure meeting you, my dear. I hope to see a lot more of you in future."

"Time will tell," she replied obliquely.

With that, the judge left. Jake shut the door behind him with pointed finality. "Quite some party you throw, Mrs. Hondo."

"It was . . . interesting," she agreed. "I suspect it will be the topic of discussion for a long time to come."

"Around here that kind of discussion is called gossip. And I'm afraid you're right. If we weren't the talk of the town before, we will be now." He thrust a hand through his hair and glanced at her speculatively. "Care for a drink? I don't know about you, but I could sure use one."

"Sounds perfect."

He led the way into a very masculine library. Steel-gray carpet covered the floor. At one end of the room was a sturdy rolltop desk and a massive captain's chair, flanked on three sides by built-in bookcases. Opposite the desk, a huge stone fireplace took up the whole of one wall.

"Do you use that often?" she asked, nodding toward the hearth.

"From Christmas on, Grandfather always kept it lit." He handed her a snifter of brandy and swept aside the wire mesh screen protecting the grate. "Care for a fire tonight?" he asked, poking at the wood stacked inside. "It hasn't gotten very cold out, but I'm in the mood for one anyway."

"Sounds wonderful." Crossing to the switch by the door, she flipped off the overhead light so the small blaze he'd started provided the sole illumination. "Better?"

"Yeah, much." He settled on the carpet in front of the hearth and took a healthy swallow of brandy. "Jeez, I'm glad that damn dinner is over."

"So am I," she said, joining him. "I'm also glad the boys weren't here. I shudder to think what they'd have done to Randolph if they had been."

"No worse than what I'd have done if he'd said one more word to you."

A topic best avoided, she decided. "It's strange to have the boys gone tonight."

"You usually tuck them in at bedtime, don't you?"

She nodded, confessing, "I like to sit and watch them sleep."

"Do they remind you of your sister? What was her name? Tracy?"

"Yes." Wynne bowed her head. "I feel closer to both her and Rob when I'm with the boys. I can . . ." She shrugged. "I can feel them nearby."

"They must have thought a lot of you to leave their kids in your care."

"They knew I loved Buster and Chick," she answered simply. "That I'd do anything for them."

"Even marry me."

Her smile held a whimsical charm. "That was the easiest decision I ever made. I realized the minute we met that you were the perfect man."

"Because I could slay dragons." Shadows concealed his expression, but his voice held a caustic edge.

"Not just that. You were the perfect man because I—" *Because I took one look and saw you more clearly than you see yourself. Because the moment I looked into your fierce golden eyes, I fell impossibly, irrevocably in love.* But she couldn't tell him that, he wasn't ready to hear it. So she offered the only response he'd find palatable. "I married you because we needed each other. We still do."

"For a little longer." His words held a grim warning.

"Jake . . ."

He released his breath in a gusty sigh. "Let me guess. What part of the evening do you want to hash out? The part about my grandfather? My parents? My untempered pillaging of the women in town?"

"I think we settled the issue of your pillaging, untempered or otherwise," she replied with a quick grin.

"Thanks to your impassioned defense."

"Don't sound so surprised. I know what sort of man you are, even if Randolph doesn't. I also know that it's ridiculous to believe you'd resort to force when you could seduce any woman in town with a single look."

His laughter sounded rusty. "It might take a little more effort than just a look."

"Maybe." She cast him a sidelong glance. "But one lesson on how to drive your truck would have overcome any lingering hesitation on their part."

He shook his head, lounging on his elbow. "No way, sweetpea. You're the only woman I've ever taught to drive a stick shift." His eyes darkened. "The only woman I'd care to teach, for that matter."

"I'm glad to hear it," she admitted with a shy smile. She scooted closer to him, sliding her hand across his thigh. Flames leapt behind the screen, the firelight branding her pale hair with crimson streaks and flickering across the pure planes of her face. "Tell me the rest, Jake," she urged. "Tell me quickly so it's off your chest and we don't have to ever refer to it again."

"You want to hear all the gory details of my life?"

"Not really. But I suspect you need to tell them to me, if only for your own well-being."

He instantly withdrew, the mental barriers slamming into place. "Why would you think that?" he asked coldly.

"It's all right, Jake. I won't run screaming in terror once I know your darkest secrets. I won't turn from you in disgust or treat you with pity. And I certainly won't sneak into your bed in the middle of the night, then pretend we're strangers come daybreak." She paused. "That is why you haven't told me, isn't it? Because you weren't certain how I'd react."

He sat up abruptly. "Damn you," he whispered.

"I know," she sympathized. "You've worked so hard to build up your defenses, secured every wall, made sure your fortress is totally invulnerable. Now you have this irritating wife, banging on the castle door and you have to open up and let her in."

"I have to?"

She gave him an impish grin. "Just this once. After that, you can sling her out into the cold and simply ignore her."

"You're a hard woman to ignore," he retorted.

"So you've said. Annoying, pesky, tenacious."

The gold of his eyes rivaled the hot glow of the fire. "And loyal as hell. Okay, wife. You've heard most of the sordid details. There's not much left to the story." He stood and tossed another log onto the iron grate. "My parents met, fell in lust, and had a summer of careless pleasure. Careless because they accidentally conceived me. When my mother found out she was pregnant, she approached my father. Sorry, he said, he'd just gotten engaged to someone else—a socially acceptable someone else—and he'd appreciate it if she'd disappear. To ensure it, my grandfather made it worth her while."

"He paid her."

"And thus helped cement her choice of careers."

"Oh, Jake," Wynne murmured.

"No pity, remember?" he bit out. "When I turned sixteen she died and I ended up on the streets. By that time, my father had also met an untimely end. His wife had never been able to bear him any children and my grandfather was desperate.

Remembering the pregnant girl he'd bought off all those years ago, he came looking for me."

"And returned to Chesterfield with a furious, resentful teenager." It wasn't a question.

"I sure as hell wasn't the grandson he'd dreamt of having. I despised him for his hypocrisy and made no bones about it. In exchange for my hatred, he gave me all he possessed. Food, clothes, a roof over my head. Everything money could buy, he provided without hesitation. The one thing he asked in exchange I refused to give him."

It only took a moment's thought to figure out what Jake had withheld. "Your name."

He nodded. "For years Grandfather begged me to change it to Chesterfield. But I refused."

She eyed him shrewdly. "It was the only way you could keep your own identity, to keep that last piece of yourself intact."

He shrugged. "I was Jake Hondo and calling me Chesterfield wouldn't change the circumstances surrounding my birth."

"But you grew to love him, didn't you, despite what he'd done to your mother?"

He ran a hand across his nape. "Yeah," he admitted. "I did. He was a proud, lonely man who'd made a lot of mistakes in his life. Not once did he ever try to justify those mistakes or place the blame elsewhere. He just stood up and said, 'I'm the one.' I respected him for that, if nothing else."

"But you didn't stay with him, did you?"

He sighed. "I presume you're asking about Lost Trail."

"Yes."

"From the minute I arrived in Chesterfield, I started working and saving so I could buy my own place."

She nodded in perfect understanding. "It's that independent streak of yours. Never depend on anyone or anything."

"Something like that," he agreed. "I got lucky. When I was in my mid-twenties, the neighboring ranch came available and

I bought it. It was pitifully small compared to what my grandfather owned, but little by little I acquired the surrounding land until I had a respectable-sized spread."

"Dusty said you didn't stay there, that you moved back in with your grandfather."

"Not long after I made the purchase, the doctors discovered he had cancer." He stared at the fire, his face an expressionless mask. "What else could I do?"

"You couldn't have done anything else," she informed him. "Another person might have been more callous."

"I'm callous enough. And just so you know how callous . . ." He gave her a cool, direct look. "I could have brought you here after the wedding. Instead I chose to take you and the boys to Lost Trail. Care to know why?" He didn't wait for her to answer, just gave her the hard, cold facts. "I didn't want you to get your hopes up about staying, didn't want you to get too comfortable living with me. That way there wouldn't be any regrets when the time came to leave."

Amusement brightened her eyes. "Do you think when I leave I'll miss the ranch more than the man?" She'd set him back on his heels with that one, she realized, stifling the urge to laugh.

"Most women would," he muttered, then held up his hands. "I know, I know. You're not most women. Maybe I should write that down so I don't forget. You have a pen handy?"

"Don't worry, I'll keep reminding you."

"I don't doubt it." He lifted an eyebrow. "Are we done?"

"Just one or two more questions," she assured. "Tell me about Randolph."

Jake grimaced. "Randolph's a couple years older. Until I appeared on the scene, he considered himself the heir apparent, despite his distant connection. It was a nasty shock to discover his error. From the minute I arrived, it became his goal to make my life a misery."

"And Evie?"

He shook his head. "Sorry, elf. That's a private matter."

"No problem. I have a pretty good idea what happened there."

"Why doesn't that surprise me?" he muttered.

He took a quick swallow of brandy, as though screwing up his courage—which was utterly ridiculous. Jake was the bravest man she knew. "What is it?" she asked gently.

His breath escaped in a harsh laugh. "You don't miss much do you?"

"I try not to," she confessed with a shrug. "Is there something else you want to tell me?"

"Not tell you exactly. I want to thank you."

Her brows winged upward. "For what?"

"For tonight." He leaned closer and cupped her face, his thumb tracing the generous curve of her mouth. "And I wanted to apologize. I should have told you the true reason for tonight's gathering. I didn't because . . . Because . . ."

She leaned into his touch. "Because you wanted to protect me from embarrassment."

He closed his eyes, a muscle jerking in his cheek. "No, damn it. That's not the reason. It's the excuse I used, but it isn't the truth. I was afraid to tell you about that clause in my grandfather's will. I was afraid of what you'd do."

She gazed at him in bewilderment. "I don't understand. You're not afraid of anything."

"I didn't think so." He looked at her then, holding her with a fathomless golden gaze. "Until I met you. You scare the living hell out of me, sweetpea."

The words hung between them, simple, brutally frank, and utterly devastating. "You're *afraid* of me?" she whispered, shocked. "Why?"

He didn't want to answer, didn't want to reveal another chink in his armor. But she deserved his honesty, if nothing else. "You're the first person ever to believe in me. To offer unconditional trust. You see people so clearly. And yet when you look at me, you see someone I don't know." His mouth twisted in a self-deprecating smile. "Don't you understand? That image, the man you've created for yourself isn't real. And the one who does exist can only hurt you."

"Then one of us is wrong. And just in case you were wondering . . ." Her eyes gathered up the firelight, reflecting its fierce heat and energy. "It's not me."

It seemed an eternity before he could respond. "What am I going to do with you?" he asked roughly.

The answer trembled on her lips, but she caught the words just in time, altering them ever so slightly. "Make love to me."

His laughter came easier now. "That shouldn't be too difficult. I can't keep my hands off you."

"I don't remember asking you to."

His hand slipped from her cheek to curve around her neck. "Come here." He exerted the slightest pressure, tumbling her into his arms.

Their mouths collided and their limbs entwined, an overwhelming urgency setting the mating dance into motion. Though he'd taught her the steps well, she'd come into her own over the past weeks, bringing a unique style and grace to the ritual. Completely unselfconscious, she rose to her knees and shed her clothing. She didn't tantalize, didn't tease, nor did she display any uncertainty in this moment of utter vulnerability. She simply gifted him with her body, offering herself, heart and soul, without hesitation or reserve. It had always been this way with her.

And it never failed to humble him.

Finally, the last of her clothes were removed and she knelt, poised before him. She was made for firelight, he determined in that moment. The glow from the leaping flames licked at the alabaster hillocks of her breasts before melting into the shadowy delta at the juncture of her thighs. He reached for her and froze.

The deep bronze of his hand stood out like a stark blemish against the pale perfection of her skin, the contrast between them as startling as it was unwelcome.

Despair filled him. How could she not have noticed? She was heavenly light battling hellish darkness, the rich, warm earth fighting the intrusion of stone and brick and cement. She offered the eternal hope of spring during the deepest despair of winter. She was all he could ever want, offering possibilities that could never be his.

"Don't," she whispered. He jerked his hand back as though burned and she laughed gently, the sound a welcome balm. "I didn't mean don't touch me. I meant—don't think. Don't analyze. Don't question it." She took the initiative, gathering him into her arms. "Just for tonight, won't you lock your demons outside? They're not going anywhere, are they?"

"No," he conceded, warning, "they'll still be waiting come morning."

"Then we'll worry about them tomorrow."

She was right. This moment offered a respite between battles, and he'd be a fool not to take advantage of it. With infinite tenderness, he rolled them onto the carpet, anointing her with mouth and tongue and teeth.

He felt the first flush of desire wash across her skin like a storm-driven tide, and he cupped her breast, the frantic pounding of her heart filling his palm. She twisted beneath him, lifting her hips to mesh with his, moving with all the sinuous grace of a sun-warmed feline.

He tried to go slow, but desire became a rapacious hunger, a demand that turned his kisses hard and urgent and made each caress more aggressive than the last. He reveled in the delicious mix of passionate heat and fluid softness, sinking into her warmth, then driving into it, compelled by a force too powerful to resist.

He heard her frantic sobs, responded to the incoherent pleas, wanting more than life itself to give her the release she so desperately sought. He angled her hips upward, melding his mouth with hers. Instantly her muscles tensed in reaction and she exploded in his arms. It was all he needed. With a harsh cry, he drove home, following her over the edge. In that instant, their eyes met.

And what he saw there knifed deep into his soul.

For in those misty green depths he saw love. A permanent love—pure and faithful and absolute. He knew then that she'd given a forever-after love to a temporary husband.

And with that terrible knowledge, the demons came storming back.

Chapter Nine

Jake woke several hours later, struggling to get his bearings in the pitch-black room. His muscles protested the amount of time he'd spent sleeping on the floor and yet he hesitated to disturb Wynne.

She lay curled on her side, tucked tightly into the protective curve of his body. The fire had died long ago and a new moon, skulking in the shadow of the earth, ducked between bits of starlight as it traversed the nighttime sky. Gingerly he eased the cramp plaguing his leg.

With a gusty sigh, Wynne rolled over to face him. "What time is it?" she murmured.

"Time for bed, wife. Do you want your own room, or would you rather sleep with me?"

She yawned. "I don't know why you even bother to ask."

"I'm asking because we're in a new place. And after the dinner party . . ."

"New or otherwise, my place is with you," she told him firmly and snuggled deeper into his arms.

Something in her words revived the memory of their earlier lovemaking. He remembered the expression in her eyes—the one that spoke of miracles and storybook endings and eternities. He didn't doubt that look had returned. It was in her voice, in her touch, in her soft, eager kisses.

The urge to distance himself became overwhelming. "Your place may be with me for now," he warned harshly, "but sleeping in my bed won't seduce me into keeping you any longer than necessary. What does that figure out to? A few days, a week, a month?"

His coldheartedness went unnoticed. "It doesn't matter how many days we have," she countered. "We also have an equal number of nights. And I want each one to be wonderful. A beautiful memory you can recall when I'm long gone and half-forgotten."

Her unstinting generosity crippled him more than any protest or tears or recriminations. He stood, sweeping her into his arms, and strode purposefully from the room. "Let's find a bed. We may only have here and now, but we can turn it into one hell of a memory for later."

"When memories are all we have left?" she asked wistfully.

He didn't answer, was incapable of answering. For even if he found the right words, he'd never have gotten them past the tight knot blocking his throat.

The boys returned late the next day, exhausted and excited, and bursting to tell Wynne and Jake all about their adventures.

"And then this big, old bull came right at Dusty," Buster told them, his feet spread wide, his Stetson tipped back on his head in perfect imitation of Jake's stance. "I thought he was a goner for sure."

Chick tugged on his brother's elbow, whispering rapidly. Buster shook him off. "But Dusty didn't budge one bit. All's he did was spit. It was *so* cool."

"You weren't in any danger, were you?" Wynne questioned in alarm.

"Naw. They made us stay clear of all the good stuff."

Chick sidled closer to his brother, whispering more urgently.

"Not now," Buster replied in annoyance. "I'm not done with my story, yet. So then Dusty whipped out his lasso and roped that critter slick as you please. See you gotta get one rope around the cow and the other around this thing on the saddle."

"Saddlehorn." Jake tossed out the word.

"Yeah. Saddlehorn. That way the horse does the work and not the cowboy. But you have to wrap the rope around so's you don't lose no fingers. Dusty called it dal—Dal-something."

"Dallying."

Buster grinned at Jake. "Yeah, dallying. Will you teach me how to do it? Huh, Dad? Will you?"

His words stumbled to a halt as he realized what he'd said and he turned white as a sheet. Shooting a stricken look in Wynne's direction, he turned and ran from the room.

Jake swore beneath his breath. "I'll talk to him," he said to Wynne.

She caught his arm. "Please, let me."

He gave a terse nod and, gathering Chick close, she followed at a discreet distance. She could hear Buster's frantic sobs coming from his room and entered, crossing to sit on the bed next to him. Chick glued himself to her other side. Gently she ruffled her nephew's sun-streaked hair. "Are you all right?"

"I didn't mean to call him that," Buster managed to say through his tears. "I know he's not my dad. You told us we're just staying with him for a little while. He's a temp . . . Temp—"

"Temporary," Wynne supplied regretfully.

"Yeah, a temporary husband. I remember you telling us all that. About how marrying Jake is like a summer job except it's during the winter. Only . . ." Tears threatened again. "Only I wish we didn't never have to leave."

"I know." Those two simple words spoke volumes.

"Why can't we stay?" He lifted his head to look at her. "I like it here. Chick does, too."

Chick nodded, his pleading gaze matching Buster's.

"I'm sorry, but that's not fair to Jake." She swallowed, struggling for composure. "You see, I promised that we'd only stay for a little while. I can't go back on my word. It wouldn't be right."

"Can't you ask him to change his mind? If he says yes, that wouldn't be going back on your word." He threw himself into Wynne's arms. "Please let us stay. We'll be good. And we won't make no more trouble. I promise."

Hearing the desperation in her nephew's voice, she closed her eyes. If she didn't see his pain, perhaps she wouldn't be tempted to give in to it. Because refusing Buster's request was the hardest thing she'd ever done in her life, especially when she wanted it as badly as did he.

"I'm sorry," she whispered, fighting back tears of her own. "Please try to understand. I can't. When the time comes, we'll have to leave."

With a silent groan, Jake leaned against the wall, his hands balled in fists, his teeth clenched. This wasn't what he'd planned. This wasn't what he wanted. He'd never intended to inflict such hurt.

Damn it to hell! Why did he destroy everything he touched? Just once in his life he'd like to be the fantasy man Wynne saw, rather than the man fate had dictated. Just this once he wished . . .

He straightened, his spine rigid, his mouth a taut line. Who was he kidding? Wishes weren't for men like him. They never had been.

They never could be.

Jake examined another receipt and checked the total, a distant sound breaking his concentration. He looked up briefly, before returning his attention to the invoices spread across his desk. Hours had passed since that incident in the hallway and he'd closeted himself in the library, focusing on a backlog of paperwork. It was a blessing not to think, not to feel, just to go through the daily grind like some computerized automaton.

The sound came again and he frowned, tossing his pencil onto the desk. Now what? He crossed to the door and opened it, the sound assailing his ears shocking him so badly, for an instant he froze.

Another heartbreaking sob sent him tearing down the hallway. He careened off the wall and skidded into the kitchen. Wynne sat crouched in the middle of the floor, her face buried in her hands, quietly crying.

Slowly he sank to his knees next to her, feeling as though he'd been sucker-punched. Except for that single, gut-wrenching tear she'd shed on their wedding night, he'd never seen Wynne cry before. Not like this. Not like her heart was breaking.

"What's wrong?" he demanded, afraid to touch her, searching frantically for an injury.

With a hiccupped sob, she thrust out her hand and shook it beneath his nose.

He took her fingers gingerly in his. No cuts or abrasions, thank heavens. No swelling. No joints out of place. His brows drew together. "Talk to me, sweetpea. Where are you hurt?"

"I'm not hurt!" she answered in tragic tones.

"Then what the hell—*heck* are you crying for?" he demanded, relief bringing an exasperated tone to his voice.

She lifted her head, her huge green eyes overflowing. She shook her hand at him again. "I *l-lost* it! It went down the *dr-drain.*"

He stared at her hand, her left hand, and understanding dawned. "Your wedding ring. Your wedding ring washed down the drain?" Fresh tears broke loose and, taking them as confirmation, he gathered her into his arms. "It's all right. Don't cry. We'll get you another one."

It was the wrong thing to say. Her crying intensified. "I d-don't want another one! I want *our* r-ring. Th-the one you gave me when we got married."

Before he could reply, Buster and Chick slid to a halt in the doorway, followed closely by Dusty. "Told you she was crying," Buster said.

"What happened to her?" the foreman demanded. "What's wrong with the girl?"

"Her wedding ring went down the drain," Jake explained tersely. "Go get a wrench, will you?"

"We'll have better luck with a shovel," Dusty replied with a snort. "Most likely we'll have to dig up the whole septic system to find the dang thing."

Wynne shuddered in his arms and Jake glared at his foreman. "If I'd wanted your opinion on the matter, I'd have beat it out of you. Just get the damn-*dang* shovel, will you?"

"I'm a-goin', I'm a-goin'. No need to git yer britches in a bunch." Dusty shot the boys a meaningful glance. "The two of you best be careful. Bad luck comes in threes, ya know." With that telling comment, he took off.

Unfortunately, he was soon proved right. Not an hour later, Jake broke his hand tearing up the plumbing.

And the day after that Mrs. Marsh arrived.

"Go to the barn and get Jake," Wynne ordered the boys, the instant their aunt stepped from her rental car. "Then play upstairs until I call you. Jake and I will speak with Mrs. Marsh in private."

"What's she here for? What does she want?" Buster questioned apprehensively.

"I'm sure she wants to meet Jake and see how you two are doing."

"Is she going to take us away?"

Wynne gave the boys a quick hug. "Of course not. Everything will be fine. She's just here for a little visit."

Chick whispered in Buster's ear. Obliging his brother, he asked, "Do we have to go to that school of hers? The one that won't let us be together?"

"Not a chance. Now hurry and get Jake."

It seemed an eternity before he finally emerged from the barn. Joining her in the kitchen, he washed up while she brewed tea. "That woman parked in the parlor is your dragon?" he questioned in amusement. "You sure her name is Marsh and not Marshmallow?"

"You'll see," Wynne predicted ominously. "Don't let all those smiles and dimples fool you. She's as tough as old shoe leather."

"Why do you call her Mrs. Marsh? Doesn't she have a first name?"

"It's Kitty, but not even the boys are allowed to use it. I have permission to address her as Mrs. Marsh or ma'am." She gritted her teeth. "Needless to say, I refuse to call her ma'am."

"And I thought taking care of your dragon lady was going to be tough." Jake picked up the laden tray awkwardly and grinned. "Lead the way, fair maiden. I have a kitty to slew. Or is it slay?"

"Just watch your back," she retorted. "Or you'll find out which it is."

It took a whole thirty seconds for him to discover the truth behind Wynne's warning.

Mrs. Marsh, a fragile-looking woman in her early forties, took a dainty sip of tea, fixed guileless powder-blue eyes on Jake and flashed her dimples. "I do hate wasting precious time on preliminaries," she announced. "Why don't we get right down to business?"

Jake lifted an eyebrow. "I didn't realize you and I had any business."

"We didn't." She stared pointedly at Wynne. "Until very recently."

He shrugged. "So talk. I'm listening."

"You have a very fine ranch here." She wrinkled her tiny nose as though smelling something unpleasant. "Assuming you like ranches."

"I gather you don't." Not that there was much doubt about her opinion.

"No," she confirmed. "But my sources say this is one of the better ones, which must be why you went to such lengths to keep it. I refer, of course, to your marriage." She returned her teacup to its saucer and lifted a finely arched eyebrow. "A condition of your grandfather's will or some such thing?"

The dragon lady had been busy making inquiries. Who had she spoken to? Or perhaps the better question was, who hadn't she spoken to? "Yeah, it was a condition of his will. So?"

"So, now that you have legal control of your inheritance, you don't need a wife anymore."

His eyes narrowed. "According to you."

"And according to most everyone in town. Wynne and the boys are excess baggage and it's only a matter of time before you toss them out the door."

"Did you hear that, elf?" Ignoring proper decorum, he propped a booted foot on the coffee table. "Folks around here think I'll be putting you out with the garbage."

Wynne muttered something uncomplimentary and he couldn't help but wonder if it was aimed at the Marsh woman or at him.

"Please, Mr. Hondo. Let's be frank." Kitty Marsh leaned back in her chair and crossed her legs. "Now that your inheritance is secure, you don't need the pretense of a family anymore. Sooner or later, you're going to get rid of them. I'm willing to make it worth your while to make it sooner."

"How much?" he asked out of curiosity.

Wynne gasped in disbelief, but he ignored her, keeping his gaze trained on the viper seated across from him. He'd learned long ago never to take his eyes off a snake poised to strike and he didn't intend to start now.

The Marsh woman smiled in triumph. "How much would you like?"

"I can't say," he confessed, running a hand across his jaw. "To be honest, I have just about all the money I could ever hope to spend."

"Then perhaps I can offer something else." Her smile turned provocative. "I'm open to suggestions."

"Don't bother trying to seduce him," Wynne snapped. "He's not interested in married women."

"Only one," Jake corrected with a lazy grin.

"Then we'll stick to material assets," Mrs. Marsh retorted, her smile fading. "What will you take in exchange for the children?"

"Why do you want them?" he countered.

She shrugged. "Why does a person want diamonds or furs or a new car? It's an uncontrollable urge. Maternal instinct or something."

Maternal instinct in a pig's eye. He'd never met a woman less cut out for motherhood than this one. "Forget it," he stated flatly, tiring of her game.

"I didn't answer that right, did I?" she asked in amusement. "Okay, how about this . . . ?" Crocodile tears welled into her eyes. "They're all that's left of my poor, dear brother. I have so much to offer them, so much to give. And since I can never have children of my own—"

"Oh, please!" Wynne cut her off. "You never wanted children. You said they'd ruin your figure, that they were messy."

Her tears vanished as quickly as they'd come. "But don't you see? That's what makes it all so perfect. No horrid pregnancy. No smelly, squally babies. And best of all, they're housebroken." She turned on Jake. "Now, how much?"

"I'm not for sale and neither are they."

"I don't think you understand." Her voice hardened. "I'm really quite desperate here. I'll do whatever it takes to get my hands on those boys."

"Brad wants them, doesn't he?" Wynne guessed shrewdly.

Fury robbed her face of all beauty. "Yes. After all these years, my dear husband has decided he wants kids and I suspect he's looking around for someone young and nubile enough to provide them. Buster and Chick are my only hope."

Jake laughed. "I'm all broken up over your marital problems, lady. But that doesn't change my mind. The boys stay here."

Her eyes darkened, the blue turning as dull and garish as fake sapphires. "Assuming that's your final word on the matter, we'll move on to threats."

He didn't look worried. "And what would those be?"

"If you don't give me the children, I'll take Wynne to court."

"On what grounds?"

"I think my concern for the safety of the children should do the trick. Since arriving in Texas, they've been forced to stay in a run-down shack when they could have been housed here. They've attempted to ride the most dangerous horse in several counties. And they've come within a breath of being bitten by one of the deadliest snakes in the country." She tilted her head to one side. "Have I overlooked anything?"

Panic appeared in Wynne's eyes. "How did you find out about that?"

Jake didn't need to ask. "Randolph! The son of a b—"

"Yes, Mr. Hondo?" Mrs. Marsh prompted with a cold smile. "You were about to say?"

He gritted his teeth. "Never mind."

"I'll be sure to add your vulgarity to my list of concerns. Assuming I can find the room. It's a very long list." She switched her attention to Wynne. "I'm here to offer you a choice. You can turn the children over to me now and I'll allow you to continue seeing them. Or you can force me to endure the cost and annoyance of a court hearing. In which case I'll make sure you never see the boys again."

"That's not a choice," Jake snapped. "It's a threat."

"Actually, Mr. Hondo, it's a promise. One I intend to keep." She gathered up her purse. "I believe that concludes our business. I'll give you some time to discuss my offer, not that there's anything to discuss. When you reach your decision, contact me at the Bluebonnet Inn. Dreadful name, but pleasant enough accommodations considering I'm in Texas."

"Don't you want to see your nephews before you leave?" Jake questioned with heavy irony.

"No need. I'll see them soon enough. I plan to have them home with me by Thanksgiving." She stood. "Please don't get up. I can find my own way."

"And do me out of the pleasure of showing you the door?" Jake snarled as he gained his feet. "I wouldn't hear of it."

She drew back. "Are you threatening me with physical harm?"

"I don't threaten, either, Mrs. Marsh. Like you, I only make promises."

Her composure shaken, she backed toward the door. "Is that how you broke your hand? In a brawl? My list gets longer by the second. And my concern for my nephews grows along with it."

Predictably, Wynne leapt to his defense. "If you think he'd ever do anything to harm them, you're sadly mistaken. He's the sweetest, kindest, gentlest man in the world."

A reluctant grin snagged Jake's mouth. "Give it up, elf. Even I have trouble swallowing that one."

"As would anyone who's met him," added Mrs. Marsh. "I look forward to your call."

Gathering the shreds of her dignity, she marched from the room. A moment later the front door banged close, signaling her departure.

The boys crept silently up the steps to their room.

"Come on, Chick. I've got a plan," Buster said with grim resolve. "She can't take us away if she can't find us. So we'll just hide out until she goes away or finds some other kids to be nice to or something."

Chick whispered a question.

"Yeah, I guess they will be worried." He brightened. "We'll leave them a note. But we won't tell them where we'll be. That way nobody can make us go with Aunt Marsh if she wins the fight."

"What are we going to do?" Wynne asked, struggling to keep the panic from her voice.

"For now, we wait."

"But what about her threats?"

Jake shrugged. "Even if she takes us to court, I doubt she'd win. For one thing, we're still together, despite local gossip."

Wynne frowned. But for how long? Too bad she didn't have the nerve to ask. "What about her other complaints—you know, about Mad Dog and the snake?"

He grimaced. "I admit, the boys got into a scrape or two, but it hasn't hurt them. As Mrs. Marsh pointed out, this is Texas. There's not a kid around these parts who hasn't been bucked off a horse or come toe to fang with a rattler. I'm hoping the judge will see her as a sweet, if unduly apprehensive relative." His expression turned sour. "I assume she can play the sweet and caring aunt when it's in her best interest."

"She's a master at it," Wynne assured grimly. "The dimples alone could convince a card-carrying pessimist that the glass is half full. And if they don't do the trick, she turns on the waterworks."

"So I saw." He shuddered. "Heaven protect me from weepy women."

Wynne glanced at her bare left ring finger and bit her lip.

He caught the direction of her glance. "I'm sorry, sweetheart," he said with a sigh. "I didn't mean you. You had cause to shed a few tears. I just wish I could have found the darned thing."

"It's not your fault," she whispered. "I should have had it sized."

He tugged her into his arms. "Let me replace it. We can go into town and buy one that actually fits. It might even help convince Mrs. Marsh—" He broke off at her expression. "I'm just making it worse, aren't I?"

Tears threatened, but she refused to let them fall. "It wouldn't be the same. That other ring was part of the Cinderella Ball, part of how we met." She gave a forlorn shrug. "I don't think I can explain."

Jake shut his eyes. She didn't have to explain. He understood better than she knew. She was hurting and there wasn't a damned thing he could do about it. She wouldn't agree to a replacement and he didn't have a hope in hell of recovering the original.

He thought about it through that long afternoon as he worked outside with his ranch hands, setting a grueling work schedule for himself in vain hope of easing his guilt. Toward the end of the day, a solution occurred to him, one he filed away for future consideration.

"Ready to call it a day?" Dusty finally asked. "Or haven't you punished yourself enough?"

Jake lifted an eyebrow in question. "The men complaining?"

"Not yet. But that's not why I'm asking." Dusty stared pointedly toward the north. "Any man who doesn't keep one eye on the weather is just askin' for trouble."

Jake followed the direction of his foreman's gaze, then stowed his tools and went in search of Wynne. He found her in the library. "Come with me. I have something to show you," he said.

She looked up from her book. "What is it?"

"Ever seen a blue norther?" he asked, tugging her from the chair.

She laughed. "I don't even know what it is."

"It's a weather front. A rather impressive weather front."

He walked out onto the front porch with her and pointed north. "That's a blue norther."

A broad bank of steel-blue clouds chewed at the horizon. Even as she watched the ominous ridge consumed still more of the crystalline sky, roiling toward them like some airborne blight.

She shivered. "Is it serious?"

"Can be if you're not paying attention. Northers come in fast and hit hard. One minute it'll be seventy, the next near freezing. Top that with a nasty wind and chilly rain and—"

"And I better have the boys pull out some warm clothing."

"Good idea." He snagged the collar of her shirt and tugged her closer, his golden eyes glittering with wicked intent. "I think this calls for another fire, don't you? That way you won't need to bother with warm clothes. Hell, you won't need to bother with any clothes at all."

She gave him an innocent look belied by a teasing smile. "How in the world will I keep warm?"

"I'll think of something." He grinned. "After dinner, how about we get the boys settled for the night, open up a bottle of wine, and celebrate the coming of an early winter?"

She slid her arms around his waist, settling into the cradle of his hips. "What sort of celebration did you have in mind?"

"We can try one of those pagan rituals. You know, the ones where the participants are all buck-naked and chase each other around in circles. You can play the woodland nymph and I'll be the wicked satyr."

She moistened her lips. "I thought that was a springtime ritual."

"Okay." His mouth nuzzled the side of her neck. "We'll also pretend it's March."

Her eyes drifted closed and a helpless moan slipped from her throat. "Call the boys and I'll get dinner started."

He pushed her collar to one side, baring a creamy shoulder. "I thought they were in the house with you." She stiffened beneath his hands and he pulled back. "They're not?"

She shook her head, apprehension reflected in her eyes. "They said—they said they were going to help you."

"When?" He shot the word at her.

"Hours ago," she whispered. "Right after Mrs. Marsh—"

He swore. Pushing past her, he charged into the house, taking the steps to the boys' bedroom two at a time. Even before he found the note, he knew they'd run. Dresser drawers hung open, clothes formed a telltale trail from closet to bed. And most telling of all, the picture of their parents was missing from the nightstand.

Wynne entered the room behind him. He watched as she crossed to Buster's pillow and picked up the note. She read silently, covering her mouth with a trembling hand. Then she turned and walked into his arms.

"We'll find them," he tried to reassure. She went cold, as though all the zest and life had frozen her into an impenetrable ball of ice. He ran his hands up and down her arms. "I'll organize the men. They can't have gotten far."

"You said those fronts move in fast. How long do we have?"

"A couple hours," he lied without hesitation.

They wasted thirty minutes searching the house and outbuildings. It didn't surprise anyone that the boys were nowhere to be found. Jake pulled Dusty to one side, speaking fast, his face set in grim lines. "Have the men mount up and fan out," he said, glancing at the sky. "That front's moving in faster than I'd anticipated. We don't have much time."

"Why don't I drive over to Lost Trail and see if they're holed up there?" Dusty offered.

"Good idea."

"Jake—"

"I know. I'll take care of it." Without another word, he turned and headed for the house. He'd delayed long enough. Now he had to act. For the first time in his life, he was going to ask for assistance. He only prayed the people of Chesterfield would be willing to give it. Snatching up the phone, he punched in a number.

"Belle Blue here. What can I do you for?"

"It's Jake Hondo." He took a deep breath and said, "Belle, I need help."

Dead silence met his request. "You want help?" she repeated. *"You,* Jake?"

He gritted his teeth. "Yeah, me."

If she found his request amusing, she hid it well. "Sure thing. What's the problem?"

"It's the boys. They've run off."

"Oh, my heavens," she said with a gasp. "Jake, there's a norther movin' in."

"I know that!" He closed his eyes, struggling just this once to keep his temper in check. "Will you round up a search party for me? We need to find those boys. Fast."

"Consider it done. And Jake?" She spoke with more warmth than he'd ever heard before. "Don't you and your missus worry none. We'll track 'em down."

"Thanks," he whispered and cradled the receiver. He didn't doubt for a minute the boys would be found. The question was . . . Would it be in time?

Chapter Ten

Evening had set in when the door to the kitchen opened. Wynne watched anxiously as Jake stepped across the threshold and tossed aside his rain-soaked Stetson. He shook his head in answer to her silent query.

She turned away, fighting for control. "What are we going to do, Jake?"

"What else can we do?" Exhaustion filled his voice. "We keep looking."

Her hands balled in frustration. "It doesn't make sense that they haven't shown up. The boys may be foolhardy, but they're not stupid. They wouldn't stay out in this weather. What about Lost Trail? Perhaps they—"

"Dusty searched it earlier."

"It's a long walk." Desperation tainted her words. "Maybe they weren't there, yet. Or maybe they hid from him."

"Okay," he said evenly. "I'll go check the house again."

She turned around, setting her chin at a defiant angle. "I'm going with you."

To her surprise, he didn't argue. Perhaps he knew how desperately she needed to act, to do more than wait, worry, and brew coffee for the search party. "Get coats," he instructed. "And some blankets. If we find them, they're going to be half frozen."

Jake's broken hand prevented him from driving a stick shift, so Wynne slid behind the steering wheel of the truck. Not wasting any time, she started the engine, ground into first gear and spun out of the driveway. Fifteen minutes later she pulled into the dirt road leading to Lost Trail. Jake leaned forward, peering through the windshield.

"Aw, hell! Floor it, Wynne. I see a light."

She stomped on the accelerator, shooting off the end of the driveway and bouncing heedlessly across the lawn. Skidding to a halt outside the mudroom door, she leapt from the truck and raced into the house. The sight that greeted her almost brought her to her knees. A fitful fire crackled in the grate of the wood-burning stove, throwing off a miserly warmth. The boys sat huddled on the kitchen floor in front of it.

They weren't moving.

"Buster? Chick?" she called, approaching with leaden feet, afraid of what she'd find. They shifted in response to the sound of her voice and she sent up a silent prayer of relief, until they turned around. She gasped in horror at their pale, blue-tinged complexions.

"Hi, Aunt Wynne," Buster murmured in an exhausted little voice. "Boy, are we glad to see you."

She fell on them, hugging them close. "Me, too," she answered, her voice breaking despite her best efforts. They were cold. So very cold.

"We tried to call, but the phone didn't work."

Jake came in then, dropping blankets and coats at their feet and Chick held up his arms. "Uncle Dad," he whispered, croaking out the first words he'd spoken aloud in a long, long time. "I knew you would gets me."

It was too much to bear. In the darkest moments of despair, a miracle was born. Wynne bowed her head and burst into tears.

Jake scooped up Chick, his hands trembling uncontrollably, and buried his face in the boy's silky hair. "Go start the truck and turn the heater on high while I wrap them up," he ordered tersely. "We need to get them to the hospital as soon as possible."

"Are they going to be all right?" she questioned anxiously.

"I hope so." Moving with swift efficiency, he carried Chick from the house. Then he returned for Buster, situating the boys so they were close to the heating vents of the truck. "Let's go."

She tried to force the clutch into gear, but stalled the engine. For the first time ever, Jake heard her swear. He caught her hand as she reached for the ignition, his steady, golden gaze holding hers. "Take it easy, honey. I know you're frightened. But it'll work out. I promise."

"I can't. I can't do it," she cried. "He's finally talking and I can't hold it together long enough—"

"They're safe," Jake said calmly. "We just have to get them to a doctor to make sure they aren't suffering from exposure."

"We're safe now, Aunt Wynne," Buster repeated sleepily. "You don't have to be scared no more."

"No more," Chick confirmed.

"Now slow and easy, just like I taught you," Jake said. "Remember? First gear is a kiss."

She nodded, fighting off tears. Taking a deep breath, she turned the key and restarted the truck. This time, she slid smoothly into first.

"Thatta girl. Now a gentle touch."

Pushing in the clutch, she shifted into second. "How far to the hospital?"

"The closest one is in Two Forks."

"Jake—"

"Don't panic. You can do it. Shift into third."

"A bolder touch," she recited in a shaky voice.

"That's right. You're doing fine. Now drop down to a gentle touch as we take this curve. Well done."

He continued to talk the entire way. First helping her through the gears, then encouraging the boys. His voice was all that saved her from insanity. Pulling up to the emergency doors, it took three tries to peel her white-knuckled hands off the steering wheel. By the time she climbed from the truck, the boys had been taken inside.

"The doctors are looking at your sons now, Mrs. Hondo," a nurse advised. "In the meantime, I have some forms for you to fill out." While Wynne wrote and worried and waited for word on the boys' condition, Jake called off the search party.

"They were all out there looking," he said when he rejoined her. "Every last man. Even Randolph."

"They're not bad people," she replied. "You just need to give them half a chance."

"You think they'd let me?"

A smile slid across her mouth. "Yes. I think they would."

Thirty minutes later, the doctor entered the waiting room. "Good news, folks. Your boys check out fine. It might have been a different story if the oldest hadn't been smart enough to build a fire. They got lucky."

"May we see them?" Wynne requested.

"Of course. We're going to keep them overnight just for observation. But you can visit for a while, if you'd like."

She found the boys in the pediatric ward, their beds side by side. Wynne climbed in with Chick, holding him so tightly he squirmed in protest. Jake sat with Buster.

"You mad?" the boy questioned nervously.

Jake didn't bother to pull his punches. "Sure am. Care to explain why you took off like that?"

"We heard Aunt Marsh say she was going to take us away. So I thought we oughta hide till she went home."

"I guess that means you don't trust your Uncle Jake," Wynne spoke up.

Buster stared at her in confusion. "What?"

She returned his look, her gaze cool and serious. "You should have trusted him to keep his promise. He said he'd protect us from Aunt Marsh and he will."

"Wynne," Jake began. "I don't think—"

"It's important that they know." She cut him off. "When you say you're going to do something, they need to trust you." She scrutinized first one boy, then the other. "Understood?"

Chick snuggled deeper into her arms. "Okay," he answered without hesitation.

"I'm sorry I didn't believe you, Uncle Jake," Buster said contritely. "It won't never happen again."

His hands firmly tied, Jake leaned against the headboard and closed his eyes. Now what the hell did he do?

Mrs. Marsh appeared on their doorstep first thing the next morning.

She breezed into the house as though she owned it, commanding immediate attention. "I heard what happened to my nephews," she began without preamble.

"And ran right over to see how they were," Jake finished for her.

Her mouth twisted. "Cute, but wrong. I'm here to issue an ultimatum."

"Another one?" Wynne couldn't help asking.

"A final one. You see, thanks to this latest episode, there's no question that I'll win custody of the boys. You've put the children at risk too many times. So I'm giving you one more—"

"Get to the point." Jake cut her off.

Her gaze grew stony with dislike. "Very well. You had a quickie Nevada marriage, now I want you to get a quickie Mexican divorce. You do that, and not only will I grant Wynne generous visitation rights, I'll put it in writing. Fight me for so much as another day and she'll never see them again." She paused, flashing shark-like teeth. "You'll understand if I require an immediate answer."

He knew what he'd like to tell her. But one glance at Wynne, one glimpse of the fear and panic she fought so hard to hide, put paid to that idea. Besides, he didn't want open warfare with the Marsh woman. Not yet. Not when another option availed itself, a choice that had to be one of the toughest he'd ever faced.

"Well?" she prompted impatiently.

His hands clenched. "My marriage in exchange for the kids, is that how it works?"

"That's it."

"I'll agree, on one condition."

"Jake, no!" Tears sprang to Wynne's eyes, tears she brushed aside with an impatient hand. "Don't do it."

"Name your condition," Mrs. Marsh said quickly. It was obvious she sensed an easy victory.

"I need time."

She inclined her head. "Very well. I'll give you three days."

"It might take longer."

"Don't let it," she retorted with curt finality. "You have money. Use it. These matters can be taken care of easily enough for the right price."

"Trust you to know that," he muttered. "Oh, and there's one other condition. I'll fly out today, but I need your promise that you won't act until my return."

"I'll hold off for three days and not a second longer. Do we have a deal?"

"I guess you could call it that."

She heaved an exaggerated sigh of relief. "Well! That wasn't so difficult. It certainly has been a pleasure doing business with you, Mr. Hondo."

"Not from where I'm standin'."

She flashed her dimples. "Next time we meet I expect it to be with divorce papers in hand. Don't disappoint me, now. You wouldn't want to make me angry." Throwing Wynne a look of triumph, she sailed from the room.

Silence reigned for a full minute. Jake stared at the floor, steeling himself to deal with the tears, the disillusionment, the pleas.

"Jake—"

He stopped her with a single look. "We don't have any choice, you realize that, don't you? We have to settle the issue of our marriage once and for all."

"But—"

He shook his head. "I don't want to hear it. Those boys have to come first. Do you want to lose them completely? Your dragon lady isn't fooling around. She's desperate, and as much as I'd like to deny it, she has a case."

"You promised," she whispered. "We had an agreement."

"I promised to take care of your dragon and that's what I'll do. But it has to be my way."

She started to speak, then hesitated. Instead she took a step closer, then another and another until she stopped right in front of him. And all the while she stared as though she could see straight through to his soul. Questions danced within her unflinching gaze, trembled on her lips. She didn't speak them. Even as he watched a quiet conviction slipped across her face, absolute trust a flame in the verdant green of her eyes.

Finally, she nodded. "I'll let you take care of it," she simply said.

"That's it?" he demanded. "No questions? No complaints?"

She managed a shaky smile. "Would it do any good?"

"No."

She clasped her hands together, her fingers unconsciously searching for a wedding band that was forever lost. The minute awareness struck, she dropped her arms to her sides.

"If you're going to be gone for three days, you'll need some clothes. Why don't I help you pack?"

"Thanks," he said gruffly. "I'd appreciate that. I'd like to speak to the boys first, though."

It didn't take long. After explaining to Buster and Chick that he was leaving on a business trip, Jake crossed to the bedroom he shared with his wife and pulled an overnight bag from the closet. Pawing through his dresser, he threw the bare essentials into the case. Wynne went right behind him, removing and folding each item before repacking it.

Finished, he turned and glanced at her. "It's time."

Her chin wobbled ever so slightly. "Have a safe trip. I'll see you in a few days." She flashed him an anxious look. "Right?"

"Yeah, you'll see me again." He picked up his suitcase and took a step toward the door, but found he couldn't leave her, not like this. His case hit the ground. "Come here."

She ran into his arms, almost knocking him over. She was steel cloaked in velvet, a delicate beauty built over indomitable strength. The breath shuddered though her as she gathered that strength, slipping her hands across the tense muscles of his chest. Her lips skimmed his cheek like a butterfly, then honed in on his mouth. With a dark groan, he kissed her, pillaging the generous warmth with a desperation she couldn't mistake. Endless moments later, he set her from him.

"I have to go."

She didn't speak, simply nodded.

He picked up his bag and this time, made it to the door. At the threshold, he hesitated, his back to her. "Do you trust me, elf?"

"I always have," came her choked response. "And I always will."

His voice dropped, sounding raspy and strained. "I've never had anyone trust me before."

He barely caught her answer. "That's because you've never been married to me before."

His shoulders sagged beneath the burden of her words. "You have no idea the risk you're taking," he informed her harshly.

And then he was gone.

Judge Graydon pounded his gavel, bringing the court to order. A silence settled over the packed room as everyone eagerly waited for the proceedings to begin.

"I'm afraid we've delayed long enough," the judge said, looking at Wynne. "Have you heard from Jake, yet?"

Reluctantly, she shook her head. "I'm afraid not."

There hadn't been a word from him, not in all of the five impossibly long days that had passed since he'd left. During that time, she'd build a protective wall around her emotions, allowing nothing to intrude—except for her nephews. All the while she'd clung to her hope and her faith, discovering in the deepest hours of the night that faith and hope made for very cold bedfellows.

The judge sighed. "Then we'll have to begin without him. To start, I want it clearly understood that this is not a legal proceeding." He glared first at Peter, who sat next to her, then at the dapper lawyer who'd escorted Mrs. Marsh into the courtroom. "We're just having a nice, friendly discussion in order see if there's room for a compromise."

The dapper lawyer popped to his feet. "Larry Livingston, Jr., Your Honor. And I can assure you there isn't any room at all."

Graydon pointed his gavel at the man. "Sit down and stay put. I'll let you know if I'm interested in your opinion. Understood?"

Deflated, the lawyer did as he was told. "Understood, Your Honor."

"Good. Now I've reviewed Mrs. Marsh's complaints." The judge's brows pulled together. "And I don't think anyone can deny that these incidents she's detailed actually happened. Heck fire, Jake himself told me about the run-in the boys had with Mad Dog and that rattler."

Livingston springboarded to his feet again. "Your Honor, I object. Your relationship with the defendant is a clear-cut conflict of interest. I request—"

"Sit down!" Judge Graydon thundered. "I've already told you this is just a friendly little discussion, not a legal proceeding."

"But, Your Honor—"

Graydon leaned across the bench. "Let me offer you a piece of advice, Mr. Livingston. Since I'm the only judge in town, I suggest you do your level best not to tick me off. It won't help your client any. Got it?"

Livingston gulped, subsiding into his chair once more. "Got it, Your Honor."

Peter cleared his throat. "If I may?"

"If you must. Keep it brief, Bryant."

"Yes, Your Honor. I'd just like to say that boys will be boys."

Graydon snorted. "Quite insightful of you, Petey. Only these incidents are a little more serious than that."

"It isn't just the danger." Mrs. Marsh spoke up, managing to sound genuinely concerned. "Although, as you say, that's serious enough. But when you combine it with the problems surrounding Wynne's marriage, I just don't see how anyone can believe my nephews would be better off with her."

The judge lifted an eyebrow. "And what problems would those be?" he asked.

Impossibly long lashes swept downward to conceal the expression in her eyes. "Everyone knows their relationship is a sham. He only married her to get his hands on Chesterfield Ranch." She glanced around as though for support. "Surely it's no secret. Just as it's no secret that he's going to divorce her." Her tone sharpened. "And once he does, she'll have no husband, no home, and no viable means of support."

Graydon frowned. "I've never put much credence in gossip, Mrs. Marsh. Nor should you. As far as I know, there's been no talk of a divorce."

She smiled smugly. "Yes, there has. In fact, that's why he isn't here. He's getting a divorce even as we speak."

The courtroom erupted.

"Wait a minute!" the judge shouted. "Quiet!" He banged his gavel until the ruckus died down. Then he fixed a stern gaze on Mrs. Marsh. "Are you telling this court you know where Jake is?"

"I suggest you try Mexico," she replied, studying her perfectly manicured nails. "Or possibly Haiti. Wherever he can get a quick divorce. Though considering how long he's been gone, I'd hardly call it quick."

Judge Graydon switched his attention to Wynne. "Did you know Jake was off getting a divorce?"

"No," she answered politely. "Because he's not."

"Well, now I'm confused. One says he is and the other says he isn't." He released a gusty sigh. "Let's get this sorted out."

Toward the back of the room, Randolph stood. "Excuse me, Your Honor. May I say something?"

"I don't believe we need your brand of help, Chesterfield," the judge retorted.

"I actually planned to speak on Jake's behalf." He held up his hands at the hoots of disbelief from the people seated around him. "I know, I know. That's a first for me. But I recently discovered that I've been wrong about him, that I've accused him of things he never did." He took a deep breath. "My . . . my cousin never laid a finger on Evie, despite what I may have told folks in the past. It was just a big misunderstanding. I saw him drop her off one night, heard her crying, and naturally assumed . . . Well, the bottom line is, I was wrong. Evie tried to explain at the time, but I didn't believe her. I guess I wanted to think the worst of Jake. Y'all can probably figure out why."

"What changed your mind?" Wynne asked.

"You did," he confessed. "And Evie. The way you both defended him. After dinner last week my wife got rather vocal on the subject. It was enough to make me stop and listen." He folded his arms across his chest, reminding her vividly of Jake. "I guess what I'm sayin' is, I'm not willing to jump to any more conclusions about the man. If Wynne says he's not divorcing her, Jake will have to say different before I'll believe it." And with that, he sat down.

"Nice speech," Judge Graydon approved. "But that doesn't change the fact that Jake isn't here and we have conflicting reports regarding his intentions. Wynne, I hate to ask this, but what exactly did he say to you before he left?"

"Do I have to answer that?" she whispered.

"I'm afraid so, my dear."

"He said . . ." She clasped her hands together, searching again for a ring that wasn't there. Taking a deep breath, she confessed, "He said that he didn't have any choice. He was going to settle the issue of our marriage once and for all."

A shocked murmur rippled through the room.

"And that didn't suggest to you that Jake is planning a divorce?" Judge Graydon questioned gently.

She shook her head, a stubborn light leaping to her eyes. "I trust Jake. He wouldn't do that to me. He knows I need a husband if I'm to keep the children."

A man in the back of the courtroom stood, twisting his Stetson between his hands. "Excuse me, Judge. But if all she needs is a husband, I'll volunteer. And I wouldn't marry her and then change my mind after the fact, neither."

"Kind of you to offer, Wendall," Graydon began. "But—"

Another man stood. "I wouldn't object to having a wife like Miz Hondo. If Jake don't come through, I'm willing to offer for her."

Three more men stood. The judge ran a hand across his face. "Let me guess. You, too?" he asked. They all nodded. "It would seem you have no shortage of husbands to choose from, Mrs. Hondo."

"Just not the one I want," she replied, her voice catching.

Asa Blue rose to his feet. "Jake's divorcing Wynne and that's a fact. We all know the man. We all know why he married. And we all know he intended to divorce his missus once he was legally wedded, bedded, and court approved."

No one argued with his assessment of the situation.

"So, let's get to the crux of the matter," he continued. "Wynne says the children were left to her in her sister's will. The Marsh lady says that without a husband, a home, or a job, the children would be better off with her. Makes sense to me that if we get Wynne what she needs, then there won't be any more problems."

Murmurs of agreement echoed around the courtroom.

"Now, here's what I propose." Asa ticked off on his fingers. "Belle and I will make sure she has a job. As far as a home is concerned, either she can live with her new husband, or we'll rent her a place in town. That just leaves gettin' her a man." He planted his hands on his hips and scanned the room. "All you who are interested in applying for the position of her husband, stand up so she can pick out the one she likes best."

"Wait just a damned minute," Mrs. Marsh snapped, leaping to her feet. "This is insane."

Judge Graydon cocked an eyebrow. "How so? You've listed your complaints and we're taking care of them for you."

"There's one small problem," Wynne interrupted. "I haven't agreed."

"But, honey," Belle called out. "What Asa's suggesting is the perfect solution."

Wynne turned to face her. "Except, Jake and I are still married."

"For your sake, I'd like to believe that's true," Belle replied compassionately. "But you have to be realistic. You know what sort of man Jake is. And you know he only wanted a temporary marriage. Heck, his own words condemn him. As tough as it is, there comes a time when you have to face facts."

Wynne looked around. Except for Randolph, they all returned her gaze with pitying looks. She bowed her head. "You're right," she said softly. "When you weigh all the evidence, I have to admit, there isn't much room for doubt. Chances are, Jake's going to divorce me."

In the back of the courtroom, shadowed in the doorway, stood Jake. He caught the arm of the woman next to him before she could reveal their presence. "Quiet," he murmured. "Let her finish."

"But—"

His eyes flashed an unmistakable warning. "For once in your life, shut the *hell* up."

He returned his attention to the scene being played out before him and folded his arms across his chest. His wife sat near the front of the silent courtroom, her head still bowed. Wisps of white-blond hair clung to her nape and more than anything he wanted to go to her, slide his hands into those silky curls and kiss her senseless. He didn't budge. He simply stood and waited, steadfast in his conviction.

After a full minute, Wynne lifted her chin. "It's obvious to everyone here he's going to divorce me," she reiterated, then stated in a firm, carrying voice, "But I still don't believe it. I think you're all wrong. I think he loves me. And I know I love him. So until he walks in here and hands me the actual divorce papers, I'll have to decline your generous offers. But I appreciate your support."

It was all he needed to hear. Dragging his companion along with him, he strode into the courtroom, never once looking right or left. The entire time he kept his gaze trained on the only person in the world who mattered to him. He stopped in front of her and without a word yanked her from the chair and into his arms. And then he kissed her. He kissed her as if there was no yesterday and no tomorrow, kissed her with all the pent-up passion of a man who'd lived a life of emptiness and despair, kissed her until the darkness of the past few days were vanquished from her soul.

He felt her hot tears on his cheeks, tasted the sweetness of her love, heard the glorious sound of his name tumbling over and over from her lips to his. "I love you," he whispered for her ears alone. "And I swear, I'll never give you cause to doubt me again."

"Excuse me!" Mrs. Marsh's jarring voice cut like a knife. "Perhaps we can get back to business?"

Jake turned, planting himself between Wynne and her dragon. "Sure thing. Mind telling me what the hell is going on here?"

"We're picking out a husband for your wife," a voice called from the far side of the courtroom.

Jake's eyes flashed dangerously. "My wife already has a husband. She doesn't need another."

"What?" Bright patches of red stained Kitty Marsh's cheeks. "You said you were getting a divorce! We had an agreement."

"What agreement is this?" Judge Graydon interrupted.

She blanched, as though aware she'd said far too much. "I—I don't think that's relevant," she stammered.

The judge's eyes narrowed. "I suspect it's very relevant. But we'll get back to that later." He switched his attention to Jake. "Mind answering a question or two, Hondo?"

Jake lounged against the defendant's table, his arms folded across his chest. "Ask away," he said with a shrug.

"We seem to have rumors of a divorce floating around here. I don't suppose you'd care to give us the straight poop."

Jake managed to look suitably shocked. "A divorce? You mean, me?" He fixed the Marsh woman with a cold, feral gaze. "Who the hell said I was getting a divorce?"

The judge glanced at Mrs. Marsh, as well, and his expression soured. "Rumor had it you were off to Mexico."

"Actually, it was Nevada."

"Well, I know for a fact you can't get a divorce in Nevada, not in just five days. What were you doing there? If you don't mind my asking, that is."

"I don't mind." He tugged two small, wrapped packages from his pocket. "I was buying my wife a couple of presents."

Judge Graydon leaned across the bench. "You spent the last five days in Nevada buying your wife a gift?"

Jake shrugged. "Couldn't get them anywhere else. And they were important gifts."

Wynne peeked eagerly around his shoulder. "May I open them? Now?"

He smiled indulgently. "Yeah, elf. Go ahead." He handed her the first, a small, square jeweler's box.

She ripped off the ribbon and paper and slowly flipped up the red velvet lid. Inside were a pair of wedding bands. Very unique, strangely etched wedding bands. "Oh, Jake," she whispered.

"Know what they're made from?"

She nodded, struggling to talk through her tears. "From the tickets to the Cinderella Ball."

He cupped her cheek, lifting her chin so he could see the expression in her eyes as he said, "You told me your ring couldn't be replaced because it was part of the ball, part of how we met."

Understanding dawned. "And so is this." She touched the larger band, moistening her lips. "There's two of them."

"About time I wore one, don't you think?" He removed the rings and slid the smaller onto her finger. "Don't go losing it. I had a hell of a time convincing the Montagues to part with even one of their precious tickets."

Then it was her turn. She took his hand in hers and gently, firmly slid the band onto his finger. "You're not a temporary husband anymore, are you?"

He shook his head. "I don't think I ever was. But just in case there are any lingering doubts." He handed her the second present, a small, flat package.

She opened it, gasping when she saw a familiar, white velvet pouch. Inside were two tickets, the words Anniversary Ball etched in elegant scrollwork on the golden metallic wafers. Tears fell, thick and furious.

Jake straightened and faced the rest of the courtroom, his face settling into savage, uncompromising lines. "Anybody have more questions about the validity of my marriage? If so, they can come up here and discuss them with my fists."

"This doesn't change anything," Mrs. Marsh insisted shrilly. "There's still the question of my nephews' safety. He's a dangerous man. He just admitted as much with his last statement. And look at his hand. I don't even want to think about how he broke it. Probably in a fistfight or something."

The judge grinned. "How did you break it, Jake?"

"Fishing for Wynne's wedding ring," he admitted reluctantly.

"Come again?"

"She'd dropped her ring down the drain and I couldn't get the pipe off." He shrugged.

"You lost your temper and tried to force the issue."

"Something like that." He ran a hand through his hair. "She was crying. I—I couldn't just stand there and do nothing."

"Faced with that choice, I suppose a busted hand is understandable. So is a five day trip to Nevada." Graydon shook his head. "The things we men do to make our wives happy."

There were a few sympathetic chuckles from the audience.

"I guess that leaves one final issue," the judge said, turning a stern eye on Mrs. Marsh.

"Your Honor—" she began.

"My turn." Judge Graydon cut her off. "Madam, I'd like to offer a few words of advice. You are, of course, welcome to pursue legal action against these people. But I strongly suggest you reconsider. Because I promise, should you take this any further I will make it my personal business to find out about this mysterious agreement Jake referred to. And when I do, I'll be sure to forward that information to the appropriate parties." He let that sink in before adding, "Enjoy the rest of your visit to Texas. I trust it will be a brief one."

The courtroom exploded with applause.

Wynne stared up at her husband, her heart in her eyes. "I love you," she said. "Thank you."

"And I must love you something fierce," he admitted wryly. "Otherwise I wouldn't have brought her with me." He jerked his head toward someone standing out of sight.

Wynne turned. "Laura!" she cried, throwing her arms around her best friend. "What are you doing here?"

"Your husband can be very persuasive when he sets his mind to it. And he persuaded me I should give Texas another try."

People began to drift over to them, offering their congratulations and saying a few kind words in the hope of making amends. But it was to only one man that Jake offered his hand. "Thanks for what you said, cousin. I appreciate it."

Randolph shrugged awkwardly. "Family should stick together."

Jake wrapped his arm around his wife and grinned, the last of his demons finally conquered. "I couldn't agree more.

Why don't you and Evie join us for Thanksgiving dinner? We have a lot to celebrate."

Epilogue

Wynne glanced at the people gathered for Thanksgiving dinner and smiled mistily. She'd never thought she'd be so fortunate, or have so much for which to be thankful. Jake met her gaze across the long expanse of the table and winked. Then, breaking off his conversation with Randolph, he lifted his glass.

"I'd like to propose a toast," he said. He looked at Wynne, his eyes gleaming like polished gold in the candlelight. "To you, elf. I've never been more grateful for anything in my life."

There was a momentary silence and then Randolph lifted his glass. "And to Jake. I'm thankful for having the opportunity to straighten out our differences after all this time. I'm especially thankful he sold some of his land to me. And though I wouldn't have minded getting my hands on Chesterfield Ranch—" He grinned to let everyone know he was just kidding.

"He's happy to settle for a parcel of fine riverfront acreage instead," Evie finished for him. "And so am I."

Laura lifted her glass next, sending Peter a blatantly besotted look. "Well, I can't tell you how thankful I am to discover that Texas men aren't nearly as bad as I remember."

"Here, here," Peter said, shooting her an equally besotted look. "And I can't tell you how grateful I am to hear her say that."

Buster grabbed his glass of milk and hefted it with two hands. "I'm thankful, too, 'cause Jake slewed our dragon."

All eyes turned to Chick, and Wynne sent up a silent prayer. Slowly he popped his thumb from his mouth. "I's thankful I can talk," he announced in a clear, piping voice. "And that I gots a uncle-dad."

After the laughter died, Jake glanced at Wynne. "And what about you? What are you thankful for?"

A slow, radiant smile crept across her mouth. "I'm thankful that this house has a nursery."

Seven sets of eyes pivoted in her direction, reflecting various degrees of shock.

Then Jake said, "You mean—"

The End

A Note From Day Leclaire

I married just five short months after I met my husband. It was a total disaster! Oh, not the marriage. The *wedding*. We wanted to elope. We even tried to elope. Only one tiny miscalculation. I may have sort of told my parents ahead of time. *Big mistake. Huge.* (Yes, that's a quote from *Pretty Woman.*)

Needless to say, they didn't like the idea. At. All. Our runaway Vegas wedding turned into a more traditional "elopement" to my parents' house, with flowers and a minister and the whole nine yards. And then we did it all over again six months later, so all our relatives could attend. Umpteen years later (yeah, too many to confess to), we're still happily married.

I really hope you enjoyed *Fairy Tale Husband!* And just a word of advice . . . If you ever decide to elope, don't tell your parents beforehand, lol!

Love, Day

FAIRY TALE WIFE

The Cinderella Ball Series:

Book #2

By

Day Leclaire

USA Today Bestselling Author

Dedication

To Frank, Donna, Keli, and Kyle Totton.
Your love and support mean the world to me.

Prologue

Park Slope in Brooklyn, New York

Nikki leaned back against the wall and closed her eyes, fighting for control.

She hadn't meant to eavesdrop on her sister, Krista. She'd simply planned to ask her about dinner plans, hesitating outside the room when she'd heard her own name mentioned. Her sister's voice continued—relentless and sincere, inflicting wounds as painful as they were unintentional.

"I'm sorry," Krista repeated. "I don't know why you bothered to phone when you already know my answer. I can't. I owe Nikki. I won't desert her now."

Why hadn't she realized? Nikki wondered in anguish. Why hadn't she noticed that Krista's needs were no longer the same as seven years ago?

"She's my sister, that's why!" Krista's voice rose in anger. "She gave up everything to take care of me. What do you want me to say? Thanks. You saved my life but now I'm out of here? I've decided to move in with my girlfriend?"

Saved her life? Nikki shook her head. She'd done so little. Offering a home after the death of Krista's husband seemed the only logical option. She'd been pregnant. What other choice was there? Family came first. Family always came first.

"Well, I can't and that's the end of it! After what she sacrificed for me, the least I can do is be there for her now. Keli and I are all she has. And we're staying until she doesn't need us anymore."

Nikki didn't wait to hear the rest of the conversation. Silently, she retraced her steps down the hallway and entered the small room she used for a secondary office. Crossing to the desk, she opened the top drawer and removed a thick, gold-embossed envelope. It weighted her hand like a lump of lead, and yet the elegant ticket inside was anything but. An engraved wafer of gold, it offered a solution to all her problems.

She had prayed she wouldn't need to resort to such a drastic alternative. A choked laugh escaped before she could prevent it. She'd purchased the ticket because the situation at work had grown so untenable. It never occurred to her that she'd have a dual reason for going ahead with her plan. Unfortunately, overhearing Krista's conversation closed all avenues but one.

Slowly, she withdrew a white velvet pouch from the envelope. Inside the protective casing, the ticket shimmered as though alive, flooding the room with a brilliant, golden promise. For many people, the ticket would represent a dream come true.

Before she could control it, a lone tear slid down her cheek.

So why did it feel like a nightmare?

Chicago, Illinois

"Oh, Jonah, thank heaven you came." Della Sanders flew into her son's arms and hugged him fiercely.

A hint of amusement lightened Jonah Alexander's grim expression. "Did you doubt I would?" he responded, wrapping his mother in a gentle embrace.

For such a tiny creature, she brimmed with passion and energy and emotion. She was also a woman who inspired unwavering devotion. Jonah had spent a lifetime watching as she charmed those around her with unconscious ease. Some singular quality reflected in her soft hazel eyes and shy, welcoming smile could soften even the most hardened men, men like her second husband, Loren Sanders. In his line of work, tough, ruthless males were the rule rather than the exception and yet she'd won over the steely, confirmed bachelor in five seconds flat.

Della peeked over her shoulder at her husband and offered an apologetic smile. "Loren wasn't certain you'd be willing to bail Eric out of his latest mess." Her breath escaped in an exasperated sigh. "And to be perfectly honest, I wasn't, either. He's really gotten himself into a pickle this time."

Reaching around his mother, Jonah offered a hand to his stepfather. "You shouldn't have waited before getting in touch, Loren. Family always comes first with me. You know that."

It had ever since Jonah had been a rebellious, angry ten-year-old who'd unexpectedly found himself graced with a stepfather who'd appealed to both his intellect as well as his emotions. Loren had become an unconditional friend. And the deep and enduring love he'd given Della for the past twenty-five years sealed Jonah's eternal support and gratitude.

"You've always been a good brother to Eric," Loren said. "But the European operation keeps you so busy, we hated to bother you with this. Besides, we didn't realize how serious it was until recently. I just hope we're not too late."

Jonah released his mother and crossed to the floor-to-ceiling windows. The Sanders' Chicago condominium commanded a stunning view of Lake Michigan—a view that under normal circumstances he'd have taken the time to appreciate. "Tell me about it," he requested, turning his back on the expanse of tinted glass.

"Eric's fallen for a married woman," Della announced starkly. "An *older* married woman."

Jonah lifted an eyebrow. Not the smartest thing Eric had ever done, but hardly the most reprehensible. "And?"

"And she works for us," Loren explained. "Their relationship is interfering with both her performance and his. Between them they almost lost the Dearfield account."

Jonah swore beneath his breath. It must be bad if Eric had put a woman ahead of their most important client. What the hell could he be thinking? Obviously, handing over the New York branch of the business to his half-brother hadn't matured him any. "Do I know her?"

"Her name's Nikki Ashton. She's—"

"Head of Special Projects. Yes, I've heard of her. I don't think we've ever met, though." Jonah ran a hand across his nape, forcing himself to focus despite his exhaustion. "You hired her right after I left for London. What's she like?"

"She's a stunning woman, one of those leggy redheads."

"Loren," Della rebuked, "you know how much I hate it when you reduce people to the superficial."

He fingered his salt-and-pepper mustache and gave an apologetic shrug. "Sorry, darling. Old habits die hard."

"Get rid of her," Jonah recommended without hesitation.

Loren cleared his throat. "I'm afraid we can't."

"Why not?"

"The company needs her. For one thing, she's brilliant," Loren admitted. "And for another, she's just been nominated for the Lawrence J. Bauman Award. The ceremony's in six weeks. How would it look if we fired someone of that caliber?"

Jonah's mouth tightened. Unfortunately, they were right. Businessmen and -women nominated for the LJB Award were the most sought after in the country. It would cause irreparable harm to International Investment's reputation if they were to dump a potential winner on some trumped up excuse. "Have you spoken to Eric about the situation?"

"No," Della admitted. "We kept hoping it would blow over. You know Eric. He falls in and out of love more often than the wind changes."

"But not this time."

Della shook her head, tears gathering in her eyes. "She must be quite a special woman to hold his interest this long."

Jonah turned to face the windows. He knew Eric well enough to suspect which qualities needed to be so "special" to snag his half-brother's attention for any prolonged length of time. If Nikki Ashton was a tenth as brilliant as Loren claimed, she'd have figured it out, as well. And she'd have used her wealth of riches to bring Eric to heel. He'd have been easy prey for a savvy—not to mention leggy—redhead.

"What about her husband?" Jonah questioned over his shoulder. "Or doesn't Mr. Ashton care that Mrs. Ashton is having a fling with her boss?"

"We don't know anything about him other than he's been out of the country for the past year," Loren confessed. "I don't even think his name is Ashton. She married about the time she started with us, but kept her maiden name. I checked with personnel and Nikki never gave them any details. He's not part of her insurance or benefit program, either. He's not even listed as an emergency contact. Only her sister is." He shrugged. "I'm afraid that avenue is something of a dead end."

"A modern marriage. How convenient," Jonah observed drily. He swiveled to face them, folding his arms across his chest. "Okay, Loren. What do you want me to do?"

"Couldn't you try to reason with Eric?" Della suggested before her husband had a chance to reply. "Or speak to Mrs. Ashton? If their relationship is causing as much trouble at the office as Loren fears, perhaps we could transfer one or the other."

"We have to be careful, Della," Loren replied with a frown. "I need Eric in New York right now. Aside from this incident with the Ashton woman, he's become a real asset to the firm."

"I've seen the reports," Jonah commented. "I'd hoped it meant he'd finally gotten his act together."

"Until this latest indiscretion he had." Loren shot his stepson a look of grim warning. "We also need to handle Nikki with kid gloves. She knows a lot about the company."

Jonah's eyes narrowed. "You mean she could do us some real damage?"

"If that's her angle," Loren confessed unhappily.

"Would you fly to New York and find out what's going on?" Della pleaded. Worry etched fine lines between her drawn brows. "Perhaps we're overreacting."

Jonah shook his head. "If anything, you're not worried enough. If Eric is serious about marrying this woman, she could be the worst thing that ever happened to him. But what if he's not serious? What if he loses interest in her? Would she want to even the score?"

Loren visibly paled. "I hadn't even considered that possibility."

"You'll fly out in the morning?" Della questioned, clutching Loren's arm.

"I'll leave now."

"But you must be exhausted," she protested. "You've just flown in from London. You need to sleep and—"

"I'm tough, Mother. Nor do I believe in jet lag." A tight smile touched Jonah's mouth. "Besides, I want to get to New York before Eric realizes I'm in the country."

New York City, New York

"What do you mean Eric's not here?" Jonah fought a losing battle with his temper. "Just where the *hell* is he?"

Eric's secretary squirmed in her chair. "I'm sorry, Mr. Alexander. He's left."

"Left." Jonah planted his hands on her desk. "Could you be more specific, Ms. Sherborne? Where has he gone? And when will he return?"

"He had to catch a plane." She risked a swift, upward glance. "But I'm fairly certain he'll be back by Monday."

"Monday," Jonah repeated. Had someone heard he'd returned from London and warned Eric? "Was this a sudden trip?"

"Very sudden. I guess—" She cleared her throat nervously. "I guess he had business out of town."

Judging by the worried quiver in the woman's tone and the telltale flush invading her cheeks, the chances of Eric's disappearance having anything remotely to do with business were next to nil. "Where is he, Ms. Sherborne?" he demanded coldly.

"I'm not certain of the specifics." She looked everywhere but at him. "I can tell you he booked a flight to Las Vegas."

"*Nevada?* What business does he have there? We don't have any clients or investments in Nevada."

It was obvious the secretary would rather be anywhere other than pinned beneath his arctic stare. "Perhaps Mrs. Ashton's assistant knows," she finally suggested, the idea of passing him on to someone else clearly appealing to her. "Her name's Jan and her workstation is right across the hall."

Jonah stilled, fury gathering in his hazel eyes. "Mrs. Ashton's secretary is more familiar with Eric's movements than you are? Why is that?"

"Oh, no," she sputtered in alarm. "You don't understand. You see, Mrs. Ashton went to Nevada, too. Mr. Sanders didn't say where he'd be staying and I thought, perhaps, since the two of them were going together . . ." She trailed off miserably.

Jonah stepped away from her desk, letting her off the hook. "You thought that since this was a business trip, Mrs. Ashton and Mr. Sanders might be sharing the same hotel, and that Jan would have the particulars. Is that right?" He made sure she caught the stern warning behind his explanation. One breath of gossip about this weekend tryst and her career at International Investment would come to an abrupt end.

Comprehension dawned in her wide eyes. Drawing a deep breath, she nodded. "Yes. That's exactly what I thought."

Without another word, he crossed the hall. Jan proved to be quite efficient. Although she didn't have any information about Eric's movements, she had all the pertinent details regarding Nikki's. Within minutes, he had a copy of her itinerary and booked himself on the next flight to Las Vegas. Which left one more vital chore, he decided grimly.

Ignoring Jan, he thrust open the door to Nikki's office and walked in, shutting it firmly behind him. He paused just inside the dim room. The November sun was fast becoming a chilly memory as the afternoon waned. It wouldn't be long before the

Friday rush hour started in earnest. He didn't bother to check his watch to see how close he risked cutting the drive to La Guardia Airport. He couldn't remember which time zone he'd set it for anyway. This little fishing expedition would have to be swift.

He glanced around, a light floral scent assailing him, a perfume he'd never smelled before. It could only belong to one person. He inhaled deeply, feeling as though he drew Nikki's essence into his lungs. It wasn't the musky odor he'd have associated with a sultry redhead. Instead of black satin and lace, her perfume brought to mind a Victorian parlor filled with fresh flowers, sunshine, and lemony beeswax.

He shook his head, amused. Clever woman. Something heavy and overtly sexual would have been too much of a cliché. Eric would have seen through that in a fast second. No, she was smart. Cloak a sexy package with an air of charming innocence and she'd bring most men to their knees.

Crossing to her desk, he switched on a high-intensity lamp. It cast a blazing circle of white in the middle of the mahogany tabletop. Files were placed in neat, orderly stacks to one side, and just outside the pool of light stood a framed photo. Intrigued, he picked it up.

The picture of a young, laughing girl jolted him. He hadn't suspected that Nikki Ashton might have a child. Career women hot to marry the boss's son rarely came encumbered. He studied the photo. The girl couldn't be much more than five or six, her tiny-boned features surrounded by a cloud of strawberry blond ringlets. A woman held the child tight within her grasp. Nikki, no doubt. He couldn't tell what the mother looked like, since the child's flyaway curls obscured most of the woman's face. Only her eyes and hair were clearly visible—china blue eyes brimming with laughter and hair a shade or two darker than the little girl's.

It wasn't much to go on.

He returned the photo to its former position on the desk and glanced around, searching for any other personal touches that might reveal more about Nikki. But the desk—hell, the entire room—was practically barren, its decor austere and stark and unrelentingly tidy.

His gaze came to rest on the one other jarring note to the office. A scraggly line of badly tended plants filled the window ledge. For some reason, the plants bothered him. A lot. They suggested some clue to her personality he couldn't quite pinpoint, but exhaustion and a relentlessly ticking clock kept the vital piece from taking shape. Later. He'd think about it later, when he had the time.

Besides, what could a bunch of half-wilted plants mean other than she'd purchased something bright and pretty on a whim and then couldn't be bothered to care for it?

Finally, he turned his attention to the appointment book centered within the circle of light. He didn't hesitate to invade her privacy. He flipped rapidly through the pages. Tucked between Wednesday and Thursday he found a thick, gold-embossed envelope, empty except for a small rectangular card. He pulled it out, scanning it swiftly.

The Cinderella Ball. The Montagues wish you joy and success as you embark on your search for matrimonial happiness.

At the bottom he found an address and the date of the ball.

It was today's date.

It didn't take long for the full impact to hit. Nikki had flown to Nevada to attend some sort of marriage ball. He thrust his hand through his hair. It could only mean one thing. Mrs. Ashton was now free of her unknown husband and available to marry. And Eric, without question, was her groom-to-be.

Jonah gritted his teeth. Well, not if he could help it. Because when he caught up with the beautiful, scheming Mrs. Ashton, she'd regret ever interfering with his family. He'd see to that.

Personally.

Chapter One

The Montagues' Cinderella Ball—Forever, Nevada

Nikki Ashton walked into the ballroom fighting to hide her apprehension behind a calm expression. There was no doubt about it. She'd clearly lost her mind.

How could she possibly believe marriage provided the solution to all her problems? And how could she walk into this room full of strangers and find a man willing to play the part of her husband for the next few months? It was crazy. Insane.

And she'd never been so frightened in all her life.

She drew in a deep breath, then another and another. Ominous spots danced before her eyes.

"Hi," said a cheery-voiced woman.

Nikki turned blindly in that direction and discovered a waif-like pixie hovering at her elbow. "Hello," she said, amazed she'd managed to return the greeting.

"Care to sit with me for a minute?"

Afraid if she didn't sit, she'd fall down, Nikki sank into one of the clutches of seats and tables dotting the outer fringes of the ballroom. "Thanks," she murmured, dropping her purse onto the small table in front of her.

"I'm Wynne Sommers," the woman introduced herself.

"Nikki Ashton."

Bright green eyes peeked at her from beneath wisps of white blond hair. "Scared?" Wynne asked sympathetically.

For the first time in what seemed like ages, Nikki answered with the truth. "Terrified." She twisted her fingers together. "I'm not sure I can do this."

"But you have to, right? People are counting on you and this is the only option available."

Nikki stared at her companion in amazement. "How could you possibly know that?"

"I thought I recognized a familiar air of determination mixed with desperation." Wynne laughed. "It's the same for me."

"You have to marry?"

"I have two kids counting on me. If I don't marry, I lose them."

"I have relatives counting on me, too," Nikki found herself confessing. "Only I'm *trying* to lose them."

Wynne nodded sagely. "Some birds won't try their wings as long as Momma's there to feed them."

Nikki smiled in relief at the woman's instant understanding. "Something like that." She glanced around the crowded ballroom, pleased she could breathe again. "Have you been here long?"

"A couple of hours. The Montagues sure have a beautiful place. Have you met them yet?"

"When I first came in. They're a sweet couple."

"And their story is so romantic. Imagine being introduced to a complete stranger at a ball, falling madly in love, and marrying that same night." Wynne sighed. "And here it is fifty years later and they're still every bit as much in love with each other as the day they met."

"I don't expect that to happen to me," Nikki insisted firmly. "I mean it's lovely of them to throw a Cinderella Ball every five years so others will have the same opportunity they did. And I'm sure there are plenty of people who find real love thanks to them. But it won't happen to me. I'm here for practical reasons. I have to get married."

"So do I. Still . . ." Wynne cupped her chin in her hand. "I don't know why we can't have it all. I'm sure going to try. And did you know there's also an Anniversary Ball?"

"A what?"

"An Anniversary Ball. The Montagues throw a one-year Anniversary Ball for everyone who marries tonight." She sighed. "I'd sure like to go to that."

"We have to get married first," Nikki reminded her. She gazed out at the glittering array of chattering men and women and fought the resurgence of her former panic. "I don't even know where to begin."

Wynne offered an encouraging smile. "The first few conversations are the hardest," she said gently. "After that, it gets easier. Honest."

"Have you had any luck finding someone?" Nikki asked hesitantly, glancing at her newfound friend.

"Oh, I have my future husband all picked out. That's him over there." She inclined her head toward a tall, fierce-looking man chatting to a hard-eyed brunette. "Nice, huh?"

Nikki shivered. "Not really."

"Don't let the tough exterior fool you," Wynne said with a quick laugh. "He wouldn't be much of a man if he didn't carry a bit of armor. He's a fighter, that one. Do you need a fighter?"

"He can't be a pushover, that's for sure," Nikki said, thinking of Eric.

"I'll tell you what. How about if you practice on my warrior? He won't mind. All I ask is that if it looks like he might be the one you want, give me the chance to talk him out of it. Okay?"

Nikki stared in astonishment. "Let me get this straight. You want to marry him, but you'll let me—"

"Have a go at him first. Sure." Wynne gave a careless shrug. "I don't think he's the man for you or I probably wouldn't offer. But he's a great icebreaker. He doesn't bother with a lot of social chitchat, just gets right to the point. Once he teaches you how to do it, the rest of the night will be a snap."

Nikki nibbled on her lower lip. "I don't know . . ."

Wynne reached out and touched Nikki's arm. "Is marrying important to you?" she asked seriously. "Is it the most important decision you've ever made? Because if it isn't, go home."

"I can't," Nikki whispered. "I don't have any other choice."

"Then focus on that. It'll help get you through the evening. Look. The brunette is leaving. This is your chance. Go introduce yourself."

Nikki took a deep breath and stood. She couldn't say how or why, but in the past few moments, she'd regained control. She glanced down at Wynne. "Thanks," she said. "I owe you more than you'll ever know."

"Just remember our deal."

With a nod of agreement, Nikki headed toward Wynne's future husband.

Jonah glanced again at the card he'd confiscated from Nikki Ashton's desk, then at the cabdriver. "You sure this is the place?" he asked doubtfully.

"The Montagues' Cinderella Ball, right?" the cabby said in a bored voice. "That's where you wanted to go and that's where I've brung you. Just follow all those people. So's long as you stay on the walkway, you can't get lost."

Jonah gritted his teeth and used his credit card to pay before climbing out. Walkway or not, it would have been impossible to get lost. The damn place was the only building for miles around. It sat in the middle of the Nevada desert, outlined against the nighttime sky by colored floodlights and looking like some sort of giant platter stacked high with white-frosted cupcakes. He stared at the ridiculous architectural confection, then shrugged. What the hell did it matter? If it allowed him to get his hands on Nikki Ashton, he didn't care if they'd built the place to resemble a bowl of whipped cream and cherries.

He worked his way through the crowd and into the mansion, pausing in the white marble foyer to get his bearings. A huge chandelier hung overhead, its soft light magnified by thousands of tiny prisms. Pine garlands embellished with twinkling fairy lights and white satin bows graced the massive Doric pillars that supported the thirty-foot ceiling. The flow of people continued around him and up twin, heart-shaped staircases. Taking a deep breath, he followed.

At the top of the steps he joined a reception line filing into the ballroom and only then realized that this ball required tickets for entry. He felt for his wallet, wondering if they took credit cards. Or perhaps he could bluff his way in. The throng moved steadily forward and within a few minutes he'd reached the head of the line. In front of him stood one of the most beautiful women he'd ever seen. She was tall and slender, her dark hair styled severely off her face. She held a basket of gold, wafer-like tickets and offered a smile of greeting.

"I'm Jonah Alexander," he began. "Listen, I have a small problem—" But before he could utter another word of explanation, she suddenly focused on the next person in line. Her rich amber eyes widened in shock.

"Hello, Ella," a man's voice rumbled from behind.

Her face turned ashen. "Rafe," she whispered, and the basket of tickets tumbled to the floor.

Dropping to one knee, Jonah scooped handfuls of the heavy metal wafers back into the velvet-lined basket. With a muffled exclamation, Ella crouched beside him to help. "Are you all right?" he asked quietly.

"Fine," she insisted, though her trembling hands betrayed her. Gathering up the last ticket, she stood. "Thanks for your help."

"My pleasure."

He rose, too, and glanced pointedly at the man she'd called Rafe. He hadn't budged, but remained rooted in place as though he had all of eternity to wait. His cold gray eyes met Jonah's, leaving no doubt whatsoever that the situation with Ella was a highly personal matter. Still, Jonah never backed down from a fight. Using his height and breadth to secure his position in front of the woman, he turned his back on Rafe.

"Anything else I can do for you?" he offered deliberately, folding his arms across his chest. Unless she asked him to move, it would take a bulldozer to shift him from his stance.

Despair filled Ella's eyes. "I'm afraid not. Welcome to the Cinderella Ball. Enjoy your visit and we wish you a . . ." Her voice wavered, but she recovered swiftly. "We wish you a joyous future."

She'd practically handed him his walking papers. As much as he wanted to remain and help her out of whatever predicament Rafe represented, he didn't dare. He'd managed to gain entrance through sheer luck. He'd be a fool to push it. To his private disgust, he lingered anyway. Old habits, it would seem, died hard.

"You're sure?" he asked softly.

Rafe stirred behind him. "Tell him to go, Ella. You know this is a private matter."

She gave Jonah a reassuring smile. "Rafe and I are old—" She hesitated, her smile turning bittersweet. "We're old associates. But thanks for your concern."

Jonah inclined his head. Sparing Rafe a final look of warning, and secretly amused at himself for bothering, he exited the reception line and plunged into the crowded ballroom. Despite the urgency of his own mission, if Ella had asked for his help, he'd have given it. He didn't have it in him to desert a woman in need. But since she hadn't asked, it was time to get down to business.

He had to find Eric and Nikki before it was too late.

Staring out across the packed ballroom, he realized what a monumental task he'd set himself. Finding his brother would be almost impossible. Eric wouldn't stand out among the multitudes, despite his slim height and gold-streaked hair. Jonah's eyes narrowed. But perhaps by zeroing in on the redheads, he could shake Nikki Ashton loose from the pack. Wherever he found Nikki, undoubtedly he'd find Eric, as well. Unwilling to waste another moment, he fixed on a possible candidate and began his pursuit.

Jonah leaned a shoulder against the wall and glared at the dancers twirling by. Damn it all! In the past ninety minutes, he'd waded through dozens of redheads in every shape, size, and shade. Not one of them was Nikki Ashton. He stifled a yawn, struggling to throw off the exhaustion dogging him. He needed more coffee and needed it badly. Check that. What he really needed was a few hours' sleep. If not for the urgency of his mission, he'd call it a night and find somewhere to crash.

But it was urgent, and tired or not, he had to get on with it.

He took a deep breath, steeling himself to chase after the next redhead who floated by, when a tantalizingly familiar scent snagged his attention. It came from a woman several feet away. She had her back to him and conducted an earnest conversation with a small, bookish individual.

He hesitated, eyeing the waist-long tumble of curls. She wasn't a bona fide redhead, at least she didn't possess the brilliant sun-streaked red from the photograph. In fact, it didn't even come close. This woman's hair reflected a subtle combination of brown and red, the color awash with vivid highlights of both in a full palate of shades.

He started to dismiss her, but she shifted her stance, and her scent drifted by once again. If it wasn't the same perfume from Nikki Ashton's office, it came damned close. Regardless, it roused his hunter's instincts. Driven to act, he resumed the hunt.

"Ah, there you are," he interrupted her conversation with a lazy smile. "Sorry to take so long."

The woman turned abruptly, her gaze clashing with his. He'd made a mistake, he decided in that instant. This couldn't be the Ashton woman.

Not only was her hair color all wrong, her eyes didn't match the china blue of the photo, either. Instead, they were a velvety pansy blue, almost violet in their intensity. She also looked far too young and virginal. Sweetly intelligent. Not bookish, she was far too beautiful for that. But contained. And about as far from the image of a femme fatal as she could possibly get.

He'd accosted the wrong woman. Again. This time he didn't give a damn. He was tired and angry and in desperate need of a ten-minute break, a break he intended to spend in the arms of a beautiful woman.

He slipped a hand around her waist. "You promised me the next waltz, remember?" he asked. Before she had a chance to argue, he inclined his head toward her companion. "Excuse us," he said without a trace of apology, and swung her onto the dance floor.

To his amusement, she didn't say a word, simply stepped into his arms as though she belonged. Even in a stunning pair of sky-high heels, she didn't come close to matching his height. The top of her head nestled just beneath his chin. Her scent wrapped around him and he closed his eyes, surrendering to the moment.

She didn't pull away. She allowed him to tuck her close, her lush curves settling into his as though they'd been specially made to fit. They danced in silence for several long minutes before curiosity drove him to look down at her.

Damn, she was a gorgeous woman, with exquisite bone structure and a creamy complexion bare of any freckles. She'd dressed all in ivory, the tailored jacket decorated with tiny seed pearls and crystal beads, and cut to accommodate her full breasts. She moved with ease, a full tulle skirt fluttering around her. Every so often it clung to gorgeous, shapely legs, just long enough to cause a momentary qualm as he recalled Loren's description of Nikki Ashton. *She's a stunning woman, one of those leggy redheads.* Jonah frowned, eyeing his dancing companion speculatively. If he hadn't seen Nikki's picture, the woman he held in his arms could fit that description.

Then he caught sight of the wedding ring decorating her left hand and his gut clenched. Nikki was supposed to be married, too.

"This might be a good time to introduce ourselves," he suggested.

She shot him a wry look. "I assume that means we haven't met before, despite what you told Morey?" Her voice matched her hair, a mix of striking color and intonation, humor adding a musical note to her question.

"You caught me," he admitted, his mouth relaxing into a smile. "But it's an oversight I'm happy to correct."

"And I suppose that also means that I didn't promise you this or any other dance?" She glanced at him, amusement glinting in her eyes. "Did I?"

Those eyes intrigued him, the color an unusual blend of lavender and blue, the lighter portion of the iris ringed by a band of indigo. "Would you have forgotten if you had?"

She shook her head, a husky laugh escaping. "I suspect you'd be a hard man to forget."

She didn't say it flirtatiously, but with the cool candor of someone stating an indisputable fact. If he weren't so suspicious of her identity, he'd find her frankness appealing. "I'm Joe Alexander," he said, using the abbreviated name he'd assumed for the evening.

"Nikki Ashton," she replied.

It took every ounce of self-possession not to react, not to haul her off the floor and level her with accusations. The music ended just then, but his arms tightened around her. He hoped to hell Eric wasn't anywhere nearby or there'd be hell to pay.

"One more dance."

Once again she subjected him to that calm, assessing stare. "You aren't asking, are you?"

"No."

She hesitated. Before she could respond, the lights dimmed and the orchestra slipped into the next song, a slow, romantic one, chosen to encourage physical and conversational intimacy. Jonah gritted his teeth and molded her close, struggling to remain unaffected now that he knew her identity. She brushed against him as they drifted across the floor and his entire body clenched in response.

He wasn't the only one affected, he realized in the next instant. Delicate color tinted Nikki's cheeks and her breathing quickened. She wouldn't react to him like this if she were in love with another man came the furious thought.

Unless, of course, she wasn't really in love. Curious to test his theory, Jonah slid his hand down the length of her spine, his palm settling into the hollow above her backside. The slightest amount of pressure set her tight against him.

And then he slowed their dance until it became nothing more than a pretext, a subtle form of foreplay. In the space of a few steps, her movements aligned themselves to his and their movements went from subtle to searing.

He was practically making love to her right there on the floor—and she to him. Each step became part of a mating dance, her breasts crushed against his chest, her hips and thighs melded to his. She moaned, the sound barely more than a breathless sigh. But he heard it. He heard it and knew what she wanted.

"You feel it, too. Don't you?" he murmured.

"Yes."

The admission seemed torn from her. As though stunned by her own daring, she lifted her gaze to his, her eyes darkening like the sky before a gathering storm. But she didn't pull away, which only confirmed what he'd suspected. If she were in love with Eric, she wouldn't be responding to him. Not like this.

Determined to have final confirmation, he maneuvered her toward a dark corner. Their movements slowed until the gentle rocking motion was no more than an excuse to maintain as intimate a contact as possible.

Her attraction was undeniable and impossible to ignore. Everything about her appealed—her full, lush mouth, her sunset-hued eyes, the rich auburn of her hair, the low, confidential pitch of her voice.

A small part of him fought to retain a clinical detachment. But as hard as he struggled to remember whom he held, that knowledge didn't change the intensity of his reaction. Whether he'd finally succumbed to jetlag or her allure outweighed his common sense, he couldn't tell.

He only knew instinct born in the male of his species millennia ago drove him—an instinct urging he abandon caution and take the object of his desire, by force if necessary. Thrusting his hand into her hair, he tilted back her head and covered her mouth with his.

He didn't ease into the kiss, didn't bother with preliminaries, but stamped his ownership in the most primitive way possible. She instantly yielded, offering sweet surrender in the face of his determined assault. It was that unexpected capitulation that almost sent him over the edge.

With an incoherent murmur, her lips softened, parted, encouraging him to plunder within. He didn't need a second invitation. He forged a union between them, mating his tongue with hers.

She trembled in his arms, clinging to him as though he alone sustained her. And he, heaven help him, worshiped her with both hands and mouth. If they'd been anywhere but in such a public setting, he'd have taken what she offered with such unstinting passion. But he couldn't allow the burgeoning fire storm free rein.

Not here.

Not now.

Ultimately, it was that thought that restored his sanity.

With a muttered curse, he dragged his mouth from hers. He'd made a mistake touching her, he realized. Desire had given her beauty a wild edge and he couldn't help but wonder what she'd look like after a night of passion. Just the thought of her in his bed, her glorious hair spread across his pillows and her white, silken limbs entwined in his sheets almost destroyed his control.

Slowly, she opened her eyes and he saw then that she'd become a flame to his moth, a bewitching siren capable of enticing him to his doom. If his little brother saw them like this, he'd know what sort of woman he intended to marry. Whether she planned to line her pockets with Sanders money or she just hoped to advance her career, her reasons for marrying Eric had nothing to do with love. Jonah fought a surge of anger. The proof of that stood trapped within his arms, evidenced by the blatant desire reflected in a pair of pansy-soft eyes.

So where the hell was Eric? he wondered savagely. Why wasn't he here to witness the duplicity of his blushing bride-to-be?

His expression must have betrayed the violence of his thoughts. With a small murmur of dismay, she attempted to twist free. Jonah caught her close, not daring to release her. Not yet. Not until he decided what to do with her.

"Easy," he soothed, stroking her back. "Take it easy."

"Joe, please."

There was a frantic note to the way she spoke his name and he knew what was coming. If he didn't act fast, she'd panic and run. And he'd never have the opportunity to uncover her plans for the evening. He slackened his hold, allowing her some breathing space while still keeping her within the circle of his arms.

"It's okay, Nikki. Just relax."

"Easier said than done." She drew a deep, shuddering breath. "Look, this was a mistake. Maybe—"

"Maybe we should make polite conversation for the next minute or two," he interrupted. "Would that help?"

She nodded in relief. "It might be wise."

"Fine. let's see..." He fingered the cluster of pearls and crystal beads decorating her lapel. "You look stunning this evening. Very bridal."

He used the word deliberately, hoping to guide the conversation toward Eric and their impending nuptials. To his surprise, her tension dissipated.

His increased.

Didn't it bother her that she'd just made passionate love to a complete stranger while her fiancé waited somewhere in the vicinity? A muscle jerked in his cheek. Apparently not.

She gave a self-conscious shrug, her gaze darting to meet his. "Isn't that the idea?"

"To look bridal tonight?" His eyes narrowed as he assessed the implications of her remark. Then he caught her left hand in his and lifted it until the overhead light sparked off her gold wedding band. "Most brides aren't already married."

"Sorry," she said with a wry laugh. "I've worn it for so long, I forgot it was there."

"I don't imagine your husband has forgotten."

"I don't have a husband. That's why I'm here."

"To get married," he clarified.

"Well, of course."

"And where is your groom-to-be?"

She'd recovered her poise and offered a cool, mysterious smile, so at odds with her fiery looks. "I haven't found him. Yet."

"And when he shows up?"

"Then we'll marry." A small frown touched her brow. "Isn't that how it works?"

His mouth quirked to one side. "Damned if I know."

"Look . . ." She moistened her lips, drawing his attention to their swollen fullness.

He'd done that, Jonah realized, or rather his kisses had. Here she stood waiting for her future husband while the taste of another man lingered on her lips. The anger that had smoldered just beneath the surface caught fire.

What sort of woman was she? And why hadn't Eric seen through her? As though sensing that something about their conversation had gone awry, she stepped clear of his embrace.

"Perhaps this would be a good time to become better acquainted."

A harsh laugh escaped before he could prevent it. "I'd say the past few minutes pretty much covered that. Wouldn't you?"

His sarcasm didn't go unnoticed. "I meant—" She broke off and wrapped her arms around her waist in a defensive gesture. "Would you mind if I asked a few questions?"

"About what?"

"About you."

He eyed her with suspicion. "What do you want to know?"

She shrugged. "Why don't we start with the basics? Where are you from?"

"Originally? Chicago."

"And more recently?"

"Abroad."

That captured her attention. "You've been living overseas?" she asked with a delighted smile. "That's perfect. Will you be staying in this country for a while or—"

"My plans are indefinite." Impatience crept into his voice. "I should be able to wrap up the situation here in a week or two."

Disappointment drained the animation from her face. "Oh. I'm sorry to hear that. Is there any possibility you might alter your plans?"

What the hell was going on? Did she hope to arrange some future rendezvous? He glared in frustration, knowing he couldn't ask without tipping his hand. But damn it all, what about Eric? He strove for patience, fighting overwhelming fatigue.

"What is it you want?" he demanded bluntly.

She stiffened. "Nothing that will fit in with your plans, I'm afraid," she said, retreating behind a remote coolness.

"How the hell do you know that?"

She took a quick step backward, distancing herself still further. Jonah grimaced in annoyance, aware their rapport dissipated with each passing second. He'd screwed up but good and didn't have a clue how to make a graceful recovery.

"I'm based in New York," she explained. "If you were willing to move there, perhaps we could work something out. But—"

Work something out? Rage made him blind to everything else. He caught her arm and yanked her close. "Lady, I'm going to ask you one last time. What is it you're asking me?"

Alarm flared in her wide eyes. "I was asking if you'd relocate to New York. But now I just want you to let go of my arm."

Slowly, he released her and stepped back. It had to be exhaustion. There couldn't be any other excuse for his behavior. "Sorry," he muttered, thrusting a hand through his hair. "I didn't mean to hurt you."

"Forget it," she retorted. "Now if you'll excuse me, I need to find my future husband" And with that she turned on her heel and walked away.

Chapter Two

Nikki swept across the ballroom, determined to put as much distance between her and Joe Alexander as possible. Never in her entire life had she lost control like that. She fought to draw a deep, steadying breath. What could she have been thinking? Control was everything to her.

And she'd lost it the instant he'd put his hands on her.

Lost it? Hah! She'd given it up without so much as a token struggle.

She shook her head. How could she have been so foolish? Since the day her parents had died, she'd been forced to take charge of her odd assortment of relatives. Krista and Keli, Uncle Ernie and Aunt Selma, her cousins. They all routinely turned to her with their problems. And with cool, calm logic, she'd resolved every single one they dumped in her lap. Even when her work situation had turned problematic, she'd found a solution without asking anyone for help.

She was proud of that. Proud of the fact that no matter how desperate her circumstances, she'd never become emotional, never failed to choose a course of action and never, ever lost her cool.

Until tonight.

She risked a quick glance over her shoulder. Joe stood where she'd left him, apart from the glittering crowd, his arms folded across his chest, watching her with a fierce green-tinged gaze. She looked away, shaken. What had just happened? One minute she'd been kissed to within an inch of her life, and the next he'd treated her as though she were beneath contempt. It didn't make any sense.

She balled her hands into fists.

More than anything, she wanted to forget him and move on to the next man. But she couldn't. Joe was too fascinating. From the moment he'd intruded on her conversation with Morey, she'd been utterly spellbound, walking into his arms as though she'd been born to do so.

Was it his eyes? she wondered. They were such an odd shade of hazel—flashing green fire one moment, before darkening to a crisp golden brown the next. Or perhaps it was the keen intelligence she'd glimpsed in his stare, the instinctive knowledge that he'd fought his way through every single one of the years marking his hard, chiseled face. Whatever the cause, it ignited an answering spark in her. Even when a cold sharpness settled in his gaze, he'd still managed to hold her captive.

"Excuse me," an earnest young man interrupted, tapping her shoulder. "Would you care to dance?"

Unable to concoct a plausible excuse for refusing, she reluctantly slipped into his arms. She'd have time for regrets later. But not now, not when she had business to attend to.

It was growing late and she still hadn't found a suitable husband. Unfortunately, Joe Alexander had succeeded in destroying what little enthusiasm she'd managed to summon for the job. She suspected it would be a challenge to find anyone else who came close to matching him.

She glanced at her current partner and struggled to muster some interests. He was a handsome man. Very handsome. In fact, his features bordered on the classic. Best of all, his rounded jaw didn't so much as hint at an annoyingly stubborn nature. Nor did he have thick, winged brows that notched upward in silent demand for answers to unreasonable questions. He also lacked that penetrating stare that stole every thought from her head.

Instead, he possessed an arrow-straight nose—no intriguing little bump to suggest a barroom brawl. Unfortunate that his lips were on the narrow side—no wide, sensuous mouth capable of stealing soul-altering kisses from unwary women. And he had a soft tenor voice—no deep, rumbling bass tones that echoed through her mind long after the words had died. But she could live with that.

In fact, he was quite, quite perfect.

And quite, quite boring.

She sighed. This had to stop! She had to quit comparing every man she met to Joe. She risked another brief look at her current dance partner, determined to find something that appealed.

His hair was a pleasant enough shade of brown, but a degree or two darker than Joe's and lacking the startling sun-bleached streaks. Nor did this man's height compare. At a guess, Joe stood several inches over six feet. Broad shouldered and built along rock-solid proportions, he eclipsed most of the men she'd spoken to so far that evening, including this one. She'd never met anyone who exuded quite such an air of power and authority.

So what in the world had gone wrong?

"My name's Dan Forsythe," her dance partner announced at length.

She broke off her analysis long enough to reply, "Nikki Ashton." Was it something she'd said that had annoyed him?

"It's a pleasure to meet you."

Something she'd done?

"Er... the song's ending."

Something she didn't say or do?

"Would you care to talk for a few minutes? Nikki?" He stopped dead in the middle of the floor. "Ms. Ashton?"

She blinked. "The song ended."

He stared at her oddly. "Yes. And I thought we could take the opportunity to talk. You know. Get better acquainted."

They left the floor together and Nikki released a quiet sigh. How different from Joe's more aggressive approach. But then, if Dan had swept her off to a darkened corner and attempted to kiss her, she'd probably have slapped his face.

"What is it you're looking for in a wife?" she asked, deciding to be blunt.

"Children," he blurted with awkward enthusiasm. His gaze slipped from her face to a spot somewhere behind her and then back again. "Do you like kids?"

"I'm afraid I'm not ready to have a baby," she confessed gently. "At least not yet."

"Oh."

His focus continued to shift to a point somewhere behind her with nervous regularity. She refrained from turning around, but couldn't help wondering if he'd found someone more appealing. She cleared her throat to regain his attention.

"The problem is, I have a career."

"Then kids are out, huh?"

She hesitated. *Forget Joe!* she told herself sternly. *Concentrate on the business at hand.*

She'd known all along that certain concessions might be necessary to achieve her goal. Her problem with Dan mirrored many she faced at work—two parties with similar ambitions but with differing needs and objectives. She just had to find an equitable solution to their dilemma.

"I wouldn't say children are out, precisely."

"Still, you're not interested in having any." He looked behind her again while at the same time edging backward. "Are you?"

If she didn't do something fast, she'd lose him. "Perhaps we could reach a compromise," she offered quickly. "If you were willing to wait a while to have children—"

"Forget it. I . . . I guess we're just not compatible. It was nice meeting you." And with that he vanished into the surrounding crowd.

She frowned. That was odd. Why had he kept looking behind her? He'd almost acted as if . . . Her eyes narrowed suspiciously. He'd almost acted as if he were intimidated by something. Or *someone.*

She spun around, not in the least surprised to discover Joe standing nearby. He held a glass of champagne, which he raised in salute when their gazes clashed. Why, that dirty, rotten . . . Hadn't he done enough harm allowing her to believe he was interested in her when he wasn't? Why did he have to chase off those who might be sincere?

Snatching the arm of the closest available male, she offered a dazzling smile. "Care to dance?"

To her relief, he didn't flat out refuse. But the next ten minutes proved to be the most arduous of her life. It didn't take any time at all to discover he was a pompous ass looking for a wife whose qualifications roughly equaled those of a maid. Worse, he danced in a tight little circle so that every few seconds she came face to face with Joe.

The instant the dance ended, she excused herself, determined to find a better scouting location—one that offered a suitable array of potential partners and yet *didn't* contain Joe Alexander.

Unfortunately, she lost out on both counts. Over the next thirty minutes, her situation progressed from bad to worse. It didn't matter whom she spoke to or where she went—there was Joe. Several times he blatantly listened in on her conversation, making her so nervous she couldn't even string a coherent sentence together.

Finally, she couldn't take any more. Determined to put an end to his harassment, she excused herself from her latest disaster and crossed to confront him. She wouldn't give up control as she had before, she told herself. This time she'd take command of their conversation. And no matter what, she wouldn't allow him to touch her.

He greeted her with a lazy smile, a smile directly at odds with the hard glitter in his eyes. "Having fun?"

"No, I'm not. And it's all your fault. Why won't you leave me alone?" she demanded. "What do you want?"

"From you? Not a thing."

"Then why are you following me?"

"Curiosity."

"Curiosity?" She blinked in surprise. "But why? You had your chance to work something out between us. You blew it. So why can't you go away and let me find a husband?"

He stilled, eyeing her intently. "Is that what you're doing? Looking for one?"

"I'm trying! But you're making it rather difficult. You keep scaring them off."

She could see him analyzing her answers, considering them as though they were puzzle pieces that didn't quite fit. His brows notched upward and she knew what that meant. Another of his impossible questions.

"Tell me this." He fixed her with an irritable glare. "Are you meeting your future husband here or not?"

"Yes, of course," she said. "Or I will be if you stop interfering."

"When and where will you meet him?"

"How would I know that?" she retorted, exasperated. "I'm not a fortune-teller."

He frowned. "I'm a bit confused. I was under the impression that you were waiting for someone specific."

She planted her hands on her hips. "I am. I have very specific qualifications, and for your information, you don't meet a single one." Honesty forced her to concede, "Well, maybe one or two. But not the important ones."

The predatory gleam returned to his eyes. "Perhaps we should discuss the ones I do meet."

"Forget it," she muttered.

Jonah came to a decision. He still didn't know whether or not she was waiting for Eric. Unfortunately, as much as he preferred the direct approach, he couldn't simply ask, not without revealing a suspicious amount of ignorance. But he needed answers. And one way or another, she was going to provide them.

"Arguing like this isn't helping either of our situations. We need to talk. Truce?"

She hesitated. "I don't know. It's getting late and I can't afford to miss this opportunity. If we can't work something out, I've lost a lot of time."

"I won't keep you long." His hand settled on her shoulder. "Why don't we go outside and talk?"

He didn't give her a chance to think of an excuse, but opened a pair of French doors leading to the gardens and ushered her through. It was cool outside, though not uncomfortably so. Slate stepping-stones marked pathways that twisted in and out of exotic trees and shrubs, their presence an incongruous touch in the Nevada desert. Splashes of moonlight revealed tables and benches half-hidden in the leafy vegetation. Few were occupied, but Jonah wanted to insure their privacy and led her deeper into the garden.

In the far recesses, they approached a table tucked snugly beneath a tree covered in twinkling fairy lights. The couple who'd been sitting there were just leaving. The man tucked a set of papers into his suit coat pocket and planted a possessive arm around the woman. She peeked out from beneath white blond hair and exchanged a smile of recognition with Nikki.

"Good luck," she whispered before being whisked along the pathway toward the mansion.

"A friend of yours?" Jonah asked curiously.

"We met earlier in the evening," Nikki confessed. "I was a bit nervous and she sat and talked to me for a while."

"Why were you nervous?"

She shrugged. "This is a pretty big step, don't you think? I suppose I was having second thoughts about the wisdom of going through with this sort of marriage."

This sort of marriage? What the hell did that mean? He waited until she took a seat before joining her on the bench. Enough was enough. The time had come for answers and he intended to get them, no matter what it took.

"This is a rather unusual party," he probed carefully.

"Until I read the article, I'd never heard of anything like it," she agreed. "Imagine throwing a ball for people who want to get married."

So he hadn't misunderstood the card he'd found on her desk. This *was* a marriage ball. Still, he suspected he hadn't quite gotten the full picture. For instance—where was Eric?

"That's how you found out about it?" he prompted. "From an article?"

"Yes. It was in our local newspaper." Her smile glimmered in the darkness. "My sister showed it to me. She found it highly amusing."

"But you didn't."

Her smile faded. "No," she admitted. "It struck me as the perfect solution."

"Solution to what?"

An innocent enough question, yet it clearly hit a nerve. She clenched her hands, the fairy lights in the trees above ricocheting off her wedding band. "It's a long story," she said at last.

"I have all the time in the world." He didn't exaggerate. He was determined to find out what the hell was going on, even if it took all night. "Talking about it might help."

She hesitated, and he could tell she was debating whether or not to answer. "I suppose complete honesty might be best, all things considered."

"I gather you don't always feel that way."

She turned her head sharply at the disapproval coloring his words. "Normally, I believe in honesty above all else," she asserted, her tone growing notably cooler.

"But whatever your story is, it involves a lie," he retorted. He didn't attempt to placate her. He couldn't. Not when she'd lied about something. Something that might affect Eric's well-being.

She didn't hesitate. "Yes," she admitted. "It does."

"Tell me about it."

He endured another brief silence while she gathered her thoughts. Even in the short amount of time they'd spent together, he had noticed that quality about her. Her control and precision. The care she took before speaking. She'd be a tough one to break, should it come to that.

"It's my own fault," she began in a low voice. "I never should have lied about being married."

Of all the possible confessions he'd expected to hear, this one didn't come close to making the list. "What did you say?"

She held out her hand, and her wedding band winked in the subdued lighting. "You asked me about this earlier. What I didn't explain is, it's pure decoration. I'm not married." A whisper of a laugh escaped. "I'd hardly be here if it were real, now would I?"

He was at a loss to answer that. Not until he found out more about this ball. "Then why the pretense?"

"The company I work for prefers married executives."

Who the hell had told her that? "So you decided to accommodate them?"

"I played with the idea. But not too seriously. At least not until—"

"Until?"

"There's a man at work. He's very sweet. Young."

"He's interested in a personal relationship with you?" Was that possible? Could Loren and Della have misunderstood the situation? Or was Nikki Ashton just a damned good liar?

"He's more than interested."

"I still don't understand. You faked a marriage because you couldn't tell him no? Isn't that a little extreme?"

"Not when the man in question is my boss."

He stood. The way she said it, with such detached candor, convinced him she spoke the truth. At least the truth as she saw it. *Damn Eric!* What the hell had he instigated?

"Why are you here?" he demanded.

She tilted her head to look up at him and the silvery moonlight caressed the pale beauty of her face. Her expression appeared calm and serene. But her eyes gathered in the shadows surrounding them, their fathomless depths hinting at untold secrets.

"I'm here for the same reason you are. To meet someone compatible enough to marry."

"Couldn't you do that in New York?"

"Possibly. But courtships are often lengthy affairs. By attending the Cinderella Ball, I can meet someone tonight, we can marry immediately, and return home in the morning. Problem solved."

He must have misunderstood. After almost thirty hours without sleep, it was a distinct possibility. His mouth tightened. He'd better have misunderstood, because he didn't like the sound of this at all.

"The people attending this party . . . That's why they're here? To marry complete strangers? They meet, choose someone at random and marry, all in *one night?*"

"Of course," she responded, surprised.

"Of course." He realized then that she was serious. Dead serious. "If that's true, you people are in desperate need of reality checks."

She frowned, her brows arching in question. "Now *I* don't understand. Aren't you here because you want to marry?"

He had no intention of answering that one. "Let's focus on you right now," he suggested. "We can discuss my situation later." He didn't give her time to respond, but continued with his interrogation. "You're marrying because your boss won't take no for an answer. Is that about the size of it?"

"There's a personal reason, as well."

"Which is?"

"As I said." Her lashes flickered downward, concealing her expression. "It's personal."

He fought to hide his impatience. "So because of this personal reason and because you can't handle your boss any other way, you're going to marry a complete stranger."

She inclined her head, the rich mix of colors muted by the darkness. "I know. It sounds insane. But you see, everyone already thinks I **am** married."

He folded his arms across his chest, a hint of sarcasm creeping into his tone. "And since they do, you're going to turn this fiction into fact. That makes sense."

"I have no choice," she retorted, stung. "I'm not interested in acquiring a husband. Ever." She drew back into the shadows, her voice low and pained. "At least not for something as illusionary as love."

That gave him pause. "If that's how you feel, then why go through with such a crazy scheme?"

"Because it's the perfect solution."

"That's open to debate."

Her temper flared again. "This isn't some half-cocked plan I've devised," she told him. "I've given this marriage idea a lot of thought. Aside from needing to resolve a private dilemma, I have a boss who thinks he's in love with me."

Jonah looked at her sharply. "And is he?"

"No. Eventually, he'll realize that for himself. But until he does, I need the protection of a real husband."

"How is this husband going to protect you from—" Damn, he'd almost slipped up. "What's his name?"

"Eric." She released her breath in a long sigh. "It won't be easy. I need someone sophisticated. Someone mature. Someone intimidating. Part of the problem is that I've told everyone my husband has been out of the country for the past year. Unfortunately, it's left the impression that our marriage is in trouble."

"So you need a man who can dispel those doubts," Jonah said slowly. "With a real husband on the scene, someone who can act the part of a passionate spouse, Eric will realize there's no future in a relationship and get over his infatuation."

"Exactly."

"So where's the problem? If you're actually committed to going through with this crazy idea, why haven't you married already?"

Her laugh was half groan. "The problem is that no one I've met so far meets my qualifications. Either they're sweet, lovely gentlemen whom Eric would rip to shreds in no time. Or they're strong, independent types with their own agendas. And those agendas don't include moving to New York for the duration of our marriage."

"I can't believe that there isn't someone—"

"No? What about you?" She leaned forward, her gaze never wavering from his. "I can offer a home, a car, and a modest salary. It doesn't even have to be a permanent arrangement. There was a man I met this evening who wanted a temporary wife. If you prefer, I'd be willing to agree to a short-term marriage, as well. I'll hire you to be my husband for whatever period of time is convenient, under whatever terms you deem fair, so long as my predicament with Eric is resolved by the time we get an annulment."

"Isn't this a little extreme? Can't you—" He broke off as a sudden thought struck him. "This Eric, is he harassing you? Has he said anything, *done* anything, inappropriate?"

"No, no, nothing like that," she answered immediately. "He's kind. Protective."

Jonah gave a short laugh. "Yes, I can see where that might be a problem."

"It's not funny! He's never touched me, at least not in any suggestive way. But I know how he feels." The iridescent seed pearls decorating the bodice of her suit jacket sparked with each agitated breath she drew. "I'm not imagining all this. I'm not!"

He held up his hands. "All right. I believe you. But tell me, how do you know it's personal? Isn't it possible you've mistaken friendly concern for something more serious?"

She shook her head. "I wish that were the case, but it isn't."

"Convince me."

Her gaze flashed to his. "I don't know why I should have to."

"You're the one desperate for a husband. Convince me you really need one."

Once again she took her time considering his request. After several tense moments, she inclined her head. "Very well. Can you tell when a woman is attracted to you?"

"Sometimes," he admitted. "If she's obvious about it."

"Well, Eric has been very obvious. Right from the start he signaled his interest."

"What did you do?"

"I told him I didn't share his feelings and that mixing business with pleasure was always a mistake. Needless to say, he thought he could convince me otherwise. And that's when I made my first mistake."

"You lied."

She released a deep sigh. "Yes. I said I was engaged. It didn't help. He stayed hopeful." She shrugged. "I guess he thought he could change my mind. So out of desperation, I showed up one Monday morning wearing a wedding ring."

"Your second mistake," Jonah informed her caustically. "Didn't the wedding ring slow him down?" Unless his brother had switched personalities this past year, it should have.

"Yes, it did. He seemed to accept the futility of a relationship."

"But something happened to alter that. What?"

"A company banquet. I came alone, claiming my husband was out of the country. Eric went along with it for the next several weeks. He'd even tease me about my husband's prolonged absence. But as time passed and I never brought him to any company functions, Eric changed." She hesitated as though searching for the appropriate description. "He became indignant on my behalf, and later angry. I think the anger changed to suspicion when I didn't share his distress. He senses I'm hiding something, and I suspect he's hoping my marriage is on the rocks."

"That still doesn't mean—"

"There's more," she interrupted. "He confides in me, although I do nothing to encourage it."

Jonah tensed. "What does he talk about?"

"His family. Mostly his older brother—how much he admires and tries to emulate Jonah, how it feels to lurk in someone's shadow. How tough it is to live up to a legend."

"Sounds like he sees you more in the light of a mother confessor than a potential lover."

"I wish that was all it were. But if I get too close to him, I can see how he fights for control. And when he looks at me . . ." She shook her head. "I can't explain it, except to say that a woman is able to sense these things."

Jonah had heard enough. "So you see marriage as the only solution."

"I don't like it, but I have no choice. I have to find a way to correct the situation before it gets any further out of hand. It's starting to affect our work. We're both making mistakes and eventually someone is going to catch on. I can't afford to lose this job. It's too important to me." She stood and clasped her hands together in an unconscious plea. "Joe, please help me. Will you . . . will you marry me?"

He knew how much it cost her to ask. But that didn't change his answer. "No."

"Why not?" Desperation crept into her voice. "What is it you want?"

"What I want isn't at issue right now. Look, Nikki, you have two choices. You can go through with this ridiculous scheme to marry or you can do the smart thing."

"And what's the smart thing?"

"Tell Eric the truth. Tell him you faked a marriage because you didn't want any romantic complications at the office. Tell him you're not interested in anything other than work and to leave you alone. Ask for a transfer."

She spun away, wrapping her arms about her waist. "I can't."

"Why not?"

"Do you really think it's so easy?" Her temper flared, stirring the passions she obviously kept under such tight control. "I'm supposed to waltz into work and make this big announcement, and then what?"

"Then you're off the hook."

"No, I'm not. By the end of the day, it's all over the office that I lied about being married because I couldn't handle the situation with my boss. By the end of the next day, our clients have heard about it, and by the day after that, so have our competitors. It would do incalculable harm to my reputation, Eric's reputation, as well as damaging the credibility of our firm. We'd be a bad joke. Thanks, but no thanks. Anything is preferable to that, even marriage."

Her attitude toward marriage bothered him. A lot. Perhaps if he'd had time to sleep on it, he might have been in a position to offer a more palatable solution. But he didn't have that luxury. "Come on." Slipping a hand beneath her elbow, he drew her close. "Let's go."

"Where?"

"To find you a man. If you're so determined to buy a husband, I'll help you shop for one."

She resisted the pull on her arm. "I don't understand. Why are you doing this?"

"Let's just say I'm a sucker for a hard luck story."

"But what about you?" she protested. "It's getting late. Aren't you worried you'll miss your chance to find a wife?"

"Believe me, finding a wife is the least of my worries." The very least. He stopped in the middle of the walkway. "What's the problem, Nikki ? Having second thoughts?"

A momentary hesitation disturbed her even expression, quickly masked by steely resolve. "No. I'm not having second thoughts."

"Then let's go."

The next hour only served to prove Nikki's point. No one they approached quite suited her needs. Most Jonah dismissed as being too weak. She was right. Eric wouldn't see them as a serious obstacle to his pursuit. If anything, he'd think he was doing her a favor. And those who would have held him at bay had their own requirements, which meant a wife to fulfill *their* criteria, not the other way around.

"There's a guy over there I haven't spoken to yet," Jonah said without much enthusiasm. The man in question was too old, too fat, and too desperate. Eric would make mincemeat of him. But time was growing short.

"Don't bother," she replied with a shiver. "How about—" She broke off, her face paling. *"Oh, no!"*

"What is it? What's wrong?"

She twisted around, practically throwing herself into his arms. "Quick! Hold me."

His arms closed around her automatically and he tucked her close. His hand skated down the length of her spine, molding her more firmly against him. She felt like heaven, soft and warm, her unique scent filling his lungs. If he hadn't believed in jet lag before, he sure as hell did now. There couldn't be any other explanation for his reaction. It was too intense, too surreal.

Her breath came in quick, panicked bursts and he lowered his head close to her ear. "What is it, Nikki? What's wrong?"

She lifted her face, her mouth inches from his. For a crazy instant he thought she intended to kiss him. Then he saw her expression. Stark disbelief registered in the pansy blue of her eyes.

"Eric's here," she whispered.

Chapter Three

"*I can't* believe it," Nikki exclaimed. "How did he find me?"

Jonah grimaced. He had a fairly good idea. The all too efficient Jan seemed a safe bet. He chanced a quick look toward the reception area. Eric stood there, an earnest expression on his face, talking to the Montagues. Undoubtedly, he was attempting to charm his way into the ball. And knowing Eric, he had every chance of succeeding. Jonah swore beneath his breath. The situation was more serious than he'd suspected.

A lot more serious.

"Come on." He dropped an arm around Nikki's shoulders and swept her through the nearest doorway.

She'd turned ashen, her eyes huge and desperate. "What am I going to do now?"

Jonah set his jaw, trying to decide. He'd been a fool to drink even a single glass of champagne, particularly when he hadn't slept for a day and a half. Right now he'd kill for a hot shower and eight solid hours between the sheets. Maybe then he could figure out an appropriate course of action. But tonight his exhaustion made that near impossible. Not that there were many avenues available to them. In fact, he'd only come up with one.

"It would seem we're out of options," he informed her. "If he's this determined, you need to marry someone he can't intimidate."

"We've canvassed just about everyone here." She scanned the assembly with an air of urgency. "Who's left?"

"Me."

It took a full minute for that to sink in. Astonished, she turned to look at him. "But you said—"

"Forget what I said."

"You're willing to marry me?" she asked in disbelief. "Why? I mean, don't think I'm ungrateful, but . . ." Skepticism gradually replaced her surprise. "Why would you be willing to help me now when you wouldn't before?"

"I ignored one damsel in distress this evening," he said with a hint of self-mockery. "It just isn't in me to ignore another."

"I won't claim to understand what you mean by that."

"That's a relief." He offered a bland smile and indicated a corridor leading to a back staircase. "Shall we get this over with? We'll need a marriage license. I overheard someone say they're being processed downstairs in the library."

A small frown puckered her brow and she shook her head, indicating she wouldn't be so easily persuaded. He almost laughed aloud at the irony. Here he risked alienating his entire family to resolve a problem *she'd* created, and she still wasn't satisfied.

If she'd just told Eric no from the start, instead of concocting this whole ridiculous scenario, they wouldn't be in their present predicament. Now, if he wanted to ensure his brother's well-being, salvage the jobs of two of International Investment's key personnel, as well as straighten out their hopelessly muddled personal lives, he'd have to take serious action.

"I know I'm not in a position to argue," she was saying.

"That's for damned sure."

She rebuked him with a look. "I do, however, have a few concerns."

He released his breath in a gusty sigh. "Naturally."

"First. I expect you to convince Eric we're a happily married couple. Can you do that?"

His eyes narrowed as he absorbed the slight. The mere fact that she needed to ask underscored her lack of faith in his abilities. Not many could have offered such an insult and escaped without repercussions.

"I'll convince him that if he approaches my wife with anything other than business in mind, he'll regret it." He allowed a hint of his displeasure to show. "Or don't you think he'll believe I'm serious?"

She held his gaze for a tempestuous five seconds before looking away, color sweeping into her cheeks. "He'll believe you," she concurred.

"Fine. Let's go."

She dug in her heels. "Wait a minute. I'm not through."

He ground his teeth. "Lady, I said I'd marry you. What more do you want?"

"I just need to make sure we understand each other."

He grimaced. "Trust me, I understand more than you realize."

"I'm talking about specifics. I don't want any dispute later on."

"Then you'd better talk fast because I'm giving you precisely thirty seconds," he informed her tightly. "After that, you're on your own."

Apparently, she took his warning seriously. Without wasting any further time, she ticked her questions off on her fingers. "Okay. You've already agreed to convince Eric we're a happily married couple. Second. You're willing to move to New York, right? You'll stay with me until the situation with Eric is resolved?"

"Yes."

"Third. You understand that your actions mustn't put my job in jeopardy?"

"I understand." He folded his arms across his chest. "Is that it? Are you through now? No fourth, fifth, or sixth on your list?"

"Just a fourth."

"Which is?"

If he hadn't caught the turbulent glitter in her eyes, he'd have thought her completely unaffected by their discussion. After all, she'd rattled off her points like some sort of human computer. But that flash of deepening violet gave her away. Whatever her final point concerned, it should have been first on her list, not last.

"I need to know your expectations."

He lifted an eyebrow, surprised by her request. He'd anticipated something far more crucial. "I expect to marry you, save your bacon, and then send you on your merry way," he replied. At the same time, he'd protect International Investment from any further business debacles and allow Eric time to come to his senses.

"And that's all?" She moistened her lips. "You won't ask any more of me?"

Comprehension dawned, and with it came a purely masculine reaction, a predator's response to spotting its prey unprotected and vulnerable. He stepped closer, his attention drawn to the pulse fluttering frantically at the base of her throat. "Are you asking if I want to sleep with you?" he questioned deliberately.

She retained her cool, although he suspected it was a hard-fought battle. "Yes. I guess that's what I'm asking."

"I don't think it's worth discussing."

To his amusement, she looked relieved. Did she misinterpret all business discussions as badly as this one? he couldn't help but wonder. He'd have to speak to her about that. He couldn't afford to have the company put at risk because of her erroneous assumptions.

"Now, have we addressed all of your concerns?"

"Yes."

"Then I suggest we get this over with before your boss succeeds in talking his way past the Montagues and tracks us down." He shot her a sharp glance. "He doesn't know the purpose of this ball, does he?"

"I don't think so. I told him I was flying out to meet my husband," she explained, then eyed him uneasily. "I don't know why he followed me. Maybe he was curious to meet you." She released her breath in an exasperated sigh. "My husband, I mean."

"Or maybe he didn't believe you were really meeting anyone. Let's just hope the Montagues don't go into lengthy explanations about their reason for throwing this little shindig or we'll be up to our necks in it." He took her arm in an iron grip. "Let's find the library."

Footmen dressed in white and gold uniforms directed them downstairs to a county clerk who processed the marriage licenses. She wore a name tag that read, "Dora Scott." On one side of her desk was a sign announcing, "For faster service, feed me hors d'oeuvres." Someone had drawn an arrow in front of the word "feed" and inserted a heavily printed "don't." A short line had formed in front of her, but by the time they'd filled out the necessary applications, the room had emptied.

"Let's see who we have here," Dora said as they approached. She held out her hand for their forms.

Realizing he stood on the brink of disaster, Jonah hastened to introduce himself. "It's Joe. Joe Alexander." Nikki might not associate the abbreviated form of his name with Eric's half-brother. But his given name was unusual enough that if Dora blurted it out, his identity would be all too evident. And he had no intention of revealing his connection to Eric until after they were safely married.

The clerk glanced at his application and chuckled. "Fine, *Joe.*" She examined the second form. "And Nicole."

"Nikki," the bride-to-be hastily corrected. She indicated the sign. "Someone give you too many hors d'oeuvres?"

"And how! One more cheese puff and I'd probably pop. Okay, folks, let's get through this." Within minutes, Dora had printeded up the necessary paperwork and handed them a thick blue-and-white envelope. "Marriage ceremonies are conducted in salons off the main ballroom. Give the envelope to whoever officiates. You get to keep the fancy-looking certificate inside as a souvenir. But it's not a legal document. That comes later in the mail." She glanced at them. "Any questions?"

"Not a one," Jonah responded.

Dora nodded. "In that case, I have one piece of advice. Take care of each other, hear?"

"Taking care of people is what I'm best at," Nikki assured the clerk.

"Funny," Jonah muttered. "That's what I was going to say."

"Swell. A pair of caring souls," Dora said with a laugh. "Get out of here, the both of you. You need to get hitched and I have work to do."

"We better make this quick," Jonah advised as they returned to the ballroom. "If Eric managed to talk his way in, I don't want to run into him at an inopportune moment."

Nikki paused outside the door to the first salon. "It seems we have a choice of ceremonies. What sort do you prefer?"

"The short-and-to-the-point sort."

He shoved open the nearest door and looked inside. Nikki caught a glimpse over his shoulder and made a small sound of disappointment. Not that he blamed her. The room was attractive, but very stiff and formal. Even when the judge beckoned him to come forward, he hesitated. For some reason, he found ice blue brocade, walnut furniture, and artificial flowers a total turnoff. Besides, it wouldn't suit Nikki.

He backed out and closed the door. "Bad choice," he announced.

"What's wrong with it?"

"Too long a line," he lied, fully aware that from her angle she hadn't seen enough to dispute his verdict. "Let's try another."

Opening the door to the next salon, he nodded in satisfaction. It was perfect. Tiny and intimate, it had an old-fashioned, almost Victorian feel to it. A dainty Laura Ashley rose print covered the walls, and the overstuffed couch and wing chairs were finished in a deep ruby velvet with ivory lace arm covers. Centered along one wall was a cherry highboy displaying an ornate silver tea service. Along the other was a fireplace with a gold-leaf beveled mirror above the mantel that captured an overview of the entire room. Fresh flowers filled delicate Waterford crystal vases, the fragrance of roses offset by the smoky scent of hickory from a gently crackling fire.

If he could have chosen the perfect setting for Nikki, it would have been one like this.

She stepped into the room behind him and caught her breath in delight. "Oh, Joe, this is wonderful."

"It'll do," he agreed with a lazy smile, not quite certain why the setting for a temporary marriage mattered so much. He must be more exhausted than he'd thought.

A minister rose from a chair beside the fire and smiled at them, his thick white hair reflecting the leaping flames. "Welcome. I assume you wish to be married?"

"Yes, please," Nikki answered without hesitation. "Right away, if you don't mind."

The minister smiled indulgently. "Very well, my dear. But before I begin, I'm required to ask that you give careful consideration to what you're about to do."

Jonah nearly groaned. If he did that, he might come to his senses and back out. No, better they get this over with and fast. "Look, we've considered, we've decided, and we're in a hurry." He thrust the envelope containing the necessary forms at the minister. "Could you just get on with it?"

The minister accepted the envelope and adjusted the wire-rimmed glasses perched on the end of his nose. "I'm afraid not," he replied, his gentle blue eyes turning somber. "You see, marriage is a serious commitment, not to be entered into lightly. So I ask that you face each other and look carefully at your partner. Make sure that your choice is the right one."

Cursing beneath his breath, but realizing it was the only way they'd get this show on the road, Jonah turned to look at Nikki, studying her with clinical detachment. At first, all he noticed was her appearance. Tall and beautifully proportioned, she was a stunning woman. Her translucent violet-flecked eyes met his without flinching. He liked that about her; he had from the start. Of course, there were other qualities he liked, as well.

Her mouth was the most kissable he'd ever encountered and her skin the softest he'd felt in an age. Even the brilliant red highlights of her hair suited her to perfection. He half smiled in appreciation as he eyed the abundant curls pulled neatly back from face and allowed to tumble down her back. Sometime during the evening, glossy tendrils had escaped to curl with fiery abandon about her temples, the shade a glorious sunset against her porcelain skin.

And that's when he saw beneath the surface.

Her hairstyle mirrored her nature, he suddenly realized. She struggled to attain the appearance of severity and restraint, but couldn't quite achieve it. Equally, she fought an unending battle between the tempestuous aspects of her nature and the need for rigid control.

On the surface, she appeared perfectly composed. But underneath smoldered an inferno that probably terrified her, that threatened the calm, orderly existence she'd built. With new insight, he looked at her again. And in the end it was those pansy-soft eyes that gave her away, betraying her uncertainty, her desperation, her passion, as well as her unwavering strength and determination.

He wanted this woman.

He wanted to feed those sparks of inner rebellion, to release the delicious fire she kept tamped inside and to be scorched by the heat of it. Keeping all those emotions bottled up couldn't be good for her, and he decided then and there to find a way to demolish her control. Hell, he'd probably be doing her a favor.

In the meantime, he had to find a way to alleviate her fears. As though in response to his thought, the scent of roses drifted to him again. He turned and crossed to the nearest vase, stripping a few sprigs of baby's breath from the arrangement.

"Come here," he ordered gruffly.

She crossed to his side, hesitating a few feet in front of him. He closed the distance between them and very gently tucked the baby's breath into the curls at her temple. Her hands slipped across his chest to cling to the lapels of his black suit coat as she waited for him to finish.

She wouldn't be happy when she discovered his identity, he realized with regret. But he hoped to convince her that what he'd done was in everyone's best interest.

At least, that's what he told himself.

Nikki stared up at Joe, scrutinizing the taut, uncompromising planes of his face. She hardly dared to breathe as he tucked the flowers in her hair. Satisfied, he looked at her, a reassuring tenderness glittering in his eyes. And with that one look, all her fears dissolved.

She'd been so nervous, the enormity of her decision almost overwhelming her. When the minister had suggested they reconsider the step they were about to take, she'd almost fled the room. Not even her desperation over Eric could have dissuaded her from backing out, even at this late hour. Only the memory of Krista, and that overheard phone conversation, held her rooted in place.

But looking into Joe's hazel-green eyes and seeing his confidence and self-possession went a long way toward easing her uncertainties. He must have known how close to the edge she'd come, for he leaned down, his breath mingling with hers.

"Don't worry," he whispered in reassurance. "I'll take care of everything."

Cupping her face, he sealed his vow, his mouth capturing hers in a gentle kiss. She opened to him, the last of her misgivings fading within the protective strength of his arms. It would all work out. With Joe at her side, she could solve all her problems.

Reluctantly, he released her. "Any more doubts?" he asked.

"None."

"Then will you marry me, Ms. Ashton?"

A tremulous smile teased the corners of her mouth. "Yes, Mr. Alexander. I will."

"Have you reached a decision?" the minister asked.

"Please begin the ceremony," Nikki requested, perfectly calm and collected. Perfectly willing. "And it's Joe and Nikki."

With a rakish grin, Jonah plucked a single rose from the nearest vase and handed it to her. At her questioning look, he shrugged. "A bride should have a bouquet."

The ceremony was surprisingly brief, as per their request. Just before the minister pronounced them husband and wife, he peered at them over his spectacles. "Would you care to exchange rings?" he asked. "We have them on hand. They're tokens, really. Just something to use until you're able to replace them with the genuine article."

"I already have a ring," Nikki told Jonah in a hesitant undertone. "Everyone would think it strange if I wore something different now."

"Give it to me."

She slipped it off her finger and dropped it into his outstretched palm. "What about you?"

"I'll need a wedding band."

The minister dutifully fetched a tray of rings. The third one Jonah tried fit. To her surprise the design on his ring almost matched her own. In fact, if she didn't know better, she'd have believed it to be every bit as real. Even more real was the moment he slipped the ring onto her finger. It was a moment out of time, a brief instant in which their marriage attained a veracity and permanence she hadn't expected.

It isn't a permanent marriage, she tried to tell herself. *It's only temporary.* But the image of their exchanging wedding bands became fixed in her mind, an indelible snapshot she knew she'd carry for a long time to come.

And as the minister pronounced them husband and wife, Nikki realized she was in deep, deep trouble.

It wasn't until they'd reached her rental car that Nikki's earlier doubts crept back. Had she done the right thing? Had she married the right man?

Had she lost her mind?

"So where do we go from here?" Jonah asked once they were confined in the dark interior of the sedan.

"I have a room at the Grand Hotel. It's not too far from here." She fought to keep her voice even and nonchalant. "I . . . I thought we could spend the night there before returning to New York in the morning."

"My ticket's open-ended," he said with a shrug. "Flying out tomorrow is fine with me."

"Are you staying at the Grand, too?"

He shook his head "I wasn't sure what to expect tonight so I booked a room in Las Vegas."

He didn't know what to expect? That didn't make sense. Surely he expected to find someone compatible and marry her. "Why—"

"How about—"

She smiled at the momentary confusion, her tension easing. "Sorry. Go ahead."

"Since your hotel is closer, why don't we stay there?"

Filing her question away for the moment, she gave her attention to the matter at hand. "What about your luggage? Would you like to pick it up now?"

"I don't see the point. We can take care of it on the way to the airport tomorrow. In the meantime, I'm sure your hotel can provide me with the bare essentials. To be honest, what I could use more than anything else is a bed."

She hoped he didn't mean that the way it sounded. Reaching for the ignition, she cast him a quick, suspicious glance, but it was too dark to read his expression.

"You must be tired," she commented pointedly.

He caught her hand before she could start the engine. "Don't let your imagination run away with you." Amusement rumbled in the deep tones of his voice. "As much as a wedding night with you appeals, sleep appeals even more."

"I knew what you meant," she snapped, annoyed that he preferred sleep over her, and even more annoyed that she'd find anything objectionable about that fact.

She started the car, the engine roaring as she gave it far too much gas. Damn it! Why had everything turned so awkward? If only she could pretend he was a difficult client. She'd always been assigned the tough ones. It was her métier and one of the primary reasons she'd been put in charge of special projects at International Investment. In every instance, she'd used her analytical skills to figure out what the client wanted, then cool, calm reason with a touch of charm to negotiate from there.

She gnawed on her lip. Unfortunately, Joe was her husband, not a client. And she suspected neither charm nor reason would cut much ice with him if he decided to be difficult.

She pulled onto the road leading to the hotel, determined to remain in control of the situation. After all, she wasn't interested in him as a man, at least not sexually. Her reaction to those kisses could be explained away as purely hormonal. That was it. It could be chalked up to a normal, healthy reaction any overworked, stressed and desperate woman would have to a virile, violently masculine, wildly sexy male animal. It had nothing whatsoever to do with a growing emotional attachment. She'd learned her lesson the hard way in that particular arena.

Emotional attachment led to pain and disillusionment and financial ruin.

Logic and control kept her world safe and protected.

All she needed was a husband to help resolve her problems with Eric and Krista. Once they were settled, she and Joe could get an annulment. Then she'd be free. Free to simplify her life and pursue her career. In fact, she'd be able to give her full attention to work and not worry about anything else. That would make her happy. Right?

"You okay?"

"I'm fine," she insisted with a too-bright smile. "I'm looking forward to starting a new life. Off with the old and on with the new and all that."

"Yeah, right."

She turned into the hotel parking lot and suddenly remembered his earlier comment. "I've been meaning to ask. Why didn't you know what to expect?"

He shook his head as though to clear it. "What?"

"A few minutes ago. You said you'd booked a room in Vegas because you didn't know what to expect at the Cinderella Ball."

"Did I?" He gave a weary shrug. "I must be more tired than I thought. I don't remember saying that."

She pulled into a parking space and turned off the ignition. "You did. To be exact you said—"

"I guess I wasn't certain I'd find anyone who would suit," he cut in decisively. "I didn't know what sort of women to expect at the ball."

It wasn't until they were in the elevator that she found the flaw in his response. "I still don't understand," she began.

"What don't you understand now?" He spoke calmly, yet she caught a betraying flash of autumn gold in his cool gaze.

"You didn't have any conditions."

He leaned against the back wall and folded his arms across his chest. "Come again?"

"Conditions." She frowned as the elevator panel blinked its way through the lower numbers. "I asked what you wanted out of the marriage and you didn't have a list. Every other man I spoke to had some requirement or request or need." She turned to look at him. "Except you."

"So?"

The door slid open and he gestured for her to proceed. "So, you're intelligent. And you're good-looking in an uncompromising sort of way," she itemized slowly. "That much would be obvious to most women who met you for the first time."

"Gee, thanks."

Recalling the passionate kiss he'd laid on her, she conceded, "Unfortunately, you're a bit on the aggressive side."

Though he certainly knew his way around a woman's mouth. She glanced at him from beneath her lashes, deciding to keep that particular asset to herself.

"I'm a man, not a marshmallow. Aggression comes with the territory."

"You're also argumentative," she shot back. "But without a list, you're easy to please. That's your best quality, in case you didn't know. So why didn't you think you'd find someone to suit?"

"I guess I have a pessimistic nature."

"So do I, but I was still fairly confident I'd find *someone*."

He stopped in the middle of the hallway and held out his hand. She stared at it blankly. "The key," he prompted in dangerously soft tones. "For the door."

"Oh. It's a card, not a key."

His hand didn't budge. "The card, then."

Reluctantly, she dug through her handbag and gave him the thin strip of plastic. "What I'm trying to say is, you never showed any interest in other women after you danced with me. In fact, you spent the whole time helping me find a husband instead of looking for a bride."

"What room?"

"Eighteen-twenty. You spent all that money to attend the Cinderella Ball and didn't find a wife."

Reaching the appropriate door, he slid the card into the slot. The light on the steel plate by the knob flickered from red to green and the lock snicked open. "I believe that wedding ceremony we just went through means I found a wife." He thrust open the door. "After you."

She hesitated. "But I'm not a real wife. And you never explained. Exactly why did you need to get married?"

A muscle jerked in his jaw. "You're a real enough wife as far as I'm concerned. And I didn't." He planted his hand in the small of her back and ushered her firmly across the threshold. "Need to get married, that is."

"You didn't?"

She spun around as the door swung closed. He stood in front of it, a large, impregnable barrier. For the first time, she realized that aggressive men could also be intimidating, especially when the man in question was her husband.

Perhaps if they were in an office instead of a hotel room and it was a business meeting instead of her wedding night, she wouldn't have felt so nervous. But he had such a grim, intimidating expression on his face. She clasped her hands together, aware that her confidence was rapidly ebbing.

She cleared her throat. "If you didn't need to marry, then why did you?"

"I didn't *need* a wife," he repeated, stepping away from the door and stalking into the sitting area toward her. "Not everyone gets married because it's the only way out of a tight spot. Some people actually marry for more pedestrian reasons. Like companionship. Or children. Or even love."

She fell back several steps, her eyes widening. "Is that why you wanted to get married? For love?"

"Why the sudden interest, Nikki?" His question had an edge she didn't like, a raspy quality that spoke of exhaustion and frustration and anger. "We had all night to talk. You could have asked these questions at any point during the evening. But you didn't give a damn about anything except solving your own little predicament. So why bring it up now?"

The sitting area that had seemed so spacious when she'd first entered the room had grown dramatically smaller. She swallowed tightly. "I just wondered why you married me." She hated how soft and breathless her voice had grown.

"Because solving your problem solves mine."

"I don't understand."

He stripped off his jacket and tossed it over a nearby chair. "I don't expect you to. Yet."

Before she could question him further, he took a final step in her direction. Retreating an equal distance, the back of her knees hit the edge of the bed and she sat down abruptly.

"It's a king-size bed," she explained in a rush, scooting backward on the quilted cover. "When I realized the mistake, I tried to get two doubles, but the hotel's full. Every room's taken. I thought maybe the couch would be acceptable." She gestured wildly toward the sitting area.

"You're not using the couch and neither am I." The mattress dipped beneath his weight. "We're husband and wife now, remember?"

He trapped her beneath him before she had a chance to roll away and she stared at him in shock. "But you claimed we wouldn't . . . You didn't intend . . ." Frantically, she searched her memory, struggling to recall his exact phrasing. "You said you didn't want to sleep with me!"

"I told you it wasn't worth discussing. And it's not. Certain issues are non-negotiable, and this is one of them." His eyes were a fierce green, glowing with blatant desire. "So no more discussion. No more negotiations. The time has come for action."

"No—"

"Yes, Mrs. Alexander. Most definitely, yes."

Framing her head with his hands, he stole a gentle kiss, confirming her earlier opinion. Dear heaven, but he knew his way around a woman's mouth. He also knew when to coerce and when to coax. And right now, he coaxed. Teased. Tempted.

Seduced.

Hot little flames flickered to life again, splashing across her skin, seeping deep within to weaken every muscle and sear every nerve ending. She tried to resist, to explain all her reasons for keeping their relationship platonic. But the words were lost, swallowed by a far greater need, a need that consumed all rational thought.

The buttons of her suit jacket fell open and his mouth drifted downward, following the length of her throat. She teetered on the edge of surrender. He was her husband. He was helping her resolve an untenable situation. And she wanted him. Heaven help her, she wanted him. Considering the circumstances, could making love be so wrong?

"Nikki," he muttered in a passion-slurred voice. "I'm sorry. I can't resist."

"I know," she whispered. "I feel the same way."

"Thanks for understanding."

His shadowed jaw rasped across sensitive skin and she held her breath, aware that she'd committed herself to folly. He cupped her breasts, nuzzling the curves above her lacy bra and then . . .

Nothing.

"Joe?" she murmured, shifting beneath his oppressive weight. He didn't respond, and as the seconds ticked by, desire waned. She moistened her lips, the return of sanity making her extremely self-conscious. "Are you sure about this?" she asked uneasily. "Don't you think we should wait until we know each other a little better? Joe? *Joe*?"

And it was then she realized he'd fallen fast asleep.

Chapter Four

Nikki stirred, two disparate sounds bringing her to full consciousness.

One was the familiar hiss of a shower.

The other was a tentative knocking at the door.

Neither made any sense to her. But then, until she'd had two strong cups of coffee, not much did first thing in the morning. She rolled onto her back and blinked up at the ceiling, struggling to recall why the bedroom looked and felt so strange.

And then she remembered. Remembered *everything*.

She darted a quick, nervous glance toward the far side of the mattress. Joe wasn't there, only a depression in the bedding confirming he'd spent the entire night beside her. That explained the sound of running water. Her—she swallowed hard—*husband* must be in the shower. Another knock sounded at the door the same instant as the flow of water stopped.

Confronting the unknown entity in the hallway seemed a safer bet than confronting the well-known entity toweling off after his shower, she decided. Kicking back the covers, she pulled on her robe and went to answer the summons. With luck, Joe had ordered breakfast before closeting himself in the bathroom. Thrusting an unruly tumble of hair from her face, she unlocked the door and tugged it open.

"Hi, Nikki." Eric stood there, an abashed grin on his face. "Surprise."

She whipped the door partially closed and ducked behind it, glaring at him through the remaining two-inch crack. "What are you doing here?" she demanded in a furious whisper. "Have you lost your mind?"

"Is that room service?" Joe's deep voice rumbled from close behind. "I'd kill for a cup of coffee."

"It's not room service," she replied without turning around. Speaking softly, she ordered, *"Go away!"*

Eric's jaw dropped. "I'm not going anywhere until you tell me what the hell my brother is doing here."

Her eyes widened in alarm. "Who? Where?"

"Right there behind you! My brother, Jonah. What's he doing in a hotel room with you? And dressed like that, no less!"

She spun around and literally went weak at the knees. Never in her life had she seen such an appealing sight. Joe stood in the middle of the room wearing nothing but a fluffy white towel. His skin was golden, his chest an endless expanse of dark brown fur, and he stalked toward her with the determination of a gladiator ready to join battle.

Everything about him exuded power. From the resolute expression in his autumn-hued eyes, to his wall-like shoulders, to his solidly muscled legs, he approached with the grace and assurance of a seasoned warrior. And all she could do was stand and wait, uncertain of the rules of engagement in this particular war.

Reaching her side, he wrapped his arms around her. "Morning, sweetheart," he muttered in his distinctively raspy voice and nuzzled the side of her neck.

She gasped at the torturous pleasure his stubbled jaw kindled. "Joe, what is—"

"Don't say a word," he cut in tersely. He spoke close to her ear, his quiet warning conveyed with a harshness that stunned her. "Just play along or I swear you'll regret it."

She opened her mouth to protest, but as though anticipating that, he kissed her. It was long and slow and deep, stealing every thought from her head. Unable to help herself, she relaxed, her body turning pliant and eager within his embrace. How did he do it? the rational part of her mind wondered. With one kiss, he demolished every hint of resistance and turned her from a reasonable, logical, intelligent woman into a helpless puppet. How was it possible?

"What the *hell* is going on here*?" Eric interrupted.*

Nikki started, having completely forgotten about his presence. But Joe—or was it *Jonah?*—didn't even twitch. Taking his time, he finished the kiss before lifting his head. He grinned down at her, flicking his finger across her rosy cheekbone.

Finally, he addressed Eric. "Hello, little brother. Here I manage to sneak off for a romantic weekend with my wife and you still find a way to track me down. How'd you do it?"

Eric fought to draw breath. "What . . . When . . ."

Jonah released a gusty sigh. "It was Jan, wasn't it? She spilled the beans." Shooting Nikki a reproving look, he ruffled her already-ruffled hair. "You've got to get better control over that secretary of yours, sweetheart. What could be so urgent that we can't have a private weekend without business intruding?"

"I—" Her mouth opened and closed like a stranded fish.

Without missing a beat, Jonah returned his attention to Eric. "And just what is it that's so urgent?"

Eric's mouth opened and closed and he finally shook his head, unable to answer.

"I'll tell you what," Jonah offered. "There's a restaurant downstairs. Order up a large pot of coffee while we dress and we'll join you for breakfast as soon as we can." He didn't wait for Eric's reply, but slammed the door shut in his brother's face.

"What the *hell*—"

Jonah cupped his palm over her mouth. "Wait!" he snapped in a curt undertone and cocked his head meaningfully toward the door. Hustling her to the sitting area at the far end of the room, he removed his hand. "Okay, finish."

"Is going on?" she concluded in a furious whisper. "Just who the *hell* are you?"

"Your husband."

"That's not what I mean and you know it! You're not Joe Alexander, are you?"

"No."

He folded his arms across his chest, drawing her attention once again to the corded muscles of his well-developed arms and the impressive width of his shoulders. Lord, he was gorgeous, she reluctantly conceded. And distracting as the devil. She closed her eyes to block out the sight, focusing once again on the business at hand.

"You're Jonah Alexander? Eric's brother?"

"Yes. I shortened my name so you wouldn't recognize it."

She'd figured out that much already, but it still came as a distinct shock to hear the casually stated confession. She sank into a chair, staring at him in disbelief. "*Why*?"

A cynical light turned his eyes a chilly golden brown. "Can't you guess?"

With his standing there in nothing but a loosely knotted towel? Not a chance. "Maybe if you dressed," she suggested faintly.

His mouth curved in amusement. "I will, just as soon as the clothes I ordered from the men's shop downstairs are delivered. No luggage, remember?"

She bowed her head to avoid looking at him. "I still don't understand," she said through gritted teeth.

"What in particular is giving you trouble?"

She could hear the laughter in his voice and resented it passionately. "What's going on? Why were you at the Cinderella Ball last night? Why did you marry me?" A sudden thought occurred and her head jerked up, her hair spilling across her shoulders in a riotous tangle of warm golden browns and heated russet. "We are really married, aren't we?"

"Oh, we're legal all right."

"But you used a fake name—"

"I just used a nickname, same as you. If you'd bothered to look at our marriage license, you'd have seen Jonah Alexander spelled out in all its glory." His tone was dry, his gaze mocking.

"From there it would have been a simple enough leap to connect me to Eric."

"If I had, I'd never have married you," she retorted bitterly.

"No doubt."

"And you still haven't answered my questions."

He ran a hand across his shadowed jaw and she remembered how his day-old beard had abraded her skin when he'd nuzzled her neck. Mild pain had melded with a more profound pleasure. The result had been electrifying and she eyed his jawline speculatively. What would it be like to feel that tantalizing scrape against her breast? An intense warmth unfurled in the pit of her stomach at the mere thought and she clenched her hands, fighting the unwanted sensation.

"Well?" she snapped.

He shrugged. "I came to the Montagues' to stop you from marrying Eric."

"*What*? I wasn't planning to—"

"I know that now."

"But you didn't last night," she stated with dawning comprehension.

"Not until after we'd conducted a rather lengthy conversation."

"The one outside in the garden." His strange behavior the previous evening began to make sense. Finally. "That's why you were asking all those odd questions and kept pestering me about my prospective bridegroom. You didn't understand the purpose of the ball."

"Not entirely," he conceded.

"What in the world did you think I was doing there?"

"Meeting Eric."

"I can't believe this," she muttered, dragging a hand through her hair.

"The evidence was damning," he explained without apology, "especially the part about you and Eric flying to Nevada on International Investment business—"

"We don't have any business interests here," she inserted automatically.

"I'm well aware of that fact." He waited a beat before adding, "And so is the rest of the office staff."

She couldn't hide her dismay. Apparently, Eric's pursuit of her had left ample room for conjecture, not to mention gossip. "But we weren't traveling together," she argued. "I didn't even know Eric had followed me until he showed up at the Montagues'."

"The bottom line is that you both flew to Nevada. You both had reservations here at the Grand. And there'd already been talk of an affair. In this case, two and two may have added up to five, but to an outsider it sure as hell looked like an elopement."

"You were leaping to conclusions," she said dismissively.

"Was I? Don't forget one other detail. The Montagues' Cinderella Ball." He let that sink in. "The few facts I'd ascertained suggested it was some sort of gala for couples who wanted to marry. And when I called the Grand, they confirmed that most of their guests were attending and gave me directions. I'd have booked a room here, but they were full by then."

Her eyes narrowed suspiciously. "How did you find out about the Cinderella Ball?"

"You left the announcement on your desk."

"You searched my desk?" she demanded, outraged.

"If you're expecting an apology, you've got a long wait," he said with callous disregard. "I had a job to do and I did it."

"So, you came out to Nevada believing Eric and I were going to marry and hellbent on stopping us, right? Why? What difference did it make if I married your brother?"

"Aside from the fact that I believed you were already married and that you have a few years on him?"

She lifted her chin. "Yes. Aside from those reasons."

"Your relationship had begun to affect your work. You acknowledged as much last night. Why do you think Loren called me home?"

Her eyes widened in alarm. "The Sanders know?"

"What my parents know, or rather thought they knew, was that Eric was having an affair with an older, married woman. The affair had become common gossip among the employees and had distracted the principals involved to the point that they almost succeeded in losing the Dearfield account."

"Oh, no!"

"Oh, yes," he responded with brutal deliberation. "I recommended they fire you. If you hadn't been a nominee for the Lawrence J. Bauman Award, you would have been."

"Why?" she demanded. "Because I had the temerity to catch the eye of the boss's son?"

"No. Because you allowed your personal life to interfere with business."

"So it was Jonah Alexander, troubleshooter, financier extraordinaire and former LJB winner to the rescue. Is that it?" She didn't bother to hide her resentment.

"That's it."

"And your solution was to marry me?"

"Not by a long shot. You were the one who settled on that as a solution. I merely accommodated you."

"*Why?*"

"What choice did I have? I couldn't change your mind about marrying and you wouldn't settle on an acceptable husband. Then Eric showed up and it was either marry or expose you as a liar." For the first time, anger disturbed the even tenor of his voice. He stepped closer, his expression falling into grim lines. "But believe this, *Mrs. Alexander,* if I didn't think that revealing the truth might damage the reputation of International Investment, I'd have given you up in a heartbeat and damn the consequences."

"I had to do something about Eric," she protested.

"You didn't have to lie. If you make such foolish decisions in your personal life, I have to wonder what the hell you're doing on the job."

The criticism struck hard and cut deep. "My work is beyond reproach!"

"Except for the Dearfield account, you mean?" came the harsh retort. "Well, we'll find out, won't we?"

"What are you saying?" she asked apprehensively.

"I'm saying that I intend to analyze your performance over the past year. And if I find anything out of sync, LJB Award or no, you'll be out on that pretty little tail of yours."

She leaped to her feet, her hands balling into fists. "If that's how you feel, why did you bother to marry me?"

"You think I wanted to?" His anger erupted with tangible force, reflected in the taut line of his jaw and the hot sparks of gold flaming to life in his eyes. "Our marriage is an inconvenient means of salvaging an untenable situation. And you, my accidental wife, are a temporary encumbrance."

"How dare—"

"Oh, cut the self-righteous indignation," he snapped.

"You used me last night every bit as much as I used you. What did you say? It wasn't just Eric but some personal matter you needed to resolve, as well?"

His reminder stopped her cold. How could she have forgotten Krista and Keli? "Yes," she conceded, her anger fading as swiftly as it had flared.

"Well, at least Eric won't be a problem any longer."

She stared in confusion. "Why not?"

"He won't poach," Jonah stated succinctly. "After this morning, there won't be any doubt in my brother's mind that not only are we married, but we share a passionate relationship. If I read him right, he'll be furious at you for not telling him the truth about us. Any feelings he might harbor should die a swift and bitter death."

She turned her back on him, blinking hard. She'd never wanted to hurt Eric, only ease an uncomfortable situation. But everything she'd done so far only succeeded in exacerbating matters. "How do we explain our marriage to him?" she asked quietly.

"We say that we became engaged before I left for London and we married a short time afterward on one of my trips to the States. We kept it quiet because we didn't want it to affect your position at work." His voice acquired a cynical edge. "We'll tell him you preferred to make it on your own. He should buy that."

Her mouth tightened. "Go on."

"We're celebrating our one-year anniversary by renewing our vows at the Montagues' party and had planned to make the big announcement to the family immediately afterward."

"You have it all worked out," she said, unable to conceal her resentment.

"Somebody had to."

"I'll have you know I had complete control of the situation." She turned to face him. "Your interference wasn't necessary."

"You had it all under control?" She couldn't mistake his sarcasm. "Which part?"

"Once I married—"

"Fine. Let's start there. Never in my life have I heard of anything as crazy as this Cinderella Ball. You really intended to marry a complete stranger?"

"Yes." She strove for nonchalance. "What's wrong with that?"

"What—" He bit off a curse. "You knew nothing about me. Not even my real name. I could have been an ax murderer. Or worse."

"What's worse than an ax murderer?" she muttered.

"Don't tempt me to show you. How could you be so irresponsible?"

"I'm sure there were no ax murderers present," she argued. "The Montagues ran security checks. They had all the guests investigated before they authorized their invitations."

"A fat lot of good that did."

His voice had become dangerously soft, the bass tones rumbling with stormy threat. His hand closed around her arm and he tugged her close. She made a small sound of complaint, not that he noticed or cared. Instead, he secured her against him, the thin cotton of her nightgown providing as flimsy a barrier as his towel. She splayed her hands across his chest, her fingers sinking into the generous pelt of hair to the taut layer of skin and muscle beneath.

"Joe— Jonah, please. You don't understand. It was perfectly safe."

"Really? Well, for your information, *wife*, I didn't have an invitation. I walked right in the front door and no one made a move to stop me. Now tell me again how everyone was investigated and deemed safe. Am I safe? Well? *Am I*?"

She stared into blazing hazel eyes, the strength of his fury impacting with stunning force. More than anything, she wanted to look away. But she didn't, compelled to meet that impossible gaze while still retaining the tattered scraps of her control.

"No," she replied tartly, remembering his attempted seduction once they'd returned to the hotel. "You aren't the least safe. Last night proved that beyond any doubt."

"Did it?" His eyes narrowed as he considered her comment and she regretted ever having made the dig. "After thirty-odd hours without sleep, some of it's a bit hazy. I don't recall much toward the end, except—"

"Nothing happened!" she broke in defensively.

A hint of jade green crept into his curious gaze, and a slow smile creased his mouth. His arms slid around her, his hands settling on her hips. "That's not quite the way I remember it," he said, easing her close.

Struggling was out of the question. She hardly dared so much as breathe for fear of the consequences. "I thought you couldn't remember anything."

A quiet laugh broke free. "I don't. At least not much. My last memory was falling asleep on the softest, fluffiest pillow I've ever set cheek to." Color flamed in her face, and his gaze drifted from there downward, settling on the agitated rise and fall of her breasts. "I wouldn't mind trying it again."

"Let go of me." If anything, his hold tightened and she was terrified he might kiss her. If that happened, she'd be lost, just like every other time he'd touched her.

And he knew it as surely as she.

"I don't recall much after that." His brow wrinkled. "I sure don't remember undressing. And yet when I woke up this morning, someone had taken off my shoes." He cocked a gold-tipped eyebrow. "You?"

"I may have."

"And my shirt?"

A sudden image of the night before came to her. Once she'd gotten over her initial shock and anger at his falling asleep, she'd been unable to just leave him sprawled on the bed, fully dressed. He'd looked too uncomfortable. The shoes had been easy. The shirt less so because he'd worn a cummerbund. Never having seen a man put on such a device, let alone attempted to remove one, she'd wrestled with it for endless moments before locating the hooks. Added to which, he'd been so huge, it had taken every ounce of strength to roll him over enough to take care of the problem.

"You haven't answered my question," he prompted.

"Once I figured out how your cummerbund worked, the shirt was a snap. I put your cuff links on the dresser, by the way."

She didn't add how unnervingly intimate the procedure had been. Finding the buttons within the folds of his dress shirt hadn't seemed so bad. His body heat singeing her through the soft cotton, though, had come as a distinct shock.

He'd lain stretched across the bed, his shirt gaping, hers to touch and care for. She'd hurried initially, desperate to get the job done. But as she'd worked the shirt off his shoulders and arms, her movements had slowed. And heaven help her, she'd been unable to resist caressing that incredible musculature.

Did he know? Did he suspect that she'd traced every hard curve, the deep furring of his chest, the taut ripples of his abdomen, the beautifully sculpted biceps?

She risked a quick upward glance, but his expression told her nothing. He held her so close the crisp hairs of his chest brushed the curve of her jaw, swamping her with desires she'd never known she possessed, desires she didn't dare communicate to him. They were the same feelings that had spilled through her as she'd unbuttoned his trousers.

She'd panicked then, just as she was almost panicking now. Last night, she'd bolted from the bed and locked herself in the bathroom for a long, hot shower. Afterward, she'd thrown a blanket over his slumbering form and crawled into bed next to him. Curling into a tight ball as far to one side of the king bed as she could manage, it had taken her a long, long time to drift off to sleep.

"Where have you gone, Nikki?" he questioned softly.

Her gaze flew to his and she shook her head, unable to answer. For where she'd been, she didn't dare allow him to follow. To her eternal relief, a knock sounded at the door, sparing her the need to invent a response.

"I think this conversation might be worth pursuing further," he said.

"I disagree." She stirred within his hold. "Aren't you going to answer that?"

"I'm debating."

"There's nothing to debate. We've been an awfully long time," she said, pulling free of his embrace. "Let's hope it's your clothes and not Eric."

It was clothing. After signing for the package, he glanced over his shoulder at her. "With any luck, Eric's put the appropriate construction on our delay and is busy inventing an excuse for being in Nevada." He tore open the package and his towel hit the floor. "You might want to get dressed, too."

With a strangled gasp, Nikki snatched up her overnight bag and flew into the bathroom, slamming the door. It took five minutes to calm down enough to dress, and a further five to dab on enough makeup to conceal the ravages of a restless night. Finally, she emerged, dressed in a businesslike fitted gold skirt and blouse, her hair thoroughly brushed and neatly gathered at the base of her neck.

Jonah took one look at her and shook his head, his mouth settling into a grim line. "Not a chance."

"What's wrong now?" she questioned defensively.

"You look like my secretary, not my wife." He approached, flicking open the first several buttons of her blouse and loosened her hair so it tumbled down her back. "Unless we're at work, you wear your hair loose."

"Why?"

"We're making a statement, remember, creating an illusion? That illusion is that we're married and can't keep our mitts off each other. When we walk into the dining room, the first thought that I want Eric to have is that we've just made love and then thrown on whatever clothes came to hand in order to join him." He examined her critically. "No jewelry except your wedding band and wear your heels from last night."

"But they're ivory. They don't match—"

"Exactly. We dressed in haste, remember? Come on. Let's go."

Jamming her feet into the shoes he indicated, she snatched up her purse and followed him to the door. They accomplished the ride in the elevator in total silence. Just before the doors slid open, he cupped the back of her head and pulled her close for a quick, hard kiss.

"I hate it when you do that," she protested the minute he released her.

"If you hate it so much, stop clutching my shirt. And when we join Eric, follow my lead. Understand?"

"No."

"Do it anyway. You ready?"

She nodded, dreading the next few minutes. He started toward the restaurant and she caught his arm. "Jonah, wait." She moistened her lips. "Please. Please don't hurt him."

His gaze turned wintry. "I think it's too late for that. Don't you? But if it makes you feel any better, I promise I won't give you the chance to hurt him anymore."

With that, he snagged her elbow and led her toward what she suspected would be the most uncomfortable conversation of her life.

Chapter Five

"What do you mean we're going to Chicago?" Nikki demanded as they entered the airport lobby. "I need to get back to New York."

"And you will," he retorted, joining the short line in front of the first-class passenger check-in counter. "Just as soon as we stop in Chicago and see my parents."

That didn't sound good. "Do we have to?" she asked faintly.

"Yes, we do." He glanced down at her, correctly interpreting her reaction. "Don't worry. I'll do the talking again."

And suffer through the accusatory stares and barbed silences she'd experienced with Eric? Not a chance. "That's what I'm afraid of. Last time you did the talking, I ended up appearing—"

"Heartless? Guilty as sin? A traitor?"

She shot him a sour look. "You do it deliberately, don't you? You twist everything I say to your own advantage."

"I don't have to twist a single thing. You've managed to tangle yourself in this little web of deceit all on your own. I'm just trying to straighten out your mess. If, in the process, you come across as less than sympathetic, it's not my fault."

"Oh, no?" She planted her hands on her hips. "For your information, I wasn't the only one being deceitful last night, *Joe*. Nor would I be in this mess if you hadn't interfered. I had everything all planned."

His eyebrows winged skyward and he made a small noise that sounded suspiciously like a snort. "You call attending the Montagues' ball a plan?"

"Yes." She ticked off her points one by one. "Go to the ball and find a husband. Make a big production out of introducing him at work. Take care of a personal situation. And let Eric down gently. *Gently!*" She glared at him. "Do you even know the meaning of the word gentle? The man I intended to marry would have."

"I see. Adding another player to the drama is supposed to simplify it. Especially someone unfamiliar with both the role and his lines. And a gentle man, no less." His voice dripped sarcasm. "Now there's a contradiction in terms."

She bit down on her lip to halt the impetuous rush of words. She knew when to beat a temporary retreat in order to salvage her pride. And that time had definitely arrived.

Besides, their breakfast with Eric had gone precisely as Jonah had predicted and had been every bit the unmitigated disaster she'd feared. Eric had offered the transparent excuse of calling on a potential customer as his reason for being in Nevada. Jonah had repeated the story he'd invented surrounding their engagement and marriage. And she'd sat there gulping coffee and trying to appear madly in love with one brother while avoiding the hurt gaze of the other.

Taking a deep breath, she asked, "What are you going to tell your parents?"

"The truth. It'll make a pleasant change, if nothing else." The ticket window cleared and he crossed to it, dumping their luggage on the scale. "Reroute these through Chicago for a one-night layover," he requested, slapping their airline tickets on the counter. "And what's your first available flight from Chicago to New York on Monday morning?"

"No! I have to get home tonight," Nikki protested. "I'm expected."

"Change your plans," he said without a trace of sympathy. "I've had to. I'm sure the incomparable Jan can reschedule your early-morning appointments with one hand tied behind her back."

Realizing further argument would prove futile, she did as he suggested and fished through her purse for her cell phone.

Stepping to one side, she called her sister first, keeping it light and breezy. "I won't be home until Monday, I'm afraid. My business took longer than expected. And I have a surprise for you."

"For me?" her sister asked. "You didn't have to do that."

"It's not for you, precisely. It's something I got for myself. But I hope you'll be pleased."

"What is it?" Krista demanded. "Tell me."

"I can't. I have to admit, I've been a bit impetuous." Nikki glanced at Jonah's broad back and swallowed. *Very* impetuous might be closer to the truth.

"*You*? Impetuous? I can't believe it."

"Believe it," Nikki retorted. "I'll see you Monday, though I'm not sure when. And I'll bring my surprise with me. You'll love him." She groaned. "*It*. You'll love *it*."

A momentary silence greeted her statement. "Oh, Nikki," Krista said in a troubled voice. "What have you done?"

"Something wonderful," Nikki insisted with a hint of defiance. She shut her eyes. Wonderfully terrifying. Terrifyingly wonderful. "I'll see you tomorrow."

"And we'll talk, right?"

Nikki winced. "Right. All my love to you and Keli. I've got to run."

"Nik, honey?"

"What?"

"It's not your fault." Krista's voice dropped, the words tumbling out in an urgent rush. "You don't have to spend the rest of your life making up for one youthful indiscretion. You have to stop blaming yourself for what happened. It isn't worth ruining your life over."

"I'm not," Nikki interrupted briskly. "I'm just trying to take care of you and Keli. It'll work out, I promise."

"Try taking care of yourself for a change," Krista shot back. "That's all I ask."

"I will." Eventually. Just as soon as she'd secured the futures of her various family members.

"Yeah, right." A sigh drifted across the line. "I love you, sweetie."

"Me, too. I'll talk to you soon."

The tears pricking Nikki's eyes caught her by surprise and it took a full minute to collect herself enough to place the next call. Despite being disturbed at home on a Sunday, Jan took the instructions to rearrange Monday's schedule with her customary composure. Just as Nikki concluded the phone call, Jonah approached.

"Finished?"

"All set."

"Good. We'll have to hustle. The flight leaves in fifteen minutes."

"Aren't you going to call your parents and warn them we're coming?" she asked in dismay.

"I'll do it on the plane. Let's go."

The flight lasted a torturous three hours, giving Nikki ample time for reflection, although she spent most of that time worrying rather than reflecting. She'd met Loren Sanders when she'd first been hired and only once or twice since. Though he seemed charming, she'd sensed he didn't suffer fools gladly.

On the other hand, she'd never met Jonah's mother and knew little of her except what could be gleaned from office gossip. Stories of Della's immense charm and appeal circulated there on a regular basis. Which might be why the idea of confronting the Sanders with her idiocy was sufficient to put Nikki in a total panic. For she knew without a doubt that that's how she'd be perceived.

As an absolute idiot.

Jonah was right. She'd made a mess of this entire situation. She should have forced Eric to listen from the beginning. Instead, she'd compounded deceit with deceit until she'd compromised herself so thoroughly, it was a wonder Jonah didn't just let her choke on all the lies. But then, as he'd so nastily pointed out, if it hadn't been for the potential harm to International Investment's reputation, as well as her nomination for the Lawrence J. Bauman Award, he would have left her to her fate without a single qualm.

At least he couldn't fault her business decisions, she attempted to console herself. Despite what he'd threatened, when he examined her record, he'd be impressed. Very impressed. And on that note, she shut her eyes and willed herself to catch up on some vitally needed sleep.

Jonah glanced at his wife. The instant she'd nodded off, she'd snuggled into his arms as though she belonged. With her head tucked into the curve of his shoulder and her fingers laced through two of his belt loops, it would be understandable for a stranger to think theirs a familiar position.

He should find it humorous, and he might have if not for one troubling detail. Even in sleep, her features had a drawn appearance he didn't like. He knew it was due to stress combined with exhaustion. Faint purple bruises beneath her eyes emphasized her pallor and a tiny line remained between her brows as though even in her dreams she hadn't found surcease from her difficulties.

He smoothed his thumb across the bothersome wrinkle, pleased when he succeeded in ironing it away. At his touch, she sighed and relaxed more fully against him.

She possessed a stoic quality that troubled him, as though she'd faced hardship on a regular basis. As though she expected life to be tough and steeled herself in preparation. And beneath it he sensed the painful vulnerability of someone who'd been hurt more than once.

He'd been hard on her. Too hard, he admitted. And he could guess why. If he hadn't returned when he had, hadn't gone to the Cinderella Ball, Nikki would have been married to someone else. Someone who had the right to touch her. Kiss her.

Bed her.

Before he could analyze why that caused his gut to clench, a flight attendant paused by his seat. "Excuse me, Mr. Alexander," he whispered. "We'll be landing shortly. Can I bring you and your wife some coffee?"

"Thanks," he said with a nod. "Black for me. Two cups with extra sugar for my wife."

He didn't bother to waken her. The rousing aroma of the coffee did it for him. She stirred, her nose twitching first, followed by the reluctant flickering of her lashes. "Tell me I'm not dreaming," she murmured sleepily. "Is that really coffee?"

"You don't even have to open your eyes. Just hold out a hand and it's all yours."

To his amusement, she did as he suggested. Halfway through her second cup, she straightened. From the flush tinting her cheeks, he gathered she was somewhat embarrassed to have awakened in his arms. And from the tightening of her mouth, he guessed she intended to pretend it hadn't happened.

Unwilling to allow the episode to pass without consequence, he reached over and combed his fingers through the spill of hair caressing her cheek, the color an autumnal explosion. If he'd hoped to disconcert her, it backfired. Badly. He'd heard of hair being compared to silk and always thought it a poetic exaggeration. Now he knew differently. Never had he touched anything so smooth and soft.

"Feel better?" he asked quietly, tucking the wayward strands behind her ear.

"Yes, thank you." She continued to avoid his gaze. "How much longer until we get there?"

"Fifteen or twenty minutes."

The faint line he'd smoothed away earlier reappeared. "We'll go directly to your parents' house?"

"It's an apartment, and yes, we'll go straight there. I don't expect the traffic to be too bad on a Sunday. It shouldn't take more than forty minutes."

"Oh." She moistened her lips, clearly working up the nerve to ask the question she'd been fretting about for the past five hours. "You said you were going to tell them the truth. What exactly do you plan to say?"

"That Eric's made an ass of himself. That you overreacted. And that if I'd had enough sleep before wading into the middle of things, I would have resolved matters with more finesse than I have."

She shot him a look of alarm. "You think marrying was a mistake, don't you?"

"It was an extreme solution to a not-so-extreme problem." For some strange reason, he felt the need to let her off the hook. "Don't worry. I'll deal with it."

A troubled expression darkened her eyes. "I didn't marry just because of Eric, remember? I do have a secondary reason."

"So you said. Care to tell me about it now?"

Her lashes swept downward, but not before he'd caught a telltale flash of violet. Whatever this reason involved, it visibly upset her. And for some reason, she didn't trust him enough yet to explain the details. Understandable, given how hard he'd been on her. What he struggled to understand was why he wanted to change that. To have her look at him with absolute faith.

"I'd rather wait, if you don't mind," she replied. "It's—"

"Personal. Yes, I know." He lifted an eyebrow and dared to tease. "I hope you're not going to make me guess. With your propensity for chaos, I doubt my imagination is up to the job."

"I'll tell you." Her mouth firmed "When I'm ready."

"I hope so. I may have difficulty resolving it otherwise."

"I don't need you to resolve it," she retorted, stung. "I can take care of my own problems."

"Now we'll both take care of them." He cut her off before she could say more. "Fasten your seat belt. We're about to land."

By the time they'd collected their luggage and caught a cab to the Sanders' apartment, the afternoon had all but vanished. Della answered the door to his knock, flinging her arms around him with customary enthusiasm.

"I'm so glad you're here. Dinner will be ready in half an hour, so there's plenty of time to freshen up." She smiled at Nikki and held out her hand, a slight reserve curbing her enthusiasm. "You must be Mrs. Ashton. Welcome."

"It's Nikki," Jonah interrupted lazily. "Nikki Alexander, to be exact. As in Mrs. Jonah Alexander."

"Oh, that just tears it!" Nikki turned on him, her taut control dissolving in the face of her fury.

As he'd hoped, the cool, reserved businesswoman vanished, replaced by an impassioned spitfire. He found the spitfire much more to his liking. Knowing his parents, they would, too.

"Something wrong?" he asked innocently.

"You need to ask?" she demanded. "You couldn't have broken the news to your mother more gently?"

"I don't do gentle, remember?"

Della's mouth fell open. "You're *married?*"

Nikki planted her bands on her trim hips, her fury a glorious sight. At least Jonah found it glorious. He slanted a quick look at his mother, relieved that she appeared more confused than shocked.

"It didn't occur to you to prepare her first instead of just nuking everyone in sight with your announcement?" Nikki continued.

He shrugged, fighting to keep a straight face. "Don't exaggerate. The only everyone in sight is my mother. And I prefer speed to delicacy."

"Well, that's obvious." She shot him a reproving glance. "Although in your line of work, I'd have thought you'd have learned something about diplomacy."

"Not much," he confessed. "I've always found making money takes talent and intelligence, not tact."

Della glanced over her shoulder. "Loren, you better get out here."

Nikki's eyes glittered with ill-humor, the color as vivid as a tropical sunrise. "That's beside the point. You told me you were going to call them."

"I did call while you were asleep." She sounded a bit grouchy, Jonah decided. Perhaps he should have fed her three cups of coffee instead of just two. "I told them we were coming for dinner."

"What's all the yelling about?" Loren questioned mildly as he joined his wife.

"That's it? Just we're coming for dinner?" Nikki stabbed a finger at Jonah. "You couldn't have added, Oh and by the way, Nikki Ashton and I just got married. I'll explain when we get there?"

"They're married," Della announced to her husband. "Jonah and Nikki."

"How can they be married?" Loren demanded. "She's already married to that Ashton fellow."

"See? This is why I waited." Jonah leaned against the doorjamb, confiding, "Getting married is the sort of happy news parents prefer to hear face-to-face."

"In the *hallway?*" Nikki fumed.

"They want to share in our joy and happiness, no matter where we are."

"They don't look the least joyful or happy. They look . . ." She spared them a brief, apprehensive glance. "Stunned."

"I'm not stunned. I'm confused," Loren grumbled to his wife. "I thought she was having an affair with Eric."

Della shrugged. "Well, now she's married to Jonah."

"You couldn't even wait until we were invited in?" Nikki folded her arms across her chest and scowled at Jonah. "Maybe work it casually into the conversation over drinks?"

He fought to assume an appropriately contrite expression. "I must have gotten carried away in the excitement of the moment. It just came out."

"You, carried away?" She snorted. "My Aunt Fanny. You never do anything without a reason."

Loren looked from one to the other, his brow wrinkling. "Who the hell is Aunt Fanny? And while we're on the subject of relatives, what the dickens happened to Mr. Ashton? Have we ever figured that one out?"

"There is no Mr. Ashton," Nikki and Jonah said in union.

Loren thrust a hand through his salt-and-pepper hair. "No Mr. Ashton? I don't understand any of this. Would someone please tell me what the devil is going on around here?"

"Maybe we should finish this discussion inside before the neighbors complain," Della suggested.

"Excellent suggestion, Mother," Jonah approved.

An awkward moment followed while they all filed from the entranceway into the living room. "What a gorgeous view," Nikki volunteered.

Della offered a strained smile. "You should see it when it snows."

"Yes, yes. The view is wonderful. Snow is wonderful. The whole damned world is just by golly wonderful!" Loren declared testily. "Now what the *hell* is going on here? Or is a reasonable explanation too much to expect?"

"It's all my fault," Nikki began.

"I believe I told you I'd handle this." Jonah's tone didn't brook defiance.

She lifted her chin. "Fine. You handle it." Turning her back on him, she crossed to stare out at Lake Michigan. What did it matter how he slanted the story? His parents were going to be upset regardless.

"I'll see if I can't keep this simple. There is no Mr. Ashton. Nikki isn't married and never was. She pretended to be married because Eric was making inopportune advances." At Della's muffled exclamation, Jonah shook his head. "No, Mother. It wasn't anything like that. He'd just allowed an understandable infatuation to get the better of his common sense." To his amusement, both Della and Nikki blushed.

Loren's brows drew together. "Let me get this straight. In order to put Eric off, Ms. Ashton, er, Nikki, invented a marriage?"

"'Fraid so," Jonah confirmed. "And that's when matters got a little out of hand."

"I'd say matters were out of hand a good bit before then," Loren inserted drily.

Jonah exchanged a silent look of agreement with his stepfather. "No comment."

"Could we get on with this?" Nikki pleaded. "I know I screwed up. It's no secret."

Jonah took up the story again. "When Eric continued to express his concern over the prolonged absence of Nikki's husband, she decided to rectify the situation. Last night, she attended a marriage ball in Nevada with the full intention of finding herself a suitable husband to present at work."

Della sank onto the couch. "Oh, my dear child. How could you?"

"It seemed like a good idea at the time," Nikki confessed.

"The suitable husband she found was me." He eyed his parents, his expression implacable. "Until Eric is past this infatuation of his and we get the situation at the New York office straightened out, Nikki and I stay married. And we all treat it as if it were real and permanent."

"Well, I think you have both lost your minds." Loren crossed to the wet bar and poured himself a Scotch. "And I want no part of it."

Jonah glanced at Nikki and his mother. "Give me a minute with him."

Della rose to her feet. "As much as it pains me to say this . . ." She smiled at Nikki. "Shall we check on dinner?"

"Do we have a choice?"

"I'm afraid not."

Jonah waited until the two women were out of earshot, then turned to confront his stepfather. "Whether you agree with my decision or not, I expect your support on this. And I expect you to treat Nikki with all the respect due my wife. If you can't, tell me now and we'll leave."

Loren's brows shot up. "Good God. You're serious, aren't you?"

"Very. You called me home to take care of a situation, and that's what I'm doing."

"It's how you're taking care of it that worries me."

"Blame it on jet lag."

For the first time, a hint of amusement touched Loren's face. "I thought you didn't believe in jet lag," he said, pouring his stepson a drink.

"I do now," Jonah replied wryly.

"But marriage?" The older man shook his head. "You don't really expect me to endorse such a crazy scheme?"

"Look, Loren, we have to protect International Investment at all costs, which means we can't fire her, and for the time being, we can't transfer her."

"So, what do you propose?"

Jonah took a healthy swallow of Scotch. "The LJB Award comes right before Christmas, so we hang tough till then. I have an excellent assistant in London who can take care of our overseas operation until after the holidays. In the meantime, I'll spend the next six weeks in New York playing the doting husband."

Loren shot his stepson a shrewd look. "What will you really be doing?"

"Looking over Nikki's track record and making sure she and Eric haven't screwed up any other accounts. As soon as I feel matters are under control, I'll return to London. We give it six more months after that. Then we encourage the lovely Ms. Ashton to either transfer far from Eric's sphere of influence or find employment elsewhere."

Loren lifted an eyebrow. "Your solution is a bit rough on your wife, isn't it?"

For some reason the exhaustion and vulnerability he'd witnessed on Nikki's face while she slept on the plane pricked at his conscience and caused anger to battle with guilt. "Unfortunately, my wife is directly responsible for this situation with Eric. If she'd told him no, or contacted any one of us when it became a problem, we wouldn't be in our current mess."

"What happens once the situation with Eric is resolved?" Loren asked.

"Nikki and I divorce," he stated baldly. So why did part of him react so badly at the thought?

"Divorce? Don't you mean get an annulment?"

Jonah's mouth tugged to one side. "I believe that falls under the heading of none of your business."

"Perhaps. But she is my employee. Come to think of it, she's also my stepdaughter-in-law. At least for the time being."

"Point taken." Jonah finished off the Scotch and set the glass gently on the bar. "When the time comes, we'll divorce."

"This time, I'm doing the talking," Nikki stated firmly.

At least she stated it as firmly as she could, considering Jonah's uncanny ability to get his own way. She found the knack quite disconcerting and suspected that not only did he know it, he took advantage of that fact.

"We'll see," he replied in a noncommittal voice. The cab pulled up in front of an attractive brownstone and he peered at it through the smudged passenger window. "Is this it?"

"Yes. I rent out the first floor and we occupy the second."

"We?"

She took a deep breath. "My sister, Krista, and her daughter, Keli. They live with me."

"Their picture is the one in your office?"

"How…?" Her eyes narrowed. "Oh, right. You searched my desk. Yes, that's Krista and Keli. I took the photo when Keli was five."

Jonah unloaded the luggage and paid off the driver. "How long have you lived here?" he asked as they climbed the steps to the front door.

"Forever." Her response sounded short to the point of rude, but she was reluctant to trust him with even such a small piece of her privacy. "Krista and I grew up here."

He paused at the top of the landing. "I assume you haven't told her about us."

"No." She caught her bottom lip between her teeth. "And fair warning, she may not take the news too well."

"No problem," he responded drily. "I'm getting used to that sort of response to our announcement. Is she the other reason for your decision to marry?"

"Yes." Taking a deep breath, she admitted, "I guess I should have explained earlier."

"That might have helped," he agreed blandly. "Although now works just as well for me. Does Krista know your first marriage was a fake?"

"Yes, but she's not to know this one is, too." Alarm flickered in her gaze. "Which reminds me. Don't, under any circumstances, tell her you're related to Eric or she'll know for sure something's up."

His eyebrow notched upward. "I take it this is supposed to be a love match?"

"Yes, yes," she said with a nervous glance at the door. "We're in love. Madly, passionately in love."

"Got it." He tilted his head to one side. "Care to tell me why we're madly, passionately etc., etc? What are we trying to accomplish?"

"You don't need to know that. You just have to act the part of the love-struck groom." Impatience edged her voice. "Can you do it?"

"In spades."

Without warning, he wrapped powerful arms around her and yanked her against a granite-hard expanse of chest. Before she could catch her breath to protest, he nailed her with an all-consuming kiss.

She should struggle came the dazed thought. She should give him hell. She should level him with a good, swift kick to the shins. Instead, she wrapped her arms around his neck and gave herself up to the illicit thrill of the embrace, only vaguely aware of his fumbling for something behind her. It took a moment to realize he was leaning on the doorbell. By the time it dawned on her, the door opened.

"Aunt Nikki!" a childish voice declared. "You're home. I've been waiting and waiting. Oh!"

"Jonah!" Nikki whispered frantically, shoving at his massive shoulders. "Let go."

The little girl began to giggle. "Mommy! Come quick! There's a strange man kissing Aunt Nikki."

"My goodness! So there is." Another voice had joined the party.

Nikki managed to wriggle free of Jonah's hold. Turning, she offered her sister a flustered smile, then had the breath knocked out of her as the child launched herself at her aunt for an exuberant hug.

"What's your surprise?" Keli demanded, wrapping her arms around her aunt's waist.

"I think that's me," Jonah confessed, lowering himself to her level. "You must be Keli. I'm your Uncle Jonah."

Nikki watched as her niece peeped shyly up at him. Even in a crouch, Jonah's impressive size tended to overwhelm, and Keli studied him uncertainly for a long moment. Wisps of strawberry blond curls floated in a brilliant halo around her face, highlighting the doubt written all over her dainty features. Then, like a shadow floating clear of the sun, the doubt vanished and she grinned.

"Hi," she said. "I didn't know I had an uncle."

"Neither did I," Krista said in a confused voice. She offered a hand to Jonah as he stood. "I'm Krista Barrett, Nikki's sister. And you are?" She lifted a winged eyebrow.

"Jonah Alexander," he said, accepting her hand. "Your brother-in-law."

"Oh, good heavens!"

"We are *not* doing this on the doorstep again," Nikki interjected.

He grinned. "I believe we just did."

"Everyone inside," Nikki snapped. "We'll talk there."

With a shrug, Jonah picked up the bags and stepped across the threshold. Keli trotted after him, studying her new uncle with unabashed curiosity.

Krista caught Nikki's arm as she started past. "What's going on?" she demanded softly.

"I'm married."

"For real this time?" Krista questioned, not bothering to conceal her concern. "This isn't another scheme you've dreamed up because of that Eric Sanders?"

"The marriage is real enough." Nikki took a deep breath and fought to put as much conviction and enthusiasm in her voice as possible. "And just so you know, I love him. In fact, we're both madly in love. And it's permanent. 'Til death us do part and all that."

Krista's brows drew together. "Uh-huh."

"I mean it!"

Nikki sent Jonah an uneasy glance. He stood with Keli, listening to her excited chatter. "And this is the living room," the child was explaining earnestly. "We keep it all picked up for Aunt Nikki. She works real hard and it helps her when I keep my toys in our bedroom."

"The one you share with your mom?" he asked.

"How'd you know that?"

"A lucky guess." An odd expression had crept into his gaze, Nikki realized with a tinge of apprehension. They'd taken on that autumn chill again, the brown-gold appearing rock hard.

"Well," Krista said in bewilderment, "I guess congratulations are in order. I'm sure we have a bottle of champagne around here someplace." She stared at Jonah. "Your name is familiar. Do I know you from somewhere? Do you live nearby?"

"No, you don't and no, he doesn't," Nikki answered with more haste than grace. "He's just back from overseas. He doesn't have any place to live, which means he'll be moving in with us."

"That's going to make it a bit crowded," Krista observed, then offered, "Why don't I put out some feelers to some of my friends? I'm sure I could find another place."

Nikki wrinkled her brow in what she hoped was a thoughtful frown. "That's a possibility. But there's no hurry."

"No hurry at all," Jonah cut in coldly. "In fact, we want you and Keli to stay put. We'll be moving into my apartment."

Nikki's mouth fell open. "But—"

"I was keeping it as a surprise wedding gift, sweetheart. Krista, the place is yours," Jonah stated in an intractable voice. "We stopped by to give you the good news and to pick up some of Nikki's clothes" His hand clamped down on her arm as she started to protest. "Didn't we?"

"I'm so pleased you let me do the talking," she bit out, watching all her plans dissipate like smoke in a high wind. Aware of Krista's worried stare, she added a terse, "Darling."

"My pleasure." He bared sharklike teeth. "Honey."

Chapter Six

"How could you?" Nikki demanded furiously.

"How could I? How could *you?*"

"You don't understand!"

"You're damned right I don't," Jonah snarled, tossing their luggage into the spacious elevator. Inserting a key in the floor-selector panel, he slammed his palm against the button for the penthouse. "Krista is a member of your family. Doesn't that mean anything to you?"

"Of course it does—"

"And yet you'd still toss your own sister and niece out of their home?"

He swiveled to confront her, and the spaciousness of the car instantly shrank. She felt as though she'd stumbled into a lion's den and found herself face-to-face with the top cat—a savage, ill-tempered beast only too happy to shred some flesh from her bones. It wasn't a pleasant sensation.

"I'd never force Krista to leave," she insisted.

"But you'd make it so uncomfortable for her, she'd vacate of her own accord, right?" The contempt in his voice ripped at her self-control. "I'll bet it's the only home those two have ever known, isn't it?"

She didn't dare answer that one, not when her response would further incite him. "Krista doesn't want to live with me anymore," Nikki attempted to explain. "She wants to move in with a friend. I'm just trying to give her a gracious way out."

His eyes flashed with gold fire. "Oh, you're giving her a gracious way out, all right. Right out the door and onto the street."

"That's not true! The problem is, she won't leave because she doesn't want me to live alone. She's got this crazy idea that she owes me."

He folded his arms across his chest, drawing her attention to the imposing width of his shoulders. Where once she took comfort in his size, now it only served to intimidate. "And who gave her that idea? You?"

She wouldn't explain, and no amount of baiting on his part could force her to. "I don't care what you think," she said tightly. "I told you from the start that I needed a husband in order to resolve two problems."

"Eric and a personal matter. I remember." He speared her with a flinty look. "If I'd had any idea what that personal matter involved or how you planned to rectify it, I'd never have married you."

"And if I'd known you'd end up interfering in something that's none of your business, I wouldn't have married you, either," she flashed back, her temper smoldering. "Krista and Keli are the two most important people in my life —"

He gave a short, hard laugh. "You have a funny way of showing it."

"I let you handle Eric the way you thought best. But you didn't grant me the same courtesy, did you?"

"There's one important difference. I have Eric's best interests at heart."

"Just as I have Krista's! If you'd let me do the talking instead of butting in the way you did, it would have all worked out fine. But now you've ruined everything I worked so hard to arrange. I went to all the expense and awkwardness of marrying for nothing. *Nothing!* And it's all your fault."

He turned to stare at the elevator doors, the muscles of his jaw flexing. "Fine. It's all my fault. I can live with that."

Fury exploded to life with all the force of a wildfire. She fought to control the rage, to dampen it with cool, calming logic and reason. For the first time in recent memory, she couldn't.

"You had no right to interfere! None. I'd planned it so carefully, taken away every last excuse she could dream up. And thanks to you, my plans are ruined."

"You think I give a damn about that?" He turned sharply to face her. "Don't expect me to apologize for protecting Krista and Keli from your machinations. I'm glad I interfered."

"You don't understand."

She closed her eyes to hide her frustration. Because of Jonah, Krista wouldn't be moving out anytime soon. That was quite clear. Why fly the nest when it was so convenient and safe to remain? Why risk the pain and sorrow of a cruel world when she could use Nikki as the perfect excuse for staying put? Nikki needed her. She owed Nikki. Nikki had saved her life.

For some reason, tears filled her eyes. She never cried. Never. But right now, she could have wailed like an infant. "Now she'll never leave."

"Tough."

"Tough?" She stared at him in disbelief, her tears instantly drying. "What am I supposed to do when our marriage ends? I can't move back in with Krista. She'll never get on with her life if I do."

"All I've done is prevent you from throwing your sister and niece onto the street." The elevator doors slid open and once again he picked up the luggage, transferring it to the door of the penthouse. "Why not let your sister. continue to use the brownstone? Kids should have a house to call their own. When we divorce, you can find an apartment. Something immaculate where you won't have to worry about a kid cluttering up your space with her toys."

"You still don't understand," she repeated.

"You're right. I don't." He keyed open the door and swept her into his arms.

"What are you doing?" she demanded in alarm.

"Carrying my bride over the threshold. Welcome home, Mrs. Alexander." Then he dumped her onto her feet. "Don't get too comfortable."

Nikki blinked hard, fighting the unexpected return of tears. Turning away so he wouldn't see how much he'd upset her, she crossed the black marble entryway into the living room. A bank of windows lined one wall, offering a stunning panorama of Manhattan. It was clearly the focal point of the room. The furniture had been artfully arranged to take advantage of the view while still maintaining an air of intimacy. It was beautiful and expensive and chillingly cold.

"It must have been pricey maintaining this place while you were in England," she commented without turning around. Though she hadn't heard him enter the room, the shiver that slid down her spine gave her all the warning she needed.

"It's not mine. International Investment uses it for entertaining," he replied. "Or we'll allow the occasional client to stay here when he or she flies in from out of town."

"Won't Della and Loren object to our using it?"

"It's my decision. Why would they object?"

She turned around, regarding him curiously. "Isn't it Loren's call? Isn't he the CEO?"

"Don't you know?"

"Know what?"

"*I'm* CEO. It's a recent change, I'll admit. But still, a woman in your position should have made it her business to stay current."

"Eric never said and I assumed . . ." She shrugged. "My mistake."

"One of many, it would seem."

She refused to allow him to get under her skin again. "So what now?"

"Now we have lunch and then go to work. I expect Eric will have gone in bright and early this morning and leaked the news of our marriage. Once there, we introduce you as Mrs. Alexander. We accept the employees' congratulations, ignore their curious whispers and stares and get down to business."

"What about after we make the big announcement?" she asked. "I mean, what happens when you return to England?"

"I don't go back until sometime after the holidays. We'll have plenty of opportunity to discuss our options."

Her eyes narrowed. "Why so long? At the Montagues', you claimed you'd only be in the country for a few weeks."

"My plans changed when we married."

"Why?" she repeated baldly.

"It would look strange if your husband missed out on your big night." At her blank look, he prompted, "You know. The LJB Award."

With all the furor of the past several days, she'd forgotten about the award ceremony. But Jonah hadn't. And with sudden, devastating insight she realized her nomination must have played an important part in his choosing to marry her when Eric made his unexpected appearance. She couldn't explain why the knowledge bit so deeply.

"It wouldn't do for International Investment to lose an LJB nominee, would it?" she asked.

"I prefer not to."

"But if the nominee isn't a winner? What then?"

He tilted his head to one side. "I'm not certain," he admitted frankly. "I'd like to see the quality of your work before I reach that decision."

"You won't be disappointed," she informed him confidently. "I'm good at what I do."

He didn't appear convinced. "We'll see."

Krista hesitated in front of the reception desk of International Investment, not quite certain whether she had to check in before going in search of Nikki's office. But since the desk wasn't occupied, she couldn't ask for either directions or instructions.

She'd never bothered her sister at work before, but the past three weeks had been odd. Something wasn't right. The few times she'd been over to Nikki's new apartment, there hadn't been an opportunity for private conversation. So she'd decided to hold the discussion here. Noticing a small crowd clustered near a huge double door at the far end of the hallway, she decided to ask one of them for directions.

"Excuse me," she began, tapping the shoulder of a tall man with golden brown hair.

"Sshh." He waved her silent without turning around. "This is too good to miss."

"What—" And then she heard it, shouting coming from the far side of the door. Her eyes widened. Good gracious, that sounded like . . .

Nikki.

"What do you mean you've reassigned the Stamberg account?" her always-in-control, emotions-on-ice sister shrieked. "That's *my* account!"

"Well, now it's Meyerson's," a masculine voice roared back. Krista's mouth dropped open. If she wasn't mistaken, that sounded very much like the brother-in-law she'd gained three weeks ago. Her brow wrinkled in confusion. She hadn't realized he worked with Nikki.

"Meyerson? That idiot? He can't tell a put from a place, much less organize a portfolio as complicated as Stamberg's. I thought you wanted to improve business."

"I do."

"Well, guess what? This isn't going to do it."

"You seem to forget who's working for whom around here," Jonah snarled.

"I doubt that will be a problem much longer."

"And just what the hell does that mean?"

"It means that a few more asinine decisions like this one and you won't have to worry about impertinent employees, portfolios, accounts, or who's working for whom at International. Because we'll all be out of work!"

"You don't know what the hell you're talking about."

"I know one thing. Appointing Meyerson is the biggest mistake you'll ever make."

"Meyerson will double Stamberg's profits."

"Don't make me laugh. Meyerson couldn't double his own age."

"Shall we make a small wager about that? Or are you all talk and no action?"

"You want action? I'll give you action. Not only won't Meyerson double so much as one of Stamberg's stock picks, but he'll lose money on the few investments he does make."

"And if you're wrong?"

"Then I'll . . . I'll . . ."

"You'll what?"

"I'll dance naked on top of your desk!" Krista heard her sister declare rashly. "But if you lose, you do the honors on top of mine."

A collective gasp rippled through the crowd, and Krista leaned against the wall, torn between shock and amusement. This was a side of Nikki she'd never heard before.

"What I wouldn't give to see that," one of the men muttered.

"Shut up, Bently," the man she'd first approached growled.

"Oh, dear, oh, dear," a balding man groaned. "What will I do?"

"You'd better win that bet, Meyerson, or Alexander will have your head on a platter," Bently warned.

There'd been several minutes of silence behind the door. Then Krista heard the sound of a chair being shoved back. "You've got yourself a deal," Jonah said. "Prepare to lose, wife."

"Hah! There's not a chance in hell you'll win this bet."

Her voice grew louder as she approached the door and everyone hastily dispersed. The man who'd told Bently to shut up turned, catching her off guard.

"Don't just stand there," he said, grasping Krista's arm. He thrust open the nearest door and practically shoved her over the threshold. "Nikki won't appreciate our eavesdropping on her conversation."

He crowded in behind her and Krista found it difficult to breathe. He couldn't be aware he still held her, she decided, closing her eyes against the unexpected warmth pooling in her stomach. Or that he'd molded her so tightly against his lean form. Feelings she hadn't experienced in almost seven long, lonely years stirred, disconcerting her.

"Please —" she began.

"Wait a sec," he murmured close to her ear. Opening the door a crack, he glanced into the hallway. "Here she comes."

"Oh, really?" Nikki was saying, fury rippling through her voice. "Well, we'll just see about that."

A door opened and then slammed closed. She swept by, rich color blooming in her face. Never had she looked so alive, or so beautiful, Krista thought.

The door opened once again and she caught a glimpse of Jonah. "Yes, we will see. And in the meantime, prepare to start stripping!" The door slamming punctuated his final taunt.

Krista wriggled. "If you don't mind," she said.

"Oh, sorry." He stepped back, his hands falling slowly away. Gazing down at her, he frowned. "You look familiar. Do I know you?"

"I don't think so." She held out her hand and gave a rueful smile. "I'm Krista Barrett. Nikki's my sister."

He blinked in surprise, then began to chuckle. "No kidding. I'm Eric Sanders. Jonah's my brother."

Startled, she stared at him. This was the man who'd been infatuated with Nikki? The man who'd made her so uncomfortable she'd invented a husband? *And* he was the brother of Nikki's new husband?

Something strange was going on here. This had to be more than a coincidence. Which meant that Nikki's marriage might not be a simple love match as her dear sister had claimed. Krista eyed Eric speculatively. Maybe he knew what was up. And maybe, just maybe, he'd clue her in.

"Listen, I know this is a bit unexpected, but would you care to have lunch with me?" Eric offered.

"I don't know," she said. "I'd hoped to see Nikki."

He grinned, a charming, boyish sort of grin. "I don't think this is a very good time to talk to her, do you?"

"I guess not." She studied him, finding his gentle appeal impossible to resist. Besides, lunch might be the perfect opportunity to pump him for a little information. "Okay. Let's go."

"Great."

Warmth gathered in his hazel eyes along with something else. Masculine appreciation, she finally discerned with bemused astonishment. It had been so long since she'd experienced it, she almost hadn't recognized that sudden, explosive attraction. He reached for the doorknob, then hesitated.

"I guess I should tell you that I used to be very attracted to your sister. Nothing happened, you understand," he added hastily.

She hid her amusement. "I understand."

"Besides, I just realized something."

"What did you realize?"

"That while Nikki's perfect for Jonah, she'd have been a bit much for me. Besides, she's a career woman and I'd really like a more traditional wife." A slow smile lit his gaze and he opened the door. "So tell me, Krista. How do you like children?"

She laughed. "Funny you should ask."

Nikki entered her office and banged the door closed behind her. Never in the twenty-eight years of her existence had she been so furious. And it was all due to one infuriating, impossible man.

Her husband.

She paced the office, trying to calm herself, struggling to regain control. It didn't work. Nothing worked. Not staring out the window and counting cabs. Not reorganizing her well-organized files. Not even tidying her already-tidy desk. Only one thing would calm her.

Grimly, she crossed to her office closet and dragged out a large carton. After removing a huge tarp from the top of the box, she spread it on the floor. It was followed by a whole array of equipment, a special blend of soil, fertilizer, gloves, snippers, atomizer, an assortment of ceramic pots and an apron. She laid everything out with military precision, then crossed to the window to gather up her plants.

They'd been given to her by various staff members, all of whom had one thing in common. Black thumbs. She took pleasure in nursing the plants back to full health before returning them. As always when she worked with her plants, the fury of her emotions eased, dissipating until she was once again in control. She worked straight through lunch, happily repotting.

An hour later, she finished. Feeling much more relaxed, she rocked back on her heels and tossed her gloves onto the tarp. She nodded in satisfaction as she gathered up her supplies.

Two of her specimens could be returned by the end of the week, she decided. And undoubtedly, there'd be several others to replace the ones she gave back. She made a mental note to sweep the office for more casualties. With Christmas fast approaching, she didn't doubt she'd be kept quite busy.

Just as she finished cleaning up the clutter, the phone rang. "Nikki Ashton," she said without thinking, then made a face. "I mean, Alexander."

"Nikki, dear. It's Selma."

"Hello, Aunt Selma." She tucked a strand of hair behind her ear and smiled in genuine pleasure. "How are you?"

"Wonderful. Excited. In urgent need of advice."

Nikki brightened. "You know I'm happy to help."

"I know you are, dear. That's why we always call on you."

"So what's up?"

"Ernie and I have had the most delicious offer." Excitement bubbled in her voice. "Of course, we want to discuss it with you before we act."

Some of Nikki's pleasure faded. This didn't sound good. But then, Selma and Ernie's ideas seldom did. "Why don't you drop by the office tomorrow? Is noon convenient?"

"No, no. It has to be tonight. We're much too excited to wait any longer. Besides, time is of the essence. We'll come to your place."

Nikki straightened abruptly. "I don't think—"

"Krista says your new apartment is gorgeous and we'd love to meet that equally new husband of yours. Shame on you for eloping, by the way, and doing us out of the pleasure of a big wedding." There was a delicate pause and then Selma asked, "What time, dear?"

Nikki thought fast. "How about six?" she suggested, unable to dream up a reasonable excuse for changing the venue.

"Six it is. See you then."

Hanging up, Nikki leaned back in her chair. It would work out, she attempted to reassure herself. With any luck, Jonah would work as late tonight as he had every other evening this week and she could meet her relatives without his interference. At least he'd better not interfere. Not again. Not when Aunt Selma and Uncle Ernie required such delicate handling.

She closed her eyes, tension creeping back. Maybe she'd better sweep the office for more plants right now. Why repot tomorrow when she could repot today?

"All we need to do is put up fifty thousand and we'll have the exclusive franchise," Selma said, clasping her hands together enthusiastically.

"But it's a limited-time offer," Ernie added. "If we don't get the money together by the day after tomorrow, we're going to miss the boat."

"This is one boat it wouldn't be such a bad idea to miss," Nikki muttered beneath her breath.

"What's that, dear?" Selma asked anxiously.

"A note. I didn't want to miss making a note of the date. The day after tomorrow," she repeated, writing Wednesday in large block letters. "And what's the name of this man who wants you to invest?"

"Timothy T. Tucker. Such a delightful man, isn't he, Ernie?"

"Really knows his way around numbers. Had our heads spinning. Why the way he has it figured, we can triple our investment in under a year."

Nikki tossed down her pen. "Uncle Ernie, even I can't do that."

He patted her hand. "Yes, sweetheart. We know. But we won't hold that against you."

"You do your best, I'm sure," Selma maintained stoutly. "We're all very proud of you."

Nikki groaned. "How did you meet this man? What do you know about him?"

"He walked into our coffee shop right out of the blue."

"A red-letter day that was," Ernie pronounced, folding his hands over his ample middle. "Looked around and knew right off we ran a profitable business."

"I'll just bet."

Nikki scowled. He'd probably watched the flow of traffic, made a few quick calculations and decided the shop kicked off plenty of disposable income. Then he'd have asked a few questions of her naive aunt and uncle and *voilà*. The birth of a scam.

"Did you tell him about your mortgage?"

Sehna looked surprised. "But we don't have one, dear."

"I know that, Aunt Selma. Does this Mr. Tucker know? Did you tell him?"

"I think we may have touched on it," Selma confessed. "But it was all very innocent. He was interested in opening a storefront in our area and wondered what the rent might run."

"Of course we had to admit we didn't know," Uncle Ernie inserted. "Since we own the property outright, we aren't all that knowledgeable about what rents go for these days."

"Why, if he's selling these franchises, does he need to rent a storefront?" Nikki questioned in exasperation.

"To interest people in buying the Miracle Box, of course."

"But that doesn't make any sense." Unfortunately, her aunt and uncle put little credence in logic and reason, much less common sense. "If you have the franchise to sell this box, why would *he* open—"

Selma reached over and patted her hand. "Don't feel bad, darling. We were confused at first, too. Dear Mr. Tucker was so patient with us, though. Wasn't he, Ernie?"

"Answered every one of our questions. Explained about the patents and our territory and made all that technical jargon sound quite sensible." He grinned proudly. "Why, I can talk about router modules and cable companions with the best of them."

"So I see." Picking up her pen and pulling her steno pad closer, Nikki started jotting down notes. "Timothy T. Tucker. The Miracle Box. Fifty grand. Wednesday. I don't suppose you have his business card by any chance?"

"Sure." Ernie plucked it from his wallet and handed it over. "Must be doing all right for himself. Cards of that quality are expensive."

"I wonder where he gets all that wealth?" Nikki asked, not the least surprised when they didn't pick up on her sarcasm.

"From ideas like the Miracle Box, I imagine," Ernie said thoughtfully.

"And how are you going to sell these boxes and still run your coffee shop?"

"Gordie and Cal are helping."

Nikki closed her eyes and sighed. She should have known her cousins would be involved. If it was an idiotic scheme and sure to cost a lot of money with little to no return, they'd be the first in line. Her aunt and uncle would be second.

"So what do you think?" Ernie asked anxiously. "May we have the money?"

"Not a chance," Nikki answered without thinking.

"Oh, Nikki. Please. It's not so much to ask. We really need the money, dear." Selma fumbled in her purse for a hankie, applying it to teary eyes. "If you won't do it for us, think of your poor cousins. It's an opportunity that will never come along again."

Nikki groaned. "I couldn't be so lucky."

"We have a CD coming due next week," Ernie reminded her. "Can't we borrow against that?"

"I have an investment lined up for that money already."

"What about our savings account?" Selma asked. "Isn't there enough in there?"

Nikki shook her head. "I thought you wanted that money so you could open up Ernie's Beanery 2."

"We can wait. Why, with the money we'll make selling—"

"No."

"But *why*?" Selma dissolved into tears. "I thought it was our money."

"It is," Nikki admitted uncomfortably.

"Then why can't we spend it the way we want?"

"You can," a new voice interrupted. Jonah stepped into the living room. "Can't they, Nikki?"

Chapter Seven

"No, they can't," Nikki retorted. "Stay out of it, Jonah. You don't understand."

"That doesn't come as any surprise." He tossed his coat and suit jacket over the arm of the couch and deposited his suitcase on the floor beside it. "I seem to have a knack for misunderstanding."

A hint of angry color washed into her cheeks, and her eyes flashed with violet warning. Jonah smiled in satisfaction. He knew what that meant. If he goaded her just a little more, she'd lose her temper as thoroughly as she had earlier that morning. He'd enjoyed their clashes over the past few weeks. He particularly enjoyed shaking her composure, watching as the icy facade melted enough to reveal the vibrant flame within.

"If you don't mind, I'm having a private discussion here."

"But I do mind, sweetheart. You haven't introduced us." Jonah approached and held out his hand, wondering who these people were and why they'd turned their finances over to his wife. "I'm Jonah Alexander, Nikki's husband."

"Ernie and Selma Crandell." They shook hands. "You sure are a busy man. We've been trying to arrange a little get-together ever since Nikki told us you two got married, but you've always had a schedule conflict."

"Is that right? I wish I'd known." Jonah glanced at his wife and said with deceptive mildness, "Sweetheart, you should have nagged me more. If I'd realized that your—" He broke off pointedly.

"Aunt and uncle," she whispered.

A deadly silence descended for an endless moment before Jonah picked up the slack. "If I'd realized your aunt and uncle had been serious about throwing us a party, I would have found the time."

"Well, since we missed out having you for Thanksgiving, perhaps we can make a try for Christmas," Selma offered tentatively. "Or do you have another commitment? Nikki wasn't certain."

Jonah's mouth compressed. Selma clearly wasn't aware that he'd never even heard their names before, let alone received any of their invitations. But Ernie didn't appear quite so obtuse.

"Maybe we've caught you at a bad time," he muttered uncomfortably. "Don't mean to be pushy relatives."

"Not at all." Jonah shot a grim look toward his wife. She made a point of avoiding his gaze, but couldn't hide the guilty color staining her cheekbones. "I'll see if I can't arrange to be free. In fact, I'll make a special note of it on my calendar."

Ernie gave a more enthusiastic nod. "Great. Since we're all the family Nikki and Krista have, we try to make the most of the holidays. My wife and their mom were sisters, you know."

"Were?"

Ernie shot his niece a curious glance. "Did she forget to mention?"

"Apparently, there's quite a bit she forgot to mention," Jonah observed drily.

"Oh. Well, Nikki's mom and dad were killed eight years ago in a boating accident," Ernie explained. "She was just a teenager, poor mite."

"Hardly a teenager or a mite," Nikki corrected crisply, jumping into the conversation. "I was twenty and a very independent college student."

"Eight years ago." Jonah glanced thoughtfully at his wife. She sat in her chair, every muscle tensed. Where only moments ago, her color had run high, she now appeared pale as a winter moon. The urge to protect her from a topic that caused such obvious pain battled with his intense curiosity. He couldn't resist probing just a little deeper. "That would have made Krista . . ."

"Sixteen," Selma supplied, shaking her head. "That year and a half after their death was such a tragic time. Perhaps if Edward and Angeline had lived, things might have been different for the girls. But with Krista marrying so young and then Nikki involved in that terrible incident—"

"I think that's enough," Nikki interrupted tautly. "I'm sure Jonah doesn't want to hear all the boring details. Besides, it's ancient history."

He pinned her with a narrow gaze. It would seem they'd pushed an emotional hot button. Interesting. "I didn't mean to upset you. We can save this particular conversation for a more convenient time."

Alarm lit her expressive eyes. "There's no need."

If she'd hoped to discourage him, she'd failed. Miserably. Instead, she'd whetted his appetite to learn more. He suspected that whatever had happened following her parents' death would shed considerable light on several aspects of Nikki's personality. Such as the tight control she kept on her emotions. It might also explain her odd attitude toward family.

"She's right," Jonah conceded with an easy smile. "This isn't the appropriate time to talk about the past. I see I've interrupted an important financial discussion." He settled onto the couch and gestured for them to continue. "Please. Don't let me interrupt."

"I believe we've concluded this discussion," Nikki announced, thrusting back her chair.

"But what about the money?" Selma turned to appeal to Jonah. "The deadline's Wednesday."

"I'm certain Nikki won't want to disappoint you," Jonah assured her. "Will you, darling?"

Nikki gathered up her notes, her color riding high once again. "I'll look into it further," she offered through gritted teeth.

Reluctantly, her aunt and uncle stood. "Well, if that's the best you can do." Selma murmured. She glanced at Jonah in desperate appeal. "It's just a small thing we're asking."

Jonah gained his feet and gathered up the coats and scarves tossed over the back of a nearby chair. "I'll see what I can do," he whispered as he helped Selma on with hers.

"Such a good boy," she said, giving him a delighted smile. "So reasonable. And by the way, welcome to the family."

"Why, thank you." He shook hands once again with Ernie. "I'm sure Nikki will be in touch soon."

"Excellent, excellent," Ernie replied in a hearty voice as he pulled on his gloves. "Took one look and knew you were the man to make her see reason."

"Uncle Ernie," Nikki began.

"Now, now." He enveloped her in a fierce bear hug. "Don't be too hard on yourself, Nikki. You do your best. But it's clear this husband of yours knows a thing or two about finances. Can't hurt to have him take a look at Tucker's prospectus."

With a final goodbye, the two left. Jonah glanced at Nikki. She stood with her back to him, her vibrant hair restrained by a wide gold clip. She'd changed out of her office clothes. Gone was the stark gray suit from that morning and in its place she'd donned ivory slacks and an oversize cable sweater in a jewel-bright emerald. He could feel the tension emanating from her and stood unmoving, anticipating the explosion. He didn't have long to wait.

"How dare you?" she demanded as she swung around. She stalked toward him, her eyes blazing with amethyst fire. "How dare you interfere in a family matter?"

"I *am* family." He smiled blandly. "Or have you forgotten?"

She halted a few feet away. "I wish I could forget," she informed him passionately, tossing her notepad and pen onto the glass-topped coffee table. "But you make that impossible."

"Good. Impossible works for me."

He watched her frustration gather, watched the struggle to control her temper. And watched her fail. "Why are you butting in where you don't belong?"

"In case you weren't aware of the fact, that marriage license you were so hot to acquire came with a few strings. I'm family now, whether you like it or not. Family is allowed to butt in."

He closed the distance between them, towering over her. He didn't care if she found his size intimidating. He hoped he intimidated the hell out of her. She smelled amazing and it took every ounce of restraint not to pull her into his arms and kiss her until all that marvelous passion found a new outlet. Only one thing stopped him.

He regarded her from beneath drawn brows, permitting a small measure of his own anger to show. "You allowed me to walk into that situation blind tonight. Do you have any idea how that felt? I didn't have a clue who those people were. Selma may not have realized, but Ernie sure as hell did. Nor have you bothered to inform me of their invitations, something else he picked up on."

She managed to meet his gaze this time, but a hint of her earlier chagrin still lingered. "I didn't think you'd be interested," she admitted.

His anger grew. "Don't lie to me, Nikki. I won't tolerate it. That's not the reason and you damned well know it. You wanted to keep me well away from your aunt and uncle."

"With good reason."

"Oh? And just what is that good reason?"

She folded her arms across her chest in a defensive gesture. "Our marriage isn't real. That's why."

He shrugged. "What difference does that make?"

She gave him an impatient look. "You know what difference. I don't want them to count on your being there when we both know it won't last. In case you didn't notice, they're a sweet couple whose affections are easily engaged."

"Mmm. I did notice," he admitted, remembering Selma's instant acceptance of him.

"Exactly. They're very trusting." She scowled at him. "Too much so."

"And I'm someone they shouldn't trust?"

To his amusement, she didn't give him a straightforward answer. "Let's just say the jury's still out," she muttered. "But that doesn't change the fact that you're returning to London soon. By the time you do, they'll have become overly fond of you. They'll also assume you've deserted me and be hurt and upset on my behalf."

"And what about you?" he questioned curiously. "Will you be hurt and upset, too?"

"Not a bit," she stated with an interesting lack of conviction. "It'll be a relief to have you gone so I can get my life back to normal."

"Does that mean you'll move in with Krista and Keli again?"

"Absolutely not. I still have hopes of salvaging that situation, despite your interference. Which is another reason I neglected to introduce you to my relatives. You stuck your nose in where it didn't belong with Krista. I wasn't about to have you do the same with Uncle Ernie and Aunt Selma."

"I told you why I interfered in your business with Krista."

"You didn't have all the facts then, just as you don't tonight. You had no right to tell Ernie and Selma I'd allow them to invest that money until you had all the information at your disposal."

"I agree."

"I —" She blinked in surprise. "What did you say?"

"You heard me. I spoke without thinking."

"Since you're being so agreeable, would you mind explaining why you jumped in?"

"Because I thought you were being unreasonable."

"Unreasonable? A fat lot you know!"

He yanked irritably at his tie as he searched for an approach that wouldn't rouse her anger again. He shook his head at the irony. For such a cool, logical female, she sure had a hot temper.

"They're your relatives, Nikki, not your clients. Maybe if you stopped treating them as if it was a business transaction and started treating them like family—"

"I'm responsible for their financial stability."

"Maybe you shouldn't be."

"You don't understand."

"You know, I'm getting really tired of hearing that phrase." He shot her a penetrating look. "How can I understand when you won't explain? And don't tell me it isn't any of my business, because as of now I'm making it my business."

She lifted her chin. "And if I refuse to tell you anything?"

"I suspect your relatives will be more forthcoming. Of course, it might be somewhat embarrassing for you when I get my answers from them. Answers my wife should have provided."

Agitation brought renewed color to her cheeks. "That's blackmail."

He tilted his head to one side in mock contemplation. "I believe you're right. It is."

"Why are you doing this?" she demanded in frustration. "What do you care? They're not your relatives."

He shrugged. "Damned if I know. I guess because I take my family obligations seriously." He waved aside her response before she could make it. "Enough, Nikki. Are you going to answer my questions or do I have a man-to-man conversation with Ernie?"

Stubborn to the end, she stewed about it for a full two minutes. Since he considered the outcome inevitable, he gave her all the time she needed. He crossed to the liquor cabinet and removed a bottle of cabernet sauvignon. By the time he'd poured them each a glass, she'd reached her decision. He waited while she gathered her composure, understanding her dilemma better than she realized. To discuss family, she had to give up a certain amount of control and trust him. And for some reason, perhaps that unspoken incident from her past, control was everything to her. Clearly, trust was something to be avoided at all costs.

"Well?" he asked, handing her the wine.

She took a disrespectful gulp and fixed him with a defiant glare. "What do you want to know?"

"How old was Krista when she married?"

Nikki dropped onto the couch. "Seventeen," she said bleakly.

He had suspected as much, but it still came as a shock. "She was pregnant with Keli?"

"Yes, though it wasn't a shotgun marriage, if that's what you're asking. She and Benjie were very much in love. Krista gave birth two days before her eighteenth birthday."

"That makes Keli, what? Six?" At Nikki's nod of confirmation, he asked, "And what happened to Benjie?"

"He died in a car accident four months after the wedding."

Jonah sucked in his breath. "Jeez, Nikki. I'm sorry."

"We all were," she said, the words a clear understatement. "It wasn't a good time."

"I'll bet. What did Krista do?"

Nikki shrugged, staring into the ruby depths of her wine. "Benjie's family wasn't in a financial position to help, whereas our parents had left us some insurance money. So, Krista moved in with me."

"And has lived with you ever since," he concluded. "You've supported them?"

"Krista has a part-time job. But I've encouraged her to stay at home with Keli. I earn enough to take care of them."

"What happened to change all that? Have you gotten tired of living in such tight quarters? Or is having a six-year-old around cramping your lifestyle?"

She set the glass on the coffee table with great care before turning on him with all the ferocity of a tigress defending her young. "Don't you ever say that again," she said harshly. "*Ever.* I love Krista and have adored Keli from the moment of her birth. If I had my preference, they'd never leave."

"Then why the hell are you throwing them out?"

Emotions chased across her expressive face—pain, sorrow, resignation. "I finally realized that Krista was using me to hide from life. She never dates, rarely goes out with friends. Her entire life revolves around Keli, and to a lesser extent, me. I overheard a phone conversation shortly before the Cinderella

Ball. She was explaining to a friend how much she owed me, how she could never leave me because I needed her. And I realized that all these years . . ." Nikki snatched up her glass and drained the contents.

Without a word, Jonah refilled it. "All these years you've protected her from life instead of forcing her to face up to it."

"Yes."

"So you've decided to set her free. In fact, you're tossing her out of the nest whether she wants to go or not."

She nodded, tears glittering on the ends of her lashes. "I've come home every day for the past six years to a hug from Keli, and now— And now— " Her voice broke and she buried her face in her hands.

He was beside her in an instant, gathering her in his arms. "Don't," he murmured. "I'm sorry. You're right. I did misunderstand."

"Keli should have a father. And Krista should have a husband." She visibly fought for control, but a stray tear escaped unchecked. "But as long as I'm in the picture, that won't happen."

"What about you?" he asked quietly, rubbing her back in slow, gentle circles. "You say that Krista's subconsciously used you as a shield, protecting herself from further pain. But haven't you been doing the same?"

She stilled. "What are you talking about?"

"I don't think Krista was the only one hurt seven years ago. Selma implied—"

"My aunt talks too much."

"There was a man, though. Wasn't there?"

"You don't under—"

He stopped the words with his mouth, tired of hearing them. She tasted of wine, the flavor far sweeter than anything he'd ever poured from a bottle. It would be all too easy to lose himself in the pleasure of the moment. But that had to wait. Right now he needed answers.

"Don't lie to me again. Not now," he muttered against her lips. "Was there a man? Yes or no."

"Yes."

He cupped her chin, forcing her to meet his gaze. Her mouth was pink and damp from his kiss and distracting as hell. "What happened? Did he desert you because of Krista?"

Her breath escaped in a harsh laugh. "You're way off."

"But you loved him and he left you."

"Oh, yes. He left."

"And for the past six or seven years you've remained as cloistered as Krista."

"I've been pursuing my career," she retorted, stung. "Not living in a convent."

He slid his hand down the length of her neck to the fragile bones beneath the neckline of her sweater. "Really? And how many men have there been since the one who deserted you?" She attempted to pull free, but he tightened his hold, refusing to release her. "How many, Nikki? One? Two? Or none?"

"None," she whispered, the fight draining from her.

"Because they all threatened to take something from you," he persisted. "They wanted pieces of you that you weren't willing to give."

"Isn't that what love is all about?" she asked cynically. "Giving up control to another person?"

"Is that how it is with Krista and Keli?"

"That's different," she denied instantly. "They're family."

"How is it different? You give pieces of yourself to them," he pointed out.

The tears had returned and she stared at him, her eyes glimmering with jewel-like brilliance. "But they don't use up those pieces," she whispered. "They cherish them, make them more complete rather than less. They don't just take. They also give."

He'd never heard a more poignant description, a description that mated the ultimate joy love could bring with the devastating possibility of betrayal. Unable to resist any longer, he drew her close. Employing infinite tenderness, he captured her tremulous mouth with his, probing the moist warmth within.

The man who'd betrayed her had been a fool, Jonah decided in that instant. To have all this and use it so cavalierly was a crime. He might not have loved her, but he didn't have to destroy her in the process.

Jonah removed the clip confining her hair and lowered her to the couch cushions. It had been weeks since he'd had the opportunity to run his hands through the silken strands. He'd found that be wanted to do it at the oddest times, like when they'd sat across each other at the dinner table. Or when he'd come into her office unexpectedly and caught her twirling a lock of hair around her finger. Even in the midst of one of their arguments, the temptation struck. But not once had he given in.

Until now.

Her hair spilled through his hands and across the white couch cushions in a cascade of autumn's most glorious shade, fire on ice. She was the most beautiful woman he'd ever seen. And as he held her in his arms, she responded so passionately to his kisses that her beauty took on a sensual wildness he found fiercely arousing.

"Jonah," she whispered, tugging at the buttons of his shirt. "Let me touch you."

He helped, yanking off his tie and ripping his shirt free of his trousers. Then he turned his attention to her, sliding his hands beneath the bottom of her sweater and along an endless expanse of baby-soft skin. Nothing hindered his progress, not even the expected scrap of lace and silk. With a husky moan, he cupped her breasts, his thumbs scraping across the sensitive crowns. The breath burst from her in frantic gasps and he drank in every minute sound.

But it wasn't enough. He wanted more of her.

Reluctantly releasing her mouth, he swept the bulky sweater over her head and tossed it aside. She froze beneath him, the chilly air momentarily bringing her to full awareness. He hesitated, reluctant to push her any further, ready to back off if she took fright. But far from panicking, she shivered at his touch, her spine arching reflexively.

"They're even softer than I remember," he commented, filling his hands with the abundance of wealth.

To his amusement, his twenty-eight-year-old wife blushed. "I thought your memories of that night were hazy."

"Not all of them. Of course, I was too tired to take advantage of my position then." He met her eyes with a determination she couldn't mistake. "But I'm not tonight."

Her eyes took on the most intense violet glow he'd ever seen and his gut clenched in reaction. He wanted her. Desperately. With a fierceness he hadn't felt with any other woman. The knowledge came as a distinct shock. He'd been aware of a nagging desire for weeks now. But he'd assumed it was a simple physical urge that would be satisfied with the inevitable bedding. After all, she was beautiful enough to attract any man worthy of the name. But this went deeper.

Curiosity ate at him, a need to see if she was as soft as he remembered, if her skin was as white, her legs as long and shapely. Like having a craving that demanded satisfaction, he found he had to explore the womanly secrets hidden beneath her clothing or go quietly insane.

He didn't just want to possess her body.

He wanted to lose himself in all of her—mind, body and spirit.

As a result, he'd pressed her hard tonight, forcing the issues she'd been using as a shield. Well, he'd stripped her of most of that armor and been pleasantly surprised by what she'd been hiding. Far from the cold, calculating creature he'd been afraid he'd find, he'd discovered a warm, generous woman, willing to sacrifice her own happiness for a member of her family. He'd seen her vulnerability. But he'd also seen her love and protectiveness. And it drew him more powerfully than he thought possible.

She felt incredibly delicate beneath him, fragile and breakable. He took his time, warming her cool skin with his hands and mouth, lighting a fire that would burn bright enough to engulf them both. When she rewarded his patience with the sweetest of responses, he peeled away her slacks, uncovering legs that seemed to go on forever.

He palmed the spot where delicate ankles met trim calves, and her eyes drifted closed, a soft sigh melting off her lips. His fingers danced higher, over her knee to the enticing curve of her thigh, pausing at the wisp of white that concealed russet-masked secrets. His breath grew harsh with need.

His control wouldn't last much longer, he realized, sparing her a brief glance. What he saw stopped him cold. Her violet-blue gaze met his with such a mix of need and anxiety, it threatened to unman him. And suddenly he knew he'd be making a terrible mistake if he didn't stop. Reluctantly, his hand slid away.

"I won't take advantage of you like this. I'm not that other man."

"I know you're not," she whispered.

"I don't want any regrets come morning and if I'm not mistaken you already look like a woman with regrets."

She moistened her lips with the tip of her tongue. "No, really. It's all right."

But the anxiety remained and he saw it. "Well, it's not all right with me."

He couldn't reach her sweater, so snagged his shirt instead, wrapping it around her. It didn't cover her completely, but it helped cool the fire to a manageable level. He pulled the collar tight beneath her chin and leveled her with a direct look.

"In case you weren't aware of it, my sweet wife, making love—not having sex, but making love—means giving up a certain amount of control. But it's control freely given by both parties."

"I know that," she began.

"No. I don't think you do. I suspect you were forced to *give* everything while your partner *took* everything. I gather some men prefer it that way. I'm not one of them. I want the woman I'm with to be a full participant. And I won't take anything I'm not also willing to give. Until you realize that and trust me, I'll pass, thanks."

"Trust you," she repeated. Her bleak laugh was heartbreaking. "You don't ask for much, do you?"

He didn't answer, just kept looking at her with those calm, hazel eyes. She struggled upright, curling her legs beneath her. It was so tempting to tell him everything—about the Miracle Box, about her parents' deaths and the aftermath. It was especially tempting to tell him about that other humiliating incident.

But he was a temporary addition to her life and she an "accidental" wife, a choice he'd reluctantly made and within hours regretted. She couldn't depend on him. She couldn't depend on anyone but herself. She'd learned that lesson the hard way and spent the past seven years making certain she didn't repeat it. She'd also spent those years compensating for that one single blunder.

Still, for the first time, she wanted someone. Needed someone. The urge to trust trembled within, like a bird desperately seeking to escape confinement. "Jonah—"

"Don't force it, sweetheart," he said gently. "I'm not going anywhere."

"Not yet," she responded bitterly.

"Not yet," he confirmed. "Go to bed. We'll talk more in the morning."

"Maybe by then I'll have come to my senses," she muttered.

He merely grinned. "I couldn't be that lucky."

Chapter Eight

Nikki awoke the next morning to discover Jonah waiting for her at the breakfast table. Over the past few weeks they'd been careful to time their comings and goings to avoid each other. Apparently, last night had changed all that.

He filled two earthenware mugs with coffee, added sugar to each and set them side by side in front of her. To her relief, he didn't say a word until she'd consumed the first cup. Then he poured some for himself, replaced her empty mug with a platter of toasted English muffins and joined her at the table.

"Don't think me ungrateful, but what brought on this sudden burst of domesticity?" she questioned cautiously, helping herself to a muffin. "Or don't I want to know?"

"You probably don't want to know."

"But you're going to tell me anyway, right?"

"Yes." He leaned back in the chair and folded his arms across his chest. The movement pulled his crisp white shirt taut across the generous spread of his shoulders. She had vivid memories of those shoulders in all their naked glory. Too vivid. "We neglected to discuss Ernie and Selma's dilemma last night," he reminded her.

"Mmm. We did get distracted, didn't we?" she murmured, burying her nose in her coffee mug so she wouldn't get distracted again this morning.

"Pleasantly so, I hope."

She didn't dare answer that one, not when she caught a glimpse of green flame smoldering deep within his gaze. "What did you want to know?" she asked, hoping to move the conversation into safer channels. It would seem talking about family now qualified as a safe topic. The irony of that fact didn't escape her.

A brief smile of awareness touched his mouth. "I want to know everything, of course. We can start, however, with your role as financial advisor. How did that come about?"

"I inherited it," she explained with a shrug. "My father was the family accountant. When he died, everyone turned to me because I was majoring in finance at the time."

He took a swallow of coffee and studied her with a thoughtful air. "You were a bit young to take on such a burden, don't you think?"

Privately, she was in complete agreement. Aloud she said, "They didn't trust anyone else."

"Ah. That old issue of trust rears its ugly head."

"Can we move this along?" she asked, reaching for another muffin to hide behind.

She wanted to get off the subject of the past. Badly. And since the future was just as uncomfortable a topic, that left the present. To her secret disgust, the idea of telling him about the Miracle Box actually held some appeal. Quite a change from how she'd felt before last night. If she wasn't careful, she really would start to trust him.

"I still have one or two questions about the past," he said, a hint of steel appearing beneath the congenial surface. "Your aunt made a reference to an incident that happened six or seven years ago and involved you. What was that about?"

"It wouldn't interest you," she replied with deceptive calm. "What's the problem, Jonah?" she couldn't resist taunting. "I thought you'd want all the gory details of how I'm being a coldhearted Scrooge and refusing to give my relatives their money. Instead, you're obsessing about a chapter of my life that's over and forgotten ages ago."

He didn't take the bait as she'd hoped. "Over, perhaps. But not forgotten." He allowed an uncomfortable silence to descend before adding, "You're not going to be able to duck a discussion of the past forever. You realize that, don't you?"

"I don't realize that at all." She fixed him with a determined look. "What I am willing to do is explain my current actions since they're of such importance to you. But my past and my future can't be of any interest."

He simply smiled. "You'd be amazed at what interests me."

Flustered, she made a production of dumping another spoonful of sugar into her coffee. "There's no point in getting too involved with each other's lives. Ours is a temporary arrangement, remember?"

"All too well." He leaned forward and caught her hand before she could spoon any more sugar into her mug. "I'll make you a deal. You stay out of the sugar bowl and I'll stay out of your past."

"Deal," she agreed instantly.

Amusement gleamed in his eyes. "At least I'll stay out for now. In the meantime, tell me about this investment."

"Right. The investment." Wriggling her fingers free of his hold, she stood and crossed to the sink, adding more coffee to her cup to dilute the abundance of sugar. "My dear aunt and uncle have been offered the unbelievable chance to own the exclusive local franchise on something called a Miracle Box."

"Never heard of it."

"Really?" she drawled in exaggerated surprise. "But it's a brilliant invention. Absolutely everyone is going to want one."

"What does this Miracle Box do?" he asked warily.

"Let's see if I can remember it all." Turning to face him, she leaned against the counter and took a quick sip of coffee. She fought to hide her grimace of distaste. It needed more sugar again, but she'd cut off her hand before reaching for that bowl. "It does everything from controlling all electronics, to taking care of all your banking needs. It makes phone calls, runs appliances, orders groceries, locks and unlocks doors, and monitors the inside and outside of your home."

"And I'll bet it washes dishes and gives change for a dollar, too," Jonah said drily.

"Not yet. But only because the inventor hasn't thought of it." She frowned. "The problem is that this Miracle Box sounds just close enough to what's already on the market or soon to be available that to people like Ernie or Selma it appears quite believable."

"Interesting scam."

She gave a short laugh. "Oh, but I haven't told you the best part yet."

"Well? Don't keep me in suspense. What's the best part?"

"My aunt and uncle can have this exclusive franchise for the rock-bottom price of fifty grand."

She'd stunned him with that one. "You're kidding."

"I'm dead serious. Not only has he conned them into believing this box will make them a fortune, but he's buffaloed my cousins, as well. Which means that everyone will be so busy selling the Miracle Box, they'll neglect Ernie's Beanery."

Jonah shook his head in disgust. "By the time they realize it's all a scam, business will have bottomed out."

"And my family will be under investigation for fraud. If neglect doesn't succeed in destroying their café, lawyers' fees certainly will. But the bottom line will be the same. They will have happily paid fifty thousand dollars to put Ernie's Beanery out of business and themselves into bankruptcy."

"I'm sorry, Nikki. I should have—"

She cocked an eyebrow. "Trusted me?"

"Something like that," he conceded.

"That's all right. I have a bit of trouble in that department, too." She dumped the remains of her coffee in the sink and rinsed the mug. "Well, I'll tell you how you can make it up to me."

"You want me to tell them they can't have the money," he said in a resigned voice.

She hid a smile. "Why, thank you. I accept. Shall we go into work now or shall I introduce you to the Beanery?"

"You say that as if I have a choice."

"The Beanery it is." She didn't bother to hide her grin. "Tell you what. I'll let *you* do the talking this time."

Jan opened the office door and poked her head in. "Sorry to disturb you, Nikki."

Nikki shoved aside the papers she'd been working on and glanced at her secretary. "What's up?"

"There's a man on line two who insists on speaking to you. He won't leave his name or number and this is the third time he's called. Do you want to talk to him or should I try to find out who it is again?"

Nikki shook her head. "No, don't bother. I'll take it, thanks." She reached for the phone and punched the appropriate button. "Nikki Alexander," she stated automatically. She'd certainly grown accustomed to using her married name, she realized with a bittersweet smile. She'd better hope she found it just as easy to get *un*used to.

"Ah, Mrs. Alexander. At last. You're a very difficult woman to get hold of."

"Who is this, please?"

"Timothy T. Tucker. I'm sure you've heard of me."

Nikki straightened in her chair. "I don't believe it. Mr. Miracle Box himself."

"The one and only. I spoke to your aunt and uncle this morning and there seems to be a small problem."

"Oh?" she drawled. "And what might that be?"

"Ernie's having trouble getting his hands on the money to invest in my proposition."

"And he gave you my number?"

There was a small pause. "Several of them," he said deliberately.

Her eyes narrowed. What did that mean? Had Uncle Ernie been foolish enough to supply this man with her number at Jonah's apartment? She stirred uneasily. And what about the brownstone? The idea of Tucker having Krista's number was very unsettling.

"What do you want?" she demanded.

"I want the money Ernie and Selma promised me. Fifty thousand to be exact."

"I'm sorry, Mr. Tucker. Perhaps my aunt and uncle neglected to mention it. They've chosen not to invest in your scam—" she deliberately paused before correcting herself "—I mean, in your invention."

"I don't think you understand—"

"No, it's you who doesn't understand," she informed him crisply. "My aunt and uncle may be gullible, but I'm not. I've examined your prospectus and plan to hand it over to the appropriate authorities."

"What the hell are you talking about?"

She swiveled in her chair to face the office window. "I'm talking about fraud. The technology you claim to have doesn't exist."

"My box—"

"Your box is as phony as you are. Goodbye, Mr. Tucker."

"I wouldn't hang up if I were you! You better give your uncle that money, or you'll regret it."

"I don't think so."

"Oh, no? Your aunt and uncle aren't just gullible. They're also very talkative. And I'm a great listener. In all my conversations with them, they were quite full of their brilliant niece." His deliberate pause was an exact copy of her own. "Brilliant now, that is."

She slowly straightened. "Get to the point, Tucker."

"You weren't quite so brilliant seven years ago, were you? I think the LJB committee would be very interested in the details of that little escapade, don't you?"

Her hand tightened on the receiver. "Are you threatening me?"

"Oh, no. I'm making you a one hundred percent guarantee. You ruin my deal with your aunt and uncle, and I expose that nasty little skeleton in your closet. Look at it as an investment in your own personal Miracle Box. Fifty grand in exchange for a box that does absolutely nothing. You have my personal guarantee that it won't make so much as a peep." He laughed raucously at his own joke. "So, is it a deal?"

Nikki closed her eyes. All she'd worked for over the past seven years, all she'd done to try to make up for that one horrible disaster would be for nothing. She knew the interpretation people would put on that incident. Not only would the award committee take away her nomination, she'd undoubtedly lose her job, as well. But to pay this slime fifty thousand in the hopes that he wouldn't say anything?

"Not a chance," she whispered. "I don't pay blackmail. Do your worst, sucker."

"I plan to," he snarled and slammed down the phone.

Nikki hung up, staring blindly out the window. So what did she do now? Without conscious thought, she crossed to the office closet and pulled out her box of gardening supplies. For the next hour, she worked and weighed her options.

Briefly, she considered going to Jonah for help. It was possible he'd understand. After all, he'd understood about Krista. He'd also understood about her aunt and uncle. He'd even gone to them and explained that Tucker was a con man, all the while handling the situation with a diplomacy she couldn't have emulated on her best day.

Then he'd taken his assistance one step further. He'd supported her advice that they use their savings to open a second Ernie's Beanery and employ her cousins to run it. By the time he'd walked out of the café, they'd fallen in love with him.

Just as she had.

The breath stopped in her throat and she closed her eyes, fighting the sudden and inescapable knowledge. No. She couldn't be that irresponsible. She couldn't truly love him. Love was for fools. Love forced a person to give up control. Love didn't work for her. Hadn't she resigned herself to that fact?

Even so, she'd never lied to herself before and didn't intend to start now. Slowly, carefully, she searched her heart. And there she saw the truth.

She didn't know when or how it had happened. Perhaps it had come on her bit by bit without her even being aware. Still, that didn't change the fundamental truth. She did love him, with a bone-deep intensity. Where once she thought her heart and soul irreparably damaged, now she saw they'd been healed. And that healing was due to one man.

Jonah.

But to have fallen in love. She shook her head. How foolish of her. Because if she loved him, that meant she trusted him. And if she trusted him, she'd have to tell him about . . .

Tucker.

She shuddered. She couldn't dump this on Jonah, couldn't watch the green fire in his gaze turn to gold ice. Perhaps if he loved her in return, she'd take the risk of telling him about the past. But the painful fact of the matter was he didn't love her. Oh, he wanted her. And he'd make sure she found their time together special, no matter how brief. But in the end, he'd leave and she'd be alone once again.

Which still left the main question unanswered.

What did she do now?

Nothing, she decided at last. She couldn't be certain Tucker would make good on his threat. By doing so, he risked exposing himself. And slime like that preferred operating in the safety of the shadows. Too much light brought too much attention.

A peremptory knock sounded at her office door. "Nikki? I wanted to talk to you about—" Jonah stepped across the threshold and stopped dead, staring at her in astonishment. "What the hell are you doing?"

"Potting plants," she replied with a self-conscious shrug. "Or rather, repotting. I do it whenever I need to think."

His narrowed gaze swung to the empty windowsill and back again. "So, you weren't killing them. You were saving them."

She glared at him indignantly and started to put her hands on her hips. Just in time, she remembered she still wore her gardening gloves. "You thought I was killing plants?" she demanded, stripping off the gloves and tossing them to the protective tarp. "On purpose?"

"You'll have to forgive my ignorance," he said gently. "At the time I came to that conclusion, I didn't know what a maternal soul you had."

His assessment gave her an odd feeling. She'd never considered herself the least maternal. She was a career woman first and foremost. Any fleeting thoughts she might have indulged regarding children had been just that. Fleeting. Besides, she had Keli. She bit her lip. *Had* being the operative word. Soon she wouldn't even have that, not if her plan succeeded.

"What are you thinking?"

She avoided his gaze. "Nothing important." Removing her apron, she began loading her supplies into the box.

"You were thinking about Keli, weren't you?"

His perception dismayed her. "Yes," she admitted, aware that denials were pointless.

"Haven't you ever considered marrying?" He edged his hip onto the corner of her desk, his trousers pulled taut across his thighs. "For real, I mean? Having children of your own?"

"Once."

"Ah. Seven years ago again. We really must clear the air about that."

"Did I mention? I'm beginning to like coffee unsweetened." She shoved the box in the direction of the closet, hoping that would close the subject. "I assume you came in here for some reason other than to annoy me."

"Not really." His large hands closed around her waist and he lifted her aside. "Allow me." With an ease she could only envy, he hoisted the box as though it were weightless and deposited it in the closet.

"Thanks," she murmured.

"No problem." Turning, he scrutinized her with unnerving intensity. Almost hesitantly, he reached out and swept a stray lock of hair from her temple. Then with a muffled exclamation, he thrust his hands deep into her topknot. Her hair came loose, spilling in heavy waves about her face. "Temptress," he muttered, drawing her close.

His name escaped in a sigh. "Jonah."

His mouth captured hers and whatever else she'd been about to say. And then his kiss stopped all thought. It had become easier and easier to give in to him, especially when his demands so closely matched her own desires. She wrapped her arms around him, not the least surprised when he crushed her along his hard length, tugging her between his legs and against the very heart of him.

"Am I interrupting something?" an amused voice asked from the doorway. They both spun around. Eric stood there, leaning against the jamb. "You took so long getting that update on the Dearfield account," he addressed Jonah, "that I decided to come looking for you."

Jonah swore beneath his breath. "Right. The Dearfield account."

Hot color swept across Nikki's cheekbones. "I have the update with my files. Let me get it for you."

"I guess the honeymoon's not over yet, huh?" Eric asked innocently.

Nikki stared at him in horror, unable to say a word.

"What the hell does that mean?" Jonah growled, shooting her an uneasy glance. "We're not on our honeymoon. We haven't been for over a year now."

Eric shrugged. "That's not what it looks like to me."

"Well, you're wrong," Nikki managed to say.

"Of course I am." He stepped into the room, grinning. "Good thing I'm not a client, though. Not very professional, you know, making love on the office floor. Or were you planning on using the desk?"

"Go to hell, little brother," Jonah snapped. "The day I need a lecture from you about professionalism—"

Eric held up his hands. "Okay, okay. Though at least allow me to suggest you lock the door next time."

Jonah's hands balled into fists. "That's enough."

"Please, the two of you stop it!" To Nikki's horror, tears pricked her eyes. Stress. It had to be stress. Between her family problems, her marriage, and Tucker, it was a wonder she hadn't gone completely insane. "Here's the update," she said, tossing the file onto her desk. "Now, if you'll excuse me?" She didn't give either man a chance to reply, but swept from the room before she disgraced herself completely.

Jonah started to follow, but Eric caught his arm. "She won't thank you for going after her. Women prefer to conduct these crying jags in private."

His brows snapped together. "She was crying?"

Eric shrugged. "I thought I caught a glimpse of tears."

"Damn." A resigned expression crossed Jonah's face. "Mind telling me what makes you such an expert all of the sudden?"

"Just using a little common sense for a change. And as long as I'm so full of it, so to speak, I'll offer you some more advice. Give her time." He paused a beat. "The first year of marriage can be tough on a couple."

"And I told you this isn't—"

"It's as good as. You can't count your first year. You didn't spend any of it together," Eric argued reasonably.

"I . . . She . . "

"Yes?"

"Forget it!"

Eric slanted him a sly look. "Your wife sure was upset."

Jonah's gaze followed the direction Nikki had taken. "Bad, huh?"

"Has to be stress, right? I mean, it can't be from sexual frustration," Eric pronounced thoughtfully. He headed for the door and paused long enough to glance over his shoulder. "Not after being married for so long." The door quietly closing punctuated his question.

"It can't *be from sexual frustration, can it?"*

In the three days since Eric had made the comment, Jonah had been consumed by that thought to the exclusion of all else. *Sexual frustration.* He pushed his fork around his dinner plate, cursing beneath his breath. Oh, he was sexually frustrated all right. Very frustrated. Very, very frustrated and getting more frustrated by the minute. He scowled across the table at his wife. Not that she noticed.

Nikki stared at her plate, struggling to work up sufficient enthusiasm to eat. For the past three days, she'd been consumed with thoughts of her husband, and of love and trust and horrible men who made horrible threats. She'd also spent the time trying to decide how to handle the predicament she'd gotten herself into. In fact, it had become a daily battle over whether or not to trust the man she loved, despite the fact that he didn't love her. She peeked at Jonah from beneath her lashes. It was *so* frustrating! Not that he noticed.

Jonah threw down his fork. If his brother were here now, he'd strangle the smart-mouthed little—

"What did you say?" Nikki asked.

"I said, I've had enough."

"I'm sorry. Don't you like it?" She glanced down at her own plate of linguini. "Too rich, huh?"

"Actually, I've changed my mind. I haven't had enough." He shoved back his chair. "But I'm about to change that. Right now."

She tilted her head to one side, the candlelight catching in the ruby streaks of her hair. "You want seconds?"

"Yes. I definitely want seconds. Seconds, thirds, and if I can manage, fourths."

Her brows drew together in delicious bewilderment. "I don't understand."

"You will." He circled the table, and without further ado, lifted her into his arms. "Catching on yet?"

"Jonah! What are you doing?"

"What I *would* have done that first night if I hadn't been so tired. What I *would* have done three nights ago, if I hadn't been trying be so damned noble." The bedroom door blocked his path and he kicked it open. "And what I'm *going* to do right now because it's what we've both wanted from the instant we met and every day since."

He tossed her onto the mattress, waiting for the inevitable argument.

She didn't say a word.

He waited for anxiety to turn her eyes the color of amethysts. They slowly changed color, but it was passion that lurked in the violet depths, not fear.

He waited for her to flee. Instead, she remained in the middle of the bed.

Her very inaction sealed her fate. He approached, unable to take his eyes from her. Her skin gleamed like ivory, while her hair was a vivid splash of glorious, life-affirming color against the black down comforter. His gaze never left her as he ripped off his shirt. His shoes came next, then his belt. Finally, he reached for the zip on his pants. Her eyes widened and the tip of her tongue appeared, skating across her bottom lip.

He wanted that lip, he decided. He wanted it for an appetizer. He wanted to nibble on it, to sink his teeth into its fullness before exploring within. And once he'd temporarily sated himself with her mouth, he wanted to taste his way downward, sampling every inch of her, course after delicious course. It would be the most magnificent feast he'd ever consumed. And for dessert, he'd return to the sweetness of her mouth.

"To hell with linguini," he muttered, settling onto the bed beside her. "Nothing can be more satisfying than this."

Nikki stared at him in utter astonishment. After three full days of endless confusion and doubt, it took a split second to realize the undeniable truth. Not only did she love Jonah, she trusted him. Totally. Implicitly. Without reservation. And with that knowledge came the most amazing sense of freedom. Joy welled within. She could tell him. She could tell him everything and he'd understand.

He gathered her close, resting half on top of her, his hands sinking into her hair. "Speak now, wife," he muttered, catching her lower lip between his teeth. "Or forever hold your peace."

"I'd rather hold you," she whispered.

Wrapping her arms around his neck, she returned the passion of his kiss. Tomorrow they would talk. But right now, there were more important matters to take care of. They had the give and take of their latest merger to work out.

Removing her clothing became a serious negotiation. The zipper of her skirt voiced a loud argument as he drew it downward. Each button of her blouse needed to be coaxed free of its hole. Her lacy garters had to be convinced to release their tight embrace on her silk stockings. And the hooks and eyes of her bra had to be rescued from their enforced closure. But she found that having a brilliant negotiator for a husband had certain advantages. With due patience and diligence, he overcame every dilemma.

And the end result was the most satisfying she'd ever known.

She lay within the safe circle of his arms, coming alive beneath his touch, on fire for him and for him alone. And she discovered the unassailable truth of his earlier observations. Making love *was* a partnership. For everything she gave him, she received tenfold in return. The more she opened to him, the more he opened to her.

To offer a delicate kiss had him returning it with a deeper one. Slipping her hands across the endless expanse of his chest led to his painting lazy circles around the rosy tips of her breasts. And when she shyly initiated a more intimate caress, he unlocked passionate secrets that had been trapped within her for years, giving her pleasure she'd never before experienced.

"Do you trust me?" he demanded at one point.

Tears welled into her eyes and she visibly fought to control them. "I—I haven't dared to," she admitted in a broken voice. Slowly, she looked at him. "Until now."

He cradled her close. "Are you sure? Very sure?"

"Yes," she whispered. "I'm positive."

And with her words still lingering between them, he mated his body with hers, taking her with exquisite care and tenderness. It was as though he sealed her pledge of trust with his body and offered her love's ultimate completion as his return promise. Without fear or hesitation, without thought to what the morrow might bring, she gave herself to him. She gave all of herself, holding nothing back, discovering the full height and depth of love.

And when ecstasy finally came, it was within the sheltering embrace of her husband, the one man she'd love to the end of time.

Nikki lay quietly as dawn lit up the sky with the promise of a new day. And in that moment of earth's gradual awakening, she listened to her inner voice, waiting for the doubt and uncertainty to return. But nothing disturbed the smooth tenor of her thoughts. She felt now as she had last night. If there was one man in the world she could trust, it was Jonah.

Rolling onto her side to face him, she discovered him already awake and watching her with an unnerving intensity. "Good morning," she whispered.

"Waking up with you in my bed is nice," he murmured in a sleep-husky voice. "The only thing better would be waking up with you in my arms."

She smiled and snuggled closer, happy to accommodate. He punched the pillows behind him, shifting to recline against them. She nestled her head into the crook of his shoulder and threaded her fingers through the thick mat of hair covering his powerful chest. His heart beat slow and steady beneath her palm.

Gently, he cupped the side of her face with his large hand, his thumb stroking across her cheekbone. She leaned into the tender caress.

It was time for the truth.

"Jonah?"

"I'm here, sweetheart."

She took a deep breath, awed at the ease with which the words came. "I need your help."

His thumb never stopped its calm, soothing motion, but the tiny tremor that shook his hand told her a very different emotion raged within. "It's yours," he answered with gruff simplicity. "What do you need?"

Chapter Nine

"Nikki? Are you home?" Jonah crushed the paper in his fist, frustrated anger darkening his eyes. "Sweetheart?"

"I'm here."

She appeared in the doorway to the bedroom, dressed in a black silk slip and damned little else. If it had been any other time, he'd have snatched her into his arms and returned to the bedroom with her. There he'd have removed that bit of nothing and made love to her until they were both too exhausted to move, think, or even speak. Especially speak. As it was, he brushed past her, grabbed a thick terry robe and held it out.

"Put this on. We need to talk."

A warm smile tugged at her full, kissable mouth, tempting him almost beyond endurance. "I can't talk to you wearing my slip?" she teased.

"It depends on the kind of talking you want to get done."

He tucked the newspaper beneath his arm and helped her on with the robe. Jerking the front closed over the plunging black neckline, his knuckles scraped over her full breasts and he stilled, caught between desperate desire and the need to give her the bad news. As much as he'd like to delay the inevitable, they had too much to accomplish if they were to avert disaster.

Sweeping her hair from beneath the collar of her robe, he gathered a handful of the silken tresses in his fist and contented himself with a prolonged kiss. Just like every other time he touched her, she melted into his arms, her lush curves settling against him in a way guaranteed to send his blood pressure through the roof. And just like every other time he touched her, she gave totally of herself, never holding anything back. Reluctantly, he ended the embrace.

She blinked up at him. Her eyes, as soft and velvety as pansies, expressed absolute faith and confidence. He stifled a groan. Heaven help him. When his wife decided to trust him, she didn't bother with half measures. It was all or nothing.

He wrapped an arm around her and headed for the kitchen. "Let's fix some coffee."

She lifted an eyebrow, a hint of concern creeping into her expression. "Coffee or something stronger?"

"I'd prefer something stronger. But we'll stick with coffee." Moving with brisk efficiency, he dumped ground beans into the filter, added the water and hit the start button. "You can even have sugar with it."

"So the worst has happened," she murmured.

"Yeah, it happened." He dropped the newspaper onto the tile counter. It was one of the more disreputable rags floating around the city. "LJB Award Nominee Swindled Family Out Of Inheritance!" the headline screamed.

She squared her shoulders and faced him. "Am I fired?"

"How can you even ask such a question?" he snapped.

"You have to protect International Investment. I understand that." She responded with such cool logic, he wanted to grab hold and kiss her until her teeth rattled. Or until she regained her senses.

He shoved his hands into his pockets to quell the impulse, settling for an unsatisfactory glare of annoyance to express his irritation. "International Investment will ride out this particular storm just fine without any noble gestures on your part."

She set her rounded chin at a stubborn angle. "I'll tender my resignation effective immediately," she said as though he hadn't spoken. "And as soon as I've dressed, I'll go in and clear out my desk."

"Stop it, Nikki."

"No, it's all right. I knew this could happen when I refused to submit to Tucker's blackmail scheme."

"Refusing to have any further dealings with that man was one of the few intelligent decisions you've made since we met. And before you ask, the other was confiding in me."

"It's not your problem," she insisted. "I'll handle it."

"You asked for my help the other night, remember? I told you then I'd deal with Tucker."

She bowed her head. "I know you did your best."

He bit back an exclamation of fury. She was determined to play the tragic martyr and he knew of only one way to snap her out of it. "What happened to all that talk of trust?" he questioned caustically. "Or was that all it was? Talk?"

As he hoped, her head jerked up, her eyes flashing with violet fire. "It wasn't just talk!"

"Then trust me, damn it. I'll stop that piece of slime if it's the last thing I do."

"But what about in the meantime? How long can you protect me if International Investment starts losing customers? What are you going to say to your clients? Yes, she swindled her relatives, but she won't do it to you?"

"You didn't swindle anyone!" he roared.

The momentary silence was deafening. Then the coffee machine gave a final, inelegant burp and she offered a watery laugh. "Thank you for your support."

"My pleasure." He filled three mugs, automatically setting two in front of Nikki. Shooting her an assessing glance, he wondered how best to break the next bit of news. "Sweetheart, there's more."

She kept her gaze fixed on the sugar, determinedly spooning it into her mugs. "Bad?"

He sighed. "I'm afraid so."

She took a fortifying gulp of coffee. "Tell me the rest."

"The LJB nomination committee has requested that you attend a special session to determine whether you should be dropped as a candidate."

"When?"

"Nine, Monday morning."

"Three days." She caught her lip between her teeth. "Who brought the charges? Or is that a ridiculous question?"

"They refused to say. But I think we both know who's responsible."

A fine line appeared between her drawn brows. "I can't do this, Jonah. I can't go before those people and talk about my past. It was difficult enough telling you." He could see the panic she fought so hard to suppress. "They're strangers. They'll never understand."

"We'll make them understand."

She stilled. "We?"

"I'll be right there beside you."

He'd surprised her with that one. Hope dawned in her eyes. "You're going?"

"You're my wife. Of course I'm going. I wouldn't let you deal with this alone."

Words eluded her. She shoved her coffee aside and covered her face with her hands.

He slammed his mug to the counter and pulled her to her feet, catching her in a rib-cracking embrace. "I have it on excellent authority that women prefer conducting these crying jags in private," he murmured against the silky top of her head. "But I refuse to leave you alone right now. So I'm afraid you're stuck with me."

"I don't want to be left alone," she responded in a muffled voice. "Please hold me."

"I'm not going anywhere," he assured her.

"Yet."

His mouth compressed at the reminder. They'd both been careful to avoid a discussion of the future and he had no intention of correcting that oversight. At least, not now. "That's right," he said at last. "I'm not going anywhere. Yet."

"Jonah," she whispered, "I'm afraid."

He swung her up into his arms, cradling her close. Her head drooped against his shoulder like a delicate rose with a damaged stem. She felt so fragile, so vulnerable. The instinctive urge to protect gripped him, the unshakable need to defend her from harm. And like a feral animal determined to keep his mate safe, he strode toward the sanctuary of his lair.

Monday arrived all too soon as far as Nikki was concerned. Choosing an outfit to wear before the committee—or "inquisitors" as Jonah insisted on dubbing them—became a major undertaking. The minute she plucked a garment from the closet, Jonah categorically rejected it.

"Too depressing," he pronounced, tossing aside the severe black suit she'd selected. "Besides, it makes you look guilty."

"What do you want me to wear?" she demanded in exasperation. "My wedding outfit? That's about all I have left."

"It's a thought. Wait a sec. Aha." He yanked a stylish ivory suit and matching silk blouse from the closet. "Here we go. This, gold jewelry, and heels."

She stared at him in disbelief. "You're not serious, are you? Jonah, this isn't a business suit. I bought it to wear last Easter."

"Exactly. I want them to take one look at you and think, 'innocent.' And this outfit will do it."

"In case you've forgotten, I *am* innocent," she muttered.

He turned, the look on his face instantly silencing her. "I haven't forgotten a damn thing. And once the LJB committee has seen and heard you, they won't have any doubts, either." He handed her the suit. "Put this on. Oh, and leave your hair down."

"Anything else?"

"Yeah." His eyes blazed with suggestive green highlights. "Make sure you wear silk and lace underwear, stockings with those sexy little seams in the back, and garters."

She planted her hands on her hips. "That's supposed to make the committee think I'm innocent?"

"No." He dropped a swift, hard kiss on her mouth. "The silk and lace is for me. The committee will just have to sit there and wonder what you have on under all that soft lamb's wool. But I'll know."

A reluctant smile tugged at her lips. "You're impossible."

She found it incredible that she could find anything humorous at a time like this. Thanks to her husband, she had. She peeked up at him. He never ceased to amaze her.

"It'll be our little secret," he said, rubbing his hands together. "Anytime I start to lose my temper, I'll think of popping those flimsy little garters. It'll wreak havoc with my self-control, but it should keep me from blowing a fuse."

"Great. And what am I supposed to think about?"

He leaned down, nestling his mouth close to her ear. "You think about what I'm wearing under my suit."

Her eyes gleamed with laughter. "You have something hidden in there I don't know about?"

"Could be. His grin was wickedly sensual. "But I'm not telling. You'll just have to find out for yourself after the meeting."

"You're going to make me wait that long? No fair!" she protested.

"Ah, but there's method to my madness. Anytime you feel panicky, I want you to think about what it might be."

"And that's supposed to calm me?"

He couldn't know how he affected her if he thought that. She couldn't look at him, touch him, listen to the deep, rough tones of his voice without a desperate need sweeping through her.

"If nothing else, it should distract you." He gave her a gentle swat on her backside. "Get dressed, wife. I'll fix breakfast."

"One cup of coffee this morning," she requested. At his questioning look, she added, "I'm jittery enough without the extra caffeine."

"Beauty combined with intelligence. We can't lose."

His comment helped her get through breakfast and the cab ride to the office complex where the nomination committee had scheduled the meeting. The first attack of butterflies didn't hit until they entered the elevator. To her surprise, Jonah must have felt something similar. Ignoring their fellow passengers, he reached out and captured her hand.

"White?" he asked.

She stared in bewilderment. "What?"

"The garters. Are they white?"

She blushed at the amused sidelong looks they received. "Ivory," she whispered. "With pink rosebuds."

He closed his eyes and grinned. "Oh, yeah."

She peeked over at him. "Boxers?"

"Not telling."

A picture of Jonah leaping into bed in a pair of Santa-festooned shorts flashed through her mind and she fought to suppress a giggle.

The elevator door opened just then, and squeezing her hand, Jonah forged a path from the back of the car. "We're on," he warned. "Be confident. We're in the right here."

"Okay." As they approached the reception area, she asked softly, "Bikini briefs?"

"Nope."

"May I help you?" the receptionist said with a congenial smile.

"Mr. and Mrs. Alexander to see the nomination committee."

"Yes, you're expected. Follow me, please." She led the way down a short hallway and paused to knock on a set of double doors.

A sudden thought occurred to Nikki and she caught Jonah's hand before he could walk into the conference room. "Wait! You do have on . . . ? You're not totally . . . ?" She couldn't say it, her gaze drifting downward in fascinated horror.

"Commando?" He gave her a slow wink in the affirmative, then thrust the doors open, stepping boldly across the threshold. "What do you say we get this show on the road?" he demanded.

Two women and three men were grouped at one end of the room. At Nikki and Jonah's entrance, the five swiveled in unison, like puppets on a string. A tall, gruff-looking man built on proportions similar to Jonah took the initiative and approached.

"Bill West. I'm the committee chairman," he said, shaking hands with each of them, before turning his attention back to Jonah. "We didn't expect to see you this morning, Mr. Alexander."

"No, I'm sure you didn't. But I'm here nonetheless." He cocked an eyebrow. "I trust you have no objections?"

"Would it matter if I did?"

"No."

A reluctant smile creased Bill's mouth. "I didn't think so," he murmured drily. "Well, you're welcome to observe. But you do understand that the accusations have been leveled against your wife and the answers will have to come from her."

"What I realize is that we're here at your request to answer unsubstantiated allegations. We're doing it as a courtesy and without benefit of counsel. Should, in the course of this *meeting,* I feel that situation should change, I'll inform you." His wintry gaze held Bill's for a long moment. *"Now* I believe we understand each other. Do you agree?"

"Oh, yes. We understand each other perfectly." The chairman gestured toward the conference table. "Make yourself comfortable. Can I get you anything? Water, coffee?"

"Three coffees. Two with sugar, one plain," Jonah ordered briskly. Turning, he escorted Nikki to the far end of the table, then held the chair for her.

"I didn't want any coffee," she whispered as she took her seat.

"I know. I just did it to tick him off. It's a power thing."

"Thanks," she said wryly. "I'm sure that 'power thing' will help the inquisition go much smoother." She folded her bands demurely in her lap. "By the way, did I mention that I have precisely five items on under my suit?"

She slanted a quick peek at him from beneath her lashes. As she'd anticipated, he was conducting a rapid fire inventory and coming up precisely one item short. She smothered a smile. Jonah wasn't the only one capable of pulling a "power thing." Wondering what she'd left off should keep him busy for a while. At least she hoped it would.

"Your coffee," Bill announced heartily, as an underling scurried in, setting cups and saucers in front of them. "Now. Shall we begin?"

"You ready, Nikki?" Jonah asked.

"As ready as I'll ever be."

Bill joined the other four members at the opposite end of the table. "First let me say, Mrs. Alexander, that we apologize for the inconvenience." A deep frown creased his brow. "Unfortunately, it's important we clear this business up. Lawrence J. Bauman nominees must be above reproach. Companies who hire our candidates demand it. Why, a nomination alone can assure a position at the most select firms."

"I already have a position at one of the most select firms," Nikki inserted smoothly.

Jonah smiled in appreciation at her comment. "And the select firm in question supports Mrs. Alexander fully in this matter."

Bill sighed. "Yes, Mr. Alexander. We're well aware of your support. We're also well aware of International Investment's standing in the business world. Nevertheless, due to the seriousness of the charges, we're forced to investigate this matter to the fullest. We don't like it. You don't like it. But we have no choice if we're to survive public scrutiny."

"What would you like to know?" Nikki asked, taking a sip of coffee and struggling to hide a grimace at the lack of sugar. Without missing a beat, Jonah switched cups with her.

"I have information here from an unnamed individual—"

"Timothy T. Tucker," she interjected again.

"You know this man?"

"Yes. He attempted to sell my aunt and uncle his invention. When I recommended against it, he threatened to publicize details of my past."

"Tell them the rest," Jonah prompted.

She didn't question his directive, but simply said, "Tucker also offered to keep quiet if I changed my recommendation and authorized payment to him to the tune of fifty thousand dollars."

The committee paused for a moment's discussion. Then Bill nodded. "We suspected Mr. Tucker's motives for providing this information were questionable at best. But that's beside the point. What we must ascertain is whether the information is accurate."

"You'll have to be more specific," Jonah requested crisply.

"Very well. Let's get into specifics." Bill consulted his notes before fixing Nikki with his undivided attention. "Did you take money belonging to your relatives and invest it in worthless real estate?"

"One moment, please," Jonah interrupted. He leaned close, gathering her hands in his. "Give them the honest truth," he instructed calmly, his thumb tracing the outline of her wedding band. "Don't hesitate in answering. Don't attempt to explain at this point. They don't want explanations, just an admission."

Her fingers tightened on his. "And you want me to give them that admission?" The butterflies in her stomach had become a swarm of hornets.

"I want you to give it to them." He met her eyes unflinchingly, the utter confidence in his gaze easing her fears. How could she have ever thought those eyes resembled the bitter chill of autumn? she wondered in confusion. She must have been blind. They exactly matched the brilliant greens and golds of a warm spring day. "Trust me," he said.

"You know I do." She glanced at Bill West and flushed. "I'm sorry. Would you please repeat the question?"

He released an impatient sigh. "Did you take money belonging to your relatives and invest it in worthless real estate?"

She didn't look at Jonah. She didn't need to. "Yes," she said.

Her answer clearly surprised him. He referred to his notes again. "And did you then borrow money from the bank in order to finance an additional purchase?"

"I did."

The questions came faster. "And did you lose that money?"

"Yes."

"Did the bank foreclose on the original property when you were unable to make the monthly payments?"

"They did."

"And did the lending institute discover that the appraisal had been fraudulently obtained and the property wasn't worth anything close to what you'd borrowed against it?"

"It was worth approximately half of what I'd borrowed," she confessed.

Bill tossed down his pen and stared in dismay. "Mrs. Alexander, I'm at a loss for words. These are very serious charges and you've admitted to each and every one of them."

"Yes, Mr. West, I'm well aware of that. But these questions were asked out of context. I assume you'll permit me to put them in context?"

"If you can," Bill retorted.

She spared Jonah a brief glance. He gave her an encouraging nod, and drawing a deep breath, she began to explain. "Eight years ago, my parents died—"

The woman on Bill's left stirred, the overhead lights picking out the iron gray streaks in her hair. "I hardly see what the death of your parents has to do with these proceedings—"

"My wife has extended you the courtesy of listening and responding to each of your allegations," Jonah cut in, his fury barely held in check. "You'll do no less for her."

"He's right, Kay. Let her tell the story her way. It's the least we can do," Bill said reasonably. "We apologize, Mrs. Alexander. Please continue."

"Their deaths have quite a lot to do with this story," Nikki responded. "I'm sure you'll understand that it precipitated a major crisis in my family. Not only did we suffer from the emotional loss, but my mother and father were also the financial advisers for a number of my relatives. Because I was studying business at the time of their deaths, that burden then fell to me." A self-mocking smile flitted across her mouth. "Youth combined with an unfortunate arrogance allowed me to think I could handle the responsibility."

"I suspect we've all been there at one point or another," Bill murmured.

"I'm relieved to hear it. In my case, I had a college professor who'd become my mentor and encouraged me in my new capacity. Whenever I had a question, he'd advise me. About the time I turned twenty-one, he left the university to pursue more lucrative opportunities."

"Real estate investment?" Bill guessed shrewdly.

"The very real estate investment for which I'm currently under investigation," she confirmed.

Jonah spoke up again. "I'd like to make it clear, since I doubt my wife will, that at this point in her life she was also supporting a pregnant younger sister who'd just been widowed. Although Nikki's parents had left some insurance money, I question that it was sufficient to cover the expenses she was incurring at that time."

"No, it wasn't," Nikki admitted. "I suppose that's why I was vulnerable to Professor Wyman's offer."

"Professor Wyman?" Kay interrupted again. "Professor Robert Wyman?"

"Yes. Although he preferred people to call him Bert." Nikki looked at her curiously. "Do you know him?"

"My daughter did." Her hand clenched around her pen. "I'm sorry. Please go on."

"Bert showed me a commercial property he felt would be a guaranteed money-maker. Funny, I still remember the name. Sunrise Center. Anyway, he was incredibly enthusiastic, said if I didn't grab it, he would." She shrugged. "So I grabbed it."

"You went to your relatives for the money?"

She nodded. "We used everything we had, my parents' insurance money, my aunt and uncle's nest egg." Her voice grew husky with remorse. "Even the funds set aside for my cousins' college tuition."

"Didn't you consider that risky?"

It took a minute to gather the emotional resilience to respond. "Not a day goes by I don't regret having taken that risk," she told them with devastating candor. "But you can't make money without risking money. Or so Bert said."

"What happened then?"

The words came more easily. "Once I'd finalized the purchase, he came to me with a second proposal. He wanted me to borrow money from the bank against the property I'd just bought."

"What did he want you to do with that money?"

"He suggested we invest it in what he called a short-term turnaround. We'd buy and sell this surefire money-maker within the space of a few months." She played with her coffee cup, remembering the naive fool she'd been. She started to pick up the cup, but her hands shook so badly, she returned it to the saucer. "I should have known it was too good to be true. Later, I learned Bert had bribed the appraiser to grossly inflate the value of Sunrise Center. As a result, the bank loaned me over twice its value."

"And the money?"

"I handed the check over to Bert." She tried to smile. "Quite the brilliant young finance student, wasn't I?"

"I assume Bert promptly disappeared with the funds?" Bill questioned gently.

"Yes."

"What in the world did you do?"

She gathered the last of her inner resources, struggling to summarize the most difficult time of her life with as little emotion as possible. "I spent the next seven years working harder than I ever had before. I learned everything I could about the business world so I'd never be taken like that again. And I gradually paid back the money to the bank, to my aunt and uncle, to my cousins, and to my sister. With interest. Last year, thanks to several legitimate investments, I was able to square all accounts."

"And what happened to Professor Wyman?"

"I have no idea. I assume he went on to scam other gullible college students."

"He did," Clara inserted softly. "But not for long. He was sent to prison five years ago."

Nikki stared at her, stunned.

Without further ado, Bill gathered his notes. "Thank you, Mrs. Alexander. That will be all."

"No, that damned well won't be all," Jonah bit out. "We'll hear your results here and now. Is she still a nominee or do I contact my lawyers?"

"Don't, Jonah," Nikki whispered, slipping icy fingers into the welcoming warmth of his huge hand. She leaned close, her lips a breath from his ear. "And just so you know, I'm wearing two stockings, one garter, a slip and one more item."

She'd managed to distract him. "Which did you leave off?" he demanded just as softly. "Top or bottom?"

"You figure it out." She raised her voice. "I don't intend to contest your decision. But in all fairness, I do think I deserve an expeditious finding."

"One moment please." There was a hushed conference among the committee. "We have no objection to giving you an immediate ruling. Assuming we find no discrepancy in the statement you've given, your nomination will stand."

"And how long will it take to look for any discrepancies?" Jonah questioned irascibly.

"The ceremony is Saturday. If Mrs. Alexander's status changes, you'll be notified by Friday."

Afraid of what Jonah might say to that, Nikki stood. "Thank you for the opportunity to answer your questions." She tucked her hand into the crook of Jonah's arm and, using every ounce of her strength, dragged him from the room. "You are more stubborn than any mule," she muttered.

His hand coasted down her spine before settling in the small of her back. Abruptly, he stopped fighting. "Come on. Let's go home," he said.

"What's the sudden hurry?" she asked, eyeing him suspiciously.

He stabbed the button for the elevator. "I think I know which item your missing."

She lifted an eyebrow. "Oh?"

"Yeah." He grinned, tugging her into the empty car. "If I'm right, it's the same item I'm missing. And I've decided I'd much rather find out for sure than argue with a bunch of stuffy committee members."

"Me, too." She snuggled into the crook of his arm, sliding an experimental hand along his hip. "Good grief, Jonah! You really aren't—"

The elevator door banged closed.

Chapter Ten

"Aren't you nervous?" Selma questioned.

"Well, I—"

"Why should she be nervous?" Krista said dismissively. "She's a shoo-in."

Nikki gave a self-conscious shrug. "Oh, I doubt—"

"Damn that Tucker anyway." Ernie glared across the width of the huge stretch limo. "Why didn't you tell us about him, Nikki? I'd have strangled the little weasel when I had the chance."

"But I did—"

"Thank heaven for Jonah," Selma inserted, offering him a dazzling smile of unabashed approval. "I don't know what we would have done without his guidance."

"Yes. Thank heaven I was there," he agreed, draping an arm around Nikki's shoulders. "After all, it's a husband's duty and moral obligation to protect his wife."

"And the little woman's family, too?" she finally erupted.

"Yes, that, too." His grin flashed in the darkness. "Feel better now?"

She nodded, the momentary anger siphoning off some of her tension. "Much."

"Good." His eyes glinted from the shadows as he shifted closer. "Have I mentioned how beautiful you look tonight, Mrs.

Alexander?" he asked, nuzzling the spot just beneath her left ear.

"Hey, hey! None of that," Eric protested. "You can celebrate after she's won."

"*If* I win," she hastened to correct. "Which is doubtful. I hope all of you won't be too disappointed."

"No one's going to be disappointed," Jonah said as the limo pulled up in front of the hotel. He peered out the window. "Good. They're here."

Nikki strained to see past his bulky shoulders. "Who? Who's here?"

"Mom and Dad," Eric replied. "They decided to catch a cab directly from the hotel instead of taking the limo with us."

"I think I'm going to be ill," Nikki said with a groan. "You didn't warn me they'd be coming."

"They're here to support you, just like we are." Jonah caught her fingers in his, squeezing gently. "Ivory?" he whispered.

She sighed, relaxing against him. "Black. Boxers?"

"Banana hammock."

A watery laugh shivered between them. "Don't tease."

"Who's teasing?"

The door opened, ending any further conversation. Loren and Della hurried forward to greet her with effusive hugs and kisses, acting as though she truly was their daughter-in-law. She found herself wishing it was fact and not just a momentary fantasy.

Once inside the hotel, they were directed to a huge, glittering ballroom where a table had been reserved for them close to the stage. Other nominees graced nearby tables. Dinner and speeches followed, dragging out the evening. By the time Bill West took the stage carrying the LJB Award, Nikki's nerves were stretched taut.

"Before I make the big announcement," he began, "I'd like to tell you a little about the winner of this year's Lawrence J. Bauman Award. The person we've selected epitomizes the standards for which the award was designed—brilliance, dedication, shrewd business acumen and, above all else, integrity. This individual possesses those qualities and a few more besides. It was those extra few qualities that allowed our committee to reach an immediate and unanimous decision."

"That's you, dear. It has to be," Selma whispered.

Tears gathered in Nikki's eyes and wordlessly she shook her head. The moment he'd used the word "integrity", she'd known they'd chosen someone else. Not that it came as any great surprise.

"This person has surmounted terrible adversity," Bill continued, "not just learning from and overcoming past mistakes, but benefiting from them, as well. No mountain proved too high, no problem slipped by until an honorable solution had been found, no moral dilemma went without the appropriate choice being made, no matter how difficult that choice might be. So, without further ado, it is my great honor and privilege to present this year's Lawrence J. Bauman Award to . . . Mrs. Nikki Ashton Alexander."

Nikki was so shocked, she couldn't move for a full minute. Jonah came to her rescue, sweeping her from the chair and into his arms. Giving her a hard kiss, he aimed her toward the stage. "You earned it, sweetheart. Now go get it."

She weaved through the tables, climbing the steps to the podium in a total daze. Bill West shook her hand, then held out the crystal-and-gold award. Accepting it, she stared blindly at the graceful design, fighting for control.

After the scandal had broken, she'd counted herself fortunate to have retained her status as a nominee. But she hadn't expected to win. She honestly hadn't. She looked up, realizing in dawning horror that she would have to make a speech. But from the moment her name had been called, her mind had gone blank.

"I—I . . ."

Her throat closed up, her self-control deserting her. Just as panic seemed her only remaining option, her gaze fell on Jonah. It only took one look at his calm, steadying features to quiet the inner tumult. Heaven help her, but she loved that man.

Taking a deep breath, she said, "My thanks to the LJB nominating committee for both this award and the opportunity to set the record straight." She glanced at Loren and Della. "To International Investment, I extend my deepest appreciation for their unwavering support in the face of overwhelming adversity. It was more than I expected and certainly more than I deserved."

Her hands trembled and she'd have given anything to flee the stage at that point rather than bare her soul to public scrutiny. But opportunities like this only came along once in a lifetime. And she owed some people. It was time they knew it.

"I'd like to thank my family for their enduring love and faith in my ability. They deserve this award far more than I. For such intelligent people, they took some foolish risks with their continued backing."

Ernie and Selma beamed. Krista just shook her head with a hint of exasperation. Nikki's gaze sought Jonah's once more. "And, finally, I want to thank my husband, Jonah." She struggled to subdue the husky catch in her voice. But she couldn't. So she just said the words, allowing the emotion to spill free. "You gave me something I thought lost to me forever. Thank you for proving it's possible to trust again. Because without trust—"

Her voice broke, destroying what little remained of her composure. The room grew hushed as everyone waited to see what she would do or say next. She caught her lip between her teeth.

Never had she wanted so badly to cut and run. But she was determined to finish. Jonah deserved no less. Gripping the award so tightly she feared it would shatter in her hands, she spoke with heartfelt sincerity. "Thank you for proving it's possible to trust again. Because without trust, you can't have love."

She didn't remember much after that. Somehow she got off the stage and back to the table. There she endured a thousand hugs and handshakes. But all she really wanted was to walk into the protective warmth of Jonah's arms and never leave. Unfortunately, she couldn't even get near him. He stood off to one side, a cryptic smile on his face, watching as she accepted the unending flood of congratulations.

"I say we all go out and party," Krista suggested, once the room began to empty. "Champagne, caviar, the works."

Eric nodded in agreement. "After all, we do have two reasons to celebrate. Nikki's award and . . ." He grinned, holding up Krista's left hand. A huge diamond solitaire sparkled on her ring finger. "We're engaged."

Nikki stared in astonishment, unable to move, unable to even draw breath.

Krista giggled, snuggling against Eric. "Your expression is priceless, big sister. I guess you didn't see that one coming."

"Now you two don't have to stay married if you'd rather not," Eric added, his gaze moving from her to Jonah.

Nikki's mouth fell open. *"What?"* she managed to say.

"The Cinderella Ball," Krista explained. "Between us, Eric and I figured out the truth about that night. We also realized that you and Jonah must have married for our sakes. You know, so we'd get on with our lives."

Eric dropped a kiss on his fiancée's cheek. "And we have. Although I'll bet you didn't expect us to do it together."

Nikki darted a quick look at Jonah. If his expression had been difficult to read before, now it was utterly impossible. "I don't understand. How did you two meet?" she asked her sister:

"I came by the office to see you," Krista explained.

"But you were busy. Then I bumped into Eric and he invited me to lunch."

"One thing led to another," he said, picking up the tale. "And here we are. So, although we appreciate what you've done, you don't have to keep pretending." A wily grin touched his mouth. "Unless, of course, you've fallen madly in love and want to stay married."

"That's enough, Eric," Jonah cut in. He offered his hand. "Congratulations. And I agree with your suggestion. This does deserve a celebration." For the first time, he turned to Nikki. "Doesn't it? After all, you finally have everything you ever wanted. Right?"

Nikki tossed her coat onto the couch and carefully placed her award on the coffee table. "What are we going to do?" she asked without turning around. She was afraid to face him, afraid of what she'd read in Jonah's cool, remote gaze.

"I don't know about you, but I'm going to hit the sack," he replied with a shrug. "You're welcome to join me if you'd like."

"That's not what I meant."

His sigh held an impatient edge. "If you're referring to our future, I don't think this is the time for that particular discussion."

Dread ran an icy finger along her spine. "Why not?"

"Because I leave for London in the morning."

"*London?*" She sank onto the couch, staring in disbelief. "You never said . . . You never mentioned anything."

"I didn't mention it earlier," he explained evenly, "because I felt you had enough to deal with."

She laced her fingers together to hide how badly they trembled. "Your return to London, is it permanent?"

He stilled. And suddenly he seemed larger, harder, tougher. "You have to ask?"

She bowed her head. "Oh, that's right. You promised Ernie and Selma you'd be here for Christmas. I assume you intend to keep that engagement?"

"What the hell do you think?" The words sounded like they'd been torn from him. "Have I ever failed to keep a promise I've made?"

"No," she whispered. "You've kept every one. And you've done an excellent job of it, too. Thanks."

His coat hit the arm of the couch and tumbled to the floor unheeded. "I don't want your damned thanks," he said with barely restrained fury.

She lifted a hand in appeal. "Then what do you want?"

"The one thing it seems you find impossible to give, despite tonight's fine speech."

"You want my trust?" she asked in confusion. "You have it."

"Do I?" He ripped the bow tie from around his throat. "Prove it."

"How?" she demanded. "You don't have a family who needs rescuing. Your reputation isn't in jeopardy. Neither is your job. You don't have any deep, dark skeletons in your past that I can magnanimously overlook. I have no way of proving myself."

But she did, and she knew it. All she had to do was speak three simple words. Tell him what she'd kept so carefully hidden within her heart. Trust him with that final piece of herself. The words fought for escape, fought to wing free. But, in the end, fear kept them locked tightly away.

He stood mute and aloof, watching and waiting as she waged her inner battle.

Desperate to give him the proof he needed without having to surrender that final bit of control, she left the couch. Reaching for the side zip of her dress, she yanked it down, the black silk puddling at her ankles. She stepped over the inky pool and approached. To her dismay, he made no move to either accept or reject her overture.

"Jonah, please." She slid her palms along the taut muscles of his chest, wrapping her arms around his neck.

His hands closed on her shoulders. For an instant, she thought he'd push her away. Instead, he pulled her close, holding her against him for several, silent minutes. Then he thrust his fingers deep into her hair and tugged her head back, gazing down at her as though memorizing each tiny detail of her face.

"Kiss me goodbye, Nikki," he whispered.

Tears gathered in her eyes. "Not goodbye," she insisted frantically. "You'll return for Christmas. You promised."

"Let's not drag this out. Kiss me, sweetheart."

"But your flight isn't until tomorrow. We still have tonight."

He shook his head. "I leave early in the morning, so I'll stay at one of the airport hotels for the remainder of the evening."

She moistened her lips, searching wildly for a way to delay him. "You—you still need to pack."

"I have a bag ready to go."

"This is it?" Her chin quivered. "You're just going to walk away?"

He lowered his head, the tenderness of his kiss almost destroying her. "What is there to keep me?" he asked.

He didn't wait for a response. Releasing her, he snagged his coat from off the floor. And moments later, he was gone.

Nikki awoke the next morning to a cold and empty bed. She also woke to discover that Jonah had kept his final promise. On the front page of the newspaper was an article reporting the arrest of Timothy T. Tucker for fraud. Credit for information leading to the arrest was attributed to an unnamed concerned citizen. But Nikki didn't need to question the identity of that "concerned citizen."

She knew it was Jonah.

The next several days were the most miserable of Nikki's existence. She'd thought signing the bank's money over to Bert Wyman had been the biggest mistake she'd ever made. But she soon discovered it didn't come close to equaling the one she'd made with Jonah.

The only excuse she'd been able to come up with to explain her idiocy was that she'd been caught off guard. The shock of Eric and Krista's announcement coming on the heels of her own emotion-laden win at the award ceremony had ended in sheer, unadulterated panic. Maybe if she'd had time to calm down, she would have been all right. Just a few days in which to get used to the idea that she and Jonah had precisely one reason left for continuing their marriage.

Love.

And she did love Jonah, despite being unable to tell him. It had taken hours of soul-searching, but she'd finally concluded that it wasn't saying the actual words she'd feared most. It was his response to her declaration. She was terrified that he didn't love her in return.

Yet he'd demonstrated over and over how much he cared. He'd helped her resolve her problems with Eric and Krista. He'd rescued her family from a con man and solidified their financial well-being. He'd salvaged her reputation, standing by her in word and deed when no one else would have.

And with each and every tender touch, he'd shown the depth of his feelings.

Prove it, he'd said. Prove she trusted him.

Prove that she loved him, was what he really meant.

Suddenly, she knew the perfect way. She could say the words, but somehow she suspected that wouldn't be enough. Not any longer. She reached for the phone, wondering if she'd have sufficient time to put her plan into action. It'd take a bit of work. Arranging for the various details would be easy enough. It was the Christmas gift she intended to have delivered that might take extra effort.

But if she could just pull this off, it would be worth it in the end.

Christmas Eve ended up being the longest day of Nikki's life.

She went into the office, running on sheer nerves. She kept wondering if Jonah had received her email, worrying she'd waited too long before contacting him, and panicking over whether or not his special gift would arrive in time. The only thing she didn't question was her feelings for him.

Or his for her.

By early afternoon, the last of the employees had left for the holidays. The building grew silent and vacant and vaguely cold. Reluctant to return to an apartment empty of Jonah's dynamic presence, she stood in the darkness staring out the window at the bustling crowd. A bittersweet smile touched her mouth. They were all rushing to get home, to share in the warmth and joy of the season. How she wanted that, too!

As she watched, the first flakes of snow tumbled through the inky night sky. Keli would be thrilled. She'd have a white Christmas. Nikki closed her eyes, desperately fighting to hold the tears at bay. But would all that beautiful snow delay Jonah?

She wanted him. Heaven help her, she needed his strength and tenderness and love. Why hadn't she just told him the truth when she'd had the chance? How could she have risked losing the single most important person in her life? She bowed her head, her breath catching on a sob.

Please, she prayed, *just let him get home safely*. It didn't matter if he was late. It didn't matter if his present didn't arrive on time. Nothing mattered, except that he return to her whole and healthy.

Behind her, something hit her desk with a soft thud. She spun around with a gasp. A file lay spotlighted in the middle of the oak surface, a file that hadn't been there moments before. Hardly daring to breathe, she crept closer, struggling to read the name through her tears.

It was the Stamberg account.

From the darkness, a shirt came flying through the air. Then a tie. And then a belt.

"Jonah," she cried, torn between laughing and giving in to her tears. "What are you doing?"

"Making good on our bet, of course."

She covered her mouth with her hand. Angels singing heavenly hymns couldn't have equaled the beautiful sound made by Jonah's rough, husky voice. "You're going to dance naked on my desk?" she demanded.

"Unless you have a better place for me to dance naked."

Laughter won out. "I have a much better place." Impatience lent wings to her feet and she raced around the desk, hurling herself against the wide, comforting breadth of him. "Did you get my email?"

"I got it, although my assistant got it first since he checks my business email. And I must say, it caused quite a stir at the office. Damn idiot couldn't keep his mouth shut after he read it." He tilted his head to one side. "Let's see, how did it read?"

"Jonah, please come home. Urgent. There's something I forgot to tell you," Nikki quoted softly.

"Everyone thinks you're pregnant." He snagged her chin in his huge hand. "You're not, are you?"

"No." A minute frown crept between her brows. She struggled with the math and realized she couldn't remember when she'd last had her period. Was it possible? "At least, I don't think so."

"Too bad. It would have simplified matters."

She rubbed her cheek against his palm. "I'm not very good at simple," she confided. "Somehow I always end up doing it the hard way."

"I've noticed," he said with unmistakable tenderness. "So what did you forget to tell me?"

She took a deep breath. "I forgot to tell you that I love you. In fact, I forgot to tell you that I love you very, very much."

A slow smile touched his mouth. From there, it expanded into his eyes, the autumn chill melting into a rich spring warmth. "I'm supposed to take your word for that?"

"Yes." She glanced swiftly at him from beneath her lashes. "Because I think you love me, too."

He cocked an eyebrow. "You think?"

"I know," she corrected hastily. "I know you love me. And I thought of a way to prove my feelings for you."

He was openly grinning now. "And how's that, Mrs. Alexander?"

"Well . . ." She tightened her hold on his neck, reveling in the delicious scent and sound and touch of him. "You'll have to wait until tomorrow. But I have a few ideas that should tide you over in the meantime."

"Do any of those ideas involve getting out of the rest of our clothes?"

She laughed. "At least one of them does. But maybe you'd rather wait until we get home."

He heaved a deep sigh. "Haven't you figured it out yet? With you in my arms, I am home." His voice deepened, filled with a rich certainty, an unquestionable commitment to the future. "And by the way, my sweet wife, I love you, too. Very, very much."

And then he kissed her, proving beyond a doubt that Christmas was still a time of miracles.

When Christmas morning arrived, it proved to be the most joyous Nikki had ever experienced. Waking up in Jonah's arms, then to his hungry kiss and finally to his urgent lovemaking got the day off to a perfect start.

Once they reluctantly left the bedroom, she showed him the changes she'd made to the apartment. Plants filled every nook and cranny. And occupying one entire corner stood a live, potted evergreen covered in lights and ornaments.

"It wouldn't be a real home without your plants," he observed quietly.

"No," she disagreed, slipping into his arms. "It wouldn't be a real home without you. The plants are just to prove that I'm here to stay."

The relatives started arriving midmorning, adding their laughter to the apartment, along with an assortment of flavorful dishes. Nikki was on tenterhooks from the moment the doorbell first rang, rushing to peek into the hallway each time she thought she heard footsteps approaching.

"Who are you expecting?" Krista asked curiously at one point. "I thought everyone was already here."

"They are—"

A knock sounded at the door just then, and breaking off, she raced to answer it. Flinging it open, she called to Jonah, "It's for you. *Hurry!*"

He didn't come quickly enough to suit her and she rushed to his side. Grabbing his arm, she tugged impatiently. Curious, the rest of the family followed, gathering in a loose semicircle behind him. In the hallway stood a messenger dressed in the same white-and-gold uniform that the footmen at the Cinderella Ball had worn.

"I understood this was urgent," the messenger said with a broad grin. He handed Jonah a beautifully wrapped package. "Merry Christmas."

"Open it," Nikki urged the instant they'd closed the door.

With an indulgent smile, he ripped off the bright gold paper to expose a small rectangular box. He removed the lid and looked inside. Nervously, she awaited his reaction, his expressionless face worrying her. At long last, he looked up. Ignoring the eager questions from all the relatives, he closed the box. Catching hold of her hand, he towed her through the living room and out onto the balcony.

It was freezing cold, but she barely noticed. "Jonah?" she questioned anxiously. "Don't you like it?"

He dug a hand into his pocket and pulled out a small square package. "Maybe you should see what I bought you."

She ripped off the ribbon and wrapping paper and slowly flipped open the red velvet lid. Inside nestled a pair of wedding bands. Very unique, strangely etched wedding bands. "Oh, Jonah," she whispered, tears pricking her eyes. "They're made from the tickets to the Cinderella Ball."

"It was odd. The Montagues said we're the second couple requesting rings like these."

She shook her head helplessly. "It's a beautiful idea. Thank you."

"I thought it was time we had real rings and couldn't think of anything more fitting." For the first time, a hint of uncertainty crept into his voice. "I didn't want there to be any question about to my feelings for you."

"That's why . . ." She gestured to the box she'd had delivered to him, fighting to speak through her tears.

Huge, puffy snowflakes began to swirl downward, catching in her hair and on the ends of her lashes. He gathered her into his arms. "That's why you gave me tickets to the Anniversary Ball."

She nodded. "It's where it all began. It's where I fell in love with you. And where I first began to trust again."

He kissed the snowflakes from her lips. "I'll never give you reason to question that trust, Nikki. I swear it."

A smile slipped across her mouth and blazed with violet certainty within her eyes. "I believe you."

And peeking through the sliding glass door at them, their entire family cheered.

The End

The Cinderella Ball Series continues with Rafe and Ella's story: *Fairy Tale Wedding* by Day Leclaire

A Note From Day Leclaire

I need to confess something. As a child, I devoured fairy tales. In fact, I still own an old, battered copy of Grimm's Fairy Tales. Even today, I'll pull it off the shelf and fall back into it for hours on end. From the age of three, I'd put myself to sleep making up variations of those tales—lovely, romantic stories of princesses meeting their prince and finding eternal love. Does it come as any surprise the idea for The Cinderella Ball Series came to me in a dream?

When I woke the next day, I still found the premise wildly romantic—a ball where men and women attended, intent on meeting and marrying the person of their dreams. The catch? To do it all in one night.

I get that the idea isn't realistic. Our rational, intellectual left brain wouldn't let us behave in such an impulsive manner. Oh, but that dreamy, impetuous right brain catches fire. In our imaginations, we picture ourselves hesitantly attending the Cinderella Ball looking for that perfect husband or wife. Who needs reality? In our dreams we sweep across the ballroom in the arms of our Prince Charming. We slip out into the adjoining garden and, beneath the romantic glow of a full moon, we tumble into the embrace of that special someone. A someone who just might be our soul mate.

I hope you fell into the fantasy of the Cinderella Ball, if only for a few hours. And I hope you enjoy the next book in the series, *Fairy Tale Wedding* which is Rafe and Ella's story. And then the series (sort of) concludes with *Fairy Tale Marriage*. Why sort of? Well, there are three more Cinderella Ball stories in another of my series, **The Salvatore Brothers**. Hope you enjoy!

Love, Day

FAIRY TALE WEDDING

The Cinderella Ball Series:
Book #3

By

Day Leclaire

USA Today Bestselling Author

Dedication

To Kathy Smith Acosta. Thank you so much for always being there when I've needed you.

Prologue

The Montagues—Forever, Nevada

"You're dreading tonight, aren't you?"

Ella Montague glanced at her mother, reluctant to hurt her feelings with an honest reply. To be precise, she'd been dreading this evening's Cinderella Ball for five long years—ever since the last ball her parents had thrown.

That bleak night had seen all her hopes and dreams thoroughly shattered. But to admit that aloud and risk causing her mother pain? She shook her head. She just couldn't do it.

"I know how much this occasion means to you and Dad," she offered cautiously.

"The Cinderella Ball does mean a lot to us," Henrietta conceded. "It's our dearest wish that others experience the sort of love and joy your father and I found in our marriage. That's why every five years we sponsor these balls. Why we've kept the tradition going for thirty-five years." She reached for her daughter's hand. "But you what we want most of all, is for you to be happy."

Happy? Ella's fingers trembled within her mother's grasp. What had once seemed such a certainty crept ever closer to the realm of impossibility. "Maybe I'm not meant to find happily-ever-after," she whispered.

"Of course you are." Alarm filtered through her mother's voice. "How could you think otherwise?"

Ella bowed her head. "I'd always imagined I'd meet the man of my dreams on a night like this and we'd fall in love and marry in the space of one magical evening. Just like you and Dad. But maybe—" She fought for control, fought to voice a possibility her parents had always refused to face. "Maybe the Cinderella Ball doesn't work for everyone."

"It works for those who believe," Henrietta insisted.

"Does it? Are you certain?"

Sadness crept into Henrietta's gentle blue gaze. "That Beaumont man hurt you badly, didn't he?"

"I'll survive," Ella said with a shrug.

"Not a day goes by that your father and I don't regret that night. It's all our fault. We should have known what was happening at our own ball." Her hand fluttered in the air like a wind-blown butterfly. "At the very least, we should have realized what Shayne had in mind."

"You weren't to blame," Ella instantly denied. "No one could have known what Rafe's sister intended to do. Shayne never told any of us what she'd planned. Besides, I didn't fall in love with Rafe at the Cinderella Ball."

"You just lost him there," her mother offered the shrewd observation.

There wasn't any point in denying it. "I'm not a naïve twenty-one-year-old. Nor am I a starry-eyed dreamer." Ella lifted her chin and met her mother's gaze resolutely. "Not anymore." The past five years had seen to that.

Henrietta's breath caught in dismay. "You've stopped believing, haven't you? Oh, darling, you mustn't give up."

"I haven't." Thick, dark lashes fanned Ella's cheeks. Not yet.

Not unless tonight ended those few remaining dreams of finding an everlasting love. She'd give it a final chance, a last Cinderella Ball in which to find her Prince Charming. And if it didn't happen, she'd know. She'd know she wasn't one of the special people meant to find that pot of gold at the end of the rainbow, one of those who discovered the happily-ever-after that turned fantasy into reality.

She stood, despair tarnishing the amber clarity of her eyes. Over the past several years she'd made up her mind. If daylight broke and she remained unwed, she'd face the inescapable truth. She'd accept that heaven never met earth. That stars were but distant pinpricks of cold firelight rather than vehicles for wishes. And that fairy godmothers didn't help dreams come true, even for little girls named Cinderella. She'd finally concede that Rafe had been right all along. Fairy tales were just pretty stories and most people never lived happily ever after—her parents the one exception that proved the rule.

"Ella? Please tell me the truth. You do still believe, don't you?"

She turned and offered her mother a reassuring smile. "It's all right. I still believe." For this one last night, she'd cling to the wispy remains of her hopes and dreams. She'd give the magic of the ball a final opportunity to work.

"I have to be certain you haven't given up," Henrietta said anxiously. "It's so important to your father and me."

"I know." Ella's smile grew. "You and Dad are incurable romantics. You always have been."

"There's no point in denying it," her mother confessed. "But that's not why I'm so concerned. There's something else. Something I haven't told you."

Ella's amusement turned to alarm. "Mother, what is it?"

"Sit with me, darling. We need to talk."

The Grand Hotel—Forever, Nevada

"You're looking forward to tonight, aren't you?"

Rafe cradled his cell phone against his ear with an uplifted shoulder. "You wish me to lie about it, Shayne?" he demanded, stabbing a heavy gold cufflink into the buttonhole of his stark-white dress shirt. "Shall I wrap up the truth in pretty falsehoods so you'll feel better about what I intend to do?"

"Yes! That's exactly what I want."

"You know I don't operate that way," he retorted flatly. "Now, did you phone from Costa Rica just to give me a hard time? Or is there something important you wish to discuss? I have a party to attend."

"Darn it all, Rafe! This is important. Please. Promise me you'll leave the Montagues alone."

"You know I can't make such a promise."

Distress crept into his sister's voice. "You mean you won't."

"Fine. I won't." He gave the words a finality she couldn't mistake. "The Montagues are going down and I intend to be there when it happens. Hell, I plan to be the one to push them off the cliff."

"But it's *my* fault! How many times do I have to tell you that?"

He stared down at the thick gold-embossed envelope he'd tossed to the bed. It contained his sister's ticket to the ball. "Maybe I would have found a different approach if it hadn't been for this latest incident. The affair five years ago was bad enough. But for them to have the unmitigated gall to send you another invitation . . ." He heard the trace of his Spanish accent seep into his words and his hand tightened around his phone as he fought for control, fought to chain the black fury that rode him so relentlessly. Only the strongest emotions caused him to regress into childhood habits. "That I cannot forgive."

"Don't you understand? *I* wanted to attend tonight's ball. I thought maybe . . ."

Rafe gritted his teeth. "You'd hoped *he'd* be there."

She didn't reply, but the heartbreaking catch in her breath bled through the static on the line.

"Ah, *pobrecita hermanita,*" he whispered. "Your pain is mine. I would do anything to spare you more hurt." He shut his eyes, a fierce determination taking hold. "And so I shall. I will resolve this matter once and for all. When I have finished with the Montagues there won't be any more Cinderella Balls to tempt you or anyone else with romantic rubbish."

"Please, Rafe." Emotion choked her words, adding to the burden of guilt he'd carried for five impossibly long years. "Don't do it."

"I must," he replied with devastating simplicity. "They cannot continue to play games with innocent lives. They cannot steal people's money with promises of love and happiness and then deliver nothing but pain and misery."

"You have to believe me. It's *my* fault, not theirs. How can I convince you?"

"You can't, Shayne, for one simple reason." He gazed out the window of his suite, watching as the sun surrendered its light and warmth to the greedy demands of the desert. "The fault is mine more than anyone's."

"I don't understand."

"You spent half your life with no one to care for you. When I finally found you, I swore I'd protect you." His mouth twisted. "It was a promise I failed to keep. I can't change the past. But I can make sure it's never repeated. I won't fail you this time."

She tried to muffle her sobs, but he heard them, the sound of her grief, soul-crippling in its impact. "We need to talk," she finally managed to say. "You don't understand."

"Ah, but I do, *mi pichón,*" he replied calmly. "I understand more than you'll ever know."

Steeling himself, he disconnected the call. His gaze returned to the envelope on the bed and he picked it up. Inside he found a white velvet pouch that held a surprisingly heavy gold ticket. He pulled the metallic wafer from its nest. It caught the last rays of the setting sun and shimmered as though alive, flooding the suite with a bright, golden promise.

"I swear to you, Shayne," he murmured. "They will pay."

Chapter One

The Montagues' Cinderella Ball—Forever, Nevada

Like a hungry mountain lion scenting its prey, awareness of Ella struck first, alerting Rafe to her presence long before he zeroed in on her location. His movements slowed as he approached and tension rippled along the length of his shoulders, radiating downward into his arms and fisted hands.

He caught tantalizing glimpses of her through the line of people waiting to enter the Montagues' ballroom. The brilliant flash of her gold dress. The deep luster of ebony hair. An endless expanse of magnolia pale skin.

And then the crowd shifted and he saw her.

His reaction came hot and swift, with all the raw power of a jaguar coiled to spring. Desire and a driving need to possess clawed through him, making a mockery of the indifference he'd thought he'd attained over the past five years. The rational part of his brain might reject her, Rafe realized bitterly, but the baser, more instinctual part still wanted her with a ferocity he couldn't deny.

Memories long suppressed flooded his mind and fed his fury. a fury aimed squarely at himself. *Dios!* To his disgust he couldn't drag his gaze from her. Five years ago he'd thought her the loveliest woman he'd ever seen. Since then she'd matured into a beauty beyond even his fertile imagination.

He shifted to one side of the line, allowing the glittering tide of guests to pass him by as he battled to overcome the perversities of fate and human nature. He was suffering from a nasty case of lust, no more than that. It had to be lust, he refused to consider any other possibility.

It was a natural reaction, one any red-blooded man would feel toward such a woman. He'd worry if he didn't have a need to hold Ella in his arms, to seduce her into his bed, to join with her in the most ancient of rituals. Still, he'd be a fool if he didn't acknowledge that this overpowering urge would complicate his mission.

His craving for her could go no further, not after what she'd done. And not considering the fate he had in store for her.

Even as he made the determination, an alternate plan occurred to him, one that would satisfy his thirst for vengeance, as well as his hunger for possession. He watched Ella with cold silver eyes as he analyzed this latest possibility. Assuming she hadn't changed since the time he'd known her, it just might work.

A humorless smile crept across Rafe's mouth. For the sake of his sanity, it had better work.

Ella had lost track of how much time had slipped away since the start of the Cinderella Ball. But she'd felt the loss of each precious moment. More than anything she longed to steal from her place in the receiving line and fight for her last chance at happiness.

Instead, she greeted the guests with a warm smile and collected the golden wafers that served as tickets to the ball. They went into the velvet-lined basket she held, building into a miniature gilded mountain of fervent dreams and wishes. And as each ticket landed with a melodic clink she added her own silent prayer that this guest would find his or her heart's desire.

She glanced up as the next visitor approached and summoned another smile. He was a large, good-looking man whose tired hazel eyes warred with a determined expression.

"I'm Jonah Alexander," he introduced himself. "Listen, I have a small problem—"

But even as he began his explanation, an odd frisson of awareness caused her to glance past him. Past him . . . and straight into the diamond-hard gaze of Rafe Beaumont.

"Hello, Ella," he said, the softly spoken words at direct odds with the threat glittering in his stormy gray eyes.

The blood drained from her face. It couldn't be Rafe! Not here. Not now. Not on the most important night of her entire life. The basket tilted in her unsteady grasp and tumbled to the floor.

For an instant, she couldn't react, couldn't move, could only stare at Rafe in disbelief. She dreaded to consider what secrets she gave away with that one single look. Knowing his uncanny ability to read her every thought and feeling, it had to be far too many.

She didn't regain control until the man at the head of the line went down on one knee and began scooping tickets back into the basket. With a muffled exclamation she crouched beside him.

"Are you all right?" he asked in an undertone.

What had he said his name was? Joe Something? Jonah? That was it. Jonah Alexander. "I'm fine," she insisted, though she suspected her trembling hands betrayed her. Gathering up the last ticket, she stood. "Thanks for your help."

"My pleasure."

Jonah rose, too, and glanced pointedly behind him. If he'd thought to intimidate Rafe, he soon learned his mistake. Rafe folded his arms across his chest and held his position as though he had all of eternity to wait. But it was the expression in his cold, bleak gaze that worried Ella the most.

She'd seen that look before, had seen men of immense wealth and power cave before it, wilting like unwatered daisies beneath the fierce desert sun. Without uttering a single word he made it clear that Jonah was intruding on a personal matter.

To her amazement, Jonah shrugged off the look. Using his height and breadth to secure his place at the front of the line, he turned his back on Rafe. "Anything else I can do for you?" he offered.

Despair filled Ella's eyes. "I'm afraid not. Welcome to the Cinderella Ball. Enjoy your visit and we wish you a . . ." Her voice wavered, but she recovered swiftly. "We wish you a joyous future."

"You're certain?"

Rafe stirred behind him. "Tell him to go, Ella. You know this is a private matter."

She gave her self-appointed protector a reassuring smile. "Rafe and I are old . . ." She hesitated, her smile turning bittersweet. "We're old associates. But thanks for your concern."

Jonah inclined his head, conceding defeat. Sparing Rafe a final look of warning, he exited the reception line and plunged into the crowded ballroom.

"A friend of yours?" Rafe asked, stepping forward to take Jonah's place.

"I've never seen him before in my life." She lifted a shoulder with an air of hard-won indifference. "I guess he just recognizes trouble when he sees it."

For the first time, a hint of amusement lit Rafe's silvered eyes. "And I am trouble?"

She stilled, searching the taut, uncompromising lines of his face. "I don't know. Are you?"

"I can think of only one way to find out."

Ella nerved herself to ask, "Which is?"

Cold resolve supplanted his earlier amusement and she shivered at the change. "Be my escort this evening and you'll have the answer to your question."

His tone made it a demand, not a request. Nor did she miss the underlying threat. *Refuse at your own peril.* The line of guests waiting to enter the ballroom had begun to build. She needed to end this unexpected confrontation and soon.

"What do you want, Rafe?" she questioned in a low voice. "Why are you here?"

"I'm a guest, of course." His gaze held everything but innocence. "Why else would I attend?" Then he opened his hand to reveal a ticket. The thin strip of gold gathered in the overhead lights, reflecting each one with blinding intensity.

"You're here to find a wife?" Ella whispered, stricken.

"Isn't that the purpose of tonight's gathering?"

With a flick of his thumb, he sent the metallic wafer spinning skyward. The ticket arced through the air, a thousand bits of fire splintering along its length. It landed square in the middle of her basket with a resonate clink.

"Welcome to the Cinderella Ball," she murmured automatically, unable to tear her gaze from his ticket. Rafe had come to find a wife! How could she bear it? How could she stand aside and watch as he chose from the vast array of beautiful women attending tonight's ball?

She lifted her gaze, anguish clouding the amber clarity of her eyes. "Rafe—"

He closed the polite gap between them, trespassing on the protective circle of air most people hesitated to violate. But then, Rafe rarely concerned himself with what most people might do. Nor was it the first time he'd violated her space. Just the first time she didn't welcome the encroachment.

"Join me," he murmured. "Assign this duty to another and dance with me, *amada.*"

"I can't." She fought to keep her voice steady and impersonal. "I have an obligation."

"You are lying, Ella. It isn't obligation that keeps you here, but fear." The words were spoken so only she heard, the breadth of his shoulders concealing her distress from the prying eyes of waiting guests. "You will have to face me sometime. Why not get it over with?"

"What do you want?" she repeated. "If you've come to find yourself a wife, why bother dancing with me?"

"This is not an issue I care to discuss in front of others. When will you be free from your duties?"

Never! "It may be some time," she prevaricated, before reconsidering.

Tonight represented her last chance for true happiness. She was still determined to give herself every opportunity to meet the man of her dreams. But how could she do that with Rafe in the vicinity? How could she stand aside and watch as he selected a wife?

Worst of all, how could she possibly find love when the man before her still held that love tight within his grasp. Until she resolved the situation with him, she'd never be free. And until she was free, she couldn't risk her heart again.

"Come, *amada,*" he insisted. "Come with me."

As though in a trance, she inclined her head. Turning to an attendant stationed nearby, she surrendered her basket. "Could you take over, please? I need to help this guest." And without a single murmur of protest, she allowed Rafe to take her arm and lead her away.

He didn't speak again until they were on the dance floor. Catching her surreptitious glances, he lifted a sooty eyebrow in question. "Have I changed that much in the past five years? I suspect I have, considering the way you keep looking at me."

"I suppose so," she conceded, using the excuse to study him more thoroughly. "Somewhat."

With his jet-black hair and piercing gray eyes, she'd always considered Rafe dangerously attractive while not quite understanding why. But tonight, she saw him with the eyes of a woman, recognizing what she'd been too young to comprehend before.

How innocent she'd been not to see the unbridled passion that fired his spirit, she marveled, or the raw sensuality that was as much a part of him as bone, muscle and sinew. And yet, perhaps she'd been fooled by the remote wariness with which he shielded his innermost emotions, the cool control he used in his dealings with those who came within his sphere of influence. She found it a deadly combination.

He lured his victims with the white-hot blaze of passion while his arctic stare warned that he'd not be easy to tame.

"Well?" he prompted. "Are the changes so bad?"

She tilted her head to one side, daring to tease, "You have a few more wrinkles." Of course the lines bracketing his mouth and creasing the corners of his eyes only emphasized his natural strength and maturity. "And you're going gray at the temples."

"Age has a way of doing that to a man," he replied calmly.

A faint laugh escaped her. "It has a way of doing that to all of us." Her laughter died, replaced by a sadness she couldn't conceal. "I suppose the most obvious change is that you've gotten harder, if that's possible. Colder."

His arms tightened. "Don't blame age for that."

"No," she whispered. "I'm to blame, aren't I?"

He didn't deny it, but cradled her in his arms as though she were precious to him instead of a woman he despised. It was too much. She couldn't bear to be this close to him and know he didn't share her feelings. She had to end this moment.

"You said you wanted to talk," she reminded.

"First we dance." His widespread hand filled the hollow at the base of her spine, stirring emotions that should have died long ago. "Then we'll talk."

Ella closed her eyes to block out the sight of him. But it only intensified her awareness. Without sight, other senses came to the fore. She could hear him. The subtle give and take of his breath close to her ear. The exultant singing of her silk dress against his tux.

His unique scent wrapped itself around her, a blend that made her think of wind and rain and rich, fragrant earth.

And the feel of him . . . The muscles beneath her hand rippled as he moved, reminding her that he wasn't a man of leisure, but one who worked the land, who came by his physique through years of backbreaking labor rather than from a high-tech gym.

Finally, the only sense left unsatisfied was taste. And just the thought of closing her mouth over his, of rediscovering the distinctive flavor of him was almost beyond bearing.

Her eyes flew open and she focused on the crisp bow tie at his throat. She forced herself to concentrate on that and only that, to ignore the other sensations rioting through her.

Not that it helped. To her horror, the temptation to tug at the ends of his tie, to rip open his shirt and taste the strong, tanned column of his throat nearly consumed her. Five years ago, she'd wanted him with all her heart and soul. And now, she could only tremble in his arms.

Dear heaven, she wanted him still.

"What is it, Ella?" he murmured. "What are you thinking?"

How could she answer when the truth was the very last thing she should entrust in his care? Fear urged her to run, just as desire compelled her to stay. Fear won the battle.

With an inarticulate murmur, she pulled free of his arms and darted around the other dancing couples, desperate to escape. She didn't understand her reaction to Rafe any more than she understood his reason for attending the ball. Both defied explanation.

The garden seemed the safest retreat and she took the back staircase from the ballroom. Already guests were making their way to the library where the county clerk busily processed marriage applications. Ella mustered a smile of greeting as she passed, envying the happiness radiating from the fortunate couples soon to be wed.

Bypassing the dining area and buffet tables, she continued through the French doors opening onto the garden. A pathway led off to the left, the trees and shrubbery glittering with fairy lights. She turned in the opposite direction, slipping between an almost indiscernible opening in the bushes.

Safe from prying eyes, she wrapped her arms about her waist and bowed her head, allowing the pain to consume her.

Rafe followed Ella at a discreet distance. It wasn't difficult to keep track of her. Her gold gown provided a shimmering beacon to hone in on. He lost sight of her when she entered the garden, but by then he knew where she'd gone. If he hadn't been through the gap between the shrubs before though, he'd never have found her. Even armed with that knowledge, he wasted several precious minutes uncovering the narrow opening.

This place would serve him well tonight, he decided. Besides offering privacy, it would allow him time to determine a course of action without the threat of outside interference. He and Ella had often hidden from prying eyes within the shelter of the Montagues' privacy glade, a small grassy area, surrounded by thick bushes.

He'd come to Nevada for a short visit, to attract investors for a hotel he'd hoped to build on the west coast of Costa Rica. And he'd hired Ella as his temporary assistant because she'd gotten along so well with his sister, Shayne.

It was the worse decision he'd ever made.

Ella had been a starry-eyed, twenty-year-old embarking on her first job. The attraction between them had been instant and mutual. The month he'd initially planned for the trip had stretched to two months and then to four.

Those had been special times, times when he'd taken her in his arms and kissed her until the world melted from existence. Back then, their love had seemed more constant than the dry desert winds and far fiercer than the scorching midday sun. How he'd wanted her! His need had become a desperation, a narcotic that had briefly seduced him into believing that magic and miracles could exist.

What a fool he'd been.

Taking a deep breath, he forced the memories from his mind. To dwell on such things now would only weaken his resolve. And he'd waited far too long for this moment to allow that to happen.

He stepped from the concealment of the bushes into the glade and that's when he saw Ella. A sledgehammer to the gut couldn't have had a more crippling impact. For what seemed an eternity he fought to keep his knees locked in place, fought to force the air in and out of his lungs. Fought to rein in emotions he'd believed forever denied to him. But his control slipped from his grasp like starshine through open fingers.

Maldito! Never had he seen such a sight. If the heavens above had parted long enough for one of their denizens to slip to earth, she could be no more pure of feature or blessed with grace than this woman before him. For the sake of his eternal soul, he should leave her untouched. He knew it as well as he knew his purpose for being here. But he was a man, not a saint, with a man's need to seize and possess. So he remained, absorbing the perfection of what soon would be his.

Moonlight washed her ebony hair with silver and gave her skin a pearly iridescence. Her Grecian-style gown clung to the supple lines of her body, lines that had both ripened and grown more defined over the past few years.

The softness of youth had been transformed into the lean fluidness of womanhood. Her breasts were fuller, her narrow waist flaring into shapely hips and a firmly curved backside.

His hands closed into fists as he fought to gain mastery over the heat pooling in his loins. He wanted her, wanted to reacquaint himself with every inch of her. Only one thing kept him in place. She stood with head bowed as though in defeat. He'd thought he could come here this evening, that without a shred of emotion he could destroy the woman who'd caused his sister so much pain.

But seeing Ella, defenseless and vulnerable, in pain herself, he found he couldn't. He couldn't take the path he'd originally planned. Not yet. Not until he'd determined whether she felt a shred of remorse for her actions five years ago. Perhaps if such an emotion eluded her, he'd be able to carry through with his intentions.

He must have made some small sound, for she stilled. With all the elegance and caution of a woodland deer, her head lifted and she turned to face him. For an endless moment their gazes met and held, the hungry, ruthless eyes of a predator locking with the wary topaz of the prey.

She held something in her hand, a shimmering strip of gold that she swiftly pocketed in the pleated folds of her gown. He couldn't be certain, but it looked like one of the tickets to the ball. "You shouldn't have followed me, Rafe," she stated in a low voice.

"I had no choice." He approached, skirting the ring of moonlight that encircled her. "You felt it, too. Didn't you, *mi alma?*"

"Don't call me that." Golden sparks leapt to life within her fiery gaze. "I'm not your soul. How could I be, when you have no soul?"

His mouth twisted. "I don't doubt you're right. But that doesn't change a rather bitter truth."

"Which is?"

"You still want me."

The breath shuddered from her lungs, the fragmented sound disturbingly audible in the stillness of the night. "I wish I could deny it," she retorted, before falling silent. She squared her shoulders, her mask of composure slipping back into place, impressing the hell out of him. She accomplished a feat few could have managed considering the stress of the moment. "I wish I could deny my feelings," she repeated. "But I can't."

The dense shadows concealed his satisfaction. "No more than I can deny wanting you." He'd surprised her, his frankness slipping beneath her defenses to touch the vulnerability he'd witnessed earlier. He lifted an eyebrow. "You don't believe me?"

"It seems unlikely."

"Why? Because we're at odds over this Cinderella Ball?"

"Yes."

His laughter held little humor. "Do you think desire is like a light switch? Do you think it's an emotion I can be turn off with a flick of the finger? Is it like that for you?"

"No."

The bleakness in that one single word impacted with devastating force. He didn't want to acknowledge her distress. But how could he avoid it? She stood so alone, a fragile captive held within a prison of moonlight. And all he had to offer was a different sort of prison, one where they shared their captivity. Unable to refrain, he reached into the silvery pool of light and caught her hand, drawing her toward the momentary freedom of the shadows.

"Desire, *mi alma,* is like an uncontrollable hunger. It must be fed before it can be sated."

He brushed his thumb along the tender fullness of her lips. They parted and for a hot instant he thought she meant to take him into her mouth. Then she turned her head as though denying her need. Deliberately he cupped the curve of her cheek, forcing her to look at him.

"We never fed that hunger," he told her. "We never feasted on our passion. Never satisfied our appetites. And now we're starving, dying for a taste of forbidden fruit."

She didn't relent. "Then we'll have to starve. Unlike Eve, I refuse to be tempted."

"You want me to seek satisfaction elsewhere?"

She flinched as though she found his words painful. "Then you were serious? You're here to find a wife?"

"I'm thirty-five years old. Don't you think it's time?"

"I'm the last person you should ask. Although I'm curious." She slipped from his grasp, distancing herself from him physically, if not emotionally. "Why come here to choose a wife? Considering how opposed you are to the Cinderella Ball, I'd think this would be the last place you'd pick."

He gave her the truth. "I came to resolve the situation between us. I can't move forward until I've put the past where it belongs. In the past."

Tension radiated from her. "What do you mean? How do you intend to settle our differences?"

"For a start, I wish to spend the evening with you. We could talk."

"No," she instantly protested. "Not tonight."

His eyes narrowed at the hint of desperation behind her words. "I'm afraid I must insist," he said with a negligent shrug. "You would be wise not to refuse me."

"And if I do?"

"Then I will resolve our differences my way. One less to your liking, I fear."

Still she stood her ground, fixing him with an unflinching gaze. His admiration for her strength and perseverance grew. She'd always been a determined woman, one who didn't back away from adversity. More often than not, she chose to champion the underdog, a circumstance that had caused conflict in their relationship. Oddly, it pleased him to discover that she'd held to her convictions.

"Why come forward now, Rafe?" she demanded. "Why after all these years?"

"Is my timing bad?" he asked in mock innocence.

"It couldn't—" Her breath caught for a revealing instant. "It couldn't be worse."

He frowned, hearing again that note of desperation. Something was very wrong here, something more than just his presence. And he was determined to discover what that might be. "Is my timing bad because it interferes with the Cinderella Ball?"

"Isn't that reason enough?"

"Possibly." His suspicion grew and with it his certainty that she was concealing something from him. "Or is there another reason, one you prefer to keep from me?"

Her pulse fluttered at the base of her throat, capturing his attention. "There's nothing," she whispered, a hint of despair flitting across her delicate features. "Not anymore."

Then it came to him in a white-hot flash. *"Madre de Dios!* There is more."

"No—"

"Don't lie to me! You were planning to marry this evening." He caught her shoulders in a bone-crushing grip. "Weren't you?"

For a moment, he didn't think she'd answer. Then her chin tilted and she looked him square in the eye. "Why so shocked? Wasn't that your plan, as well? You've suggested as much."

He forced himself to ease his hold, to caress the bared shoulder beneath his palm instead of crushing it. Something felt off kilter, but he couldn't seem to work through his fury to discover what. "Why, Ella?" he questioned gently. "Why would you do such a reckless thing?"

"Reckless? The Montagues' daughter meeting the man of her dreams at the Cinderella Ball isn't reckless." An impenetrable calm encased her as she spoke, an icy reserve he felt compelled to breach. "I find it quite appropriate."

"Don't be ridiculous." Anger flashed within his silver gaze. "There's nothing at all appropriate about marrying a man you've only just met this evening. And you damned well know it. If I had my way there would be no more Cinderella Balls."

"I'm well aware of that. I'm also well aware that you've done everything within your power to bring an end to them."

A humorless smile cut across the angled planes of his face. "Not everything, or I wouldn't be here."

"What do you mean?"

He sensed her alarm, but did nothing to ease it. "I mean there were one or two methods I chose not to implement."

"You mean you choose not to implement them . . . *yet*." He inclined his head in agreement and her mouth compressed. "I'm surprised you were willing to show such restraint."

"I prefer to employ less absolute options," he retorted. "Unfortunately, they haven't worked. Which leaves me with a small dilemma."

Ella lifted a dark eyebrow. "Is that so? You amaze me. In the past you never would have hesitated to do your worst. Don't tell me you've learned compassion or forgiveness in the last five years."

He tugged her closer, bitterly amused that he failed to intimidate her. But then, why should she fear him? No matter how angry he became, he could never harm her. She had to know that.

"If I'm a man without compassion or forgiveness, you have only yourself to blame."

A surprising softness glistened in her tawny eyes. "I don't believe that any more than I believe you'd carry through with the various threats you've made over the past few years."

"That may prove a costly mistake on your part." He allowed a grim warning to infuse his voice. "The fact that I have not exercised all the options at my command shouldn't be mistaken for weakness, *mi amada*."

She laughed, the sweetness of the sound quenching a lengthy drought. Once upon a time he'd lived to hear her laughter. But he'd purged that need long ago. His mouth compressed. Too bad abstinence hadn't purged his other needs as well—the ones that demanded a more physical expression.

"Trust me, I've never considered you weak. Far from it." Her amusement faded, replaced by an apprehension he was hard-pressed to resist. "Why have you come, Rafe? Why have you *really* come?"

It was time to reach a decision. His choices were clear. He could carry through with his original plan and extract a revenge that would put a fast end to any further Cinderella Balls. Or he could achieve the same result while satisfying the need burning between them.

By his presence alone, a fire had been set. As he'd danced with her, the sparks had fallen on dry kindling. It wouldn't take much to fan it, one kiss and the flames would rage out of control.

From there he knew the progression well. Once the fire had been fed for a time, it would settle into a delicious, hot flame. Too bad it couldn't last, but such was the nature of fires. From hot flame it would slowly burn down, dying to warm embers before the inevitable fade to cold ashes.

The choice before him took little thought. The final outcome would be the same regardless. Tonight would see the last Montague ball. As to how he went about it?

His hungry gaze feasted on Ella. He'd be a fool if he didn't take that which would fall so easily into his grasp. She wished to marry. He could save her from such foolishness. And he could prove to her, as well as to her parents, that the Cinderella Ball was a dangerous illusion.

"Why have you come?" she repeated. "What do you want?"

His decision made, he tugged her into his arms. "I want a wife, *mi alma*. And you shall provide one for me."

Chapter Two

Ella stared at Rafe in disbelief. He was destroying her. Bit by bit, piece by piece he dimmed the light of hope she'd guarded with such care. The hope she'd experience a love as eternal as the one her parents had found.

Did he really expect her to provide him with a wife? How could he, after the past they'd shared? He must have some idea of the pain that would cause. Or didn't he care?

She moistened her lips with the tip of her tongue, praying she'd misunderstood. "You can't be serious."

"I'm very serious." He continued to hold her in an embrace that made intelligent thought a sheer impossibility. The one time she attempted to pull free, his hand settled on her hip, anchoring her more firmly in the harbor between his thighs. "I want you to find me a woman."

"And how do you propose I do that?" Stress added a husky edge to her voice, but if Rafe heard he didn't let on. "Scurry from room to room, making an announcement?"

"Nothing so drastic," he replied in amusement. "I would think after all these years, you'd have some idea of how to go about it. Isn't the purpose of your Cinderella Ball to play matchmaker to a host of lonely individuals?"

"Well, yes. But—"

"Then be my personal matchmaker. How do the other guests find their mates?"

"I don't know." At his skeptical look, she insisted, "Really, I don't. I've never participated in the process."

He didn't take the hint. "You will tonight. Now answer my question. How is it done?"

"I suppose the guests introduce themselves to each other," she told him. "Most seem to have some preconceived notion of the sort of person they'd find compatible." She searched her memory of past balls. "Some even bring lists."

"A list? How distressingly practical." His eyes glittered like raindrops on a windowpane. "Is that the way you intend to find a husband, by making a shopping list?"

"Not exactly." How had she gotten herself into this conversation? "I have certain qualities and characteristics I consider important—"

"That sounds like a list to me." When she started to contradict him, he added, "But if that's what it takes, who am I to argue? You have far more experience than I."

This was ridiculous! "Rafe, please—"

"No, no. We must do this right. If a list is necessary for a successful pursuit, than a list it is. What shall we choose as our first requirement?" He snapped his fingers, the retort as sharp as a hunter's rifle. "I know."

"She has to be of the female persuasion, right?" Ella interrupted, the glib remark escaping before she could prevent it.

His only response to her baiting was a slow smile. "Not just any female. She must be special, *amada*. Very special." His thumb swept the arch of her cheekbone and his voice softened, the faintest of accents giving his words a seductive lilt. "One with eyes like a desert sun."

Anger kindled as she fought to throw off the spell he wove with such skill. Did he think her without any feeling at all? He held her in an unbreakable hold, subverting her already fragile defenses with every look, word, and touch until her emotions were in a state of total chaos. And then he had the unmitigated gall to describe the woman of his dreams in that calm, rational manner of his? A woman she was expected to find for him?

"Desert sunshine?" Ella questioned dryly. "You expect me to run around and see if any of the women here have hot eyes? That should make for an interesting evening."

His mouth twitched. "I have every confidence in your ability."

She released her breath in a silent sigh. Why did she bother goading him? She'd never won such a contest in the past. It seemed unlikely that she would now. "Is that it, a hot-eyed woman? Or is there more?"

His arms tightened a fraction, realigning her smooth curves to fuse with his sharper angles. "I have quite a few requirements. She should also be elegant and warmhearted. She should have a bite to her, tempered with compassion for those less fortunate."

"This is a woman we're talking about?" Ella asked dubiously. "Because it's beginning to sound an awful lot like you should get yourself a dog, instead."

This time she did get a rise out of him. A hint of annoyance gave his reply a grating edge. "Your attitude isn't helpful," he informed her. "You wish to find a husband tonight, yes?"

"Yes." *Maybe.* After seeing Rafe again, she wasn't as certain as she'd been this afternoon.

"Until I find a wife, you won't be free to do so. Now, I suggest we get on with this."

Ella gritted her teeth. She'd love to tell him to go to hell. But she didn't dare ignore his earlier warning. If she didn't cooperate, he'd choose his own way of settling their differences. There was still time for her to find a husband, she tried to console herself. Not much, but some.

All she had to do was locate the wife of Rafe's dreams. The woman had to be around here somewhere. Surely it wouldn't be that difficult to find her. Once Ella had unearthed this paragon for Rafe, she'd be free to give her heart to another. She bit down on her lip to keep it from trembling.

Assuming she had a heart left to give.

"You're right," she conceded. "Let's get this over with. What else do you want in a wife?"

"Let's see. She must be intelligent. And strong."

"So, you want a muscle-bound genius with the attributes of a dog." She offered a guileless smile. "Have I got it right?"

"Amada," he said dryly. "You're not getting into the spirit of things." He tilted his head to one side, fixing her with eyes capable of piercing clear to her soul. "Or don't you believe the Cinderella Ball can provide me with an appropriate woman? What's happened to your faith? Don't you believe anymore?"

"Of course I do!"

But his question had hit with pinpoint accuracy and she prayed that he didn't suspect the truth. Had he any idea how close she'd come to giving up? Did he know she considered this her last chance to experience the magic of the Cinderella Ball?

"I still believe," she insisted, as though the mere act of speaking the words aloud would give them validity. "I do."

For a heart-stopping moment his eyes narrowed. Then he inclined his head. "I never doubted it." His hand crept upward, brushing the wispy curls from her temple. "Let's see, where were we?"

He continued to hold her far too close, his touch making it more and more difficult to breathe normally, let alone respond in a natural fashion. "We were discussing the qualities you'd like in a wife," she prompted, fighting to conceal her distress.

"So we were. I wonder what else we should add to our list?" He paused to consider and his hand drifted from her temple to stroke the side of her throat. Supple fingers slipped beneath the sleek knot at the nape of her neck, sending a riot of sensations shivering through her.

She drew a short, panicked breath. "I think your list is long enough," she managed to say.

"You could be right." Humor rippled through his satiny voice. "Though I confess I have a preference for dark-haired women. You will keep that in mind, won't you?"

"I'll do my best. Anything else?" she demanded.

His touch grew bolder, more provocative with every passing moment. If he didn't release her soon, she'd thoroughly disgrace herself by clinging to him and begging that he never let her go.

"I can think of just one more requirement."

She closed her eyes in a mixture of relief and regret. "Which is?"

His fingers played a tantalizing dance down the length of her spine to cup the curve of her hip. "When I kiss her, her response must be as abandoned as this."

Before she realized what he intended, he lowered his head and captured her mouth with his. The heat simmered between them exploded, consuming her in a fire she had no hope of containing.

An instant later she realized she didn't want to contain it. She wanted to feed the flames, burn higher and hotter and brighter, until nothing mattered but the pleasure that could be gained from this timeless moment.

She caught his shirt in her hands, tugging him close, satisfied only when she could feel the swift, strong beat of his heart beneath her palms. His arms felt like corded steel, his hold as unrelenting as his nature. After all this time, she shouldn't still want him so desperately. She should resist, fight the trap he'd sprung. But the truth was, she'd been waiting for this to happen since he'd first appeared in the entranceway to the ballroom.

It had been so long since they'd last kissed. To her amazement, she discovered she hadn't forgotten a thing. Not his smooth, intoxicating flavor. Not the firm, warm feel of his mouth. Not the soul-jarring response of her body to his bold touch.

She traced the tiny scar on the left side of his bottom lip knowing by his shiver that he found their embrace as affecting as did she. For a fleeting instant, it gave her hope.

"You understand now, don't you?" he whispered against her mouth. "This is how it should be between a man and woman. How can you think of giving yourself to another when you still burn like this for me?"

His words ripped into her heart. "What about that perfect woman you described in such detail? You may object to my plan, but you intend to marry a stranger tonight, too." Her regard turned caustic. "Or is it different for men?"

"For some men, perhaps."

He didn't say whether he was one of them or not. But the stark need in his gaze told its own story. He wouldn't be satisfied until he'd had her. The knowledge became a certainty, leaving behind a disconcerting bewilderment. There was only one way he could satisfy that desire. Only one way she'd consent to giving herself to him.

As though reading her thoughts, he said, "Yes, *amada*. I know the price I must pay to have you."

"But what about the woman you wanted me to find?" she demanded. "Remember? The hot-eyed brunette?"

His lids drifted downward, concealing the expression in eyes that had gone smoke-gray. "Ah, yes. Her."

"Yes. *Her.*"

"Could you not tell?" When he looked up again it was with a lazy amusement that sent time tumbling backward. "It was you I described."

It took a full minute for his meaning to sink in. "I'm the muscle-bound genius with the attributes of a—" She couldn't say it.

He grinned. "Regrettably, yes. But I'm willing to be generous and overlook such obvious failings."

Disbelief warred with an uncontrollable surge of hope. "You can't be serious."

"Very serious. You wish to have a husband. I wish for a wife. What could be more natural than we each fulfill the other's desire?"

Ella felt as though she teetered on the brink of a perilous abyss. To believe in Rafe would be the same as flinging herself over the edge into arms that might fail to catch her. If she misjudged him, she'd end up free-falling with nothing below to impede her plunging descent. Nothing to catch her before she hit the unforgiving chasm floor.

Her composure slipped, revealing the vulnerability beneath. "What are you asking?"

"I am asking you to marry me." His soft, persuasive words filled the moon swept glade, adding to the magic of the setting. "Marry me, Ella. You know it's what we both want. What we've wanted for years. We can't look at each other, touch each other, without being torn apart by our need."

She shook her head. It wasn't possible. They couldn't just start over. Not after all this time, not after the past they'd shared. "You don't love me. You can't. Have you forgotten—"

"I have forgotten nothing!" For an instant she caught a glimpse of rekindled fury, of a man still thirsting for vengeance. Then he visibly reined in his anger, banking the blazing fire storm once more. At least, for the moment. "What happened between us is in the past where it belongs. You must forget all that for a moment, Ella, and answer my question. Do you intend to marry tonight?"

"I'm considering it."

He captured her face in his hands, his work-roughened palms sparking a delicious friction along the length of her jaw. "Your expression gives you away," he warned. "However you choose to qualify your response now, your original plan was to marry. Admit it, Ella. Is that not true?"

"All right, yes!"

A dozen warring emotions swept across his countenance, too swift and confusing for her to follow, their passage like snowflakes driven by a savage winter wind. "Something has pressured you into taking such a desperate gamble. What is it?" he demanded.

In that instant her motivations crystallized and she hated him for forcing her to face the truth. For a split second she saw her decision through his eyes, recognizing the desperation that spurred her actions. Fear had driven her to take such drastic measures, not that she could admit that to him.

"I planned to fall in love this evening and marry," she evaded the question. "Just like my parents. Just like a thousand other couples who have found happiness at the Cinderella Ball. Is that so wrong?"

His fingers played a delicious melody across her bared shoulder. "But this can't happen, *mi alma,*" he informed her gently. "For how can you go to another man when you have nothing to give him?"

She stared in confusion. "I don't understand. What do you mean?"

"Just what I said. You have nothing to offer this man. Do you not realize?" He paused for a devastating instant. "I still hold your heart."

"No!"

"You can't lie to me. Not after what we just shared. I know the truth."

How could she have given so much away with a single kiss? She couldn't bear it, couldn't stand to have him that intimately aware of her deepest, most guarded feelings.

"Please let me go, Rafe," she begged, knowing the words were futile even as she uttered them. Clearly, he'd already determined the path their future would take.

He had no intention of releasing her.

"I can't," he said, confirming her worst fears. "I can't allow you to marry another. It would be dishonest, the marriage a sham. He would come to hate you for it. You must realize that?"

Her throat closed over and she shook her head, incapable of speech.

"Listen to me," he insisted. "What exists between us is something neither of us planned. When I came here tonight, I didn't expect to look at you and feel what I do." Shadows carved his face into harsh, uncompromising lines. "Can you think otherwise?"

"No," she agreed tightly. "I'm sure you didn't attend the ball because you still had a romantic interest in me."

"Just as I can presume that when you decided to find someone of your own this evening, you believed what was between us had ended long ago." His wry expression acknowledged the vagaries of fate. "But it hasn't. It's still there."

Tears of defeat gathered in her eyes. She'd lost. She'd sworn she'd give the Cinderella Ball a final chance, that she'd give love a final chance. And in one devastating move, Rafe had stolen that possibility from her.

"So what happens now?"

"It's quite simple. We take the same path all the other guests follow in a situation like ours. We marry."

He'd suggested as much before, but she still couldn't believe he was serious. Her hands tightened around the unyielding muscles of his arms. He was pure, indomitable strength, she a fragile barrier in his pathway. Still, she had to summon the fortitude to stop him, to prevent him from carelessly doing that which could not be later undone.

"No, Rafe. It wouldn't work."

"It would. It's practical. Logical. And I promise . . ." His mouth feathered across hers in a tantalizing caress. But even as he wrung a helpless response, his lips were gone, leaving her frustrated and unfulfilled. "I promise, you'll find our marriage quite satisfying."

She looked down so she wouldn't be swayed by the desire that turned his eyes to silver flames. She had to fight him, had to alter the course he'd set. "After all that's occurred in the past, how can you even suggest that we build a future together?"

"This is the Cinderella Ball. A night of fantasy and magic and miracles," he had the nerve to remind. "I thought that meant anything was possible."

"With another man, perhaps," she flung back. "But not with you. You don't believe in fantasy or magic, let alone miracles."

"I'm here, aren't I?"

"You didn't come because you wanted what the Cinderella Ball had to offer. You came here to cause trouble. Well, congratulations. You've succeeded."

He gathered her in his arms, tucking her head in the hollow of his shoulder. He'd held her like this more times than she could count. But never had it seemed so right, so natural. His touch felt more solicitous than provocative, the overt sexuality still there, though muted. And while his kiss had successfully destroyed most of her defenses, his tenderness reached far deeper, to the inner core she'd hoped he'd never breach.

"*Amada,* don't you understand that we have no choice? You may have wished to find a husband, but it wouldn't have worked. You say you believe in the magic tonight brings to special couples. Can you not believe that magic was meant for us, as well? Is it not possible that, regardless of what prompted me to come, the end result was preordained? We were meant to be together."

She lifted her head, forcing herself to reject what little comfort he offered. "If you were a different sort of man, I might believe such a thing could happen. I've always considered the Cinderella Ball capable of changing any man." She broke off, deciding for once to choose wisdom over valor.

A bleak emptiness settled over Rafe's rigid features, like winter over a barren plain. "Finish it," he ordered. "This night can change any man. Any man, except me?"

She looked at him unflinchingly, sorrow dimming the brilliance of her gaze. "Yes, Rafe. Except you. You're too hard. Too ruthless and self-contained. You don't trust anyone. You keep suspicion as your constant companion and hold all emotion at bay."

The first natural smile of the evening broke through his grim facade, the sheer beauty of it only adding to her misery. "But, you haven't mentioned any of my faults. There must be one or two you can think of."

"You see?" She attempted to lever herself off the brick wall of his chest. "What I consider negatives, you see as positives."

"A most fortunate circumstance." He tucked her back into the curve of his shoulder. "It'll bring balance to our relationship."

She gave up the struggle to win her freedom and relaxed against him. Her could only hope sober reasoning countered the intoxication of desire. "I'm serious about this, Rafe. You're a man without faith and I haven't enough for the both of us. I couldn't bear the eventual outcome."

He lifted an eyebrow. "And what outcome is that?"

"That once you'd satisfied your curiosity, you'd be furious with yourself—and with me—for allowing moonlit madness to overrule common sense."

"Curiosity?" Sudden anger rippled through him and his hand sought the swell of her breast, carefully palming its weight. "You think this is mere curiosity?" he countered. His gaze held hers as his thumb grazed the straining tip. "You can't be that innocent, *amada*."

The breath exploded from her lungs in short, uneven bursts. Heaven protect her, but his touch awakened a deep, helpless yearning. She fought for control, to conceal the torturous craving he'd stirred to life, a craving that stripped away the thin veneer of civilized behavior. She grasped his wrist, tugging futilely. She couldn't think when he touched her, and he knew it. Knew it and used her defenselessness to emphasize his point.

"This isn't fair!" she protested. "I don't deny that I want you. How can I?"

A blistering fever raged deep in his eyes, one that matched her own. "You can't. It's as evident as my desire for you." He urged her tight within the cradle of his thighs to prove his point. "And it makes me just as vulnerable."

Ella gathered what remained of her inner resources. She had to stand firm. To give so much as an inch invited disaster. "That doesn't change the facts," she argued. "And the fact is that if we married you'd wake up one morning and realize sex hasn't rid you of your anger. You'd feel trapped and you'd resent me. Little by little your resentment would grow until it consumed every aspect of our lives. Don't you understand? I couldn't live like that, waiting for the inevitable to happen. I think it would destroy me."

Tension radiated from him. "You see far too clearly," he whispered.

"Then you'll end this?" Emotion threatened to choke her, relief vying with disappointment. "You'll let me go?"

She could see the debate seething within, his face drawn taut from the effort. Slowly he shook his head, an air of implacability cloaking him. "If you had no feelings for me, I might consider it. Despite what you think, I couldn't force myself on you." He'd come to a decision, she realized, a decision she didn't have a hope of altering. "But that isn't the case."

"You would sacrifice our future for a momentary pleasure?" She tried one final time.

His expression turned fatalistic. "The moment is all we have. No one knows what tomorrow will bring. You predict only one possible future."

"The most likely one."

He didn't deny it. "I will not allow you to marry another," he replied instead.

His calm assertion infuriated her. "You won't allow? How do you plan to stop me?"

"Suffice to say, I will prevent it."

"But, I have to marry tonight!" The words were out before she could stop them, revealing far too much by the passion they contained and by the depth of despair they reflected.

He stilled, fixing her with the full force of his attention. "Marrying tonight can't be that important."

This time she kept carefully silent.

His brows snapped together. *"Dios!* It is that important to you. Why, *amada?* Why is it so vital you find a husband?"

"It's none of your business, Rafe. It stopped being your business a long time ago."

His anger dissipated, replaced by a tenderness which almost proved her undoing. "I regret to inform you, that has now changed."

"Don't do this to me, Rafe. Please."

"What is wrong?" he questioned gently. "Why this urgency to leap into marriage?"

"You wouldn't understand." She made a helpless gesture. "I have to find a husband tonight, that's all."

"You *have* to?" A frown creased his brow and he caught her shoulders, holding her at arm's length. The lines beside his mouth deepened as his eagle-eyed gaze swept her from head to toe. "You are with child? You must find a father? Is that why you're so anxious to marry tonight?"

"No, of course not!"

His tension dissipated. "I'm relieved to hear it. A baby would complicate matters."

"Because you wouldn't want to raise another man's child?"

He shrugged philosophically. "By the time you gave birth, the baby would be ours, regardless of how it came to be conceived."

His casual acceptance of such a possibility caught her by surprise. "Then—"

"The complication arises from the problems that still exist between us," he explained patiently. "We have enough on our plate to deal with, don't you think?"

She couldn't deny it. "Yes."

"Enough, Ella. It's time to come to a decision. If you wish to acquire a husband this evening, there's only one possible solution. We will marry. If, on the other hand, you feel there is too much between us, then I'll walk away. I leave it up to you."

"And if I elect to marry someone else?"

His eyes darkened to a steely gray. "It won't happen."

It would be pointless to argue further. No matter how hard she fought to deny it, he was right. She couldn't bring herself to marry another. Not after seeing Rafe, being held and kissed by him. That just left one final determination.

Did she marry Rafe or commit herself to a life alone?

As though aware of the dilemma she faced, he released her and stepped backward. If he'd said it aloud, he couldn't have made his feelings any clearer. The choice was hers. He wouldn't try and sway her any more than he had already.

The surrounding darkness enclosed him in a tight embrace. She could still make out his silhouette, tall and lean and muscular. But his features remained shrouded, only his quicksilver eyes glittering from the black depths of the night. They held her with a steady calmness, already accepting her verdict.

If she refused him, he'd walk away and she knew with an instinctive certainty she'd never see him again.

And if she accepted him? How would her life change? For it would change, there could be no question about that.

She closed her eyes. In the end all that mattered was one vital fact. She loved Rafe, loved him with all her heart and soul. The Cinderella Ball had wrought its magic after all, offering her a final opportunity to discover happily-ever-after. Now it was up to her to take advantage of that opportunity. She just had to reach out and accept what Rafe offered. Just reach out.

Slowly she opened her eyes, her decision made.

"Yes, Rafe," she whispered, extending her hand. "I'll marry you."

Chapter Three

Once Ella agreed to marry Rafe, he didn't give her a single second to reconsider. Perhaps he didn't dare. Sweeping from the shadows, he captured her hand and escorted her toward the bright lights of the house.

It was late, Ella realized in surprise, taking note of the almost deserted garden. Far later than she'd suspected. The crowd had thinned during the time she'd been secluded in the glade, until only a trickle of couples remained. She peeked at Rafe. Thank heavens he hadn't been serious about finding a wife among the guests. The choices would have been limited.

As limited as her choices for a husband, came the disconcerting thought.

"Where do we marry?" he questioned briskly, as they entered the dining room and skirted the buffet tables.

"We have to get a license first. There's a county clerk stationed in the library with the necessary applications." She cast a wistful glance at the wide selection of delicacies they bypassed. Nerves had prevented her from eating very much today and she was beginning to feel the effects. Perhaps she could nibble after they were married. She slanted another look at Rafe's set features.

Or perhaps not.

Rafe hesitated outside the dining room to get his bearings and then turned down the appropriate hallway. Opening the door to the library, he ushered her inside. They found the county clerk stationed behind a massive oak desk wearing a name tag that read, Dora Scott. In front of her she'd propped a sign that had originally announced, "For faster service, feed me hors d'oeuvres." But at some point during the evening, the word "don't" had been squeezed in as an afterthought and underscored twice in heavy black ink. And beneath that she'd written, "Under penalty of not receiving a license."

Rafe studied the sign and grinned. "Don't feed you hors d'oeuvres? You're certain?"

Dora returned his smile, falling for his charm as thoroughly as every other woman Ella had ever known. "Not if you want my help. That sign seemed like a brilliant idea at the beginning of the evening. But as the night's worn on, it's drifted from brilliant to uncomfortable to downright nauseating."

"Perhaps we could arrange for something to ease your problem," Rafe suggested. "Would that be acceptable?"

The clerk sighed in relief. "You take care of that for me and I'll have your forms processed in triple time."

"Done."

Rafe crossed to speak to one of the white and gold liveried attendants stationed in the hallway. While he made the arrangements, Dora whipped through her paperwork. By the time she'd finished, a small bottle of pink medicine rested at her elbow.

"You're a lifesaver," she told Rafe gratefully. She held out a blue and white envelope. "Give these forms to whomever officiates at your wedding ceremony. There's a souvenir certificate inside that you can keep. But it's not real. That comes later in the mail."

"Thanks for your help," Ella murmured.

Dora fixed her with a curious gaze. "You're the Montagues' daughter, aren't you?"

A flush mounted Ella's cheeks. "I guess the application I filled out makes it a dead giveaway, doesn't it? A name like mine has a tendency to stand out."

"It is rather unusual," Dora acknowledged with a sympathetic smile. "Will your parents be surprised when they discover you're getting married?"

Ella glanced uncertainly in Rafe's direction. "You could say that."

Shocked and horrified might be closer to the truth. When she'd agreed to marry, she hadn't taken their reaction into consideration. Now she wondered how on earth she'd explain it to them.

But then, maybe it wouldn't be so difficult after all. They knew how she felt about Rafe. They had every confidence in the magic of the Cinderella Ball. And more than anything, they wanted her to be happy. Besides, it would only take three simple words to reassure them: *I love him.*

Once she'd told them that, their fears would be allayed.

"Well, good luck to you," Dora was saying. "I'll give you one piece of advice before you go, if you don't mind." She grinned. "Or even if you do mind."

"Which is?" Rafe asked.

"Do right by each other and you can't fail."

For a fleeting instant darkness shadowed Rafe's features. And then it was gone. "Sound advice," he said in an equitable tone. But the words sounded as short and clipped as exploding bullets.

"I thought so, or I wouldn't have offered it. Now go get married and let me polish off this pink stuff." Dora brightened. "If it works, maybe I can enjoy some more appetizers."

Laughing at her expression, Ella slipped a hand in Rafe's and left the library.

"Where do we go next?" he asked.

She hesitated, her brows drawing together in response to the terse nature of his question. What had happened to upset him? she wondered in dismay. He'd been fine until . . .

Until Dora had advised that they do right by each other. Would that advice be so difficult to take? Did the memory of past events still stir his anger? Did he still blame her for what had happened to Shayne?

"We go upstairs," she finally said. "The wedding ceremonies are conducted in the salons off the ballroom." She slowed her steps, forcing him to slow down, as well. "Rafe, we don't have to go through with this. No one is forcing us to marry. If you need more time to consider, I won't be upset."

"We're getting married. *Now.*" He indicated an archway. "Through here?"

"Yes," she confirmed, realizing the futility of any further discussion.

He didn't speak again until they'd reached the appropriate rooms and even then it was only to say, "We appear to have a choice of services."

"Any kind you'd like. We'd hoped to make the occasion as special as possible by offering a full selection. Something the couples would remember for the rest of their lives."

"I imagine it would be difficult for them to forget," he murmured. "Let's try this room."

He thrust open the first door and stepped inside. Ella followed, her breath catching in dismay. Her family called this the Blue Room, an elegant, rather formal parlor filled with dried flower displays, walnut end tables, and blue silk-covered furniture. In front of the drawn drapes stood a podium behind which a justice of the peace conducted a generic wedding ceremony.

Rafe shot her a quick look. "What is it?"

Was she that easy to read? "Nothing," she insisted with a shrug.

He muttered a nasty-sounding word in Spanish, something she suspected she was better off not understanding. "I don't believe you, Ella," he stated flatly. "Tell me what bothers you."

"It's just . . ." She released a tiny sigh. "It's just that whenever my Great Aunt Mavis visited, we'd all come in here to talk."

"It brings back uncomfortable memories?"

"Only because I had to be so *good.*"

His expression lightened unexpectedly. "I can see where that must have been a strain."

She made a small face. "Don't laugh. I had to sit on the edge of that couch with my back straight, my hands folded in my lap and my ankles crossed for hours on end. Talk about torture! You try doing that at five years of age."

"At five I was hunting jaguars with my friends in the jungles of Costa Rica."

Shock held her rigid. "Your parents allowed you to do that?"

"There was only my father. My mother had died a number of years earlier and he hadn't yet remarried."

She glanced at him, curious. "I remember Shayne mentioning them. Your father came from Texas, didn't he?"

"A Texan with French grandparents. An interesting combination, don't you think? My mother was half Tico. Costa Rican. I've always suspected my father escaped from his former life by marrying her. All I know for certain is he didn't give a damn about anything, except growing coffee."

"That's why Spanish is your first language, isn't it?" she guessed shrewdly.

He shrugged. "It was the predominate language spoken." Before she could ask any more questions, he drew her from the room. "Since this place has such bad memories, we'll go elsewhere."

He opened the door to the next salon and Ella stared in disbelief. "When did my parents do this?" she marveled, crossing the threshold. "It's like we've stepped into a different era."

"Do you like it?"

"It's beautiful."

And it was. Huge wrought-iron holders stood in all four corners of the room, studded with thick white candles. Heavy chains held a chandelier made from a wooden wheel hub suspended from the ceiling. The only lighting in the room came from the massive stone fireplace and the countless candles scattered atop every available surface. They walked further into the room, the wide oak-pegged flooring echoing with each step they took. Between the tapestries hanging from the wall and the weaponry mounted above the mantel, it felt as though they'd wandered into a scene from the Middle Ages.

A minister rose from his seat by the stone hearth, the lenses of his wire-rim glasses reflecting the firelight. "Good evening and welcome. Would you like to be married?"

To Ella's relief, the tension faded from Rafe's face. Whatever concerns had plagued him earlier had apparently been laid to rest. "Yes, we would," he replied. "But we need a minute first." Not waiting for a response, he drew her off to one side.

"Is there something wrong?" she asked.

"You know what's wrong, *amada*. We can't marry like this. You'd always regret it."

She hardly dared ask. "My parents?"

"They should be here," he confirmed. "Would you like to send someone to notify them?"

"You're certain you don't mind?"

"I don't approve of their decision to hold another Cinderella Ball after what happened last time. But they should be present when their only daughter marries."

Tears pricked her eyes. "Thank you, Rafe. I'll send for them right away."

He turned back to the minister and surrendered the envelope Dora Scott had given him. "We'll marry as soon as the Montagues arrive."

After sending the message, Ella came to stand at his side. "They should be here in just a few minutes."

The minister inclined his head. "Very well. Before we begin, I'm required to ask that you give careful consideration to what you're about to do." His gentle blue gaze held theirs with grave deliberation. "Marriage is a serious commitment, requiring serious thought and consideration. So while we wait for the Montagues, I ask that you face each other and look at your partner. Make sure that your choice is the right one."

Ella turned to Rafe, surprised by his stoic expression. He held perfectly still, his features carved into harsh lines, his eyes a dark, stormy gray. And he waited, as if braced for a blow. It was almost as though he expected her to change her mind. Which was ridiculous. She never would. She tilted her head to one side and studied him. Or perhaps he didn't fear her changing her mind so much as . . .

The truth struck with stunning force. He worried that standing in such a reverent setting she'd finally see what lay behind the mask he held up to the world.

She almost laughed aloud. Didn't he realize? Didn't he suspect? She'd seen behind that mask long ago.

He was an intriguing combination of elements, his singular background laying the foundation for the diverse set of qualities that had forged him into a man. When it came to his half-sister, Shayne, she saw someone of compassion and integrity. A concerned brother who would do anything to protect the one he loved.

But she'd also seen the ruthless streak in him. She'd learned from hard experience he prowled through life like a lone wolf, wary of his fellow man, constantly on the alert for threat or weakness. Few dared cross him and those who did paid a stiff penalty. The fact he didn't forgive easily made their marriage all the more surprising. For to marry her he had to first come to terms with their past.

Still, that didn't change one small fact.

Over five years ago she'd fallen in love with him, flaws and all, and nothing he'd said or done since had altered that.

She offered Rafe a reassuring smile. "I know the sort of man you are and I'm still willing to marry you."

Rafe froze, his hands knotting into fists. If she'd slapped him full in the face, he couldn't have been more stunned.

What the hell did she mean? She knew the sort of man he was? Did she suspect? Had she figured out his plan? If so, why would she still be willing to marry him? She couldn't be so foolish as to ignore the ramifications.

Once married, he'd keep her only so long as their passion burned hot. He'd prove to her once and for all that happily-ever-after lasted for about *cinco minutos* and not a damned second longer.

He'd make it clear that what they felt was lust, no more.

He'd fought for five long years to weed this woman from his life. And like some sort of tenacious vine, she'd wrapped herself around his heart and soul and held on with a strength that baffled him. Vines like that were dangerous. They didn't allow for mobility. Their roots sank deep into the earth while their tendrils burrowed through brick, stone, and mortar, crumbling any and all resistance.

Still, that didn't change one small fact.

He wanted her. It was wrong. He'd regret his actions one day, he didn't doubt that for a moment. And that he'd pay an eternal penalty for the crime he intended to commit he accepted as just and proper. But at least he'd have brought closure to their relationship. Bitterness burned like acid in his belly. Why bother with lies? He wanted revenge as badly as he wanted Ella. Through marriage, he'd get both. Only one thing troubled him.

Looking into her clear golden eyes, seeing the sweet dreams that sparkled within their depths, he realized he couldn't exact that sort of revenge. For Shayne's sake, he had to bring a certain death to any future Cinderella Balls. But to destroy Ella in the process—

"We're here!" Henrietta bustled into the room, Donald following behind at a slower pace. She drew to an abrupt halt when she saw Rafe. "Oh, dear," she murmured faintly. "Mr. Beaumont! What a . . . what a surprise."

Rafe inclined his head. "Mrs. Montague."

"What are you doing here?" Donald demanded with far less civility.

Before Rafe could reply and end a situation fast becoming a farce, Ella stepped into the breach, catching his hand in hers. "He came for me. We're going to be married and he asked that you join us."

"*Amada,* perhaps this isn't such a—"

"*You* asked that we witness the ceremony?" Donald interrupted sharply. "Not my daughter?"

Rafe shrugged. "To exclude you would have made Ella unhappy. And I prefer her wedding be a pleasant memory."

Donald didn't appear convinced, but Henrietta breathed a sigh of relief. "It's a dream come true," she exclaimed. "It's what I've prayed for with all my heart."

And just like that, completely counter to what Rafe had anticipated, the Montagues gave their full approval. He closed his eyes in exasperation as the two descended on Ella, sweeping her into their arms for tearful hugs and kisses. When they'd finished with her, they turned to him. Henrietta gave him a warm embrace before linking arms with her daughter and crossing to the far side of the room for a private conversation.

Donald offered his hand. "I'm relieved all this nonsense is over between us," he said gruffly. "You almost broke Ella's heart holding her responsible for Shayne's actions."

"I still hold her responsible," Rafe retorted. "Don't think this marriage changes my views on that. Nor have I changed my mind about the Cinderella Ball. I marry your daughter in spite of these objections."

Donald remained silent for a long moment, his steady gaze holding Rafe's. "I think I understand," he murmured at last. "You regard this marriage as a means to several ends, don't you?"

Montague's insight didn't come as a surprise. As foolishly blind as he might be about the Cinderella Ball, he was still an intelligent man, aware that a person's nature contained as many flaws as strong points. As clearly as he saw those positive aspects, he also saw the negative. Saw and accepted?

"You understand?" Rafe emphasized, folding his arms across his chest. "All of it?"

Donald released his breath in a long sigh. "Yes, Mr. Beaumont. I'm afraid so. You wish to have my daughter as well as your revenge."

"That's more than your daughter knows. You realize that, don't you?"

"She's in love with you. She's also a woman who prefers to see only the good in people. She undoubtedly hopes the good in you will overcome your need for vengeance. I, on the other hand, am more realistic."

Rafe lifted an eyebrow. It would seem that Ella's father truly did discern his reasons for marrying. "How do you intend to use this knowledge?"

"Dad?" Ella interrupted uneasily, leaving her mother to join their conversation. "Is something wrong?"

Donald slid an arm around his daughter's shoulders and dropped a reassuring kiss on her brow. "Nothing at all. Just renewing my acquaintance with your husband-to-be. Sweetheart, would you mind sending for refreshments?"

"Champagne?" she suggested.

"That would be perfect." He waited until she'd moved out of earshot before continuing. "And to answer your question, Mr. Beaumont—"

"Rafe."

"If you prefer," Montague allowed. "What I plan to do is quite simple. I plan to celebrate my daughter's marriage."

"That's all?" Rafe frowned. "Now I am confused. You will stand by and say nothing?"

Donald's regard held calm resignation. "Believe me, I understand what you hope to get out of this marriage. Whether you succeed or not is another story."

"Do you doubt it?" Incredulity laced his question.

"Yes, as a matter of fact I do," came the composed reply. "Because there's something you've neglected to take into consideration."

The older man's assurance gave Rafe pause. Had he forgotten some vital point, missed some minor detail that Montague had spotted? He swiftly analyzed every aspect of his plan, searching for the hidden flaw. His eyes narrowed. There was nothing he hadn't already anticipated.

Nevertheless, wisdom dictated he be certain. "What have I overlooked?"

"You've neglected to consider that the head doesn't always rule the heart. If it did, you wouldn't be marrying my daughter."

It took every ounce of restraint for Rafe to maintain his cool. Fury simmered through his veins, desperate for an outlet. "You are mistaken," he snapped. "I never allow emotion to influence my decisions."

Ella's father inclined his head. "In that case, I look forward to having this conversation again at the Anniversary Ball. By then we'll both know who's correct."

Rafe stiffened. "What Anniversary Ball?"

"I assumed you knew," Donald said in surprise. "One year from tonight all the guests who wed are invited to return to celebrate their first anniversary with us. It's a tradition."

In a lightning-swift move, Rafe pivoted to insure Ella didn't overhear their conversation. "Shayne?" he demanded softly. "She knew of this ball?"

Compassion darkened Donald's gaze. "I'm sorry, Rafe. She did."

"That's where she was going the night . . . ?"

"I'm sorry," Montague repeated, regret and sincerity implicit in his voice. "If it's any consolation I swear to you that Ella didn't know of those plans. We heard about the accident after the fact, but decided not to tell her."

"I half expected Ella to call," Rafe admitted. "Not that I would have put her through to my sister."

"And Shayne? I heard she's recovered. How is she doing?"

"As well as can be expected." It wasn't a precise answer, but it was the best he could give.

"I hope you understand why we didn't tell Ella. It wouldn't have solved anything, only added to her burden." A hint of censure crept into his tone. "It's a burden she's carried for five years. Undeservedly so."

Rafe just stared at him. He felt cold, as cold as an arctic wasteland. When would he get it right? When would he save those in his care instead of destroying them? He couldn't stop his gaze from tangling with Ella's. She was a pure golden flame, promising to warm even the most frozen heart. His teeth clenched so hard his jaw ached. There was only one small problem. To warm a heart, there first had to be a heart.

"I cannot do this," he whispered.

"You *can* do it. And you *will* do it," Donald retorted in a forceful undertone. "Oh, don't look so shocked, my boy. I have my own reasons for wanting to see this marriage go through."

Rafe stared rigidly ahead. "Which are?"

"She wants you. Why, I can't say. But not once has her love faltered over the past five years. Can you claim as much?"

"You know my plans," Rafe said, ignoring the question. "So you must realize this marriage will not fulfill her dreams."

"That's a possibility, one I'll deal with if it happens."

"When it happens."

"Perhaps. Time will tell."

Rafe kept his gaze fixed on Ella. "Then so be it. You will accept the consequences of your inaction?" he queried in a stony voice.

"Just as you'll have to accept the consequences of your action."

Rafe inclined his head in acknowledgment and without another word, crossed to Ella's side. "You may begin," he informed the minister, capturing her hand in his.

The ceremony turned out to be relatively painless. The only glitch occurred when it came time to exchange rings. "I'm sorry, *amada.* I don't have a ring for you," Rafe confessed.

Ella nodded as though she'd anticipated as much. "You didn't plan to marry when you came here."

He refused to lie. "No."

"We have rings on hand," the minister offered. "You could use them until you're able to purchase the genuine article."

After a momentary hesitation, Ella shook her head. "If it's all the same to you, I'd rather not."

Reaching into the folds of her gown, she pulled out a thin golden rectangle—one of the tickets to the ball. The truth struck Rafe, as undeniable as it was painful. She held his ticket. Before she'd ever discovered the purpose of his visit, she'd stolen the gilded wafer from the basket as a keepsake.

He knew then what she intended to suggest, knew and wanted to shout a harsh refusal. But he couldn't. He couldn't be that cruel. For her sweet act left behind a crushing impression. No one had ever made such a romantic gesture before. Not for him. He fought a silent battle between a restless yearning for the impossible and bitter acceptance of the actual, struggling all the while to maintain an impassive front.

Heaven protect him from sentimental angels.

Ella warmed the ticket between her palms for a long minute then glanced at him. "Do you happen to have your pocketknife with you?"

"In my tux?"

His irony didn't divert her. She simply smiled. "If memory serves, you carry it everywhere."

Giving in without further protest, he reached into his jacket pocket and removed the folded knife. "Is there something I can help you with?" he asked politely.

Anticipation turned her eyes the color of sunlit honey. "Yes, please. Could you cut this ticket into two, one piece a little larger than the other?"

"And then?"

"I'm hoping they'll be malleable enough to roll into rings," she said with devastating simplicity.

A sharp pain twisted in the vicinity of his chest. "I'll see what I can do." He glanced at the minister and indicated the ballpoint pen lying on a nearby table. "Would you mind?"

"Please. Help yourself."

Unscrewing the pen, he removed the copper ink cartridge. His blade made short shrift of slicing the ticket in two, but the metal wasn't pliable enough to bend. Crossing to one of the candles scattered about the room, he utilized the scissor accessory on his knife to hold the smaller half of the ticket above the flame. In no time the metal had softened enough to mold. Using the thin ink cartridge as a guide, he rolled the ticket into a neat cylinder. A final twist curled it into a finger-sized circle.

"Perfect," Ella whispered in delight. "Now make the other half of the ticket into a wedding band for yourself."

He started to refuse, wanting to reject such a touching request. But looking into her face and seeing her anxious expression, stopped him cold. What did it matter if he wore a ring? Let her enjoy the moment, let her revel in all the small marital rituals, meaningless as they were. It wouldn't change the eventual outcome. It would only add greater impact to the lesson she'd soon learn.

Without a word, he fashioned the second ring and gave it to her. He couldn't bring himself to look at his bride as she placed it on his finger, though. His instinct for self-preservation was too strong for that. Instead he focused his full attention on the odd-looking ring. It burned into his finger like a brand. It must still be hot from the flame, he tried to tell himself, knowing all the while that it had cooled long ago or he'd never have allowed Ella to touch it.

As though from a distance he heard the minister impart the solemn vows. Heard a sweet, joyous voice repeat them, followed by another voice, one lower and rougher. Then the ceremony ended and Ella Montague no longer stood by his side, but his wife.

Ella Beaumont.

"You may kiss the bride," the minister prompted with a smile, his bright blue eyes glittering from behind his glasses.

Rafe gathered his wife's face between his hands, intent on bringing a swift end to the ceremony. He had no problem with this part of the ritual. He'd have preferred a little more privacy, but he schooled himself to patience. He could wait until they returned to his suite at the Grand to bring this night to its natural conclusion.

He lowered his head to deliver a swift, hard kiss. But instead of taking her mouth in a stamp of ownership, he found himself bestowing a kiss of infinite tenderness. She opened like a flower to the heat of the sun and like a hungry bee, he chased after her sweetness.

In that instant, he felt his control slip.

With a half-bitten exclamation, he released her and stepped back, furious with himself for letting down his guard for even so brief a moment.

Ella gazed at him in confusion. "Rafe?"

"My apologies, *amada,*" he said roughly. "I got carried away. If you would say goodbye to your parents, we should go."

He silently endured another round of hugs and kisses, his tension mounting with each passing moment. If he didn't escape soon, he'd explode. He dragged air into his lungs, willing himself to hold on for the few remaining minutes before they could leave.

At the door, Donald offered his hand again. "I'll be interested to see which wins in this game you've started," he said as a farewell. "Your head or your heart."

Rafe flashed him a look of grim warning. "You would be foolish to bet on the heart."

"For my daughter's sake, I hope you're wrong."

"For your daughter's sake, you should hope I'm right," he growled in reply.

With that, he dropped a possessive arm around Ella's shoulders and swept her from the room.

Chapter Four

"The suite is beautiful," Ella informed Rafe.

She glanced at him from beneath her lashes, wondering for the umpteenth time if he'd begun to doubt the wisdom of their marriage. He'd barely spoken a word since they'd arrived at the Grand Hotel.

He didn't reply and she suspected private demons consumed him to the point he hadn't heard her comment. Yanking at the bow tie constricting his throat, he prowled a sitting area that would have been spacious if not for his presence.

She crossed the room, joining him as he came to a restless halt in front of the floor-to-ceiling windows. The full moon had begun a slow descent, gilding the desert's stark features with silver. She turned from its cool beauty to confront the far starker features of the man beside her.

"What's wrong, Rafe?"

He rested his forearm against the plate-glass window and stared blindly at the surrounding landscape. "Your father puzzles me," he said at last.

She sighed in relief. So it wasn't their marriage that troubled him, but something her father had said. "I noticed you two were having a rather intense conversation before the wedding."

"I thought he would stop the ceremony," Rafe stated unexpectedly.

Nervous dread feathered a path along her spine. "Did you hope he would?"

"No."

"Then why—"

He swung around to confront her, folding his arms across his chest. He'd opened the top portion of his dress shirt and the soft cotton parting to reveal the bronzed skin beneath. A thin white scar sliced across the left side of his collarbone, snagging her attention. It hadn't been there five years ago.

Before she could ask about his injury, he said, "I thought he'd stop the ceremony in order to protect you."

She blinked in surprise. "Protect me? From what?"

His shoulders lifted in a casual shrug, but his eyes glittered darkly, seething with a desperate intensity. "Protect you from the man you planned to marry. Who else?"

Her gaze cut to the scar again and she frowned. "He knows as well as I that you'd never hurt me."

The bitterness of his laughter shocked her. "You don't honestly believe that, do you?"

She met his gaze with a calm assurance that came from the very bottom of her soul. "Did you marry me in order to hurt me?"

"I married you because I want you," came his oblique reply. He swallowed the distance between them, catching her arm in an iron grip. "I married you because it was the only way I could get you in my bed. The only way to keep you there until we'd had our fill of one another."

Her eyebrows shot upward. "Our fill? You mean making love is like quenching a thirst or—"

"Or sating a hunger," he interrupted forcefully. "Yes."

"I don't know about you, but a while after I've eaten I'm hungry again," she dared to tease.

"Don't mock me," he warned through gritted teeth. "Do you think I have never desired a woman before? Do you think I have not taken her to my bed and, once satisfied, left without a backward glance?"

She tilted her head to one side. "No. As a matter of fact I don't believe that. The affair may have ended because you weren't right for each other, but you'd never just take what you wanted and then leave. Not without making sure she was satisfied, as well."

"Do not shape me into someone I am not!" His accent deepened. "It will make the truth that much harder to endure."

"What truth are you referring to? That once we've made love, that's it? It's all over?" She laughed, genuinely amused. "Do you think our feelings for each other are so superficial?"

"Si! No hay duda."

She wondered if he realized he'd answered in Spanish. Probably not. It only happened when he came under extreme duress. In fact, she'd only witnessed his losing control to that extent once before—which meant he considered this issue serious. Very serious.

"Did my father know you felt this way?" she asked. "Is that why he should have stopped the wedding?"

Rafe swung around, the edge of his fist hammering against the window casing. The glass shuddered beneath the impact. "He knew why I married you and still he stood by and did nothing. Why? *Why* would he do that?"

She thought carefully before answering. "Perhaps because he loved me and wanted what was best for me."

"No! That is not right." A muscle jerked in his cheek and he stabbed his index finger in the air to emphasize his point. "If he loved you, he would have dragged you from that room. He would have taken you as far from me as physically possible."

"But, why?"

"So I could not hurt you." He thrust a hand through his hair. "Don't you understand? He must make sure that no harm comes to you. It is his duty. His responsibility. Why does he shirk it?"

For some reason her father's actions, or rather, inaction, infuriated Rafe. And though the reason for that fury eluded her, she felt an obligation to try and explain her father's point of view on the subject.

"You must realize that I'm a grown woman," she began.

His eyes flashed in dark amusement. "I have noticed."

"Then you must also realize I make my own choices and my own decisions. Dad knows that, just as he knows if my choices are wrong, I'll learn from them."

He made a sound of disgust. "Does he stand aside and allow you to wander into the path of an oncoming truck, confident in the knowledge that once it hits, you'll have learned not to make such a mistake again?" His sarcasm intensified. "Of course, you are injured beyond repair, but no doubt you have learned your lesson."

"Are you comparing yourself to a truck?" she asked. Despite his anger, a smile tugged at her mouth.

He set his jaw. "In this case, yes."

"It certainly makes for an intriguing image," she murmured. Not giving him an opportunity to vent a reply, she hastened to say, "Seriously, Rafe. My father will always be there to comfort me when I need it. But he can't wrap me in cotton wool in the hopes that I'll never injure myself. It would be pointless. He can't look after me every minute of every day. He can only do his best."

Rafe closed his eyes, visibly waging an inner war. She waited patiently until he looked at her again. The darkness had fled from his gaze, at least for the moment, and his eyes had turned from blackest slate to a brilliant silver-gray. He reached out and cupped her cheek, tracing her lower lip with the rough surface of his thumb.

"I could not do as your father has," he told her. "I could not stand aside while one I cared for was threatened."

"You're not a threat," she repeated.

His mouth twisted into a self-derisive smile. "And you, *amada,* are far too innocent. Too trusting."

"Because I believe in you?" She shook her head, her steady regard never wavering. "You're my husband. I'd trust you with my life."

A sigh shuddered from the depths of his chest. "Then heaven protect you, for I cannot."

"I don't need heaven's protection. All I need is you."

He drew her into his arms, the tenderness of his touch betraying far more about his true nature than he realized. Lowering his head, he rested his jaw against her temple. "Have you any idea what I have planned for you?" His words brushed the side of her face in a feather-light caress. "Do you?"

When had her ear become so sensitive? she wondered hazily. Or was it Rafe that made it so? "What have you planned?"

He nuzzled the side of her neck beneath her earlobe, warming the sensitive skin with his breath. "I plan to hold you in my arms while I strip away every scrap of your clothing."

A smile trembled on her lips. "How shocking. And then?"

"Then I'll carry you to the bed. And there I'll make you mine while the moon and stars look on."

"I see why you thought I needed protection," Ella whispered. "It sounds like a fate worse than death."

She slid her hands into the thick blackness of his hair and gave in to the temptation that had plagued her from the moment she'd set eyes on him. Pressing her mouth against the hollow of his throat, she tasted his unique flavor.

He tilted back his head to give her greater access. "Ah, *amada*," he muttered harshly. "I will regret this night. I will pay a thousandfold for what I do to you."

"Why such a steep price?" Hunger gave her voice a husky edge. "When it's what I want, too."

"Be very certain," he warned.

"I've never been more positive of anything in my entire life. Is that certain enough for you?"

He didn't need any further urging. The single shoulder strap of her Grecian-style gown parted beneath his hand and the bodice drifted to her waist, baring her. For a brief instant, a virginal fear kept her frozen in place. Then her breath escaped in a soft rush.

This was Rafe, the man she'd wanted since she'd first learned what it meant to be a woman. She could no more fear him than she could fear the passing of night into day.

"*Dios,*" he breathed. "I am afraid to touch you. My control is shaky, *amada*. Very shaky."

"It's all right. I still trust you."

A near-silent groan spilled from his throat. "That may not be wise."

She stepped free of his embrace intent on proving her words with action. Reaching for the zip at the side of her gown, she tugged it downward. "According to you there's very little I've done this evening that's wise."

"Very little," he concurred, giving her every movement his strictest attention.

"And also according to you, there's little I've done that's smart." For a breathless moment the silk clung to her curves with nothing to hold it up but sheer defiance. He reached for her dress as though itching to lend gravity a helping hand. "Starting with our marriage."

"A bad decision." His graveled response betrayed how close to the edge she'd pushed him.

"And ending with this." Surrendering to the inevitable, her gown drifted to the floor like flaming fingers of gold.

His gaze could no more resist the pull of forces beyond his control than her dress. His breath hissed through his teeth as he looked his fill. "Ending? Oh no, *mi alma,* this is not an ending but a beginning."

She dropped her arms to her sides in a gesture of total faith. "In that case, I leave the rest to you."

"Your first wise decision." He reached for her, stopping mere inches from her breast. His hand quivered ever so slightly and with a muttered curse, he curled it into a fist. "I am but a schoolboy around you. Thank heaven I did not know how little lay beneath this dress."

"Or?"

He didn't evade the truth, but looked her square in the eye. "Or we would have been further delayed in that glade tonight."

"I'm not sure I would have minded."

His mouth tightened. "It would not have mattered if you had," he replied in a clipped, strongly accented voice. "I realize it does not speak well of my self-control. But to have seen you like this and left you untouched?" He shook his head. "It would not have happened."

He opened his hand again. This time his fingers were rock-steady. And when he reached for her, he didn't draw back as before. His eyes contained the silver flash and sizzling heat of summer lightning, his desire like a ferocious storm drawing her into its fiery center. Now it was her turn to tremble, for her thoughts to twist and scatter like leaves in the midst of an autumn gale.

At his first velvety caress, a startled cry escaped before she could prevent it. "Easy," he murmured. "You set the pace. I won't push faster than makes you comfortable. Tell me what you want. Tell me, *esposa.*"

She knew that word, considered it the most beautiful she'd ever heard. *Wife.* "Kiss me, Rafe." She wrapped her arms around his neck. "Just kiss me and I'll know it's all right."

He sank his fingers deep into her hair, pulling the ebony curls free of its elegant knot. "A kiss to make you feel better about what's to happen this night?" he demanded. The silken strands spilled through his open hand like a midnight tide, swirling around her pale shoulders. "Is that what you want from me?"

Did he think her a child in need of reassurance? "No, not a kiss like that," she corrected unsteadily, her mouth teasing the tension from his jawline. "I want the sort of kiss a husband gives his wife on their wedding night. For the first time in my life, I want to experience a lover's kiss. A beginning without end."

The air seeped from his lungs. But instead of his tension easing beneath her tender caress, it increased, communicating itself to her in the tautness of his arms and the heavy beat of his heart. *"Mi amada y mi alma,"* he whispered the husky words. *"Te adoro."*

Then slowly, powerfully, he cupped her bottom in his calloused hands and lifted her against him. Her breasts slid along the soft cotton of his shirt, the friction a delicious torture. It was incredibly erotic, her near-nudity a shocking contrast to his formal attire. For a breathless moment his hot silver gaze lay claim before his mouth captured hers. He held nothing back, rejecting the preliminaries to invade the warm interior, taking her with the desperation of a man too long denied.

Her hunger rose to match his, boundless in its need. She put every last bit of her heart and soul into the kiss they shared, saying with hands and mouth what he'd have rejected if she'd dared to speak aloud. She loved him. Dear heaven, how she loved him.

He released her mouth, seizing her lower lip between his teeth in a brief hungry bite. "Is that the sort of kiss you wanted?"

"It's a start."

She didn't know where she found the presence of mind to goad him. But it had an extraordinary effect. He reacted to the challenge with the swiftness of a hawk swooping toward its prey.

He swept the legs out from under her, lifting her high in his arms. A few rapid strides carried them from the sitting room to the bed. Her high-heeled sandals thudded to the floor at the same instant as her backside hit the mattress. She bounced once before tumbling against the pillows.

He stood over her, his chest heaving beneath his gaping shirt. His eyes burned with an ardent promise that fueled her own painful need. "I've waited an eternity for this. But no longer."

Without a further word, he jerked the gold cufflinks from their holes and dropped them unheeded to the carpet. His shirt and cummerbund followed. And that's when she saw them, a dozen silver scars striping his chest and shoulders. With a shocked gasp, she bounded from the bed and flew into his arms. Now it was her turn to touch him with a shaking hand.

"Oh, Rafe," she murmured sorrowfully, tracing each jagged line with a gentle finger. "What in the world happened to you? Were you in an accident?"

"No."

"But—"

"I witnessed a car crash."

It took a split second to understand. Her gaze shot to his. "Dear heaven. You received these pulling someone from a wreck, didn't you?"

He gathered her close, catching her mouth in a soothing kiss. "Don't give me too much credit. It was Shayne trapped in that wreck. I feared the car would catch fire. If it had been a stranger" He shrugged. "I may have had second thoughts about lending assistance."

Tears leapt to her eyes. "I know you too well to believe that. You would have helped no matter what," she disputed unevenly. "And Shayne? Is she all right? Was she badly hurt?"

"She has scars as I do, but she's recovered for the most part."

"I'm sorry. So sorry. I didn't know or I would have gone to see her." Ella pressed her lips to the thin white line that ran the length of his collarbone. "It terrifies me to think how fragile our lives are. How brief a time we have and how suddenly it can all end."

Rafe inhaled the sweet feminine fragrance of her hair and skin. The scent intoxicated him, eclipsed every thought but one. "Then we shouldn't waste another minute."

Palming her breasts, he paid reverent homage with his tongue and teeth to the delicate peach-tinted tips. They peaked sharply in response, pearling from the pull of his mouth. It wasn't enough. He wanted more of her. He wanted all of her. He slid downward, warming her belly with his breath as he stripped her of the final lacy bits of underwear. He smoothed the taut skin of her thighs and buttocks, feeling the supple muscles quiver in response.

"Rafe, please! I need you."

Gently, he slipped his fingers into the very heart of her. Her soft cry broke above him, shivering like frost-tipped leaves. She was all liquid warmth, a devastating combination of passionate purity and demanding sensuality. It wouldn't take much to push her over the edge, to feel her flame to life within his hands. Already her breath had grown shallow and rapid, an exquisite tension building beneath each stroking touch.

He released her, lifting her onto the bedspread, silk on silk. She looked at him, her eyes the color of molten gold, her need a silent cry. "Soon, *amada,*" he soothed. "Very soon."

His gaze never left her as he swiftly stripped. She stiffened as he shed the last of his clothing, vulnerable in her innocence, strong in the power of her femininity. Finally he came to her, gathering her close. Passion rode him hard, threatening to break what little remained of his patience.

He wanted to go easy with her. He wanted to be the honorable man she thought him, instead of the vengeful one he was. Just this once, he wanted to fulfill her dreams before she awoke to the brutal harshness of reality.

"Don't be afraid," he whispered. "I'll try not to hurt you."

"I'm not afraid." She cupped his face and he sensed she was gathering the nerve to speak. "I know you don't want my love. But you have it anyway. When I give you my body, I also give you my heart."

Words of rejection leapt to his tongue. He didn't want to hear this. Not now. Not if he had a hope in hell of finishing what he'd started this night.

"Don't—" he began.

She sealed his lips with her fingers. "Please don't stop me. What I have to say is long overdue. You have no idea what it's been like these past five years. I thought I'd lost you forever. I thought I'd never have the opportunity to tell you what's in my heart."

He tried again, catching her wrist and dragging her hand from his mouth. "Some things are best left unsaid. This is one of them."

"No, it isn't. I love you," she repeated in soft wonder. "Don't you understand what a miracle that is?"

He turned his head, rejecting the slice of heaven she offered with such unstinting generosity. "It's no miracle."

"But it is." She laughed, the sound a silvery ripple. "You see, tonight was my last chance to discover that miracle. You didn't know that, did you?"

He tensed, swinging back to look at her. "What do you mean?"

"I mean that tonight was my last chance to experience the magic of the Cinderella Ball."

"Why?" He heaved himself onto an elbow, gazing down at her with all the hostility of a caged jaguar. "Why do you say that?"

"Over the past few years . . ." She gave a self-conscious shrug. "I'd begun to lose faith."

She couldn't mean what he thought. It would be too bitterly ironic. "Lose faith, how?"

"It must seem odd coming from me of all people. But I'd almost stopped believing in the Cinderella Ball," she confessed hesitantly. "I'd almost stopped believing in magic and miracles and everlasting love. So, I decided to give it one last night in order to determine if those things really exist."

"This night? This was your last night?" At her nod, he demanded, "What if you didn't find love?"

"I made myself a promise. If I wasn't wed come morning, then I'd give up. I'd have proven that I was never meant to find happily-ever-after. That I wasn't one of the special people destined to receive the miracle of love." She traced the tense curve of his cheek, her eyes shining like golden stardust. "And then you walked in."

He shook his head in fierce denial of her words. "No."

"Oh, Rate. Don't you see? It was fated."

"Ill-fated, you mean."

"No!" Her full mouth tilted in a tremulous smile. "You restored my faith. If you hadn't come tonight, I would have given up. I know I would have. And then I'd have realized you were right about the Cinderella Balls."

"I am right about them, Ella," he told her forcefully. "They're just foolish pipe dreams for desperate people."

"You're wrong, Rafe. You must see that now. If it hadn't been for you, I'd have spent the entire evening searching for a man to love. But it wouldn't have worked. I'd never have found him."

She was destroying him, inch by agonizing inch. "You don't know what you're saying."

"Yes, I do. You warned that I had nothing to offer anyone else and it's true." She clung to him, pressing close, the softness of her breasts branding his arm. "You have it all. My heart, my love, my future. It's all in your keeping."

"Basta!" He thrust her away and in one swift motion rolled to the side of the bed. He sat on the edge, the broad expanse of his back turned toward her.

"Rafe, what is it? What's wrong?" She scooted closer, laying a cool hand against his fevered skin.

"Don't touch me!" He tossed the curt words over his shoulder. "If you have so much as an ounce of self-preservation, you will not touch me."

The final rays of a dying moon cut a harsh path across his bowed head, catching in the deep crevices marking his face. He gulped air, his chest heaving beneath the effort. His muscles stood in high relief, corded into taut ridges, as though he fought to sustain an unbearable weight.

"Rafe, what is it?" she whispered in concern.

His throat moved convulsively and his hand fisted on his knee. "Just give me a moment to regain my control." Drawing on battered inner reserves, he stood. In one swift motion, he snatched the silk comforter from the bottom of the bed and tossed it at her. "Cover yourself," he ordered.

She caught it automatically, wrapping herself in its concealing folds. "Please tell me what's wrong." Fear wove a shaky path through her words. "What have I done?"

"I can't go through with this," he replied, deciding to give her the truth, straight and unvarnished. "I thought I could, but I was wrong."

"You can't do what?"

He turned on her, thoroughly disgusted with himself but also irrationally furious with her for being so naive and trusting. When would she realize he didn't deserve her trust, let alone any of the finer emotions with which she'd gifted him?

"Why the hell do you think I married you?"

"You've told me that already. Because you want me." She held out a hand in appeal. "I know you believe it's only a physical attraction. But I think given time—"

"Time will not change anything," he cut in, determined to end this farce. "Nor does it explain my presence at your home this evening. Perhaps you would care to guess my reasons for that?"

She groped for a response. "To resolve our differences?" she offered tentatively.

"No, Mrs. Beaumont. Try again."

He waited, holding her gaze with an implacability she couldn't escape. He steeled himself to watch the comprehension dawn, to watch as disillusionment drained the animation from her delicate features. It didn't take long.

"Rafe, please. Don't do this."

"Answer me," he commanded. He kept his emotions rigidly in check, refusing to be swayed by the tiny spark of hope still reflected in her expression. "Why did I come this evening?"

The light of hope faded. "You came to get revenge," she whispered painfully.

"That's what has driven me all these years," he confirmed. "But my main purpose for attending tonight was to put an end to the Cinderella Balls."

Her chin lifted with the first hint of angry defiance. "By marrying me? How would that have ended the balls?"

He didn't answer. He couldn't. He couldn't put into words the plan he'd devised nor the manner in which he intended to execute it. She remained silent for several long minutes, lost in thought. Then once again comprehension dawned and he strove not to flinch as her face turned ashen.

"You . . ." She moistened her lips with the tip of her tongue. "You thought once we'd made love our feelings for each other would die. And that when they died, so would our marriage."

"I see you understand now."

"No," she whispered, shaking her head. "You're wrong. That's not what would have happened."

"We will have to agree to disagree on that point," he said gently.

"You're serious?" She hugged the comforter tighter against her breasts. "You were going to make love to me and then leave?"

"Not quite. I wanted you for longer than one night," he confessed with brutal candor. "A month or two would have seen the job done. By then you'd have realized marriage isn't the miracle of love you seem to think. And you'd have run home to Mommy and Daddy a disillusioned but wiser woman."

"You believed my parents would have been so upset by my failed marriage, so disillusioned themselves, they'd have stopped the balls?" she questioned in disbelief. "Well, I have news for you—"

He cocked an eyebrow. "It wouldn't have worked? *No problema, amada.* I still have an alternate plan should they prove stubborn."

She seemed to hesitate, as though compelled to speak, but deciding at the last minute to remain silent. "You're referring to one of those alternatives you mentioned earlier in the glade?"

"Qué coqueta. But then you always were clever, when you weren't allowing your emotions to interfere with your reason. I hesitate to take such drastic measures," he felt compelled to add. "But make no mistake. I will end these balls."

"Because of Shayne?"

His control broke and he caught her arm, yanking her close. *"Yes,* because of Shayne! I'd do anything. *Anything,"* he stressed, "to protect others from her fate. You don't understand, do you? But then, how could you? You live a life of illusion. Nothing about your existence is real."

She twisted free of his grasp, scooting toward the center of the massive bed. "That's not true!"

"No? When you return to your fairy tale existence, *princesa,* open your eyes and take a good look around. Your cupcake castle has so many rooms even you are unfamiliar with them all. It sits in the midst of a desert and yet is filled with plants and shrubs better suited to tropical climes. I doubt they could survive without the protection of a fleet of gardeners and enough water to quench a small city. You hide from strife in a private glade with verdant sod to comfort your dainty feet and leafy trees to shade your fair skin. Well, real life isn't like that." His voice reflected his contempt. "Ask Shayne."

Tears glittered in Ella's eyes, tears she fought valiantly to conceal. "You still haven't answered my question. What happens now?"

"If I have a written guarantee from your parents that the balls end, nothing happens. You go home and the marriage is annulled."

"And if they don't agree?"

"If they refuse, they will soon find themselves without the financial ability to throw another Cinderella Ball. And I warn you, it is well within my powers to do as I threaten."

Shock held her rigid. "That's what you came tonight to tell us?"

He didn't bother to wrap it up in pretty paper. "Yes."

"And then you decided—"

"That I still wanted you," he replied, determined to be blunt and brutal to the bitter end. "To my surprise, I discovered you also wanted me. Our marriage was an alternate means to a similar end."

"While at the same time satisfying our," she cocked her head to one side. "How would you refer to it? Our mutual desire?"

"Exactly."

"So why didn't you go through with it?"

He gazed into her brilliant golden eyes. They gleamed like the last few rays of sunlight, fighting against the relentless push of night. He basked in those final moments of warmth, knowing it would never again be his. He gathered his strength. It was time to finish what he'd started.

"I discovered revenge is not as sweet as I thought. In fact, it tastes quite bitter." He gave a careless shrug. "Besides, my point has been made. You spout sentimental nonsense about true love, about the magic of this inane ball. But you haven't found love or magic or a Prince Charming this evening, have you my *pobrecita* Cinderella? You found vengeance."

She didn't look at him, but remained crouched in the center of the bed, clinging to the comforter as though to a lifeline. "You're going to leave now," she said at last.

It wasn't a question.

"It would be pointless to stay." It took every ounce of control not to drag her into his arms, to set right the terrible wrong he'd done. Instead he retrieved his clothing from the floor and dressed. "I will give you time to reach your decision about future Cinderella Balls," he said as he gathered his belongings. "But I suggest you not wait too long before reaching that decision."

"No," she whispered. "I won't wait too long."

"The room is yours until morning. There's no hurry to vacate."

"Thank you," she responded, unnervingly polite.

Rafe found the five minutes it took him to complete his packing more agonizing than any of the injuries he'd received rescuing Shayne. He almost wished the harm he'd caused could take on physical expression. Wounds that did not kill eventually healed. But in his heart of hearts, he knew fate had no intention of being so kind. He'd bear these scars the rest of his life.

At the door, he turned and looked at Ella and his pain surpassed anything he'd ever felt before.

The golden sunshine had fled her gaze and the blackness of night consumed her.

And in that moment, the gates of hell opened to welcome him.

Chapter Five

"He's not coming, is he?" Ella asked quietly as her father approached from the direction of the house.

She stood in the middle of the glade, the one Rafe had described in such caustic terms, and gazed at the moon. It would be full in another week, the second full moon since the Cinderella Ball. And it would offer yet another painful reminder of that disastrous night. Silvery light caressed her upturned face. Was Rafe in Costa Rica, also staring at a midnight sky? The thought caused her throat to close.

"No, my dear. He isn't coming back," Donald finally replied. He didn't offer his sympathy and she was grateful for his restraint.

"I'd hoped—" She broke off, bowing her head.

She'd hoped that Christmas might bring with it the miracle she'd prayed for with every fiber of her being. But just moments ago the huge grandfather clock in the hallway had laid that fantasy to rest. On the final stroke of midnight, Christmas Day had passed without a word from Rafe.

"No matter how it might look, he cares for you," her father insisted. "There's no doubt in my mind."

"What makes you say that?" She turned to confront him. "Do you think he cares because he called you the night we married? You'll have to excuse me if I don't find that a very convincing argument."

Donald sighed, the sound like the tired creak of a pine. "When Rafe phoned from the Grand's lobby, I'd never heard a man more tortured. He didn't just ask me to interrupt the ball and bring you home. He ordered me to." Her father dropped a hand to her shoulder, squeezing gently. "If I hadn't done as he'd demanded, I suspect he'd have come after me personally."

"I doubt that." Her laughter sounded shaky and she broke off, aware that it revealed far too much of her inner turmoil. "He was well on his way to Costa Rica by the time you arrived."

"No, Ella. He wasn't."

Her head jerked up. "What do you mean?"

"I doubt it would have made any difference if I'd told you two months ago." He hesitated for a brief moment. "But perhaps it will now."

"Told me what?"

"When I arrived at the Grand Hotel, I saw Rafe sitting in a cab outside. Just sitting and waiting while he smoked a cigar. Waiting for me to come for you, I suppose."

She shook her head. "You must have seen someone who resembled Rafe. It couldn't have been him. He doesn't smoke."

"He did that night. I saw him quite clearly."

"What are you saying, Dad?"

"Just this. If ever a man needed his faith restored, it's Rafe Beaumont."

"You're mistaken," she said with a slight smile. It amazed her that she could still find anything humorous about her husband. "He doesn't want his faith restored. He doesn't even believe in such a thing. Just like he doesn't believe in magic or miracles or love."

"Oh, he believes. That's why he fights so hard to deny it. You see, to believe in the untouchable, one must give up control."

She frowned. "I don't understand. What do you mean?"

"Rafe is a man who briefly lost control of his life a long time ago. When he regained that control, he swore never to lose it again."

"When was this?" she asked in confusion. "He never mentioned—"

"I'm not surprised. Perhaps someday he will. In the meantime, what you need to understand is when you love someone, you gift her with your heart and your body, even your soul. You are forever connected to that person, and therefore vulnerable. You can't control what that person may choose to do with your gift." He smiled, a sad, wise smile. "You've discovered that for yourself, haven't you?"

The first hint of hope dawned in her gaze. "You think Rafe loves me, don't you? But he denies it because it would mean giving up control."

"I can't answer that," Donald admitted. "Only he can. But I do believe he needs you. And I think you may be the only one capable of reaching him." He lifted a snowy eyebrow. "If that's what you want."

It didn't take any thought. "It's what I want," she said without hesitation.

Her father smiled, giving her a quick hug. "In that case, you have a suitcase to pack and a flight to schedule."

She gazed at him in wonder. "Yes, I believe I do."

Rafe stood outside, staring up through the tropical foliage at a midnight moon. His thoughts were consumed by Ella. Always by Ella. He took a deep drag on his cigarette, cursing himself for a fool.

"I wish you'd put that thing out," Shayne said, approaching from the direction of the house. "It's going to ruin your health."

He shrugged. "Death is inevitable."

"Maybe so," she said, linking arms with him. "But you don't need to hasten its arrival."

He dropped his cigarette butt to the ground and extinguished it beneath his boot heel. "What keeps you up so late, *hermanita?*"

"I'm worried about you. You've been so distant. So closed in. And I wondered if it might not have something to do with this." She caught his hand in hers, running a finger over the crude wedding ring he still wore. "You've never explained its presence, you know."

"There's nothing to explain."

"But you're married, aren't you?"

He hesitated briefly before giving a curt nod. "It need not concern you. The marriage is a temporary measure."

"Your ring has a familiar design." She glanced at him from beneath her lashes. When he kept stubbornly silent, she prompted, "It's made from a ticket to the Cinderella Ball, isn't it? *My* ticket?"

He didn't bother with pointless denials. "Yes, it's yours."

"And who wears the other?" When he didn't answer, she closed her eyes. Moments later her breath caught. "Oh, dear heavens. You married Ella, didn't you?"

"As I have said, this does not involve you," he said quietly. "All that matters is I have put an end to them, Shayne. Soon there will be no more balls to tempt you."

"I don't care about the balls. I care about Ella. How could you?" she demanded. "How could you do that to her?"

"There was no other option." He thrust a hand into his pocket, dragging free the crumpled pack of cigarettes. Only one remained. He lit it, drawing the acrid smoke deep into his lungs. "I married her. And I left her, taking with me her hopes and her dreams, leaving behind pain and despair." He tilted his head to one side, his expression colder than the icy peaks of Mt. Everest. "It was a fair exchange, don't you think?"

"*Why*, Rafe?" Shayne unhooked her arm from his and swiveled to face him. "Was it really necessary to hurt her?"

"It was the only way."

"But to hurt Ella, of all people." For the first time in years, he saw temper flash in her dark, liquid gaze. "I think I hate you for that, Rafe." Without another word, she turned and stormed back to the house.

"It's all right, *mi pequeña.*" He lifted the cigarette to his mouth and drew an uneven breath. "I would expect no less."

Early in the afternoon of New Year's Day, Ella pushed open the door exiting the Juan Santamaria International Airport in Costa Rica. Instantly, she found herself surrounded by a pack of young boys.

"Carry your bags, *Señora?*" the first asked, hefting a piece of her luggage.

"You need Tico money?" requested the next.

"Taxi?" offered still another.

She glanced from one eager face to the next and smiled. "Yes, please."

Two of the boys peeled off, scurrying to take care of her needs. The third gathered the rest of her bags. "You come this way," he urged.

"Perhaps I should help you—"

He shot her a look of such indignation, she murmured a quick apology. "Come, *Señora,*" he repeated, jerking his chin in the direction of the curb.

She followed, feeling guilty at allowing a child barely ten years old to carry so much luggage. But glancing down the sidewalk, she realized it seemed to be the practice here. School-age children littered the area, all offering their assistance to arriving tourists.

Bright sunlight assaulted her eyes and she slipped on a pair of sunglasses and jammed a floppy straw hat onto her head. After living for so many years in Nevada, protecting her eyes and skin had become a habit.

"I need to take a cab or a bus to the town of . . ." She pulled a copy of Rafe's marriage application from her purse and swiftly scanned it for the information she needed. "I need to get to the town of Milagro. Do you know where that is?"

"*Sí.*" He raised his voice, signaling to one of the boys who'd initially greeted her. "Diego! *Ve, trae a* Marvin."

The boy who'd offered to exchange her money returned just then with a young man in his early twenties. "You wish to buy Tico money, *Señora?*" the latest arrival asked.

Tico, she remembered Rafe explaining, meant Costa Rican. "Oh, yes. Please."

The transaction went smoothly, although she couldn't help wondering if Rafe would consider it a foolish risk to use a moneychanger instead of a bank. No doubt she'd find out when next they spoke. By the time she'd tucked the thick wad of *colones* into her wallet, Diego showed up with the taxi driver in tow.

"Marvin, he take you to Milagro," Diego said.

A wide grin split the cabbie's face. "*Sí, no problema.* I live in Milagro." He signaled the boys to load her luggage into the trunk of his dusty orange cab. "I get you there very fast."

"Thanks. I'd appreciate that."

Tipping each of the boys who'd helped her, far too much if their enthusiastic reactions were any indication, she climbed into the back of the taxi. They pulled around the circle fronting the airport and onto a highway heading away from San José. Ella leaned forward.

"Diego said your name was Marvin. That's not a Tico name, is it?"

"Is *Norte Americano.*" He glanced in the rearview mirror, his dark eyes bright with amusement. "*Mi madre* give me this name. It makes *las turistas* laugh when they hear it so they remember and hire me again"

She returned his smile. "And does it work? Do you get more business than the other cabbies?"

"Two times as much," Marvin boasted.

The highway narrowed as they continued toward the mountains. "How far is it to Milagro?" Ella questioned. "Will we be there soon?"

"Not far. Two, three *horas. Más o menos.*"

"Three hours!"

"Es problema?" He looked in the mirror again and stomped harder on the accelerator. "For you, *Señora*, I drive *muy rapido.* Very fast. But most the roads, they are dirt and gravel. We go very fast, very slow so we miss all the holes. Okay?"

"No! That's not what I meant."

"It is not the roads that worry you?"

"No, not really." Although right at this moment, they did. But only because he spent more time looking in the mirror at her than at the road in front of them. "You can slow down. I don't mind."

"It is the money that worries you?" he guessed shrewdly, his foot easing a fraction from the accelerator. "The price of my taxi?"

Ella sighed. "I guess we should have settled on a fare before we left the airport."

"No problema," he claimed, in what she was fast realizing must be a stock reply. "You give me all your *colones* and I drive you to Milagro."

For one horrible, stomach-churning moment, all her worst nightmares about a woman alone in a foreign country sprang to life. Then Marvin began to chuckle.

"You're kidding, right?" she asked, the faintness of her voice a dead giveaway.

His grin widened. *"Sí."*

"Thank heavens."

"Is good joke, yes? Very funny."

She returned his smile. "Hysterical."

"I no charge you much. I have to go to Milagro anyway. We share a ride. Okay?"

"Thanks, I appreciate that."

"See those mountains?" He pointed in front of them toward a purple range of toothy crags. "We go there. I tell you all about them. You like that, yes?"

"I'd like that, thanks," she confirmed.

"Okay. The mountains, they are made of volcanoes. You know about our volcanoes? It makes good soil for *las fincas*. These are farms. You understand?"

She nodded, doing her best to listen attentively. But the stress of the last several weeks had taken its toll. Only a dozen more sentences registered before exhaustion overcame her and she fell sound asleep.

The screeching of brakes brought Ella violently awake. Marvin jerked the wheel to one side to avoid a pothole, sending her tumbling from one end of the seat to the other.

Clipping the edge of a pit large enough to consume an entire fleet of trucks, they slewed precariously close to the edge of the gravel road. For a horrifying instant Ella stared out the window into a brilliant green abyss before Marvin brought the taxi back to the middle of the single lane. Struggling to right herself, she shoved the straw hat off her face and repositioned the sunglasses from the tip of her nose to the bridge.

"Ah, *Señora*. You are awake," he greeted her. "This is good."

"I—I must have been more tired than I'd realized." Insomnia had a way of doing that, she'd discovered over the past two months. "Have I been sleeping long?"

"Long time, but that is good. We get to Milagro very soon now."

"Oh, that's wonderful."

"See the coffee fields?" He waved his hand out the open window toward a blur of bright green they were passing at top speed.

She peered curiously at the tall bushlike trees, the first she'd ever seen. They climbed the hillside at an almost vertical slant. How anyone could possibly pick the bright red berries clustered among the shiny leaves, she couldn't begin to imagine.

"You are visiting someone in Milagro?" Marvin asked. "I know ever'body. I take you there."

"*No problema*, right?" she teased. "Actually, I'm here to see my husband."

Marvin swiveled to stare, his amazement almost comical. "You have a husband in Milagro?"

"His name is Rafe Beaumont. Do you know him?"

The words had no sooner left her mouth than Marvin slammed on the brakes and jerked hard on the wheel in an exact reenactment of his earlier maneuver. With a painful squeal, the taxi skidded to a halt at the side of the road. He jumped out of the car, his Spanish coming in such a torrent, she didn't have a hope of deciphering so much as a word.

"What is it? What's wrong?" she demanded.

He pointed at the coffee fields on the opposite side of the road, then said Rafe's name before launching into another irate deluge of Spanish. The way he practically spat out her husband's name suggested Marvin might be even more ticked off with Rafe than she was. With a final exclamation of fury, he circled the cab and threw open the trunk.

This could not be good.

Ella bolted from the backseat just in time to see him dumping her luggage on the side of the road. "Hey, wait a minute! You can't do that."

Marvin set his chin at a belligerent angle. "*Sí*, I can do that." He kept offloading her bags. "*Y tambien...sí*, I keep doing it."

She grabbed the nearest bag and tossed it back into the trunk, reloading as quickly as he unloaded. "What happened?" she panted. "What did I say?"

"Lo siento," he claimed, in what was clearly a lie. As far as she could tell, he didn't look the least bit sorry at all. "I cannot take you to Milagro."

"Why? What's wrong?"

"Is your fault, okay?" He stopped unloading and faced her, planting his hands on his hips. "Your husband. You no tell me who he is."

"My fault!" She imitated his stance, fighting for breath in the higher elevation. "How was I to know it would make a difference? What does it matter if Rafe Beaumont is my husband? What did he do to you?"

"Not to me. *Mi sobrino.* My nephew. He fire Manuel."

"And because of that, you can't take me to Milagro?"

"Sí. It would be an insult to Manuel."

"How would it be an insult?" she questioned in exasperation. He didn't answer, simply went back to offloading her luggage. She hastened to switch tactics. "Look, you can't just strand me here on the side of the road. No one knows I'm coming."

Marvin's head emerged from the trunk to peer at her. *"Señor* Beaumont? Does he not know?"

"I wanted to surprise him." She pressed her advantage, small as it was. "What if no one else comes along to help me? Or what if the person who does come decides to rob me? Then it'll be your fault."

He hesitated. Clearly it went against the grain to leave a woman in such a precarious situation. "I cannot take you. It is a matter of honor. *Comprende, Señora?"*

"No! I don't understand."

"You are his wife. His honor is your honor."

"Whatever Rafe has done has nothing to do with me, honor or no honor." She folded her arms across her chest. "And consider one more thing. If you think you had trouble with my husband before, it will be nothing compared to the trouble you have with him after this."

Marvin launched into another incomprehensible tirade. Finally, he calmed enough to say, "I go to Milagro and send someone for you. It is best I can do. You wait here."

She glared at him, though with her sunglasses concealing her eyes, it lost most of its effectiveness. "Where would I go?"

"You wait here," he repeated. "Someone come very soon."

He climbed back into the cab and gunned the engine. Skidding away from the side of the road in a thick cloud of dust, he promptly dropped his rear wheel into a pothole. This one didn't appear quite large enough to swallow entire trucks, but it was sufficient to bring the cab to a grinding halt. Once again Marvin jumped from the vehicle, roundly cursing his fate and, if she didn't miss her guess, her, as well.

"It's your own fault," Ella told him. She pulled off her straw hat and used it to swipe at the dust clinging to her white sundress. To her dismay she only managed to transform the accumulated grime from ugly brown speckles to uglier brown streaks. Damn! "You shouldn't have left me behind. It's . . . it's divine retribution."

He scowled at the buried wheel, then at her. "You push, okay?"

She stared at him for a full minute. "You've got to be kidding."

His chin poked out again. "I do not kid with you. You push the car or I forget to send help from Milagro."

"I don't believe this." She tossed her hat in the direction of her luggage. "Buster, you just lost yourself a really good tip."

"Okay, but you push."

A big, fat raindrop plummeted from the sky, splattering in the dusty road midway between them. They both looked up at the same instant. Thick black clouds roiled above them, blotting out the brilliant blue sky. A chilly wind caught at her loose hair whipping the ebony strands across her throat and face. For an endless moment neither of them moved.

"Uh-oh," Marvin understated their predicament.

"That does it." Ella crossed to where her luggage had been dumped and seated herself on the largest of the suitcases. She removed the sunglasses she no longer needed and dropped them into her purse. Then she fixed Marvin with the steely gaze she'd learned so well from Rafe. "I'm not moving until you agree to take me to Milagro with you. If I'm going to get soaked, so are you."

He stared at her, his mouth dropping open. *"Madre de Dios! La Estrella!"*

She lifted an eyebrow. "Excuse me?"

"La Estrella! You are *La Estrella."*

"No, I'm Ella Beaumont."

"Sí, sí. Señora Beaumont." He bobbed his head up and down and beamed as though she were the answer to all his prayers. *"La Estrella. Lo siento,* Estrella. I did not know it was you."

She regarded him with deep suspicion. "Who is this Estrella person?"

"It is you. You are *la profecía."*

"The prophecy?"

"Sí. The prophecy." He slanted a nervous glance skyward. "Hurry, please. The rain come very hard. We must go."

Ella gnawed on her lower lip. She didn't have a clue what had just happened, but she'd be a fool not to take advantage of it. "Load my luggage first."

"And then you push, yes?"

"You won't leave me?"

He covered his heart with his hand. "My word of honor, Estrella."

By the time the luggage had been returned to the trunk, it had begun to rain in earnest. Within seconds, she was soaked through, her hair plastered to her neck and the side of her face. Great. Now she'd show up on Rafe's doorstep looking little better than the proverbial drowned rat.

Marvin climbed behind the wheel of the taxi and peered back at her. "Push, Estrella. Push!"

Flattening her palms against the filthy rear panel, she obediently shoved with all her strength. The wheel spun, kicking up a stream of mud and grit that covered her from head to toe. Just as her strength gave out, the cab bounced free. With the abrupt loss of support, Ella fell forward, plunging into the mud and water choked pothole. With a shriek of frustration, she scrambled out the other side, minus one sandal.

"Damn you, Rafe Beaumont," she muttered beneath her breath. She stood in the middle of the road, soaked to the skin and dirtier than she'd ever been before in her life. "If you don't fall in love with me after this, I swear I'll make you pay big time."

Marvin stuck his head out of the window. "You do good work, Estrella! Hurry. Get in before the road washes away."

Slogging with uneven steps through the rapidly deepening muck, she reached the taxi. "I'm really dirty, Marvin," she warned.

"My cab, it will clean. Get in. Get in."

She didn't waste her breath arguing further, but climbed in and collapsed against the backseat. Marvin thrust the car into gear and took off. Water runneled from her hair and dress forming a muddy pool around her half-shod feet and she wondered idly if Rafe would even recognize her. She fingered her wedding band. Grit filled the creases and she took the least dirty corner of her skirt and wiped it clean. Seconds later it gleamed a golden promise and she smiled in spite of herself.

"Not long until we get there, Estrella," Marvin reassured. He shot her an anxious glance in the rearview mirror. "If you don't let the road wash out, it would help."

"Excuse me?"

"The road, you keep it from washing down the mountain, okay?"

"And just how am I supposed to do that?"

"You are *La Estrella*," he said reasonably. "You must know how."

"Oh, really? Well, I have news for you. I haven't a clue." She peered outside and shivered. The rain was coming down so hard she couldn't see the coffee trees any longer. What she wouldn't give for a hot shower and some dry clothing. Or even a spare sandal. "Tell me about this prophecy," she requested through chattering teeth. "How did I get involved? I've never even heard of Milagro until just recently."

Marvin fiddled with the controls for the heater and a blast of warm air issued from the vents. "The prophecy has been here a long time. It says that when the two golden *estrellas*—stars? When the two golden *estrellas* appear in the midnight sky, happiness and *prosperidad* will return to Milagro."

"I don't understand. How does that make me this Estrella?"

"It is your eyes, *Señora*. They are the golden stars. And your hair. It is the color of a midnight sky."

"Uh-huh." She waited for the punch line. When it didn't come, she prompted, "Because I have dark hair and odd-colored eyes, you think I'm the one who fulfills this prophecy? You're kidding, right?"

"No, *Señora*. To the people of Milagro the prophecy is no joke. They have waited a long time for you. We have many problems you must put right." He flashed her a quick, deferential look in the mirror. "First you must convince *Señor* Beaumont to hire Manuel once again."

She stared in alarm. "I'm not sure I can do that. *Señor* Beaumont is a very stubborn man."

"We have noticed that about him. But you will find a way, Estrella. The villagers, we depend on you."

She closed her eyes, too exhausted to figure a way to set him straight. She had enough problems with Rafe without taking on the town's troubles, as well. "How much longer?" she asked.

"Not far." Marvin whipped around a curve guided, she guessed, more by instinct or memory than sight. Four hairpins later he said, "This is Milagro. We go just a little further to the top of the ridge."

She squinted out the window but didn't see a town, let alone a ridge. It wasn't until they'd reached a tall stucco wall and a set of iron-wrought gates that the rain eased enough for her to realize they'd arrived at Rafe's home.

"La Finca de Esperanza," Marvin announced.

The gates stood open and he pulled through them. A long drive ended in a formal circle in front of a sprawling ranch house. The minute Marvin cut the engine, the rain stopped and the sun broke through the clouds.

"Gracias, Estrella. You kept the road from washing away and have brought the sun."

"Look. I had nothing to do with ending the rain or I'd have taken care of it a lot sooner than this." She glared at her ruined sundress. "A heck of a lot sooner."

She'd wasted her breath, she realized. Marvin had moved out of hearing range and busily stacked her luggage on the tile entranceway. Ella stepped from the cab and gathered her energy for the next battle.

The one she'd undoubtedly wage with her husband.

As though the thought alone had summoned him, Rafe appeared in the doorway. Without a word of acknowledgment, Marvin deposited the last of her suitcases and disappeared around the side of the house. Apparently, his odd view of honor kept him from hanging around.

Ella drew in a deep breath, wishing she looked a little better. At the very least, a little cleaner. "Hello, Rafe."

Chapter Six

Rafe stood for a long moment without speaking, a lit cigarette held negligently between his fingers. He lifted it to his mouth and inhaled, his gaze switching from Ella to the damp luggage at his feet.

"You want to come in?" he asked with gentle irony, flicking the still-burning butt into the garden. "Or would you prefer I hose you down first?"

"That might be wise. Pushing cabs out of potholes during a downpour can be a bit ... messy." She glanced in the direction he'd thrown the cigarette. A thin plume of smoke drifted up through the bright red hibiscus blossoms decorating a nearby bush. "Dad mentioned you'd taken up smoking. I told him he must be mistaken."

"You always did have too good an opinion of me, *amada*. I'll have to see what I can do to correct that." He stepped from the threshold and gestured toward the open doorway. "Welcome to my home. You can shower and change before we talk."

"Thanks, I'd appreciate that."

"After which I'll return you to the airport."

A dozen arguments leapt to her lips, but she suppressed every one of them. She had no intention of quarreling on the front doorstep. She'd save that for his study or library or wherever else he conducted private discussions.

It turned out to be an office.

"You look much better," Rafe commented when she joined him a full hour later.

"Thanks. I feel much better, too."

She'd taken her time preparing for this meeting, keenly aware she'd only have this single opportunity to convince him she should stay. The outfit she'd chosen was one of her favorites, a short, fitted skirt in bridal ivory and a matching silk shell. To counterbalance the rather formal effect, she'd kept her hairstyle loose and simple by brushing it into a glossy cloud that framed her shoulders. She also kept her jewelry simple, limiting herself to a pair of gold earrings and her wedding band.

"I think that shower rated as a religious experience," she commented, glancing around the room.

It was decisively masculine, trimmed in mahogany, starkly furnished and smelling of smoke. By conducting their interview here, Rafe had trapped her within the boundaries of his territory. It was a calculated maneuver, she realized, one designed to make it more difficult to turn the tables on him.

Still she had no choice but to try. "I appreciate your hospitality."

"I'm pleased I could accommodate you." He gestured toward the chair in front of his desk. "Have a seat and tell me why you've come. I assume it's to discuss my plan in regard to your parents. If so, you're wasting your breath."

She did as he requested, glancing at him curiously. "Plan?"

"You're right," he conceded with a shrug. "To call it a plan is an inaccurate assessment of my intent. Perhaps *threat* would be more precise."

Comprehension dawned. "You mean your threat to destroy my parents financially if they don't end the Cinderella Balls."

He cocked an eyebrow. "Have I made any other threats?"

Her mouth quivered on the verge of a smile. "No. I believe that's the only one. At least toward us. I can't speak for anyone else, however." She tilted her head to one side. "Have there been others?"

"Not that I can recall." Amusement lit the stormy depths of his eyes. "To the best of my knowledge, you and your parents have the honor of being the first."

"I'm relieved to hear it," she murmured dryly. "Of course, I'd be more relieved if we were also the last. Better yet, I'd prefer for you to give up the practice altogether."

"I'm sure you would. But enough of this, Ella," he said with a hint of impatience. "If you haven't come in an attempt to change my mind, or to offer me a written guarantee that the balls will end, then why have you come?" He reached for the half-empty pack of cigarettes littering his desk and shook one free.

"It's quite simple, Rafe." She fought the nervous dread knotting in the pit of her stomach. If she didn't miss her guess, her gallant host was about to become an infuriated husband. "I've come home."

His brows lowered ominously and he froze in the act of lighting his cigarette. "Pardon me? Did you say, home?"

"Yes, home." She stood and leaned across the desk, plucking the cigarette and match from between his fingers. "I always thought smoking a nervous habit. A crutch. But that can't be right. You aren't in need of a crutch, are you, Rafe?"

Keeping her gaze fixed on him, she snapped the cigarette in two and blew out the match, tossing them both into a nearby ashtray.

Her perfume drifted toward him like the smoke from the match, filling his lungs with a seductive scent instead of an acrid one. With a muttered exclamation, he shoved back his chair, leaving his pack of cigarettes behind.

"What the hell are you doing here, Ella? And I want the truth."

She took her time reseating herself. "It's quite simple." She crossed her legs and smoothed the silk skirt along her thighs, keenly aware he watched her every movement. "You married me. Now you're stuck with me."

"You know why I married you," he informed her through gritted teeth.

"Yes, I know. You want me. Well, guess what?" She held his gaze, her feelings reflected in that one forthright look. "I want you, too."

He reached for his cigarettes again, freezing at the betraying gesture. With a growl of annoyance, he grabbed the pack and viciously crumpled it. "This isn't going to work," he announced, tossing the crushed remains into the trash. "I'll arrange a return flight for you first thing in the morning."

She shook her head, her hair swirling in a graceful arc around her shoulders. "I'm not going anywhere. Not yet. Not until we've sorted this out."

His fist crashed against the teak tabletop. And that's when she saw it. He still wore his wedding band. It caught the rays of sunlight streaming in the window and sparkled in a bright, golden promise.

"We sorted out our differences two months ago," he rasped. "If you'll recall, our marriage ended as rapidly as it began."

"That's where you're wrong." She steeled herself to deliver her next little bombshell, somewhat bolstered by the sign of commitment he carried on his finger. "You see, I have no intention of releasing you from your vows until I'm convinced you have no feelings for me."

"Feelings? Our marriage has nothing to do with feelings," he practically roared. "Our marriage is a travesty, one of my own making, I admit. But at least I had the good sense to walk away before it went too far."

She leaned forward in the chair, her hands clutching the armrests in a white-knuckle grip. "Well, I refuse to walk away. I've loved you for years and I'm not going to ruin my one chance for happiness because you're too pig-headed to take a chance. If you want to get rid of me, you'll have to physically throw me out."

He surged to his feet. "Do you think I won't?"

"You may try." She stood, as well. "But we both know what will happen the minute you put your hands on me. If you carry me anywhere, it won't be out the front door. It'll be to your bed to finish what we started two months ago."

"Don't tempt me to prove you wrong!"

"Let me make it easy for you." She opened her arms. "Go ahead, Rafe. I'm all yours. Pick me up and we'll see whether we end this on the front steps or in your bedroom."

Fury exploded in his diamond-hard eyes, along with a blazing passion. He started around the desk toward her, his strides eating up the distance separating them. She knew a momentary twinge of fear, but it died as swiftly as it was born. He could fight and struggle and snarl all he wanted. It wouldn't do any good. What existed between them couldn't be denied any more than it could be controlled. A single kiss would shatter every purpose but one.

To finish what he'd started on their wedding night.

He slung a hand around her waist, hauling her against him. "You shouldn't have come back. I swear, you'll regret it."

"Don't you understand? That's a chance I'm willing to take."

With a frustrated groan he seized her lips with an avid greed and gave back a wealth of passion. If he'd thought to employ restraint, it was rapidly lost beneath the ardent response his touch elicited. Her desire was as genuine as it was unchecked. Not once in all the time he'd known her had she tried to conceal her feelings for him. Never coy, never shy, never reluctant, she gave with unstinting generosity.

"Rafe, please."

Her urgent whisper scorched the air between them. He backed her toward his desk, ripping her blouse loose from her waistband. She didn't protest. He lifted her onto the edge, thrusting the short skirt to her waist and stepping between her legs. She held him tighter. With a harsh groan, he palmed the pale expanse of thigh between the top of her stockings and her lace-trimmed panties. Her silken lips beneath his mouth threatened to destroy him, just as her silken skin beneath his fingers nearly unmanned him.

She was everything he could ever want in a woman. If he could wrap himself in this moment, he would. But he couldn't bring himself to take her on his desk with such callous disregard. "Not here," he muttered with a groan.

"You know I won't refuse you." Her eyes burned with her need. "You're my husband."

"And you're my wife. At least in name."

"You could change that."

"Not here," he repeated. "And not now."

He closed his eyes and leaned into her softness, gathering the remnants of his control. Her breasts cushioned his face and he could feel her heart fluttering beneath his cheek. He took a deep breath and reluctantly pulled back. Holding out his hand, he helped her off the desk.

To Ella's dismay, her fingers were notably unsteady as she straightened her clothing. Not that she was the only one affected. From the corner of her eye she caught Rafe reaching for his cigarettes. It took a split second for him to remember what he'd done with them. When he did, he released a harsh sigh of frustration.

Tucking her blouse into her skirt, she gave Rafe a direct look. "Well?" she asked with a determined show of mettle. "Did we settle that particular question?"

Furious color raced across his peaked cheekbones. *"Eres mío!"* he whispered roughly. "You are mine. And your fate is sealed. I give you one week. You understand? One week!"

Before she could decide whether to consider that good news or bad, a brief knock sounded on the door behind them before bursting open. Marvin and a small, lovely Tico woman stood there, their mouths agape.

"Perdone, Señor," the woman said with a gasp. She started to leave, but then stole a second, closer look at Ella. *"Marvin! Tiene derecho! Es La Estrella. Está aquí! Por fin, está aquí."*

"Chelita, what's going on?" Rafe demanded. "What the hell are you talking about?"

She gestured toward Ella, a becoming flush tinting her cheeks. "The *Señora*. She is *La Estrella*. I did not believe Marvin, but he is right. She has come to fulfill the prophecy. She has finally come."

"The prophecy? You think Ella—" Rafe turned and glared at the cabdriver. "What are you up to, Marvin? What rumors are you spreading about my wife?"

"They are not rumors, but truth," Marvin protested. "Look at her, my friend. She is the prophecy, come as promised. Just because you are too blind to see what is right before your eyes, does not mean the rest of us are."

"She is not the fulfillment of some prophecy, she's Ella Mont—" He shut his eyes, cursing beneath his breath. "Ella *Beaumont*. My wife. Not *La Estrella*."

But he was talking to thin air. Chelita and Marvin had vanished from the doorway, the sound of their excited, chattering voices growing ever more distant.

"I guess I should have mentioned that," Ella said hesitantly. "Marvin got it into his head that I'm the fulfillment of some prophecy and I haven't been able to convince him otherwise."

"That's just great." He paced the room like a caged beast. "Marvin and my housekeeper are two of the biggest gossips in the area. By the end of the day it will be all over the village that I harbor *La Estrella* beneath my roof."

"Is that so bad? If it gives them hope—"

"Hope? What good will hope do them?" Rafe questioned caustically. "Will it fill their children's bellies with food? Will it get the coffee crop picked? Will it put *colones* in their hands? I don't think so."

"The coffee crop?" She frowned. "Marvin seemed terribly upset about something to do with the coffee fields. But he spoke in Spanish and I didn't understand."

Rafe sighed, his mouth set in grim lines. "The workers are on strike. Marvin's nephew, Manuel, has told them not to pick the beans."

No wonder Manuel had been fired. And how interesting that Marvin had neglected to mention that part. "Why are they striking?"

"Because I plan to sell Esperanza."

"Sell your plantation?" She stared in disbelief. "But, it's your home. It's been in your mother's family for generations. Why—"

"Enough, Ella." He cut her off brusquely. "This need not concern you."

"But it does concern me," she argued. "If I'm to live here—"

"Which you are not."

"A matter still open to discussion," she corrected. "If I'm to live here, then I'd like to help."

"You can't help. Don't you understand? This prophecy they speak of promises happiness and prosperity to the people of Milagro."

"I know. Marvin explained it to me."

"Then you must realize how impossible the situation is. How do you plan to fulfill this prophecy? They expect you to perform miracles." His tone turned sardonic. "Or did you just happen to pack a dozen or so in your suitcase?"

"Don't be ridiculous."

"Ridiculous? Be careful where you point fingers, amada. I'm not the one claiming to be *La Estrella*."

"I never claimed—"

"Nor have you managed to deny it." He rested a hip on the edge of his desk, the dark material of his trousers pulled taut across his muscled thighs. "What happens when you are unable to give them what they expect?"

"Is happiness and prosperity so difficult to achieve?" she asked gently. "If prosperity is dependent on picking coffee beans, than all we need to do is find a way to return the workers to the fields."

He lifted an eyebrow. "Oh, really. Is that all? How little you know."

"How can I know any more, if you won't tell me?" she flung back.

"I'm telling you now. There is no room for compromise with the villagers. They will not work. So much for their prosperity. And their happiness? What will you do to gain that, *princesa?*" He folded his arms across his chest. "Wave your magic wand and grant their dearest wish."

She shrugged. "It might be just that simple."

"Then you are as foolish as they."

"If you consider it foolish to believe in the possibility of happiness and miracles, then yes. I'm a fool."

"That's not what I meant."

"I suspect it's exactly what you meant. But I don't mind." She leaned against the door leading to the central corridor and regarded him intently. "Do you realize it's New Year's Day?"

"Is it?" He thrust a hand through his hair. It was longer than when she'd last seen him, falling heavily across his forehead and along the nape of his neck. "As a matter of fact, I'd forgotten."

"Then I'm glad I'm here to remind you. Because today offers the chance for a new beginning."

"Meaning?"

"Meaning as of today I start my campaign to restore your faith. I suspect you're too cynical to convince right away. But eventually, I hope to change that."

"It won't happen," he stated with cold assurance. "Not in a week. Not in a month. Not even if you had a full year."

"You're so certain?"

"I'm positive."

"Well, I don't agree." She thought fast. "I'll bet that before I leave I can perform a few miracles on you, too. Like restoring your trust and your faith. And maybe, just maybe," she suggested daringly, "I can even restore your belief in love."

A bitter coldness swept his expression, his eyes turning a bleak, slate gray. "You will lose this bet, *amada.*"

"But if I win—"

He nailed her with an unyielding gaze. "Let us be clear. If I could, I'd send you home right now. So much for faith and new starts. Unfortunately, to return you to Nevada is no longer possible. At least, not yet."

"Because of the prophecy?"

His mouth twisted. "I'd rather not be the one to drive *La Estrella* away. Better she be run off by the good people of Milagro once they realize she's a fraud. My guess is that will take about a week, which is fortunate since that's all the time you have."

"You're far too generous."

"More generous than you know."

"In that case, it looks like I have my work cut out for me. Which reminds me." She shifted from her stance at the door and approached with a concerned frown. "Perhaps you can help me perform my first miracle. I'm supposed to convince you to rehire Manuel."

He laughed, the sound deep and sincere and incredibly appealing. "For that, *amada,* you will need a true miracle. I have vowed that Manuel won't be rehired unless the workers return to the coffee fields. They won't return unless I promise not to sell the plantation. And that I will never do. In fact, I meet with the buyers in the morning to finalize the terms of our agreement."

"You never did say why you want to sell." A sudden thought struck and alarm darkened her eyes. "You're not in financial trouble, yourself? You don't have to sell, do you, Rafe?"

"Yes, I have to sell. But not for financial reasons."

"Then—"

"It's personal. And as I've said before, none of your concern." He walked past her and stood by the door. "Come. I'll make sure the rest of your luggage has reached your room. Would you like Chelita to help you unpack?"

"I can manage to transfer my clothing from suitcase to dresser drawer without assistance, thanks." She joined him at the door. "Despite what you think I'm quite self-sufficient."

"I'm relieved to hear it." He stared down at her. "And just so you know. You may claim to love me, but they're just words. There can only be one explanation for your presence. And that's to prevent me from harming your parents. Any other excuse is a smoke screen."

"That's not true. Besides, if you can actually do as you claim and affect their finances, that means you could have done it at any point over the past five years. But you didn't" She smiled up at him. "If you'd really wanted revenge, you'd have taken it long before this."

"Is that what you think?"

"It's what I believe."

"You consider me incapable of harming your parents?" he questioned curiously.

"Of course. I—"

He cupped the side of her face, sealing her lips with his thumb. "Listen to me now. And listen carefully. I will not be diverted from my purpose by you or anyone else. To think otherwise is to risk more disillusionment. Will your parents give me my agreement?" He caressed the length of her mouth before releasing her.

She moistened her lips. "I haven't asked them to, no."

"Then fair warning. Their fate is in your hands."

"No, Rafe," she countered. "It's in yours."

He didn't respond. Instead, he opened the door and stepped to one side, bringing the interview to an end. She'd both lost ground and gained ground, she realized as she returned to her bedroom.

She'd won the right to remain at Rafe's *finca*. For the moment. But only at the risk of her parents' financial security. If she were smart, she'd give him what he'd demanded and leave. Unfortunately, to do that meant relinquishing any chance of a future with him. She didn't doubt that her marriage would last only as long as she continued to have something he wanted.

A light tapping at the door interrupted her thoughts. "Ella?" Shayne peeked into the bedroom, tucking a strand of honey-blond hair into the formal twist at the nape of her neck. She gazed at Ella, her huge, dark eyes oddly expressionless. "May I come in?"

"Shayne!" Ella ran to greet her, enveloping the younger girl in a warm embrace. It was returned with a surprising fierceness before Shayne pulled sharply away. "It's been so long."

"Five years. Five very long years." Aside from a nervous knotting of her fingers, Shayne's composure appeared picture-perfect. "It's lovely to see you again."

Tears pricked Ella's eyes. "And just look at you." She scanned her one-time friend for changes, astonished by how many there were. "You're taller, I think, and—" Cooler. More remote. More like Rafe. "Why, you're all grown up," she finished lamely.

"It was bound to happen sooner or later." Shayne took a hesitant step into the room. "I stopped by to apologize. This entire situation with Rafe is my fault."

"Your fault?" Ella moved away from the door. "Come in and talk to me while I unpack. Why do you think any of this is your fault?"

Shayne perched on the edge of the bed, her posture stiffly erect, her attitude far too reserved for someone who'd just turned twenty-three. "The ticket Rafe used to attend the ball was mine."

"Yours!"

"He had a fit when he found out what I'd planned, as I'm sure you can imagine."

Ella shook her head in confusion. "I don't understand. How did you manage to get a ticket? Guests have to fill out an application well in advance. We have everyone screened by a security company. I'd have known if you had applied."

"Oh, I circumvented that," Shayne revealed. "I talked a friend into applying for me. I planned to use his ticket once he received it, but I'd forgotten that you use special messengers to deliver them. It was a foolish error."

"The application was in his name?"

"Yes." A strand of hair came loose again and with an impatient grimace, she tucked it behind her ear. "When the messenger arrived to deliver the ticket, it caused quite a commotion in the village. Eventually word reached Rafe. He realized at once what I'd done."

"I see." Ella gazed at Shayne in concern. "Why in the world did you apply?"

"I'm sure you can guess. I thought Chaz might be there." Her response was stark. To the point. And utterly devastating. "It's the same reason I tried to attend the Anniversary Ball. If it hadn't been for the accident . . ." She trailed off and shrugged.

Ella inhaled sharply. "That's when you were hurt? On the way to the Anniversary Ball?"

Shayne glanced at Ella uncertainly. "Didn't you know about it?"

"Not until recently." She crossed to sit on the bed, catching Shayne's hands in her own. "Sweetheart, I wish you'd called instead of going to so much trouble. I could have told you Chaz wouldn't be there."

A hint of dark emotion flitted across the younger girl's face before vanishing beneath a mask of composure. "You're certain?"

"I checked the list myself."

Shayne bowed her head. "It was stupid, I know. If I'd just left well enough alone, Rafe wouldn't have bothered to go after you again. That's why he's so determined to end the Cinderella Balls. Because of me."

"You let me worry about that. He might still surprise you."

"For your sake, I hope so." Shayne hesitated before rushing into speech. "There's something else I've been meaning to ask." Again came that flash of emotion and again she brought it under swift control. "You never told Rafe what happened, did you?"

"At the Cinderella Ball five years ago?" Ella clarified. "No, I didn't."

"Why didn't you just tell him I'd lied? That you hadn't invited me?"

"For one simple reason. I'd never do anything to harm your relationship with Rafe."

"I—" She bit her lip. "Thank you."

"Don't thank me." Ella's gaze held a flash of fire. "I didn't do it for your sake, Shayne. I did it for his."

"I see." She seemed to gather herself. "I owe you an apology. A long overdue apology. I took advantage of you. Worse, I ruined your relationship with my brother. I realize nothing I can say now will ever make up for the wrong I did. But I am sorry."

"You were only seventeen. I understood."

"That's more than Rafe would have," Shayne said candidly. "Still, I hurt you both. Terribly. I hope you can forgive me one day."

Ella smiled. "I forgave you long ago." She tilted her head to one side. "You've never told him the truth, either. Have you?"

"I've tried," Shayne replied. "I've gotten as far as admitting it was my fault. But he won't listen. I'm not sure he wants to hear the truth."

"And what truth is that?"

For a brief instant, her composure shattered and Ella caught a glimpse of a grief-torn woman. "I still love Chaz McIntyre. It's been five years and nothing's changed."

"Is that why you keep coming back? You hope to find him again?"

Shayne nodded. "Rafe had the marriage annulled because I was underage. You want to know the funny part?" A heartbreaking smile chased across her mouth. "If the ball had been just one day later, I'd have been eighteen. And the ending to my story might have been very different."

"Shayne—"

She stood abruptly, pulling her hands free. "I can't talk about it anymore. Excuse me, won't you?" She paused at the door, her back rigid, her hand clinging to the knob. "Dinner's at seven. I'll see you then."

The door shut softly behind her.

Ella closed her eyes. There had to be something she could do. Some way she could help to put Shayne's life right again.

It would seem that *La Estrella* had yet another miracle to perform.

Chapter Seven

"I'm so pleased you've come, Ella," Shayne attempted to break the silence at dinner that evening. She darted a swift glance in her brother's direction. "Is this a prolonged visit?"

"Yes. Very prolonged."

"No," Rafe retorted at the same instant. "It will be very brief."

Chelita paused in the act of pouring him a glass of wine, her expression patently horrified. "Oh, *Señor* Beaumont, you will not make *La Estrella* leave! The villagers, we need her."

"*La Estrella*?" Shayne questioned, glancing from one to the other. "What's she talking about?"

Rafe released his breath in an impatient sigh. "I have no intention of making her do any such— Chelita, the wine?"

The housekeeper hastened to right the bottle before it overflowed the glass. "Oh! *Lo siento, Señor* Beaumont. It's just that we are so happy. She has finally come after all this time and—"

"No one told me she'd finally come," Shayne complained. "Where is she? Who is she? Would someone please tell me what's going on?"

"Um. I'm what's going on," Ella confessed. "I guess I forgot to mention it earlier. It seems that Marvin and Chelita have gotten it into their heads that I'm *La Estrella*."

Shayne's mouth dropped open "You're—"

"Chelita," Rafe interrupted with a frown. "Unless I'm very much mistaken, this wine tastes suspiciously like champagne."

"*Sí, Señor*. I knew you would want to celebrate the arrival of *La Estrella*."

"You knew this, did you?"

"It is obvious," she said, missing his sarcasm. "Everyone is so excited. Now will come the happiness and prosperity her arrival promises. We should celebrate such a miracle."

"Unless, of course," Shayne said in an innocent-sounding voice, "my dear brother sends her home."

"Damn it, Shayne!"

"Send her home?" Chelita slammed the bottle onto the table, suspicion swiftly replacing her earlier enthusiasm. She glared at Rafe. "You will take *La Estrella* from us, *Señor* Beaumont? You would do that to the people of Milagro?"

A muscle leapt in his jaw. "I have no intention of sending her anywhere."

"Then I'm permitted to stay?" Ella inserted smoothly. "For longer than a week?"

All eyes pivoted to Rafe.

He drained his glass in a single swallow and set the flute on the table with enough force to make the fragile crystal vibrate in protest. "I am not accustomed to being interrogated in my own home."

"But, *La Estrella*—" Chelita began in protest.

"*La Estrella* is free to come and go as she pleases." His gaze switched to Ella, a silent order glittering in the wrathful gray depths of his eyes. "Before long, I expect it will please her to return home. End of discussion. Chelita, serve the dinner, *por favor*."

The housekeeper folded her arms across her chest. "Not until you promise to keep her."

"Chelita!"

"Fine! I will serve the dinner. And I will bring a wine more to your liking." Snatching up the bottle, she headed for the kitchen, continuing to voice her complaints in rapid Spanish.

"Gee, I sort of liked the champagne," Shayne murmured. "I thought it a nice touch."

"I believe you've caused enough trouble for one evening," Rafe said, frowning at his sister. Then his eyes softened. "But it is good to see you so animated. Perhaps Ella's visit has had some benefit, after all."

"Three cheers for me," Ella muttered.

Her comment drew his attention. "May I suggest you change the subject to something less volatile, *amada?* Or would you care to return to my office and continue our previous discussion? We could pick it up where we last left off."

Choosing the safer of the proffered choices, Ella addressed her sister-in-law. "How's your mosaic work going? I look forward to seeing your latest pieces."

It was unquestionably the wrong topic to choose. The color bleached from Shayne's cheeks and she copied Rafe's example, swallowing her champagne in a single gulp before returning the flute to the table. Once again, the fragile crystal sang in protest.

"I haven't done any mosaic work since . . . In a long time. I'm studying to be an accountant now."

"An accountant!" Ella couldn't conceal her distress. "But you're so talented. How could you—"

"Dinner, it is ready," Chelita interrupted, pushing a wooden serving cart into the dining room. After replacing the wine, she removed a silver cover from the first dish and set a steaming plate in front of Ella. "For you, Estrella, I have made a special Tico meal called *casado.*"

Shayne began to laugh. "That's meant to be amusing, Ella. A Tico joke. You see *casado* in Spanish means a married man. The dish is supposed to be what a husband can routinely expect from his wife once he's safely caught and wed. It's sort of a potluck—a little of everything. There's rice and beans—"

"Y picadillos," Chelita added.

"That's a mixture of potatoes, string beans, meat, and tomatoes. Oh, heavens. Just about everything minced and thrown together with some spices. Let me see, what else has she given you? Spaghetti, salad, eggs and— Is that *corvina*, Chelita?"

"*Sí, corvina.*"

"And sea bass."

Ella smiled her appreciation. "It looks wonderful."

"It tastes wonderful, too," Shayne assured her. "Chelita is a marvelous cook."

The housekeeper served Shayne next and finally Rafe. Crossing to her cart, she began to swiftly roll it toward the kitchen.

"Chelita. One moment, if you please," Rafe said mildly.

Ella glanced up in alarm. She knew that tone of voice. It didn't bode well for any of them. Apparently, Chelita knew it, as well.

"I must get to the kitchen," she began.

"First you will explain this." Exerting some effort, he managed to spear a cut of meat on the end of his fork. "Would you mind telling me what this . . . this black item is, please?"

"Steak," Chelita whispered, her gaze glued to the floor.

"Steak," he repeated, lifting it off the plate for a closer examination. "How interesting. And have you discovered a new method of cooking it, perhaps?"

She cleared her throat. "*Sí, Señor.* It is a new method."

"I see. And this new method, is it one that involves leaving the meat on the grill until it shrivels up into an inedible lump of coal?"

"I believe that is how it is prepared." She peeked at him from beneath her lashes. "*Gusta usted?*"

"No, Chelita. I don't like it. If this is your clever way of preventing *La Estrella*'s eventual departure, it has failed." He returned the steak to the plate. "Be so kind as to take this to the kitchen and bring me a fresh meal."

"*Sí, Señor,*" she replied in a subdued voice.

"And, Chelita?" He waited until he had her full attention. "No more experiments of this nature. I have told you *La Estrella* is welcome to stay as long as she wishes. Burning my dinner will not succeed in keeping her here any longer than she chooses to remain. Just as it didn't succeed in convincing me to rehire Manuel. Is that understood?"

With a quick nod, she fled.

The minute the housekeeper cleared the room, he turned on Ella. "This is your fault," he informed her.

"My fault? How could it possibly be my fault?"

"She wouldn't dare risk her job in such a manner if she didn't believe prosperity and happiness awaited just around the corner. She undoubtedly expects *La Estrella* to remedy everything that goes wrong in her life. Including the loss of her employment."

"Well, I wouldn't let you fire her, that's for sure."

"Really?" He leaned back in his chair and fixed her with a curious gaze. "And just how would you go about stopping me?"

"I would hire her myself."

"A novel idea with only one unfortunate flaw."

"Which is?"

"You forget, *amada*. This is my home. Who works within its walls is up to me."

"And your wife has nothing to say about it?"

"No," he stated succinctly. "She doesn't. That being the case, may I recommend you do nothing to encourage Chelita or any of the others in their misguided beliefs. You are not this prophecy come to life. Nor can you fix their various problems. To attempt such a thing will only further complicate matters."

After a few moments of awkward silence, Shayne offered a new topic for them to pursue. Ella seized it with relief. She sympathized with Rafe's position in regard to the villagers and his dismay at their eagerness to believe in the prophecy. She just didn't agree. But until she could change his mind, the less said, the better. Once they'd finished eating, Chelita served *tacita de café*—a small cup of coffee—which Ella discovered typically concluded the meal.

"It's the estate's own blend and absolutely wonderful because it's processed with more care than larger commercial operations," Shayne said. "Our coffee is classified as an arabica strictly hard bean which makes it one of the finest products in the world."

"I've always wondered how coffee was produced," Ella commented. "I saw the trees on my way here, but I didn't see any beans, just berries."

"The beans are hidden inside, two to a 'cherry,' except for the occasional peaberry which contains only one," Rafe explained. "When they turn red, they're ready to pick."

"I assume you don't wake up one morning to discover a field full of ripe cherries?" she teased.

He smiled. "No. It's an arduous job, requiring several return visits to the same tree. Once the coffee beans are picked, our particular variety is washed through several machines to remove the pulp. The beans are then left to ferment for a day for a variety of reasons, one of which is to add sharpness or acidity to the flavor. It makes a superior cup of coffee, don't you agree?"

"It's delicious," Ella said truthfully.

"I'm pleased you like it." He stood and to her utter astonishment leaned down and snatched a quick kiss. "I apologize for deserting you, but I have a phone call to make."

"That's all right," she said faintly. "I understand."

After he'd left, Shayne grinned. "So, how did you like your first lesson on coffee production?"

"It was fascinating." Ella poured herself another half cup and added a large dollop of warmed milk from the earthenware pitcher Chelita had provided. "In fact, I'd enjoy learning more."

Shayne made a face. "That's what you think. You're lucky Rafe decided to give you the shortened version or you might have found it far less fascinating. It's more complicated than he's making out."

"I can imagine."

"Listen, I have an idea." Shayne shifted her empty cup to one side and stood. "Why don't I take you to see the mosaic in the courtyard? My dear brother would probably discourage my showing it to you if I suggested it. But since the mosaic is of you I think you might enjoy seeing it."

"Of me?"

Shayne laughed at Ella's expression. "I'm kidding, or perhaps only half kidding. Actually, it's supposed to represent *La Estrella*. Would you like to see a rendering of your namesake?"

"I'd love to." Ella followed eagerly as Shayne led the way through the corridors toward the center of the ranch house. "Is it one of your designs?"

A momentary darkness slipped across Shayne's features. "No, though I did work on restoring it at one point."

"Shayne, what happened?" Ella asked gently.

They stepped out into the central courtyard. Deep purple bougainvillea arched overhead and ferns leaned across the pathway. Flaming heliconia and bright pink torch ginger turned the area into a blaze of color.

Shayne remained silent and Ella slipped her arm around the younger girl. "Why did you give up something that meant so much to you?"

A coolness settled into Shayne's dark eyes. "Creating mosaics is a pipe dream, not a profession. Studying to be an accountant is much more practical."

"That's your brother speaking."

"Yes, I suppose it is."

"What happened to the girl I knew?" Ella questioned sadly. "Where has she gone?"

Shayne pushed free of Ella's hold, her pace increasing. "She doesn't exist anymore. She grew up."

"Growing up doesn't mean letting go of dreams."

Shayne laughed, the cynical sound particularly harsh in the serene beauty of their surroundings. "That's exactly what it means. You'll discover that for yourself if Rafe has anything to say about it."

"I hope you're wrong."

"I'm not." Shayne gestured toward an open area skirting a large fountain. "This is it. I'd stay, but I have some computer work to finish before morning. Excuse me, won't you?"

She'd blundered, Ella realized. She shouldn't have pushed so hard. At least, not this soon. "Shayne, wait. Please, don't go—" But she was ignored.

She didn't attempt a pursuit. There'd be time enough to make amends at a later date. With a sigh of regret, she turned her attention to the mosaic beneath her feet.

It was a fascinating piece. A brilliant rainbow of colors coiled around the fountain seemingly at random, bright at one end and fading to black at the other. At length, she began to discern a pattern. And what she saw took her breath away.

The bright swirl of colors was a woman's gown and had been designed to wrap around the fountain as though she knelt in prayer. The black section was her hair, the mosaic tiles dusted with specks of silver so it did indeed look like a midnight sky. And the two golden stars... They were the woman's eyes—an oddly familiar shade between gold and amber.

When the two golden stars appear in the midnight sky, happiness and prosperity will return to Milagro.

Ella hadn't understood why Marvin thought the prophecy referred to a person instead of a celestial event. But now she did. If Marvin had seen this, it was no wonder he'd mistaken her for *La Estrella*.

Whether it was Shayne's restoration work or the interpretation of the original artisan, the woman depicted in the tiles bore an uncanny resemblance to the face Ella saw in the mirror each morning.

A small sound captured her attention and she turned to peer toward the denser shadows in the far corner. Rafe stepped into the dusky light, a brandy snifter in hand. He gestured toward the mosaic. "The two of you have a lot of work to accomplish."

"So it would seem." She glanced at him uncertainly. "I thought you had a call to make. Have you been standing there long?"

"Long enough. My call was brief so I came out here to enjoy the sunset. If I hadn't so rashly disposed of my cigarettes, you'd have detected me the instant you and my sister arrived."

"That's unfortunate."

"Because I overheard Shayne's comments?" He took a healthy swallow of brandy. "She said nothing I didn't already know."

"Rafe, there must be some solution to all these problems. You can't honestly believe Shayne is better off as an accountant than doing the work she loves?"

"It doesn't matter what I think." He shoved his hand into his trouser pocket, and though he shrugged almost negligently, she noticed his fingers bunched into a fist.

"After the accident, she lost the heart to design. That's what your Cinderella Ball did to her."

"Isn't there anything—"

"Enough, Ella! You are not *La Estrella*. You cannot solve all the problems that exist here. To try risks more than just disappointment."

"Why do you say that?"

"Being the fulfillment of a prophecy is a dangerous business."

"Only to those who don't believe."

"Dios! Don't tell me you are buying the fairy tale, as well?" he demanded. "You're not here to bring happiness and prosperity to Milagro. Nor are you here to restore my faith or Shayne's. To try such a thing is to risk doing more harm than good."

"How can it hurt anyone to give them hope?"

"Because they believe in you. They trust you. Which means they can be led astray by you."

"Led?"

"You must realize that wherever *La Estrella* leads, the villagers will follow."

She lowered her gaze to the mosaic, digesting his words. They offered some intriguing possibilities.

As though sensing the path her thoughts took, he warned, "Don't be diverted from your purpose, Ella, or you'll regret it. You've come to Esperanza for one simple reason. To try and reach a compromise regarding your parents' situation. Stick to that and you have a chance of achieving some limited success."

"That's not why I'm here," came her instant denial. "I came because I—"

"Don't say it." The words were torn from him. "Not again."

"Is it so difficult to hear?" she asked regretfully.

"You confuse lust with love. Don't tempt me to show you the difference."

She glanced at him from beneath her lashes. "I wish you would."

He lifted the brandy snifter to his mouth and tilted it, draining the contents. Then he set it on the rim of the fountain and approached, grim purpose in every line of his body. She didn't wait. Taking the initiative, she slipped into his arms and caught his face between her hands.

The gathering of night was kind to him, gentling stark lines and softening taut planes. But the need torching his eyes rejected even that slight kindness. His gaze burned with the harsh light of necessity. Determined to give him what he craved, she tugged his head toward hers and kissed him.

He tasted of warmth and brandy and heady passion. Tilting her head to one side, she deepened the kiss, parting her lips and surging into the sweet, tangy warmth. His groan slipped from his mouth to hers, full of primitive demand. It touched a primal chord she'd never known existed, resonating with a power that left her with no option but one.

To give herself body and soul to this man.

In the brief space from one breath to the next, he took control. His mouth consumed hers. It wasn't a gentle loving, but a hot, urgent mating. Taking. Plundering. Invading. His hands settled on her hips, cupping the narrow bones. With each frenzied kiss, his hold grew more aggressive. He surged against her, rocking rhythmically, fighting to get closer than cotton and silk would allow:

Her reaction was as instantaneous as it was violent. She shuddered in his arms, a desperate moan catching in the back of her throat. "Oh, please, Rafe," she whispered. "If this is lust, I'll take it."

He reared back as though she'd struck him. Thrusting her away, he snatched the brandy snifter from the rim of the fountain. For a split second she thought he meant to hurl it against the side of the house. Instead it shattered explosively within his grasp. For a long, shocked moment, he stared at his hand. A trickle of blood spread across the palm and he pulled the air into his lungs as though it were a great effort.

"Rafe!" She started toward him, but he shook his head, warning her off.

"You should not have come to Esperanza," he rasped.

He looked her full in the eyes. Where once passion had blazed like a thousand candles, a terrible darkness had descended, snuffing the light.

"How can you say that?"

"It is so simple, a child could see. You have no one to protect you from harm as long as you remain here." His mouth twisted. "No one to protect you from your husband."

She held out a hand. "I don't need protection. I just need you."

"No! Don't you understand? I will use you. I will hurt you." He drew in on himself, raising an impenetrable wall between them. "I cannot allow that to happen."

"For the love of heaven, Rafe. Explain it to me. You can't allow *what* to happen?"

"I have destroyed a life once before by failing in my duty, by failing to protect one of my own. I won't destroy another. And that's what would occur if this went any further. I'd destroy you."

"You wouldn't. You couldn't."

"I will, *amada,* because it is in my nature to do so. And nothing you can say or do will change that." He inclined his head in an oddly formal manner. "Excuse me while I see to my hand." And with that he turned and disappeared into the night.

Ella didn't move for a long time. He'd destroyed a life once before by failing to protect one of his own? That could only refer to Shayne and the Cinderella Ball. She shook her head in confusion.

She still didn't understand. Something more motivated his anger, his fierce drive to protect those he cared for. And until she found out what, their marriage didn't stand a chance.

Releasing a sigh of frustration, she took a final look at the mosaic. "Well, Estrella. It looks like Rafe was right. We do have a lot of work to accomplish. But thanks to him, I believe I've figured out how to perform our first miracle."

Bright and early the next morning Ella trekked down the dirt road to the village of Milagro. It was a beautiful day, the air dry, but far softer than the aridness she'd grown accustomed to in the desert. The amount of green also astounded her. If she didn't have a job to accomplish, she'd have stopped every few feet to examine a new tree or bush or flower. She grinned. Or ant trail. The first person she ran into when she reached Milagro was Marvin.

"Estrella," he greeted, clearly surprised by her presence. "You have come to visit us?"

"Actually, I've come for some help."

"But, of course. How may we assist you?"

"I'd like to pick coffee beans and I don't know how to do it. I'd hoped someone from the village could explain the process and loan me whatever equipment I might need."

His mouth fell open and he stared in astonishment. "You play a joke on Marvin, *sí?*"

"No. I'm quite serious." She glanced over his shoulder at the people who'd begun to gather in the street and offered her warmest and most confident smile. "Hello."

The response was typically Tico-friendly. Returned smiles and an occasional *"pura vida"* came from the ever-expanding crowd. Marvin turned and relayed her request in rapid Spanish. After several minutes of debate, he switched his attention back to her.

"You understand, we are on strike," Marvin began uncomfortably.

"Oh, I understand. I don't expect anyone to help me. But it's past time to pick, isn't it? And somebody has to do it." She shrugged. "I guess I'm that somebody."

Another man stepped forward. "It is my fault, Estrella. I am the one responsible for this strike."

"You must be Manuel." She looked at him, secretly surprised. She'd expected an angry activist. Instead she found a sincere young man with a bright smile and lively, intelligent eyes. She held out her hand. "I'm Ella Beaumont."

He took her hand in his. "It is a pleasure to meet you."

"Perhaps you could help?" she suggested. "If you would equip me with the supplies I need and then explain whatever I should know in order to pick the beans, it'll give us a chance to become better acquainted."

"I'd like that," Manuel instantly agreed. Intense curiosity crept into his nut-brown eyes. "You'll need a *canasta*. A wicker basket. And to protect your clothing, an apron would be wise."

Both were almost instantaneously produced, along with a straw shade hat. Ella accepted each with a pleasant smile and sincere thanks. Once outfitted, she started back up the hill with Manuel at her side.

"Why do you wish to pick the beans?" he asked. "Is it your hope to bring an end to the strike?"

"Yes," she admitted readily. "From what I gather, both you and my husband are stubborn men, each too proud to back down once you've taken a stance."

"That is an accurate assessment," he confessed with a charming smile. "However, there are reasons why we are forced to take opposing positions."

"Both are valid reasons, I'm sure," she said, trusting he'd catch her underlying meaning. Although she sympathized with the villagers, she wanted to be clear she supported her husband above all else. "I'm hoping if the villagers see *La Estrella* picking beans, they'll decide to help."

He glanced over his shoulder. "I expect you're right."

A quick look confirmed that they were being followed by a large crowd. "Once they're back at work, I'll try and convince Rafe to rehire you."

He lifted an eyebrow. "And how do you plan to do that?"

"Oh, I have an idea or two that might do the trick."

"I applaud your incentive. However, you must realize I cannot follow my friends and family into the fields. *Señor* Beaumont would not stop the others from working. But he cannot allow me to do so until our differences are resolved. I must respect that, Estrella."

With each moment that passed, he impressed her more and more. She sent him a hesitant look. "You do know that I'm really not this *La Estrella*."

"Who is to say?" he replied with a shrug. He paused beneath the shade of a banana tree on the edge of the fields. "The people believe, which is the most important consideration. Your actions, as well as any inaction, will have a tremendous impact on them."

"Rafe said something similar," she admitted. "But surely it's better to do something than nothing."

Again he shrugged. "Time will tell."

"Your English is excellent, Manuel," she probed delicately. "What do you do aside from pick coffee beans? When you're not on strike, that is?"

He chuckled. "I am a botany student at the University of San José."

A sudden thought occurred to her. "And do you also provide love-struck young women with tickets to Cinderella Balls?"

"Guilty, I fear. Shayne wished to find her husband and I could not refuse her request." A faint flush tinted his angled cheekbones. "Especially when Chelita added her pleas to those of your sister-in-law."

"I see," Ella said, struggling to keep a straight face. She slapped the wide-brimmed hat onto her head. "I guess I'm ready. What do I do?"

Amusement flashed in his eyes. "It's quite simple, Estrella. You pick anything that's red. Put it in your basket. And watch out for snakes." With a friendly smile and a cheerful *"buena suerte,"* he turned and trotted back toward the village.

"Manuel, wait a minute!" she called after him in alarm. "Snakes? *What* snakes?"

Chapter Eight

"Señor Beaumont?" Chelita knocked on the door before stepping into his office.

"Yes?" He glanced up from his papers. "What is it?"

"Los hombres malos son aquí."

He sighed, capping his pen and dropping it onto the blotter. "Just because they're interested in purchasing Esperanza doesn't make them bad."

"You are right. It makes them very bad," she retorted. "We will all lose our jobs when they take over *la finca*. Then the villagers will have to leave their mountain homes or they will starve. We will end up begging on the streets of San José." She shot him an ominous look. "Or worse."

He struggled to contain his annoyance. "I've told you a hundred times, the new owners won't do any such thing. Life will continue just as it always has."

"Of course, *Señor*. I am sure you are right. Should I let them in?"

His brows lowered. "You've left my guests standing outside?"

"I did something wrong?" she asked innocently. A little too innocently.

This was getting out of hand. Never had he dealt with such blatant defiance. Never, that was, until his darling wife had arrived on his doorstep.

"You know damned well you did something wrong!" He fought to lower his voice, a task becoming increasingly difficult with every hour his wife remained his wife. "Please admit the visitors and then ask Ella to join us."

"Who?" she asked in feigned bewilderment, her grasp of English miraculously vanishing.

"La Estrella. Remember her? The bearer of happiness and prosperity? Where is she? I'd like to introduce her."

Chelita blanched. "I'm not sure that is such a good idea."

His suspicion grew. *"Mi esposa,"* he rasped. *"Dónde está?"*

"I, ah, I have forgotten your guests. I go let them in." She ducked out of the room.

"Chelita!"

She peeked nervously around the corner of the door. *"Sí, Señor?"*

"Where. Is. She?"

"In the coffee fields," Chelita whispered, wringing her hands.

"The coffee fields."

He fumbled for his pack of cigarettes with his bandaged hand, remembering an instant too late that he'd thrown them away. How could he have been so foolish? Of course, he knew how. One glance from a pair of pleading golden eyes and. his common sense drained straight into his trousers. *Dios!* It was enough to drive a man to drink. He eyed his housekeeper.

"Chelita, would you be so good as to tell me what the hell my wife is doing in the fields?"

Her voice grew even softer. "Picking coffee beans."

Rafe's hand closed into a fist as he fought for control. It was a long time coming. Finally, he shoved back his chair and stood. Chelita edged toward the door, her eyes wide with apprehension.

"Señor? What do you intend to do?"

"I intend to go fetch my wife. You are to invite my guests in and serve them a cup of coffee while they wait. Is that clear?"

"Café. Sí, Señor. I will use the estate blend. And I will be polite. Very polite."

"What a novel idea."

He left the room and took the back way to the coffee fields. To his utter astonishment, the workers were all there, laughing and joking . . . and picking beans. He was keenly aware of the sudden silence and surreptitious glances he received as he strode along the row of bushy trees. It took him several minutes to discover which wide-brimmed hat concealed his wife.

"Oh, hello, Rafe. Isn't it a beautiful morning?"

She greeted him with remarkable nonchalance for a woman about to be strangled.

"I would like to speak with you, please."

"Sure. Go right ahead."

"Someplace more private, if you'd be so kind."

"Okay. But I should warn you—"

"You may warn me when we're alone."

He stripped off the basket harnessed around her waist, seized her arm and escorted her through the crowd of avidly watching villagers. As she passed, they quietly removed their baskets and sat down.

"I tried to warn you," she began breathlessly. "If I don't work, neither will they."

"That does not concern me at the moment. What does concern me is that my wife is picking coffee beans like a—"

"Like a common peasant?" she inserted blandly.

He clamped his jaw closed, waiting until he had sufficient mastery of his anger before continuing. "It is not appropriate for you to be here. The villagers know this, which is why they chose to go into the fields rather than continue with their strike. They cannot in good conscience allow you to work unaided."

She smiled at him from beneath the shade of her straw hat. "I assumed as much."

His eyes narrowed. "If you knew this, then why are you here?"

"To try and end the strike. As a matter of fact, you gave me the idea."

He stared at her as though she'd taken leave of her senses. "*I* did?"

"You told me last night that where I led, the villagers would follow." Her smile turned impish. "So I just led the way to the fields. And you were right. It worked."

It took every ounce of willpower not to grab her by the shoulders and give her a good, hard shake. "Explain to me how this solves the basic problem."

"That's what I'm hoping you and I can do now."

He folded his arms across his chest. "I'm listening."

"You want me to leave the fields, right?"

"Of course I want you to leave."

"Perhaps we can reach a compromise. If you'd rehire Manuel—"

He shook his head, finally seeing the path her convoluted thinking had taken. "I cannot. It is a matter of honor."

"But—"

"It was a good try, *amada,*" he said gently. "Unfortunately, it won't work."

Resentment crept into her gaze. "Only because you're unwilling to make it work."

He thrust a hand through his hair, thoroughly exasperated. "I refuse to argue the matter with you. Not while standing in the middle of a coffee field. And not while the entire citizenry of Milagro listens in."

"As well as your buyers?" she asked innocently, glancing at a point somewhere over his shoulder.

He restrained the urge to turn around. *Madre de Dios!* What more could go wrong? "You will pay for this, my love," he murmured for her ears alone. "I will see to it. Personally."

She inclined her head. "I look forward to the experience," came her impudent retort. "In the meantime, I'm afraid your wife will continue to pick coffee beans. It's a matter of honor for me, as well."

"Whose honor do you speak of?" This time he did grab hold of her, ignoring their fascinated spectators. He pulled her close so she would see his anger and determination. "Do you refer to the honor of *La Estrella?* She doesn't exist. What you are attempting will end in disaster. You will bring harm to the villagers and to yourself. End this now, Ella. Before it's too late."

"It's already too late."

"I can force you to leave," he warned. "I can physically remove you from this place."

"But you won't." She stepped back and he released her, his silence confirming her guess. "It may not be a perfect solution, Rafe. But at least the beans will get picked and the villagers will be paid. The rest is up to you." She started to leave, then hesitated.

He lifted an eyebrow. "Was there something else?"

"Are—are you all right?" she asked awkwardly, gesturing toward his bandaged hand.

A momentary softness gleamed within his silvery gaze. "I am fine. Thank you for your concern."

Still she hesitated. "You're sure?"

"Quite certain."

She sighed. "In that case, I'd better get back to work."

With that, she turned and headed into the fields. Picking up her basket, she fastened it around her waist and adjusted the brim of her hat to shade her face. Then she plucked a violently red cherry from amongst a cluster of green berries.

And as she led, so the people of Milagro followed.

Rafe approached the door to Ella's room. It was closed and he couldn't hear her moving around. He tapped on the wooden panel. When she didn't answer, he pushed it open.

"Ella? It's time for dinner," he called.

And then he saw her.

Apparently working all day in the coffee fields had exhausted her, for she lay in the middle of the bed, sound asleep. She'd showered beforehand, wrapping herself in nothing more than a lightweight robe. A reluctant smile touched his mouth as he noticed her damp hair. She would have a job taming it when she eventually awoke. It fanned out behind her, the tumble of inky waves a sharp contrast to the crisp white pillowcase.

Unable to resist, he approached, staring down at her. She'd curled into a snug ball, her thin, silk robe pulled taut across her pertly rounded bottom and slender thighs. Her hands were folded beneath her chin, cushioned by her breasts, but he could still make out faintly stained fingernails. His smile grew.

Marvin had told him that she'd pried open a fair number of cherries. From what he could gather she'd repeatedly examined the twin beans inside, each time hoping to find a peaberry. If her rosy lips were any indication, she'd tasted her fair share of the sweet pulp, as well.

He crossed to her dresser and opened drawers at random until he found the one he sought. Removing a frothy silk nightgown, he crossed to the bed and eased her into his arms. Her lashes quivered for an instant and then she sighed, burrowing against him.

He held her for several long minutes, absorbing her warmth and sweet feminine fragrance. With a sigh of reluctance, he untied the robe and briskly stripped it from her.

She was as beautiful as he remembered, full-breasted and narrow-waisted, her skin softer than a quetzal plume. He ignored the ache building in his loins and pulled the nightgown over her head. Just as he'd finished easing her arms through the appropriate openings, her eyelids fluttered and she blinked up at him.

"Hello," she said with a wide yawn.

"Buenas noches, amada." To his relief, the lemon-colored silk drifted downward, concealing what tempted him almost beyond endurance.

Her head dipped to his shoulder again. "Did the buyers leave?" she asked sleepily.

"Long ago."

"Were they upset that your wife was working in the coffee fields?"

"Intrigued would be a more accurate description. They wondered if I were forcing you to pick the beans as a means of discipline."

She laughed, the sound low and husky and unbearably intimate. "The perfect excuse. I hope you took it."

"Tempting as it was, I did not."

Curiosity glittered in her gaze. "What did you tell them?"

"The truth."

"Oh," she murmured. "What was their reaction?"

"They were upset. Naturally, news of the strike did not please them."

"I'll bet."

He shifted her in his arms so her head rested more comfortably in the crook of his shoulder. "They requested that I bring in migrant laborers from Nicaragua to complete the job."

She tilted her head to look at him, alarm registering in her golden gaze. "Did you agree?"

"No. The villagers have traditionally picked Esperanza beans and they will continue to have that opportunity as long as I am owner of this *finca*."

"And when you're no longer the owner?"

He shrugged. "It is too early to say. I will do my best to protect them."

"I'm relieved to hear it." Another yawn caught her by surprise, blurring the end of her words. "Is it dinnertime? I guess I should get dressed."

"There's no point since I have just undressed you."

She glanced down, clearly amazed to discover herself wearing her nightgown. The tip of her tongue crept out to moisten her lips as she peeked up at him. "You undressed me?"

His gaze grew fiercely possessive. "Do you think I'd allow anyone else the pleasure?"

Disconcerted, her lashes flickered downward. "But dinner—"

"Chelita will bring you something on a tray."

"I can come down," she objected.

"Don't bother. You'd only end up falling asleep in your *olla de carne.*"

"My what?"

"Your beef stew."

"But—"

"Do you intend to return to the coffee fields in the morning?" At her stubborn nod, he swept back the covers and deposited her between the sheets. "In that case, you will need your rest. Make sure you put on strong sun protection tomorrow. At this time of year, a little exposure can prove quite painful. If you need lotion, ask Chelita when she brings your meal."

Ella plumped the pillows behind her with unnecessary force. "Why do I feel like a child who's been put to bed early for acting naughty?"

"I can't think of a single reason," he retorted in an even voice. "Can you?"

She curled into a ball again, her lids drifting closed. "No," she muttered crossly. "I can't."

He brushed her hair from her cheek and feathered a kiss across her temple. "Goodnight, *amada,*" he whispered. "Dream of me."

By the time he'd reached the door, she'd fallen asleep again. He frowned in concern as he headed for the kitchen. This stalemate had to end or *La Estrella* was likely to collapse. And that wouldn't help anyone. He released his breath in an exasperated sigh, forced to concede the inevitable.

The time had come to have a serious talk with Manuel.

The next morning Ella dragged herself from bed and headed for the coffee fields before she could think of a good excuse to avoid it. She hurt. Badly. In fact, there wasn't a muscle in her body that didn't ache. Who would have thought picking coffee could be so difficult?

Not that a few sore muscles would change her mind. Not a chance. She'd decided to attempt this particular miracle. And by heavens, she'd see it through to the bitter end. The villagers were waiting for her on the outskirts of the field. The moment she plucked the first cherry off the first tree, they immediately followed suit. Not five minutes passed, however, before nervous whispers warned that Rafe had once again come after her.

She turned to welcome him with a jaunty smile, praying her exhaustion couldn't be seen on her face. Her prayers weren't answered. A frown crashed down on his brow.

"You look like hell, *amada.*"

"And good morning to you, too."

"Fair warning," he leaned close to say. "Today this ends." Then in a louder voice, he announced, "I've come for my wife."

Before she could draw breath to ask what he meant, he yanked his switchblade from his pocket and flicked it open. In one easy move; he sliced through the harness.

The attached basket upended, spilling ripe beans into the dirt at her feet.

"Rafe!"

His name ended in a panicked shriek as he picked her up. Tossing her over his shoulder like a sack of potatoes, he spoke in rapid Spanish to the workers. To her utter astonishment, they burst into loud cheers. Twisting around to look, her hat snagged on a nearby branch. It was lifted neatly off her head, while her loosened hair tumbled free, clouding her vision. Planting her hands on the solid wall of his back, she shoved upward.

"What's going on?" she demanded furiously, shaking her hair back from her face.

His only response was to wrap one arm around the back of her knees and bounce her to a more secure spot on his shoulder. Her breath left her lungs in an audible gasp. Catching hold of the back of his belt, she hung on for dear life as he strode from the fields. Once they were well out of view of the villagers, he dropped her to her feet. She staggered and he caught her elbow while she steadied herself.

"You want to explain what all that was about?" she questioned grumpily. She attempted to bring some sort of order to her hair, but soon gave it up as a lost cause.

"That was about saving face."

"I figured as much." She glanced back at the fields. "Why did they cheer?"

"Because I ended the strike."

She swiveled to look at him. "You—You're not selling the *finca*?" she questioned hopefully. "You've changed your mind?"

He shook his head. "I warned you it wasn't that simple. I fired Manuel for a very good reason. I'm not about to rehire him just because you've been rash enough to step in where you don't belong."

"Then how did you end the strike?"

A cold smile touched his mouth. "As a matter of fact, you gave me the idea that night at dinner."

"*I* did?"

"You said you'd hire Chelita if I fired her." He inclined his head in response to her dawning comprehension. "It seemed fitting to turn the tables on you. I may not be in a position to hire Manuel, since I'm the one who fired him. But you can. The distinction isn't lost on the workers. It appeases them so they're willing to return to work—"

"While still allowing you to save face." She nodded ruefully. It wasn't quite what she'd hoped to achieve, but it was a start. "What am I supposed to do with Manuel? I don't really need an employee."

Rafe shrugged. "That's your problem. But in future, I'd appreciate your staying out of my business. No more miracles. Are we clear?"

Her brows drew together. "I'm not sure we are."

"Allow me to clarify. I leave for San José within the hour. A problem with the sale of Esperanza has cropped up and must be dealt with. Don't look so hopeful," he was quick to add, accurately interpreting her reaction. "The problem is nothing that a few days' discussion won't correct."

She smiled sweetly. "I'm sorry to hear that."

"I'm sure you are." His expression might have been carved from stone. "While I'm gone, give your future plans careful consideration. Stop worrying about matters you can't change and start worrying about matters you can."

"Meaning?"

"Your own position is somewhat precarious at the moment, far more so than the villagers. At least they have my protection. You do not, as you discovered last night. I recommend you think about ways to correct that."

"You mean the agreement you want from my parents."

"Yes."

"One conversation can straighten that out," she assured him calmly.

"I'm relieved to hear it." He waited a beat before adding, "We'll have that conversation on my return. Now are we clear?"

"As crystal."

"Excellent."

And with that, he turned and, once again, walked away.

Over the next several days, she considered what Rafe had said. But it didn't change her mind. It just made her more determined than ever to find a way to get through to him, as well as to find out why he was so hell-bent on selling Esperanza. Once she discovered the answer to that, perhaps she could prevent the sale and help the villagers.

And then there was Shayne. Ella knew she couldn't wave a magic wand and make Chaz McIntyre reappear, she just might be able to give some assistance in another area.

Shayne's mosaics.

Manuel had told her about an art gallery in San José that specialized in unique artworks by local artisans. It sounded perfect for what she hoped to accomplish. If she showed a few pieces to the proprietor, perhaps an expert could convince Shayne her talent shouldn't be wasted. Unfortunately, in order to put her plan into motion, she needed to go into the city while Rafe was away.

It took hours of arguing to convince Manuel to help. "You don't understand," he protested. "I cannot bring you back. I have to return to school."

"I can drive myself back. I'll watch the route we take."

He shook his head. "It's not that simple. The mountain roads can be very confusing. And they're dangerous. There are rock slides. We get sudden downpours where entire sections of road wash away. Not to mention the potholes. If something happened to you—"

"Nothing will happen. Not if you draw a map and not if I'm careful. Please, Manuel. It's important. I wouldn't ask you to do this if it were just for me. But it's for Shayne. Or do you want her to spend the rest of her life working as an accountant?"

"What's wrong with being an accountant?"

"Nothing, if that's what Shayne really wanted. Can you honestly say it is?"

"No," he admitted. "Creating mosaics has been her obsession since she was a teenager. She even had a few commissions before . . ." His shrug spoke volumes. "Just the other day, when she thought no one was watching, she sketched a new design for her portfolio."

His words confirmed what Ella already suspected. "Then you'll help?"

He sighed. "I will help. But if anything goes wrong, you could work in the coffee fields until doomsday and still not salvage my job a second time."

That gave her pause. She wouldn't want to do anything to harm Manuel's future. And though that future wasn't picking coffee berries, she didn't doubt Rafe had a long reach. Not to mention a propensity for vengeance. "I promise. I'll be very careful."

And she was. The entire way to San José the next morning, she paid close attention to the route. Even after they arrived in the city, she reviewed the map Manuel had drawn and thoroughly familiarized herself with it. Next, they located the art gallery.

"The owner is away on a buying trip," explained the assistant, a friendly young woman, with an appealing smile. "But I'd be happy to show him your mosaics when he returns."

"I can leave them with you?" Ella asked. "You wouldn't mind?"

"Not at all." She examined them appreciatively. "They're stunning. I'm certain *Señor* Jiménez will be most impressed."

After leaving a phone number and address where Shayne could be reached, Manuel drove to the outskirts of the university. He insisted on reviewing the map once more before he was satisfied she could find her way to Milagro.

"I'll start back right away," she assured him. "Don't worry. I'll be home well before dark."

"It won't matter. Your husband will have my head for this regardless," he predicted gloomily. "Even if it is for a good cause."

Ella grinned. "Well, Chelita will appreciate the effort you've taken even if Rafe doesn't"

Once again dusky color tinged his cheekbones. *"Hasta luego,* Estrella. *Vaya con Dios."*

"The same to you. And thank you, Manuel."

Taking a deep breath, Ella put the car in gear and pulled into traffic. To her relief, the trip progressed without incident. She took her time, managing to avoid most of the potholes she came across and all of the oncoming cars. They passed at such high rates of speed she suspected they'd end up finding their way down the mountain by the fastest possible route—off a cliff and straight to the bottom. To her relief, the kamikaze traffic vanished once she turned onto the side road that led to Milagro.

Two thirds of the way home, she skirted a pile of branches dumped in the middle of the road. And rounding the next curve she ran into trouble.

Serious trouble.

Chapter Nine

Rafe stood by the side of the road, leaning against his car, a jacket hooked over one shoulder. Ella immediately applied the brakes and pulled in behind him. He stared for a moment, then shook his head and walked toward her.

"Why am I not surprised to see you?" he asked, resting his forearms on the edge of her open window.

She couldn't help smiling. "I don't know. Why?"

"Perhaps it's because I so frequently find you where you don't belong."

"Maybe you should just change your opinion of where I do, or rather, don't, belong."

"I have reached a similar conclusion," he admitted wryly. "Is there any point in asking what you're doing here?"

"I'd rather discuss what you're doing," she replied candidly.

"Broken water pump. I've been waiting for a Good Samaritan to come to my rescue."

Her smile grew. "And here I am. The answer to your prayers."

"The answer to many prayers, I fear," he said with resignation.

She thought better of responding to that one. "If you're willing to drive, I'd be happy to give you a lift."

He raised an eyebrow. "Don't you like our roads, *amada?*"

What would be the most delicate way of phrasing her reply? "No."

"In that case I'd be happy to offer my services. Let me get my luggage and briefcase and we can be on our way."

He returned a moment later and dumped his bags and suit coat onto the backseat. Climbing behind the steering wheel, he shot her a curious glance. "You still haven't told me what you're doing here." Pulling onto the road, he carefully skirted his abandoned car, the narrow lane leaving little room to spare.

Around the next bend she spotted another pile of branches. "I saw those on the last curve," she commented. "Why would someone just dump them in the middle of the road, like that?"

"I put them there to indicate a hazard ahead. It's a common practice. And you haven't answered my question."

She hadn't expected to successfully divert him. Still, it had been worth a try. "I went into San José."

He frowned. "On your own?"

"No, Manuel drove me." His frown grew fiercer and she hastened to emphasize, "As my employee, he could hardly refuse my request for a driver. Although to give him credit, he tried."

"I suspect if he hadn't consented, you'd have gone on your own," Rafe guessed shrewdly.

"True enough. He needed to go back to the university, so we drove in together."

"Leaving you to return to Milagro by yourself?"

She took instant exception to the implied criticism. "He drew a very detailed map and went over it several times." Her mouth tightened. "I'm a twenty-six-year-old woman, Rafe. Not a child. I'm perfectly capable of driving myself from point A to point B without a man along to help."

He let that pass. "What were you so anxious to accomplish in San José that it couldn't wait until I'd concluded my business?"

"Actually, I didn't think you'd be willing to take me," she confessed.

Comprehension dawned. "Once I knew what you wanted, you mean?"

"Yes."

"And the purpose for this trip was what?"

She shot him a nervous glance. She'd been most concerned about his reaction to this part of the story. Best to get it over with quickly. "I took several of Shayne's mosaic pieces to an art gallery for an expert opinion on their quality."

"Performing more miracles, Estrella?" he inquired with surprising tolerance.

"Just a very tiny one."

Before he could say anything more, the car gave an odd coughing sound. Muttering a curse, Rafe pulled to the side of the road once again. With a tired wheeze, the engine died.

"What's wrong? What happened?" Ella asked.

"Give me a moment to see." He attempted to restart the car, without success. Next, he opened the door to get out, then paused. "Ah, *amada?*"

She didn't care for the tenor of his voice. "Yes?"

"When you were busy being this independent twenty-six-year-old woman capable of driving herself from point A to point B, did you by any chance check the fuel level?"

She cringed. "We're out of gas?"

"Yes, we're out of gas!"

"Oh."

"Oh? That's all you have to say?"

"Um. I'm glad you're here to keep me company?"

He climbed from the car and slammed the door closed. "Sit tight and don't move."

"Where are you going?"

"I'm going to put more branches in the road."

"I can help."

He spun around and strode back to the car. "No. You can't help. And, no. You won't help. You will sit without moving so much as an inch. Understand? The way our luck is running, you're likely to gather up some manzanillo branches and poison yourself."

She folded her arms across her chest and glared. "Even you couldn't be that lucky. Besides, they only grow by the ocean and you know it."

He poked his head through the open window. "First of all, there would be nothing lucky about losing you to the tree of death," he informed her in no uncertain terms. "And second, I don't care where it grows. With your propensity for sticking your nose where it doesn't belong, you'd manage to find one. Now don't move."

Ten minutes later he returned to the car. "It may be a while. I don't suppose you have any bottled water?"

"Actually I do. Manuel insisted," she informed him, hoping to score a few points on the student's behalf. "I also have a thermos of left-over coffee and a bag full of Tico snacks I couldn't live without. Or so Manuel informed me."

Rafe picked up the large bag she indicated and looked inside. "I may have to forgive his lapse in judgment in taking you to San José. He has made some excellent choices. We won't starve, that's for certain."

"What's in there?" She peeked over his shoulder. "I haven't even checked."

He shifted toward her side of the seat so she'd have a better view. "Are you hungry?"

"Very."

"Well, we have *tortas* and *chorreados.*"

"Which are?"

"*Tortas* are a bread containing meat and vegetables. And *chorreados* are a corn pancake." He rummaged through the bag. "It would seem Manuel has a sweet tooth. Half the bag has been filled with cajeta, pañuelos y tapitas."

"All right. I give up. What's a cajeta?"

"It's fudge."

"And *pañ—*"

"*Pañuelos.* The literal translation is handkerchief. But it's a pastry."

"And *tapitas?*"

"A small chocolate wrapped in foil." He gave her a lazy smile. "Is this a Spanish lesson? Perhaps there are more words you'd like to learn."

His question sparked her curiosity and she slowly nodded. "As a matter of fact there are." She gazed at him intently. "What does *esperanza* mean? I keep forgetting to ask."

His jaw tightened, his amusement vanishing with frightening speed. Clearly, he hadn't expected that particular question. "It means hope," he said without expression.

She stared at him, stunned. "Your *finca* is named hope?"

"Not from choice."

"That I can believe." Her curiosity grew. "And the town? What is Milagro in English?"

"Miracle."

She drew a shaky breath. "And *amada?*"

He gazed out the front windshield and shrugged. "It is a form of endearment. One not often used." He tossed the bag into her lap. "I thought you were hungry. Have the *cajeta.* It's quite good."

"*Amada,*" she repeated deliberately, shoving the bag aside. "What does it mean?"

His voice was so low and rough, she had to strain to catch his response. "Beloved." He thrust his hand into his pocket. "What the hell have I done with my cigarettes?"

"You threw them out, remember?" she murmured, badly shaken.

"The day you arrived. How could I forget?"

"Don't change the subject." She touched his shoulder, drawing his gaze. "All this time, that's what you've been calling me? Beloved?"

"You must have realized it was a form of endearment," he said testily.

"Not really."

"What did you think I'd been calling you?"

"I don't know. Dark-haired woman. Most annoying one. Silly twit. I was afraid to ask."

Amusement turned his eyes to points of silver light. "Silly twit?"

"I think I prefer beloved."

"I would hope so."

She snuggled closer, dropping her head to his shoulder. "I missed you," she confessed.

"And I, you. It has been a long few days." His fingers grazed her cheek. "I trust you've stayed out of the coffee fields while I've been gone?"

"Yes. Have you changed your mind about selling the *finca*?"

"No."

"Is it because you can't bear to live on a ranch called hope outside a town called miracle?"

"I have lived there for a good portion of my life." His hand shifted from her cheek to ruffle her hair. "I would not sell my home for such a trivial reason."

"Then why?"

He hesitated. "I'm doing it for Shayne's sake," he finally said, answering the question that had plagued her since she'd arrived.

"Shayne?"

"You aren't the only one who has seen changes in her," he responded indirectly. "She isn't the same girl she was five years ago. Everything she ever held dear, she has pushed away."

"Including you?"

He didn't spare himself. "To a certain extent. Yes."

"Because you took her from Chaz McIntyre?"

"There could be no other reason." He released his breath in a ragged sigh. "I have tortured myself over that decision for years, wondering if I made a mistake. I've analyzed it again and again and each time I come to the same conclusion. She was a child who'd only known this man for a few short hours. To have left her in his care would have been wrong."

"Why did she marry him? Do you know?"

"Yes. I know." He gave her a straight look. "She wanted the fairy tale. She wanted your life, *amada*. A life she'd never had."

"My life?" Ella repeated, taken aback. "But she lived a fairy tale existence of her own. Why would she think mine better than the one she already had?"

He hesitated. "Her life was not a fairy tale."

"I realize you lost your parents, but—"

"Our father and her mother were killed in a boating accident when I was sixteen. Shayne was three."

She stared at him, stunned. "I hadn't realized you were so young. Were there relatives to help?"

"No."

Ella stared in shock. "What in the world did you do?"

"What could I do? I tried to keep our life together, to take care of the coffee *finca*, to take care of my little sister, to protect all those who depended on me." He shrugged as though it didn't matter. But she knew better. "I failed. I lost everything— the estate and what little money I inherited from my parents. But worst of all, I lost Shayne."

Ella recalled the conversation she'd had with her father on Christmas night. He'd said that Rafe had once lost control of his life. That he fought an ongoing battle to ensure it never happen again. This must be what her father had referred to. Though how he'd uncovered the story, she couldn't begin to guess.

"What do you mean, you lost her?" she asked gently. "What happened to Shayne?"

"When I realized I could no longer care for her, that soon we'd be without a home or enough food to survive, I called my stepmother's sister. Jackie lived in Florida. And though she'd been violently opposed to the marriage, I decided to take a chance, thinking that under the circumstances she might help."

"I assumed Shayne's mother was Tico," Ella said in surprise.

"No. Ironic, is it not? I am but one quarter native, Shayne not at all."

"So, did Jackie come?"

"She came. And then she left with Shayne."

It took a moment to absorb the significance. "Just Shayne?" Ella asked softly.

Again came that careless shrug. "We weren't related, Jackie and I. Therefore she was under no obligation to help 'a filthy Tico peasant.'"

"Oh, Rafe. I'm so sorry."

"Save your sympathy. It was not I who needed it."

"Your sister?"

He stared through the front windshield as though peering into the distant past, lost in dark memories. "She was gone from my life, but not a day went by that I didn't think about her, wonder and worry about whether I'd done the right thing by giving her to Jackie."

"What else could you have done?"

"That question has haunted me from the moment I placed Shayne in that woman's arms."

"What did you do after they left?"

"I worked for the next ten years rebuilding my finances. When the price of coffee bottomed out in the mid-eighties, Esperanza came on the market again and I bought it. Soon afterward, money was no longer a problem." His mouth tightened. "So I went looking for Shayne. I had to make sure I'd done the right thing by giving her to Jackie."

She dreaded asking the next question. "What did you find?"

"That I'd made a terrible mistake. I gather feeding and clothing and raising a child, even one partly her own flesh and blood, was not how Jackie wished to spend her life. She made certain that Shayne paid every day for having been 'rescued' from her previous existence." He closed his eyes. "My sweet *hermanita* had gone from a bright extroverted child to a shy, nervous teenager starving for love and affection."

Tears stung Ella's eyes. Poor Shayne. "What happened then?"

"Jackie sold my sister to me."

"Sold her?"

"Sold her like a commodity. I took Shayne back to Costa Rica and I swore I'd protect her from that day on. I succeeded. I succeeded, that is, until one terrible night five years ago."

"The Cinderella Ball."

He nodded. "She was so susceptible to its allure. It offered all that she'd been denied as a child. Love, happiness, and happily-ever-after. How could she resist such a temptation?"

"She couldn't," Ella acknowledged.

"Perhaps she'd have been better off if I'd left her with McIntyre. But she was so young. And I had failed to protect her from Jackie. I couldn't fail again."

"I'm sure Chaz didn't know her real age."

"To his credit, I don't think so, either."

"You've explained about Shayne. But you still haven't told me what that has to do with selling the *finca.*"

He frowned. "As long as Esperanza is her home, she will continue to hide from life. You have seen her, have seen the changes in her. She is a woman who has lost her direction."

"I thought she was studying to become an accountant."

"She studies so she can help me. It's as though she's paying penitence for a sin she never committed. I once offered to finance whatever dream she cared to fulfill. But she will take nothing from me. It's as though she's lost her love for life."

"And the funds from the sale of Esperanza? Why would she accept that when she wouldn't take the other money you offered?"

"I never told her I'd lost the estate. All she knows is that it was left to both of us equally on the death of our parents, which is true. She'll consider herself entitled to those funds. At least, I hope so. Even if she does not, she'll be forced out into the world."

"You won't be able to protect her in that world," Ella felt obligated to caution.

He rubbed the crease furrowing his brow. "A seventeen-year-old teenager needs adult protection to avoid a painful fall. I am forced to concede, however, that a twenty-three-year-old woman should be permitted to stumble once or twice. By skinning an occasional knee, she'll be in a better position to protect her own children when the time comes."

"But it's difficult to let go, isn't it?"

"Perhaps the most difficult thing I've ever done."

"That's why you weren't upset when you found out I'd taken her mosaics to the art gallery."

"Yes." His gaze held a warning. "She'll be angry when she discovers what you've done."

"At least if she's angry, she'll be feeling something."

A car horn blared just then. They looked up to see Marvin's cab skidding around the curve toward them. He honked again in greeting, then stopped in the middle of the road. "It is a good thing I have come along, *sí?*" he called.

Rafe climbed from the car. "A very good thing, my friend. Are you here by luck or by design?"

"A bit of both. Manuel left instructions. He said that if *La Estrella* didn't show up by midafternoon, I was to come looking for her. Just in case." He grinned. "It was a good plan, I think."

"It was an excellent plan," Ella said dryly. "Thank you."

"De nada," Marvin rubbed his hands together. "So, what is the problem?"

"We're out of gas," Rafe told him succinctly.

Marvin's gaze switched from one to the other. He struggled to conceal his amusement and failed. *"No problema,"* he said. " I will have you on your way *muy rapido."*

"I'd like to take Ella to see the sunset at *Abrazo de Amante.* Do you have enough gas to spare?"

"Por supuesto. It would be my pleasure." In no time, Marvin had the gas syphoned from one tank to the other. "I will warn Chelita of your late arrival," he offered when he'd finished.

"I'd appreciate that," Rafe said.

"And I have something else you might appreciate." Marvin opened the trunk of his car and pulled out a large folded blanket, tossing it to Rafe. "Take this and enjoy your embrace."

Color tinted Ella's cheekbones. "Why did he say that?" she demanded.

"Abrazo de Amante. It means lover's embrace. He was just making a little joke."

"Oh." She slanted another look in Rafe's direction. "Why is it called that?"

He smiled cryptically as he started the engine. "You'll see."

Further down the road, he turned onto a small side track that dipped back down the mountainside. It was little more than two ruts slicing through the thick foliage. He drove carefully, allowing her to get a good look at the variety of birds that winged across their path.

"That's a motmot," he said, pointing to a bird whose long electric-blue tail flicked back and forth like the pendulum of a clock. "And a pair of toucans are hiding in that tree there."

At the next turn, he pulled to a stop so she could watch the noisy antics of several howler monkeys shaking the branches overhead. But the most breathtaking sight of all was the brief glimpse she caught of the spectacular Morpho butterfly, its cobalt wings flashing like iridescent jewels against the vivid green canopy.

They rounded a final curve and she stared in astonishment. A huge rock pool spread out before them, fed by a spring. Steam rose from the glassy surface, wafting off the water to fog the surrounding forest. It was primeval, stirring a response that felt as ancient and elemental as the jungle itself.

"Abrazo de Amante," Rafe said softly, turning off the engine.

"Now I understand why Marvin gave you the blanket."

He left the car and she followed, unable to drag her eyes from temptation. She itched to shed her sticky clothes and climb into the hot tub nature had so kindly provided.

Drifting closer to the pool, she asked, "Can we . . . Can we go in?"

He came to stand behind her, so close his breath stirred her hair. "Take off your blouse," he directed, the warmth of his body radiating along the length of her spine.

She didn't hesitate. Continuing to stare at the steaming water, she lifted a hand to work the buttons. One by one they slipped through the holes. When she'd finished, she shrugged the lightweight cotton off her shoulders. It never hit the ground. Rafe snagged it as it fluttered earthward.

"Your skirt."

He didn't move any closer, but simply waited. Keeping her back to him, she obediently lowered the side zip. Still without actually touching her, he bunched her skirt and slip in his fists and pulled them both to her waist. Then he swept them over her head before stepping back once more.

It was the strangest striptease she'd ever done. The *only* striptease she'd ever done. Erotic and yet innocent. Touching without touching. It made her keenly aware of her own sexuality, that she was removing her clothing for the pleasure of a man. The fact that the man in question happened to be her husband made it all the more tantalizing. The fact that they'd never made love before, made the tension almost unbearable.

"What next?" she whispered.

"Your bra."

She unhooked the scrap of white lace. Lowering her arms to her sides, she crooked her elbows slightly so the straps caught there. He reached around her, his hand so close to her skin, she could feel the heat he generated. He leaned in, his warm breath teasing across her shoulder and down the slopes of her breasts, furling the peaks into tight little rosebuds. He hooked his finger around one silky strap and waited until she dropped her arms. The lace fell into his grasp.

"And now?" she asked.

"There's only one thing left."

"Do I take it off or leave it on?"

His voice grated. "Take it off."

This would be the most difficult part of all. She closed her eyes, debating whether or not she should end the game now. Never in her life had she felt so vulnerable.

But her decision boiled down to two simple words. Trust. And love. It was Rafe standing behind her. The man she loved with all her heart and trusted with her very soul. He'd never hurt her, despite what he'd threatened. And she wanted him, wanted to be his wife in fact as well as name.

Without further hesitation, she kicked off her sandals and slipped her thumbs into the elastic waistband, inching the lightweight silk down her hips. She could hear the sharp intake of his breath followed by the ragged release, sensed he teetered on the knife's edge between restraint and raw instinct. Once her underpants slid past her thighs, they floated to the ground. She took a step forward, leaving them behind.

She smiled, knowing he couldn't see her expression, and lifted her hands to her hair, removing the clip restraining it. With a quick shake, the strands tumbled free, veiling her neck and shoulders in a thick dark curtain.

She glanced behind her then, allowing him to witness her smile. Before he could act on the savage need burning in his eyes, she darted toward the pool. She hesitated for an instant at the rocky rim, testing the temperature with her toe. It was perfect. She slipped in, the warmth of the water sheathing her like a velvet glove. *Abrazo de Amante*. The name made perfect sense to her now.

"Feel good?" he called to her, his voice stark with desire.

"It's unbelievable."

"Have you ever gone swimming in the rough before?"

"Never. It's—it's . . ."

A hard grin slashed across his face. "Yes, it is." The pool was deep, well over her head, and full of large black rocks. The heated water felt like a lover's hand, swirled over her breasts and between her legs in the most sensuous caress she'd ever experienced. She drifted toward the center, watching Rafe.

He hadn't taken his gaze from her. At a distance his eyes appeared black instead of gray, but there was no mistaking the intent registering in that scorching look. He wanted her. Badly. Every line of his body, every ripple of compact muscle underscored that desire. He swiftly shed his shirt and shoes, and in one easy move, ripped his belt from the loops. Then he reached for his zipper.

A light breeze stirred the steam so warm spray kissed her skin and caught in her hair, sparkling like stardust. Kicking lightly to one side of the pool, she dove deep into the heated heart. It was sheer bliss. She glided underwater toward the edge closest to Rafe, hoping to surface and surprise him. But as she started up, her hair snagged in a narrow crevice between the pile of rocks.

She tugged, expecting the strands to pull loose. Instead, they held fast. She tugged again, harder this time, the first glimmer of panic radiating through her subconscious. But no matter what she tried, she couldn't work her way free. She couldn't even get enough leverage to plant her feet against the slippery rocks and use her leg muscles to rip the hair from its anchor. Her chest burned, lending urgency to her actions. In sheer desperation, she kicked toward the surface as hard as she could, stretching out her hand in an effort to break the plane of the water and alert Rafe. Her trapped hair yanked her backward.

She was going to die. She knew it. Her mouth opened in a silent scream and water poured in.

Chapter Ten

Rafe placed his clothing on the front seat of the car and turned, staring across the pool with a frown. Something was wrong. Very wrong. He could feel it. And then it hit him.

He couldn't see Ella.

Driven by pure instinct, he reached back into the car. Snatching his switchblade free of his trouser's pocket, he pivoted, sprinting flat-out for the pool. What he found there turned his blood to ice. Ella's hair had become caught in the underwater rocks and she was trying frantically to pull the strands loose.

Flicking open his knife, he dove to her side. Her hands were in his way and he yanked them clear. Panicking, she fought back, too desperate for air to understand his intent. Finally he wrapped an arm around her, locking her flailing limbs tight against his body. Dragging her as far from the deadly rocks as possible, he slashed his knife through her trapped hair. Not wasting another second, he kicked toward salvation.

She tried to inhale the minute they broke the surface. Instead she choked, the water filling her lungs making breathing an impossibility. Rafe tossed his knife onto the rocks and heaved himself from the pool, hanging on to her with one hand. Reaching down, he hauled her up and into his arms. She collapsed against him and he bent her at the waist, squeezing her ribs until she'd dispelled enough water to breathe.

Weak tears spilled from her eyes. "Rafe," she whispered hoarsely. "Oh, Rafe. Hold me."

"I'm here, *amada*. I have you." He cradled her more tightly in his arms, sweeping her hair from her face. "Easy, *pobrecita*. Take it easy."

She fought to speak. "I thought I was going to die."

"I would not let that happen," he said simply.

"I didn't think you saw." She shuddered. "I couldn't reach you. I couldn't let you know I needed you."

His mouth caressed her temple. "I knew. Somehow I knew." She shivered again and he started to stand. "You're cold. Let me get the blanket."

Tears welled up in her eyes again. "No! Don't leave me."

"Just for a moment," he soothed. "I'll be right back." Even the few seconds it took to reach the car and grab the blanket seemed an eternity. As soon as he returned, he wrapped the heavy cotton around them both and sat with her on the edge of the rocks. In time her shivers eased and her breathing grew more relaxed.

"Come," he said at last. "Let's get dressed and go home."

"No, not home. I'd rather go back in the water."

Her request caught him off guard. "I don't think that's a good idea."

"I know it sounds crazy, but, this is too beautiful a place to leave with such bad memories." She gazed at him, her eyes vibrant bits of gold. "Please, Rafe."

He couldn't argue with her, not after what she'd just experienced. If she had the courage to return to the water, who was he to object?

"Then come," he said.

He drew her toward the rim of the pool, absorbing the shiver that rippled through her as they paused at the edge. After a few endless moments, her fear evaporated, absolute faith implicit in the glance she sent him.

"Take me in with you."

"Do not look at me like that, *amada,*" he demanded.

"Like what?"

"With such trust."

"But I do trust you. With my life, as it turns out."

His mouth tightened. "You should not."

To his irritation, she gave a soft, knowing laugh. Gritting his teeth, he helped her into the water, never allowing her to drift further than arm's length. But there was a steep price to pay for such close care.

Every few minutes she brushed against him. Her lush bottom drifted over his hip. Her full, ripe breasts danced along his forearm. With unerring accuracy, her unguarded foot found the taut length of his thigh. When he felt the pebbled tip of her breast scrape across his back, he could stand no more.

"We should get out before I do something we both regret," he said, barely restraining a groan.

"What is it you think I'll regret?" She smiled. It was a revealing sort of smile and understanding crashed in on him.

"You play a dangerous game," he informed her tightly.

"And you don't play at all."

It was the last straw. With a guttural snarl, he lunged. Wrapping her in an unrelenting hold, he kicked to the far side of the pool.

"You have been begging for this."

"Since the night we were married," she confirmed without hesitation. "Are you finally going to give it to me?"

He closed his eyes, his anger dissipating as swiftly as it had emerged. "Yes, *amada*. Since it's what I want, too, it will be all too easy to give you what you wish."

Ella hesitated, catching her lower lip between her teeth. "If I say I love you, will you leave like you did on our wedding night?"

He shook his head, but deep furrows carved a path from his cheekbones to the tense line of his jaw. "I don't have that much control. Not anymore."

"In that case . . ." Cupping his face, she took his mouth in a tender kiss. "I love you, Rafe. Please make me your wife."

"I cannot give you all that you ask," he whispered.

"But I will give you all that I have."

Mist rising off the pool dewed his hair with diamond droplets, matching the silver glitter of his eyes. She splayed her hand across his collarbone, tracing the ragged scars she found there. With a murmur of regret, she bent and kissed each individual mark of valor. His muscles knotted beneath her fingers and she followed the taut lines down his chest to the corrugated surface of his belly.

"Do not go any further," he warned roughly. "Or this moment will end before it has begun."

"Tell me what you want."

"Why don't I show you, instead." He slid his hands beneath her arms and lifted. His breath came rapidly, hot against her damp skin. "You are so beautiful. The most beautiful woman I have ever known."

Water sluiced downward, beading on the tips of her breasts. She whispered his name, half in encouragement, half in protest. With a low groan, he caught the tears of moisture with his tongue. She gripped his shoulders, her eyes drifting shut. Then his mouth closed on her, each tiny love bite more pleasing than the last.

"Good?" he murmured, his jaw a delicious abrasion against her sensitive skin.

"Do you need to ask?"

"I can make it better."

She laughed, the sound low and husky. "I don't think that's possible."

"You will see. Grab the rock above you, amada."

She looked up. A fingerlike outcropping jutted directly overhead and she reached for it, latching onto the rough surface so she hung half in, half out of the water. Her weight pulled her taut and he took full advantage of the exposed landscape, wandering over creamy hillocks and into delicate hollows, exploring rich deltas and moist caverns. And always he drove her. Past curiosity. Past budding desire. Relentlessly pushing her toward an all-consuming desperation for fulfillment.

Her breathing grew labored, her body heavy with need. "I can't hold on any longer."

"Wrap your legs around my waist and let go."

She did as he requested and he caught her as she fell, slowing her descent. Palming her bottom, he sheathed himself within her, burning heat melding into innocent warmth. When he could go no further, he lifted her again, starting the slow, stormy slide all over.

She trembled helplessly, filled with such joy and wonder that tears flooded her eyes. This was what she'd waited for, refusing to settle for less, knowing it wouldn't be right without Rafe. As though sensing her thoughts, he whispered tender words, striving to make each moment sweeter than the last. Bit by bit their pace increased until the hot water washed over and around them, slapping, splashing, churning. And then came the moment that fused them into one, shattering in its impact.

In that instant, Ella felt as though anything was possible. The villagers would receive the prosperity and happiness they'd long awaited. Shayne would find satisfaction and contentment through her mosaic work. The *finca* wouldn't have to be sold. And, Rafe . . .

Rafe would end his vendetta and allow love into his life.

At long last, she'd receive the magic of the Cinderella Ball. And with that magic, she'd discover happily-ever-after in the arms of the man she loved with all her heart and soul.

Rafe and Ella returned to Esperanza just as the sun set. "Why don't I ask Chelita to fix a salad for us?" he suggested, wrapping an arm around her shoulders. "After working our way through Manuel's bag of snacks, I'm not very hungry."

"I'm not, either. A salad sounds perfect." She paused within the cool shelter of the entranceway, her quiet voice amplified by the slate flooring. "I'll go shower, then meet you in the dining room. All right?"

Chelita appeared just then. *"Disculpe, Señor,"* she said nervously.

"Yes?"

She spared a swift glance for Ella. *"El padre de la Señora està aquí. Quiere hablar con usted solo. Solamente usted."*

"Adónde?"

"En la oficina."

He frowned. "Thank you, Chelita. I'll deal with it."

"Is something wrong?" Ella asked. She'd recognized a word or two of the housekeeper's rapid-fire Spanish, but not enough to follow the conversation.

"Go ahead and shower. I have some business to attend to." He hesitated. "Perhaps you should come to my office once you've changed."

"There's something wrong, isn't there?"

"That's what I'm going to find out."

"Why don't I come now?"

He shook his head, his expression adamant. "Give me a moment first. It may be nothing."

She didn't argue. But an inexplicable fear seized her. In sudden need of reassurance, she caught his face between her palms and tugged him toward her. He didn't require any prompting, but covered her mouth in an ardent kiss. One hand bunched in the damp curls of her hair, his other followed the length of her spine, molding her against him. She felt his desire return, felt the desperate need reassert itself.

"We can't," he muttered.

"I know." She sighed, catching his bottom lip between her teeth and tugging gently. "Thank you for today. Maybe tomorrow—"

"Do not say it, *amada*." He closed his eyes, deep lines slashing along the sides of his mouth. "Today might be all I can give you."

"I don't believe that," she protested. "I *won't* believe it."

He started to speak, then shook his head. "Go and shower. I was wrong to say anything. This isn't the appropriate time."

She shivered, suddenly cold. "I hope that time never comes."

He didn't respond, but stood motionless and silent, his eyes an unreadable sooty gray. Standing on tiptoe, she planted a quick kiss along the taut line of his jaw and headed for her room.

She didn't rush her shower. Although part of her wanted to hurry back to Rafe, a more rational part urged caution. Something had happened in the entranceway. Something that had changed his attitude toward her. And she wasn't in any hurry to discover what that might be.

She needed a second to herself. A brief moment in which to relive the past several hours. A brief moment in which to believe that dreams could come true.

Once she'd finished dressing, she made her way to Rafe's office. After knocking, she pushed open the door. Rafe sat behind his desk. And leaning across it, speaking in irate tones, was her father. Clearly, they hadn't heard her knock.

" . . . idea what you're doing!" Donald was asserting.

Rafe stared at him coldly. "I know precisely what I'm doing."

"Dad," she said in astonishment. "I didn't know you were here."

They both looked up at the same instant, conflicting expressions on their faces. Her father looked furious. Rafe appeared resigned. "Come in, *amada*. And close the door."

"I don't want her involved in this," Donald protested.

"It is far too late for that."

She glanced from one to the other. "What's going on?"

"Go ahead," Rafe ordered. "Tell her."

After a momentary hesitation, Donald said, "It's a financial matter. It has to do with our mortgage. It comes up for renewal soon." He shrugged in resignation. "There's no easy way to say this, so I'll be blunt. The company who owns the note—the Phoenix Corporation—won't renew it. And the banks I've approached have been less than helpful."

Ella fought to control her alarm. "The banks weren't helpful in the first place. That's why you went to Phoenix. When does this note come due?"

"In three days."

She spared a brief glance for her husband. "What does this have to do with Rafe?"

"I've come to ask his advice."

Her father was being evasive, she could tell. "Why *his* advice?"

"If I can't get the loan extended, our only option is to sell the house."

"Sell?" She turned to Rafe. "You have to help."

"What is it you'd like me to do?" he inquired politely.

"I don't know. Come up with something!"

"Ella—" her father began.

Rafe cut in. "I would think the funds generated from these Cinderella Balls would be more than sufficient to meet several years' worth of loan payments."

"They would," Ella said impatiently. "If my parents kept the profit instead of donating it to charity."

He frowned. "Charity?"

"You didn't think we kept the money, did you? Look, could we get back to the matter at hand? What if you talked to this Phoenix Corporation on their behalf?"

"And?"

"And tried to convince them to renew my parents' loan."

"Ella—"

Once again Rafe cut Donald off. "Why would I do that?"

She glared at him. "Because they'll ruin my parents. They'd be stealing your idea. You have to stop them."

He stared at her in utter astonishment. Then he gave a short, rough laugh. "Ah, *amada,*" he murmured. "You never cease to amaze me."

She lifted an eyebrow. "I gather that's not a compliment."

"No, I'm afraid not." He drummed his fingers on the tabletop. "Hasn't it occurred to you that I could be the one behind these financial difficulties?"

"No."

He looked intrigued. "Why not?"

"Because I trust you," she said simply. "You promised to give me time and you will."

"Ella—" her father began yet again.

"One moment, please," Rafe interrupted. All expression had dropped from his face and he stared at Ella with winter-gray eyes. "Then let me ask you this. Why would I step in? What difference does it make who takes your parents down when the end result is exactly what I'd hoped?"

She stalked across the room. Planting her hands on his desk, she leaned over the polished teak surface. "I'd think it would make a lot of difference. This Phoenix Corporation will have robbed you of your revenge. Besides, it's one thing for you to make the threat. We can discuss it like two rational adults and eventually I can get you to see reason. But this corporation—"

"Ella, you don't understand," Donald cut in.

She glanced over her shoulder. "What don't I understand?"

Rafe sighed. "I believe what your father is trying to say is that *I* own Phoenix Corporation. I'm the one causing your parents' financial woes. I did warn you I had the means, if you'll recall."

She straightened, stepping back from the desk. "No, I don't believe you."

Rafe glanced at Donald. "Would you excuse us for a moment? This won't take long. I'm sure Chelita is hovering nearby. Feel free to ask her for a cup of coffee."

The minute the door closed behind her father, Ella broke into speech. "Stop this, Rafe. I know you can."

"I can. But I won't."

She fought to keep her voice even. "If I gave you my word that there wouldn't be any further Cinderella Balls, would that be acceptable?"

"It isn't your word I need, but your parents'."

She stared at him as though she'd never seen him before. "Have you any idea why I came to Costa Rica? Any idea at all?"

He released a tired sigh. "We've been over this ground before. You're here to stop me from harming your parents. It's the same as I would have done if I'd been in your predicament. It's what I've been trying to do for Shayne ever since I took her away from Jackie."

"And this afternoon? Was making love to you another way of protecting my parents?"

His eyes narrowed. "If it was, it won't work."

"That you'd even think I could—" Every scrap of color drained from her face. "After all we've been through, you still don't trust me, do you?"

"I don't trust easily. You know that."

"But do you trust me?"

His control snapped and he surged to his feet. "Do you think I don't want to? I trusted you once before, remember? I let down my guard and trusted you with the one person who meant the most to me. And you betrayed me by inviting her to the Cinderella Ball. Is it any wonder I hesitate to trust again? Is it any wonder tht I'd do anything to stop these balls?"

"I guess not," she whispered.

He held out his hand. Where once his wedding band had glittered with a bright promise, now it appeared dark and somber. "Ella, our marriage doesn't have to end, if that's what concerns you. Once your father has given me the guarantee I've requested, we can be done with this matter. Our marriage can continue as before."

"Exactly how long will it continue? Forever?" He didn't answer, which was answer enough. "That's right. You don't believe in forever. Or miracles. Or love. Or happily-ever-after. Do you, Rafe?"

He closed his eyes. "No," he said bleakly. "I don't."

"I could make this so easy for you," she murmured. "But I refuse to do it."

"What are you talking about?"

She shook her head. "No, Rafe. I don't want half measures from you. It has to be all or nothing, which I guess leaves me with nothing. Now, if you'll excuse me, my father's waiting. I have to go."

"Go? What do you mean, go?"

She paused at the door. "I'm leaving, Rafe. I'm returning to Nevada. As far as your guarantee is concerned . . . She looked over her shoulder with tarnished gold eyes. "You can go to hell."

A bitter smile touched his mouth. "It's too late, *amada*. I'm there already."

Shayne stepped from the shadows shading the courtyard fountain and approached Rafe. "You're staring at that mosaic of *La Estrella* like she holds the solution to all your problems," she commented.

"I wish that were so." He glanced down at what he held in his hand—Ella's unfolded wedding band. It was the only thing she'd left behind, a symbolic gesture that gleamed dully within his palm. "But it isn't."

Shayne watched him apprehensively. "You still don't trust her, do you?"

"Don't you start, too. Not now."

"Is—Is it because of what happened at the Cinderella Ball?"

Rafe glanced at his sister, something in her voice capturing his full attention. He slipped the ring into his pocket. "Yes, the Cinderella Ball has a lot to do with it." He paused before asking with grave deliberation, "Or is it a mistake to hold that against her?"

Slowly Shayne nodded. "Yes," she whispered. "It is."

His gut tightened as the blinders were wrenched from his eyes. "She didn't invite you to the ball, did she? She didn't know you intended to find a husband."

"No," his sister confirmed, her voice almost inaudible.

But he heard. Heard and was forced to believe. *"Ah, mi pobrecita pichón.* Why have you kept this from me for so long?"

Her chin quivered and she made a helpless gesture. "Because I was afraid."

"Afraid? Afraid of what?"

"Afraid that if I told you the truth, you'd hate me. That you'd get rid of me the way Jackie did."

"Dios mío, nunca!" He vaulted off the bench, sweeping her into his arms. "I'd never do such a thing. Surely you must realize this?"

She burrowed against him. "I'm sorry. It was wrong, I know. But I couldn't take the chance. You were all I had left."

"I swear, I will always be here for you." He caught her chin in his hand and forced her to look at him. "Nothing will ever change how I feel about you."

Tears filled her eyes. "I think I know that now."

"But you didn't then."

"No."

Jackie had a lot to pay for, far more than his wife ever would. "I can understand your remaining silent. But why didn't Ella tell me?"

"I asked her once. She said it was for your sake. That she didn't want to harm my relationship with you."

He swore beneath his breath, bitterly aware of how he'd misjudged his wife. If she were here now, they'd have a lengthy discussion on the subject. Unfortunately, he'd have to deal with that at a later date. For now he had other, more pressing concerns to address.

"Why did you do it?" he demanded. "Were you so unhappy with me? Was your life so terrible that you felt you had to marry in order to escape?"

"No, no. Just the opposite." Her tears spilled over. "My life was that wonderful. Don't you see? You came all the way to Florida looking for me. I wanted to find a man just like you, Rafe. Someone who would love me so much he'd go to the ends of the earth in search of me."

It was several minutes before he'd regained his control enough to speak. "You are mistaken," he told her hoarsely. "I am not such a man."

"Aren't you?" Shayne pulled free of his arms and fixed him with huge, dark eyes. "You think there's no such thing as happily-ever-after. But don't you get it? That's exactly what you gave me as a child."

"No. I failed you. Jackie—"

"Everything you've ever done has been out of love and the desire to protect me. Even Jackie."

"And McIntyre?"

"I found happily-ever-after with him, too. Briefly. Someday I'll find it again. And this time, I won't let anything take it from me."

Her admission ate at his soul like acid. "You still love him, don't you?"

She didn't spare his feelings. "With all my heart. Even if I never find love again, at least I had that one night." She gripped his hand. "I'll bet Ella feels the same way."

"Perhaps once," he said. "But no longer."

"You can't be certain of that. Don't lose this opportunity, Rafe. You'll regret it the rest of your life."

"I have no faith," he whispered, staring at the mosaic with empty eyes. "I don't believe. And she needs someone who does."

"Ella believes enough for the both of you." Her voice grew urgent. "Listen to me, Rafe. You have a decision to make. A very simple decision. Either you love and trust Ella enough to try and win her back. Or you don't. Now which is it?"

His hands folded into fists. "I don't think I can say the words she needs to hear."

"Then show her. Show her by making things right."

"You ask the impossible."

"Because of the Cinderella Balls? They're no longer an issue now, are they? Or is it that you suspect her motives for coming here? That's it, isn't it? You think she came for her parents' sake instead of for yours." She made an impatient sound. "Honestly, Rafe, I could slap you for being such a fool."

"What the hell are you talking about?"

"Do you really think Ella's feelings for her parents are any less than your feelings for me?"

He shook his head decisively. "No. They mean everything to her."

"And yet she put their future in danger by trying to gain your love instead of giving you an agreement to end the Cinderella Balls. Would you have been willing to risk as much if your positions had been reversed?"

It came to him then, with all the raw power of a lightning strike. Shayne was right. There could only be one reason Ella would put her parents in such financial jeopardy. And she'd been shouting it loud and clear from the moment he'd first walked back into her life. He just hadn't been listening.

His mouth twisted. "It would seem Donald Montague will have the last laugh, after all."

"About what?"

"He said it would be interesting to see which won out in our marriage—the head or the heart."

Shayne laughed in genuine amusement. "And you, of course, said the head."

Rafe gave a self-derisive smile. "Only because I was so certain I had no heart."

"Which just goes to prove what we've all known." She shot him an impish grin. "You aren't so perfect after all. I'm sure Ella will be vastly relieved to hear you admit it."

Ella stood in the middle of the glade behind her parents' house. She'd spent more time here in the week since she'd left Costa Rica than ever before.

She bowed her head and studied her ring finger. Where once there'd been a wedding band, now only a pale mark remained to underscore painful memories. It hurt to her very soul to discover she'd been wrong about Rafe and the Cinderella Ball.

She'd wanted so much to believe in magic and miracles and fairy tales. But the time had come to face a bitter truth. She wasn't Cinderella any more than she was *La Estrella*. To pretend otherwise only led to heartbreak, as she'd so recently discovered.

"I thought I might find you here."

She lifted her head at the familiar-sounding voice, afraid to look, afraid to discover her imagination had played a nasty trick.

"Aren't you even going to say hello?" Rafe asked, amusement rippling through his deep voice.

Steeling herself to face him, she turned. "Why have you come? Or is that a foolish question?"

"A very foolish question, *amada.*"

Her mouth tightened. "Don't call me that. Not anymore."

"What would you rather I called you?" He raised an eyebrow and approached. *"Dulzura? Mi alma? Mi corazón?"*

"Stop it, Rafe. You don't mean any of those endearments, so just stop."

"Or perhaps it would be more fitting to say . . . *La Estrella*."

Her chin quivered. "I'm definitely not that."

"Have I stolen all your dreams, then?" he asked gently. "Have you no more faith?"

"Wasn't that the idea?" She drew a deep breath, fighting for composure. "You must be here for your agreement."

He shook his head. "I no longer need it."

"I see." That could only mean one thing. He knew about the Cinderella Balls. Disappointment filled her. She'd hoped he'd come because his love for her was so overpowering it had surmounted all the obstacles that stood between them—his anger, his mistrust, even his hunger for revenge. But then, what had she expected? A miracle?

"In that case, I assume my father's already spoken to you."

"Not yet, although we have quite a few matters to discuss, I would imagine."

"But you found out, didn't you? That's why you've returned?"

Slowly he shook his head. "You have lost me, *amada*. What is it I'm supposed to have discovered?"

"I'm talking about—" Her breath caught unexpectedly in a tiny, revealing break. "I'm talking about your finding out the truth."

His eyes narrowed. "And what truth is that?"

"That there aren't going to be any more Cinderella Balls. There never were!"

His brows snapped together. "Again, Ella. And more clearly this time."

A tiny flutter of some emotion, an emotion precariously close to hope fought for rebirth. "You're positive my father didn't say anything to you?"

"I've just told you that we haven't spoken," he replied impatiently. "Now what's going on? What has happened?"

"The night of the last Cinderella Ball, my mother revealed that she and Dad had decided to put an end to them. They'd gotten to an age where it was too difficult and stressful to organize such elaborate events." She gazed at him uncertainly. "You really didn't know?"

"Madre de Dios! This is true?" he rasped. He reached her in two swift strides and caught hold of her shoulders. "You knew from the beginning there would be no more balls?"

"Yes."

"Why did you not tell me? Why did you keep it a secret once I'd threatened—"

"Can't you guess?"

He closed his eyes and grimaced. "Hell. It's because you thought the truth would bring a rapid end to a hasty marriage, yes?"

"You'd have walked away and never looked back," she agreed.

"You're wrong. I was as consumed by you, as you were by me. If I'd walked, it wouldn't have been far, nor would I have been long returning." He gazed at her, his eyes like twin silver flames. "You were afraid, weren't you? Afraid that if you didn't marry, you'd lose your last opportunity for the Cinderella Ball to work its magic."

She glanced away. "I was a fool."

"Ella—"

"No! I don't want to hear it. You only came back because you wanted to see if your threat had worked."

He cupped the nape of her neck and forced her to look at him. "You will hear me, *amada*. I am not here for any such reason. No, don't argue with me. Just listen. As far as I was aware, you'd refused to give me my agreement and were willing to lose your home rather than cave to my demands."

It took every ounce of willpower not to lean forward and surrender to his warm strength. "You weren't wrong. We would have given in," she admitted. "In fact, Dad's been trying to reach you ever since we arrived home."

"To inform me there aren't going to be any more balls?"

"Yes." She closed her eyes. "I should have told you the truth before we left Costa Rica. For that matter, I should have told you right from the start. I—I was wrong to put my parents at risk."

"You were lucky it didn't go any further," he concurred. "And just so you know, I've paid off their loan."

"Saying thank you hardly seems adequate. But I do thank you." She eased from his arms and away from temptation. "We each have what we want now, don't we?"

"So there's no reason to continue our marriage, is that what you mean?" He wrapped an arm around her waist and pulled her back where she belonged. "Is it, *amada?*"

The tears fell then. "Please, Rafe," she whispered. "I can't bear any more. You have what you came for. Can't you just leave it at that and go?"

"No, I can't. You see, you took something that belonged to me when you left. It was something I didn't even realize I possessed until I'd lost it."

"I have nothing of yours," she instantly denied.

"You hold it tight within your grasp even as we speak."

She splayed her fingers. "I have nothing," she repeated.

He caught her wrists in an iron grip. "Please look again. For somewhere in these hands you've hidden my heart. And I would like to know that it is in safekeeping."

A sob tore at her throat. "Why have you come? Why have you really come?"

"It's difficult for me to say the words," he confessed in a low voice. "But I had hoped this might speak them for me."

Reaching into his pocket, he removed a small, square jeweler's box. She took it, shaking so badly she could barely manage to pry open the lid. Inside she found the wedding band she'd left behind. Only it had been repaired—and six colored gemstones encircled the ring, the largest a diamond.

He lifted the band from its velvet nest. "The smaller stones are for each of the Cinderella Balls that have been held since your birth."

She spoke through the tears blocking her throat. "And the diamond?"

"It is for the ball deserving the most recognition. The one where we wed. There's an inscription inside." She tilted the ring and in that instant hope dawned anew.

It read, *Happily-ever-after*.

This time she couldn't stern the tears. She gestured toward his wedding band. "You've fixed yours, too."

He shrugged. "I am a rather crude jeweler. My ring kept snagging and I was afraid I would damage it."

"Does it also have an inscription?"

"It says . . ." He dragged air into his lungs, his eyes black with emotion. "It says, *Forever*. For if such a thing exists, I would spend it with you."

She gazed up at him, her eyes as brilliant as the stars found in a midnight sky. "I promise you it does. And if you'll trust me just a little, I'll spend the rest of my life proving it to you."

"Ah, *amada*, my beloved wife." He lowered his mouth to capture hers. "I will trust you to keep that promise."

Epilogue

"Rafe, I'm fine," Ella insisted. "It's just a stitch. Nothing to worry about."

"Perhaps we should cancel the festivities." His accent deepened with worry. "You are in no condition—"

"We can't cancel the Anniversary Ball!" she protested. "It would disappoint so many people. They've been looking forward to this event for a full year. Besides, it's too late to cancel anything. Our guests are due to arrive any minute, whereas our baby isn't due for another two weeks."

He pulled her into his arms. "Naturally I would regret disappointing those who have come to celebrate their first anniversary with us. But my concern is for you and only you." He rested his hand on her swollen belly in a gesture as intimate and tender as it was familiar. From the day he'd learned of her pregnancy, he'd made a habit of holding her like this, his long fingers splayed across the gradually increasing expanse of her stomach.

"Our baby is active tonight," Rafe murmured. "Anxious to join the world."

"Anxious to meet his father, you mean."

"His? You assume a lot, *amada*. Perhaps we'll have a girl." A slow smile of satisfaction crept across his mouth. "To hold a daughter in my arms would make me a happy man."

She gazed at him anxiously. "Would a son also please you?"

"Very much, as you well know."

A light knock sounded at the door and Shayne peeked into the room. "Ella, your parents sent me. It's time. The first guests are just arriving."

"We'll be there in a moment," Rafe said. He waited until his sister left before adding, "She looks better, don't you think? Contented."

"She'll be fine, Rafe." Ella caressed the taut line of his jaw, feeling his tension ease beneath her loving touch. "Her mosaics are in constant demand. She just picked up three new commissions."

"Thanks to *La Estrella*," Rafe inserted. "You have been a busy woman performing all those miracles. Shayne has a career she adores. Milagro has become happy and prosperous—"

"That's just because you changed your mind about selling Esperanza. As for Shayne's personal life, give her time. That will come, too."

"With you working your magic, how can I doubt it?" He pulled Ella closer, resting his jaw against her temple. "I made a mistake six years ago," he confessed. "I took from her the one man she ever loved. That was wrong of me."

"You don't know that for certain," Ella replied gently. "None of us do. She was only seventeen. A mere child. You did what you thought necessary to protect her from harm."

"I should have given this McIntyre a chance. Perhaps it would have worked out between them."

"Regrets won't change the past." She kissed the worry from his expression. "Let it go, sweetheart."

"If you wish. For now." Rafe slipped a supportive hand around her waist and looked down at her, his eyes a brilliant shade of silver. "Come, *amada*. It's time to greet our guests. I have arranged for a chair to be placed at the head of the receiving line for you. You are to tell me if you experience so much as a twinge. Understood?"

She smiled, a smile full of love and joy. "Understood."

"Chick, if you'd let me get a word in edgewise I'll tell you how we first met," Jake Hondo groused.

"But is this where you got married? Is it?" the six-year-old demanded. "Right here?"

"They didn't get married on the sidewalk," Buster scoffed. "They did it inside. In that palace, over there." He waved a hand toward the cupcake castle in the distance.

"We did first meet on the sidewalk, though," Wynne inserted, ruffling Chick's pale blond hair.

"And I told her to get lost," Jake added dryly. "Not that she listened. Come to think of it, she still doesn't listen all that well."

Wynne chuckled. "You should be used to it by now."

"Damn—I mean, danged straight," he muttered soft enough that only she heard. "Though it's come as one heck of a shock to find my life ordered around by a pint-sized elf and three noisy kids."

She just grinned. "You can't fool me. You love every minute."

His gaze softened. "You've got that right. Every second of every minute of every hour of every day."

"You haven't finished the story," Chick complained, tugging on Jake's suit jacket.

"You've heard that story a thousand times," Wynne protested. "You don't really want to hear it again, do you?"

"He likes it. And so do I," Buster explained, before taking up the tale. "Then Uncle Jake married Aunt Wynne and found out about us. Boy howdy, he was ticked. You prob'ly don't remember 'cause you was too little."

"I do so remember! He cussed and Aunt Wynne yelled at him for cussin'."

Jake heaved an exaggerated sigh. "She still yells at me."

"There's a simple solution to that," Wynne retorted. "Stop cussin'."

"Spoilsport."

"I'm not done with the story!" Buster complained. "And then Uncle Jake saved you and me from freezin' to death. And got rid of mean Aunt Marsh. Then they had Tracy. And last of all named her after our Mom once she got borned. Isn't that how it happened?"

Jake grinned. "Something like that." As though in response to hearing her name, his three-month-old daughter gurgled in delight. He shifted her to his other arm and she fixed him with bright spring-green eyes beneath a mop of satiny black curls. He flicked her snub nose with a gentle finger. "Well, folks? We gonna stand out here jawing all day or do we go in and join the party? As I recall they have some mighty fine desserts in there."

"Desserts!" Chick and Buster shouted in unison.

A greedy light dawned in Wynne's eyes. "I'll second that. Lead the way."

"*Jonah,* there's something I want to tell you," Nikki began.

He wrapped an arm around her and pulled her close. "There's something I want to tell you, too. Care to guess?"

Her gaze slid downward, examining the line of his trousers. "You didn't—"

A suggestive grin spread across his mouth. "No, as a matter of fact, I didn't. But that's not what I wanted to tell you."

They reached the entrance to the ballroom and he brushed her mouth with a quick kiss. "Afraid it'll have to keep."

"But, I—"

"Hang on, love." Jonah offered his hand to Rafe Beaumont, then introduced Nikki. "So, we meet again."

"Under more congenial circumstances, I hope," Rafe replied.

Jonah glanced at a very pregnant Ella and his grin widened. "Most definitely. I'm relieved to see the two of you worked out your problems."

Amusement crept into Rafe's voice. "Or added to them."

"With children, you never know," Jonah acknowledged. "Scares the hell out of me."

"You aren't alone, my friend," Rafe said wryly. "Enjoy your visit."

Jonah caught Nikki's hand in his and guided her into the crowded ballroom. "Come on, honey. Let's dance." His hazel eyes gleamed suggestively. "Remember the last time we danced here?"

"Is that what you call it? I thought it was a blatant attempt to seduce me."

He gave his most innocent look as he swung her onto the floor. "Isn't that the point?"

"It certainly was a year ago." She sighed as their bodies melded, moving together in perfect harmony. "Jonah, we never did finish our conversation."

"Too true, my love. What were we discussing? Ah, I remember. Undergarments."

"No, you were discussing undergarments. I was discussing—"

"Well, hello there," a cheery voice interrupted from the edge of the dance floor. "Remember me?"

Nikki turned, searching her memory for a name. "Of course I remember. Wynne, isn't it? Wynne Sommers?"

"It's Hondo, now."

"I was nervous about finding a husband and you let me practice on—" Her gaze switched to Jake and she gave a chagrined laugh. "Oops. Hi, again."

"She let you practice on me, did she?" Jake asked dryly. "Why doesn't that surprise me?"

"It was harmless," Wynne insisted blithely, cradling their baby against her shoulder. "You weren't ready to admit defeat and marry me. And Nikki needed to get over her nervousness. Hey, have you tried the desserts yet? They're—"

"Hang on, elf," Jake interrupted. "I think there's a lady behind you who needs some help."

Nikki glanced over her husband's shoulder, her breath catching in a soft gasp. "Oh, Jonah. It's Ella Beaumont."

"Looks like she's gone into labor," Wynne predicted. "Let's go see what we can do."

The four hurried to Ella's side. She stood in the doorway between the ballroom and the salons, clinging to the wooden frame as though her life depended on it.

"Easy, Mrs. Beaumont." Jake gently lifted her into his arms. "Looks like you could use a ride to the hospital."

"My husband," she gasped. "I need Rafe."

"You need to get to the hospital," Wynne corrected gently.

"I'll find your husband and let him know what's happened," Jonah offered. "We'll be in the next car out of here. I promise."

"You do enjoy playing the knight in shining armor," Ella murmured with a pained smile.

"I'm not sure it's a role I enjoy. Just one I seem to get stuck with." Jonah glanced at Jake. "Can you get her to the hospital?"

"No problem. Wynne, drag the boys away from that dessert table and we're out of here."

"Do you mind if we stick around a while longer?" Nikki asked a short time later. She took a seat in the waiting room. "I don't want to leave until I'm sure Ella and the baby are both okay."

"Mrs. Beaumont seemed to be handling it like a trooper." Jonah ruffled her auburn curls and chuckled. "If you want to worry about anyone, save your concern for Mr. Beaumont."

"Did you understand anything he said?"

"Aside from *rapido?* Not a word. My Spanish is a bit rusty, which I believe is just as well." He shook his head. "This is not an ordeal I'm anxious to experience."

Nikki gripped her hands together. "Listen, Jonah—"

"Hi, again," Wynne greeted them, excitement sparkling in her bright green eyes. "Did you decide to hang around, too? Do you mind some company?"

"Not at all," Jonah replied. "The more the merrier."

"Jonah—"

"With all these kids, I can supply the more," Wynne said with a chuckle. "If you'll supply the merry. I wonder if Ella will take as long to deliver as I did. I swear, I was in that labor room for a solid week."

Jake leaned against the door jamb between the waiting area and the hallway. "Doesn't look like we'll have quite that long to wait. Beaumont's on his way right now."

"Jonah," Nikki tried again, exasperation edging her voice.

Rafe walked in and grinned. "I just wanted to stop by and tell you Ella had a boy. I'd offer cigars, but I fear my wife would not approve. So instead I offer you my most sincere thanks and appreciation."

"Jonah—"

"Congratulations, Beaumont." Jonah stuck out his hand. "We were happy to help."

"Honey—"

"I guess we'll be leaving now," Wynne said. "It's time we got our troop to bed. Please give Ella our best."

"Jonah!"

Rafe inclined his head. "Of course. If you'll excuse me. I have a wife and son waiting me."

"Jonah!" Nikki shouted. "I'm pregnant, dammit."

"Hey, lady. You're not supposed to cuss," Chick informed her earnestly.

"I know and I'm sorry." She looked at Jonah apprehensively. "I've been trying to tell you all evening. But we keep getting interrupted."

"In that case, we'll be going," Wynne said firmly. She gave Nikki a quick hug and kiss. "Take care of yourself. And stay in touch."

And then they were alone.

"You're pregnant?" Jonah demanded. "With a baby?"

"That's the normal procedure," Nikki said tearfully. "Unless you know something I don't."

"Why didn't you tell me? I mean, before tonight. You must have known."

"I've been trying to work up the nerve. I—I didn't think you wanted a baby."

"Didn't want . . . ?" He closed his eyes. When he looked at her again it was with such fierce desire her tears overflowed. He hauled her into his arms. "I'm sorry. I'm sorry I ever gave you that impression since it's the furthest thing from the truth. I love you, Nikki. And the thought of you carrying my child" He touched her with gentle tenderness, his enthralled expression giving weight to his words. "This is the best gift you've ever given me."

"Even better than tickets to the Anniversary Ball?" she teased.

"Those come close." His hand sank into her hair and he feathered a kiss across her mouth. "But only because this is where it all began for us. And where, it would seem, it continues."

"Isn't he beautiful?" Ella whispered, stroking her son's cheek with a gentle finger.

Rafe peered over her shoulder. "If you like things that are small, red, and squished, he's attractive enough I suppose."

"Rafe!"

"I am joking. He is the most beautiful son I've ever had. Of course, he's also the only son I've ever had." He hesitated, tucking a stray lock of hair behind her ear. "There is something I have been meaning to tell you for a very long time."

Busily counting fingers and toes, Ella simply nodded.

"I love you, *amada*. I love you with all my heart and soul."

She stilled, instantly losing count. "What did you say?"

"I said, I love you." He frowned pensively. "I do not know why I found the words so difficult to say when actually, they come with ease. *Amada,* why are you crying? Is there something wrong? Should I call a nurse?"

She shook her head, wiping her cheeks before she soaked the baby. "No, you just caught me by surprise. I love you, too, Rafe."

He stole a slow, gentle kiss. "I am finding that it is as good to hear the words as it is to say them."

"I'm glad you finally came to that conclusion. You have a lot of catching up to do, you know."

"I'll go to work on it right away, I promise."

"We should call my parents and Shayne and let them know about the baby." She caught his frown and understood the cause. "Don't worry. Her chance will come again. The happiness we've found, she'll find, too."

"It is possible." He took a deep breath and then said, "It is possible she will find love at the next Cinderella Ball."

It took a full minute for his words to sink in. "What did you say?"

"The next Cinderella Ball. Maybe Shayne will—"

Tears welled up in her eyes again, turning them to molten gold. "Do you mean it? You're willing to carry on my parents' tradition?"

"How could I not? The money goes to a good cause. And from the research I've done these past months, there has only been one marriage to fail in all the years your parents have held the ball."

"Shayne's?"

"Technically, it cannot be considered a failure, since the marriage was not legal."

"Rafe?"

He sighed. "I am willing to give it a try, *amada,* if you are. And perhaps . . ."

"Perhaps?"

"Perhaps we don't have to wait a full five years."

The End

A Note From Day Leclaire

Can you guess the most frequent questions about **The Cinderella Ball Series?** It's A) is the Cinderella Ball is based on a real event? and B) where they can get tickets?

Yup. Seriously. I'm sorry to say that the idea was *not* based on a real event. But I have to admit, I'm really curious. If there really were a ball, would you attend? What would have to be happening in your life in order to purchase a ticket?

Ella Montague grew up on fairy tales and happily-ever-after endings. So is it any wonder that she would expect the magic of the Cinderella Ball to work for her? Unfortunately, Rafe Beaumont doesn't believe in faith or hope or miracles. Worse, he's determined to prove how wrong Ella's dreams are by making this the very last event of its kind.

I've really enjoyed writing the Fairytale Weddings series. And I hope you'll enjoy sharing in the romance and fantasy of the Cinderella Ball just one more time.... A very happy, healthy and prosperous New Year!

Love,   Day

FAIRY TALE MARRIAGE

The Cinderella Ball Series:

Book #4

By

Day Leclaire

USA Today Bestselling Author

Dedication

To Frank, my Forever Love

Prologue

The Beaumonts—Forever, Nevada

Ella Beaumont rolled onto her hip and stared at her husband. A full moon made that job a little easier, burnishing the room in silver and painting a swath of gentle ivory across Rafe's hard-chiseled features.

"Are you sure we're doing the right thing, Rafe? Maybe we shouldn't interfere."

"My interference is what put my sister in this situation to begin with. I stayed out of it for the past nine years, hoping against hope Shayne would find someone. But there's never been anyone else for her. Not one single man who's captured her heart."

"Except McIntyre," Ella said softly.

Rafe nodded. "Except McIntyre."

"How do you know he's not married? How do you know he'll come?"

"I've made it my business to keep a watchful eye on him since I had their marriage annulled."

She took a moment to absorb his comment before very gently informing her husband, "As much as you might want to, you can't play God."

"I'm not playing at anything." He set his jaw in a manner she recognized all too well. It spoke of rock-solid determination. It also warned she wouldn't sway him. Not on this point. "I'm attempting to set right a wrong. If it succeeds, Shayne will finally have her happiness."

"And if it doesn't?"

Grief silvered his eyes. "Then at least I will have given her the chance I stole all those years ago."

Lullabye, Colorado

"You can't be serious!"

Doña Isabella inclined her head in a regal fashion, her grip tightening on her gold-tipped cane. "I am quite serious, *Señor* McIntyre. You knew those were my terms when I contacted you last month. Yet, you have done nothing about implementing them."

"You expect me to find a wife in one short month?" he demanded savagely.

"No." Black eyes flashed above a strongly hooked nose. "I now expect you to find a wife in one short week."

And that said it all.

He paced the length of his office, fighting for control. Reining in his temper proved as difficult as reining in a wild stallion bent on freedom. He didn't doubt for a minute *Doña* Isabella fully expected him to have a bride on his arm at the end of the allotted seven days.

It didn't matter that marriage was the last thing he wanted. It didn't matter there wasn't a chance in hell that a woman within a hundred miles of his ranch would take him on or that he had nothing to give a wife. All that mattered was she'd decreed he do as she demanded or she'd refuse to give him the one thing he wanted most in the world.

Forced to admit he'd run out of options, he acted in the only way he could under the circumstances. He shot her a cocky grin. "I don't suppose you have any candidates available?"

Doña Isabella's mouth thinned. Apparently, a sense of humor wasn't a characteristic she openly embraced. "I leave for Mexico in one week, *Señor* McIntyre. If at that time you've met all my demands, I'll give you what you wish. If not . . ." She shrugged, her black eyes coldly implacable. "The choice is yours."

His grin vanished. "No, madam. It's not," he assured her, just as coldly. "If it was, we wouldn't be having this discussion."

A brief knock sounded and Chaz's foreman, Penny, pushed the office door open a scant inch. No doubt fear of the intimidating *Doña* kept him from opening it any further. "Hey, boss?"

"I thought I told you not to—"

"Yeah, I know. Sorry about that. But there's a really strange guy out here and I'm afraid if you don't see to it your own self and get him out of here, somebody's like as not to shoot him purely on the principal of the thing."

Damn. "Excuse me," Chaz said to his guest.

He received another of the *Doña*'s regal nods and amusement vied with frustration. As though he needed permission from her to run his own household! He swore beneath his breath. Unfortunately, that was precisely the case. *For now.*

Stepping into the entrance hall, he confronted a sight he thought he'd put behind him nine long years ago. A man stood there, a man who looked about as uncomfortable as a body could. Dressed in white and gold satin, his uniform sported braided nonsense on the shoulders and down the front of his short bolero jacket. Honest to God lace decorated his womanish shirt and the end of his sleeves.

He clutched a gold tray with hands encased in spotless white gloves—hiding sweaty palms, no doubt—with a thick embossed envelope propped in the center. The death grip the man had on the flimsy piece of metal suggesting he expected to have to use it to defend himself. Smart fella. Something about fancy duds and a ranch just didn't go together, and all three of them were painfully aware of that fact.

"I'm looking for a Mr. Cassius McIntyre," the man announced.

"It's Chaz. And you found him."

The footman didn't attempt to disguise his relief. "Allow me to present you with a special invitation to the Cinderella Ball." He offered the thick, gold-embossed envelope on the tray.

It took everything Chaz possessed to keep from laughing. But he managed. "Didn't apply to the ball."

"No, sir. The application was made in your name."

Chaz's eyes narrowed, the laughter draining right out of him. "Now who do you suppose would have done such a foolhardy thing?"

"I wouldn't know, sir."

"Well, you can take that envelope and—" He broke off, painfully aware of two infuriating facts. First, this just might provide the solution he needed. And second, the people providing that solution were the very last he'd ever wanted to see again. Fate, it would seem, had decided to take another swing at him.

"Go on," Penny encouraged eagerly. "Tell him to shove it where the sun don't shine."

"Get back to work, old man." Of course, his foreman instantly obeyed by digging in his heels and folding his scrawny arms across an equally scrawny chest.

"I'm instructed to leave it," Mr. Fancy Pants informed him. "What you choose to do with it is your business. But under no circumstances am I to return the envelope to the Beaumonts."

Chaz's gaze sharpened. *"The Beaumonts?"* The question had more bite than he'd intended. The footman took a hasty step backward, raising the tray like a shield. "Rafe Beaumont?"

"Yes, sir."

"What happened to the Montagues?"

"The elder Montagues have retired. Their daughter, Ella, is now married to Mr. Beaumont, and they host the balls."

"Give me the envelope. *Now.*"

"At once, sir." With a quick nod, the footman extended the tray once again. It trembled notably. The second Chaz took the envelope, the footman turned around and hotfooted it out the front door toward a waiting limo.

"What's in the envelope?" Penny questioned suspiciously.

"An invite."

"What sorta invite?"

"It's for a lot of things."

To revisit the past. For revenge. But most importantly, it was an invitation that would allow him to satisfy *Doña* Isabella's demands.

"Huh?"

"You heard the man, Penny." Chaz fixed his attention on the envelope, sensing the winds of change sweeping across the Rocky Mountains. Dry, harsh winds originating from the unforgiving desert surrounding Forever, Nevada. "It's for a ball. A marriage ball. Meet the woman of your dreams and marry her, all in one night."

"And you're going to this ball thing the idiot was talking about?" his foreman asked incredulously.

"Yeah, old man. I am." A remote coldness filled the crags of a hard-lived face. "Not only am I going, I'll be bringing back a wife."

The Beaumont Residence—La Finca de Esperanza, Milagra, Costa Rica

Shayne stared up at the starlit Costa Rican sky. The moon hovered overhead, as full and white and beautiful as any she'd seen. She opened her hand and stared at the gold ticket that had arrived by special messenger earlier that day. It glittered gently beneath the moon's softer light. But even so, it had a brilliant flash and fire she remembered well, one that spoke of hope and love . . . and dreams long lost.

"Why did he send it?" she asked aloud.

Of course, no one answer. Not that she expected any. She didn't have a single doubt her brother was behind the gift. Was it a prompt? A suggestion that she get on with her life?

She'd done that already. Okay, so she wasn't happily married like Rafe and Ella. Still, she had a satisfying career. She ran the coffee *finca* when her brother was absent. And she was content, if not perfectly happy. What more could she want?

Chaz McIntyre.

His name came as easily to mind now as it had nine impossibly long years ago. Where was he? What was he up to? Did he ever think about her and what they'd once experienced? Or had he moved on with his life?

For a long time she stood sheathed in white light, the ticket glowing in her palm like a living entity. Finally, she closed her fingers around it and lifted her face to the moon.

"I'll do it. One last time, I'll attend the Cinderella Ball."

The ball would be the key to her future. She'd move forward by stepping into a new life. She'd finally put the past behind her once and for all. And never again would she look back with regret.

Chapter One

To My Long-Lost Bride,

I don't know if this will ever reach you. Whether you will ever know how I've searched for you over the past two months—ever since the night we married at the Cinderella Ball. But I have searched.

Everywhere.

The Montagues won't give me any information, even though I've shown them our marriage license. I spoke to Ella. She's hurting because of your brother, too. It's like you've vanished off the face of the earth. I'm thinking of hiring a private investigator to find you, but I don't know where to tell him to look. All you said was you lived on a coffee plantation. But where? *Damn it, it never occurred to me to ask! I thought we'd have all the time in the world to find out the details of our past.*

Know this, light of my soul . . . The one thing that won't vanish is what I feel for you. You are my life and my love, my one star in a dark night sky. Fight for what we had. And come back to me.

Until that day, you live in my heart, my Forever Love.

The Beaumonts' Cinderella Ball—Forever, Nevada

Chaz McIntyre propped a shoulder against the wall as he waited for the reception line to move forward. What the hell was he doing here? Here, of all places.

This had to be the one corner in Hades guaranteed to hold the worst memories of any he'd ever experienced. And yet here he stood, like some sort of fool, begging Rafe Beaumont to stick it to him one last time.

He swore viciously beneath his breath. He'd spent years protecting himself from the sort of hurt Beaumont specialized in doling out. Still, with one unreasonable decree, an arrogant old woman had done the impossible—put him right back where he least wanted to be.

The line inched forward a little farther and he caught a glimpse of the man who'd taken such delight in screwing with his life. Amazing. Nine years had passed and yet the SOB hadn't changed a lick.

He couldn't help wondering about Shayne? Had she changed? She'd have had to. When he'd last seen her, she'd been a seventeen-year-old child pretending to be an adult. Now she'd be . . . what? Twenty-six? Almost twenty-seven. Would she be here tonight? Is that why Rafe had sent the ticket?

A coldness seeped deep inside, relentless and all-pervasive, consuming him with comforting familiarity. Shayne didn't matter. Nothing mattered except achieving his goal.

It took another few minutes before he reached the head of the line. Ella Montague stood at Rafe's side. Correction. Ella *Beaumont*. She'd been a Montague when they'd last met. So Rafe had gained a wife, while robbing Chaz of his. The sheer irony made him bare his teeth in a parody of a smile.

"McIntyre," Rafe greeted him with a stiff nod.

"Beaumont." Chaz caught the wary look in the older man's eyes and allowed his smile to grow, edging it with animosity. "Fancy meetin' you here."

"You came. I wasn't sure you would."

"Mind telling me why you sent the ticket?"

Rafe hesitated and then inclined his head toward an area where they'd have more privacy. Once they were clear of the reception line, he said, "I thought I owed it to you."

"Now why would you think you owe me anything?" The soft question had an unexpected bite.

A muscle rippled along Rafe's jawline, acknowledging the hit. "You wish me to admit it? Very well. I interfered in your marriage, in your relationship with my sister. Does that satisfy you?"

It should have. But for some infuriating reason, it didn't. He checked his anger, aware it would be a mistake to allow it too much freedom. Once released, it would be near impossible to contain.

"You were just protecting your family. I can understand that. I'd probably have done the same thing if I'd found my seventeen-year-old sister shacked up with an older man."

"You weren't shacked up. You were married. There's a difference."

"Nah, we weren't married. Not legally." The wrath Chaz had been struggling to control surged to the surface. It shocked him to realize he still reacted with such unchecked fury, even after all these years. "You saw to that, right?"

"She was a vulnerable child! She slipped into the ball when no one was looking. And then she attached herself to the first man to smile at her." Apparently, Chaz wasn't the only one still harboring hard feelings. "What did you expect me to do?"

"I expected you to give us a chance."

"How? Why?" Rafe's voice dropped, the sound raw with frustration. "I was due to return to Costa Rica. You expected me to leave my seventeen year-old sister behind with a man she'd known only a few short hours? You were a footloose cowboy without home or roots or goals. What if something had gone wrong? What if she'd needed me?"

"She was my wife, damn it. Did you really think I'd do anything to harm her?"

"How would I know? You admitted you had attended on a whim. You didn't even have a ticket. You simply slipped in through the garden. You could have been anyone. A security check hadn't even been run on you. You were a self-confessed drifter."

That stung. "I was a wrangler."

"Who hadn't remained in any one place for longer than a season. What sort of life is that for a young girl?"

"You weren't willing to give me a chance to make a home with her. You barged into our hotel room, knocked me on my backside without waiting for an explanation and took my wife from me."

"My sister!"

Chaz caught himself in time and exchanged glares with Rafe. This was ridiculous. He refused to get into a slanging match over events nearly a decade old. It wasn't worth it. Besides, he had other business to take care of tonight.

"Forget it, Beaumont. It's not important anymore."

After a long moment, Rafe nodded in agreement. "Very well. I appreciate your coming."

"I'm sure." Chaz shifted impatiently. He didn't have time for social niceties, particularly those coming years too late. "Now, if you'll excuse me—"

He'd only managed two short steps before Rafe stopped him in his tracks. "Aren't you even going to ask about her?"

Chaz didn't bother to turn around. "No."

"Then why the hell did you come?"

Ella approached just then, laying a restraining hand on Rafe's arm. "Easy, darling. You weren't going to lose your temper, remember?" She turned her attention to Chaz. "My husband's question is a good one. If you didn't come back to find out about Shayne, why are you here?

He turned. Interesting. Apparently the Beaumonts had a hidden agenda. Now why didn't that come as a surprise? Unable to resist, he slashed at his opponent. "I came for the

same reason all your other guests have. To find myself a wife."
He cocked an eyebrow. "I assume you don't have any
objections?"

"Not a one." Rafe's expression gave lie to his words, his
mouth tightening. It was a dead giveaway. Apparently, he had
plenty of objections, though none he intended to state. "I won't
bother giving you the usual rundown since this isn't your first
visit. I'm sure you remember where to find food and so forth."

"Not to mention the women." He offered a slow, insolent
smile. "Think I'll stick to the more enjoyable aspects of your
shindig. Food can wait."

"In case you weren't aware, it's a masked ball this time."

"Yeah, I read that. Guess I forgot mine."

Rafe inclined his head as regally as the *Doña*. "You'll find
extra masks on the table behind you. Help yourself."

So stiff. So arrogant. So damned in control of his world
and everyone in it. Chaz longed to take some of the stuffing out
of his former brother-in-law. But he didn't dare. As much as he
resented it, he needed Rafe's help. Or rather, he needed what
Rafe's ball so amply provided.

Women.

"Thanks. I'll do that." Chaz glanced at his hostess. "It's
been a pleasure, Cinder-girl."

Snagging a mask, he headed for the ballroom. And all the
while he cursed himself for a fool. An odd warmth sparked
close to the inner core of ice that protected him.

He should have let Beaumont tell him about Shayne.

Shayne stood on the balcony looking down at the
crowd. This was it. Her last Cinderella Ball. The last time she'd
allow herself to remember, to allow regret to overshadow all

that life had to offer. To hide from pain and sleep, when she should be living. As this night waned and the sun rose on a new day, she'd confront the future, instead of constantly looking over her shoulder toward the past.

She glanced at the reception line. Her nephew, Donato, had long ago been put to bed and yet there was still a steady stream of visitors arriving, though the crowd had lightened somewhat. Perhaps she should go over and offer to take tickets again. Rafe had insisted she should enjoy herself, but she felt guilty dumping all the work on her brother and sister-in-law.

Studying Rafe, she frowned. Who was he talking to? If she didn't know better, she'd swear he was annoyed. Possibly, more than annoyed. His shoulders were rigid, his hands opening and closing into fists. What in the world had set him off? The crowd shifted and then she saw what had caused him such distress.

Chaz McIntyre stood at the head of the line.

Shock rolled over her like storm-driven waves, threatening to sweep her feet out from under her. From a great distance she heard the urgent clamor of silver-toned chimes and realized she must be trembling, setting off the strings of bells decorating her mask. She gripped the banister to keep from falling and the bells quieted.

Dear heavens, how could it be? After all these years, her husband had returned. Why? Why now when the time had come to move on? What did he want? Or should she be asking . . . who? She watched Chaz walk over to the table holding the spare masks. Selecting one, he plunged into the ballroom.

Understanding struck with as much pain and power as a fist to the chin. Finally, her prayers had been answered. Her husband had come back. The painful irony was . . . In all likelihood, he hadn't returned for her.

For the first time in years, Shayne acted without thought. Her mask hung from her arm—an elaborate beaded and feathered affair decorated with the tiny bells that announced her slightest movement. It covered most of her face, making it almost impossible to identify her.

She slipped it over her head, the bells singing a song of urgency. Crossing to the staircase leading to the ballroom, she lifted the wide skirts of her gold dress and descended the steps, searching the crowd for a tall, well-built man, brown hair highlighted with streaks of sun-bleached gold, dressed in a western-cut brown tux.

It took her forever to reach the ballroom. Three different people required assistance and she didn't want to abandon them until their needs were met. Finally she reached the dance floor.

She spotted Chaz almost immediately, standing to one side, calmly scrutinizing the three women who ringed him— a dainty blond, a willowy redhead and a sultry brunette. It stopped her dead in her tracks.

What in the world was he up to? Her pulse picked up. He couldn't be here to find a wife, could he? Slipping close enough to observe, she watched as he swept first one of the women, then another onto the dance floor. He still moved as gracefully as she recalled, his movements sure and powerful.

A man appeared at Shayne's elbow. "Excuse me, would you care to dance?"

"No, thanks," she demurred.

"Please?" He smiled with unexpected charm. "Just one?"

What could it hurt? She'd help a guest and it would give her the opportunity to study Chaz without his noticing. "All right."

"The name's Sotherland." He swung her around in an easy circle. "August Sotherland."

"Hello, Mr. Sotherland. I'm Shayne."

"So you're hoping to get married?"

"No, I'm afraid not."

She'd caught him by surprise and his step faltered for a split second. "No?"

"I'm sorry," she apologized, instantly contrite. "My brother and his wife host the Cinderella Ball. I'm simply observing. I guess I should have explained sooner."

"A shame." He recovered with impressive speed. "Well, I guess a single dance isn't against the rules, right?"

"Not at all."

She glanced over his shoulder toward Chaz. The blond and the redhead had disappeared and he now danced with the sultry brunette. She wore a Cleopatra outfit, her skirt so tight Shayne wondered how could move at all. Perhaps that explained why she found it necessary to drape herself over Chaz—so he could drag her around the dance floor without having to do more than shuffle her feet.

" . . . but if you were looking for a husband, what would you want him to be like?"

She forced her attention back to August. What should he be like? Her gaze drifted to Chaz once again. "Intelligent. Straightforward. Protective. Honorable." Her husband had been all those things. At least, when she'd known him.

Sotherland grinned. "So far, so good."

So far, so good? Surely, he didn't think she'd changed her mind about marrying? No, he hadn't, she realized in relief. She could see it in the teasing gleam in his eyes. Cute.

She decided to play along. "Oh, but there's more."

He lifted his eyebrows. "Do tell."

"If I were considering a husband, he'd have to be tall, broad-shouldered, have brown hair with whitish streaks, and intense blue eyes. Oh! And a tiny chip in his left canine tooth."

"Darn. Not a chip to be found." He grinned to prove it.

"Oh, dear." She gave him a regretful look. "I'm afraid that will never do."

He shook his head with a soft click of his tongue. "I guess that means we weren't meant to be."

"I guess not," she responded with a sigh of regret.

"But I notice that fellow behind us has rather intense blue eyes."

A hint of warmth washed across her cheekbones. "Really?"

"Sure enough." He maneuvered them in a tight circle to get a better look. "I admit I'm not the best judge, but he appears on the tall side, too. Not to mention broad-shouldered."

"How interesting," she murmured.

"Isn't it?" August murmured. "Too bad his streaks are gray—"

"They are not gray!"

"No?" he asked innocently. "My mistake. Now if only we could discover if the poor man has chipped teeth." Before she could protest, he swerved into the path of the oncoming couple. "Gee, didn't see you folks," he quickly apologized.

Chaz swung around and looked at them. For a breathless moment, Shayne was certain he'd recognized her. That he, too, felt the hot, sweet emotions that lingered, charging the air between them. But after subjecting her to a swift, impersonal examination, he turned his attention to August. "No damage done."

"Hey. Is that a chipped tooth you have there?"

Chaz's jaw locked and a warning glitter appeared in his eyes. "What if it is?"

"Amazing coincidence, wouldn't you say, my dear?" he asked Shayne. "White streaks, blue eyes, chipped tooth. It's downright magical."

Chaz folded his arms across his chest—a chest that seemed even broader than she remembered. "Buddy, you're startin' to rub me the wrong way. Maybe you should move on before you end up with a few chipped teeth of your own."

"Right you are."

He gave Shayne a surreptitious wink, captured Cleopatra in an enthusiastic embrace and half-dragged, half-danced her across the floor.

A silent moment passed while Shayne scrambled for something to say. Chaz's eyes behind his mask were every bit as piercing as she recalled and having them fixed so steadily on her didn't help her conversational skills.

"Mind telling me what that was all about?" he finally asked.

She fought to speak normally. "August was just trying to be helpful."

"Helpful."

"Yes. He asked me to describe the man I'd want to marry." She shrugged, confessing with painful honesty, "I described you."

"Why?"

"You remind me of someone I once knew." Knew, and considered to be the perfect man. Had August sensed her feelings and decided to do a bit of matchmaking? Gratitude vied with nervousness. "When my friend saw you and made the connection, he took matters into his own hands."

Chaz's eyes narrowed. "Were you trying to blow him off? Is that why you described me?"

She sensed a harshness in him that hadn't been there before, a molten core tamped under tight control. What would happen if that control ever slipped? She didn't think she'd like to be around as a witness.

"I wasn't lying to him, if that's what you're asking."

His eyes narrowed. "Why describe me? It can't just be my resemblance to this other man."

The molten core splashed closer to the surface and Shayne realized she'd have to respond very, very carefully. "I thought we might be compatible." They had been, once upon a time.

"What about me made you think that?"

Everything. Their past. The way he'd made love to her. The fact that he stood before her after all these years. "It's just a feeling."

The chill coming off him froze her out completely. "I don't trust feelings."

That alarmed her more than anything else he could have said. Had he changed so much? "What do you trust?"

"Not much. I want to see and touch it to believe in its existence. And even then I have my doubts."

Unbidden tears pricked her eyes. Had she and Rafe done that to him? Were they responsible for the coldness that iced his every word? "Why are you here?" she asked helplessly.

"To find a woman."

For a split second hope raced through her. "What woman?"

"Doesn't much matter so long as we can come to terms."

She turned abruptly, the air escaping her lungs in a desperate rush. It hurt to inhale, hurt to blink, hurt to think. "What are your terms?" she asked thinly.

"Lady, we're standing in the middle of a dance floor. Do you really want to negotiate a marriage contract here?"

"We could go downstairs and have a cup of coffee." She desperately needed the warmth to counteract this first, brief bitter-cold conversation. "Would that do?"

"Sure."

Realization struck and she almost burst into hysterical laughter. Her ex-husband—were they considered ex-husbands when the marriage had been annulled?—wanted to sit down and share a cup of coffee with her while discussing what he needed in a new wife. Did life get any stranger than that?

She glanced over her shoulder to where August had stranded Cleopatra. She'd already picked up a new swarm of admirers. "Am I taking you away from someone?"

His hand settled at the base of her spine, filling the hollow with surprising heat. "No one important." As though realizing how callous he sounded, he added, "We weren't on the same wavelength."

They left the floor and the bells decorating her headdress and mask swayed, colliding with soft, excited jangles. For some reason the melodic sound reassured her. It announced change and spiritual awakening, both of which she needed very badly.

Chaz flicked one of the golden strands. "I won't lose you in the crowd with these."

The words seemed prophetic. "It's easy to become lost."

"No problem," he claimed without hesitation. "I'd find you again."

He hadn't last time and hurt made her reckless. "That's assuming you want to find me."

His careless grin contrasted with the dead seriousness of his gaze. "Oh, I'd want to find you."

As they left the ballroom, Shayne glanced toward the reception line. Rate and Ella were no longer there. What would they do if they discovered her with Chaz? Or was that the idea? Had her brother sent tickets to both of them in the hopes of sparking this meeting?

Once in the dining room, they bypassed the tables loaded with every conceivable delicacy and found a discreet table tucked away in the corner of the room. "I'll get coffee," Chaz said. "Looks like they have every sort in creation. What's your preference?"

"Plain and black, please."

"A hot water and beans woman, huh? And here I'd had you pegged as one of those fake coffee lovers."

"You think I look like the cappuccino type?"

He cocked his head to one side as he assessed her. "I'd say a latte or perhaps a mochaccino."

"Doubled or tripled?"

He regarded her in amusement. "Oh, a grande, at the very least."

"Heavens, no! It has to be a tall skinny halfway between a flat white and a cap. No foam." Her brows drew together as she gave it further consideration. "On second thoughts maybe I should go with a lungo or a poophead."

He held up his hands in surrender and a smile pulled the harshness from his face, hinting at the boyishness she'd once known so intimately. "One black coffee, it is."

"The thicker, the better?" she teased.

"I drink the type you have to cut with a knife and fork. But I'll be a nice guy and make yours a bit weaker if that's what you prefer."

"You want a strong cup of coffee? Maybe you should try—" She'd almost suggested the Costa Rican *tacita de café,* but caught herself at the last minute. Bringing Costa Rica into the conversation would be a dead giveaway.

"Try . . . ?"

"Try asking the barista," Shayne replied instead. "I'm sure she'll know which will offer the best jolt for the sip."

To her relief, he appeared to accept her comment at face value. Thank goodness! She didn't want Chaz to know who she was. Not yet. Not until she'd had a chance to spend some time with him. She wanted to discover what had happened over the past nine years and see if they could regain what they'd once shared.

It was a ridiculous dream, as foolish as it was reckless. But she couldn't help herself. Just as she'd been instantly attracted to him that infamous night so long ago, she found that attraction every bit as immediate and powerful the second time around. A few minutes later he returned and took the seat across from her.

"Here we are. Two coffees. Both black." He set Shayne's in front of her. "I don't believe we've introduced ourselves." He offered his hand. "I'm Chaz from Lullabye, Colorado."

He hadn't volunteered his last name. That would simplify matters. "My first name's Marianna." It was the truth. She'd only adopted her middle name, Shayne, when Rafe had rescued her from her hellish existence in Florida.

"Marianna. Pretty. And why are you here?"

She lifted a shoulder in a brief shrug. "The same reason most of the people are. I'd like to find a husband." One special, long-lost husband. "What about you?" She struggled not to appear too anxious.

"I'm looking for a wife."

"Why?" she couldn't help asking. "Why here?"

He hesitated for an instant. "Someone sent me a ticket."

Rafe! "So you came? Just because you received a ticket?"

"I had another reason." He toyed with his coffee cup. "I recently bought a ranch."

So the wanderlust had finally left Chaz McIntyre. "And this ranch requires a wife?"

"Yes." Bald. Abrupt. He spoke the word in a tone that warned he wouldn't take kindly to questions.

Too bad. She had questions and a lot of them. Did he really expect to show up at the ball and entice someone to the altar with just his good looks? He'd be satisfied married to such a shallow, undemanding woman? "Why do you want a wife, Chaz?"

He took a long drink of coffee, as though debating how much to say. She suspected it would be as little as possible. "The ranch is in need of repair. I can handle the structural changes, but not the rest."

"What rest?"

His mouth compressed. "It's a bachelor's residence. There isn't a female within miles. The place needs a woman's touch."

She stared at him in disbelief. "You're getting married so you'll have someone to coordinate throw pillows?"

He slammed his mug to the table. "No! I need someone who can create a ho—" With a muttered oath, he looked away, tension vibrating along every line of his body.

"A home?" she finished in a gentle voice.

"Yeah."

He hadn't meant to admit so much. Dusky color rode his angled cheekbones and his features compressed into taut lines, etched there by more than the sum total of thirty-one years. No doubt they'd been a hard thirty-one years, filled with disillusionment and pain, his face weather-beaten into the sort of creases women found irresistible on men and dreaded seeing in their own mirrors. He thrust a hand through his hair, combing the sun-kissed streaks on top into the crisp nut-brown strands beneath.

"I gather you prefer more than a housekeeper or interior decorator?"

"A lot more."

"And what are you willing to give in return?"

He didn't like the question. "What do you want?" he asked warily.

"That isn't what I asked. I assume you're offering a home and basic creature comforts."

"I'm not a rich man," he warned.

She regarded him steadily. "Then it's a good thing I don't need riches, isn't it?"

He returned her look. No doubt his years of wrangling had helped him sum people up with swift accuracy. "Lay it out for me, Marianna. You're after something. What is it?"

She thought about it, sitting so quietly even the bells on her mask fell silent. He wanted a wife to create a home for him. He'd offered to provide physically for that wife. But what about her emotional needs? What about his? "Will we share a bed?"

"Yes."

"Tonight?"

He answered without hesitation. "Yes."

"And you expect a woman to hop into bed with you after such a short acquaintance?" she asked curiously.

"We'll be married."

"So you gift her with your worldly possessions and she gifts you with her body and a home. That's your idea of a marriage?"

"If you're looking for more than that, you're sitting at the wrong table."

"No love? No affection?"

"I'll treat you well. I'll never hurt you, at least not intentionally."

He was lying. She sensed it with every instinct she possessed. He was a man in desperate need of love, though he'd undoubtedly deny it, just as he'd undoubtedly fight long and hard to hold it at bay. So the real question was, did she have it within her to give him that sort of unconditional love?

It was an even greater risk than the one she'd taken nine years ago. Then, he'd been open and carefree, all-too willing to surrender his heart, to give every bit of himself to a woman. She couldn't be certain that man still existed, that once he uncovered her identity, he'd ever come to trust her enough to allow love into his life again.

"Are you interested?"

He asked the abrupt question as though her response were of no particular interest. But his hands clenched around his coffee mug and his eyes remained carefully blank. That, more than anything, gave her hope. He was a man determined to keep love out of his life, and yet he'd come to the Cinderella Ball to find a bride capable of creating a home for him.

"Yes, I'll marry you."

Coffee sloshed over the rim of the cup. "I don't recall askin'."

"Now who's playing games?" She didn't give him time to respond. "Do you want to marry me or not?"

He paused for an infinite second. "Okay, fine. But you have to do something for me, first."

"What's that?"

He leaned across the table toward her, his eyes an incandescent blue, full of fierce determination and tightly controlled passion. "Take off your mask."

Chapter Two

To My Long-Lost Bride,

I'm counting the days until I see you again. It's been almost a year and I can't get you out of my head—or my heart. Your brother sent the annulment papers, but I don't care what they say. You'll always be my wife, the woman who will bear my children, my Forever Love, the person I'll adore until the day I die. You are my sweetness in an often-bitter world.

I've been working hard these long, lonely months, saving every penny. I know one of your brother's concerns was that I couldn't support a wife. But I've been smart. I invested my earnings and am planning the perfect home for you. It won't be much to start, but it'll be all ours.

The Anniversary Ball is just a week away. It's to celebrate the first anniversary of those who married at the Cinderella Ball, and even though our marriage was annulled, I know you'll be there and that this time when we become man and wife, no one can part us. Keep fighting, Shayne. And come back to me.

Until I hold you in my arms again . . . you are my Forever Love

To Chaz's private amusement, the bells on Marianna's mask clattered together in discordant protest. "Take off—"

"Your mask. Yes." He lifted an eyebrow. "Problem?"

"I'd rather not," she admitted.

Something about such devastating honesty had him regarding her with acute suspicion. "And why's that?"

"What does it matter what I look like?" It was her turn to clench the coffee mug with white-knuckled desperation. "I don't recall your mentioning that as part of your requirements. You wanted someone who'd turn your house into a home, who'd be willing to live with you in Colorado, who'd—"

"Sleep with me."

It was a wonder the cup didn't shatter in her hands. Did she find the idea of being intimate with him so overwhelming? He'd soon ease her past that particular concern.

"Yes," she acknowledged. "And to sleep with you."

He stood and approached her side of the table. "Don't you think we should have a peek under the masks to make sure we can face each other over the breakfast table every morning?" he asked.

She held him with inky dark eyes, eyes that stirred memories he'd sooner forget. "And if my looks don't appeal, we go our separate ways?"

Damn it! Did she think him so heartless? "I didn't say that."

"So it's not whether or not I can make a home for you that's important. It's whether or not I'm attractive enough to share your bed?"

He stooped beside her, taking her hands in his. "Honey, in case you didn't know it doesn't much matter what your partner looks like once the lights are out, so long as part A fits pleasurably into slot B."

He'd insulted her. It hadn't been intentional. He just had an unfortunate knack for brutal frankness. Hell, he wanted a wife. Or rather, he needed one. If he were perfectly honest, he didn't care how plain-faced the woman he married, so long as she could satisfy his requirements.

He'd had beautiful. If he was forced to take a wife, then this time around he wanted practical.

Chaz studied his prospective bride. He could see her intention to walk away as clearly as if she'd spoken it aloud. But something held her back. Something he couldn't quite understand. Still, he saw it in the slight softening of her chin and the gentling of the anger darkening her passionate brown eyes. A smile flirted with her mouth, a smile as feminine and appealing as any he'd ever seen. Warmth pooled in his gut, stirring a reaction he hadn't felt in far too many years.

"If it doesn't matter, then the mask stays," she said. "You decide. Are you willing to marry, sight unseen?"

Aw, hell. He carefully disengaged their fingers. "You're asking me to take a lot on faith."

"You're not a man with a lot of faith, are you?"

"Not a scrap."

"What happened?" she asked with the sort of kindness he couldn't handle, the sort of kindness he didn't deserve.

"I lost it long ago."

"Perhaps someday you'll find it again."

"If that's what you're holding out for, you're going to be sorely disappointed." He straightened, towering over her, and thumped his index finger on the linen-covered surface for emphasis. "I'm offering you a house. I'm offering you a warm bed. The closest you'll get to faith is that I'll remain true to our marriage vows for as long as they legally last. And I'll see that you don't want for anything it's within my power to give. Take it or leave it."

"Just don't expect love?"

"Not a chance in hell."

Her mouth drew together as she weighed his statement, gathering into an unconscious half-kiss that proved a gut-tightening temptation. If she hadn't chosen that moment to speak, he'd have leaned down again and sampled those rosy lips to see if they tasted as luscious as they appeared.

"Why should I agree to that sort of a marriage?"

"Frankly, I can't think of a single damned reason." He picked up his coffee cup and downed the contents. Studying the dregs, he considered his words. "Look, sweetheart, I came here to find a wife." He set the mug on the table with a finality she couldn't mistake. "I've given you my reasons and I've been honest about what I can offer in return. Brutally honest. If what I'm selling doesn't coincide with what you're buying, tell me now. There's still time to find new partners."

She stood, as well. "I'm not interested in finding someone else."

"You sure?" Chaz regarded her with unflinching deliberation, allowing just a hint of his annoyance to spill into his gaze. She'd pushed him as far as he intended to be pushed. If she didn't back off soon, he'd take a walk and scout the area for an alternate bride. "I'm not in the mood for games."

"Neither am I. In fact, I only have one last question."

"And what's that?"

"How do you feel about children?"

He took a deep breath. It was a reasonable question, all things considered. "The first thing I packed were several guarantees to avoid that particular complication." He held up his hand before she could interrupt. "I'm not opposed to them. I'm just trying to be sensible. Let's work out the kinks in our marriage before introducing babies into the mix."

"But you don't rule them out at some point in the future?"

"No." He studied her with unrelenting intensity. "How do you feel about kids?"

"I love them." She smiled. "If you don't want to have any right away, I'll be happy to adopt any of your employees' children until you are."

That won his approval. "Young ones are in scarce supply around the ranch. But I'll see what I can do."

"I'm curious."

His mouth twisted. "Now why don't I find that surprising?"

"I can't imagine," she teased.

"Go on," he said with a sigh. "Spill it. What are you curious about?"

"How do you decide whether I'm capable of turning your house into a home? What qualifications does your wife need?"

"I think this might be a good time to take our discussion someplace more private. There's a small balcony on one side of the garden. It's probably off limits, but I'm willing to risk it, if you are." He held out his hand, palm up—a hand that mirrored its owner, work-roughened and callused into painful hardness. "Would you mind if we go there?"

Shayne stilled. She remembered that balcony all too well. That's where she'd first met Chaz. He'd appeared in the garden beneath and, spying her, had done a very poor imitation of Romeo, spouting an amusing "cowboy" version of Shakespeare.

And then he'd come after her, scoffing at the circular staircase hidden behind the bushes and instead climbing the trellis adjacent to the balcony. One look into laughter-filled blue eyes set above a cocky grin and she'd been lost. He'd vaulted over the wrought-iron railing and captured her heart the same instant he'd captured her lips.

They'd talked for hours, planning a dream-life that on the stroke of midnight they'd turned into a reality by speaking vows she'd kept to this day.

She inclined her head, ignoring the clamor of protest issued from silver-voiced bells. "The balcony sounds perfect."

He led the way into the garden, finding the steps concealed behind the shrubbery with unerring accuracy. She preceded him without a word, afraid if she spoke, she'd give herself away. Did he even realize that behind the French doors at the top of the stairway he'd find the bedroom she'd used whenever she and Rafe visited the Montagues on business? Of course, the bed and furniture were now draped in dust covers, the room as asleep as she'd been all these years.

"Okay, Marianna. Let's get down to specifics."

She fought not to react to the name. It seemed such a sham coming from his lips. Worse, it brought back memories of her aunt and of Florida, memories she'd rather not have resurrected. "Go ahead."

"I already told you I live on a ranch. It's a fair size which means it takes up a good bit of my time."

"So you won't be around much?"

"It depends on the season and the workload. I'm just giving you notice there'll be occasions where you'll spend more hours alone than you might like. Can you handle that?"

"It shouldn't be a problem. I have art commissions I can work on when I'm at a loose end."

"You're an artist?"

"On the days I'm not managing the family farm."

She'd surprised him. "Then you're familiar with the lifestyle?" he asked in relief. "You understand it'll be isolated."

"I understand going to town is an all-day affair." At least, it had been on Rafe's coffee *finca* in Costa Rica. "I assume many of the chores will be similar, even though I doubt our farm is the same as your ranch. If so, I can handle your accounts, schedule employees, take care of payroll, and run a household."

"Anything you can't do?" he asked in amusement.

"Well, there is one rather notable failing. But I'll give just about anything a try. Is that good enough?"

He folded his arms across his chest and lifted an eyebrow. "Care to tell me what that failing is?"

She shook her head. "Not really."

Instead of annoying him, he must have found her confession amusing. A broad grin revealed the tiny chip in his tooth, a chip she'd found quite by accident when they'd first kissed. "I'm supposed to marry a masked woman with one serious failing. More and more interesting."

"It'll give us plenty to learn about each other over the course of our marriage."

"So I've found a woman who likes mystery in her relationships." The amusement died. "Okay. Have it your way."

Astonishment held her silent for a split second. "Then, you agree?"

"Fair warning. I have a few secrets of my own. If a bit of mystery between a husband and wife doesn't bother you, it doesn't bother me."

A nerve wracking thought struck. "This secret of yours isn't anything illegal, is it?"

To her astonishment, his mouth tightened. "Nothing I can be jailed for."

"Oh, Chaz," she whispered, moving close enough to touch his arm. "Is your secret really that serious?"

"Serious enough, masked lady."

What in the world had he done? "Do you regret it?"

"No." His answer was swift and unconditional and all the response necessary in order for her to make her decision.

"Then that's all that matters."

"Not quite. I'm willing to take you sight unseen and accept this serious flaw you possess. But there's one important aspect of our relationship we have to explore before we make a final commitment."

She could guess what that might be. "Is that why you brought me here?"

"Yes."

"So we'd have some privacy?"

"Yes."

She refused to be coy. "Privacy to make love."

He didn't back down beneath her direct gaze. "We need to know for sure. It's an important aspect of a marriage."

The sex had to be good, but wasn't to involve emotions. Didn't he see how wrong that was? "And if we're not compatible?"

"We reconsider."

The bells on her mask issued a quick, urgent warning. "I'm nervous, Chaz," she confessed. "Is that so surprising?"

His eyes were black in the darkness of the night, the distant fairy lights strung through the garden not enough to touch them with color. He turned and leaned against the railing, folding his hands along the top and stared out at the starlit night.

She saw his gaze drift past the fanciful gardens and outward toward the stark, uncompromising landscape of the desert. The full moon washed down, blessing it with softness. But the night's shadows cut across the silvery light in hard, harsh strokes, giving lie to the pastoral gentleness. It was a fitting match for the man at her side.

"I noticed you when you first arrived," he said after a bit. "You didn't know that, did you?"

Alarm filled her. Had he seen her unmasked? "When I first arrived?"

"A few minutes before you danced with Sotherland. You came down the steps into the ballroom. Your mask hides a lot, but it didn't hide your eagerness, your impatience to join the party."

To find him, she almost corrected. "And?"

"Before you could reach your goal, a rather elderly man stopped you."

She remembered. "He'd twisted his ankle and needed help."

"You helped him."

"That impressed you?" she asked in disbelief. "Anyone would have done the same. It's common decency."

"No one had helped him until you arrived." He glanced at her over his shoulder. "He wasn't the only one, either. There was a young girl sitting by herself,

"She reminded me of someone I once knew," Shayne admitted.

"You sent her home, didn't you?"

"She didn't belong. She'd only come because she wanted to escape her home life. I suggested some alternate ways she could accomplish that without marrying a perfect stranger."

"Unlike you?"

The question hit home. "I'm not eighteen, nor am I trying to escape an unhappy home life."

"What are you trying to escape?"

"Nothing." She took a deep breath, struggling to open herself to him. Once upon a time, she'd have shared her innermost thoughts and feelings with ease. But over the years, she'd become more cautious. "I'm not trying to escape anything, Chaz. I'm trying to find something."

Tension built along his shoulders and tautened his spine. "Find what?"

Respite from the past. A love she'd lost long ago. "My future."

"And you think that future's with me?"

"I haven't decided, yet," she admitted with perfect candor.

"If you're looking for some sort of fairy tale romance, you're talking to the wrong man. I'm not interested in love. I'm after someone who's interested in a practical relationship. Who's willing to help create a home. A woman with a sense of humor and a generous spirit who'll stick by me when life gets tough." He turned and faced her. "Are you that woman?"

"Let me get this straight. I can share a life with you, but not love?"

"Not unless you want a world full of hurt."

"And that's supposed to induce me to marry you?"

"No. That's supposed to make you think long and hard. Are you in the market for practical, or are you Cinderella waiting for the prince? Fantasy or reality?"

Didn't Chaz realize? He was that prince, their hearts and souls joined on a fateful night nine impossibly long years ago. He might regret ever having met her, but what they'd shared had been special. She refused to believe otherwise.

Their joining had been a delicious combination of fantasy and reality. Otherwise, the feelings would have faded over time, brought to mind on rare occasions, to be examined unemotionally with a sigh of regret or a smile of distantly remembered pleasure.

She faced him, feeling impossibly small and fragile beside his indomitable strength. She had to win this battle of wills. There was no other choice. She had to make him believe in dreams again.

"Why don't you kiss me, Chaz, and we'll see whether it's fantasy or reality."

Something dark and powerful moved in his gaze. "All right, sweetheart. Have it your way." His words were pragmatic enough, but the tone told her something far different. It warned of a man fully roused, a man who took what he wanted, no quarter given. "Let me prove that it isn't Prince Charming you're kissing, but the real thing."

"Or perhaps it'll be a little of both."

"Don't fool yourself, darlin'." He captured her in his arms, his hands strong and firm on her back. Then they slid to her hips, settling on the gentle swell flaring beneath her narrow waist. "I intend to see to it that you go into this marriage with your eyes wide open."

"They're open."

"Keep them that way."

Reaching up, he ripped off his mask, revealing the features that had haunted her memory all these years. The boyishness had given way to leaner angles, emphasizing his blade-straight nose and cheekbones set at an interesting slant. His mouth was broad, the lips wide enough to be considered sensuous, yet decidedly masculine. And his chin warned of a man set in his way. But his eyes . . .

His eyes held her, drew her in, denying the coldness of his words. Somewhere behind the barriers of pain, buried beneath years of denial, lay a heart capable of a love so deep, so indomitable, she'd do anything to find it again.

As though sensing the direction of her thoughts, he reached for her mask. "Still intent on keeping this on?"

"Please, don't!" She evaded his hand with a quick twist that stirred her bells to life. She had no choice but to hide her face. Any chance of establishing a relationship with him would end the instant he saw who she was.

Chaz reacted without thought. She shouldn't have run. The primeval urge to hunt forced him to give chase. He couldn't explain what ancient cravings drove him—whether it was the mystery of her features, or the fleet grace of her movements, or the generous womanly curves set in a dainty frame. Perhaps it was something far more basic, man scenting a woman's desire. All he knew was he had to have her.

Now.

She paused mid-flight, trapped by the railing, and spun to face him. Her gown belled out around her and he could hear the nervous give and take of her breath. For a long moment, she stared at him. And then her arms dropped to her sides in unconditional surrender. She was his for the taking and they both knew it.

He offered his hand and she pleased him by slipping willingly into his embrace. She was a contradiction that enticed, her pale hair bound into repressive order at the nape of her neck, while her dark eyes warned of an intensely passionate nature.

"Will you let me keep my mask on?" she asked.

"Keep it, if it's important to you. But if I can't see you, at least let me taste you."

Her eyes fluttered closed, eyes that haunted him in unsettling and unexpected ways. "Chaz . . ."

Her whisper was sheer temptation, a siren's call pitched to beguile even as it pleaded for his seduction. Her breath mingled with his, the honeyed warmth pulling him closer, demanding he sample the lush flavor. He wanted to take her mouth, hot and fast. Instead, he drove them both insane with slow and thorough.

He drank, deeply, his thirst ravenous. Her mouth was every bit as soft as he'd anticipated, opening to him without hesitation. They began the ageless dance of lips and tongue and teeth, first gentle, then rapacious. Teasing. Then deadly serious. He wrapped a hand around her neck, feeling her desperate moan vibrate against his palm. The sound licked through him, piercing straight to a non-existent soul. He knew that distinctive feminine whimper. Knew what it meant. Knew what it demanded of him.

"It's coming, my sweet. I have what you need."

He felt for the zipper at the back of her dress and lowered it. The metallic rent meshed with the urgent babel of bells. Their mouths melded again and again while his fingers slipped along the smooth expanse of her spine to the hollow above her buttocks. He backed her away from the railing, deeper into the shadows of the balcony. Moonlight cut across her mask, highlighting the ivory beads and golden bells, and revealing the liquid darkness of her eyes. Black eyes. Familiar eyes. Eyes that haunted.

"I'm no prince, sweetheart. I'm all man, blood and bone and as tough as they come."

She shook her head, hair loosened from their embrace slipping in a pale curtain about her shoulders. "You're a man who holds honor dear and protects those in his care."

"You couldn't possibly know that."

"I know."

"You're putting your faith in a man who doesn't believe in such things. Blind faith isn't smart, honey. Not with someone like me."

"That kiss erased any doubts I might have had."

His gaze shifted to her mouth. Her lips were kissed into plump ripeness—damp and swollen and ready to be taken again. "Don't kid yourself. That kiss was lust at its best."

He cupped her upper arms, nearly groaning aloud when her dress slipped downward, draping over his hands in silent supplication. Ivory-toned skin peeked through her curtain of hair, stirring an urge so dangerously primitive, he shook with it.

He pushed out the words. "At least our marriage won't be lacking in one area."

"It won't lack in any area. Not if you're willing to give it a chance."

He closed his eyes, speaking through gritted teeth. "A wife. A home. Sex. That's all I want."

"It won't be. Not for long."

"You play a dangerous game, lady."

"It's no game."

Her arms lifted free of her dress and encircled his neck. She was like some untamed mythological goddess. Masked, her hair tumbled in an appealing tangle, bared to the waist, her mouth lifted to his in generous invitation. He unleashed his control and allowed her spell to consume him.

She branded him with her delicate touch, igniting him, setting a wildfire that wiped clean all thought He leaned into her, fell into her, filling his hands with her lush breasts, filling her mouth with fierce, uncontrolled sweeps of his tongue.

The scent of her drove him wild, her taste a distant, yet strangely familiar memory that had him acting on pure instinct. He bit her lower lip, tugging on it. And then he found the fine-boned joining of her neck and shoulder, and finally the pebbled tips of her breasts.

Her soft cries of pleasure drove him onward, had him lifting the wide skirt of her gown to give her the completion they both so desperately sought

"Wait." She stayed his hand. "We can't. Someone might see."

"Don't stop me." His breath labored in his chest and he trembled with the strain of speaking when the moment called for sheer physical expression. It had been so long since he'd had a woman, so long since he'd wanted a woman that he was almost mindless with need. "I don't think I can stop now."

"You don't have to. But we can't make love here." She fumbled behind her for the doorknob. "This room's been deserted for years. No one will find us."

If he'd been paying attention, he'd have known the truth, known whom he held in his arms, understood why her kisses were so familiar, why they made him so frantic, why he could anticipate her every craving and she his. But he simply accepted her comment at face value, accepted that she would know the room was empty, that no one had used it for years, and that it lay silently in wait for the joining of two time-lost lovers.

Moonlight led the way inside and then deserted them, forcing him to rely on scent and sound. For some reason it intensified his arousal, drove the imperative to mate. The rustle of her dress pinpointed her location and he came after her, snatching her from the arms of darkness into his embrace. Her dress was a hindrance soon discarded.

"Where?" he demanded.

Somehow she understood his question. "This way."

Three swift steps led him to a sheet-covered bed. He lowered her to the cool cotton, stripping away her nylons and panties. For a brief instant the moon unveiled itself again and he saw her clearly.

She was white on white, her skin a lustrous pearl on a bed of milky innocence. The only color provided by the hint of gold in the long strands of hair pillowing her head and textured between her thighs.

And her eyes. Huge and black and filled with a woman's vulnerability. For some reason her mask only added to that vulnerability, adorning her with shy mystery.

"I won't hurt you," he whispered.

"I know."

"I'm going to make you mine. Now. But I swear on what little honor I possess I'll marry you afterward."

"I know that, too."

Her certainty cut with whip like brutality, biting deep and leaving a scar he'd carry for years to come. He didn't deserve such faith. But he wanted it. He wanted it as urgently as he wanted to sink into her softness.

The moonlight dimmed, like the slow giving of day into the dusky embrace of night. Before it slipped away, he intended to be in her arms, to hold her close so she wouldn't be alone in the dark.

His clothes hit the floor with decisive haste. Once finished, he came to her, wrapping her in warmth as the blackness descended, rolling onto his back with her on top of him. Her mouth scoured his chest with kisses of fire and her hair blanketed him, the strands long enough to cloak him all the way to his hips. He shuddered, tortured by a pleasure so intense he thought it just might kill him. If he could have found his voice, he'd have begged for mercy.

Instead, he flipped her onto her back. His kisses were too hard, too demanding. But rather than complaining, she cupped his face and lifted her mouth for more.

"Tell me this isn't your first time," he said, his voice raw to the point he barely recognized it as his own.

"It's not my first time."

He bowed his head, straining for control. "I don't know if I can— It's been so long that—"

"I want you. Very badly."

The urge to fill her, to take her, to make her his in the most basic way possible clawed at him. But he fought it. From somewhere he found the few remaining shreds of decency.

He touched her with exquisite care, instinctively finding the deliciously feminine spots that would give her the most intense pleasure. The sides of her breasts, the burgeoning tips, the sensitive skin at the lowest point on her belly, the backs of her knees, the upper slope of her buttocks and the creamy softness of her inner thighs. He found them all, anointed each and every one until her body wept for his possession.

And when he'd finished, he took her, filled her, rode the wildness that exploded between them. Only once before had he ever felt such divinity in an act, known such completeness in a physical joining.

Memories stormed back, memories he was helpless to rein in. They possessed him as surely as he possessed the woman beneath him. The bells from her mask pealed, as though in joyous welcome. Unable to resist, he gathered her up, sent her surging toward ecstasy. And then he followed her into that glittering realm, at one with her. At one with nature. Heart, body and soul in perfect accord.

But it was an accord not meant to be.

From a great distance he heard the door open and harsh light impaled them. "Oh, excuse me," a voice gasped. Ella's voice. And then ... "Oh, dear heaven. Chaz? Is that you? And ... Shayne?"

Chapter Three

To My Long-Lost Bride,

It's taken a full year before I could sit down and write this letter to you. I was so sure, so certain you'd be at the Anniversary Ball. I waited for you. Waited until dawn broke through the night sky. And then I left.

I'm not even sure why I'm writing this. Maybe it's my way of saying goodbye. Maybe it's because I never know when to let go. And I confess, I rarely give up. What did I tell you on the balcony that night? Fight until you're unconscious or the other fella gives up. Well, I'm not out, yet. And I won't have won this particular fight until you're in my arms again.

I sold the property I'd bought for us and I'm back wrangling. The ironic thing is, I made a ton of money off the sale. Even your brother would be impressed. Ah, hell. What does it matter? There's only one thing I care about.

Damn it, wife. Why weren't you there? Where have you gone and how do I find you again? Or was what we shared pure fantasy? Maybe it was just a dream, a foolish fairy tale. And perhaps I'm the biggest fool of all for still believing.

Shayne. Sweetheart. My Forever Love. Where are you?

Chaz jerked as though he'd been sucker-punched. "Shayne!"

"I can explain," she began as Ella made a hasty retreat.

He grabbed the mask and yanked it from her head, flinging it across the room. The elaborate confection caught the moonlight as it soared through the air, glittering with soft radiance while the bells clattered in nervous panic. It hit the floor with discordant finality, sliding into a tangle of painful silence.

Light from the hallway had revealed a lamp on a bedside table, and he fumbled for the switch. Seventy-five watts of incandescent power stabbed through the room with punishing swiftness, darting into every corner and across every object, including her.

Never before had she felt so naked. Without her mask, she lay in the middle of the bed still flushed and replete from Chaz's lovemaking, her every thought and expression totally exposed to his unforgiving gaze. She snatched at the bedcover to hide herself. Fortunately, his attention remained fixed on her face, overlooking another of her secrets, a secret that would have been revealed if he'd paid closer attention.

The unnatural calm stretched into an unbearable minute, the tension as punishing as the light. Then he swore, the words harsh and crude, stealing the lingering traces of sweetness from the room.

"It was a trick!" He erupted from the bed. "From the beginning you and your brother have made a fool of me."

"No, Chaz." She held out her hand in supplication. "Please. Let me explain."

"What's to explain?" He prowled the room, his nudity making his rage all the more unnerving. "Big brother ripped us apart nine years ago. And now, for some damn reason he's decided to thrust us together again. The master puppeteer yanking the strings."

"That was my fault. You were the only man I ever loved and—"

He approached the bed, magnificent in his rage. "And so now I'm good enough for him? Now that I have property and a home and money, I'm an acceptable husband for his sister?"

"He didn't know you had those things. I didn't know."

"He had me investigated, Shayne. There's no other explanation." He snatched his trousers from the floor and thrust his legs into them. "That explains both the ticket and your presence. Well, thanks, but no thanks. I had my strings chopped off by the Beaumonts before. I won't allow it to happen again."

So history would repeat itself. Once more she'd share a single night with the man who'd captured her heart all those years ago. And once more, she'd lose love. No. No! She'd been passive for too long, afraid for more years than she could count. And what had it gotten her? She swept from the bed, wrapping the cover around herself like a sarong. Her hair tumbled in a wild tangle about her shoulders, but she didn't care. She faced him down, anger and determination burning within.

"You're not leaving without me."

"That's where you're wrong, Shayne."

"You promised."

"Only because I didn't know who you were."

She had to convince him, no matter what it took. It was their only chance at happiness—a chance he needed as desperately as she, whether he realized it yet, or not. "You came for a wife. Or had you forgotten that minor detail. There's not enough time to find someone else."

"There's time." He thrust his arms into his dress shirt, shoving the tails into his trousers. It hung open, revealing the bronzed chest she'd taken such delight in kissing less than an hour ago. A shudder ran through her at the memory. "There may not be a lot of choices, but it's not morning, yet."

"You're going to walk away from what we just shared?"

"As much as I appreciate your generous sacrifice—"

"Don't!" The pain was so intense she swayed with it. "Don't tarnish what happened in that bed. Leave if you want. But don't destroy something so miraculous on your way out."

For an instant his expression softened and she caught a glimpse of the Chaz she'd once know, the man who'd made her his with a fierce adoration that she'd never forgotten. Would never forget. "Shayne . . ." Her name whispered through the air, ripe with memory.

Behind them the door thrust open. In one instinctive move, Chaz pivoted, planting himself squarely between her and the perceived threat.

"Shayne?" Rafe called out. "Are you all right?"

She drew a ragged breath, overwhelmed by what Chaz had revealed. Whether he wanted to admit it or not, he still had feelings for her. No doubt they were buried deep. And no doubt he'd weed them free, if he could. But they were there, nonetheless. "I'm fine, Rafe. Chaz and I were just getting—" If it weren't so tragic, she'd laugh. "We were getting reacquainted."

"Ella was concerned. I am also concerned."

"This is between your sister and me, Beaumont," Chaz snarled. "Or were you planning on interfering again?"

"I wanted to make sure she was unharmed."

"She's a big girl now. A few bumps and bruises aren't going to kill her."

Fury glittered in Rafe's eyes and he took a step into the room. "If you mark her in any way—"

This time Shayne took a protective stance in front of Chaz. "It's an expression, Rafe. He didn't mean it literally. Chaz would never hurt me."

"You're pretty confident," he murmured in her ear. "Considering I was on my way out of here when big brother arrived."

Rafe inclined his head. "I'll arrange to have a wedding salon made available." The tiniest of accents had drifted into his voice, warning that he wasn't feeling as equitable as he let on. "Do you have a preference as to the ceremony?"

"Yeah." Chaz bent down and snagged his cummerbund from the floor. "None. I got what I came for."

Rafe drew in a harsh breath and Shayne knew if she didn't act fast, someone was going to leave the room in a lot more pain than when they entered. She turned into Chaz's arms, catching him by surprise.

"We can make it a temporary marriage," she said in a low, desperate voice, praying her brother didn't hear. "Just until we find out whether or not I'm pregnant. That'll give me enough time to give you the home you want."

He looked like she'd sucker-punched him. "What the hell are you talking about?"

"You told me you'd packed plenty of protection against that possibility." Her eyes flashed with temper. "Perhas you should have taken a moment to unpack before coming here."

"I didn't expect to take my bride before taking a wife!"

For some reason that struck Shayne as funny and she couldn't help smiling. "We never seem to get it quite right, do we?"

"Pregnant," Chaz repeated, a shade too loudly. "Damn."

"Preg— *Basta!*" Rafe roared. He stabbed his finger at Chaz. "You will finish dressing and present yourself in the library within the next five minutes. I will have a priest standing by."

"And if I refuse?"

"You would allow her to bear your bastard? It is your style, yes?"

Chaz went white, his hands collapsing into fists. Shayne stared from one man to the other in alarm. Something unspoken passed between the two, something she didn't have a hope of understanding. Whatever it was, it locked them in a battle of wills, an explosive edge of violence burning between them, fighting for expression.

Without knowing what had set them off, she had no hope of diffusing the situation. Still, she could try. "Could we calm down and discuss this rationally? What's going on?"

"Nothing that need concern you," Rafe replied. "Your husband-to-be and I are simply reaching an understanding. Do you agree to my terms, Mr. McIntyre? You will marry her?"

"You'll regret this, Beaumont."

"I don't doubt it." Rafe's mouth pulled to one side and he shrugged. "But she is my sister. I'll do whatever it takes to make her happy. For some strange reason, she thinks you're capable of doing that. Five minutes." Without another word, he turned and left the room.

"Chaz...?"

"Don't. Don't say another word." He searched the room for his boots. Finding them kicked beneath a drape of sheet, he sat on the edge of the bed and pulled them on. "You heard your brother. You'll have your heart's desire in five short minutes. Do you plan to dress for your wedding or is that bedcover your gown of choice?"

"I didn't intend to deceive you, Chaz, any more than I intended to end up—" She gestured toward the bed. "I just wanted to have time to get to know you again before you found out who I was."

"Honey, I recognize a setup when I see one. A willing woman, a convenient bed, a relative at the door. It's as old as the hills."

"But—"

"Enough, Shayne." He shot her a look that silenced her more effectively than anything else could have, one that combined a bitter cynicism with an underlying fury. "You have precisely thirty seconds to put on some clothes, or I swear I'll drag you downstairs the way you are."

She didn't waste any more energy talking. In one swift move, she dropped the bedsheet while sliding her gown over her head. Underpants and heels followed. She didn't bother trying to wiggle into her stockings. Beneath her floor-length skirt, it was doubtful anyone would notice. Except for her hair, she'd pass muster. Chin held high, she started for the door.

Chaz stepped forward to block her path. An odd expression slipped into his gaze, an expression she'd known long ago, one that was protective and caring and almost loving. Tears of longing pricked her eyes.

"Shayne." Even her name came on winds from the past. "We can't go back."

"I know." She returned his look, regret and hope mingling as one. "But we have the future. We can choose which path we take from here."

A tender smile touched his mouth even as he shook his head. "That path was decided a long time ago. I'm not the man you knew. What you're doing will only cause a world of hurt."

"Only if you choose to hurt me."

The tenderness seeped away, leaving behind desolation. "I can't do anything else. It's not too late, Shayne. Tell your brother you've changed your mind."

"I haven't changed my mind, Chaz. Not in nine years. Not in ninety."

"What you feel is a dream. It isn't real."

"Then I hope I sleep forever." The truth was, she'd been sleeping. She'd slept for the past nine years. But she was awake now, brought to life by a single kiss. She couldn't go back to that other existence, even if she wanted to. Life awaited her, a life with Chaz.

His mouth settled along grim lines. "So be it. Let's hope your dream doesn't turn into a nightmare."

Thrusting open the door, he gestured for her to precede him. As she passed she had the crazy impression that he feathered a kiss on top of her head. Of course, she was mistaken. He was furious with her. Furious at her deception, at Rafe's insistence that they marry, at being caught in the machinations of the Beaumonts once again. Any feelings he might have for her, she'd destroyed when she'd opened her heart, while cautiously masking her face.

Her mask! Spinning around, she darted past him and back into the room. She didn't know why it felt so urgent to recover the mask, but it did. The bells chattered an urgent greeting as she looped the elastic band over her arm.

"What are you doing, Shayne? You don't need that any longer."

"I know. I just wanted to have it."

He lifted an eyebrow. "A souvenir?"

She lifted her chin, refusing to back down. "Is that so difficult to believe?"

"I thought souvenirs were to mark occasions you want to remember. Not those you'd rather forget."

"And you'd rather forget tonight?" she demanded in a rare display of anger.

"There's only one thing about this evening I care to remember." He lifted the mask dangling from her arm and plucked free a strand of bells. "The rest will haunt my memory without any reminders. Now do we join your brother, or do we put an end to this farce?"

"We join my brother." She touched his arm as he drew level with her, feeling the heavy cording of work-hardened muscle beneath her hand. Tension radiated from him. Did her mere touch do that? If so, there was hope for them yet. "You had a reason for marrying, Chaz. That hasn't changed. I promise I'll do whatever I can to help you achieve your goal. But I was serious earlier. If I'm not pregnant, I'll leave if that's what you want. All I'm asking is that you give us a chance."

As close as they stood, she could see the implacable set of his jawline, the tight swallow that moved the bronzed column of his throat. A flare of emotion sparked in his eyes, before being swiftly doused. "It won't work, sweetheart," he said ever so gently. "Maybe, long ago. But not now."

"Why?"

"Because I have nothing left to give. If I ever knew love, it was so long ago I can hardly remember."

A fierce determination seized hold. "Then I'll find it for you. I can. I will!"

"No, Shayne. You won't."

She could scarcely contain her frustration. "I don't understand. Why won't you let me help you? We could find what we once had. I know we could."

His gaze fastened on hers, the expression cold and clear and absolute. "Because I don't want this thing you call love. Not from you. Not from anyone. It's all a lie. And I swear. If you wrap up those lies in pretty declarations of undying love, I'll send you back to your brother before the words even hit the air. Are we clear about that?"

As clear as the sound of her heart breaking. She shivered and the bells pealed a mournful dirge in response. "Yes, Chaz. We're clear."

Chaz stood in front of the priest, deaf to the words being spoken. Only one thought filled his head. He shouldn't have told Shayne the truth.

He could have made his objections clear without being so harsh. Maybe then he wouldn't have seen the desolation that filled those huge, dark eyes of hers. Or felt the physical blow her pained gasp had caused. Or heard the jarring clash of bells as she'd jerked free of him, walking away with a fragile dignity that nearly unmanned him.

He slipped his hand into his pocket and fingered the strand he'd stripped from her mask. Honesty was best, under the circumstances. That way she'd know right from the start what to expect from their marriage.

Chaz suddenly realized there'd been an interminably long silence. While he'd been lost in thought, something significant had happened. Something that had caused everyone in the room to turn and glare at him.

"Er . . . I do?" he said hopefully.

"Oh, Chaz," Shayne whispered, tears filling her lush brown eyes, eyes he could lose his soul in.

He sighed. "Damn it, Shayne. What have I done now?"

Rafe slammed his fist against Chaz's bicep. "*Imbécil!* She said no to you."

"She said . . . ? Excuse us for a minute." He grasped Shayne's elbow and hustled her off to one side of the room. "What's going on?"

She bowed her head. "I can't go through with this. I can't allow Rafe to force you to marry me. I won't force you to marry me."

"You don't understand."

"Yes, I do." She spared a quick glance at her watch. "There's still time. I can help you find someone else. Someone who could—"

"Not a chance," he interrupted. "We're doing this here and now."

"But you said—"

"You were right earlier. You could be pregnant."

She had trouble meeting his eyes, a blush blooming across her cheeks. "If I am, we can deal with it then."

"We'll deal with it now." He released his breath in a rough sigh and bent his head closer to hers. Her scent threatened to drive him crazy, but he rather no one overhear their conversation. It wouldn't be fair to Shayne. "Listen to me, sweetheart. Once I realized the consequences of what we'd done, I'd have forced you in front of a priest, whether you and your brother agreed or not."

"No!" she instantly denied. "When you found out it was me, you were going to leave."

"Yeah, I was. I admit it. If your brother hadn't stopped me, I'd have taken off. But not to find another bride. You have to believe me, Shayne. I'd have come back for you. It was only the shock of discovering who you were and having to deal with your brother again that caused me to react the way I did."

"You don't want to marry me, Chaz. I know you don't."

He leveled her with a single hard look. "Honey, I don't want to marry anyone. I didn't have any choice before I got here and I sure as hell don't have any choice now. Neither do you. The minute you tumbled into that bed with me, you sealed your fate."

He'd said too much. Curiosity dawned in her gaze. "What do you mean you didn't have any choice before you came?"

"I warned you that I had a few secrets of my own."

"Rafe knows your secret, doesn't he? That's what you two were talking about."

"I'm guessing he does. Not that that changes anything." He jerked his head toward the cluster of people waiting for them. "Time to finish what we started."

"And if I say no again?"

"You won't. You're bent on redeeming me, remember?"

"I thought you were beyond redemption."

"I am." He offered a crooked smile. "But you're a woman. So you'll try, anyway." He'd insulted her again. Unfortunately, he suspected it wouldn't be the last time.

"Once we know for certain I'm not pregnant, I'll end the marriage," she assured.

Her promise should have relieved him. Perversely, he found himself thoroughly annoyed. "You'll stay until you've fulfilled your promise to make a home for me. Then you can go if that's what you want." Maybe.

"It will be."

"Fine. Now get back over there and tell them you've changed your mind. It's a long drive to Colorado. I'll want to leave for the ranch as soon as you're packed."

This time when they resumed their positions in front of the priest, he paid attention. Several minutes into the ceremony, another painful nudge from Rafe's fist prompted him to repeat his own vows. Not that he needed any prompting. He hadn't been lying to Shayne. Once he'd realized the potential results of their rather enthusiastic reunion, he'd have been back on her doorstep demanding marriage.

Gathering her hands in his, he spoke the required words. If anyone noted that he omitted the word "love" they didn't call him out on it. But he knew Shayne felt the impact and silently cursed again.

Why did she leave herself open to such hurt? She was a fool to marry him. And he was an even bigger fool to let her. In her heart, she was still that naive seventeen-year-old, believing in miracles and fairy tales.

Well, life with him would soon disabuse her of that notion.

"You have rings you wish to exchange?" the priest asked.

"Sorry, I don't—"

"Allow me," Rafe interrupted, slipping his hand into his pocket.

Chaz forced himself not to move, not to knock loose a few perfect white teeth set in an arrogant mouth. Any doubts that he'd been set up vanished. "All the details planned, right down to the rings, is that it, Beaumont?"

"I like to be prepared."

Chaz swiveled, lowering his voice so only the two of them could hear. "Then start preparin', brother. Next time we meet, you and I are going to exchange more than words. And one of us is crawlin' away from the meeting wishing he'd never played God with my life."

"If that will make you feel better, you may try to make me crawl. So long as you treat my sister well, what you do to me is immaterial." Rafe forced the ring box into Chaz's hand. "But if you hurt her, I will make your life a living misery."

"Too late, Beaumont. You did that already."

Beside him, Shayne caught his arm. "Chaz? Is everything all right?"

He bit back the words he longed to vent. Words that would make a mockery of the vows they'd just uttered. "Everything's fine."

Thumbing open the jewelry box, he silently swore. Beaumont had taken tickets from the Cinderella Ball and fashioned them into wedding bands. Of course, they fit perfectly.

The minute their union had been blessed, Chaz gathered his wife into his arms. She lifted her gaze to meet his and he saw there an inner strength that had been barely perceptible nine years ago. Time and experience had forged that strength with steel. He wasn't the only one who'd walked the painful side of life and fought back. And yet she still retained the full depth of a woman's heart, open to the possibility of love, no matter how remote.

"I'm sorry," he murmured beneath his breath.

"Sorry that you married me?"

"No. Sorry that our marriage will hurt you."

Leaning down, he captured her mouth, drinking in the taste of her, knowing she'd soon live with him as his wife. That for a few short weeks he'd have the fulfillment of a dream, a painful irony now that he no longer believed in dreams. But for some reason, he found his cynicism fading, found that all he could think about was the woman in his arms and the sweetness of her kiss. She opened to him, giving what he refused to take by force, offering all of herself despite the threat he posed.

Ever so gently, he released her. "You need to pack. We'll leave as soon as you're ready."

"I'll help," Ella offered.

Rafe stepped forward and embraced his sister. "Your husband and I will wait for you in my office."

She returned his hug with unmistakable enthusiasm and Chaz nearly groaned aloud. It annoyed him no end to see her bestowing her affections on such undeserving recipients. First him. Now Beaumont. Did the woman have no sense of self-preservation?

"No fighting," Shayne warned in a whisper that carried to all corners of the room.

"We'll behave." Rafe shot Chaz a pointed look. "At least we'll try."

Chaz shook his head. "One of us will try."

The other would beat the living hell out of an arrogant coffee farmer at the first wrong word. He cheered up as they left the room. With any luck at all, that word would come within minutes of them gaining some privacy. He worked hard on stoking his temper as they traversed the maze of corridors to Rafe's office.

"It's fascinating, the information one can acquire," Rafe announced the moment they'd entered his office. "Wouldn't you agree?"

Chaz flexed his fist. That sounded remarkably like a wrong word to him, "Such as my ring size?"

"Ring size, hat size, boot size." Rafe indicated a thick folder centered on his desk as he moved out of reach. "It is all documented. Would you care to see the file?"

Somehow, it seemed undignified to chase the man across the room in order to sock him. Chaz decided to hang tight a bit longer. The instant Beaumont came close again, he'd pop him one. In the meantime . . .

"You had me investigated." It wasn't a question. "That's damn personal information you've got there. If I didn't know better, I'd swear your PI slithered into bed with me."

Rafe regarded Chaz without amusement, his silvery eyes like splinters of ice. "Perhaps she did. I didn't inquire as to her methods. I merely paid well for the results she provided." He crossed to the liquor cabinet. "A drink?"

Chaz bared his teeth. Yeah, sure. Bring it on over. He might even take half a second to drink it down before knocking Beaumont's teeth out. "Whiskey. And for the record, I didn't sleep with your investigator." Now why the hell had he said that? He didn't owe the man an explanation. If anything, Beaumont owed him. And he'd be only too happy to collect.

For the first time, Rafe's expression eased. "I know. I also know precisely how many women you've been with since my sister. That information is the only reason you are now married to Shayne, my friend."

Fury seized hold, satisfyingly hot and just begging for expression. "You had no right!"

To his intense annoyance, Rafe inclined his head in complete agreement before crossing to hide behind his desk. The coward! He set the two glasses on the mahogany surface and nudged one in Chaz's direction. "So Ella has told me and on more than one occasion."

Aw, hell. Now why did he have to go and be friendly? "Glad we got that straight," Chaz growled. "Can't go nosing around in a man's private business."

"I would feel precisely the same if our positions were reversed," Rafe commented with disgusting affability. He opened the humidor on his desk and finding it empty, released his breath in a disappointed sigh. "It is just as well. My wife doesn't approve and I would pay the consequences if she were to catch me."

Chaz grinned, despite himself. "It's one vice I've managed to avoid. Probably the only one."

"Quite self-destructive," Rafe conceded. "Ella calls it a nervous habit, a crutch. Ridiculous, of course. Still, I have the urge to indulge, particularly in moments of stress. So perhaps she is right, after all."

"I gather this is a moment of stress."

"Hell, yes. Don't you think so?"

They shared an instant of perfect accord, an accord bound to be destroyed the moment one of them chose to speak again. Chaz waded on in, only too happy to have them back on more familiar footing. "It didn't have to be that way. If you'd just butted out—"

"You don't know the whole story, McIntyre. You don't know the life Shayne has lived or you'd understand why I protect her so fiercely."

"That's no longer your concern."

"That's where you are wrong, my friend. Shayne will always be my concern. But I am willing to give her into your keeping. For now."

"Damn it, Beaumont. She's a woman, not property. She's not yours to give any more than she's mine to take."

"But she is yours to protect." The warning glitter had returned to silver-gray eyes. "See that you do so."

"More threats?"

"Yes."

At least he didn't bother with false denials. "I wouldn't let anything hurt her."

"I believe you." There was no doubting Rafe's sincerity. "But I am more concerned about your hurting her than any outside force."

Chaz tossed back his whiskey and slammed the glass to the table. "I won't hurt her," he lied desperately.

"Not on purpose, perhaps. That doesn't change the fact that you have become a hard man, a ruthless man. Hard, ruthless men can crush tender young things beneath their boot heels without even realizing it."

"Not Shayne."

"Let us hope not." Rafe fingered the folder on his desk. "There's one other subject I wish to address before she joins us."

Damn it all! "What now?"

"Relax, McIntyre. It's simply an offer."

"Fine. Say what you need to and let's end this farce."

"My investigator has turned up quite a lot of interesting information."

"And?"

Rafe looked at him. "And if you ever need my help, you have only to ask."

Chaz released his breath in a harsh sigh. He could take insult at the suggestion. Hell, it would be easy. He could allow his pride and anger to drive him to offer the sort of physical response he'd been longing to since he'd first set eyes on Rafe Beaumont. Didn't his hands ache to curl into fists and pummel something?

Instead, he stood and leaned across the desk, offering the hand of friendship to his brother-in-law.

"Thanks," he said, and meant it. "I'll do that."

Chapter Four

To My Long-Lost Bride,

I dreamed of you last night. Three years have passed, and yet still, I dream of you. Your scent surrounded me, consumed me, made me believe for just one short instant that you lay beside me. I could hear your voice, shy and yet edged with a woman's passion. I could see your eyes, as dark as the night sky, filled first with laughter and then with warmth and finally with a love I've never seen before . . . or since. Does it sound trite to say your skin was like satin? Your hair a silken waterfall that streamed over us like golden sunshine in a moonlit room?

Have you any idea how you linger in my mind? How, until I hold you in my arms again, I'll never know peace? Have you any idea how many nights I've awoken, desperate for one last touch, one final word? Desperate for the completion no other woman can provide? You haunt me, my love. You steal my soul and make me long for the impossible. Whenever I look at a woman, all I see are the ways she doesn't compare to you.

I love you, sweet wife. My Forever Love. There will never be anyone but you.

Late afternoon sunshine slanted across the Colorado landscape and settled on a structure as hard and rough as the man beside her.

"This is your home?" Shayne asked.

"No," Chaz corrected in a tone curiously void of expression. "This is my house. It's your job to turn it into a home."

Shayne studied the sweeping lines of the huge ranch house with ill-concealed apprehension. Structurally, it needed work. The porch steps sagged and the roof had been patched more than once. The clapboard siding hadn't seen fresh paint in years and the overflowing gutters looked like they provided hearth and home for any number of woodland creatures. The grounds surrounding the house weren't any better. The patch of earth that might have been a garden long ago was unkempt and gasping beneath dead weeds and thatch. But that particular project could wait until spring.

Assuming she was still here come spring.

She touched her belly with a tentative hand. Had Chaz's child taken root from their one explosive encounter? In a few short weeks she'd know. In the meantime, she could only hope.

"Tell me what you'd like done."

"Nothing out here. I'll take care of that part. Your skills are needed inside."

Shayne eyed the warped front door. If the inside was as bad as the exterior, she was in deep, deep trouble. She took a steadying breath. She could do this. If she wanted to build a life with Chaz, she would damn well find a way to whip this slapped-together concoction of wood and nails and pasteboard into a home.

"Show me," she replied.

He led the way, climbing the steps and forcing the door inward with his shoulder. Shayne followed. She hesitated on the threshold, then stepped boldly across, not held in her husband's arms as a newlywed might expect, but trailing behind, about as welcome as a barefoot guest arriving at a black-tie-and-tails dinner party.

Any bride-like feelings she might have harbored vanished with that single step. For the first time she wondered why creating a home was so important to Chaz. Why did he need a wife, when an interior decorator would have done just as well? She struggled to recall what he'd told her. Not much. And yet, it had seemed so important to him.

Important enough to enter into a marriage he clearly didn't want.

A short, grizzled cowpoke appeared from the bowels of the house. "Boss, we got trouble and more trouble."

Chaz sighed. "Now why doesn't that surprise me?" He inclined his head in her direction. "Shayne, this is my foreman, Penny. Penny, my wife."

The foreman ran a hand over his stubbled jaw, studying her with open curiosity. "Maybe she oughta take door number one."

"Door number? Aw, hell. What's behind door number one, old man? Or should I say who?"

"The Donna woman's in your office. Gave her that room since I figured she wouldn't do too much poking around behind your back. Can't see her riffling through your desk on the sly, can you?"

"Not really. And behind door number two?"

"Mojo."

This time Chaz's curse was a bit more virulent. "What's his problem now?"

Penny drew himself up to his full height, which wasn't much. But what little he possessed was all attitude. "He heard you went and got yourself hitched."

"Heard it from you, no doubt, since you're the only one I told."

"Be that as it may, he got hisself in a real snit over it. If you want, I'll get Jumbo to deal with him. Jes' don't ask the boys to go up against the Donna woman. She scares 'em spitless."

"But not you, right?"

"Keep it up, boss man," Penny warned. "Ride me a little harder and I'll hightail it over to the Winston spread. That little Cami girl said I could have a job whenever I wanted."

"Working for their foreman?" Chaz folded his arms across his chest. "Now that I'd like to see. You and Gabby couldn't agree on the color of the sky. Hell, you'd claim a cow was a bull, just to avoid being on the same side of an argument with him."

Shayne stifled a groan. No doubt these two could exchange insults until— Until the cows came home seemed an appropriate expression, given the circumstances. And if it avoided dealing with the individuals waiting for her husband's attention, no doubt they'd still be standing here come Christmas. Time to take charge.

"Chaz, if you'd go talk to Mojo, I'll speak with Donna. Penny, do you think you could bring us some coffee while we wait?"

The man took instant umbrage. "I'm no cook."

"I'm well aware of that. But I doubt there's a foreman alive who doesn't make a better cup of coffee than the resident cook."

Wicked amusement lit the old man's expression. "Best not be sayin' that anywhere around Mojo."

"The Mojo who's in the kitchen in a snit?" she asked fatalistically.

"The one and same."

"And he is . . . ?"

"The resident cook. Mojo, git it? More joe? Not meanin' to point out your ignorance, but joe's coffee, in case you was wondering."

Great. Just great. She hadn't spent two minutes on the premises and already she'd insulted someone. "Would you mind terribly getting the coffee since I doubt Mojo will?"

"Yes, ma'am, I would mind." Heaving a tremendous sigh, he relented. "But seein' as how you're new here and all, I'll fetch some. Jes' this once, though. Hear?"

"Thank you. That's very sweet of you."

Penny scowled. "Do something nice for a body and see how they repay you." He stomped down the hallway. "Insult you, that's what they do. Sweet. Hah!"

"I don't think this is a very good idea," Chaz began.

"You'll join us as soon as you've spoken to Mojo, won't you?"

"Shayne—"

She ran her hand along his arm. She'd been aiming for reassurance and came away with a sweep of desire so strong she trembled with it. How was that possible? The nine years they'd been apart should have lessened those feelings. Instead, she couldn't look at him, couldn't touch him, without wanting to find her way back into his arms.

And into his heart.

"You married me to act as your wife. At least, I think that's one of the reasons. Let me do my job, Chaz. I can sit with Donna for a short time and share a cup of coffee without turning it into a disaster."

"Don't count on it," he muttered.

"Either you trust me or you don't."

"It's not a matter of trust." He thrust his hand into his hair, tumbling the nut-and-wheat-colored strands into attractive disorder. "First off, her name isn't Donna. It's *Doña* Isabella. *Doña* Isabella Madalena Vega de la Cruz."

Interesting. "And second?"

"And second." He closed his eyes. "Aw, hell, Shayne."

"She's one of your secrets, isn't she?"

Lines of tension bracketed his mouth, confirming her guess. "She's part of one. I just don't want her telling you something that should come from me. You don't deserve that."

He was protecting her! The knowledge ignited a tiny spark of hope, hope that she'd nurture with every bit of determination she possessed. "Then I'll make sure she doesn't tell me. Will that do?"

"I guess it'll have to."

"Where's your office?"

He gestured toward a door off to her left. "Through there. I'll join you as soon as I can."

She smiled. "It'll work out, Chaz."

"Not likely." He cupped the nape of her neck and drew her close. His mouth slipped across hers in a brief kiss. An instant later he returned for another, this one harder, edged with unchecked passion, a plea and a promise and a demand all wrapped up in one.

"I have an idea."

For some reason her eyelids refused to lift. "What's that?"

"Why don't we let our unwelcome visitors sit and stew awhile. We can sneak upstairs and catch up on nine years of waiting. With any luck, they'll be gone by the time we return."

Her eyes flickered open at that. "Am I the lesser of two evils?"

"No. You're the escape from two evils." His mouth scalded a path along her jawline, found her ear and unhinged her with the warmth of his breath. "You're an oasis, water in the middle of an endless desert, life in a barren jumble of rock and dust."

Oh, God, she knew this man. He wasn't the Chaz she'd married, but the one she'd fallen in love with once upon a time. She silently rejoiced at his return, relieved beyond measure to discover that he hadn't totally disappeared. With a little effort, perhaps she could coax him from the hard, cold shell in which he'd encased himself. Maybe. If she were very, very careful.

"I wish we could go upstairs and hide there forever," she confessed with devastating honesty. "Just the two of us."

"We can." He urged her closer into a sweet tangle of arms and legs. "Put on your mask, wife, and we'll pretend we're two strangers with no past and no future to torment us. Just the pleasure of the moment, for as long as that moment lasts."

Pain returned, swift and sure. "And when it ends?"

"We'll deal with that. But, later. Much later."

"I wish—"

"Wish what?"

She fixed her gaze on him, wondering if he sensed all she found so difficult to express. "I wish last night meant more to you than a quick tumble in bed. I wish today could, too."

She'd said the wrong thing. His expression closed over and he pulled back, a wintry breeze washing away the heat of passion. Any cracks in his shell had been swiftly repaired. The abrupt change brought tears to her eyes, tears she hid beneath a protective sweep of lashes.

"I warned you before we married."

"I know."

"Don't ask for more than I can give."

Her mouth tilted to one side, tender amusement easing the pain. "Sorry to disappoint you. But I'm going to keep asking."

"Then brace yourself, sweetheart. Because I'm gonna keep refusing."

"That's up to you." She gathered what remained of her self-control. "Why don't we take care of business? I suspect it will make our time together all the more special when we do finally indulge."

He snagged the front of her blouse and tugged her close again, branding her with a final kiss. "Count on it. And count on the fact that I intend to indulge at our earliest convenience."

A ferocious hunger sparked deep in his eyes, like that of a starving animal stumbling across an unexpected cache of food. Understanding dawned. A starving animal would fall on the food with a voracious appetite that demanded instant gratification, knowing it could be taken from him at any minute.

"You think that what we feel for each other is going to vanish, don't you?"

"There's not a doubt in my mind," he confirmed. "One day we'll wake up and all we'll have between us is hot desert and hard rock."

"If that day ever arrives, you won't have to ask me to leave. I'll go of my own accord."

He inclined his head in agreement, but something held her in place. Something that urged her to take him in her arms and swear her undying love. To promise the love she felt would survive anything. That now they'd found each other, nothing would ever part them again. But caution rode her every bit as hard as it did him.

She stepped away, finding it more difficult than she thought possible. "I'll go introduce myself to *Doña* Isabella."

"I won't be long."

They went in opposite directions, an irony not lost on Shayne. Opening the door to Chaz's office, she braced herself to face the *Doña* and whatever secret Chaz was protecting. It only took a single glance to recognize the woman as a formidable presence.

She sat perfectly erect in the chair opposite Chaz's desk, her spine so rigidly straight, Shayne suspected it could be used as a measuring stick. She didn't turn, but kept her attention focused on a point square in the center of the wall across from her, her hands folded in her lap, her chin set at an imperious angle. It wasn't until Shayne came into her line of sight that the woman cast a black-eyed glance in her direction, her magnificent gaze filled with a rebellious life at direct odds with her inflexible frame. How curious.

"*Doña* Isabella, I'm Shayne McIntyre, Chaz's wife. I apologize for keeping you. We've only just arrived."

"Wife?" That captured the woman's full attention and a hint of emotion moved across sharply proud features. "So he has done as I requested. I confess I'm surprised."

Instead of taking the chair behind Chaz's desk, Shayne chose the adjoining one. It was a small gesture, but one she hoped the *Doña* would take as a conciliatory sign. "Why does our marriage surprise you?"

Her raven-like eyes fastened on Shayne, quick and clever and glistening with a shrewd intelligence. "I did not think he would find a woman willing to join with him."

"I was more than willing."

Her hooked nose was perfectly shaped to emphasize her sniff of disdain. "That does not endear you to me."

Shayne regarded her in amusement. "Do I need to endear myself to you?"

"If you wish my cooperation, you will do everything within your powers to make me happy."

Curiouser and curiouser. "I've ordered coffee. Would that be a good start?"

"No. I drink tea."

"A shame," Shayne said calmly, seeing through the woman's game and playing along. "I suspect Penny would consider it an offense to the cowboy way of life if I were to ask him to fix you some."

A spark of laughter flickered briefly before dying an icy death. "He is a rude old man."

"I quite like him. He struck me as someone who offers an honest opinion."

"Offers it freely and often. Hardly an appropriate attitude for an employee."

Shayne lifted an eyebrow. "Do you want me to speak to him about his attitude?"

"Would it do any good?"

"None."

"Then what would be the point?"

Shayne leaned closer, lowering her voice. "Sheer wicked enjoyment."

Doña Isabella released a snort of laughter just as the door opened behind them. Penny entered, carrying two steaming mugs of coffee.

"The coffee's black. Don't believe in ruining a good cup o' Joe with anything but whiskey." He thumped the heavy porcelain mugs onto the desk between the two, eyeing the women suspiciously. His grizzled brows drew together. "What? Whatcha lookin' at me that way fer?"

The two women shared a moment of pure feminine understanding. "Thank you for the coffee, Penny," Shayne said as demurely as she could manage. "I hope it wasn't too much trouble."

"Yeah, it was. Not that you two give a hot da—" One glance from the *Doña* had him backpedaling toward the door.

"Dang. A hot dang. If the boss wants me, I'll be out in the barn where the critters don't look at ya funny."

The instant the door slammed behind the foreman, *Doña* Isabella gave a sharp nod. "I've reached a decision," she announced. "I have decided you will do."

Shayne's brows drew together. "Thank you, seems the appropriate response. Though I'm not quite sure why."

"McIntyre has neglected to tell you about me, I assume?"

"He hasn't explained. Yet."

She gave another snort of displeasure, which impressed the heck out of Shayne since the *Doña* somehow managed to retain her regal air while making the sort of noise capable of cracking glass. It was quite a feat. "Then I'll wait until he does before rendering my verdict."

"And you'll wait because . . . ?"

"Because I want to be certain that you'll remain his wife once you know why I'm here."

"I see," Shayne murmured.

It was a lie and they both knew it, but apparently the *Doña* intended to let it pass. Clearly this had to do with the secret Chaz had mentioned on the balcony the night they'd made love.

When she'd asked him if it was anything illegal, he'd replied, "Nothing I can be jailed for." Somehow it involved this woman. The question was . . . how.

" . . . and do what I pay you to!" Chaz's voice roared through the thick oak door. A loud thwack punctuated his shout. "Is that the best you can do? Hell, you can't even throw straight, you ham-fisted excuse for a cook!"

Shayne started in alarm. Now what? "Excuse me, please."

Hurrying to the door, she yanked it open. Chaz stood with his back to her, shaking his fist at a huge, muscle-bound giant of a man who rapidly disappeared down the hallway. From the way her husband's muscles were knotted beneath his shirt, he'd soon give physical expression to his anger. She hastened to close the door.

It didn't take any great mental acuity to realize Chaz and the *Doña* were at odds. No point in giving her more ammunition to use against her husband. Now she just had to figure out why he was also at odds with Mojo.

"What's going on?" she whispered.

"Just explaining the facts of life to my mule-headed idiot of a cook." He raised his voice. "My mule-headed, idiot, soon-to-be-unemployed cook."

"I don't understand. Why is he so upset over our marriage?"

Chaz glanced at her over his shoulder, his expression reflecting a wariness that cut to the quick. At a guess, he didn't know how she'd respond to the situation and if there'd been time, she'd have blistered him for it.

"I guess I should have spoken to him before I left and warned I might be bringing home a wife. But since I didn't know for sure I'd find someone, I—"

"Chickened out?" she interrupted without giving due thought to the ramifications of her comment. "Considering the size of him, I don't blame you."

Chaz's eyes narrowed, irritation vying with amusement. To her relief, his sense of humor got the better of him. "You think that's intimidating, you oughta see him with a meat cleaver in his hand." He nodded to the front door off to her right.

The sight of a meat cleaver imbedded deep in the wood stopped Shayne's breath in her throat. Her knees wobbled. "He—" She gulped. "He threw that at you?"

"Aw, hell, honey. He wasn't serious or I wouldn't be standing here. He was just punctuating some of his choicer remarks."

Shayne closed her eyes and whispered a Spanish prayer her Costa Rican nanny used to repeat each night to chase away the demons hiding under the bed. Of course, once she'd been taken to Florida, she'd had to say those prayers all on her own. Not that they'd worked.

"Why is he upset that you married me?" she asked again.

"He's afraid you'll try and change things. He's sort of possessive about his kitchen."

Was that all? She felt instantly better, though she had trouble communicating that fact to her knees.

"Hey, you okay?" Chaz gathered her into his arms. "He won't hurt you. Honest."

If only she could believe that. She buried her face against his shoulder. His arms wrapped around her replacing the chill with sweet heat. She drew in a deep breath, his spicy cedar scent filling her lungs. Held like this, she did feel safe.

His hands snagged in her hair, tipping her head back. Fierce blue eyes focused on her with explosive need. He murmured something, something that sounded remarkably like "my love." But that couldn't be.

And then she couldn't think. His hands tangled deeper in her hair, forcing her up into a scalding meld of lips and tongues and heated breath. She slipped her hands beneath his shirt, reacquainting herself with the flesh embodiment of strength and power.

"Everything will work out," Chaz muttered against her mouth. He drank deeply once more, drugging her with his taste. "You'll see. I'll take care of it."

How typically male. He had a lot to learn about the woman he married, if he thought he could cut her out of the loop. "Is Mojo one of your secrets?"

"No."

No? "Now I'm really worried. I think we're overdo for a talk, don't you?"

The door to Chaz's office opened on her words and *Doña* Isabella appeared in the doorway. "I agree. We are long overdo for a talk," she announced, her raven-black gaze raking them both with sharp reprimand. "Do you intend to stand there all day cooing like lovesick turtledoves or do you plan to grace me with your presence sometime in the near future?"

"I'm so sorry," Shayne said. How could she have forgotten the *Doña?* Not that it took much thought. First Mojo and his meat cleaver and then Chaz's embrace. It was enough to make her forget everything else—even a woman as formidable as this. "We're coming right now."

"I apologize for keeping you waiting," Chaz said as soon as they took their seats. "I see Penny brought you coffee."

"It is cold."

"That's what happens when you don't drink it when it's hot."

"*Doña* Isabella prefers tea," Shayne hastened to interrupt.

"Funny. Last time she said she detested tea."

The *Doña* dismissed his comment with a sweep of her hand. "An old woman is permitted to change her mind. It is one of the few pleasures left at my age."

"Yeah, and you take to it like a duck to water, don't you?"

Laughter gleamed. "If you are asking whether I enjoy being difficult, the answer is yes. I enjoy it quite thoroughly."

"I can tell." He planted his hands on top of his desk. "Let's get down to it, shall we? You've met my wife. I've given you what you requested. Now give me what I want."

The *Doña*'s mouth compressed, her thoughtful gaze settling on Shayne. "She is a lovely choice. I didn't expect you to show such wisdom."

"Then what's the problem?"

She sighed. "You haven't told her, have you?"

"I planned to tonight." His voice hardened. "You've jumped the gun a bit by showing up today."

"Tell her now."

His eyes flashed in warning. "Don't push me, old woman."

"Tell her now so I can be certain she won't leave you once she knows the truth."

"You have no right—"

Doña Isabella slammed her cane against the floor. "I have every right."

"Go ahead, Chaz," Shayne prompted. "If it will satisfy the *Doña*, get it out in the open."

"Honey, I really did plan to tell you," he explained regretfully. "Just not like this."

That meant it was bad. She took a deep breath and fought for calm. She'd spent most of her life practicing self-control, learning to hide her thoughts behind an impassive mask. The years she'd spent with her aunt had honed that skill. And after her aborted marriage to Chaz, when her brother's guilt had threatened to overwhelm them both, she'd worked hard to maintain a cheerful facade so he'd have peace. Whatever Chaz's secret, she'd greet it with calm acceptance.

"It's all right," she assured. "I told you before we married I'd accept your secret. I meant what I said."

"Very well." He seemed to gather inward, as though drawing his emotions under tight control. "*Doña* Isabella has something I want."

"I gathered as much."

"In order to get it, I had to meet her demands. The first was that I acquire a house."

"Her other demand was a wife?"

"Yes."

"And in return, she'd give you . . . what?"

He hesitated for a split second, then said gently, "In return, she'd give me my daughter."

Chapter Five

To My Long-Lost Bride,

Another year has passed without you in my arms. How many has it been? Four? Four long, impossible years. How I miss you, my Forever Love. Are you still waiting for me? Or have you found another? That thought haunts me, twists me into knots so I can't think straight.

Was it only my imagination that made me believe we were joined that night, that we're two parts of one whole? Can you still picture me, see my face in misty dreams, as I see yours? Do you hear me, Shayne, as clearly as I hear you— your voice whispering on the night wind, calling with every birdsong at day's break, murmuring in the streams as spring breaks through winter's icy hold? Or am I nothing but a faded memory?

I'm losing you, my sweet, I can feel it. And I know if that happens, I'll also lose the part of me you kept alive.

Come back to me! I need you.

It took every ounce of self-possession for Chaz to remain in his seat. He wanted to leap across the desk, gather

Shayne in his arms and carry her off to his bedroom. To explain about his daughter in private, with a gentleness that might have helped ease the hurt somewhat.

But *Doña* Isabella had forced the issue, had taken the timing out of his hands. And instead his newlywed wife sat as rigidly as the *Doña,* her chin set at a desperately proud angle, her eyes two huge, dark pools of anguish, her wide, lush mouth compressed to hide the slightest of quivers.

"What's her name?" she finally asked, her voice ripe with pain. "Your daughter, I mean."

"Sarita."

"It's a lovely name." She said it with a generous sincerity that left him helpless to respond. "How . . . how old is she?"

"Three last August."

"The same age as my nephew, Donato. And Sarita's mother?"

If this didn't end soon, Shayne would end up in tears. He refused to let that happen, refused to give the old woman the satisfaction of knowing how badly he'd hurt his wife with his silence. He stood and came around the desk. "We'll discuss that later. Well, *Doña?* Are you satisfied now?"

The woman recognized the double-edged question and inclined her head. *"Lo siento, Señor* McIntyre. My timing was unfortunate. I should have allowed you the opportunity to explain in your own way."

"Yes, you should have." He offered his hand. "I'll see you out."

"What about Sarita?" Shayne asked.

The *Doña* rose to her feet with Chaz's assistance, leaning heavily on her cane. "I'll bring her by at the end of the month for a visit."

He didn't like the sound of that. "You said—"

"You have done all I've asked, so far," the *Doña* interrupted tartly. "I do not expect the rest of my requests to cause you any great hardship."

"Requests? Or demands?"

She shrugged. "I try always to be polite." Her cane shot out and she used it to maneuver him clear of her path, showing remarkable agility for someone so crippled up with arthritis. "You often make common courtesy a most difficult task."

"I aim to please," he sniped right back, though for Shayne's sake, he probably should attempt to curb his annoyance. "I don't suppose you'd care to list the rest of your demands so I know there's an actual end in sight. Or do you make them up as you go along?"

She didn't like that. Her remarkable eyes flashed with dark warning. "Use care, McIntyre. Sarita is not yet in your possession."

"She will be."

Doña Isabella paused in front of Shayne. "And what about you, *Señora?* Are you willing to accept Sarita as your own?"

Shayne didn't hesitate. "She will be my own."

Her words shook Chaz to the core. They implied a permanence he couldn't handle if he hoped to maintain a safe distance. It was his daughter he wanted, not a wife. Especially not a wife with a heart as soft as Shayne's. Only Sarita mattered. But even as he made the silent assertion, it echoed through his mind, sounding rife with desperation rather than ripe with certainty, mocking his conviction.

He fought to remind himself of the man he'd become. Once upon a time he might have had something to offer a woman like Shayne, when he was young and foolish and believed that love was a solution instead of a tribulation. But he no longer believed in such an emotion. Not in its purity, not in its goodness, and sure as hell not in its durability.

Nine long, lonely years had cured him of that particular fantasy. What he knew of love was dark and painful, the emotion nothing more than a shadow that stole across a man's heart and snuffed his soul. If he kept Shayne for his wife, she'd discover that darkness, too, and he'd end up hurting her again—just as Rafe had warned.

"I want my daughter, *Doña,*" Chaz interrupted. "I've been patient long enough. I've given you everything you've requested. You wanted me to provide a home for her. I have. You wanted a mother for her. Here she is."

"And now I wish to assure myself that this home you have purchased and this woman you have taken for a wife will be suitable for my Sarita."

"Don't push me, Isabella."

For a split second, her regal facade cracked, revealing an old woman's vulnerability. All pretense had been forcibly ripped away and her internal battle to do what was best for Sarita waged across a network of lines cut deep into a once handsome face.

"She is my only female great-grandchild," she offered in a pained voice. "She is not a stray cat or a dog in need of a good home. If I decide you are unsuitable, I will return with her to Mexico. I can provide her with everything she requires there."

"Can you?" Something didn't ring true about the *Doña's* statement. "Then why did you come to me? Why tell me of her existence when your granddaughter went to such pains to keep me in the dark? You could have returned to Mexico with no one the wiser. So why ask me to take Sarita if you're capable of providing for her so well?"

She didn't reply. Instead, the battle ended and her face smoothed into an implacable mask. She turned and marched relentlessly across the office before pausing in the doorway. "Sarita is in need of some culture, if she is to live in such an isolated place," she announced. "We leave for San Francisco in the morning. I will return at the end of the month. And I shall be interested to see the progress your wife has made toward turning this house into a suitable home for my Sarita."

Shayne followed, slipping a hand beneath Isabella's arm. "I'll do my best." She opened the door and offered the sweetest of smiles. "Why don't I see you out?"

Doña Isabella inclined her head. "If that is your wish."

Damn Shayne's kindness! Chaz thrust a hand through his hair, thoroughly exasperated. Great. Just great. The woman who'd haunted him for more years than he cared to remember coupled with the woman who'd plagued him nonstop for the past three months. Nothing good could come out of that combination.

"Jumbo!" he roared.

With more speed than grace, Jumbo lumbered into the office. He was a massive man, his skin bronzed to a coppery sheen by a heritage as diverse as it was interesting. His instant response suggested he'd been hovering nearby. No doubt he'd gotten quite an earful, all of which he'd pass on word for excruciating word to his brother, Mojo, and to Penny, as well as to anyone else who'd pause long enough to listen. Jumbo might be one of Chaz's hardest-working employees, but he was also an inveterate gossip.

"You bellowed?"

"Get supper on the table. And make sure there's plenty of liquid refreshment, if you catch my drift."

Jumbo shook his head in disgust. He folded arms that could have passed as tree trunks across his chest and lifted a single, thick black eyebrow that extended, unbroken, from one side of his face to the other. "You gonna drink yourself into a stupor on your wedding night?"

"It's not my wedding night." Or was it? Did their pre-wedding celebration count? Damn. Probably not. Nor did the overnight drive it took to get here. "And don't give me that look. I'm not the one in need of stupefying, not that it's any of your business."

A knowing gleam drifted into Jumbo's odd gold eyes. "Got it. Champagne for the lady? Or wine?"

"Not champagne." She'd probably kill him. "Wine. A nice merlot, I think. And keep her glass full, though I doubt it'll help." Nothing would help except to change the events of the past. Unfortunately, if his life had taken a different course, he wouldn't have Sarita. The knowledge unsettled him. "And keep Mojo in the kitchen. No point in scarin' my wife off her first day here."

"He'll want a peek at her."

"Tough."

"Okay, but fair warning. He might not be willing to cook for your wife, especially if she starts messin' around in his kitchen."

"We'll deal with that if it happens." Since Shayne might not be staying long enough to mess with anything, Chaz decided to back-burner that particular problem. Hell, he had enough other, far larger worries looming over him. "Now will you take care of your brother or do I have to do it?"

Jumbo held up his hands. "Don't sweat it. I'll deal with Mojo." And with that, he returned to the kitchen.

"Offer her more wine," Jumbo advised.

Chaz shot his employee an infuriated look. Not that it did any good. The man was as immune to the finer points of authority hierarchies as Penny.

He gritted his teeth. "More wine?" he asked Shayne.

"No, thanks."

"You sure? It's got quite a pleasant flav—"

"I'll pass, thank you."

Right. She'd pass. Again. Just like she'd passed on the salad, and the bread. And no doubt just like she'd pass on most of her dinner and Jumbo's eventual offer of dessert, and most frustrating of all, any and all attempts at conversation. He reached for the glass she'd refused, before slamming it to the table in sheer frustration. Purple-red wine sloshed over the rim and stained the one good tablecloth he could call his own. Good linen had never seemed important.

Until now.

"Shouldn't push her, boss," Jumbo advised cheerfully, dropping a dinner plate in front of him. "Maybe she doesn't like wine. If you're still hopin' to get her drunk, I can fetch some of that hard stuff you have hidden in your desk drawer. We could lace her coffee with it."

"Repeat that word."

Jumbo's face collapsed into lines of contemplation. "What word?"

"The 'b' word."

"What? Boss?"

"Yeah. That word. I want you to reflect on it and all its many connotations before opening your mouth again. That way you might keep your job past the end of the meal."

Jumbo's impressive eyebrow bunched together, like a fuzzy caterpillar rolling into a ball to escape a predator. "What? What did I say?"

"First, you're buttin' in where you have no business buttin'." Chaz fought to keep his voice down, with only limited success. "Second, you're giving out far too much information. And third, I'm not trying to get my wife drunk."

"Oh, yeah? You give up on that plan? Didn't much care for it, myself."

"Jumbo!"

Perhaps it was the volume that finally penetrated. "You want me to shut up?"

"Either you can do it, or I'll do it for you." Chaz flexed his hands, just in case.

Jumbo's caterpillar brow thrashed around in apparent death throes before rippling into a straight mortally wounded line. "Won't say another word."

"Good."

He set an overloaded dinner plate in front of Shayne. "Anything else I can get you?" He shot Chaz a defensive look. "And just so we're clear, I wasn't buttin' in. Asking her that is part of my job. Can't very well fetch her something if I don't know what needs fetching."

"No, thanks, Jumbo," Shayne hastened to say.

"But you're gonna eat all I brung you, right?"

Shayne blinked in surprise. "To be honest, I'm not very hungry."

Jumbo planted his massive fists on his equally massive hips. "Not a good idea."

Her eyes widened. "No?"

"Not even a little. If you kept this up, Mojo's gonna come charging out of the kitchen with a meat cleaver in hand, demanding retribution. He doesn't take well to people giving his food such short shrift."

"Jumbo!"

His employee spun around, his right elbow missing the top of Shayne's head by a scant inch. "Do you want your wife chopped into itty-bitty pieces, boss? I'm just trying to protect your property."

"She's not my property!" Chaz roared.

What was it with people considering his wife property? First Rafe and now Jumbo. Couldn't they tell by looking at her that she was as strong and independent as they came? Perhaps it was because she appeared so fragile and was possibly the most delightful bit of femininity to ever grace his home. No doubt it roused the protective instincts in the male species.

"She's a woman with a will of her own," he explained, painfully aware of Shayne's attentive regard. "Not to mention, the ability to make her own decisions."

"Now, see . . ." Jumbo took a seat. "There's your first mistake. You tell a woman stuff like that and things get way out of control."

"Jumbo's not the most enlightened of men," Chaz explained to his wife. "Perhaps that explains why he's never been married."

"You want my advice?" Jumbo asked. Not that it was really a question.

Chaz sighed. Clearly, he needed to redefine the word "employee" again. This time he'd do it with his fists. "Not even a little."

"When you went to that fancy-pants ball you should have bought yourself an obedient sort of wife. Not that there's anything wrong with the one you did buy. It's just that with a different sort, you could tell her straight out that she's to mind the house and take care of your kid and she wouldn't get her feelings hurt."

"I did not buy a wife! I never said that."

"Not in so many words," Jumbo concurred. "But we caught your drift."

To his alarm, Shayne shoved back her chair and tossed her napkin to the table. Aw, hell. "Honey, I did not tell anyone I bought you. I swear."

"Would barter be a better word?" Jumbo asked pensively. "You know. You agree on a trade-off. You give her a home, she gets to take care of it. That sort of thing."

She shot to her feet. "Excuse me, please."

Damn and double damn. "Honey, wait—"

She listened to him as well as everyone else in his household, doing precisely the opposite of what he requested. She didn't run, but she did move at a good little clip, hastening into the hallway and toward the bedrooms at the rear of the house. He'd lay odds that she was crying.

Chaz turned on his employee. "Have Mojo put together a light meal that'll keep. Then you stick it on a tray outside my bedroom door. And do it quietly, or I swear, you won't see another dawn." He slammed his finger into Jumbo's chest. "Tomorrow, you and I are going to conduct a little experiment."

"What sort of experiment?" Jumbo asked warily.

"We're going to experiment with how many times I can punch you in the jaw before all your teeth fall out."

Not waiting for a reply, Chaz left the dining room and gave chase. He found his wife at the end of the hallway, looking around, clearly without a clue which door to try. He settled the issue by swinging her into his arms and carrying her into their bedroom. Twilight had settled in, bringing a deepening gloom. But when he reached for the light switch, she stayed his hand.

"Don't," she whispered.

Now he knew she'd been crying. Chaz fought for patience, fought to be the sort of man she deserved instead of the one she'd ended up marrying. "Honey, we have to talk."

Darkness filled her voice. "Not really."

"Yeah. Really."

"Then talk. But no lights."

"I can't see your reaction to what I say without lights," he argued.

"I know."

Okay, fine. They'd do this her way. All things considered, it seemed only fair. He settled her onto the bed before moving away, giving her a bit of space. He snagged a ladder-back chair from against the wall and brought it closer to the bed. Spinning it around, he straddled the seat and folded his arms along the back.

"I'm sorry, Shayne," he began. "First for the things Jumbo said. But also because I should have told you about Sarita before we married."

She curled up in the center of the mattress, hugging his pillow in a way that sent white-hot desire bolting through him. She'd hugged him like that the night of the Cinderella Ball. Of course then she'd been wearing only three things—a mask that sang of her desire, her petal-soft skin and the secret scent of a woman's passion.

"Why didn't you? Why keep Sarita a secret?"

"Because I was good and pi—"

His wedding band caught the final rays of fast-dying light and he broke off, rethinking his language. The irony wasn't lost on him. Forty-eight hours ago, he'd have blistered the air with his opinion. Now he was learning the fine art of husbandly caution. Amazing.

"I was good and ticked at your deception. I didn't feel I owed you a thing at that point, sure as hell not an explanation."

"I see." She lowered her head and her hair spilled forward, the deep reds and purples filling the evening sky catching in the pale gold color, like a molten sunset embracing a field of wheat.

"Look, Shayne. I know I hurt you. Not only didn't I tell you about Sarita. But I hurt you through the mere fact of my daughter's existence."

"We weren't married." She wrapped herself so tightly around the pillow it was a miracle the seams didn't burst. "You weren't under any obligation to remain faithful to me. I understand."

"Do you?" The question slipped out before he could stop it. But once spoken, he had to know the answer.

She tossed the pillow aside, as though throwing off a crutch. "I'm sure you'll find this hard to believe, but yes. I do understand." Even her voice had gained strength. "What you don't want to hear is why I understand."

No. He didn't. They were forbidden words, words that tied him in knots of restless anger and despair. "Her name was Madalena," he said with forceful deliberation. "And she made life a little easier during a tough time."

Shayne looked at him. Not that it did any good. Without any light to gauge her expression, it remained as unreadable as if she'd been wearing her mask. Even her voice held a cool, even quality that threatened his sanity. "Did you love her?"

"Do you really need me to answer that?"

"You don't think you're capable of loving anyone, do you?"

Her question whispered through the darkness, chilling him. Perhaps it was the lack of emotion in her voice. Or perhaps it was the quiet acceptance. He didn't want to hear either one. Cursing beneath his breath, he came for her, following the sweetest of scents with unerring accuracy.

He caught her in his arms, her small gasp revealing that she hadn't anticipated his approach. "I loved you once upon a time. Isn't that good enough?"

"No!" She fought him, shoving at his chest and squirming in a way that sent heat scalding through his veins. "You're afraid to live, Chaz. I wouldn't have thought it possible, but you are."

"Not afraid, wife," he whispered close to her mouth. "Cautious. Suspicious. And more than a little cynical."

She turned away from that almost-kiss, her rigidness spurning his touch. But he refused to release her. Or perhaps he simply didn't dare. "What happened to Madalena?" she asked when it became clear that he wouldn't let her go.

"It was a temporary diversion."

"For you or for her?"

"Both," he replied evenly. "She was the youngest in her family and a natural-born rebel. They tried to box her in and she fought back in the one way they couldn't forgive."

"Did her family find out about you?"

"Yes."

"And they took her from you, too?" She relaxed ever so slightly, turning into his warmth. "Oh, Chaz!"

He'd have laughed if it wasn't so tragic. "No, Shayne. They didn't react the way Rafe did. Their response wasn't loving outrage. They cut her off without a penny."

"They disowned her?" He could hear the shock ripple through her voice. "How could they?"

"Misplaced pride. Inflexibility. Who knows? The only one to stand by her was her grandmother, *Doña* Isabella."

"Couldn't you have done something to help? Couldn't you have married her?"

"I didn't know she'd been thrown out. Even if I had, Madalena didn't want marriage any more than she wanted me." He rested his chin on top of Shayne's head. "I told you. It was a temporary relationship. When it became apparent that our feelings for each other had changed, Madalena packed her bags and wished me well. *Doña* Isabella showed up the next day and they left. A week later, I moved on to my next job."

"They didn't tell you about Sarita?"

"Not then. Not until a few months ago. *Doña* Isabella dropped in to inform me that Madalena had died in a car accident. She brought Sarita with her."

"Quite a surprise. Or is that too mild a word?"

His mouth curved into a faint smile. "I think 'shock' might be closer to it."

"Isabella must have felt you should be told about your daughter. Why else would she have brought her?"

Shayne had keyed in on the one issue that didn't make any sense. "I'm still trying to figure that one out. If Doña Isabella doesn't want me to have Sarita, why tell me about her? Why all the games?"

"I gather she offered to let you raise your daughter?"

"To adopt her. But only if I could provide a home for her."

"And a wife?" The hurt stormed back into Shayne's voice.

He released his breath in a sigh. "That, too."

She fell silent for a long moment and he felt the tension building in her, thrusting against his chest and arms, rejecting him with unspoken, yet clear determination.

"Perhaps this would be a good time to discuss what you require from me," she said.

What the hell did that mean? "What the hell does that mean?"

"Jumbo wasn't far off, was he? We did make a bargain. You told me you wanted a wife who could create a home." She slipped from his grasp before he could stop her. "You just neglected to mention the home was for your daughter, rather than for us."

She was killing him by inches. "And?"

"And I'd like to know precisely what that involves. What do you want from me?" she repeated.

He didn't have a clue how to answer that one. Rolling off the bed, he crossed to his dresser and removed a T-shirt. "Here." He tossed her the improvised nightgown. "We're both exhausted and I don't know what Jumbo did with our suitcases. Wear this tonight and we can unpack tomorrow."

"I'm not sleeping here."

"Then pick another room. Doesn't matter much to me where we bed down."

"I mean, I'm not sleeping with you."

He'd already figured that out. Not that it altered his decision any. "We sleep together." He said it in a tone he rarely used, but one that made even the most ornery cowpoke scramble to obey. "Now get changed."

He thought he heard a word he'd have sworn his precious wife didn't know. Between that and the rustle of clothing being shed, he knew he'd won this particular battle. Trying to ignore the surge of relief that one argument had finally gone his way,

Chaz opened the door and recovered the tray Jumbo had left. A shaft of light slipped into the room and as he turned, he saw Shayne.

She knelt in the center of his bed, her legs curled beneath her and her arms lifted as she prepared to drop his T-shirt over her head. She'd removed her clothes and the light licked across her profile. Time paused for a breath, gifting him with a second that seemed to last an eternity, enabling him to look his fill.

Golden hair streamed down her back, the ends stopping just shy of the full, lush curves of her buttocks. Creamy thighs joined with narrow hips, shadows taunting him by throwing a modest hand across the golden delta beneath her flat belly. Her breasts were high and round, the rosy tips pearling in reaction to the cold kiss of the surrounding air. Her face was turned toward him, the vulnerability revealed in her wide, dark eyes burning a permanent path to his very soul.

He kicked the door closed, returning her to the protective embrace of the darkness. And then he fought to breath, to force air into badly depleted lungs. Desire clawed at him, demanding that he toss the tray aside and take the woman on his bed, to brand her with his possession.

"Chaz?"

Her voice slipped through the darkness, ripe with apprehension, and he knew that he couldn't do anything that would hurt her. He'd caused her enough pain. Fighting as he never had before, he slowly regained his self-control. Memory guided his footsteps to the end of the bed and he set the tray on the mattress.

"You didn't eat your dinner, so I had Jumbo leave this."

"You didn't eat, either."

He snapped on the bedside lamp. Shayne had retreated beneath the covers, the blankets pulled to her chin. He'd suspected that she'd been crying earlier and one look at her face confirmed it.

Her lashes formed damp spikes and he could make out the faint track of dried tears on her cheeks. Helpless rage swept through him—anger at himself for provoking her tears and anger at her for opening herself up to hurt.

If she'd just realize that love wasn't all it was cracked up to be, if she'd just deaden her emotions, life would be a hell of a lot simpler. They could take pleasure in each other's company without all the angst.

And without the guilt.

He recovered the tray and settled next to her. Mojo had put together a huge romaine salad liberally sprinkled with mesquite chicken, sweet red peppers and croutons. Chaz speared a sliver of chicken and fed it to his wife. She took it without protest, which was either a testament to her exhaustion or to her hunger. Whichever, he wasn't about to complain.

He waited until she'd eaten a decent-sized portion of the salad and the crispy rolls before speaking. "Here's the deal, sweetheart. I'll do anything to get my hands on my daughter. Unfortunately, Doña Isabella holds all the cards. If she decides to hightail it out of the country with Sarita, there's not much I can do about it. At least, not without a lengthy legal battle. I'd rather avoid that, if at all possible."

"And I'm the means by which you'll get Sarita." Her dark eyes were trained on him, filled with some unnamed and unwanted emotion. "That's why you married me, to gain custody of your daughter?"

He steeled himself to say the unforgivable. "That's about the size of it."

Her lashes swept downward, concealing the warmth of her gaze and shutting away feelings that shouldn't matter. So, why did her cool reserve annoy the hell out of him? Why was he tempted to catch her chin in his palm and force those beautiful brown eyes to look at him, to see if he could coax free the expression that had glittered there when they'd made love? He forced himself not to touch her, knowing he'd be unable to restrain himself if he were foolish enough to put his hands on her.

As though sensing his thoughts, Shayne wrestled the blanket closer to her chin. "You expect me to guess what the *Doña* wants and give it to her?"

"Yes. Though as to what that might be . . ." Desperate for something to do, he picked up the tray and dropped it onto the chair by the bed. "I gotta tell you, your guess is about as good as mine. Better, I'm willing to bet."

"Then you're giving me a free hand?"

Uh-oh. "Looks like I don't have a choice."

"And what happens once you have Sarita?"

He didn't pretend to misunderstand. "What happens to you?"

"Yes." She curled up against the pillow in a protective ball, small and vulnerable beneath the protective prickles of antagonism. "If I'm not pregnant and once you have custody of Sarita, what happens to me?"

Chapter Six

To My Long-Lost Bride,

I've made a decision. It's a foolish one, I don't doubt that for a minute, but one I can't seem to resist.

Another Cinderella Ball is coming up and I've decided to attend one last time. I had a friend apply, so Ella wouldn't see my name on the guest list and warn your brother. But count on it. I'll be there.

I don't know. Maybe it's so I can say goodbye. Or maybe I'm just kidding myself and I'm hoping to find you again. Part of me expects to find you there. Strange, isn't it? After all these years?

I guess I need to know for sure. I need to be able to put you behind me once and for all and make a new start. I keep telling myself that even if you are there, we're not the same people we once were. There's a good chance that we'll take one look and run the other way.

But I have to know. I have to be certain that going forward in life without you at my side is the right thing to do. If you're there, we'll have another shot at it, won't we, my Forever Love? And we'll take it.

If you're not there, I guess I'll have my answer, won't I?

Wait for me, wife. I'm coming.

Pregnant. Ripening with his child. The image was so strong, Chaz shook with it. "Why don't we wait and see?"

"No. I'd like an answer now." He could tell Shayne wasn't going to let go of this one until he responded. He'd never met a woman so determined to get herself hurt. "If I'm not pregnant, what happens to our marriage?" she repeated.

"Hell, sweetheart. I'm not going to throw you out."

"But you won't need me. You won't want me. Is that it?"

She had him good and cornered. "You're asking for answers I don't have." Naturally, he'd said the wrong thing. He'd managed to wound her again. Damn. He did some fast backpedaling. "If you're pregnant," he persisted doggedly, "then, of course, you stay."

It was still the wrong thing. "But only if I'm pregnant." Her mouth quivered, begging for a kiss he knew she'd reject. "If I'm not, the marriage ends."

"I didn't say that!" He closed his eyes, wishing he were one of those silver-tongued charmers who could spill lies as fast as a wild bronco spilled riders. "Honey, I'm so tired, I don't know what I'm saying. It's been at least two days since I got any shut-eye, and you have to agree, today's been a bit of a trial."

His efforts to soothe must have lacked something. She rolled onto her side, confronting him with her back. "I think I'll go to sleep now. Maybe you should, too."

"Good idea." He stood and stripped off his clothes before joining her. He started to slip an arm beneath her shoulders, but she stopped him.

"We don't have to touch, do we? I don't think I can—" Her voice broke, tearing him apart. "I think we'd sleep better if we didn't touch."

She was hurting, he reminded himself. And she was exhausted. The last two days hadn't been any easier on her than they'd been on him. "No. We don't have to touch," he assured gently.

"Okay. Good."

But it wasn't okay. He lay beside her and waited, waited until her hiccuped breath grew slow and steady and the tension fled her muscles. And then he rolled her over, easing her into his arms. Her hand slipped across his chest, settling close to his heart, and her head nestled into the crook of his shoulder. She curled up against him as though she'd done it a thousand times before, one leg thrown over the top of his, the soft probing of her knee giving him fits. He gritted his teeth, determined to endure.

But the final victory, the one that gave him peace enough to rest, came with the sleepy kiss she pressed against his jaw and the murmured words he shouldn't want to hear. Only then did he allow sleep to claim him.

Shayne awoke gradually, with the disconcerting realization that something wasn't quite right. She'd been warm and comfortable and lost in the most delicious of dreams—one she seemed to have been chasing for a lifetime. But it had vanished with the coming of morning, along with her heat source.

The clanging of a loud, brassy bell trembled through the room and Shayne pried her eyelids open. Chaz stood at the end of the mattress by the bedpost. As she watched, he slapped his Stetson on top of his head and aimed his penetrating blue gaze in her direction.

"Mornin'," he greeted warily.

He continued to stand there, rocking back on his heels as if he had all the time in the world. Apparently, he was waiting for her to respond. Considering the downhill slide their last conversation had taken, she wasn't too eager to start another. Still, she supposed she should try.

"Did I hear a bell?"

"Just Mojo letting us know breakfast is ready." He hesitated, as though he had something more on his mind, but lacked the proper words to address it. "I'm sorry about last night," he said at last. "It wasn't quite the wedding night I'd planned for us. I'll—I'll try and do better."

"Better?" she managed.

"Yeah. Better." The muscles along his jaw knotted. "Less . . . less hurtful."

All that escaped her throat was a tiny squeak of disbelief. She must have looked a sight, her hair in a wild tangle, his T-shirt drooping off one shoulder, her eyes bulging, her mouth hanging open. He apparently took her mouse imitation as agreement, because he gave a nod of satisfaction and left the room. *Less hurtful?* What did that mean?

She remained in bed for a full five minutes mulling over his words, until it suddenly dawned on her that she'd been sleeping dab-smack in the center of the mattress. A slight depression remained where Chaz's body had been, a depression that she overlapped by a good foot. No question. At some point in the night, she'd slipped over to his side of the bed and turned him into a surrogate pillow and bed warmer. What she'd denied while awake, she'd revealed in her sleep.

Less hurtful. The words trailed her into the shower and around the room as she pulled clothes from the suitcase that had been dropped off at some point in the wee hours of the morning. It wasn't much, but it was a start. It meant Chaz was willing to try. A spark of hope sprang to life, a warm, determined glow lighting a path toward the future. Maybe, just maybe, their marriage had a chance.

Shayne found Chaz sitting in the dining room, nursing a cup of coffee. A second cup was steaming at the place setting next to his. She slid into the chair and buried her nose in the mug.

"So what are your plans for today?" he asked.

"I thought I'd figure out how to change this place into a home."

"Any ideas?"

Her nose dug deeper into the mug. "None."

"Don't panic. I'm sure something will come to you." He waited until she'd taken another couple sips of coffee before suggesting, "How about taking a day to familiarize yourself with the place? See if anything strikes your fancy. You might want to take a look at the bedrooms and choose one for Sarita."

He'd made an excellent suggestion. "How many employees can you spare to lend a hand once I'm ready to start?"

"You can have Jumbo. He turns his hand to most anything that needs doing around here. I'm down to the bare minimum of help, right now. But we can hire in town. There's always people looking for extra jobs before the holidays. Tell Jumbo what you want and he'll take care of it."

As though Chaz's comment had summoned him, Jumbo appeared in the doorway, two steaming plates in hand. "Mornin'," he said, greeting them with a wariness that made her smile.

They hadn't gotten off to the best start yesterday. Perhaps she could help them do a little better today. "Boy, I'm hungry," she announced.

Jumbo positively beamed. "Well, then, little lady. I have the perfect start for your day." He slapped a heaping platter in front of her. "I have more if this isn't enough."

Her smile weakened at the sheer amount of food and Chaz choked back a laugh at her reaction. "Thanks. I think this will be plenty."

"Don't tease me now. This little ol' helpin' would hardly satisfy a gnat."

"No, really. It's plenty."

He clicked his tongue. "Mojo's gonna come out here, for sure," he warned sorrowfully. "Hope you weren't too partial to your wife, boss man."

"She's mine. I'm keeping her. And if Mojo wants to have words with me about it, I'll be happy to oblige."

Chaz's spirited defense perked her right up. Dropping her napkin into her lap, she won a grin from Jumbo by seizing her fork and tackling the mountain of scrambled eggs. It wasn't until she'd made a dent in one corner that she gave Chaz her attention again.

"I have my first request," she informed her husband.

"Yeah? What's that?"

"I want a dog. A big, hungry wolf of a dog."

His mouth eased into a broad smile. "And where would you like him, wife?"

"Right under my chair," she replied, returning his grin.

"I'll see what I can do."

Twenty minutes later, she shoved her plate away and groaned. "I can't eat another bite."

"But you're only halfway through. Mojo—"

"Mojo! And more Mojo. This is getting ridiculous." Tossing her napkin onto the table, she stood and started for the kitchen.

Chaz came after her. "Honey, this may not be a good idea."

"I think it's an excellent idea."

She shoved open the door to the kitchen. Jumbo sat on a bar stool that fronted a huge, long counter. Standing at the sink, his back to her, was the giant of a man she recognized as the infamous Mojo. He made Jumbo look like a shrimp.

"Hello," she said brightly.

Mojo's spine went rigid. Apparently, with one simple word, she'd managed to say the exact wrong thing. "That the missus?" he asked his brother.

"Yeah. That's her."

"What does she want?"

"I don't know." Jumbo eyed Shayne. "What can we do for you, missy?"

"I though Mojo and I should become better acquainted."

"Mojo doesn't get acquainted."

Shayne folded her arms across her chest. "He does now."

Ever so carefully, Mojo set the frying pan he'd been cleaning on the draining board and wiped his hands on his apron. He turned, revealing a face slashed into pieces and just barely stitched back together again.

She didn't flinch as she suspected every other person confronted with Mojo's disfigurement did. Instead, she openly studied the vivid red scars. Then she crossed to his side. Ignoring the way he stiffened at her approach, she stood on tiptoe and pushed aside the thick black hair covering his brow, exposing a particularly nasty cut shaped like a Harry Potter lightning bolt. It split his brow in two before racing toward the corner of his eye.

"Boy, were you lucky," she commented. "A fraction of an inch lower and you could have done a great pirate imitation. Black patch, snarl and all. What happened? Car accident?"

"Let's just say my horse doesn't have a windshield anymore."

Shayne choked. "Horse?"

Jumbo chuckled. "It's a joke. Me and Mojo don't ride."

"Maybe because there isn't a horse born willing to carry you," Chaz offered from the sidelines.

Mojo scowled. "We get by with our Jeep."

Shayne managed to figure out the punch line on her own. "I assume you named your Jeep Horse?"

Jumbo looked impressed. "You got it. One day Horse decided to toss ol' Mojo on his face by running itself off a mountainside and into a big ol' spruce."

"That sounds familiar."

Shayne moved to the nearest countertop and lifted herself onto it. She peeked at her husband from beneath her lashes, wondering how he'd handle this next part. Well, he'd have found out sooner or later. Better sooner. Better still, she could show him her secret someplace where they weren't alone and he'd be forced to control his reactions. She unbuttoned the left sleeve of her blouse. While the men watched curiously, she rolled it up, exposing a faint, jagged scar of her own.

"It goes right up to my armpit," she announced. "I'm lucky I can still lift my arm. I still get odd tingles when the weather changes."

Chaz inhaled sharply and Shayne glanced his way, nerves strung taut. He looked gut-punched.

Mojo whistled. "Nice."

"That's nothing." She yanked the blouse from her the waistband of her jeans and revealed a network of silvery lines along her ribs. She managed a flippant grin. "I've got them all over this side of my body. I'd show you some more except my husband might object."

"What the hell happened?" Chaz demanded.

"Car accident. Same as Mojo."

"How? When?"

"A while ago, by the looks of them." Mojo came close enough to whistle over a few of the more impressive ones. "How long were you laid up?"

The question enabled her to evade her husband's shocked questions. "A couple months. Not including the cosmetic surgeries to get rid of some of the worst ones."

"Hah. Got you beat. Six months," Mojo boasted. "The first week I flat-lined three times. The doctors didn't think I had a chance."

"Yeah? Well, I lost half my blood volume."

"No!"

She grinned. "Okay. Maybe not half. But it was a lot. If my brother hadn't gotten to me so quickly, I'd have been a goner for sure."

Chaz's mouth had acquired an odd, white-lipped appearance. "Rafe was there?"

She chose her words with care. "He was following me at the time."

"Where?"

"Costa Rica. Those mountain roads can be really hazardous."

"Then we'll make sure you stay off the ones around here."

Relief vied with annoyance. "That'll be a little tough to do living in the shadow of the Rockies."

"You'll stay off them," he repeated in a voice he no doubt hoped would end the subject.

She simply shrugged and returned her attention to Mojo. "Now, about the kitchen . . ."

The cook scowled. "What about it?"

"That seems to be an area of concern. Or so I understand."

He folded his arms across his massive chest. "You have something to tell me?"

"I sure do. Since I'm so busy revealing secrets today, I thought I'd reveal another."

"What's that?"

"I don't cook."

It took a moment for the words to sink in, but the second they did, Mojo positively beamed. "No cooking? For real?"

"No cooking. For real. Our housekeeper in Costa Rica tried to teach me a number of times, but finally gave it up as a lost cause."

Chaz relaxed enough to smile. "How many dinners did you burn?"

"Too many to count. Rafe was amazingly equitable about the whole thing. Maybe because he'd just rescued me from—" Her mouth snapped closed an instant too late.

"Rescued you from . . . ?" Chaz repeated softly. "Who? From me?"

"No! No," she repeated again, so there wouldn't be any doubt. "You know full well I didn't need rescuing from you."

"Then who?"

"My aunt." She hopped off the counter and offered his employees a brilliant smile. "So have we resolved the kitchen crisis? You'll continue cooking for us, Mojo?"

"You got it. And if there's something special you want some night. Well, hell. I'll even consider fixing it."

"I appreciate the offer," Shayne said gravely. "And I'll try not to take you up on it."

He patted her on the back, his meaty hand nearly leveling her. "I knew I liked you. A bit on the scrawny side, but I can take care of that."

Chaz stepped in before Mojo pounded her into the ground with his enthusiasm. "She's fine how she is."

"Not if she's eating for two."

Chaz whipped around. "What did you say?"

"I have the eye," Mojo insisted proudly. "Got it from my momma. She could see things like that and so can I."

Shayne caught Chaz's hand and tugged him toward the door. "Come on. Mojo's just teasing. It's too early to know for sure."

He allowed himself to be drawn from the kitchen. "Mojo's gonna find himself out of a job if he's not careful."

"Trust me. You don't want to do that."

He cocked an eyebrow. "Oh, yeah? You really that bad?"

"Worse." She shot him a grim look. "Far, far worse."

"But, you don't understand, boss."

Chaz didn't look up from his accounting book. "There's nothing to understand. Jumbo. She's in charge. If she says to move something to the left, you damn well pick up the house by the foundations and move it to the left. Got it?"

"But . . . But she has a clipboard."

That caught Chaz's attention. "A what?"

"You heard me. It's one of those official ones with a pen hangin' from it." Jumbo's single eyebrow knotted into a ferocious scowl. "And it gets worse. I don't know how to tell you this, boss. So I'm gonna come right out and say it. But I want you to brace yourself."

Aw, hell. "I'm braced."

"She's makin' a list. Just like she was Santa friggin' Claus."

Chaz put down his pencil. "A list, you say?"

"Don't that beat all?" Jumbo began to pace, eating up the huge room in three short strides. He turned and rumbled toward the desk again. "It wasn't very nice of me, but I peeked at the damned thing. And it's numbered and everything."

Chaz ran a hand across his jaw. "Numbered." He shook his head. "That sounds serious."

Jumbo planted massive fists on his equally massive hips and glared, his eyebrow doing a mambo from one side of his face to the other. "Whatcha gonna do?"

"Looks like I'll have to talk to her. Any idea where she is?"

"In one of the bedrooms." He shuddered. "I'll just wait here until you turn her from the devil's spawn back into that sweet little lady you married."

"I'll get right on it."

Chaz ran her to ground in the spare bedroom he'd considered using for Sarita. His wife was curled up on the padded bench in the bow window that overlooked the pasture, cradling something in her arms. Tossed to one side was the clipboard with its ominous list and he couldn't help but grin. She'd even changed for the role she'd taken on, dressing in neat black wool slacks, crisp black blouse and power jacket. And she'd tortured that glorious hair into a business-like knot.

He came up behind her and made short work of the knot, allowing the straight, pale strands to slide free. Then he slipped his hands beneath the golden waterfall and massaged the stiffness from her neck.

"I didn't think it was possible, but you actually scared Jumbo."

She kept her back to him, leaning against his chest and staring out at the snow-peaked Rockies. "So I gathered. I suspect it was the clipboard that put him over the edge."

"He's in my office trembling like a scolded puppy. I'm standing here prayin' he doesn't wet the carpet."

A hint of laughter touched her voice. "I'm sorry. I was just trying to be organized."

"Do me a favor, will you? Try a little less organization so you don't chase off the help." She nodded in agreement and he asked, "Come up with any brilliant ideas?"

"A few." She straightened away from him. Ever so gently she took the box she held and set it on the window seat next to her. "I decided this would be the perfect room for Sarita. I gather you did, too."

Damn. He'd forgotten he'd left that here.

Shayne turned the box around, revealing the doll he'd bought Sarita, the sort he hoped a little girl would find irresistible. The face was porcelain, the hair long with shiny black curls. She was dressed all in satin and lace, her dress poofed out over layers and layers of petticoats. Long silky lashes framed big brown eyes that stared solemnly up at him.

He cleared his throat, aware that something had gone terribly wrong, but not quite sure what or why. "I heard little girls like dolls that share their coloring."

Shayne closed her eyes, suddenly exhausted. How could a man who acted with such thought and care think himself so heartless? It didn't make sense. "It's absolutely gorgeous," she said. "Sarita will love it."

"Will she? I picked it up for a Christmas present or as a little special something to make her feel more at home when she moves in here. What do you think?"

It was the first time she'd ever heard him sound uncertain. He must want his daughter very badly. Part of her rejoiced for him, that he'd go to such lengths to make a home for her. But another, far less noble part, wept that he'd never made such an effort for his long-ago wife.

She collected her clipboard and stood. "I think it's the perfect present, whenever you choose to give it to her."

He caught her arm as she started past. "Have I done something wrong?"

"No, of course not."

"You're upset. Why?" He studied her intently. "Is it this clipboard business?"

"Don't be ridiculous."

"Is it because of last night? Are you afraid I'm going to dump you once I have Sarita?"

She didn't have the energy for another confrontation. How could she explain to a man who didn't believe in love that she'd spent her entire life searching for it? That once upon a time, she'd found it in his arms. And how could she explain to a man who didn't believe in love that it was the one thing his daughter would crave more than anything in the world, including beautiful, porcelain-faced dolls?

Shayne had once been a little girl who'd lost her parents, and been left in a cold, sterile environment without love or laughter or reassurance. They'd been the worst years of her life, a full decade that had left scars more permanent then the ones she carried on her body. As a result, she'd learned that, without love, life was a wasteland.

She stared up into her husband's eyes, those gorgeous blue eyes that could be as hard and cold as a winter's day one minute, and gentle and concerned and brimming with kindness the next. Right now they were summer-warm. *Are you afraid I'm going to dump you once I have Sarita?* he'd asked. Didn't he understand?

"No, Chaz. I'm not afraid of that." She fought to keep her mouth from trembling, to reveal how heart-wrenching she found their situation. "I'm afraid—terrified, actually—that you're serious. That you really don't know how to love, anymore."

And as she watched, winter descended, sweeping into the harsh lines bracketing his mouth and darkening the sunshine of his gaze. "No need to be afraid of the truth, honey," he said, coupling his exaggerated accent with a humorless smile. "Just face right on up to it."

Chapter Seven

To My Long-Lost Bride,

I went to the Christmas Ball. It goes without saying that you didn't.

I don't know what to write anymore. I don't know what to feel I guess that's because there aren't any feelings left. I never thought I'd give up. But right now . . .

I met someone, Shayne. I don't love her, but then, I don't think I'm capable of experiencing love anymore. Madalena and I have reached an understanding and she seems happy enough, even though I don't have much to give her. Hell, if I were honest, I'd admit I don't have anything to give her, not that she's asking. But she fills a void that's grown larger with each passing year. A void I suspect will someday consume me.

So why do I feel like I'm cheating on you?

I've failed you, honey, and I'm truly sorry for that. But this is it. I can't take anymore. And so, my long-lost bride, I'm saying a final goodbye.

If I could have found a Forever Love, it would have been with you.

Chaz remembered the exact second the realization struck. He was on a ladder, pulling all manner of debris out of the gutters around the house. He could have lost her.

He'd spent years searching for Shayne and she could have been permanently lost to him ages ago, killed in a car accident on a twisty mountain road in Costa Rica. And he'd never have known of her fate. Despite the frigid temperatures, he broke out in a cold sweat. He climbed off the ladder before he fell off and walked into the house. He found her upstairs, ordering the general destruction of all three spare bedrooms.

She paused mid-order and looked at him, an eyebrow raised in question. "Do you need something?"

"Yeah," he said roughly. "I do."

He waved the workers from the room, then stripped off his work gloves and dropped them to the floor. The second they were alone, he backed her up against the nearest wall and cupped her face in his hands. For a long moment, he simply looked at her, drinking in the delicate features.

She had such soft, creamy skin, the healthy flush of exertion. highlighting her arching cheekbones. As he watched, she moistened her full, lush mouth and fixed him with velvety dark eyes. Eyes that had haunted him for years. Eyes that continued to haunt him even when he stood perched on a ladder, cleaning out gutters.

"Chaz?" she whispered.

"Shh. I just had to do this."

"Do what?"

Words escaped him so he let his actions answer instead. He slipped his hand around the nape of her neck and drew her up toward his mouth. And then he tumbled into sheer pleasure, the fall long and hard and endless. But it wasn't painful. Not when he was caught by the most delectable set of lips he'd ever kissed. He inhaled her, consumed her, ate her up in quick, hungry bites.

She could have died.

But she hadn't and the evidence was lifting on tiptoe to return his embrace. His fears subsided, if not his desire. If anything, his desire had become so strong, he could barely think straight. He scooped her closer, relishing the feel of her soft breasts flattening against his chest and the rounded hips snuggling into the cradle of his. If there hadn't been people nearby, he'd have taken her then and there.

Would she have wrapped her slender legs around him and allowed the wild storms to consume them? Or would modesty have prevailed? Their passion deepened with flash-burn intensity and he had his answer.

But how long would that passion last? How many days would he continue to crave the woman in his arms? How long would it be before his heartlessness destroyed their marriage? How many nights would pass before one or both of them became sated into dissatisfaction?

He kissed her again, harder and more uncontrolled this time, desperate to hold the future at bay and focus on the delights of the moment. He harbored her safe within his arms—if his arms could be deemed a safe harbor. Not that Shayne seemed to share his doubts.

For his wife, his sweet, precious wife, gave her mouth with such unstinting tenderness and generosity, so open to his every desire, that it threatened to utterly destroy him.

If she lived to be a hundred she'd never understand the man. "I don't understand you, Chaz. I thought you wanted me to fix the place up."

"Yes. Fix it." His jaw worked in an odd way. "Fix means paint. Fix means doodads on the furniture. Fix means—" His arms made a few pinwheels in the air. "It means a rug here and there and maybe one or two of those useless colored pillows. It doesn't mean this!"

"I wasn't going to leave the bathroom without plumbing for long. I just had to pick fixtures more suitable to a little girl."

"Little girls need railings on their tub?"

She avoided his gaze. "And in the shower. Along with one of those cute seats in the corner. They're perfect for holding all the shampoo bottles. Little girls use lots of different shampoo bottles. A whole seat covered with them."

He crammed his Stetson further down on his brow and clamped his back teeth together. "Fine. Have a shower with a seat. But two sinks? What does she need two for?"

"Yes, well . . ." Inspiration struck. "It's obvious you've never had a house full of females before."

"One little girl is not a house full of females."

"It is when she has friends over for her birthday or a slumber party."

Chaz paled. "Slumber party?"

"They're essential," Shayne stated firmly. At least, they had been for the girls she'd gone to school with. Her aunt had never allowed her to attend any, let alone throw one, so her knowledge of sleep overs was painfully limited. But even so . . . "Why, as soon as word gets out that you have a daughter, I suspect you'll be overrun with hordes of little girls."

"Hordes," he repeated faintly.

"Giggling and shrieking and putting on makeup."

For the first time in her entire life, she saw Chaz look downright terrified. "Makeup? Sarita's only three!"

"They do grow up fast," she replied cheerfully.

"No." He shook his head. "Oh, no. Not my daughter."

She wrinkled her brow in thought. "I seem to remember Rafe saying something similar about me. Except it was in Spanish and there was some sort of threat involving the first man who tried to date his little sister."

Chaz slumped against the wall in defeat. "Date?" he croaked.

She patted his arm. "We'll talk later. Right now I have a meeting with the electrician. Little girls need lots of electrical outlets for their stereo systems and electrical outlets for their private phone lines." Giving his arm a final pat, she started down the hallway. "Now, what did I do with my clipboard?

I really should make a few notes so I don't forget to arrange for the satellite TV hookup."

"What the hell happened to my floor?" Chaz roared.

Jumbo held up his hands in surrender. "Don't look at me. This was all your wife's idea."

"My—" He should have known. "And just where is my dear wife?"

"In your office."

Chaz frowned. That didn't make him any happier. A man's office should be sacrosanct, even from wives. He jabbed Jumbo's chest with his finger. "Don't cut any more holes in my floor. Got it?"

"Sorry, boss," Jumbo replied cheerfully. "I'm not taking orders from you these days, remember? You told me to do everything Shayne said and that's what I'm doing. Including six more holes."

A growl of frustration rumbled deep in Chaz's chest. "Keep it up, big man, and I'll have you riding fence line until your . . . your ears freeze off."

"My ears, huh?" Jumbo whistled. "Marriage sure has done strange things to your grasp of the English language. You aren't anywhere near as colorful as you used to be."

The fact that his employee was right only served to aggravate Chaz all the more. "Oh, yeah? Well, your colorful days will soon come to a screeching halt, too, my friend. The second my daughter hits this house, I don't want to hear a single word not meant for a child. And that goes for Mojo, too."

Jumbo grinned. "You gonna tell him that or you wanna tie a note to a rock and heave it in the general direction of the kitchen?"

Momentary laughter glittered in Chaz's eyes. "Think I'll let my wife handle that particular duty."

"And he'll take it like a lamb. Hell, he'll probably even smile at the scolding." Jumbo shook his head in disgust. "Never thought I'd see the day when a woman would lead my little brother around by the . . . er . . . ears."

"You haven't seen anything, yet. Wait until my daughter moves in. She'll have him tied up and put in his place within the hour."

Assuming she moved in. Which brought him right back to Shayne. Chaz glanced at the door to his office. A closed door. A closed door behind which sat his precious wife getting into heaven only knew what sort of mischief. Damn it it all, he had work to do. He couldn't afford to spend all his time dealing with a wife.

Giving in to the inevitable, he thrust open the office door. "Shayne, what the hell have you done to my floors?" he demanded.

She sat behind his desk, her glorious mane of hair once again constrained in a painfully tight knot at the nape of her neck. His hands itched to ease the tightness, just as he longed to ease her toward their bedroom and kiss his way down all those silvery scars. Of course, he hadn't been given the opportunity.

The only time she'd allowed his touch in the past two weeks had been the far too infrequent kisses they'd exchanged during the day or when she'd been sound asleep. Only then would she curl into his arms and wrap herself around him. Only then would she kiss his jaw and whisper her forbidden words of love, allowing him to join her in sweet oblivion. Only then did he find true peace.

Their marriage was killing him, bit by bit, chipping him into pieces he'd never be able to put together again. Not that his wife noticed. Hell, no. She remained frustratingly oblivious.

Glancing up from the papers scattered across the oak surface of his desk, she cupped a hand over the microphone of her cell phone. "I'll be with you in a minute."

"We need to talk, Shayne—"

Of course, she ignored him. "The ones I want are all three foot square and labeled FT dash one through twelve. Could you have them crated and shipped to me? Air express the package, if necessary. Yes, I know it'll be expensive, but send them anyway. See they get through customs yourself, Chelita. Or have Marvin take care of it. He'll make sure there's no hang-up. He and I have an understanding."

Say, what? "Who are you talking to?" he demanded. And what the hell kind of an understanding did his wife have with a Marvin?

"Thanks, Chelita. Talk to you soon."

He didn't wait for her to hang up. "Who the hell is Marvin?"

"A friend. He grew up in the village outside Rafe's coffee *finca.*"

"And what is he bringing through customs?"

"Some of my artwork."

"Oh." Damn. Here he'd worked up a good bluster and she'd managed to drain it right out of him. He switched to a different subject, one that would allow him to bluster all he wanted. "Now, look. About my floors—"

The door opened and a man with a tool belt dragging his pants in the general direction of his knees walked in. Swearing beneath his breath, Chaz shifted to block the worst from Shayne's sight. Damn it all! Here was something else he'd have to take care of before returning to work. Couldn't have some strange man wandering around like that in full view of his wife. It wasn't proper. And he'd make sure the fella knew it, too.

Shayne shifted her chair so she could see around him. "Hi, Tim. What can I do for you?"

"Punched those holes in the walls you wanted. No problem." He hitched his pants up. They stayed for a whole two seconds before gravity tugged them downward again. Another inch and serious action would be needed. "But would you mind taking a look before I frame it up?"

"Wait one damn minute here," Chaz interrupted. "Not more holes!"

Shayne gave Tim a smile that Chaz would have killed to have turned on him, full and natural and tastier than anything Mojo had ever dreamed of serving up. "Thanks, Tim. I'll be right there." The door banged closed and she glanced at him, her smile fading. "I thought you put me in charge of the house."

"I did. But—"

She cut him off. "I don't recall their being a 'but' as part of our agreement. You said I was in charge and when you said it, there was a period at the end of your statement."

"I'm fairly certain I shoved a 'but' in there someplace," he retorted through gritted teeth. "Along with a comma so I could make amendments should someone put holes in my house!"

"You're shouting."

"I'm allowed to shout." He began to pace, needing some outlet for his energy other than snatching his wife out from behind that desk and giving full rein to every physical expression he could think of. Considering how long it had been since he'd physically expressed himself, he could think of a goodly number. "And I'm allowed to swear. And I'm allowed to complain like hell when my wife entertains half-naked men."

"You can't mean Tim."

He whipped around to confront her. "Yes, I mean Tim! If his pants drooped any lower you'd know him better than his doctor. You're supposed to be getting the place ready for my daughter. We only have a couple short weeks before Satan's sister sweeps in on her broomstick."

She tilted her head to one side. "Now there's an interesting image."

Chaz slammed his Stetson onto the desk, biting back some of the choicer words burning a strip off his tongue. "You know what I mean. Instead of fixin' stuff, you're ripping it down around our— Our—"

His wedding band flashed a warning. Damn it all! Enough was enough. His life wasn't his own, anymore. His employees had turned traitor, his wife treated him like an annoying little brother, and he couldn't speak his mind without checking each word before he uttered it. But worse of all, he had an ache that wouldn't go away.

Well, there was one thing he could do. He could march out to the barn, oust the dang animals from their dang stalls, and turn it into a cussin' room. A place for men only and the fouler-mouthed, the better. No women. No holes in the walls. And no watching his language. Hell. He'd stick a refrigerator in there and stock it with beer and have himself more than just a room. He'd have a whole cussing bar. Of course, he'd have to put a lock on the damned place or his spread would be overrun with drunken cowboys.

Shayne lifted an eyebrow. "You were saying? I've been ripping the house down around our . . . ?"

He balled his hands into fists. "Around our *ears*."

"That's what I thought you were going to say."

She stood and circled the desk. To his everlasting disgust, she ended their argument by cheating. She wrapped her arms around his waist and slid every female inch she possessed along every male counterpart she could find. She said something else, but he didn't have a clue what it was. He was too busy dealing with far more serious problems.

At her first touch, every piece of hardware in his body went into instant overload. Massive system failure followed. Autonomic systems short-circuited and his brain shut down in an effort to recalibrate. He fought to breathe. Only one system remained on-line and in excellent working order. Her hip bumped it, threatening him with the very real possibility of total annihilation.

"Don't. Do. That."

She pulled back and looked up at him with a puzzled expression. "Is something wrong?"

Aside from the fact that he felt like he'd just been poleaxed? His jaw moved in an effort to imitate speech. She waited patiently, blinking wide brown eyes at him which forced him to recalibrate a few more brain cells. Maybe if he didn't look, he'd summon an answer to her question. It was there somewhere. Just one simple word. All he had to do was force the air from his lungs and the word from his mouth. "No."

"Okay." She gave him another brain-splintering hug and then trotted toward the door. "I'm going to check with Tim. Catch you later."

He didn't know how long he stood there. But when mobility returned, he used it to stagger in the general direction of the barn. The frigid winter temperature knocked him to his knees, but he had the air blistered nice and hot in no time, the curses sliding off his tongue faster than rainwater off a grease-dipped duck. If his wranglers thought his behavior at all strange, they were too smart to say anything. All except Penny, who swaggered over.

"Gotcha where it hurts, don't she, boy? Wives sure are good at that. Or so I've heard." He braved Chaz's wrath with a knowing smirk, then risked his neck further by adding, "Never been stupid enough to find out, myself."

"Okay, this is it. This is where I draw the line."

Shayne blinked up at Chaz in confusion. From her kneeling position on the office carpet he managed to loom as impressively as Jumbo. "What line?"

"The one I'm drawing right here, this very minute." He shoved his Stetson to the back of his head and folded his arms across his chest. "Now, I didn't fuss about your tearing apart one of our bathrooms, which I think is damned decent of me. I barely said a word about that crazed electrician, even though I should have had him arrested for indecent exposure. And I've been the most understanding man in the world about the holes you've punched in the walls and in my floor."

"You have?"

"I've taken it like a lamb. And honey, that's saying a lot in cattle country." He gazed at her with such earnest sincerity, it forced her to accept he truly believed every word he'd uttered. "Why, there's not another man on this planet who would put up with the general mayhem going on around here the way I have without losing his cool and banging a few heads together."

"There's not?"

"No way." He turned to scowl at her latest efforts on his behalf. "But this is going too far."

She looked around in bewilderment. "If it's because I'm using your office floor, it won't be for much longer."

"I can't get to my desk."

"I can." She half rose. "Is there something you needed? I'd be happy to get it for—"

"That's not my point." She sank back onto her heels as he gestured to indicate the strings of fairy lights gaily twinkling in neat lines on the carpet "This looks suspiciously like Christmas."

Her brows drew together. His tone sounded utterly outraged, as though she'd committed some horrible sin. "That's because it is for Christmas. I thought I'd put up a few lights and decorations before—"

"Not in my house you're not."

"I'm not?"

"Not a chance in this world or the next. I don't do Christmas."

She stared at him, nonplussed. "What do you mean you don't do it?"

He ticked off on his fingers. "No lights. No tree. No silly ceramic angels or Santas cluttering up the place. No ribbons or bows or anything remotely red or green." He paused to consider. "Unless it's edible. Don't want to be unreasonable about this. But no Christmas. Got it?"

"No."

Anger crackled in his eyes, intensifying the blue. "Come again?"

"You heard me."

Before matters could escalate further, Jumbo appeared in the doorway carrying an armful of tangled outdoor lights. He looked from Chaz to her and groaned. "Uh-oh."

Shayne turned to him for confirmation. "Boss man says he doesn't do Christmas. What's going on?"

His eyes widened and he shuffled his feet, practically tearing the carpet loose at the seams. "I couldn't say. I just work here, ma'am."

"You can't say, or you *won't?*" She gave him her sternest look. "Come on, Jumbo. Spill it. No Christmas? Not ever?"

His eyebrow began twitching nervously. "'Fraid not. Leastwise, not as long as I've known him and that's going on five years. He usually locks himself in his office with a bottle of Jack Daniels and a stack of writing paper and drinks himself into a stupor."

Chaz whipped his Stetson off his head and slammed it to the floor. "Jumbo!"

The tangle of lights tumbled from his massive arms. "What? What did I say wrong this time?"

"If I want my wife to know about my little fling with JD, I'll damn well tell her myself." He jammed his finger into the Dwayne Johnson-like chest. "Don't forget who signs your paycheck or it'll be my pleasure to remind you."

"Shoot, boss. You keep forgettin' you assigned me to her. I have to answer her questions."

Time to interrupt before blood got spilled, Shayne decided. She rose to stand nose-to-chest with her husband and did a little finger-jabbing of her own. "And my next question is, why do you dislike Christmas so much? Would you care to respond to that or shall I take it up with Jumbo?"

He didn't want to answer, Shayne could tell. The reason escaped her, though she'd get to the bottom of it eventually. He could be darned closemouthed when he chose. But then, she could be darned stubborn. He glared at Jumbo and jerked his head toward the door. Sounding remarkably similar to a herd of cattle in full stampede, Jumbo bolted from the office.

"Spill it, Chaz. What's going on?"

"If you have to know the truth, Christmas holds some bad memories for me," he confessed.

At one point in her life, it had for Shayne, too. All the more reason to replace the bad with some good ones. "Is it anything you can tell me about?" she asked sympathetically.

His jaw set. "I'm sorry, Shayne. I'm not ready to do that."

She fought to conceal her hurt, reminding herself that the "why" of his refusal wasn't as important as getting him to change his mind about the decorations. "Chaz, I can understand your reluctance, but surely you must see that you can't avoid celebrating Christmas. It's not fair to Sarita."

Lines sank into his face and his gaze turned flat and hard. "Don't bring my daughter into this."

She wouldn't give up. Even if it meant suffering his wrath, she'd push him on this to the bitter end. "Do you really think you can simply ignore the season into nonexistence?"

He gave a callous shrug. "Works for me."

"Well, it doesn't work for me. Nor will it work for Sarita. And I guarantee it won't work for *Doña* Isabella."

"Considering that the *Doña* won't be around come Christmas, what she doesn't know won't hurt her."

"And me? Will I still be here? Or don't my wishes count?"

"Whether or not you're still here hasn't been determined, yet. Are you pregnant?"

His hard-edged question stole her breath, the reminder delivered with all the brutality of a backhanded slap. She fought against the tears burning for release. This wasn't the man she'd married nine years ago, she tried to tell herself. Circumstances had replaced him with the stranger standing before her, one with a heart as frozen as the peaks outside her bedroom window.

What in the world had happened? What had caused him to become so cold and remote? And what could she do to coax free the Chaz she'd married all those years ago?

It took a full minute to regain control enough to speak. "I don't know whether or not I'm pregnant," she lied.

He held onto his coolness for a moment longer, then seemed to thaw ever so slightly. "I'm sorry, Shayne. That was uncalled for."

"Is Christmas when Madalena left you?" she asked gently. "Is that why it holds such bad memories?"

She half expected him to freeze her out again. Instead, he shook his head. "This doesn't have anything to do with Madalena. I don't like the season. End of subject."

"So that's it? That's your final word?"

"That's my final word."

Chapter Eight

To My Long-Lost Bride,

I can't even begin to explain why I'm writing to you again this year. Habit? Or am I just a glutton for punishment? I don't love you. I don't. I don't love anyone, anymore. What feelings I had died long ago.

But still I look at other women and think ... They're not you.

Shayne, what happened to our Forever Love? Why can't I get you out of my mind?

"What part of my final word—no Christmas— didn't you understand?" Chaz roared.

Shayne sat perched high on a ladder placed dab-smack in the middle of the hallway, clutching streams of ivy to her chest. She blinked down at him with the most innocent expression he'd ever seen. Too bad he didn't believe any part of it. Not the thick, fluttering lashes that surrounded killer fudge-brown eyes. Not the lush, moist lips parted with such innocent seduction. And certainly not the spine-tingling, husky way she said, "Whatever do you mean?"

"You know damn well what I mean." He swept his arm through the air to indicate the latest changes to his surroundings. Dramatic changes that seemed to come faster with each day that passed. "These Christmas decorations. The ones I said you weren't to bring into my, I mean, *our* house."

"*Our* house?"

His altered phrasing elicited a delicious smile, one that melted him for a whole two seconds before he remembered why he was so flat-out furious with her. "That smile isn't going to cut it, sweet stuff. Now, I want all these decorations out of here. Pronto."

"Don't be silly, Chaz. These aren't for Christmas," those lush lips lied with brazen disregard.

"You have twinkly lights up! If that's not—"

"Oh, that." She dismissed them with a wave of her hand. "Those aren't Christmas lights."

His jaw worked. "They're not?"

"Goodness, no. Would you like to know how I can tell?"

"Please. Tell me." Reining in his anger, he folded his arms across his chest and braced his shoulder against the doorway leading to the dining room. "This I've gotta hear."

With blatant disregard to her personal safety, she wriggled her pert little bottom more firmly onto the top step of the folding ladder, not showing the least concern when the aluminum legs wobbled alarmingly beneath her. "See, Christmas lights are red, green or white. These are blushing tea rose pink."

"Blushing tea rose pink."

"Exactly. And those bows? The ones holding up the ivy?" To his relief, she stopped squirming around, reducing the ladder's wobble to a mild shimmy. "Well, they're not Christmas bows, either."

He ground his teeth, amazed they weren't down to useless stumps by now. "No, of course they aren't. Let me guess. That's because they're purple."

"Don't be ridiculous. They're puce. And I haven't used any pinecones or greenery or mistletoe or anything remotely Christmas-like."

He pointed to the garland of ivy twisting a graceful path around his door frames. "So, what do you call that stuff?"

"Cosmetic work. You said I was supposed to take care of that, right? Heck, the ivy isn't even green."

"Then what is it? Salamander red?"

She chuckled. "Now you're teasing. You know perfectly well it's blue. Bluegrass pine, to be exact."

"Are you trying to tell me the 'pine' and 'grass' part aren't green?"

"Not even a little." She swiped her arm in an expansive gesture, nearly tipping herself over backward. "The blue overrides any other color."

"Uh-huh." He straightened away from the door frame and approached her ladder. "First, when I said no Christmas decorations, that's what I meant. And that includes all this stuff. Second, when I asked you to oversee the cosmetic work, I meant for you to slap a coat of paint on the walls, not drape ivy all over the place. And third, if you don't fill in the holes in the floor soon, someone's libel to fall in and never be found again."

The ladder trembled rather violently. "There's a subfloor," she explained. "It's not likely anyone will fall through that."

"No, they'll just trip and break something."

Strands of ivy fluttered from her hands, snaking affectionately around his boots. "It's funny you should mention the holes. Jumbo will have them taken care of by the end of the day."

"Would you care to tell me how Jumbo will take care of it?"

She cleared her throat. "I think I'll leave that as a surprise."

He frowned. Reaching up, he plucked her off the ladder before she fell off and set her in front of him. She stood there, her expression so full of hope, he found it painful to witness.

"And will it be as much of a surprise as your un-Christmas decorations?"

"Count on it."

"I was afraid you'd say that."

He leaned down and carefully untwined the strands of ivy from around his ankles before he found himself nose-down in one of Shayne's holes. As tempted as he was to rip the garland apart, he didn't think he could face her expression if he accidentally damaged it. Winding the garland into a neat coil, he set it aside. Then he eyed the twinkling fairy lights—the tea rose blush pink twinkling fairy lights—the puce-purple bows and blue ivy that looked amazingly green to his eyes.

"Honey, I hate to tell you this, but it's all got to go."

Her soft mouth quivered in a way he longed to ease with a kiss so hard and time-consuming it would wipe every other thought from her head. "But, why?"

Before he could explain even one of his objections, a knock sounded at the front door. No doubt sensing a reprieve, Shayne darted around him and tugged it open. *Doña* Isabella filled the doorway. And hovering at her side, her tiny hand clinging to the *Doña*'s, stood Chaz's daughter. She gazed at them with huge, apprehensive eyes, shrinking closer to her great-grandmother.

Shayne greeted them with a huge grin. "*Doña* Isabella. What a pleasant surprise." She stooped to the little girl's level. "And this must be Sarita. Hello, sweetie."

Sarita buried her face against the old woman's skirts, then peeked at them, the prettiest smile Chaz had ever seen slipping free.

The *Doña* looked around inquisitively. "I hope we haven't arrived at an inconvenient time."

"How can it be inconvenient since I'm sure you planned it that way?" Chaz asked dryly.

Shayne chuckled. "You just ignore him. It's not inconvenient at all." She threw the door wide and gestured for them to enter. "Now don't trip on the holes in the floor. We'll have those covered up before the end of the day."

The cane paused mid-tap. "Holes in the floor?"

"That's just what Chaz said when he first saw them. Of course, he said it a bit louder."

"Shayne!"

"Just like that, as a matter of fact."

Sarita tugged on her great-grandmother's hand and pointed to Shayne's latest "cosmetic" contributions to his house. *"Abuelita, mira! Qué bonita."*

Abuelita? Chaz fought to suppress a grin, with only limited success. Somehow he'd never pictured anyone having the nerve to call the austere *Doña* Isabella "little grandmother." But apparently his baby girl was an exception. One look at his nemesis, however, killed his grin dead.

Once she deemed him appropriately cut down to size by her razor-sharp glare, she turned her attention to their surroundings. "What beautiful Christmas decorations," she commented with admirable sincerity. "You have done a lovely job."

Shayne shot Chaz an uneasy glance before addressing their guest. "Oh, they're not for Christmas. Goodness, no. I just thought they looked pretty. But if you notice, I didn't use any Christmas colors, which means they're not."

She trailed off dispiritedly and Chaz felt like an utter heel. She'd worked so hard to get the place spruced up and ready. And all for his daughter. All so he'd be granted custody by the black vulture hovering beside Sarita.

He gave in to the inevitable. "Glad you like it. Shayne deserves all the credit. She's worked hard on making the place perfect for the holidays. I assume you're here for the grand tour?"

"If it wouldn't be an imposition."

"Now why would you think that?" he asked dryly.

"How about if I show you around?" Shayne hastened to suggest. "That way you can make suggestions for any changes that occur to you."

Doña Isabella graciously inclined her head. "That would be acceptable."

"Great! Where would you like to start?"

"Have you prepared a bedroom for Sarita?"

"That was my first project. Come this way." She stuck her hand behind her back and waved Chaz off. Then she held out that same hand to Sarita. His daughter spared him a brief, wistful glance, before slipping her fingers into Shayne's and trotting down the hall with the two women.

To his dismay, that single look squeezed something he thought long dead. Chaz closed his eyes. He really needed to do something about opening up that cussin' bar. Right now, he had the overwhelming urge to cuss up a storm while swigging down a gulp or two of rotgut. Anything to ease the unexpected pain centered in a forgotten place deep in his chest.

"Keep in mind that we can change the colors of the walls if you don't care for them," Shayne offered as she led the way deeper into the far recesses of the house. "And the furniture can be replaced, too."

"You are very accommodating," *Doña* Isabella murmured.

Something in the woman's tone caught Shayne's attention and a small frown etched a path across her brow. "You make that sound like it's a bad thing."

"It could be, if it's not sincere."

Shayne pushed open the door to the room she'd prepared for Sarita and waited until the little girl was preoccupied exploring her surrounds before turning to the *Doña*.

"I'll make you a promise, Isabella," she stated with quiet conviction. "I'll never lie to you. And I'll never pretend to feel something I don't. I'll also treat that little girl as if I'd brought her into this world myself. She'll never have a moment's doubt that she's both loved and wanted. And she'll never, ever be made to think she's a burden."

"A burden?" *Doña* Isabella's eyebrows drew together over her hooked nose. "What an odd suggestion. Explain where it comes from."

Shayne didn't want to answer, but gaining this woman's trust and understanding was paramount. Reluctantly, she opened a small part of her soul that she'd rather have kept far from prying eyes. "I lost my parents when I was three. My aunt raised me."

"It was not a successful relationship?" *Doña* Isabella asked delicately.

It took a full minute before Shayne could reply. "My brother, Rafe, rescued me when I was thirteen."

"I see." No doubt she did, too. *Doña* Isabella hadn't lived so many years without witnessing what life had to offer, both for good and ill. "And you will see to it that my Sarita does not share your fate?"

"You have my word."

For a long moment, hard black eyes held her, boring straight through to her heart. And then the *Doña* inclined her head. "I believe you." Turning her attention to the bedroom, she sighed with pleasure. "This is quite lovely."

Shayne had worked hard on the room, trying to turn it into a safe retreat for a little girl. Feeling safe when torn from the only family a child had ever known was vital. Even after all these years, she still remembered that.

She'd chosen creamy white furniture to match the soft wool carpet. The walls were a sunny yellow with the bedding in yellow and white pinstripes trimmed in Swiss lace. She'd also gone out of her way to provide lidded boxes in bright colors and secret cubbyholes for storing private treasures. But what had instantly captured Sarita's attention was the doll propped up on the window seat. She'd not dared to touch, but instead had knelt beside the box, staring with great dark, hungry eyes.

Shayne joined her on the window seat. "Your daddy bought that for you. Would you like to open it?"

With an excited nod, Sarita picked up the box and carefully pried open the lid. The packaging defeated her, so Shayne gave her a hand. From that point on, the doll never left

Sarita's arms, the object of periodic hugs and whispered conversations.

Shayne indicated a door on the far side of the room. "There's a bathroom that opens onto an adjoining bedroom," she explained to the *Doña*, before pointing out the huge walk-in closet to Sarita. "If you go in there, you'll find a secret tunnel hidden in the far back.

Doña Isabella lifted an eyebrow in question. "We will take another route, I trust?"

"We'll go through the bathroom," Shayne reassured with an understanding smile. "You can make sure the fixtures are acceptable."

The *Doña*'s keen gaze didn't miss a thing about the way the plumbing had been set up. And though she lifted an eyebrow in question at some of the features Shayne had chosen, she contained her curiosity. Tapping her way into the second bedroom, she looked around, wordless.

Facing south, the room embraced the sunlight, glowing with vibrant gemstone colors. Although Shayne had wanted to use a thick, luxurious carpet that could be difficult for people with canes, so she'd settled for a short, tight weave that wouldn't catch at unwary feet. But she'd compensated for the loss with the accessories, making them rich in texture and restful to the eye. The bed and dresser only took up a small portion of the room. Against one wall, she'd set a cozy love seat, perfect for snuggling with a little girl and in another section, a roomy play area with comfortable chairs, an inlaid wooden card table, and a generous entertainment center.

Shayne shot *Doña* Isabella a quick, nervous glance, before erupting into speech. "There's a private landline and your own TV with a satellite hookup so you can watch American shows or one of the Spanish channels."

"Indeed."

She couldn't quite read the *Doñas* reaction. "Since this room is larger than Sarita's, I've put an itty-bitty kitchenette in one corner, in case you don't care for Mojo's cooking. Though, my goodness, he's quite a wonder with a skillet. Just don't let his face scare you the first time you see it. He's a little sensitive."

Isabella continued to remained silent, so Shayne pointed to a long, blank wall, begging for some pictures and chattered on. "Maybe this spring I can convince Chaz to poke a whole in the wall over there for a door and build you a small outdoor patio. He's sort of funny about poking holes in the walls, but don't let that worry you. We can also add on a private bath, if you'd rather not share. Now, there is a third spare bedroom which has its own, but it's further away from Sarita and right next to our bedroom. It's more of a nursery, if you catch my drift. So, I thought . . ." Her words finally trailed off and she finished in a rush. "I thought this room would be best."

Doña Isabella waited another endless moment before asking, "You designed this for me?"

Shayne twisted her hands together. "I understand you probably have relatives clamoring for you to live with them back in Mexico. But I also know how it is to lose the one person you love most in the world. It would make Sarita happy if you stayed." She couldn't tell how the *Doña* was taking the offer. "Or if you must go, we can keep this room for whenever you visit."

Sarita poked her head out of the walk-in closet. Seeing them, she beamed. *"Abuelita!* I came through the tunnel."

Doña Isabella stared at a point just above the wrought-iron headboard of the bed. "What is this tunnel?"

"Oh, that." Shayne looped a strand of hand behind her ear. "You see, the closets were back-to-back, so I had a passageway knocked through so they'd connect.

Tears filled *Doña* Isabella's eyes. "You did this for me?" she whispered. "You truly wish me to stay?"

Shayne didn't hesitate. "Yes, please. I think family's important and you're all Sarita has left of her mother."

The old woman fought for composure. "McIntyre will not approve."

"Oh, well. We'll just tell him it's temporary until he gets used to the idea."

"That may take quite a while."

"He'll come around. He pretends he's heartless, but his heart's in there somewhere." It had to be. "We'll root around until we find it. What do you say? Want to help?"

A single tear followed the network of lines down *Doña* Isabella's face, though a fierce, innate pride kept her from breaking down completely. "It may be interesting to remain, if only for its amusement factor."

Uh-oh. That didn't sound good. "Perhaps you won't mind if I break the news to him?"

A hint of laughter replaced Isabella's tears. "I would like to be a fly in the wall for that conversation."

Shayne grinned. "Somehow I suspect I'm the one who'll be in the wall."

Gnarled fingers reached out to touch Shayne's cheek and the *Doña* murmured softly in Spanish, "Are you very certain you want to do this, child?"

"Quite certain," she replied in the same language, wondering how the *Doña* knew she was fluent. Perhaps Rafe wasn't the only one capable of hiring a private investigator. Considering how protective the Doña was of Sarita's well-being, Shayne could see her taking every possible precaution. "I'm in charge of creating a home. I wouldn't be doing a proper job, if that home didn't include you. Please stay with us. Chaz doesn't realize it, yet, but we need you."

"Walk me to the front door, if you will." *Doña* Isabella tucked her hand into the crook of Shayne's arm and signaled to Sarita who obediently followed, whispering secrets to her new doll. "You may tell *Señor* McIntyre I have agreed to let him have custody of his daughter. Perhaps that will ease his anger a trifle when he learns the rest. Tell him also that until I'm satisfied that my great-granddaughter is properly settled, I will stay for a visit."

"An indefinite visit."

"Yes." Isabella broke down and smiled, a smile of unexpected beauty. "Most definitely indefinite."

They found Jumbo in the hallway, carefully filling one of the holes in the floor with the first of the mosaic squares she'd had shipped from Costa Rica. It was from a set of twelve, each a depiction of one of the months of the year. Beside her, Isabella drew an astonished breath. "Where did you get this piece?" she asked, still speaking in Spanish.

"I made it."

Isabella stilled. "You are an artisan?"

"In my spare time."

"And your name before you married?"

"Shayne Beaumont."

"I have seen your work, Shayne Beaumont. There was a mosaic piece I viewed quite recently." Her brow drew together in thought and she rapped her cane sharply against the floor. "But of course. On loan to the museum in San Francisco. It was quite striking. A man, half in darkness, half in light."

"It took me quite a while to create that one. To be honest, I didn't think I'd ever finish it. But, I have to admit, it's my very favorite."

"Does your husband know?"

Shayne shook her head. "And I'd rather it stayed that way, if you don't mind."

Isabella shrugged without offering any promises. "I remember thinking at the time that the man reminded me of someone. Now I realize who. The resemblance to McIntyre is quite striking."

"Thank you."

"I was a foolish old woman not to see it before." *Doña* Isabella's eyes narrowed, as something else occurred to her. "You said this work took you a while to create. How long a while might that be?"

"I worked on it sporadically over an eight-year period. At one point I gave up on it altogether. But my sister-in-law helped me through some tough times and encouraged me to finish what I'd started."

Isabella released her breath in a gusty sigh. "Then you knew McIntyre long ago. Before my Madalena came into his life."

"We were briefly married," Shayne confessed, wondering how the *Doña* would receive the news. "But my brother thought I was too young and had it annulled."

"This explains much that I did not understand."

Apprehension filled her. "Has it changed your mind about coming to live with us?"

"No, my dear." To Shayne's delight, *Doña* Isabella leaned forward and embraced her. "It has proven to me that I made the right decision. But you should tell your husband about this artwork and allow him to judge it for himself."

"I can't."

"Because it is too revealing," *Doña* Isabella guessed shrewdly. "It is sad to see two people so much in love and so afraid to show it."

"You're wrong," she insisted steadily. "Chaz doesn't love me."

Isabella regarded her with open amusement. "When you are as old as I, you will see the folly of your words, as well as this decision regarding your artwork. And when you do, you will either laugh with your husband over your foolishness. Or . . ."

"Or?" Shayne prompted, dreading the response.

"Or you will cry in your lonely bed, filled with regrets that come far too late." And with that, she took Sarita's hand in hers and tapped her way to the front door.

"**What do you mean** she's left? Where's Sarita?" Chaz shot from behind his desk, ready to chase them down. Damn it all, he'd drag the old crow back by her hooked nose, if necessary. In fact, he half hoped it would be. "I didn't even get the chance to say goodbye."

His response was so telling, it took a moment to speak. "It's all right," Shayne attempted to soothe. "She'll be back."

"What did the witch tell you? Will she let us have Sarita?"

"Pretty much."

"Pretty much? What the hell does that mean?" He thrust a hand through his hair, his gut twisting at his wife's sudden nervousness. "Let me guess. More conditions?"

"Just one. I promise, it's the last."

"I'd feel better if *she* promised it was the last." He propped his hip onto the corner of his desk and fought to control his impatience. Over the past month, he'd found that particular skill more and more difficult to master. "Let's have it, sweetheart. What's the catch?"

To his concern, she wandered toward the far end of his office where a large picture window faced out the front of the house. "This would be a perfect place for a Christmas tree," she murmured.

"We already had that discussion, remember?"

She wrapped her arms around her waist, looking suddenly small and alone. "I was hoping you'd changed your mind."

"Not even a little."

"But Sarita—"

"Forget about the damn tree, Shayne, and tell me what the *Doña* wants."

She turned, taking unfair advantage of his soft nature by allowing huge, glittering tears to fill her eyes. "She's a child, Chaz. She doesn't understand that you have some personal reason for hating Christmas. All she knows is that she's alone and without family—at least family she recognizes—and it's Christmas. Only there's no music and no laughter, no tree or presents."

He straightened and cautiously approached. There was something going on here, something that escaped him. "Why do I have the funny feeling we aren't talking about Sarita, anymore?"

She paled and he knew he'd struck a nerve. "I . . . I'm sorry." She clasped her hands in front of her and tilted her head to look directly at him. Her chin quivered in a way that twisted him into knots, but she didn't back down, refusing to give in to her distress. "You're not the only one who has bad memories of past Christmases. But I'd never take them out on a child. I'd do everything I could to give her happy experiences, hoping that they'd give them to me, as well."

He reached for her with a gentle hand and brushed away a tear that had tumbled loose. "What happened to you, sweetheart? Why all this commotion over a silly tree?"

"I just want Sarita to be happy."

His eyes narrowed. "I don't think so. Why is it so important for you to decorate the house? Come on. Spill it."

The quiver had spread to her sweet, vulnerable mouth. "I—I'm not feeling well. I think I'll go lie down for a little while."

"Honey—"

She shook her head, backing away from his outstretched hand. "Please, Chaz. Give me a little time alone."

"Wait a minute. We need to talk. You haven't told me about the *Doña*'s condition. And damn it all, Shayne, I want to discuss this Christmas business with you."

"I don't think I can." Her voice broke. "Not right now."

With that she turned and fled the room. Every instinct he possessed urged him to give chase, not to wait until she'd had time to deal with whatever demons haunted her, but instead force them into the open. He hesitated, suspecting he was listening to raging male hormones, the sort that wanted to sweep her into his arms and fight those demons for her, instead of the more rational part of his brain that urged him to abide by her wishes.

He checked his watch. One hour. He'd give her one hour and then they were going to have a long talk about their past and about Sarita, about their marriage and about their future.

And then he'd give in to those raging male hormones.

Chapter Nine

To My Long-Lost Bride,

Another year has gone and winter has arrived again. Or has it always been here? Sometimes it feels that way. I look outside and see a blanket of white as beautiful and untouched as you were the first time we kissed. So many years have passed and yet the memories haven't dimmed.

I don't understand that. Our love died long ago, the embers long since turned to ash. And yet I look out my window and there you are, as clear to me as the first time I saw you in the Montagues' garden.

You'll stay in my thoughts, wife of my heart, a sweet memory I'll allow myself to recall just once a year. You linger in the far recesses of my mind. A laughter-filled voice. A tantalizing scent. A heart-stopping smile.

I'm keeping you there, where you'll be safe, where we can visit in my yearly dream, where you remain my wife from long ago, the only one I've ever loved. A Forever Love.

Chaz eventually found his wife in their bedroom, curled up on the mattress, fully clothed and sound asleep. An hour had come and gone long ago, but an emergency with one of his animals had intruded.

Gazing down at Shayne, he wondered again why she'd been so upset earlier. He frowned over the protective way her arms were folded, the fetal position she'd assumed, and the slight reddening of her nose. And suddenly he knew the truth beyond any shred of doubt.

He sank onto the edge of the bed. She'd discovered she wasn't pregnant and thought it meant a fast end to their short marriage. That's why she hadn't told him, because she'd suspected he'd send her away. He sat there for a long time, struggling to understand the disappointment that ate at him. He didn't want more complications in his life, did he? And yet . . .

A soft knock sounded on the door and Chaz opened it, surprised to find Mojo standing there, holding an overloaded tray. "The little missy just picked at her dinner, so I thought I'd drop this off," the cook explained with an abashed expression. "Maybe you can get her to eat something."

It amazed Chaz to realize how quickly she'd found a place in the hearts of his men. But then, hadn't he tumbled just as hard at their first meeting? "I'll see what I can do," he promised.

Taking the tray, he set it on the dresser and glanced at his wife. She looked frighteningly vulnerable, adrift in the center of their mattress. Perhaps he'd slip her into a nightgown. If she woke, he'd feed her as he had their first evening together. Only this time, he'd try not to make her cry.

For some strange reason, her tears worked him into an uproar, something he'd prefer to avoid, if at all possible. He opened one of the dresser drawers he'd cleared out for her use, intent on finding the briefest scrap of nightwear he could find.

The drawer was empty.

What the hell? One after another, he yanked them open, finding every last one bare. For a horrifying moment he thought she'd decided to leave him. That instead of telling him she wasn't pregnant, she'd just go. Fury gripped him.

This was all Isabella's fault! She'd agreed to turn over his daughter and Shayne had taken that to mean he didn't need her anymore and packed her bags. Only one thing had kept her from disappearing into the night. She'd fallen asleep before she could make good her escape.

He crossed to the closet and ripped open the doors. A single dress hung there, but it was enough to loosen the fist like knot forming in his chest. And then he saw it. Shoved off to one side on the floor of the closet he found her suitcase. Bits and pieces of silken underclothes spilled haphazardly over the side and she'd draped a knit shirt on top. The clothes were in reasonable order, but something about the way they'd been pushed around told him they weren't packed in anticipation of a hasty departure. A frown pulled his eyebrows together as understanding slowly dawned.

She'd never unpacked.

For one full month she'd lived out of her suitcase and he'd never even noticed. His breath expelled in an audible hiss. He knew what it meant. She'd known practically from the start that she didn't carry his child. This was her silent acceptance of the impermanence of their marriage.

Her unstated fatalism nearly brought him to his knees. She planned to leave. Not today. But sooner or later, she'd neaten those bits and pieces of silk and lace, zip up her case and he'd lose her, just as he had all those years ago. Only this time it would be permanent.

No. No way.

He didn't know when it had happened, but at some point in the past few weeks, he'd gone from wanting a swift end to his marriage, to wanting to keep her

He stared at the bed with hungry eyes. Maybe he could give a gentle hint, tell her without words how he felt.

The idea appealed immensely. Removing the suitcase from the closet, he carried it to the ladder-back chair and set it on the seat. The sun had given way to dusk and he wouldn't be able to see for much longer without switching on a light. But he didn't want to wake Shayne until he'd finished.

Quietly, he opened the drawer to the nightstand table and removed the matches stocked there. Winter storms frequently knocked out the power and the first time he'd fumbled for a flashlight and found the batteries dead, he'd made a habit of keeping a hurricane lamp filled and ready. He lit the wick and turned it low. The soft glow barely kissed the small mound Shayne made in the middle of the bed. Satisfied that it wouldn't disturb her, he turned his attention to the suitcase.

Yanking open the first dresser drawer, he loaded it with delicate scraps of temptation. He stood there for a full minute trying to decide whether he'd be considered perverted if he folded her female fripperies instead of leaving them in a jumbled heap of pastels. Gingerly, he sorted the pile, not quite folding, but carefully arranging the tiny scraps into sections based on usage.

That finished, he made short work of the rest, either stacking the articles of clothing into a drawer or hanging them in the closet, the decision based solely on its wrinkle-ability. At the very bottom of the suitcase, he found the mask she'd worn to the Cinderella Ball.

The bells greeted him with happy, silvered voices. Lifting his Stetson off the top of the bedpost, he draped the mask there, slapping his hat on top. The combination of hat and beaded mask made him grin. Then he turned and eyed the suitcase, his amusement fading. He picked it up and crossed to the nearest window. Shoving up the sash, he sent the case hurtling out into the frigid night air, taking a perverse delight in his actions.

"Chaz?" Shayne lifted onto one elbow, blinking at him with huge sleepy eyes. "Was that my suitcase you just threw out the window?"

"Yup." Supreme satisfaction edged his voice.

She sat up, shoving a tumble of pale hair from her face, looking quite delightful in her confusion. "But, why did you do that?"

"I was making a statement." He crossed to the dresser and picked up the tray and placed it near her on the mattress. "Hungry?"

"I don't understand." She drew her knees toward her chest and wrapped her arms around her legs. "What sort of statement?"

"You're a smart woman. You figure it out."

Her lashes flickered downward, then lifted. An expression every bit as hungry as his lit the darkness of her gaze. "Should I assume I won't be going anywhere soon?"

"Good guess."

"Even though Isabella will let Sarita stay? Even though you won't need me much longer? Even though . . . Even though we don't know for sure whether or not I'm pregnant?"

Oh, he knew. And he intended to take that excuse away from her right this very second. "I'm changing the conditions of our marriage agreement." He thrust out his jaw. "Any objections?"

"To be honest," she admitted wistfully. "I sort of liked the clothes I had in my suitcase."

"I didn't throw out your clothes, just the case."

To prove his point, he opened one of the drawers and removed a particularly fine bit of black silk. If he were honest, he'd admit he'd had a few perverted thoughts about this particular piece of nothing while putting it away. With any luck at all, he'd turn those thoughts into action.

"See? All your belongings, safe and sound." Safe and sound until he ripped them off her.

"You know this doesn't change anything, don't you?"

Returning to the bed, he removed the plastic wrap covering one of the plates. He passed her the sandwich Mojo had prepared and waited until she'd begun nibbling on it before continuing.

"This place needs a bit of work, but it's in a good location and has serious possibilities. I've worked on some of the ranches around here before and like the area. This is where I want to raise my daughter. The people are friendly and the town wholesome."

Shayne slanted him a quick glance from beneath her lashes. "Are you trying to sell me on the place?"

She planned to leave him. The certainty took hold. "Do I need to?"

"It occurs to me that we've never settled certain issues." She picked at her sandwich, scattering crumbs across the spread. If their conversation hadn't turned so serious, he'd have teased her about it. "Maybe we should discuss them now."

He didn't want her telling him about the baby she wouldn't bear. Not tonight. "And maybe we should take things one day at a time."

A flash of pain flickered across her face and she returned her sandwich to the plate, half-eaten. "Did you ever look for me, Chaz?"

Damn. Where had that come from? He didn't have the energy for this sort of discussion. "I looked," he stated briefly.

"But Rafe made it impossible for you to find me, didn't he?"

He thrust a hand through his hair. "Do we have to talk about this now?" He didn't want to open old wounds, to discover whether or not anything still festered there. Some matters were best left untouched. It was safer that way. "I looked. I didn't find you. End of subject."

"How long did you look?"

"Shayne—"

"A day?"

A ripple of anger raced through him. "Let it go, honey."

"A month?"

"Yes, damn it. A month."

"A year? Did you keep looking for a whole year?"

Each question sliced deep, ripping toward that dark, bitter place, a place he didn't dare touch. "You don't know anything about it, Shayne," His tone was too low, too harsh. Too close to the edge. She planned to leave him. He had to get her to stop before he did or said something he'd regret, before he drove her away. He forced a deadly note in his voice. "Be smart. Drop it. Now."

"Was it longer than a year? Or did those twelve months pretty much cover it?"

"Did you hear? *Stop!*"

Her dark eyes flashed with a contradictory mixture of velvety softness and sharp reprimand, as though her emotions were at war with her reason. "You gave up, didn't you?"

For an instant he didn't move. A distant roaring filled his head, preluding the coming of an anger so deep and so old and so relentless, it drowned out every other feeling or consideration. He exploded from the bed, the bells on her mask startled into a frantic jumble of sound. Rational thought vanished, the thin veneer of civilization stripped away and replaced with sheer animal rage. With a guttural shout, he snatched the tray from the bed and threw it with every ounce of strength toward the nearest wall. Dishes shattered.

He caught a glimpse of himself in the mirror over the dresser and flinched, seeing a man reduced to his most primitive state. Vivid color scored his cheekbones, the wild glitter in his eyes fired by deadly intent. Even the atmosphere in the room had changed, burning with the scent of fury, as though ancient pheromones had been released, igniting the urge to attack. He sucked air into his lungs, desperate to regain his control, shaking with the effort.

"I searched, damn you!" The raw words howled from a bottomless well of pain. "He bought off my private investigators. I sent you letters. You never answered. Where were you, Shayne? Why didn't you come to me?"

"I came." She approached, adorable, foolish woman, braving his wrath with gentle hands and soothing words. "At least, I tried to."

The coldness returned, sweeping over him and he welcomed it. Embraced it. Clung to it. It would protect him from feelings he refused to acknowledge. "What stopped you, Shayne?" He turned on her like a wounded animal, intent on inflicting as much damage as possible before giving in to his own agony. "What possible excuse could you have?"

"I . . ." Sadness shadowed her expression. "I had a small accident."

He discovered in that moment he had a heart and this woman controlled its every beat "An accident," he repeated stupidly. An accident. *The* accident.

He shook his head. No. Not that. Not the car wreck that had scarred that sweet, beautiful body. Not while she'd been coming to him. Not the one she'd told Mojo about, all the while shooting him quick, nervous glances, as though half-expecting him to reject her because of a few scars.

"I did that to you?" he whispered. "Your scars were my fault?"

"No!" She was in his arms, wrapping him in warmth. "It wasn't anyone's fault. It was a freak storm and a small rock slide on a bad corner. I lost control of the car."

"Rafe. He was trying to stop you, wasn't he?"

"He wasn't chasing me, if that's what you were thinking. He'd discovered what I'd planned and attempted to intercept me at the airport. I was lucky, Chaz. If he hadn't come down the mountain when he had—"

"Don't!"

She broke off, pulling back ever so slightly. "You're shaking!"

"You're damned right I am." In one swift movement, he yanked her knit shirt over her head and tossed it aside. "And in a minute, you will be, too."

Her bra came next, neatly removed with a flick of his fingers. As much as he wanted to fill his hands with her softness, he had more important duties to take care of first. Like getting her naked and on the bed where he could feast on her at his leisure. Unfastening her slacks, he worked his thumbs into the waistband and tugged everything not skin off her legs.

In less than thirty seconds, he had her exactly as he wanted her, the way he'd fantasized since that first passionate encounter before their wedding. Hell, if he were honest, he'd admit he'd clung to the desperate memory for nine long years. Sweeping her into his arms, he carried her to the bed.

He set her down, her body barely denting the mattress. She stared up at him without a hint of shyness and he found he appreciated that calm, direct gaze, relieved her scars hadn't stolen that from her, hadn't filled her with self-loathing or embarrassment.

The instant his clothes hit the floor, he joined her on the bed. The kerosene lamp filled the room with shadows, but now that he knew what to look for, he found the network of scars with ease. Before this night ended, he'd kiss the full length of each and every one. They were a testament to his history with Shayne, to what they'd gone through to finally come together again. They were a silvery road map that had led to this moment in time.

"Chaz . . ." Her voice slipped through the dusk, filling him with longing.

How he wished he could love her as she deserved. That the deadness inside him would burgeon with new life. That the heart he'd just discovered was capable of more than shoving ice-cold blood through his veins. "I'm here, sweet. And you're safe. Nothing will hurt you, I promise."

Except him, the knowledge taunted.

Shayne's gaze followed the gentle fingers of light that traced across the impressive width of her husband's shoulders, chasing the shadows deep into the crevices of his work-hardened muscles.

She couldn't see all of him. Darkness ate into their circle of privacy, concealing him from the waist down. But the lamp-light fell full on his face, turning his eyes to an impossible shade of blue. It also highlighted the sharply angled cheekbones and the sun-weathered creases that told of a man who'd ridden a long, hard road.

He returned her look in full, taking his time about it. Then he clasped her wrists in one hand and lifted them over her head, anchoring them there while he studied her even more closely. Without a word, he dipped toward her, finding the jagged line that ran from wrist to the tender inner curve of her upper arm. She shuddered at the first touch of his mouth, shivering helplessly beneath each rasping lap of his tongue. Inch by torturous inch, he followed the scar until he reached the end. Only it wasn't the end.

He rolled her onto her side, her hands still shackled above her, allowing the light to fall on all of the other scars, ones only her doctors had ever seen. And then he kissed them one by one, a thousand kisses of tenderness.

"How old are they?" he demanded.

"Old."

"How old? Five years?"

"Yes."

"Six?"

"Yes!"

"Or is it eight years?" He released her wrists and cupped her face, forcing her to meet the sorrow burning in his eyes. "How about eight years and one month. Could that be how old they are? You were on your way to the Montagues' Anniversary Ball, weren't you? To try and find me and start our life again."

Tears threatened, tears of regret and longing, tears of sorrow for one careless jerk of the wheel on a rain-slick mountain road. "Yes," she cried. "I'm sorry, Chaz. So sorry. I did try to get to you. I did."

He stopped her words with a kiss of such passionate poignancy that the tears flowed unchecked. "It's in the past," he said with unmistakable finality.

He found the scars with his mouth again, but instead of filling her with a shivery pleasure, they roused an unbearable tension. His hand accidentally brushed her breast. Or was it accidental? His callused fingers grazed the softness of her lower belly where there no scars marred her skin. Her muscles rippled tight. A fluttering started there, centered deep in the most feminine core of her. With each careless touch, it intensified, causing a throbbing between her legs and driving the crowns of her breasts into tight, painful peaks.

"Please," she gasped, unable to stand another minute.

"I plan to please you, sweetheart. I plan to please you every which way I can, plus any others that come to mind in the next few hours."

He cupped her breasts, giving them his full attention. Her breath quickened, just as her body quickened, drawing taut with need. He lay heavily over her, slipping his hands beneath her thighs and parting them. He found the center of liquid warmth, dipped into it, intensified it, gorged on it, reveled in it. And when they were both mindless with desire, he filled her, riding with her to an ecstasy that made them inescapably one. One mind. One heart. One soul.

Joined in a perfect, shattering union.

It wasn't until much, much later, until the darkest hours of the night when nightmares roam and uncertainty cavorts, that he awoke and knew the truth. She planned to leave him and there wasn't a damn thing he could do about it.

"You've done what?"

Shayne sat up and dragged the covers around her, glaring at Chaz. "I knew you'd overreact when you found out. That's why I didn't tell you sooner."

"You listen up, wife, and you listen up good. It will be a cold day in hell before I allow that old bat to live under my roof. Do you have any idea the months of torture she's put me through?"

"She's only trying to protect Sarita."

He thrust a pillow behind his shoulders and glared at his turncoat wife. "Bull. She's trying to drive me insane."

"Sarita needs her. Besides, it's too late to tell her no. I've already said yes."

"Find a way."

"How am I supposed to do that?" she demanded in exasperation.

"Lie to her. Be honest with her. Explain that we don't have a room for her. Frankly, I don't give a damn. But you make sure Her Worship and that cane of hers are on the next outbound transport to Mexico."

"There's only one small problem with your plan."

His jaw made a prominent appearance again. "And what's that?"

"I can't tell her we don't have room." She gulped. "Because she's already seen it."

"What do you mean, she's already seen it? Seen what?"

"I mean . . ." Her voice dropped to a barely audible level. "I fixed up one of the bedrooms for her and let her see it."

"You did *what?*"

She refused to take all the blame for this. "If you'd bothered to take a look at the improvements I've been making, you'd have seen it, too. I didn't hide anything I was doing."

He erupted from the bed. "Are you trying to tell me you planned this from the beginning?"

"I'm not *trying* to tell you anything. I *am* telling you."

Why was it that every time she got him naked, he left the bed angry? She cupped her chin in her hand. She must be doing something terribly wrong. Maybe if they didn't use a bed next time, these arguments would turn out different. His chest distracted her, rising and falling in a way she found entirely too provocative. No doubt he did it deliberately.

"Let me get this straight," he said. "You remodeled one of my bedrooms specifically for *Doña* Isabella?"

"Yes."

"So she'd . . ." He closed his eyes. "I can hardly bring myself to say this. So she'd *stay?*"

"Yes and yes."

"Why?"

Finally. A question she could answer. "Because Sarita needs her."

"Sarita will have us."

"It's not the same, Chaz. Believe me, I know." Before he could follow up her statement with any unwanted questions, she continued. "*Doña* Isabella is someone your daughter's known since birth and the only family left on her mother's side. At least, the only family who'll accept her. Isabella hasn't said anything, but I suspect the reason she didn't want to take Sarita back to Mexico with her was because of the reception your daughter would have received from the rest of Madalena's family."

Damn it! He hated when Shayne was right. "I hadn't thought of that," Chaz admitted, adding stubbornly, "but that shouldn't keep Isabella from going."

"Have you any idea what it's like to be three years old and torn from the only family you've ever known?"

There was an odd quality to her voice, something that captured his attention as nothing else would have. "Of course not." He deliberately paused a beat. "Do you?"

She moistened her lips, her nervousness a dead giveaway. "Yes." She rushed into speech. "Granted, Sarita will be with people who love her. But it's not the same as being with the woman who's raised her from birth."

"This has something to do with your aunt, doesn't it? The one Rafe rescued you from."

Shayne nodded, her delicate features lined with dread. "I never talk about that time. Not even with my brother. But for Sarita . . ." She closed her eyes. "I will for Sarita's sake."

Aw, hell. "No, honey—"

"Rafe and I have different mothers. Did you know that?"

"You don't have to say another word," he tried again.

But she didn't listen. Her focus had turned inward. Even her body seemed gathered in on itself, balled tight to offer up as little surface space as possible. A horrifying thought occurred to him. It was almost as though she'd curled herself into as small a target as possible. Is that how she'd learned to protect herself as a child?

"Our father and my mother were killed in a boating accident when I was three. Rafe had just turned sixteen. Despite being so young, he tried to keep us together. He worked the coffee fields, ran the household, cared for me. He did everything possible to keep his family intact."

"I had no idea," he said gently. He sat next to her and drew her close, massaging the rigidness from taut muscles and offering what little comfort she'd allow.

"He lost it all, Chaz. Our home. Our money. By the end, he was desperate. He couldn't even put food on our plates."

"What did he do?"

"Right before Christmas, he used his last penny to call my mother's sister, Jackie, and ask if she'd take me in. Jackie had never approved of my parents' marriage, but she did her duty. She flew to Costa Rica and took me back to Florida with her."

"What about Rafe?"

Shayne's mouth twisted. "She left him behind. He wasn't her responsibility. According to her, he was some filthy peasant child from Costa Rica, related only through an accident of marriage. For years, she wouldn't even say his name. Just that disgusting description."

Chaz found it difficult to reconcile the man he knew with the boy Rafe must have been. "She abandoned him?"

"I wish she'd left me, too, even if it meant living on the streets," Shayne whispered. "It would have been kinder."

Chaz stilled. "What the hell did she do to you?"

If he hadn't been holding her, he wouldn't have felt the tiny tremor that rippled through her body. "Nothing overt. Nothing child welfare could use to remove me from the home. But I paid the price for what she regarded as my mother's sins. The first thing she did when we arrived in Florida was to burn all my possessions, including the doll Rafe had given me for a Christmas present." She attempted a smile, the tremulous pull of her lips so vulnerable and so sad, it utterly unmanned him to witness it. "You asked me why having a tree is so important to me? I never had one the entire time I lived with her. I was the original Cinderella. Isn't that a riot? And Jackie relished the role of wicked stepmother."

Stark stories followed, ones he knew with soul-crippling certainty she'd never revealed to another person, not even Rafe. Stories that had him clutching her convulsively, helpless to protect the child she'd been. "What about your brother?" he asked, when her throat grew hoarse and the words ran dry. "He found you, didn't he?"

"Yes, he found me."

But it hadn't been in time. Not nearly in time, Chaz realized. "How old were you?"

"Thirteen."

Ten years. Forever to a helpless child. And almost as long as it had taken Chaz to find her. "So Jackie just turned you over?"

"Oh, no." Shayne looked at him then, her eyes huge, wounded smudges in her tightly drawn face. "She sold me to him."

A roar of fury welled up inside, one even more tortured than before. His throat worked as he forced it down, forced himself to offer succor for a wound that couldn't be healed. He held her in his arms and rocked her, murmuring meaningless words of comfort.

"You don't understand, Chaz. I didn't tell you this for my sake."

"Shh. Everything will be all right."

"No, it won't." She eased back and captured his face within the softness of her palms. "I know you can't love me anymore. That doesn't mean you can't love Sarita. She's an innocent child. Don't let her go through what I did. She needs Isabella just as I needed Rafe. But she needs you even more. Please, Chaz. Do this one thing for me and I won't ask you for anything else."

"Don't, Shayne."

"I'm begging you. I promise I won't cause you any more trouble."

He couldn't bear it. "Sarita doesn't have anything to worry about."

Shayne expelled her breath in a relieved sigh and Chaz closed his eyes, fighting an almost incapacitating fear. "I promise I won't cause you any more trouble,"

It was a farewell, if he'd ever heard one.

He needed to swear, to vent his frustrations with a truly nasty word. He fought to come up with one, even a mild one. Just something to blister the air. Just a single oath to ease the confusing tumble of emotions that muddled his brain. But nothing came to him. Nothing but a single jittery warning, ringing with all the clarity of silvery bells on a winter's breeze.

She was going to leave him.

Chapter Ten

Chaz paused outside the door to the parlor, startled to find his foreman sitting with *Doña* Isabella. Now there was a sight he'd never expected to see. Neither of them noticed him, so he shoved his Stetson to the back of his head and blatantly eavesdropped.

"Now, Izzy," Penny said. "I don't want you to be upset when I put my cards down."

"I won't be the least upset."

"It's jes' that I've noticed you don't take well to losing."

"Carry on with the game, *Señor* Penworthy. I believe I called?"

"So you did. But, Izzy, I warned you about calling me Penworthy. If word got out that was my legally binding name, I'd be a laughingstock."

"As you wish, *Señor* Penny."

"That's better." He spread out his cards. "Read 'em and weep, precious. Full house, aces and kings."

"Very impressive." She stayed his hand as he reached for the pot of matchsticks with the gold-tipped handle of her cane. "But not so fast."

"You can't have my full house beat. You drew four cards!"

"Ah, but they were four excellent cards." She plunked down a fistful of queens and actually grinned. "My pot, I believe."

Chaz shook his head in disbelief. He never thought he'd live to see the day when those two would get chummy. It gave him an odd feeling. As odd as when he'd walked into the kitchen earlier.

His daughter had been perched on Mojo's lap slapping balls of cookie dough onto a metal tray. She'd waved at him, her fingers studded with bits of chocolate chips, chattering at great length in a mixture of Spanish and English while Mojo sat there, not understanding a word, a big, sloppy grin on his ugly mug.

It was the same sappy expression he'd worn ever since the two had first met, the day Sarita had darted into the kitchen before anyone could stop her. Mojo had been at his worktable, frozen in place, a potato peeler poking out of his massive paw.

Sarita had skidded to a halt at his side. But instead of running shrieking from the room or reacting with fear, she'd studied him with open curiosity. Then she'd climbed onto his lap, and there she'd stayed. From that moment on, they'd been the best of friends.

So why did Chaz feel so out of sorts? He should be delighted. He'd assembled all the various pieces necessary for the life he'd always wanted and Shayne had put those pieces in order. The end result was a home more perfect than he could have ever imagined.

So what the hell was bothering him?

He wandered into his office and stood by the window overlooking the front of the house. He knew what it was. Shayne and that damn Christmas tree. Shayne and the hideous childhood she'd barely survived. Shayne and her unending search for love.

He suspected what hurt her the most about their relationship was that he'd let her down, first by failing to find her in the years that had passed since their marriage nine years ago. And second, and most importantly, because he didn't love her the way she so desperately needed.

She was going to leave him.

Now that she'd created a home for him, she'd go, and there was only one thing he could think of to stop her. He could prove that he'd done his best to find her. And he could let her know that once upon a time, he had loved her.

His next decision took no thought at all. Rifling through his desk drawer, he searched for the business card he'd tossed in there close to a month ago, a card he'd never thought he'd have occasion to use. Finding it, he punched in the series of numbers printed in the corner. The phone only rang once.

"Beaumont."

"You said to call if I ever needed help."

"McIntyre? Is that you?"

"Got it in one, big brother. I've decided to take you up on that offer." Chaz released his breath along with his pride. "I need your help."

Chaz found San Francisco cold and

gray, the misty rain bringing a chill far more cutting than the fiercest winter his mountain home in Colorado could offer up. He stood outside the museum, silently cursing Rafe for forcing this out-of-the-way meeting. Couldn't he have just sent the packet? Why all the games?

"McIntyre. Glad to see you could make it."

Chaz turned and greeted his brother-in-law with a handshake. "I don't recall you leaving me any choice."

"I didn't. There were things I wanted to say I'd rather Shayne not overhear."

"So you dragged me all the way to San Francisco? That sister of yours must have incredible hearing."

A cool smile touched Beaumont's mouth. "There might have been one other reason I chose this place. Come. As long as we're here, we might as well take a look around."

Chaz struggled to hang onto his temper. Rafe had a regrettable tendency to take charge. Well, he'd let the man run things this time. Since he had the bit between his teeth, it would be tough to stop him. But it would only continue until Chaz had what he'd come for. Then their "brotherly" relationship would screech to a halt and they could go back to a more natural mutual antagonism.

After wandering through the museum for a good fifteen minutes, Rafe paused near a huge mosaic. Reaching into his suit jacket, he removed a packet of papers and stared down at them with a dark frown.

"Would you mind telling me why you wish to give her these? Is it to drive us apart?"

Chaz took instant umbrage. "Hell, no! Just what kind of man do you think I am?"

"My apologies. But if it isn't to drive a wedge between the two of us, then why? Why after all these years?"

"Because she needs to know I did try and find her. That I didn't just give up on her."

"Ah. I see. That means she's told you about her aunt."

Chaz nodded. "She told me."

"Did she also tell you about her accident, that she was on her way to the Anniversary Ball—to you—when she crashed?"

Even though he already knew what had happened, hearing it stated so baldly filled Chaz with a helpless rage. He hadn't been there to protect her. Maybe if he'd tried harder to find her, the accident could have been prevented. "I know about the car wreck and the scars it left behind."

"And did she also tell you she bought a ticket to the next Cinderella Ball, the one four years ago?"

Chaz didn't even try to conceal his astonishment. "I went to that ball. She wasn't there."

"That's because I took her ticket and attended in her place. Ella and I were married that night."

Chaz balled his hands into fists. "So you kept her from me again."

"It was wrong of me. I know that." Rafe lifted silvery-gray eyes, eyes filled with regret. "But consider this. If events had transpired differently, you wouldn't have Sarita."

"That's the only thing that keeps me from knocking your teeth down your throat."

Rafe wandered further down the corridor. "Then perhaps it isn't too late to recapture the love you once shared with my sister."

"It is too late," Chaz stated coldly. "Far too late."

"Are you sure that's not your pride talking?"

Damn the man! "I have no pride where Shayne's concerned. Otherwise, I wouldn't be standing here having this conversation. Nor would I give her those papers."

Rafe shook his head. "No, my friend. There's something more. Something you haven't told me. What is it?"

"You really want your pound of flesh, don't you?" Chaz gritted his teeth. "Fine. You'd have figured it out, eventually. I need what you're holding, Beaumont. If I don't give it to her, she'll leave me."

To his fury, Rafe actually chuckled. That did it! Brother-in-law or no, this time Chaz planned to beat the living tar out of the man. Before he could do more than cock his fist, Rafe paused in front of the mosaic and inclined his head toward it.

"It took her eight years to complete this."

Chaz glanced at the piece and then took a second look, then a third, stunned by what he saw. His arm sagged to his side. *It was him!*

He stepped back so he could fully appreciate the scope of the piece. In the mosaic, he was climbing a trellis, just as he had all those years ago when he'd first met Shayne, half of him in shadow and half in light. His hand, the one caught in the light, reached toward a woman's hand. Shayne's hand. And in the background, the darkness gave way to a rainbow of color. He'd never seen a more beautiful piece of artwork. Never.

He peered at the title and it impacted like a blow to the gut, as did the name below it. *The Coming of a Forever Love* by Shayne Beaumont.

Shayne Beaumont *McIntyre*, he wanted to shout. *His wife*.

Beside him, Rafe released his breath in a pitying sigh. "My poor sister. You don't even realize you still love her, do you?" He held out the papers. "If you hurt her, McIntyre, I'll make you pay."

Chaz took the packet without a word, barely noticing. Rafe's departure. *You don't even realize you still love her, do you?* He shook his head. No. It wasn't possible. He hadn't felt love since . . .

He closed his eyes, his throat moving convulsively. He hadn't felt love since he'd last held her in his arms. His eyes opened and he stared at the mosaic with desperate hunger. He'd first found love in her arms. He'd also considered it a forever love. Only he'd been too afraid to admit it.

He never knew how long he stood there. A minute. An hour. An odd feeling deep in his chest finally propelled him into motion. A flicker of warmth. A burgeoning.

A resurrection.

He'd told Shayne he'd died inside years ago, but he'd lied. Instead, those emotions had lain dormant, waiting for the return of spring. And spring had come storming through, wearing a bell-draped mask, a tender smile and velvety eyes filled with a love so generous and so absolute that it brought humbling tears to his eyes. She'd come, sweeping aside the bitterness of winter, her kiss coaxing life where none should exist.

His jaw worked as he forced himself to face the soul-stripping truth. He loved her. He had the first time he'd set eyes on her over nine years ago and he'd continued to right up until this very second. And he would for the rest of his life. There'd been only one thing that had kept him from admitting it.

Fear. Fear he'd lose her again at some point in the future. Fear he couldn't handle it if anything happened to her. But most of all, fear she wouldn't love him as utterly as he loved her. Well, the proof of her enduring love stood before his eyes, an eight-year labor of love.

"Well, you love-crazed fool," he muttered to himself. "What the hell are you doing sanding here?" He tucked the packet Rafe had given him into his coat pocket. Tomorrow was Christmas Eve and he had a home and a daughter, a grandmother and a handful of crazy employees to get back to.

But most important of all, he had a wife who loved him. A wife he loved with all of his newly discovered heart.

"What's he doing?" Shayne demanded in an undertone.

Jumbo shook his head morosely. "Doin' what he always does on Christmas Eve. He's holed up in there with a bottle and a stack of writing papers."

"But why?"

"Can't say, missy. Now why don't you get along to the kitchen? I'm sure Mojo can find something to keep you busy."

She shook her head. "No, thanks, Jumbo. I don't feel like burning any food right now."

"Well, maybe you'll be in the mood a little later."

Staggering her with a gentle pat on the back, Jumbo lumbered on his way. Desperate for something to occupy herself, Shayne pretended to buff the mosaic pieces set into the floor along the hall, but really she used it as an excuse to hang around outside Chaz's office door.

After another ten minutes of halfhearted polishing, she glanced around, assuring herself the corridor remained empty. Then she tiptoed to his door and pressed her ear to the wood. She couldn't hear a sound. If he sat in there drinking himself into a stupor, he was being darned quiet about it.

"Somethin' I can help you with, little lady?"

Shayne whipped around, blushing at the amused twinkle in Penny's eyes. "Oh, no. I was just . . . . Just . . . ."

"Waxing the door with your ear?"

She sighed. "Something like that."

"Well, then. Carry on. But you should know." The laughter died from Penny's eyes. "He won't be out until morning. Never is."

"Oh."

Shayne gave the door a final forlorn look before slipping away to her bedroom. She had a few last-minute presents to wrap, even though Christmas promised to be decidedly strange this year. Still, she couldn't allow Sarita to be affected. She just hoped a box brimming with hair ribbons and combs and barrettes would be enough. She spared a brief glance toward her gift for Chaz. She sniffed, distressed to find herself in tears yet again.

Topping the small box with a colorful bow, she pushed it aside. Dam it all! Curling up on the bed, she allowed herself a good cry, hoping to get it out of her system. She was being foolish, she knew that. But tomorrow would mark the end of any chance to win Chaz's love. Once he opened her gift, her dreams for being loved for herself would end.

Surely that deserved a few tears, didn't it?

"Keep your voices down, damn it!"

"You try and wrestle a tree this big into a room half its size and see if you don't give a yelp or two," Penny complained.

Chaz gave the base of the tree a tremendous shove, sending his foreman tumbling into his office. "If you wake up my daughter or my wife, yelping is the least you'll be doing."

"Where do you want it, boss man?" Mojo asked.

"By the window." Shayne had haunted that spot for the past week. "Is the tree stand ready?"

"I've got it." Jumbo got down on his hands and knees. "Bring 'er on over. That's right. Stand her on up. No, no! More to the left. Forward. Now toward the back."

Chaz gritted his teeth. "Jumbo, if you don't get the trunk into the stand in the next three seconds, I'm gonna stick you in that thing and hang ornaments from your ears!"

"There he goes with those ears again," Mojo said. "Somehow, Jumbo, I don't think it's your ears he's gonna decorate."

Penny hooted. "You got that right."

"What part of *be quiet* don't you three understand?" Chaz demanded, heaving the tree into position.

"Still can't believe you're sober enough to put up a tree, boss. What happened to your date with Jack Daniels?"

"JD and I have had a parting of the ways."

Penny grimaced. "I knew marriage would ruin you."

Chaz just grinned. "And you were right."

He stood back and eyed the tree. Not bad, if he did say so himself. Not too crooked. Maybe if he lopped off a few branches nobody would notice the slight starboard list.

He nodded toward his men. "Thanks for your help. I'll take it from here."

"You don't want us to help put silly little doodads on it?" Penny grumbled.

It didn't take any thought at all. Chaz shook his head decisively. "Nope. That's my job." Actually, it was more than that. "It's my pleasure."

Shayne awoke early the next morning and rolled over, knowing before she even looked she wouldn't find her husband beside her.

Quietly, she left the bed and pulled on a robe. She needed to talk to him before anyone else in the household stirred. It was Christmas morning and she had to find a way to make him understand the importance of the day to a small child, something she'd obviously failed to do so far.

She slipped through the silent house, heading straight for Chaz's office. The door stood ajar and she gave it a little push. Hovering there, she could only stand and stare. Her husband lay sprawled on the floor, sound asleep. At the sound of her gasp, he pried open an eye, wincing at the bright sunlight filtering into the room. He muttered something beneath his breath, something she tactfully pretended not to hear.

"Oh, Chaz," she murmured. "What have you done to yourself?"

"'Mornin', sweetheart. Merry Christmas."

She blinked, not quite certain she'd heard him right. "You know what day it is?"

"Of course I know." His eyes were red-rimmed, but alert, his smile as devastating as ever. If he'd indulged last night, it had been with something other than a bottle of bourbon. "Don't you?"

"Well, yes, but—" She walked further into the office and then she saw it. A huge tree filled one entire end of the room. She stared at it in disbelief. "That . . . that looks like a Christmas tree."

Chaz folded his arms behind his head, still sprawled on the floor. "Naw. That can't be. I don't do Christmas, remember?"

She took a step closer and fingered one of the needled branches. "It feels like a Christmas tree," she said unevenly. "It even smells like one."

His brow wrinkled into a frown. "Well, I'll be. Now isn't that the strangest thing."

She released the branch and it swayed ever so slightly. An excited chorus of silver-toned bells filled the air, ringing out a happy greeting. They were the bells from her mask, she realized, tears flooding her eyes. He'd strung them, one by one, on the tree.

"It—" Her voice broke and she swallowed hard, trying again. "It even sounds like a Christmas tree."

"Well, heck. Then it must be one. Don't know how the silly thing found its way in. Guess I'll have to drag it on out of here before anyone sees it."

The tears that had become such a natural part of her day overflowed her eyes. "You even decorated it."

In addition to the bells, he'd taken green and red ribbons—the colors made her cry all the harder—and tied them on the ends of each branch. The fact that the bows were a bit lopsided and imperfectly tied endeared them to her all the more.

"Honey?" He sat up. "You aren't crying, are you?"

"No," she sobbed. "I'm not."

He was on his feet in a flash. Crossing to her side in two swift strides, he pulled her into his arms. "Please don't cry, sweetheart. I did this to make you happy. Not to upset you."

"I'm not upset," she wailed.

"You sure sound upset." He bent at the knees so their height matched and peered at her face. "And if all that stuff comin' out of your eyes is any indication, you look upset, too."

"Don't you know anything?" She wrapped her arms around his waist, pressing her lips to his chest. "This is my happy face."

He smiled at that, his tension slowly easing. "Now there's a scary thought." And then he kissed her, kissed her with a passion she couldn't mistake. It was a touch that spoke of love and forever and permanence and commitment, words that were once forbidden, but now seemed imperative. "Merry Christmas, wife."

It took Shayne several minutes to recover, her lids lifting reluctantly. "I don't understand a bit of this. You put up a tree and decorated it."

"So I did."

"You must have worked on it all night."

"Just about."

She could scarcely take it in. "But why?"

"Because I was wrong. Dead wrong. You and Sarita deserve a proper Christmas."

"You even have presents." She was dreaming, she had to be. But it appeared real, beautifully, incredibly real.

"They're nothing much." The wicked light that appeared in his eyes instantly alerted her.

"What have you done?"

"Now, honey. If I told, it wouldn't be a surprise."

Before she could ask any more questions, they heard the patter of feet outside the door. A moment later, Sarita burst into the room. Spying the tree and presents, she released a squeal of delight and threw herself into her father's arms. Chaz closed his eyes, clutching her close, the expression on his face almost painful to witness.

Then he tossed her into the air, laughing at her helpless giggles. "Merry Christmas, princess."

Mojo and Jumbo plowed through the doorway next, with Penny and *Doña* Isabella not far behind. "Check the tree! Not bad, boss man."

The next few hours were the most pleasurable Shayne could remember in a very long time. After changing and grabbing a quick breakfast, everyone gathered in Chaz's office to open presents. That day Sarita solidified her relationship with her new parents, racing back and forth between Shayne and Chaz, dispensing hugs and kisses with such utter generosity that if Shayne hadn't already fallen in love with her brand-new daughter, she'd have tumbled head over heels right then and there. And Chaz's expression was filled with such an abiding joy that tears were never far from the surface.

Doña Isabella and Chaz's men were also the recipient of Sarita's affections. She darted from one to the other as they each opened their presents. She oohed and aahed over everything, no matter how ridiculous, from the meat cleaver for Mojo, "since he has a tendency to throw his away," to the first-class clipboard that turned Jumbo pale with fright.

Chaz didn't spare any of his employees from his warped sense of humor. For Penny, he'd wrapped up a huge box of matchsticks and a deck of marked playing cards. "So you can win a few." And when Shayne dared to scold him, he'd simply laughed and whispered he'd also put a fat bonus in their paychecks, a surprise they'd appreciate far more than any other gift he could have chosen.

He'd kept his present for *Doña* Isabella more serious, giving her a beautiful quilted dressing gown and cozy slippers. Shayne had drawn a sketch of the mosaic patio she'd build for Isabella come spring. And Sarita took one look at the fancy new dollhouse her daddy had brought back from San Francisco and disappeared into the corner, happily playing. She only emerged on those occasions she wanted her new "momma" to change her hair ribbons, rhapsodizing over the many choices.

At long last, Chaz drew Shayne away from the others, a small, flat box in his hand. "I'd rather do this next part in private," he said.

She glanced around the room. Everyone was preoccupied and wouldn't miss her if she slipped off with Chaz for a while. Tucking her hand into his, she drew him toward their bedroom.

"Is this private enough?" she asked.

His smile felt as tender and loving as a kiss. "This is perfect."

"So who goes first?"

"Open mine." He handed her the box.

She could see a hint of uncertainty dimming the blue of his eyes and lines of tension bracketing his mouth. He didn't know how she'd react to his gift, she realized. She stared at the box for a long moment before she carefully unwrapped it. Removing the lid, she found a stack of letters.

Her brow furrowing, she lifted out the first one. Her name was scrawled across the envelope and it had been sent care of the Montagues. And then she saw the date. Christmas Eve, nine years ago. Slowly she turned over the envelope. It was sealed.

"Open it," he said.

Without a word she removed the letter and read it. And then she reached for the next, dated Christmas Eve, a year later. And then the next, until she'd read his testament to a decade of enduring love.

The final one wasn't postmarked. "You . . . you wrote this last night, didn't you?" she asked unevenly. "When you were locked up in your office with Jack."

"No Jack, I swear. Just a stack of writing paper and a pen. It takes me a while to get the letters right. Most of the night, usually. But for some strange reason, I found this one a lot easier. Which left plenty of time for a few other chores."

He meant the tree and decorations, she realized. As she had with all the others, she turned the envelope over and pried it open, removing the single sheet of paper.

To My Newly Found Bride,

There's only one thing left to say. Only one thing I've neglected to say. Only one thing that would have been said if I hadn't been so afraid.

I love you.

My wife. My one true love. My Forever Love.

By the time she'd finished reading, she was so overcome with emotion, she couldn't speak. "There's one last item," he said. "It's in the bottom of the box."

Barely able to see through her tears, she pulled aside the tissue paper. Two golden tickets glittered in the subdued lighting. Tickets to next year's Anniversary Ball. "Oh, Chaz," she whispered.

"I know it's ten months away, but I thought maybe we could make it a date. Right now."

"I don't understand." She stared at him in bewilderment. "You were so sure you couldn't love anyone."

"I was wrong. I loved you from the first moment I set eyes on you. I've always loved you. Fear held me back." His mouth tightened. "I never thought of myself as a coward. But denying how I felt for you was easier than facing the truth. Safer than admitting that without you I was only living half a life. And I was furious, Shayne. Down to the bones, raw with anger. Angry at your brother for parting us. Angry at you for not coming back to me. Mostly, angry at myself for not finding you."

She offered a look of utter understanding. "I know all about fear and anger, remember?"

He met her gaze then, straight and earnest and totally frank. "I love you, Shayne. I always have and I always will. I'm sorry it's taken me so long to come to my senses."

She slipped into his arms and kissed him, a kiss of love and forgiveness. A kiss of promise. A kiss of passion. When they drew apart, she handed him the present she'd wrapped for him. "I don't know how you'll take this," she confessed.

"I'm sure I'll love it, whatever it is." He used far less care than she had opening the box. He ripped the paper away and pulled off the top. And then he simply sat, not uttering a word.

She regarded him apprehensively. "Aren't you going to say something?"

He picked up the baby rattle. "You're pregnant? For real?"

She nodded. "For real."

Without a word, he tipped her backward onto the bed and pushed up her sweater, baring her stomach and cupping the slight swell with gentle hands. "This—" He blinked hard. "This is the best present you could have given me."

"Are you sure?"

A blissful smile touched his mouth. "Oh, yeah, sweetheart. I'm real sure." Then he frowned. "There's only one problem."

"What's that?" she asked nervously.

"You don't suppose . . ." He broke off and shook his head. "Naw. It's too ridiculous."

"What?"

"I just had this terrible thought."

"Chaz!"

He slanted her a teasing glance. "You don't suppose this means Mojo really does have the 'eye,' do you?"

She chuckled. "I'll tell you how we'll know for sure."

"Yeah? How's that."

She sat up and wrapped her arms around his neck. "We'll know for sure if he 'sees' our next baby before Mother Nature confirms it."

"Our next baby? You mean the one after this?"

"That's generally what 'next' means."

Laughter rumbled through Chaz's chest, a happy, contented sound. "Okay. You're on."

Epilogue

Shayne sat curled up in the leather chair behind Chaz's desk and grinned at her husband, blinking a suspicious moisture from her eyes. He lay on the floor in front of the Christmas tree, overwhelmed by a flurry of pigtails and giggles. Even Sarita, so grown up at eight years, wasn't too big to wrestle her daddy to the ground. And she was such a loving big sister to Caitlin and the babies—twin girls that Mojo had "seen" long before the doctors. Despite his original terror at the notion, Chaz had gotten his house full of girls, after all.

The past five years had been the best of Shayne's life, years of love and laughter and incomparable joy. Years of richness with Chaz and the girls, Isabella and Mojo and Jumbo and Penny. Her youngest toddled over to her, looking for her mother's lap, and Shayne was only too happy to accommodate.

Nibbling the end of her pen, she returned to her yearly letter. By Christmas morning, Chaz would find the envelope hidden somewhere on the tree, a tradition they'd started on their first anniversary. She didn't doubt the tradition would continue for the rest of their lives. Cuddling her daughter close, she rested her cheek against the silky curls and put pen to paper.

To My Forever Love . . . she began.

The End

Thank you for reading **The Cinderella Ball Series** by Day Leclaire. Look for more Cinderella Ball stories in **The Salvatore Brothers Series!**

A Note From Day Leclaire

Christmas has always been my favorite holiday. Even better than my birthday, definitely better than the Easter Bunny. I love the renewed spirit of faith and joy and love, and sharing that with friends. But most of all, I love being with my family.

Okay, I'll be honest. Family can be a mixed bag, at times exasperating, especially when they get up in your business, lol. But I wouldn't trade a single second of my time with any of them. Those moments end up being the most precious and before you know it, they're gone.

I guess that's how Nikki and Jonah's story evolved. They're two people who'd go to any lengths to keep their families happy— even attend the Cinderella Ball and marry a total stranger.

So, even when you get caught up in the craziness of the holiday season, considering taking a moment for yourself, and enjoy a few hours of romance. Hope you enjoy Nikki, an independent, career-minded redhead, and Jonah, the family "fix-it" man on their path to finding true love.

And have a joyous holiday season!

Love, Day

Meet Day Leclaire

I love family first and foremost, which is why writing a family saga is so much fun. Maybe you can tell that from my books since they always feature the warmth and joy that comes from having a close-knit family. I also love animals and have taken in rescue dogs and cats and fostered dogs for the local animal shelter. And of course, I love writing. All I need is a functioning brain (batteries not included), a pen, and paper, and I can write anywhere. Please don't let a conversation with me lag because my imagination takes over and I. Am. Checked. Out!

USA Today bestselling author, Day Leclaire is the author of more than 60 novels and has received an impressive eleven nominations for the romance industry's most prestigious award, Romance Writers of America RITA© Award. Day lives in Charlotte, NC and spends her days obsessively writing while vaguely remembering to pay attention to her adorable husband, busy son and daughter-in-law, two tiny grandchildren, and two even tinier Teddy Bear dogs. Not to mention a whole lot of dust!

Thank you so much for taking the time to read **The Cinderella Ball Series:** *Fairy Tale Marriage*. I hope you enjoy this romantic series. I love hearing from my readers. For a personal response, please contact me at Day@DayLeclaire.com. And be sure to visit my website at https://www.DayLeclaire.com. Would you like a ***free book?*** Sign up for my newsletter on my website for your copy, as well as the latest exclusive updates and specials.